THE
HUNDRED-YEAR
HOUSE

ALSO BY REBECCA MAKKAI

The Borrower

THE
HUNDRED-YEAR
HOUSE

REBECCA MAKKAI

VIKING

VIKING
Published by the Penguin Group
Penguin Group (USA) LLC
375 Hudson Street
New York, New York 10014

USA | Canada | UK | Ireland | Australia | New Zealand | India | South Africa | China
penguin.com
A Penguin Random House Company

First published by Viking Penguin, a member of Penguin Group (USA) LLC, 2014

LIBRARY OF CONGRESS CATALOGING-IN-PUBLICATION DATA
Makkai, Rebecca.
The hundred-year house / Rebecca Makkai.
p. cm.
ISBN 978-0-525-42668-4
1. College teachers--Fiction. 2. Family secrets--Fiction. 3. Artist colonies--Fiction.
4. Eccentrics and eccentricities--Fiction. I. Title.
PS3613.A36H85 2014
813'.6--dc23   2013047855

Printed in the United States of America
1 3 5 7 9 10 8 6 4 2

Designed by Nancy Resnick

This is a work of fiction. Names, characters, places, and incidents either are the product of
the author's imagination or are used fictitiously, and any resemblance to actual persons, living
or dead, businesses, companies, events, or locales is entirely coincidental.

for
—but not about—
Ragdale and Yaddo
with boundless gratitude

Nothing of her was left, except her shining loveliness.

—Ovid's *Metamorphoses*, "The Transformation of Daphne"

CONTENTS

PART I

1999

I

For a ghost story, the tale of Violet Saville Devohr was vague and underwhelming. She had lived, she was unhappy, and she died by her own hand somewhere in that vast house. If the house hadn't been a mansion, if the death hadn't been a suicide, if Violet Devohr's dark, refined beauty hadn't smoldered down from that massive oil portrait, it wouldn't have been a ghost story at all. Beauty and wealth, it seems, get you as far in the afterlife as they do here on earth. We can't all afford to be ghosts.

In April, as they repainted the kitchen of the coach house, Zee told Doug more than she ever had about her years in the big house: how she'd spent her entire, ignorant youth there without feeling haunted in the slightest—until one summer, home from boarding school, when her mother had looked up from her shopping list to say, "You're pale. You're not depressed, are you? There's no reason to succumb to that. You know your great-grandmother killed herself in this house. I understand she was quite self-absorbed." After that, Zee would listen all night long, like the heroine of one of the gothic novels she loved, to the house creaking on its foundation, to the knocking she'd once been assured was tree branches hitting the windows.

Doug said, "I can't imagine you superstitious."

"People change."

They were painting pale blue over the chipped yellow. They'd pulled the appliances from the wall, covered the floor in plastic.

There was a defunct light switch, and there was a place near the refrigerator where the wall had been patched with a big square board years earlier. Both were thick with previous layers of paint, so Doug just painted right on top.

He said, "You realize we're making the room smaller. Every layer just shrinks the room." His hair was splattered with blue.

It was one of the moments when Zee remembered to be happy: looking at him, considering what she had. A job and a house and a broad-shouldered man. A glass of white wine in her left hand.

It was a borrowed house, but that was fine. When Zee and Doug first moved back to town two years ago, they'd found a cramped and mildewed apartment above a gourmet deli. On three separate occasions, Zee had received a mild electric shock when she plugged in her hair dryer. And then her mother offered them the coach house last summer and Zee surprised herself by accepting.

She'd only agreed to returned home because she was well beyond her irrational phase. She could measure her adulthood against the child she'd been when she lived here last. As Zee peeled the tape from the window above the sink and looked out at the lights of the big house, she could picture her mother and Bruce in there drinking rum in front of the news, and Sofia grabbing the recycling on her way out, and that horrible dog sprawled on his back. Fifteen years earlier, she'd have looked at those windows and imagined Violet Devohr jostling the curtains with a century of pent-up energy. When the oaks leaned toward the house and plastered their wet leaves to the windows, Zee used to imagine that it wasn't the rain or wind but Violet, in there still, sucking everything toward her, caught forever in her final, desperate circuit of the hallways.

They finished painting at two in the morning, and they sat in the middle of the floor and ate pizza. Doug said, "Does it feel more like it's ours now?" And Zee said, "Yes."

At a department meeting later that same week, Zee reluctantly agreed to take the helm of a popular fall seminar. English 372 (The Spirit in the House: Ghosts in the British and American Traditions) consisted of ghost stories both oral and literary. It wasn't Zee's kind of course—she preferred to examine power structures and class struggles and imperialism, not things that go bump in the night—but she wasn't in a position to say no. Doug would laugh when she told him.

On the bright side, it was the course she wished she could have taken herself, once upon a time. Because if there was a way to kill a ghost story, this was it. What the stake did to the heart of the vampire, literary analysis could surely accomplish for the legend of Violet Devohr.

2

Doug worked in secret whenever Zee left the house. The folders on his desk were still optimistically full of xeroxed articles on the poet Edwin Parfitt. And he *was* still writing a book on Parfitt, in that its bones continued to exist, on forty printed pages and two separate diskettes. The wallpaper on his computer (Zee had set it up) was the famous photo of Parfitt kissing Edna St. Vincent Millay on the cheek.

But what Doug was actually sitting down to write, after a respectful silence for the death of both his career and the last shred of his manhood, was book number 118 in the *Friends for Life* series, *Melissa Calls the Shots*. He hid the document on his hard drive in a file called "Systems Operating Folder 30." This book, unlike the Parfitt monograph, even had an actual editor, a woman named Frieda who called once a week to check his progress.

Doug's stopover in the land of preteen literature was only the latest in a wretched chain of events—lack of money, paralysis on the monograph, failure to find employment, surreal indignity of moving into the coach house on Zee's mother's estate—but it would be the last. He would get this done and get paid, and then, because he'd be on a roll, he'd get other things done. He would publish the Parfitt book, he'd land a tenure-track post, and somehow along the way his hair would grow thicker.

He'd found Frieda through his friend Leland, a luckless poet who wrote wilderness adventures at the same press for "two grand a pop." Leland talked like that, and he drank whiskey because Faulkner had. "They give you the entire plot," he said, "and you just stick to the style. Really there *is* no style. It's refreshing." Leland claimed they took a week each, and Doug was enchanted with the idea of shooting out a fully formed book like some kind of owl pellet. He hadn't written fiction since grad school, when he'd published a few experimental stories (talking trees, towns overcome with love) that now mortified him, even if Zee still adored them. But these publication credentials, plus Leland's endorsement, landed him the gig. He knew nothing about wilderness adventure, but the press was suddenly short a writer for their middle-grade girls' series—and desperate enough to hire a man. And so. Here he was.

The money would be nice. The coach house was free, but not the food, the car payments, the chiropractor. And that last wasn't optional: If Dr. Morsi didn't fix Doug's back twice a week, he'd be unable to sit and work on anything at all. Frieda sent him four other books from the series, plus a green binder labeled "THE FFL BIBLE" with fact sheets on each character. "Melissa *hates* dark chocolate!" came several bullet points above "Melissa's grandfather, Boppy, died of cancer in #103."

"The first chapter," Frieda told him on the phone, "introduces the conflict, which is the Populars on the team, will Melissa ever be goalie, *et cetera*." He'd never met Frieda, but imagined she wore pastel blazers. "The second chapter is where you recap the founding of the club. Our return readers skip it, so you can plagiarize chunks from other volumes. The rest will be clear from the outline. Everything's wrapped up at the end, but there's that thread you leave hanging, 'What's wrong with Candy,' which is where 119 picks up; 119 is being written already, so—as we tell all our writers—it's important you don't make uninvited changes to the world of the series." Doug took comfort in the fact that this was clearly a memorized speech, part of the formula.

He dumped the books at the thrift store, hid the "Bible" pages among some old tax forms, then went to the library every day for a week to skim the series.

And meanwhile, the little house was strangling him, tightening its screws and hinges. There was an infestation of ladybugs that spring, a plague straight out of Exodus. Not even real ladybugs but imposter Japanese beetles with dull copper shells, ugly black underwings jutting out below. Twice a day, Doug would suck them off the window screens with the vacuum attachment, listening as each hit the inner bag with a satisfying *thwack*. The living ones smelled like singed hair—whether from landing too close to lightbulbs or from some vile secretion, no one was sure. Sometimes Doug would take a sip of water and it would taste burnt, and he would know a bug had been in that glass, swimming for its life and winning.

There was a morning in May—notable only for Zee storming around in full academic regalia, late for commencement—when Doug, still in bed, nearly blurted it all out. Wasn't it a tenet of a good marriage that you kept no secrets beyond the gastrointestinal? Hundreds of movies and one drunken stranger in a bar had told him as much. And so he almost spilled it, casual-like, as she tossed shoes from the closet. "Hey," he might have said, "I have this project on the side." But he knew the look Zee would give: concern just stopping her dark eyes from rolling to the ceiling. A long silence before she kissed his forehead. He didn't blame her. She'd married the guy with the fellowship and bright future and trail of heartbroken exes, not this schlub who needed sympathy and prodding. When she dumped her entire purse out on the bed and refilled it with just her keys and wallet, he took it as a convenient sign: *Shut the hell up, Doug.* He might have that tattooed on his arm one day.

Zee's mother, Gracie, would sometimes include the two of them in her parties, where she'd steer Doug around by the elbow: "My son-in-law Douglas Herriot, who's a fantastic *poet*, and you know, I think it's *wonderful*. They're in the coach house till he's all done writing. It's my own little NEA grant!" Doug would mutter that he wasn't a poet at all, that he was a "freelance PhD" writing *about* a poet, but no one seemed to hear.

The monograph was an attempt to turn his anemic doctoral dissertation on Edwin Parfitt into something publishable. Parfitt was coming back into style, to the extent that dead, marginal modernists can, and if Doug finished this thing soon he could get in on the first wave of what he planned, in job interviews, to call "the Parfitt renaissance." The dissertation had been straight analysis, and Doug wanted to incorporate some archival research, to be the first to assemble a timeline of the poet's turbulent life. In her less patient moments, Zee accused him of trying to write a biography—academically uncouth and unhelpful career-wise— but Doug didn't see what harm it would do to set some context. And the man's life story was intriguing: Eddie Parfitt (Doug couldn't help but use his nickname, mentally—after nine years of research he felt he knew the guy) was wealthy, ironic, gay, and unhappy, a prodigy who struggled to fulfill his own early promise. He committed suicide at thirty-seven after his lover died in the Second World War. Parfitt had left few personal records, though. Nor had he flitted about the Algonquin Round Table and cracked wise for posterity. Entire periods—the publication gap between 1929 and late 1930, for instance, after which his work became astonishingly flat—lacked any documentation whatsoever.

Not that it mattered now.

Each morning, as Doug switched off his soul and settled in to write (*"Twelve-year-old Melissa Hopper didn't take 'no' for an answer,"* the thing began), he imagined little Parfitt stuffed in the bottom desk drawer on those diskettes, biding his time between the staplers, choking with thirst. The ladybugs hurled their bodies against his desk lamp, and it sounded like knocking—like the ghost of Parfitt, frantically pounding against the wood.

In the brief window between commencement and the start of
Zee's summer teaching, Gracie invited them to the big house for
brunch. They ate on the back terrace overlooking the grounds—
the paths, the fountain, the fish ponds. It was like the garden
behind a museum, a place where art students might take picnic
lunches. Bruce, Gracie's second husband, had conveniently excused himself to make his tee time when Gracie announced that
she had invited Bruce's son and daughter-in-law to move into the
coach house too.

"It's really a two-family house," she said, "and what was done,
way back, was to keep the gardener's family there as well as the
driver's, and they all shared the kitchen. Can you believe, so
many servants? I couldn't manage."

Zee didn't put the butter dish down. "Mom, I've met Case
twice. We're strangers." Bruce's children had always lived in Texas.

"Yes," Gracie said, "and it's a shame. Didn't you dance with
him at our wedding, Zilla? You'd have been in college, the both
of you. He's quite athletic."

"No."

"Well he's out of work. He lost five million dollars and they
fired him. Miriam's a wonderful artist, but it doesn't support them,
you know how *that* is, so they need the space as much as you."

Doug managed to nod, and hoped Zee wouldn't hold it
against him.

"So they'll both hang around the house all day," Zee said.

"Well yes, but it shouldn't bother you, as you'll be at work. It
only concerns Douglas. He could even write about them!" Gracie
rubbed the coral lipstick off her mug and smoothed her hair—
still blonde, still perfect. "And something will open up at the
college for Douglas, I'm sure of it. Are you asking for him?"

"Really," Doug said, "I don't mind. I can get used to anything."

That afternoon, Doug watched his wife from the window above his desk. She stood on the lawn between the big house and the coach house. Anyone else might have paced. For Zee, stillness was the surest sign of stress. She stared at the coach house as if she might burn it down. As if it might burn *her* down.

She wouldn't let herself pitch a fit. At some point she and Gracie had come to the tacit agreement that no actual money or property would pass between them. It was the apotheosis of that old-money creed that money should never be discussed: In this family, it couldn't even be *used*. Doug had doubts whether Zee would even accept her eventual inheritance, or just give it directly to some charity Gracie wouldn't approve of. She was a Marxist literary scholar—this was how she actually introduced herself at wine and cheese receptions, leaving Doug to explain to the confused physics professor or music department secretary that this was more a theoretical distinction than a political one—and having money would not help her credibility. But she had accepted the house.

And now this.

The Texans were just *there* one Tuesday in June when Doug returned from the gym. He picked a box off the U-Haul lip and carried it up to the kitchen, which sat between the two second-floor apartments. Doug loved the feel of an upstairs kitchen, of looking out over the driveway as he flipped pancakes.

A woman with curly brown hair stood on the counter in cutoffs and a tank top, arranging plates in a high cupboard. He put the box down softly, worried that if he startled her, she'd fall. He waited, watching, which seemed somehow inappropriate, and he was about to clear his throat when she turned.

"Oh!" she said. "You're—Hey!" He offered a hand, but she shook it first, then realized what it was for and held on tight as she hopped to the floor. She was a bit younger than Doug and Zee, maybe twenty-eight. And tiny. She came to his armpit. "Miriam, obviously. I hope we're not in your way. I had to scoot some glasses over."

"Doug Herriot," he said, and wondered at his own formality. "I can clear out the lower cupboards. You'll never reach that."

"I'm not so tall, am I! But Case is. We'll be fine." She opened the box on the table, saw it contained clothes, and closed it again. "This is a hell of a place."

He looked out the window and laughed. "Yeah, it's not subtle."

"Oh, I meant *this* place!" She tapped the open cabinet door. "This is quarter sawn oak!"

Doug had no idea what she meant, but he nodded. He wasn't surprised that the kitchen should be well built; the same architect had designed both houses, and presumably the same carpenters and brick layers had constructed them. The stone wall that bordered the estate also formed the eastern wall of the coach house, or at least its ground floor. The second story rose above that, making the structure look from the road like a child's playhouse perched atop the wall. Really it was quite large. The ground floor had at first been open garage space, with two arched entrances for cars. Gracie and her first husband, Zee's father, had the arches filled in with glass panels, and stuck a sunporch on the back. Why they bothered was unclear, except that in the post-chauffeur sixties they'd wanted an attached garage on the big house and felt they ought to transform the old one into something useful and rentable.

The estate had belonged to Gracie's family all along—the Devohrs, though Gracie never used her maiden name. The Devohrs sat firmly in the second tier of the great families of the last century, not with the Rockefellers and Vanderbilts of the world but certainly shoulder-to-shoulder with the Astors, the Fricks, and were lesser known in these parts only by virtue of their Canadian roots. Toronto was hardly Tuxedo Park. Of those families, though,

only the Devohrs were so continually subject to scandal and tragedy and rumor. An unkind tabloid paper of the 1920s had run a
headline about the "Devohrcing Devohrs," and the name had
stuck. So had the behavior that prompted it.

   Before that infamy, back in 1900, Augustus Devohr (unfocused son of the self-made patriarch), wanting to oversee his
grain investments more closely, had built this castle near Lake
Michigan, thirty miles straight north of Chicago. By 1906, after
his wife killed herself in the house—the suicide that had so bothered an adolescent Zee—he wanted nothing more to do with the
Midwest or its crops. In either a fit of charity or a deft tax dodge,
Augustus allowed the home to be used for many years as an artists' colony. Writers and painters and musicians would stay, ex-
penses paid, for one to six months. And—a knife in Doug's
heart—Edwin Parfitt himself had visited the colony, had worked
and lived right behind one of those windows, though Doug would
never know which one. It was the real reason Doug had even
agreed to move into the coach house: as if the proximity would,
through some magical osmosis, help his research.

   Miriam climbed back on the counter, her small legs folding
and then unfolding like a nimble insect's. She redid her ponytail.
She wasn't exactly attractive, Doug decided (he'd been deliberating, against his will), but she had an interesting face with a jutting chin, eyes bright like a little dog's. And as soon as he thought
it, he recognized it. It was the beginning of a thousand love stories. ("She wasn't beautiful, but she had an interesting face, the
kind artists asked to paint.") And uninvited, the next thought
bore down: He was supposed to fall in love. It wasn't true, and it
wouldn't happen, but there it was, and it stuck. Anyone watching
him in a movie would *expect* him to fall in love, would wait patiently through the whole bag of popcorn. He tried to push the
thought away before she turned again, before she saw it on his
face. He excused himself and left the room.

3

Doug was reading in bed when Zee got home. She closed the door. "Did you see them?"

"I met her—Miriam—and she's okay. She's small. But then I stayed in here working. I'm sure we don't have to whisper."

It was probably true—the two bedrooms were at opposite ends of the second floor. Each apartment had a large entry room, which would once have been the sitting area but which Doug and Zee used as a study, desks under both windows. Before the Texans came, they would use the other apartment for laundry folding or exercise or sex.

"You just hid in here? Did you meet Case?"

"I didn't want to make them feel they were invading. You know, like if I sat and watched them unpack. Right?"

She was disappointed. She'd wanted the whole story, the gruesome details. Something concrete at which to direct her anger.

She had managed to stay calm and pleasant all day. She had forced herself to smile when Sid Cole had called to her across the lawn—in front of students—that "Marxists don't drink cappuccino!" She'd even raised her coffee cup into the air. She had laughed out loud: Ha!

The irony was not lost on her that she, willfully mistaken for a Communist by her most obnoxious colleagues, should be allergic to communal living.

"Does she have a Texas accent?"

"No, actually. I don't think so. Not really, more like—I don't know."

What was wrong with him?

She said, "Did she take Case's last name?"

"I have no idea."

"That would have a horrible sound. Miriam Breen. It's too ugly."

"Yes, it's ugly."

Zee changed and found her glasses and lay on top of the covers, underlining an article in *The New York Review of Books*.

"It should give you some impetus to write," she said. "The more annoying these people are, the better."

"I'm writing every day."

She hoped it was true. The worst part of her wanted to stand over his shoulder as he wrote, to suggest commas. Once, early in grad school, she'd tidied up a paper of his when he was out for the night. He'd never noticed.

Doug flipped himself around on the bed and started rubbing her feet.

"Doug," she said. "Stop it."

"I can't hear you."

"I have stuff to do."

"I'm sorry, I'm way down here by your feet, and I can't hear you."

He peeked over the crest of her knees like a groundhog, then ducked down. He did it till she laughed. She put the journal down, and he worked his way up.

4

ase and Miriam and Zee were at the table when Doug
came out the next morning, fortunately having remembered to put on pants. Case was tall, as Miriam had said,
and deeply tan with big, straight teeth. Polo shirt and flip-flops.
In a movie, Doug thought, he'd be the guy who beats up John
Cusack. The men shook hands, and Doug found himself giving
Miriam a ridiculous little salute. He began making eggs, just so he
had something to do.

Zee was dressed for teaching her summer session class, silk
blouse tucked into her skirt in such a tidy way that if he hadn't
known better, Doug would have imagined her morning routine
involved duct tape. "So," she said, "I hear you're searching for a
job, Case."

Case looked up from his cereal, leaned back, and regarded Zee
as if she'd ruined his beach vacation by asking where he planned
to be five years from next Thursday. "I'm in no rush," he said. And
then he laughed, releasing them all abruptly from whatever contempt he'd held them in. Doug decided, in that moment, that he
despised Case Breen.

"He needs a few weeks to recoup," Miriam said. "We're aiming
for September."

"Gonna get some exercise. Might shop for a new car."

Zee said, "What's wrong with your old one?"

Miriam put her hand on Case's shoulder and said, "I hope we

won't be in the way. I know you're making a sacrifice. I was going to set up on the sunporch to work, but only if it's okay with you."

Doug gestured to the constellation of ladybugs on the ceiling. "You won't be more trouble than our other houseguests." No one laughed.

"Or the ghost," Zee added, and smiled as if she'd just played some kind of trump card, as if Case and Miriam would now spring up and flee. "Violet mostly sticks to the big house, but you'll hear her knocking on the windows some nights. You'll get used to it."

Miriam said, "Oh, I *love* ghost stories. I do."

Zee picked up her keys. "I'm kidding, of course."

She left, and Doug ate his eggs standing up. Case asked if Doug wanted to join him for a run, and he managed to bow out, blaming his bad knees.

"Suit yourself," Case said, and (Doug could have sworn) glanced at Doug's paunch before leaving the room.

Doug started scrubbing dishes, and a minute later Case appeared down on the drive, changed and stretching his calves. Miriam came over to rinse and dry, and they talked above the sound of the water. He learned that Miriam's art was mixed-media mosaics.

"Most people would call it detritus collage," she said. "But I use classical mosaic techniques. Just using found pieces. I'm always cutting up Case's clothes." She pushed her curls from her face with a wet hand. "Tell me about your poetry."

"No," he said, which she didn't deserve. "Sorry. I'm not a poet. I'm writing *about* a poet. Gracie's mixed up. I didn't mean to shout at you."

She smiled, as if it were regular and amusing for people to make idiots of themselves in front of her. "What poet?"

"Oh. Edwin Parfitt? He was a modernist."

"Sure, right, that one poem! From high school! I mean, not—"

"'Apollo on the Mississippi.'"

"Yes! 'Whose eyes' bright embers gleam.' That one!"

"He was a one-hit wonder. It's his worst poem, but it's all any-one knows. That and his suicide note. He drowned himself in a lake, and the note had instructions for his friends to burn his body on the beach just like the poet Shelley. And they *did* it." He let the soapy water out and sprayed down the basin. All because of that inane thought yesterday, he was aware of the distance between their bodies.

"I'd love to read it," she said. "Your book, not the suicide note." She dried her little red hands. "Well, both."

5

Z ee took two aspirin, forgetting they'd just make her sicker
to her stomach. The cramps might have been from
dehydration, or from the hell of teaching summer school
English to the seventeen-year-olds who were supposed to be experiencing college-level academics but were more interested in
college-level drinking. But the headache was definitely from having her home invaded.

She gave up on grading ("Most people," began one essay on
Heart of Darkness, "will encounter water at some point in their
lives") and stacked the papers neatly on the corner of the desk, so
it would look like a planned installation rather than an abandonment. On top she put the strange metal thing she'd found in the
woods behind the big house that spring. It was probably some sort
of machine part, but she loved the design of it, the waffled roundness, and she loved its thick and ancient rust. She thought of it
as a metal daisy top: six hollow petals around a hollow center. She
stuck a pencil in one of the holes, and now the stack looked complete.

She checked mail and got coffee in the English office. Chantal, the department secretary, was on the phone, so Zee lingered
over a sabbatical notice on the board.

Zee was obsessive about the bulletin board, and about the
campus papers and the department calendar. She figured her job
had two parts: the work part and the career part. The work part

right now was teaching, publishing, flying to petty conferences in depressing university towns. The career part was showing up at concerts and sitting behind the college president, keeping in touch with everyone from grad school. If she could, she'd have hosted dinner parties. It was easy enough to tell her colleagues she and Doug were renting a coach house in town, but it would be far too risky to bring them so close to the Devohr family history. She couldn't imagine the jokes Sid Cole would make if he knew she'd been to the manor born.

Thank God the "Devohr" was buried under her father's name, Grant. She'd been tempted to take Doug's name just to inter the Devohrs one layer further, but she refused to part with that last scrap of her father. She told colleagues, if they asked, that her mother had stayed home, and her father had been a journalist and a recovering alcoholic, all of which was true. Really, she felt she could say "recovered" alcoholic now, in defiance of all the careful AA jargon, because he'd never have the chance to fall off the wagon again, and never had in the twelve years she knew him, not even on the night Nixon was reelected and he was the only man in town hurling books at the TV. He had a lifelong habit of sucking coins—popping a nickel in his mouth and flipping it with his tongue while he wrote or thought—that she figured must have been some kind of crutch. A reminder not to drink, maybe.

Chantal hung up and crossed her eyes at Zee. "Are we working out?" she said.

"I need to punch someone. But working out will suffice."

Chantal had a thousand little braids, and not one was ever askew. She was the most competent person Zee knew—a filing system to rival the FBI's—and Zee liked her better than any actual department member. They did the ellipticals side by side, and Zee told Chantal about the Texans moving in. "I never get along with southern women," she said. "I'm always offending them.

What I see as debate, they see as assault. The worst part is, Doug will fall in love with her." She was whispering. There were students all around.

"Is she pretty?"

"The point is she's *there*."

Chantal was cheating, taking her hands off the grips. "But he's not like that, is he? Your husband?"

"He's so desperate not to work on the Parfitt thing, he'd fall in love with a zebra. He might not *do* anything about it, but he'll fall in love." A woman like Miriam, with the wild eyes and chewed-off fingernails, would fall for anyone who listened to her emote—especially Doug, whose half smile was a sort of magical charm. It had disarmed even Zee. But Doug wouldn't recognize the difference between love and a diversion, would think that just because he hadn't been distracted like this before, there was destiny involved. "You know what his nickname was, in school? Dough. Because he was Doug H., but also because he's just—he's malleable. He's suggestible."

Chantal pushed the button to up her speed. "Keep him on his toes. Not to tell you what to do. But a bored man is—I don't know, isn't there an expression for that?" She laughed. "A bored man is not a good thing."

6

Doug walked to the library, even though he was more inclined to watch morning TV and do half-hearted yoga downstairs. The Texans might not irritate him into working harder, but they would embarrass him out of doing anything else. He even stayed up in the adult section, something he hadn't done since he'd started the *Friends* book.

"I wondered if you had anything on Laurelfield," he said to the reference librarian. "The old artists' colony." He'd asked just a few months ago, but there was always the chance something new had appeared.

Laurelfield was still, technically, the name of the house. Those olden-day Devohrs had named their homes like pets. When Zee and Doug were first dating, Gracie had sent out Christmas cards with an artist's rendering of the estate on the front, the word *Laurelfield* in script beneath. "It looks like the logo of a ham company," Zee had said. "Thank you for buying Laurelfield smoked sausages." It was the first time Doug had fully stopped to think what it meant that his girlfriend's family had spawned five Canadian MPs, that they had namesake buildings and foundations all over Ontario.

The librarian led him to the glass-front cabinet and pulled out four books on local history. The only helpful one was the photo book of local estates he'd seen before, but he sat anyway in a computer chair staring again at the grainy photo dated 1929.

Designed in the English country style by Adler Ross in 1900 for the Devohrs of Toronto, Laurelfield was home to the Laurelfield Arts Colony from 1912 to 1954. Notable residents included the artists Charles Demuth, Grant Wood, and Emil Armin; composer Charles Ives; and poets Marianne Moore, Lola Ridge, and Edwin Parfitt. The home is now again a private residence.

These seven guests, while impressive, were the only seven he'd ever seen listed—and were, in other words, the only ones of note. Perhaps this was why there were no archives, no coffee table books of photographs and reminiscences.

The picture was taken from high up. It showed the north end of the big house, plus the space between the two buildings, filled by a massive, long-gone oak. Doug squinted at the windows, hoping to see lord knows what. Parfitt making out with Charles Demuth, maybe. There, in the bottom right corner, sat the coach house, two cars on the gravel drive in front, the ground floor still open to motor traffic. A man in knickers leaned against the eastern wall near the cars, his hand raised to his mouth. Smoking. By his feet, a blur of a dog. Doug knew the man wasn't Parfitt, though he couldn't say exactly why. The prosaic hat, perhaps, or some intangibly heterosexual angle to the hips, or the fact that here he stood by the cars when Parfitt would be upstairs on his bed, ankles crossed, gin in his left hand, black fountain pen in his right.

Doug had no idea when Parfitt was actually in residence at Laurelfield. He visited both Laurelfield and the MacDowell Colony in New Hampshire throughout the twenties and thirties, but the Parfitt archive at Princeton mentioned Laurelfield only once, in a letter from 1942: "I haven't been as sick since one summer at Laurelfield," he wrote to his niece, "and this time it's worse because I'm getting old, Annette, I am." When Doug had found that reference, he was already dating Zee, had already seen the

Laurelfield Christmas card. He double-checked with her, as casually as he could ("Didn't you say your house was an artists' colony?
At some point?") and when Zee confirmed, it wasn't that Doug
saw her as a ticket to Laurelfield but that he took the connection
for a sign. Here was this woman whose childhood bedroom might
have been the very room in which Parfitt had written! The stars
were aligned, and he should marry her. Zee, no Parfitt fan, was
less impressed by the coincidence. "Lots of people stayed there,"
she said. "He was probably in Grand Central Station at some
point, too. That doesn't make it hallowed ground."

Doug xeroxed the picture and started home. It was blazing
hot, the time of day when more reasonable nations took a siesta.
He felt productive, for a moment, the xerox folded in his pocket,
until it hit him that *this* was his way of "getting to work" on what
should have been hard-nosed textual analysis: copying a picture
of a house that he could see out his bedroom window anyway.

Halfway back, Case passed him running, on the opposite side
of the street. Shining in the sun. Looking like he belonged in this
town, in a way Doug never would.

7

Z ee decided not to drink at the lunch.

The eight department members still in town were squeezed into the back room of Pasquali's with spouses. Zee did not invite Doug to these events, preferring to talk him up in his absence. She'd created, over the past year, a mythical Doug whose earth-shattering book would soon be completed, whose thesis adviser wanted him to return to teach in Madison.

The celebration of Sid Cole's twentieth year at the college (his thirty-fifth year teaching overall) had been put off for a few weeks by Sid's gall bladder surgery. But now here he was, with his caterpillar eyebrows and obsessive lip-licking, as sprightly and malevolent as ever. Old age turns the most horrible people into "characters," their misanthropy masquerading as crustiness. Sid was known to offer students a five-minute break in the middle of long afternoon classes, then mock anyone with the nerve to leave. The adoring faithful stayed and gleefully jotted "Coleisms" in their notebooks.

Cole was to blame, in Zee's mind, for Doug's joblessness. Two years ago, right after the college hired her, they offered Sid Cole's job to Doug. Cole had announced his retirement, and Doug was the perfect fit. Then, the day before Doug was to meet with the dean and talk salary, twelve of Cole's students showed up at the old man's house with a bag of letters. They quoted Milton and Frost and Thoreau. They convinced him to stay. Zee's contract was already signed, and Doug's only other leads were on the east coast. Now, even if Cole retired, Doug—two years and zero publications later—was significantly less qualified for the job than he'd been back then.

Two things were necessary: a vaguely Doug-shaped hole, and a Doug who could account, impressively, for the past two years. The latter she had some control over; he'd finish the book this summer, even if she had to write the damn thing for him. The former was harder, but there were two small colleges in this town alone and a dozen more in Chicago, any one of which might become an option. It seemed even the adjuncts had sunk in their teeth, though, and weren't budging.

And Cole announced, regularly, that now he was in for life. "They'll have to carry me out on my desk chair," he said, "exams clutched to my chest with rigor mortis."

Zee sat between Ida Hayes and Jerry Keaton, grateful at least for her free pasta. Golda Blum, the acting chair, made a toast to "Sid's illustrious decades of terrorizing students and baffling his colleagues." It was an unspoken rule that to toast Cole was to roast him, and that he in turn would grunt and curse like the village drunk. Hoffman and Grasso stood to read a poem they'd written in a fit of Chianti-induced cleverness: "Old King Cole was a Derrida soul, and a Derrida soul was he—and he called for his Yeats and he called for his Poe and he called for his lady-friends three!"

Cole stood to give a brief speech about how he planned, in his twenty-first year at the college, to scare each and every student out of his classes, until he was left with "exactly one attractive and intelligent specimen that will grade its own papers and massage my neck." When even Golda laughed, Zee pretended to as well. Cole must have felt his age protected him against rumors of impropriety, though Zee understood there were plenty of whispers about the man back in the eighties. She'd heard a senior boy claim he knew "for a fact" that the policy of leaving office doors cracked during student conferences could be traced to Cole's misbehavior some fifteen years earlier. He had been married once, briefly, but by the time he came to campus he'd long been a swinging bachelor—attractive, back then, too—so rumors were bound to follow him. The fact that the rumors *stuck*, though, spoke to his behavior, not his erstwhile good looks. Jerry Keaton, for instance, with his kind eyes and soft voice and pictures of his toddler son all over his office, would never attract such talk.

Zee got through lunch by pretending it was Cole's retirement party. And when that fantasy failed, she imagined relaying one of her own less amusing Cole anecdotes. She might tell about his sophomore advisee who came to Zee crying, after she'd shown Cole a course list including Stage Makeup for her double major in theater. "So you're learning to put on makeup?" he'd asked. The girl had shrugged and said, "Basically." He took her face in his hand, turned her head to the side, and said, "Well, it's about damn time." But even if Zee had worked up the nerve to tell this story, to say "Let's raise a glass to the most insensitive man in Illinois," the others would have chuckled, waiting with bated breath for the old man's reply.

Cole, she realized, was talking to her from down the table, pointing his empty fork at her chest. "Comrade Grant is uncharacteristically withdrawn today," he called. "I suspect she's planning her Marxist revolution!" Before the laughter died down, he continued. "This is why I'll never leave. She'll replace me with her minions and all the seniors will take 'Why Dickens Was a Stalinist.'"

She felt, as she often did around Cole, like a child outwitted by a clever uncle for the amusement of other adults. Mercifully, the conversation swelled again, and the waiter brought coffee. Zee wished he would sweep her up with the empty wine glasses and carry her back to the kitchen and plunge her into the sink, where she could remain till the lunch was over.

The other day, her mother had called her office number. "I was thinking," she said. "Why couldn't Douglas work in Admissions? Because that doesn't require you to publish, does it?"

"Admissions is bubbly twenty-four-year-olds with diverse backgrounds."

"Well he's diverse. He certainly didn't grow up here." Zee had said she had to go, and her mother said, "It's not going to fall in his lap, dear. To be perfectly frank, I don't know what good that biography will do. There are so many books nowadays! But we'll think of something."

Sitting there sober with her drunken department, Zee *did* think of something. Doug was a man who needed a job. Cole was a man who did not deserve the job he had. And here she was, passively wishing. And leaving Doug home alone all day with that woman. When Chantal had said to keep him on his toes, she'd probably meant something along the lines of meeting him at the door in lingerie. But Zee had more at her disposal than underwear. And she knew how to do more than grade papers and wait.

She turned her tiramisu slab on its side to cut it better. She had nearly forgotten who she was.

8

They were all due at the big house at six, for cocktails and dinner to welcome the Texans "officially." The Breens, Doug tried calling them in his head, but to him Bruce and Gracie were the Breens, so Texans it was. Maybe if he started calling Case "Tex," he'd like him better.

In the two weeks they'd shared the house, the couples had fallen into a routine of cooking separate dinners, perhaps overlapping in the kitchen for five or ten awkwardly sociable minutes. Doug and Zee found themselves eating takeout downstairs more and more.

Zee came into the bathroom when Doug was brushing his teeth. She said, "I have some motivation for you. I think something might be happening with Cole. This might be his last year."

Doug made a mouth-full-of-toothbrush noise. Zee wasn't often prone to wishful thinking, but Doug knew enough about Cole not to get his hopes up.

They all four walked up the drive together, Doug carrying a bottle of wine too cheap for Gracie and Bruce to drink. They passed Case's new car: a black 2000 BMW 3 Series convertible, liquid-shiny, parked beside their own weathered Subaru. Doug had gladly joined in Zee's eye rolling, wondering how Case thought he could blow through his savings, how weirdly sure he was of landing a new job the moment he started looking. How a convertible would get him through a Chicago winter. But privately, all Doug wanted to do was lick the hubcaps.

He marveled anew at the way the thick ivy turned the big house into an organic entity. The house turned brown every fall, it died every winter, and by late spring it was in full foliage.

The front door was locked, and so they stood waiting as Hidalgo, Gracie's standard poodle ("Is there something bigger than standard?" Doug had asked Zee several times now. "Because he's really not normal") flung himself at the window again and again, claws scraping the glass.

"Oh God," Miriam said, "I *hate* poodles."

"Just wait," Doug said.

Bruce answered the door himself, tossing Hidalgo peanuts to keep him at bay. "Welcome!" He gave each woman a long kiss on the wrist like a lecherous Austrian prince, pumped Doug's hand, and slapped his arm around Case. "My boy!" he shouted, as if he'd never talked to his son before in his life.

Bruce was red-faced, with big cheeks and a ring of white hair and a belly of hardened fat. Later, he would bully Doug into smoking a cigar with him out back. But he was a good man, and Doug hadn't really had a father, so the handshakes, the cigar, the talk about bumping into the Clintons on Martha's Vineyard—he found them weirdly thrilling.

Doug saw Hidalgo advancing and kneed him in the chest before the claws could make contact with his shoulders, before the beast could leave welts down his arms again. Hidalgo was not one of those poodles with the haircuts. He was shaggy, fur the color of a rotten peach, breath like hot compost. Bruce threw another peanut.

Gracie stood waiting in the library, in a long, gauzy green thing that Doug's mother would have called a Hostess Dress. Zee kissed her cheek. "So you're locking us out now?"

"Bruce," Gracie said, "did you lock the door? The ghost must've done it."

"The ghost only ever does three things," Doug whispered to Miriam. "Closes doors, knocks on things, and flushes toilets."

Miriam whispered back: "Maybe it died from getting locked out of the bathroom."

Bruce mixed everyone gin and tonics without asking, and poured himself his standard glass of Mount Gay rum. "Let me tell you something, though," he said, in a voice that wasn't at all asking permission to let it tell you something. "We're going to need new locks anyway. Y2K, December thirty-one, these fancy security systems are worthless. Crime will shoot up, credit cards won't work, and are you aware, even your *car*, your *car* has a computer. I'm buying a '57 Chevy. No computer, and I've always wanted one anyway. But I'll tell you, no one should be out celebrating that night. *Nuclear power plants*, think about that. Best we can do is hunker down with the canned goods and barricade the doors."

"How festive," Gracie said. Bruce had given the same speech at every opportunity for the past year, but this was the first time he'd mentioned the nuclear plants. "Let's change the subject, shall we? Something less apocalyptic. Case, how's your job search?"

Case, sprawling on the couch, stretched his legs out. "I got some fish in the water," he said.

Zee said, "Some lines?"

"One could say that, Zee. One could say that."

Bruce said, 'I'm going to introduce him to Clarence Mahoney. Big guy in Chicago. Lots of projects, and none of this dot-com nonsense. Watch what happens to those dot-com folks, January one."

Case turned to Doug. "Tell us what your poems are about," he said. "Nature, or what?"

Doug tried to hide the ice cube under his tongue while he talked. "I'm actually writing a monograph. A book. On a poet named Edwin Parfitt. He stayed here a few times, at the arts colony."

"Just imagine," Gracie said, gesturing around the room. "This place filled with painters and musicians!"

"I've been meaning to ask," Doug went on, willing himself not to look at Zee. "What about back in Toronto? There wouldn't be anything from the colony up there, would there? Archives or photos? That got taken back?" He'd asked it before, but her answers were always so evasive that he held out hope she might blurt something different if she was in a good mood, if the weather was right, if she'd had enough to drink. (Once, after champagne, she'd volunteered the story of Zee's birth in fairly graphic detail.) Plus she never seemed to remember that she'd already turned him down.

"Oh, dear God, no. The colony was such a burden to my father, he'd have shredded all that. The woman who ran the place, you know, turned out to be a Communist. And the drinking! It was always in the papers, someone driving into a fence. He was glad to be rid of the whole mess."

Zee would bawl him out when they got home. Not just for bothering her mother, but for grasping at straws. Zee so often had to defend, to people like Sid Cole, her own interest in historicity and context, that she ought to have been sympathetic to Doug's search for something archival. But she saw no similarity.

"So that's when you moved here?" Miriam asked. "After it closed?"

"More or less."

There had been profound resentment in the artistic community back in the fifties, when her father reclaimed the house and moved Gracie in here with her new husband, George, Zee's father. When Doug was engaged to Zee, he had secretly ordered a history of the Devohr family through interlibrary loan. That was the only mention of Gracie at all—the strong implication that her father closed Laurelfield just to get the drinking, womanizing George Grant out of Canada.

"So your job is to write the story of this guy's life?" Case seemed to find this hilarious.

"It's really an analysis of the poems. How his life affected his work."

"Like a term paper," Gracie offered.

"Yes," Doug said, after he drained his glass. "Like a really long high school English paper."

Zee, to his relief, smiled sympathetically from the other couch. She was stunning in her blue sundress, and her collarbones were a work of art.

"Refills," Bruce announced. "Would anyone care to climb Mount Gay with me?"

Doug had been prepared for the line, was always prepared for it, but it was still a struggle not to lose it. And it was a struggle not to look at the flaming, shaking, red spot next to him that was Miriam's face.

Doug stayed quiet through dinner. Sofia, the housekeeper, shuttled back and forth with plates of swordfish and asparagus, lemon sorbet, pineapple cake.

Case was telling them all a story about sailing, something about his buddy getting lost in the Gulf, when he leaned the whole chair back and hit the sideboard behind him, sending a green china vase to the floor and into a million pieces. "I'll—oh, God, I'll—hey, I'll pay for that," Case said.

"With what?" Gracie muttered.

Miriam convinced Sofia to surrender the dustpan so she could sweep the shards herself.

"He gets his coordination from me!" Bruce shouted. "That's why they kicked him off the football team!"

Case looked like he didn't know what to do with his hands, or how to arrange his mouth.

Doug searched for a way to change the subject, but Zee beat him to it. "You do realize that's the ghost behind you," she said to Miriam. "The painting, I mean."

Bruce gave the ancestor a look most men reserved for center-folds. "She's a beauty, isn't she? A *natural* beauty. Nothing fake back then."

"Except the paint," Zee said.

Doug didn't know much about art, but he could recognize that it was a great picture. If he ran into this woman on the street in modern dress, he'd recognize her instantly. Gorgeous, it was true, by any standards. Black hair and dark eyes, like Zee, balanced by the shoulders of a black gown. But somehow profoundly evasive. Some paintings seemed to follow you with their eyes, but this one had the opposite effect: No matter where you stood, Violet woudn't meet your gaze. He couldn't figure out why—he just knew he didn't want to be alone in this room at night.

"Do you mind my asking how she did it?" Miriam said. "How she died?" She was still down on the floor sweeping, a disembod-ied voice.

"I always imagined hanging," Gracie said. "But my family never spoke of it."

"Maybe that's why I'm getting a vibe on the staircases! Maybe she did it from a railing."

Doug hadn't contemplated this before in detail. He'd always imagined her drinking poison quietly in bed. "She might have jumped from a window."

"She'd make a better ghost if she wore white," Case offered.

Miriam stood up with her dustpan and looked at the painting. "She's got me fully convinced."

9

They were all back in the solarium with coffee, windows open, hot night air rolling through. Hidalgo slept on his back. Zee wanted to be home and asleep, but she forced herself to smile at Miriam. "I've peeked at your new project," she said. "I hope you'll hang some of your pieces around the coach house."

"Anything that doesn't sell."

Zee wondered if Miriam had ever sold a piece in her life. The new one was an atrocious swirl of orange with blue and brown things sticking out.

"Tell me, what inspired that orange piece?"

"Oh, it's a fractal! It's basically math, so don't ask me to explain! You can just *see* they're amazing, the colors and symmetry." Zee wanted to shake her. It was her greatest fear for her female students, that they'd end up giggling and apologizing at everything.

Case grinned. "You know what I call those? The barf pictures. It's the barf series." He'd been drunk for a while.

"I'm starting a new bunch, though. Unloved dresses. I'm butchering them and doing tessellation around the forms. If you have any old prom dresses or anything . . . And I have to say, I've never worked better in my life than I have the past few days. This place must have a magic spring under it."

Gracie patted her knees and sat forward. "Miriam, we've got

the perfect little consulting job for you. There's a painting I want to rotate out of storage, and Bruce hates it. The signature is unreadable, so we have just no idea. It's raw, but I think it's sweet."

Bruce loped behind the far couch and returned with a gilt frame, the farmhouse and pasture inside all awkward angles and illogical sunlight. Like the product of an art therapy class at a nursing home. Bruce said, "We should be paying for her opinion. She's an expert, you know."

"We'll pay her with old dresses!" Gracie said. "She can take Zilla's cotillion dress. It's still up in the closet. Remember the yellow one, with the shoulder pads? Oh, it was ghastly! I told you at the time."

Something came to a boil inside Zee's head, some irrational sibling rivalry she'd never had to develop skills for dealing with. She did not need a yellow silk dress from an arcane ritual she'd been forced through at age fifteen, even if Greg Stiefler had kissed her in that same dress on the lawn of the Chippeway Club. "You can't give away my dress," she said.

Bruce said, "I thought you were for the redistribution of goods to the proletariat!"

"Where did you get this?" Miriam asked. She rested the frame on her lap, squinting down at the corner, running a finger over the paint. She pulled her curls back.

Gracie said, "I believe it's left from the colony. *There* you go, Doug! Something from the colony!"

"It *could* be . . ." Miriam said. It obviously pained her to be critical. "This person might have had some natural skill, but no training. The perspective is off."

Case squinted over her shoulder. "Isn't that what the modernists did?"

"Well, not like *this*. I'm just saying it's not likely from the colony."

Gracie flushed and took the painting off Miriam's lap. "Oh,

don't worry, dear. We value your opinion. It's funny, though. George, Zee's father, seemed awfully fond of it. And he was an art critic! He must have seen something there. I wouldn't know one way or the other. Sofia!" Sofia was clearing the sugar and cream. "Can you run to the northwest bedroom, the flowered one, and see if Zilla's old yellow formal dress is still in the closet?"

"Oh, please don't—" Miriam started, but she swallowed her words. Sofia was already gone.

10

(The white skin
Of his inner arm

The back of his neck, where
His hairline rubs his collar

His hipbones

I could drag him to me
By the beltloops)

11

The house had settled into a peaceful rhythm, everyone happily ignoring everyone else. (Sofia, fortunately for all, hadn't found the yellow dress that night. She'd come down with dust in her hair and sweat on her upper lip. "I even look in the old things from forty years ago, all the long gowns!" On a certain level, Doug was disappointed. He'd pay for a glimpse of this ugly dress.)

And then, on Saturday, Case had been out for a long run when Doug and Zee heard him scream so loudly from below that they'd both leapt from the table. They found him crumpled in the doorway. He'd simply missed the step into the house, landed terribly, and his Achilles tendon had snapped and "rolled up like a window blind," according to the medic.

Doug was in the kitchen one morning a few days later when Miriam came up, filled a glass with ice and whiskey, and headed downstairs again. Doug followed a minute later (victim to a potent mix of curiosity and procrastination) and found Case with his leg propped on the ottoman in its blue medical boot, the drink half-drained. Miriam sat cross-legged on the floor, and they were watching a black and white movie. Doug knew Miriam had been renting them all summer—*Sunset Boulevard* and *Top Hat* and *The Big Sleep*—but this was the first time he'd seen Case join her.

"Mind if I take a break down here?" Doug said. Case shrugged
and Miriam said, "Please do." He sat on the arm of the couch,
across from the Morris chair Case had claimed, the one Doug had
come to think of as his own. Doug guessed the chair had been in
the coach house all along. A brass bar for adjusting its hinged
back; worn, cracked leather. He could picture the beleaguered
chauffeur who once sat there to read the paper and dream of sailing to Siam.

Doug said, "What are we watching?"

It was *Bluebeard*, Miriam explained, the 1930 MGM version.
"It was a cursed movie," she said, a few minutes later. Case didn't
seem to mind when she turned the volume down. He was watching his glass, anyway, not the screen. Doug didn't mind either, as
her narrative was more interesting than the film. "Absolutely everyone in it was dead within seven years. That's Renée Adorée,
the French one, and she died of something normal. But the other
one, playing her sister, that's Marie Prevost. She died alone in her
apartment, and her dachshund started to eat her."

"Jesus."

"And John Gilbert, Bluebeard, he was married to Greta
Garbo, but he drank himself to death. And then the German
maid, the one giving the dirty looks?" Miriam usually moved her
hands when she talked, but right now she kept them wrapped
around the remote, as if the actors onscreen were doing the gesturing for her. "That's Marceline Horn. She died the day after
Bluebeard wrapped, and they realized it was from poisoned
makeup in her dressing room. Someone put arsenic in her lipstick. The sicker she got, the worse she looked, so she put on more
and more makeup to cover it up."

"Seriously?"

"There's a scene—I'll show you—in one scene, you can see
she's sick. She was supposed to eat the food, but she couldn't."

Case cleared his throat and said, "You done, babe?"

Miriam stood. She took a moment to tighten her body, to compose a smile. She handed Case the remote and went to the sunporch. Case switched to CNN, where the news was about people building survival shelters in Colorado, taking their millennial fears a few steps further than Bruce.

"Look," Doug said, "I had knee surgery a while back. I know it's—you feel kind of trapped. I know."

Case didn't answer.

12

If she hadn't already decided to take action, two things would have made up Zee's mind. The first was Sid Cole knocking on her office door. He'd climbed all those stairs just to ask if she'd noticed that Jerry Keaton was calling his seminar "The Gay Canon."

"You were at that meeting," she said. "Weren't you?"

"I'm going to teach a class called 'Milton the Marginalized.' How about 'Chaucer, the Forgotten Poet'?"

Zee knew better than to pick a fight, even on someone else's behalf. She said, "If it makes you feel better, I think he's got some Shakespeare sonnets on the syllabus."

"Haaa!" Cole made a great show of collapsing against her wall. "Shakespeare, that famous queer. The Pansy of Stratford-on-Avon."

The second thing was that Doug had begun working harder on the monograph. The very day after she told him something might be happening with Cole, she came home to find him still at the computer at five thirty, still in the boxers and undershirt he'd slept in. He'd forgotten to eat lunch. It almost broke her heart, to see him working this hard on something no one really cared about, something no one but Zee was waiting for. (The book wasn't for the masses, but for the fifteen people in the world who already knew everything about Parfitt, and the hiring committees that would never read it but would care that he'd written it.) She couldn't bear if his effort were all for nothing.

It was funny how much she'd hated Doug when she met him in grad school. He had that lingering, sideways half smile that so often presaged trouble: Here was a man who'd make you feel like the center of the universe, until, just after you'd become hopelessly attached, you realized he looked this way at all women. Besides which he had questionable taste in both shirts and poetry (Edwin Parfitt was a poet her father had once rightly called "miniscule"), and he'd somehow conned all the professors into believing he was the greatest student ever to walk through the program. She invited him to her February spaghetti party along with everyone else, but she'd been rude enough to him over the past six months that she was shocked when he showed up. He held out a bottle of sake, which he told her he'd brought precisely so she couldn't serve it with spaghetti. "You have to save it for yourself."

Much later, as the lingerers helped clean up, his wayward elbow knocked a picture frame off her end table, and although the glass was fine, the frame, made of porcelain, had cracked into quarters. The picture was the one of herself, age five, reading *Green Eggs and Ham* to her father. She didn't want him to fix it. "I *know* you have superglue," he said. "Don't lie to me." And long after everyone else had gone, he sat on the couch holding pieces together until the glue was set and the thing was whole, if spiderwebbed. "She's not quite seaworthy," he said. He put it in the middle of the coffee table, a sort of offering.

It was certainly not his macho insistence on solving her problems that won her over—she did not see herself as a fragile thing that needed fixing—but the fact that he seemed so determined to make her not hate him. It became hard not to root for him. It was another six months before they became romantically involved, but the dots weren't hard to connect. Was there much distance between rooting for someone and loving him? Was there any difference at all, even now?

13

Five weeks in (and a week overdue) Doug was still stuck on the soccer team tryout, so he was going back to chapter two, which he'd saved because it was easiest. This was the plagiarism bit, the part that necessitated the presence of the actual *Friends for Life* books. He'd borrowed several from the library, and he placed pens across the pages of each to hold them open.

The first sentence of chapter two was always something like "It seemed the club had been together forever, thought Candy [or Molly, or Melissa] gazing at the faces of her five friends." Doug started with, "They had so many memories together, these six friends, and as Melissa looked into their faces, she was transported back to that day when they first formed their club."

He moved on to his descriptions of each girl. By the time he got to Cece ("She was the crazy one of the group," the others uniformly read. "She even showed up at school once wearing her brother's army jacket as a skirt!") he was punchy and decided he'd venture into new territory. "Crazy old Cece," he wrote, "had started a business of writing poems on her friends' hands. She charged ten cents a line and had already made enough for a new pair of earrings!"

And so of course it would happen to be this particular day that Miriam knocked softly behind him. He managed to close the computer window, but not the books. He swiveled, hitting his knee on an open drawer.

"I'm on a quest," she said. She held out a small, orangish-red piece of glass. "I'm searching for absolutely anything in this color."

"Let's look." He led her quickly into the bedroom. Of course there was nothing orange, and now he was just staring at the unmade bed. Doug knelt to examine the stack of books under his nightstand. He rifled through his own laundry basket, hoping not to be faced with the dilemma of dirty boxers in just the right shade. He moved to Zee's dresser—as if she'd ever let Miriam use her jewelry—but Miriam was gone. He found her back in the study, in his desk chair.

"I used to love these!" she said. She was holding *Candy Takes the Cake*. "God, these have been around forever!"

Doug sank to the floor, where all he could do was laugh. "Don't you want to know why I have them?"

"I figured it wasn't my business. I was looking for orange covers, but I see they're library books. Is this . . . research for the monograph?"

"Oh, Christ. Yeah. So. The monograph is apparently titled *Melissa Calls the Shots*," he said. "Number 118. I've never done this before. It's just for the money."

"I'd *hope* so."

"You're the only one who knows. Zee would kill me for not working on Parfitt. There *is* an actual book I'm neglecting. A serious book."

"You don't call this serious? Listen: 'Lauren might have forgotten a lot of math that summer, but one thing she learned was this: She would never take the Terrible Triplets camping again.' That's poetry!"

He stood and swiped at the book, but she held it out of reach. "Please don't say anything."

"We'll make a deal. Get me something orange, and promise to let me read your Parfitt thing *and* this thing too. It's hard to sit on such juicy gossip."

Doug found her an orange bank-logo pencil and an orange ad page from *The New Yorker*, and he suggested she might scan the storage room downstairs for seventies-vintage upholstery.

He couldn't concentrate after that. He spent the rest of the morning vacuuming ladybug carcasses from behind the furniture.

14

Zee knew Sid Cole would be out to dinner with the pro-
vost. And she guessed correctly that he'd fill the time between his late class and the seven o'clock reservation with
the office hours he always complained were unnecessary for summer students. He sat snacking and grading and growling at any
hapless teenager who dared disturb his peace. Zee stuck her head
in to ask if he had any papers she could recycle for him. The man
had famously refused the college-issued bin and threw everything
from root beer bottles to old issues of *PMLA* into the black can
under his desk. He smiled up at her, his mouth full of pretzel.

"You are a hardboiled egg, Zsa-Zsa. A hardboiled egg." Last
spring he'd started amusing himself by supplying ridiculous endings for her initial, as if he'd never seen her full name on articles
and campus directories

She made three more trips down from her office and past his
second floor one, returning from the student snack bar with a
newspaper, then a coffee, then a brownie. By six forty-five his was
the last light on, and by six fifty he had gone, leaving his door
closed but unlocked. It was lucky, but it also meant he'd be back:
For years he'd done all his writing in his office at night. She had
an hour though, at least.

His computer was on, as she'd hoped. The air-conditioning
blasted. The rumor, according to Chantal, was that he kept the
room cold so he could see the girls' nipples through their shirts.

"Has anyone reported it?" Zee had asked.

"Oh, it's just what the kids say. How would they prove something like that?"

Zee jiggled the mouse to wake the computer, and went online, relieved that his Internet was even hooked up. Cole was largely computer illiterate, using his new, department-purchased iMac for nothing more than typing.

She spent the next hour downloading the most explicit free pornography she could find. She was careful to avoid anything potentially illegal (as much as she loathed Cole, she didn't want him arrested), but focused on college-aged girls, on sites that claimed "She Just Turned 18 and She's Wet for You!" The downloading was painfully slow, but she managed to save thirty pictures in a folder labeled "Photoedit"—easy enough to find if someone was searching, but nothing Cole would notice himself.

It was funny: As she slunk out the door, she felt some feminist guilt over the pornography itself, the girls who probably weren't eighteen at all but sixteen with drug problems, but she felt no moral guilt about the act of sabotage, about advancing her husband's career by less than legitimate means. She felt less like Machiavelli than Robin Hood, taking from the rich and giving to the poor. And helping the department, too, and the students. Cole was a parasite, a toxin, a cancer cell. Zee wasn't upsetting the universe, but balancing it.

She did the same thing on Thursday, when Cole simply left his office unlocked for the night, and again the following Wednesday. It would look better if they were downloaded on more than one occasion—less like sabotage, more like porn addiction.

Meanwhile, she told the following story to her classes, to Chantal, to three different colleagues, and to all the college students she could find who'd stayed in town as lab assistants or nannies: "You won't believe this, but I've heard one of our

summer kids has Cole using the Internet! He needed to buy
pants, but he hates running into students in the stores, so apparently this lovely young woman showed him how to shop online
at L.L.Bean. Really she did it *for* him, but he was sitting right
there. He was worried about getting lost on the Internet, so she
showed him the 'Home' button. He goes, 'So I just click my heels
together three times?' He said he was going to look up White Sox
scores. I think he might be hooked!"

Her colleagues believed it, even Chantal believed it, because
despite Zee's abiding hatred for the man, she'd been careful never
to say a quotable word against him, careful to throw him an acer-
bic line when she passed his office.

If anyone teased Cole about online shopping he'd respond that
he never used the Internet—but they'd take it as another of his
jokes, more crustiness on top of the crust that was Cole.

On Sheridan Road, the traffic was stopped. No way to turn her
Subaru around. She waited and cursed her luck and tried to see
what kind of flashing lights those were, so far ahead.

When the cars finally oozed forward, she rubbernecked with
everyone else. A fire truck, and, in front of it, a little black BMW,
its hood charred and smoldering. No collision, no dents. Just one
of those burst-into-flame scenarios.

She wouldn't have recognized the man who sat folded on the
curb, head in his hands, if it weren't for the blue medical boot on
his foot, the crutches stacked neatly at his side.

15

Doug turned in *Melissa Calls the Shots* just twelve days overdue, and after he'd finished some quick revisions for Frieda he received an actual two thousand dollar check in the mail, followed by the contract to complete two more books before the end of summer. One was another Melissa book, this time about her work backstage at the school play, and one was a Cece book. "I loved the detail about her poetry business!" Frieda said. "I think you'll have a great ear for her."

The whole week had been hot, but Doug made himself exercise anyway, circling the grounds and stretching. Behind the big house, he stopped to do the back releases Dr. Morsi taught him, then stepped on the fountain lip to stretch his hamstrings.

Miriam had been digging at the back of the fountain, and he nearly stepped in the hole. Apparently she'd been out here breaking old plates when she noticed a different shard, a red and white one, sticking out of the dirt. She'd pulled it out and dug around and found more—not just that one pattern but dozens of other colors of porcelain and glass and terra cotta. She'd excavated about two cubic feet back there. Her own archeological dig. "It's like the house is giving me pieces," she said. "Like they're growing from the ground." ("Or like someone had a really bad temper tantrum once," Zee said. "And broke all the china in the house.")

He'd remembered to bring bread crumbs, and he dropped them in the three koi ponds. How long did koi live? Eighty years?

These ones were enormous and mottled and drowsy, and he liked to imagine Edwin Parfitt feeding them his leftover breakfast.

At the south end of the property, he toed helplessly at the foundations of the studios Gracie tore down in the seventies, when they were past repair—the long one that must have housed several artists, and the small one behind that. Both lay far enough back that the remains weren't eyesores, and Gracie seemed content to wait for erosion and vegetation to swallow them. Even farther in the woods stood a granite statue of a squatting bear, about three feet high, moss covering its right flank. Doug sometimes rubbed its head for good luck. What else were statues for? The one surviving studio, on the other end of the property behind the vegetable gardens, had long ago been converted to a groundskeeper's shed, but Zee remembered her father referring to it as the composer's cottage—which was the only reason Doug hadn't cut through the padlock and scoured the walls for Parfitt-era graffiti.

As he rounded the big house, he saw Sofia heaving paper grocery bags from the back of her van to the garage floor. The driveway was eerily empty: Gracie and Bruce off on separate golf dates, the Subaru with Zee in the city, Case's BMW zapped by the Greek gods. Doug offered to help, but Sofia shook her head. Then she said, "This is ridiculous that Mr. Breen wants."

There must have been twenty bags, from several different stores—Jewel, Dominick's, Sunset, Don's. He righted a Jewel bag that had fallen and saw it was full of blue cylinders of Morton's table salt. So was the next bag over, and the next.

"He is for the end of the world," Sofia said. "On the New Years."

"He's . . . stockpiling salt for the end of the world?"

"Is for take the water out of the food."

"Wow."

"Yes, is wow."

Doug held up his hands as if to say, Hey, he's your employer, not mine. Although Sofia probably saw them all as family, saw Doug as part of this entitled clan as much as anybody. And really, he was. Who was he kidding? Yet as he headed back to the coach house, he felt the urge to call over his shoulder that he'd gone to a crappy public school, that he never had a decent bike, that he was raised on off-brand TV dinners.

Up in the kitchen, he opened a beer and watched Sofia out the window. He could hear her grunting from all the way up here. No, that wasn't right. She was too far, and it was coming from downstairs.

He went back down and found Miriam sobbing on the sun-porch, her face folded into her arms on her card table. He tried hard to walk away.

"Hey," he said, "hey."

"I'm sorry, this is so embarrassing." Miriam sat up, still sobbing, and wiped her face with the bottom of her T-shirt. He was surprised she didn't leave makeup on it—he'd been told women from Texas wore makeup at all times. "This is so stupid."

"I can leave," he said.

"It's—did you hear what happened?"

"Case's car? Yeah, we all heard."

"Oh. No, not that. John F. Kennedy Jr. He was flying his own plane last night, with his wife, and it crashed in the ocean."

"They died?"

"This is the silliest thing to be crying about. I guess I was just a little bit in love with him. Like everybody else, right? I mean, I just always thought someday I'd at least get to *meet* him, and we'd have a really great conversation."

Doug was thinking, on one level, about the Kennedys, about little John-John saluting his father's coffin. On another, much louder level, he was realizing: Miriam is crazy. Miriam is absolutely bat-shit crazy.

He should have seen it before, in the bizarre, clashing mosaics covering the sunporch floor, in her cutting scraps from cracker boxes, her smashing empty wine bottles and saving grape stems. He looked closely now at the two big pieces on the floor. The one that was nearly finished centered around a blue sundress covered almost entirely by other, tiny things—paper, wood, broken plastic toys, beads, a clock hand, pen caps, dried flower petals, paper clips—so that they constituted another dress, a beautiful one, with swimming lines and arcs of light. But there was something insane about it, something that screamed "outsider art," the kind of work made by someone who lived in a cabin and produced her best pieces when she went off her meds.

"You must think I'm crazy," she said.

"No, no, not at all! It's a sad event. That's horrible, that whole family. There was the one who just died on the skis, right? And now this. And he was the best one."

She sniffed wetly. He wanted to leave, but she'd be hurt. So he said, "Did you see what Bruce is making Sofia do?" and told her about the salt for the end of the world.

"Oh, he asked us to store the canned goods! Did you know that? He goes, 'You have all that room on the ground floor, how about we fill you up?' He's worried about mice in the basement at the big house."

"Mice that bite through cans?"

She smiled a little, which was a relief. "Apparently. I mean, I guess there's pasta boxes and stuff. And their pantries are packed already, and he said the attic is full of old furniture and file cabinets Gracie won't throw out."

He laughed, trying to make her laugh. "What *files* could Gracie need? I've never seen that woman touch a piece of paper that wasn't a note to the staff."

"Maybe they're from that arts camp. He said the furniture was. He said there were at least twenty mattresses up there, and headboards and dressers."

"*Really.*" He'd been leaning against the door frame, but now he sat on the floor among the heaps of cloth and shredded magazines.

The vague promise of some artifact of Edwin Parfitt's had hit Doug in the solar plexus, and he felt like a man meeting his former lover on the street, someone he believed he'd forgotten but whose overwhelming effect indicated otherwise.

"Christ," he said. "That old bitch! Listen, you know first of all it wasn't an arts *camp*, it was a major arts colony. Okay, so, no, a minor one, but extremely important, at least in the twenties. I mean, you're an artist: Charles Demuth? Grant Wood? There could be—think what could be *up* there!"

"What do you mean, Charles Demuth? He stayed here? I adore him!"

"I mean his stuff's in the attic."

She looked as if he'd told her JFK Jr. had just swum to shore, shaken but still dreamy.

"Potentially," he added. "But didn't artists do that, sometimes? They'd leave paintings as payment?"

She sunk her head again. "I don't know, Doug, this isn't what it sounded like, with Bruce. He just said there were disgusting file cabinets and the furniture. If there were anything valuable, he'd know."

"But if someone like Demuth just doodled on an envelope! Bruce would have no idea what that even was!" Doug wasn't sure why he was trying to get Miriam interested, since he didn't want her messing this up for him. Maybe he was just irrationally insulted that she wasn't as excited as he was.

He refrained from mentioning Parfitt. If she'd been paying any attention that night at the big house, she'd have heard him say Parfitt stayed there. But then she hadn't even seemed to register that it was a real arts colony. In her short time here, she hadn't struck him as someone terribly curious about much outside her jungle of beads and scraps. She hadn't been out to explore the town, and she never talked on the phone. It had all seemed vaguely charming before, but now, for some reason, it upset him.

He left her to her collages and her weeping, and asked her not to say anything about the files.

"More secrets!" she said. He couldn't read her tone. "What fun."

(There was a man
I wanted to kiss
On the eyes
And there was a man
I needed to pin down.
There was a man
I wanted to smash
Into my breasts and there was a man
Whose lips were pillows. Here
Is what I want to do
To you: throw you to the floor and lick
The crease behind your ear.
It is a part of yourself
You have never seen.
I see it every day.
I want to leave you
Diminished.)

Zee needed to get off campus for her own sanity, which was the only reason she'd agreed to meet Gracie at the Chippeway Club. It was one of those places she'd rather not be seen, on principle, by some faculty member who'd wrangled an invitation.

Gracie reclined by the pool in a pink one-piece, her limbs tan and slim. Zee joined her and watched the lunchtime calm at the kiddie end as children sat by their nannies to digest their grilled cheeses. Between the pool and the golf course stretched a field of browning grass decorated with three white teepees, some kind of sick and inaccurate homage to the Chippewa, who hadn't really lived here anyway. Zee herself hadn't set foot at the club till after her father died, when her mother shocked her by saying they'd been members all along, and now that her father couldn't object they were free to go there and wouldn't Zee like to learn golf? As a teenager she knew that the other kids, the fun ones, would sneak out to the teepees during weddings and graduation parties to deflower each other and finish the wine they'd stolen.

Zee ordered a Long Island iced tea. The club served them notoriously strong.

"Mom, we need Case and Miriam out of that house. It's distracting Doug." Her mother's expression behind the big sunglasses was unclear, but she kept talking. "The whole point of moving in was the peace and quiet." She hadn't planned on bringing this up today, but then this morning at breakfast, Doug had asked Miriam if she wanted the used coffee filter for her "art," and she'd folded it in fourths and tucked it in her shorts pocket.

"Are they loud? I suppose it's cultural."

"Miriam has that whole porch covered with the trash for her collages. I mean literally, *garbage*."

Gracie shook her head. "Bruce is convinced of this Y2K fiasco, and he won't throw his son on the street with the world about to end. And the poor thing. His tendon! And now they have no car. How would they even leave? On horseback?"

The waiter handed Zee her drink in a frosted glass. She hated how good it felt to be taken care of. Zee drank like someone was timing her and then lay back to feel the sun tighten her skin. She remembered her father's objection to the club name: "Chippeway," he said, every time they passed the sign, "in that context, suggests nothing so much as poorly played golf."

Zee kept her eyes closed and said, "I'll make a deal with you. After the New Year, if the world doesn't end, Case and Miriam need to leave. His ankle will be better. If you get them out, I promise Doug's book will be done and he'll be at the college by next fall. If they stay . . . I don't know."

"I can work on Bruce, but I don't see how you can guarantee anything about poor Doug."

"I've always been lucky."

18

All the cars were gone, and Doug let himself into the big house through the garage with the emergency key.

As often as he'd been on the ground floor, he hadn't ventured upstairs since the days when he was dating Zee and she'd bring him home for Thanksgiving and set him up in a guest room with a set of fluffy towels. He dragged his hand up the railing. This must be what people meant by *patina*, this buttery softness. The house seemed as much alive on the inside as on the leafy outside—the way the wood of the door frames contracted in winter and expanded in summer, the way the glass on these staircase windows was thicker at the bottom than the top, from the slow, liquid pull of a century.

Hidalgo hadn't met him at the door, and Doug assumed the beast was in his crate. There were clicks, though, and creaks, all around him in the hall, and he reminded himself about houses settling. He tried to recall which was the door to the attic stairs. It must be this one, at the north end: next to a closet, but not a closet, the brass keyhole made for one of those toothy old keys with a loop handle. He tried the elliptical little knob, but it just clinked tightly back and forth. He knelt, his eye to the inch of gap at the bottom of the door. It wasn't dark—he remembered the dormers running along both the back and front of the house—but all he could see was tan. The riser of the bottom step.

Something crackled behind him. Doug's back had been turned on the hallway for a long time, as if he'd never watched a spy movie in his life. He rose and turned, certain he'd see an angry Bruce or a frightened Sofia. But there was just afternoon light from a high window, magnifying a million specks of floating dust. Now that he'd become aware of his back, of the fact that he couldn't turn his head like an owl, he was uncomfortable whichever way he faced. He wanted to flatten himself against a wall. Instead he walked calmly down the stairs and out the garage door.

19

After one more Long Island iced tea, Zee left her car at the club and Gracie drove her home, a Bobby Darin CD playing and the windows down.

"Aren't we living it up?" Gracie said.

Sofia was unloading the dry cleaning from her van. Miriam, barefoot, sat on the bench by the coach house with a book in her lap. And, bizarrely, Doug was emerging from the big house's garage, staring at everyone. As Gracie got out, Miriam rose and hopped across the hot gravel. They formed a little group of four on the driveway, which Zee watched from the car for a long, blurry second. Something was off. The pieces of the world were not where she'd left them.

Her mother waved her out of the car, and by the time Zee stuck her head into the heat Sofia was backing toward the big house. "You see! I get, I get!" Zee wanted to form a question, but she couldn't decide which one, and her lips were asleep.

"Thought I heard Hidalgo freaking out in there," Doug was saying, and "wanted to be sure he was okay," but Gracie wasn't listening.

Sofia returned, butter-yellow fabric in her plump arms.

"This is the one? I find it on the floor of the flower bedroom, behind the bed. This is whose?"

Zee blinked at the thing. It was her cotillion dress, shoulder pads and ruched waist, but wadded and wrinkled.

"I haven't seen that in nineteen years," Zee managed to say. And yet she felt she somehow had—but no, it was just that they'd talked about it so recently.

Gracie clapped her hands, as if chunks weren't falling out of the universe and onto guest room floors. "Well, that's just the luck of Laurelfield! Miriam, you need to know that this is the distinctive legacy of the house: ridiculous luck, whether good or bad. We've had tragedies here too, but then magic things like this happen! Now you have to make a *wonderful* mosaic out of it."

Sofia held the dress out, but Miriam looked at the thing like it was tainted. "I don't understand," she said.

Sofia shrugged. "Maybe was the ghost."

Zee took it from Sofia herself. It wasn't dirty, just creased in a thousand places. The sun was too hot, and even the dress was hot, and she felt she might melt into it. "Maybe it was Doug," Zee said, not looking at him. "Maybe he was trying to help Miriam find it."

Doug made a startled, choked noise, a refutation and a laugh at once.

Gracie said, "Why on earth would he do that? And leave it on the floor? He's not a raccoon, dear."

Zee draped the dress over Miriam's arm. "Here," she said. "Clearly it was meant to be."

She wondered if this would all make sense once she sobered up, but she doubted that. She wanted to stomp, to scream, to ask why things would rearrange themselves just when she'd got them straightened out. Instead she walked back to the coach house, trying not to sway. Doug caught up and whispered: "What the hell was that? Was that a joke?"

"Covering for Sofia. She probably went back to look, and it was on the closet floor. My mom would pitch a fit about the wrong hangers or something." She wasn't certain she'd made sense, but she hadn't slurred. Doug stalked past and turned on the TV.

Could that have been it? Or could Doug really have snuck into the house days ago to find the thing, to present it to Miriam like a dog with a bone? And then, when he heard footsteps, stuffed the dress behind the bed. Then he'd gone back to retrieve it today, only it wasn't where he'd thought it would be.

When Zee saw from the upstairs window that Miriam had gone back to her bench, the dress folded neatly beside her, she went down to Doug on the couch. She straddled him and unbuttoned her blouse and yanked his head back by the hair. She knew he wanted to be mad at her, and she knew he wanted to fall in love with Miriam, but for the next ten minutes he'd be unable to do either.

20

On the hottest day of August, Doug met up with the friend who'd gotten him started on *Friends for Life* and the lucrative but soul-sapping Melissa Hopper in the first place. Doug and Leland had taught high school together in Ohio, in the hazy few years between college and grad school— the same years when Zee was off on her Fulbright, saving the world. Leland had recently begun wearing black button-downs with the collars wide open, so now Doug was a little worried, meeting him in a Highwood bar, that they'd be mistaken for a gay couple. Leland taught poetry classes all over the suburbs, living not off the paychecks but off the wealthy women who preferred him to their CEO husbands.

"It's on me today," Doug said. "You saved my ass. You saved my pocketbook."

"And they're fun, right? You get to be the adolescent girl you never were."

"I will never admit to that."

There was a bowl of nuts on the bar. It was good to be out of the house, and it was good to be eating nuts and drinking and watching the Cubs. When they started tanking in the fourth, Doug filled him in on Case and Miriam. He described the scooter Case was now using to get around town—how he'd prop his bad leg up on a little shelf and push off with the other. He'd had a few job interviews set up in the city, but he'd canceled those, worried how he'd look showing up sweaty from the train and cab, on top of wounded.

"Tex and the crazy lady," Leland said. "Tex and the Wreck. That's a country song, right there. This woman, is she of the attractive persuasion?"

"Fortunately no. I mean, maybe a six. The craziness doesn't help. Six point five."

"This kid's an asshole." He was talking about the Cubs. "But then, your wife makes everyone look like shit, right? Tell me something: The Victoria's Secret catalogue gets to your house, you even bother to look? Or is it like, hey, I got better stuff upstairs?"

Doug was glad there seemed no obligation to answer. Leland had met Zee only once or twice, and he hadn't looked at her with any more interest than most men did. Doug knew what he was really saying, what everyone was really saying when they commented on her beauty: They weren't sure how she'd ended up with Doug. He wasn't shorter than her, or bad looking. He'd always gotten plenty of girls. It was more what people presumed about women as intense as Zee, about what they were after and what they could get. Women like Zee did not pick nice guys with average golf games who occasionally forgot to brush their teeth. They picked jackass publishing executives with famous ex-wives and ski houses.

"And can we get the bullpen up?" Leland said.

Partly to keep him from talking about baseball when Doug knew relatively little about the Cubs, and partly because this was why he'd called Leland in the first place, Doug told him about the files in the attic. He told him too about the past month of unsuccessful fishing. In the days after he tried the attic door himself, Doug tried wheedling a key out of Sofia, who apparently didn't have one, and out of Bruce, who'd laughed and said, "You want Gracie to kill me? I been up there *once*, to trap a squirrel. Look, I don't even open the crisper drawer without her say-so. You know? This is called marital peace."

"Do you *have* a key?" Doug had asked, and Bruce had clapped him on the back.

"It's not really my house, right? And—Doug, my friend—it's definitely not yours." Bruce turned to go, then came back. "Hey. Don't let me hear you bothering Gracie with this. She's had enough stress with the landscapers."

And before all that he'd asked Zee—as she lay there with her head on his lap, in those lovely, sleepy minutes after she came down and fucked him on the TV room couch—if her mother might ever let him explore the attic and basement for colony artifacts. She'd given him the look the question deserved. "*I've* hardly been in that attic," she said. "And I can tell you exactly what's in the basement, and right now it's supplies for Armageddon."

Leland had turned on his bar stool so his back was to the TV. "Marianne *Moore*," he said finally. "Christ. I know you're gay for Parfitt and all, but do you realize what someone could do with unpublished Moore documents? Jesus God, I'm *drooling* here. Fuck. I mean, if she stayed there, it'd be late in life. She never went anywhere without her mother while the mother was alive. So this isn't early shit. This isn't *juvenilia*. This is, like. *Fuck*." He slid his empty glass to the bartender. "I mean, just a draft. A photo!"

It was sublimely gratifying to see Leland's reaction, after Miriam's calm pessimism. "I know. It's gotta be *something*. Otherwise why the evasion, you know? That's what I'm saying."

"So you gotta get it out of there."

"Sure. I know. It's keeping me awake."

"You tell Zee?"

Doug shook his head. With each day he knew he was less likely to. He wasn't sure if she would laugh and tell him he needed real source material, not old phone bills, or if she'd storm the attic herself and take over the whole enterprise, but something in his bones rebelled against what should have been spousal transparency.

Maybe the secret of the *Friends* books had indeed been a tiny wedge.

"So you're going to help me."

"I'm—okay, what, we're breaking in? I wear a ski mask?"

"You pretend to be a photographer."

Leland laughed and shook his head. "No, no, this is sounding like a sitcom."

"Listen: Any Moore documents, any correspondence, you can have it. You can publish it, sell it, it's yours."

"Huh. Christ."

"I just want the Parfitt stuff."

What he asked Leland to do was call Gracie pretending to be with the Adler Ross Foundation. Adler Ross was the architect of the place, just famous enough for someone to care about his attics. Leland was going to be sad and sweet and claim this was the last attic he needed to photograph to complete the records. He'd take pictures of the windows, throw around some jargon, get out of there. "It's reconnaissance," Doug said. "You just see if there are file cabinets. And if everything's going well, maybe ask if you can move one to get a better picture, then you say, 'God, these are heavy, what's in these things,' right? And meanwhile you're watching what key she uses on the attic door, where she puts it when she's done."

"This is insane, Doug. I'm not a good liar."

"Marianne Moore. Marianne Moore's undiscovered poem about her secret affair with Mickey Mantle."

"Well, yeah. Okay. True."

21

Zee had waited patiently through the whole summer session, through one sweltering reception on the president's lawn, and the first two weeks of class. She finally let herself go to the science building computer lab to type up the letter. She sat with her back to the windows and typed in eight-point font, then blew it up only for proofreading.

Dear Dean Shaumber and Prof. Blum,

I write on behalf of myself and two other female students who feel disturbed by the photos on Dr. Cole's computer. We are sure you are familiar with the photos, as they are common knowledge. Although he closes that file when we enter the office, it is unnerving to know he has been looking at the photos, and that he is in a state of mind to degrade women.

We simply wish him to consider the effect this behavior has on those women who visit his office. We are also upset about his continual use of the word "coed," but this is old news and we understand nothing is going to be done about it, and furthermore we and the other students we have spoken to are far more disturbed about the pornography.

Respectfully submitted by three women who wish to remain anonymous.

Zee went back and forth on the spelling of *effect*, but figured the three imaginary girls would be imaginary English majors, and would get it right. She left two copies in the printer trays where they could be found by students, then stuck one copy in Shaumber's mailbox and one in Blum's.

This last she did right in front of Chantal, but there were plenty of other papers in there already. She turned calmly and asked Chantal to make some copies. Her mother had always maintained, back in the days when Zee and her father had played hide-and-seek around the house, her father as gleeful as any eight-year-old, that plain sight was the best place to hide. They'd talk Gracie into hiding, and when they found her she'd been sitting in the kitchen right where they'd left her, smoking a Virginia Slim. "But it took you five minutes!" she'd say when they complained. That was in the days before her mother put on airs, back when the estate was just a ramshackle shell for a regular, sloppy family, entire guest rooms given over to Zee's Lego configurations. Friends from the art world—George's reviews eventually went beyond the local scene, and the house became a pit stop for artists passing through Chicago—would play Mastermind with Zee at the table while Gracie cooked eggs. The only formality was her father's predilection for folding the dinner napkins into sailboats on special occasions. Things hardened after his death. It was later that year— Zee was still twelve—when her mother saw her take a spoonful of chocolate frosting from the container and said, "That's how girls get fat." Her mother had gotten a manicure, had wallpapered the bathrooms, had joined the Presbyterian church, all new things Zee didn't understand except to know that everything was different now, that without her father's laugh dismissing the rest of the world, there were appearances to be maintained.

On her way out of the building she ran into Cole, who held the door open. Those eyebrows: long white hairs among the dark short ones. Someone had planted them in the wrong garden. "Smile!" he shouted, and because her every interaction with the man was a charade anyway, she did just that. He didn't let her past, though. He poked a bony finger into her sternum, right above her blouse. "Do you know why I like it when you smile?"

"I do not," she said, still grinning, though her ears were hot now, and her neck.

"You resemble someone I used to know. It's uncanny. The ears and chin."

"Why, thank you," Zee said, and leaned back so she could get around his finger without it grazing her breast.

"A man, mind you!" he called after her. "It was a man!"

22

D oug had been much more confident about the soccer chapters in the previous book—he'd played varsity in high school, three lifetimes ago—than about the theater business here. He was flummoxed by the parts of Frieda's outline where the Populars and the Friends shared a dressing room. In the back of an old notebook, he'd begun listing things he needed to research:

Would have bra?
Purse? Backpack?
Stage makeup?
Undress in front of each other or hide in stalls?
Chairs backstage? Benches?

They read like a pedophilic stalker's notes, and he wanted them scratched out as soon as possible. He could maybe use the Internet for the theater parts, but he shuddered to think where an AltaVista search for "twelve-year-old, brassiere" would lead.

He started down to look for Miriam, but she was on the landing of the stairs, cross-legged, sorting through an ice cube tray of colored beads. She said "Oh!" and some of the glassy blue ones splashed out and rolled down the steps. Doug bounded down, picked them up with the sweat of his fingertips, then shook them into Miriam's outstretched palm.

"I'll tell you why I'm here," she said, as Doug sat on the step above her. He regretted his choice of seat immediately. She wasn't wearing a bra, and he could see too far down her green tank top. He leaned back and looked instead at the ceiling. Miriam said, "I wasn't sleeping well, so I thought I'd spend time in the ghostliest part of the coach house. Just to dare something to happen. If it does, I'll know. And if it doesn't, I'll sleep better."

"Why is this the ghostliest part?" He hoped she didn't have a good answer.

"Oh, you know. Doorways, staircases, attics, windows. You never see a ghost in the middle of the room."

"I've never seen a ghost at all."

"Well, yes. That."

"But Doug," she said. "I found out. How she died."

"What, Violet?" He sat back up despite himself.

"I went to the library and they got me set with microfiche. There was an obituary with no information at all—But did you know she was born in England? I love it! English ghosts are scarier, right?—so I was about to give up. But then there was this weird article a few days later that was like, 'Husbands, pray for your wives!' You know, very 1906. And then it talks about 'to perish by starvation, in this land of plenty.' And it was clearly about her. *Starvation.*"

"Seriously. Wow. Wait, I thought she killed herself."

"Exactly. Something doesn't add up."

"Was anorexia a thing back then?"

Miriam tilted her head. "That's the boring version. I think Augustus killed her. I think he starved her."

Doug let out a low, slow whistle and laughed. "So I need your help on something less serious," he said. "Since you're already in on my secret." He decided not to ask the bra question, in light of current circumstances. "Do twelve-year-olds carry purses?"

She put the bead tray down. "Oh, fun! Well, the Populars

would have *chic* purses. The Friends should have backpacks. Cece probably has an army surplus bag, something cool that she stenciled on." Doug scribbled in the notebook as she talked, and twenty minutes later most of his problems were solved.

She said, "Just pay me back when you find that original Demuth painting."

And then, before he could fathom why he was doing it, he told her about the plan with Leland, who had conceded to go undercover next week. Maybe it was for the same reason he hadn't shared the news with Zee: One secret, whether shared or kept, begot more.

"I want to help!" she said. "I won't get in the way. It's just that nothing exciting has happened to me for such a long time."

"You'd be handy for identifying art," he said. "Not that my hopes are up. I'm skeptical. But just a list of who stayed here and when, if Parfitt were on the list—it would be huge. You know, who was with him, that kind of thing."

Miriam rubbed her bare arms. "See, don't you feel the ghosts around you when you say things like that? All those people, all that creative energy—it had to go *somewhere*. And Parfitt was another suicide. People like that are the most probable ghosts."

He stretched his legs, which had fallen asleep.

"Oh!" Miriam said. "You have scars!" She was eye level with his knees and the thick white scars below each kneecap, and to Doug's surprise she reached out her finger and traced down the length of the left one, as if it concerned her greatly.

Doug knew he ought to run for his life, but he did the next best thing. He said, pointedly, "How did you and Case meet?"

"Oh, he bought one of my pieces. And I thought he was so *old*, because he was twenty-eight! Can you believe that? I was still in college."

"He's had a rough go here." He laughed in what he hoped was a friendly way.

She said, "I wonder about this house. This whole place. Gracie said it's lucky and it's unlucky. It's been lucky for me. I've never done so much good work in my life."

"Don't take philosophical advice from Gracie."

Miriam picked a red bead out of the container. "I've seen an astrologer do a birth chart for a house, just like a person." She saw the look on his face. "I know, *stars*, but it's no weirder than genetics or pheromones telling us what to do, right? It's just the genome of a place."

"But *you* like it here."

"It's like—did you ever play with magnets as a kid? You know how if you have them turned to the wrong pole it pushes away, but you flip the same magnet around and it clicks together? I feel like Case is the wrong pole, the one that gets pushed. And I'm the right one."

It wasn't till he was back in his room, silently mouthing her words just to feel their strangeness on his lips, that he felt they almost made a kind of sense.

One Twix and two beers later, he was on fire. He found the bra information in the *FFL Bible*. He was stupid not to have looked there first. Candy got a bra in book 60, apparently, then Molly, but not Melissa. He spun his chair to celebrate, and got back to work. With Violet's unexplained starvation fresh on his mind, he decided (why the hell not? The books could use some edge) to give one of the Populars an eating disorder. He showed Amelia Wynn, the sixth-grade dictator, eating a glass of salted ice. He showed her counting her ribs in the dressing-room mirror. Her arms were as thin as tapers.

23

(I wrap my ankles around chair rungs
So I don't spring out and bite your shoulder.

Your thumb and finger
On the edges of a CD

Your tongue
Makes its way between your teeth
In time with music

I want to be
That music

The hair just below
Your navel
Curls to the left.
Let me untwist it)

24

By October, there were rumors. Cole was rarely in his office, and one afternoon Zee saw Jerry Keaton pull Bob Grasso into the seminar room and close the door. She asked Chantal if she knew what was going on, and Chantal shook her head—but she did not ask what Zee was referring to. And that was confirmation enough.

Her seminar kids were already calling themselves The Ghostbusters and had written wonderful essays on *The Turn of the Screw* and *The Haunting of Hill House*. They'd been quick to point out that these stories weren't so much about ghosts as madness, and our slippery hold on reality. Good kids. She was surprised to find she was having more fun with them than with her Fictions of Empire students.

After class, Fran Leffler followed Zee to her office to talk about grad school. Fran was a major, a sorority girl with dimples. Zee told her to sign up for Literary Theory, then leaned across her desk: "Listen, Fran, this is under wraps, but I'm sure you've heard about Professor Cole?"

Fran looked concerned, like Zee was about to tell her the man had cancer.

"I'm just asking because I believe this sort of thing is important to talk about, and you seem like someone who might hear if—Well, I just want to make sure people feel comfortable coming forward."

"Coming *forward?* Did he, like—"

"Oh, no! No, not that. It's just his computer. I guess—I shouldn't say this, but I've probably said too much already, and I don't want your imagination getting the best of you. Apparently some students, some female students, have been made uncomfortable by the images on his computer. They were, you know . . . explicit."

Fran shook her head in horror, but her eyes were lit with gossip. "Is he in trouble?"

"He'll be in trouble if he *needs* to be. Who knows if it's even true. But, as a senior—if you heard anything from younger women, anyone in your sorority—I hope you'd let someone know. At this point they're just gathering information. And you didn't hear it from me, please."

As Fran left, Zee took her shoes off and stretched her feet. Later that same day, she watched Golda Blum and some man she'd never seen before, a dumpy guy in a communist-green polo shirt who could only work for IT, go into Cole's office without him.

"It's marvelous," Gracie said. They were at the breakfast table in the big house late that afternoon. Zee had just told her she could stop worrying about Doug, that there *would* be openings by the fall, as long as he could finish his book in an unshared house. (The debate would take months, of course, and they'd let Cole finish the year. But they'd start the head hunt soon to replace him.) Hidalgo, under the table, breathed hot air on Zee's legs. "Do you think the school will really remain open, though, after this whole computer thing?" It took Zee a few terrifying seconds to realize she meant the Y2K bug. "Bruce reads absolutely all the news, and the smartest people are saying it's just the end of everything."

Sofia was cleaning out the refrigerator, tossing old containers of deli salads Gracie and Bruce had never gotten around to eating. Zee wanted to ask her more about that dress, that yellow dress that had no reason to be on the floor, but now was not the time. It had been bothering her for weeks now, and the more she thought about it, the more she felt that somehow she'd seen it very recently, and remembered touching it. She'd started to consider that she might have done something in her sleep, walked to the big house and found the dress, crumpled it and hidden it from Miriam.

But this was ridiculous, and she'd long ago trained herself not to second-guess things to the point where she lost the reality of them. She used to worry all the time about losing her mind. In the library at boarding school she'd found a book, *The New World Barons*, published in the 1960s, with sections on the Palmers and Carnegies and Devohrs, among others. "The Devohr history is not one of summer estates and long lineage held taut by familial love; it is one of scandal, Diaspora, insanity." She spent hours on the floor between shelves, reading about the Devohrs who killed themselves, the ones who vanished into Mexico, the one they found buried under old newspapers. She returned to the book many times, to trace the lines of the small, gray jaws with her pinky. Great-aunts and distant cousins. Her grandfather, Gamaliel, as a long-haired boy in a dress. (His mother, Violet, not a Devohr by birth and not a Devohr for long, merited mention only as "another suicide.") Zee had never met any of them. Gracie's parents died before Zee was born, and Gracie's brothers were all "degenerates" to whom she no longer spoke. No cousins ever visited, no aunts. The Devohrs weren't people so much as sea turtles that laid their eggs and then crawled back to the ocean, not particularly invested in meeting their progeny ever again. That she and Gracie were relatively close was a miracle.

Gracie said, "Do you think the college might find a job for Case as well? Something in the business office?"

Zee was still contemplating what kind of response this merited when Gracie's phone rang. She answered it and handed it to Zee. It was Doug.

"Hey!" he said. "You're at your mom's!" He was a terrible actor.

"What's wrong?"

"Nothing, no, I just wondered. So you won't be back for a while?"

"Maybe an hour."

"Okay. Like, a whole hour? Okay!"

She hung up and told her mother she needed to get going right away.

"It's just as well. Some poor fellow's coming over to take pictures. The architects are sending him. I don't know what on earth he wants."

Zee put her teacup in the sink, kissed her mother's cheek, and ran out the side door. A car was pulling up to the front, the beat-up black Saturn of the architectural lackey, who had no idea what Gracie would put him through.

In the coach house, it seemed eerily like a normal Thursday afternoon. Miriam on the sunporch, fully clothed, working on her unloved dress collages. Case sulking at the kitchen table. Doug sprawled on the bed with *Sports Illustrated*, smiling, as if he'd been expecting her.

25

On the phone, Leland had said the pictures turned out but he wasn't sure what the hell he was looking for. Doug didn't know why this was disappointing. He hadn't really believed Leland would find a cardboard box labeled "Parfitt's Memoirs." But somewhere between getting Leland into the attic, and getting Zee out of the house in time, and arranging this meeting down at the beach, Doug had come to assume there would be a major payoff. He'd stopped considering the possibility that Bruce was wrong about the file cabinets. That there might be nothing there but a pile of dusty bed frames. He'd forgotten that even if there *were* colony files, they might have just been heating bills.

It was a cool, sunny day, and Lake Michigan was Caribbean blue. Doug found Leland and Miriam at separate picnic benches on the grass between the sand and the cars. He introduced them, and Leland poured out an envelope of snapshots: windows, bureaus with missing drawers, piles of headboards and desk chairs, and yes, four black metal file cabinets, each two drawers high, with no visible locks.

"They were old enough. You see the script on the logo?" He'd managed to sneak a close-up of the manufacturer's plaque on one cabinet. "Looks like what, forties? Fifties? That fits, right?" Leland attempted to lay the photos into the general shape of the attic. "It wasn't easy," he said. He was taking up one whole bench, his legs spread wide, looking at Miriam in her yellow shirt in a way that implied Doug had sold her short. "I didn't tell her it was the attic I wanted till I'd thanked her a million times, told her what a jackass my boss was, how I was afraid I'd get fired. So by the time I said 'attic,' she'd feel bad saying no. Oh, and I told her my girlfriend was from Toronto. That helped. I don't have a girlfriend, but hey. So she *did* say no, she told me there were bats and she hadn't been up there in years. So I go, 'Oh, well if it's hard for you to climb, I can go by myself.'"

"Oooh, brilliant!" Gurgle of southern laughter, toss of curls.

"So twenty seconds later she's marching up the stairs. And here." He shuffled through the photos and found two of the attic door—one from outside, one from inside. "It's a simple old lock. The key was just two prongs."

"But she had the key *on* her?"

"No. I mean, I was exaggerating about the twenty seconds. Really she disappeared for five minutes and came back with the key. So sue me. I'm a poet. I'm prone to exaggeration." He grinned at Miriam, who was too absorbed in the photos to notice.

"Here's what I think," she said. "I doubt there's anything valuable there. No one would put a rolled up painting in a file cabinet."

"But a poem!" Leland said. "A poem that was part of someone's application!"

"Slides," Doug said. "Letters of recommendation. Project proposals. Listen: Just this summer? The New York Public Library bought the archives from the Yaddo colony for some huge amount, and they're saying there's unpublished Carson McCullers in there. We're not in the same league, but still."

"So how do we convince her to let us look?"

Doug sighed and watched the joggers going past. He wasn't sure if Gracie's persistent and decisive evasion of Laurelfield history had to do with her guilt at having displaced the colony, or her shame at being associated with so many unwashed artists, but she hadn't budged. At Bruce's birthday dinner last week, when Doug had asked if historians had ever shown interest in documenting Laurelfield, Gracie had said, "Douglas, isn't there something more productive you ought to focus on? Perhaps you could publish a novel." ("What is her *problem*?" Miriam had whispered later. "Her energy is so off.")

"What if we talk her into donating it to a library?" Leland said. "Or the college?"

Doug said, "I think she'd sooner donate her kidneys."

"It doesn't seem that Gracie's the right person to make the judgment call," Miriam said. "She's not a writer, she's not an artist, she's not a historian. And didn't you say"—she turned to Leland—"it's an easy lock to pick?"

When a man sat down at the next bench with his laptop they began whispering, but what they came up with over the next hour was a hypothetical scenario so risky that Doug knew he'd never pull the trigger on it. They were having fun though, and so he let Leland and Miriam plot.

They agreed that the best time to break into the attic would *not* be on one of the rare occasions when both Gracie and Bruce were gone. Sofia was usually around, as were Bruce's personal secretary and the guy who came to walk Hidalgo. If someone met them on their way out, they'd have a hard time explaining the armloads of files. Miriam was the one who remembered the Democratic fund-raiser Gracie and Bruce were hosting in early December, which Doug and Zee and the younger Breens would be expected to attend. They could easily smuggle Leland in. Sofia would be working downstairs with the caterers. It would be loud. No one would hear if they had to bust down the attic door.

"It'll be like *Notorious*!" Miriam said. "Only we won't get caught like Ingrid Bergman." Seeing how her hands flew around her hair and her nose flared out, how her whole face was pink and bright, Doug wondered if she'd actually been depressed all summer. Those other times she'd seemed happy, like standing on the counter that first day with those plates, it must have been something fake. It was nothing like this.

Doug finally shook his head. "Zee would never forgive me," he said. "Not for going after the files, but—I mean, Gracie would kick us out." He could imagine his mother-in-law smiling thinly, saying that now that he'd found a new career in espionage, he could surely afford his own home.

"It's five weeks away," Miriam said. "You have time to decide. Don't say no just yet."

When they finally disbanded, Doug felt they should all put their hands in a heap and chant something, like a field hockey team. But he let it end with Miriam heading down the beach for pebbles and he and Leland trudging all the way back to town for coffee.

"You jackass," Leland said as they crossed the train tracks. "I can't fucking believe you."

"What?"

He shook his head in a rueful way that he must have stood in front of the mirror and practiced, a poet's astonishment at the varied and exasperating world. "You rate a woman a six point five and go off about how crazy she is."

"Oh, she has her moments. I probably didn't do her justice."

"That's not what I meant. You're in love with her."

Doug almost ran into the guardrail. So they were starting, the inevitable assumptions. He decided to wait long enough that his answer wouldn't seem defensive, because it wasn't, and he needed Leland to understand that.

They were all the way across the street by the time he said "I am sincerely not."

"I'm just saying, the only reason I can think to sell a lovely person like that so short is that maybe you're fighting something."

"Or maybe she's really crazy. You walk in when she's working, and she looks like a homeless person. She's got pencils behind both ears, and pins sticking from her mouth, hair frizzed out. Her pupils are fully dilated."

"Okay, sure. Sure. But let me ask you this: Why do you keep walking in when she's working?"

Doug considered punching Leland in the face, but decided against it.

26

As Zee sorted handouts before class, the talk grew shrill in the corner. "It was right there on the screen," Meghan Dwyer said. A smart, sweet girl who could actually write. Everyone was turned toward her. "And I wouldn't say it was underage stuff. But it was graphic. I know some people are picturing just, like, a topless woman leaning on a car. But this was, like—" she looked around, saw Zee immersed in her papers, and mouthed the words "—*butt-fucking.*"

Zee wondered, in brief amazement, if it *had* all been true, if she'd simply set things in motion. But no, this was her own creation, her own monster. She had willed this into being.

Near the end of class, Dev Kapoor raised his hand, a look on his face like he was trying to fend off a headache. He said, "How come ghosts are always from the past? I mean, why are they never from the future?" The class snickered. Zee suspected his peers had a different impression of Dev than she'd gotten from his workmanlike papers.

"Go on," she said.

"A ghost from the future would have a lot more at stake. Ghosts from the past are always in the Hamlet model, right? Like, remember me and avenge my death. But a ghost from the future is going to be desperate. If things don't go right he won't be born."

"Time doesn't work that way," Fran Leffler said, and then they all started in, telling him he'd watched too many movies.

"Maybe I don't mean a ghost. More like a spirit or a force. But anyway, my point is, a ghost from the future *wouldn't* be scary, right?"

Zee said, "So we're afraid of the undead, but not the unborn."

Sarah Bonheur thrust her hand definitively into the air and didn't wait to be called on. "*A Christmas Carol*," she said. "By Charles Dickens. The ghost of Christmas Future is the scariest of all."

Dev said, "Oh. Right," and collapsed back in his chair.

But Antwon Haynes picked up the ball. "That's an exception. Maybe it's like what we're afraid of isn't death, but the *past*. No one walks by a crime scene the very next day and feels a ghost. It takes twenty years, right?"

They were on to something, Zee thought. We aren't haunted by the dead, but by the impossible reach of history. By how unknowable these others are to us, how unfathomable we'd be to them.

She started writing on the board.

Cole had been making himself scarce outside of class, so Zee was caught off guard when, as she passed his office, he stuck his head out and motioned her in. It was the first time she'd set foot there since the sabotage, but here were the same books stacked on the floor, same Post-its covering the Indiana University diploma.

"Zenobia, my dear, I need your advice," he said. He sat on the front edge of his desk, which left Zee choosing between the student chair, three inches from Sid Cole's crotch, and his own desk chair, inappropriate in a different way. She opted for leaning against a bookcase. "As a communist, you're interested in intellectual freedom, no?"

"I'm not a communist, I'm a Marxist scholar."

. "Here's my point: The administration should not be able to access the computers of tenured faculty. Let's imagine you were looking at some Web site of a communist politician, and then you're hauled in front of a committee. When the whole point of tenure is the freedom."

"I'm not tenured."

"You've heard what's happening, I'm sure."

Zee attempted to look bewildered, but he shook his head.

"You hear everything. You know what the deans ate for breakfast. You know when Blum takes a crap. And what I want to know is, when did we become afraid of sex? We ask them to read *Lolita* and Chaucer, but a nude picture is going to warp their minds? They're *adults!*"

Zee genuinely *was* bewildered now, by what seemed a confession, but she reminded herself that this was just Cole, that he was the kind of man who would argue against the Dalai Lama, simply for the thrill of battle. So she said, "I think if you believe strongly in this, you should fight it. whether you did the thing or not."

"Ha! I'm not asking your permission. What I'm wondering is this: You always have your finger on the pulse, so to speak. How many faculty do you suppose would back me?"

"It depends what you're planning to do."

"If I say, either you stay out of my computer or I quit my job and take this very public. How many people would support me on that?"

"You're not asking them to quit *with* you."

"No. Write letters, shave their heads."

She picked up a little jade monkey from the shelf and felt its smooth back with her thumb. A strangely delicate object for Cole to possess. "I imagine you'd have some support. Just don't count on all the feminists."

"Isn't everyone a feminist now? I thought that was the point of Women's Studies."

"I can probably help with the feminists."

Despite everything, when he winked at her right then, she could see why he charmed the kids. It was so hard to get on his good side that once you got there, even under false pretenses, it felt validating, like the hard-won respect of a difficult father.

Doug looked much younger asleep. It was comforting, in a way. A reminder that she was the one with the plans, that she was the one keeping things together.

You could only lose control if you let go. You could only lose *anything* if you let it go. She said to herself.

From the shoulder of Doug's T-shirt she pulled a long, curly brown hair.

27

The ivy on the big house had yellowed, to disturbing effect. The vines seemed somehow malevolent now, a strangling, draining force, all roots and tendrils, fused with the stone. Doug thought all through the rest of October about the risk involved in going behind Gracie's back once and for all. He considered, too, that a political fund-raiser might involve Secret Service in some way. He asked Zee, casually, if there would be guards. She said, "It's more like a Tupperware party."

But the real threat wasn't Gracie or even men with earpieces. It was Zee, who had surely already noticed how antsy he was lately. If they went through with it, he wouldn't be able to look her in the eye for weeks.

He knew Zee wanted, more than anything, for him to finish the monograph—but she'd see this as more procrastination, as chasing fingerprints when he ought to be engaged in hard-nosed analysis. He could imagine her forehead creased, her hands on his shoulders. "You thought," she'd say, "that you could finish your book by breaking into my mother's attic? *That* was your plan? Show me how much you've written."

He felt, bizarrely, that he was choosing between Edwin Parfitt and his wife—and not for the first time. The night he met Zee, at a welcome cocktail party at the graduate dean's house, and she'd learned he was planning to write about Parfitt, she'd said, "*Parfitt.* Wow. Oh dear. I put him in a category with Joyce Kilmer."

Doug had been blinded by the shine of her black hair, by the thin straps of her dress, but he'd managed to call her out. "That's because you know exactly one poem by each. You know Kilmer's 'Trees,' and you know Parfitt's 'Apollo on the Mississippi,' and they're both sappy. They were completely different poets in every way. They weren't even writing at the same time!"

"Yes, they *are* different. They're both trite, but Parfitt is also opaque. And my God, you could march to his rhythms, right?"

Doug was holding a bacon-wrapped scallop that he had no idea what to do with. "He just had this one cheesy period: 1930 to '32. Everything got all happy and rhymey. I mean, happiness is bad for poetry. And 'Apollo' was from that time. But that's the stuff that got famous. You need to read his early sonnets. The Persephone series, and the Aeneas ones. And his last poems are devastating. Have you read 'Proteus Wept'? Or 'Pond's Edge, Forgotten Girl'? It's so different from what you think."

"I've read it. He loved to eroticize those drowned women, didn't he?"

Doug had decided by this point that he hated this bitch, this sharp-chinned bitch who was looking over his shoulder for someone better to talk to. "Well, he was gay," he said. "If drowning turns you on, that's *your* issue." He'd stalked away.

Over the next year, as hatred melted into repartee and then to lust and sex and dating and engagement, he'd managed to convince her that Parfitt was someone she *ought* to like, though she never did become a fan. "You have a similar worldview," he told her.

"What worldview is that?"

He couldn't answer, but he wanted to say: Both of you—you feel so small that you'll never realize the volume of your own voice.

28

Miriam stood at the counter, prying a small pumpkin open with a kitchen knife. She was making soup to go with the lasagna Doug had prepped that afternoon, or so she had announced, but Zee had yet to see so much as a pot. It was already six thirty, with the older Breens due at the coach house in half an hour.

Doug was in a suspiciously good mood, bouncing around and inviting Case to join him for a beer on the tiny, precarious balcony off the kitchen. Zee almost stopped them, almost said that if Case stepped on the balcony, it was sure to be hit by lightning and break clean off the house. His ankle should have healed twice over by now, but he'd strained the tendon again leaping from his flaming car. So here he was, four months after the initial injury, still in the boot, still in pain. If things continued this way, one day Case would just combust like his car had. Miriam would wander back to Texas alone with her garbage. Problem solved.

Now that things were going so well with Cole, Zee was meditating, that night, on the one issue remaining: how to guarantee that Doug finished saying whatever he had to say about Edwin Parfitt so the monograph could be under contract by spring. Despite his improved work ethic, whenever she asked how much he'd written it was never more than a hundred words, and he was never ready to show her.

With everyone occupied, Zee walked quietly back into the apartment.

Getting into Doug's computer was so easy, compared with the risk of hacking Cole, that her pulse hardly rose. She looked first, optimistically, in the "Recent Documents" menu. The list included "In the last months of," "To Whom It May Concern," "Budget 99" and "Systems Work Folder 30, B." She checked the first, the only one with any promise, hoping the document would refer to the last months of Edwin Parfitt's life. It did. It read, in its entirety, "In the last months of Parfitt's short life, these five poems comprised not only the (don't repeat w/ thesis, but + PATHOS of Apollo on Miss. and Peonies)."

She knew he saved chapters individually, and he claimed he'd completed at least four, but this fragment was not encouraging. And if he hadn't been writing, what had he been doing every day? Zee's head began throbbing. The anger was there, strongly—the urge to throw the computer through the window and watch it shatter on the gravel—but more overwhelming was the sensation of the entire universe backfiring. Here was the precise opposite of everything she'd fought for. No: It was as if some malevolent genie had twisted her wishes into realities she couldn't handle. Cole was imploding—confessing, even!—but Doug wouldn't be ready to take the job. The job would open up just in time to go to some wunderkind who'd hold it for fifty years.

She should look at the other documents to make sure, and she should look at everything saved in his "Diss." folder, no matter how old, and she should look on all the disks she could find, just in case he'd been an idiot and neglected to save his work on the hard drive. With twenty minutes before her aggressively punctual mother and stepfather would arrive, she began searching in earnest.

29

Miriam's soup, she announced, wouldn't be ready for another hour, but it was worth the wait. Doug served Bruce from the bottle of Mount Gay purchased specially for the occasion. The rest of them got to work on a Pinot Noir. Zee was still hiding in the bedroom, sleeping or seething or grading papers, and nobody proposed calling her into the kitchen.

Gracie wandered, inspecting the cabinet hinges and the chipped tiles by the oven. She paused by the old panel right next to the refrigerator, about three feet square, that they'd painted over that spring with the same light blue as the rest of the kitchen.

"This was cheaply patched," she said, "wasn't it? Long before my time. I believe it's where they cut to install the electricity. My grandfather had the big house all wired up just as early as it was ever done, but he left the colony director living here with no lights until, I don't know, the thirties. He was never one to think of his employees."

It was the first time Doug heard Gracie refer to the colony with anything other than complete disregard. Apparently her disregard for her father was stronger. Gamaliel—a name Doug found suitably villainous for the man who'd shuttered the colony. When he'd mentioned him to Miriam, she'd said, "Oh, let's call him Gargamel! Like the bad guy from *The Smurfs*!" And ever since, Doug had pictured a man skulking around in a black robe, plotting the demise of the little artists. The real Gamaliel had suffered a nervous breakdown following the 1929 stock market crash, and although his fortunes had recovered, his mind never did. At least this was what Doug had gathered from *The Devohrs of Toronto: A Family Portrait*, back in graduate school.

"Miriam, *there's* a commission for you!" Gracie said. She was still examining the panel. "You might as well make yourself useful. Couldn't you paint it or something? A landscape?"

Miriam had perched on the counter, bare feet swinging, wine glass in hand. "I don't paint much. How about a traditional mosaic? In glass and little tiles?"

Case said, "Hey, see?" He turned to Bruce with a sharp, unfriendly grin. "That's how it's supposed to work. Hooking people up with gigs. What are you doing for *me*?" Joking, but of course he wasn't.

Bruce looked at his son with what Doug took for deep irritation. "My friend Clarence Mahoney will be at the fund-raiser. That's what I'm doing for you."

The art project, at least, was quickly settled, and Bruce told Gracie she was "a regular Medici." Miriam was already eyeing the piece of wood like something she planned to ravish.

There was a small crash from Doug and Zee's rooms, and a grunt of what sounded like frustration. They ignored it.

"Oh, just think!" Gracie said. "This might turn out to be your best artwork ever, and I thought of it just by happensack!"

Case let out a quick burst of laughter, and Miriam quickly stuck her head into the oven under the pretense of checking the pumpkin. Bruce beamed like Gracie was the cutest thing.

"Just by happensack," Doug repeated, and managed to keep a straight face. "And of course you'll pay Miriam for the tiles," he said, because he knew Miriam wouldn't say it, and he knew Gracie wouldn't think of it. "Unless you want it made of snipped up shirts and compost." He looked at Miriam to see if he'd offended her, but when she emerged from the oven she was smiling appreciatively.

"Oh, of course. And something extra for the labor. Shall we see what's keeping Zilla?" There was a horrible scraping sound just then, though, and no one volunteered.

By the time the soup was blended, the orange mess sopped from the counter, the remains served, and the lasagna finishing in the oven, they were all in high spirits. Maybe not Case, but certainly the rest of them. Gracie was more and more talkative with the wine, and Doug and Miriam couldn't stop giggling. The soup was delicious.

Gracie said, "I'll have you know we hung that farmhouse painting in the solarium regardless. I realize it's a bit naïve, Miriam, but it's *innocent*, and I like that. I don't like *violent* art. And my late husband, as I mentioned, adored it."

"Good King George," Bruce said. He was sloshed. "George the Late. George the Infallible."

Miriam took a big breath and glanced—apologetically, it seemed—at Doug, and then said, "Speaking of things I could be doing with my days. Bruce mentioned there were old filing cabinets—up in the attic? Those must be a burden. Wouldn't you like help cleaning those out?" Doug's first inclination was to panic, to kick Miriam under the table, but he supposed it was all right. Zee wasn't there to hear, and Case didn't care, and Bruce's presence might force Gracie's hand. "I mean, I want to earn my keep."

Gracie didn't look at Bruce at all, just blinked at Miriam. She said, "I can't help but think it's a shame you never had braces, Miriam. It really does mark a person. I always say, if you want to know someone's lot in life, look at the teeth."

Zee returned to the kitchen as the main course was served, and there was something about her smile, her slow pace, that made her look like a drunk trying to walk a straight line. She kissed her mother's cheek, and Miriam scrambled for another place setting.

Gracie was going off about the Internet, and Zee joined the group of baffled, nodding heads. "What's so horrifying is they can just put your name on there, and there's nothing you can do about it," Gracie said. "Even for the phone book they have to have your permission! And correct me if I'm wrong, but I have the impression they can even show photographs. I don't know if you need a special computer to get them, but just think! Miriam, have you seen this? In your work with the computers?"

Miriam protested that she was a technophobe in disguise, and Doug could practically hear the creak of Zee's eyes rolling beside him. "Some of my *planning* is on the computer," Miriam said, "but then it's all hand work."

"Tell them about the secrets!" Bruce said. "All her secrets are under there!"

Miriam's neck turned red. "Oh. Behind the materials," she said. "After I've outlined my shapes, and before the mortar, I write a secret in paint. People like knowing it's there, I think. If a buyer asks, I'll sometimes tell what it said."

Case said, "Secrets about me, right babe?"

"I didn't know it myself, till we read that article last year," Bruce said. "Miriam, have they seen the article?"

Zee said, "It's amazing the secrets people can keep. Isn't it." There was something wrong with her. Doug put his hand on her knee and she jerked away. "I used to think I could tell when someone had a secret. I really did. And it turns out—"

But Gracie shrieked and they all turned to her. "There was a ladybug!" she said. "Right on my plate."

30

Zee rose from bed like a heavy animal, her legs slow and numb.

Out at the table, the two of them giggling over breakfast. "Happensack—the luckiest town in New Jersey!" Miriam could hardly get her breath.

Doug: "It's the karma that gets you stuck on the turnpike!"

Zee couldn't look at them.

Miriam: "It's a sack full of four-leaf clovers!"

"It's when someone accidentally kicks you in the nuts!"

Doug's book bag lay on the floor. He was headed to the library, he said. She wanted to tear the zipper off, to see what was really inside. Books about adolescent girls, love letters to Miriam, a hundred bags of cocaine. The possibilities were endless.

Instead she said, "Miriam, why don't you meet me for coffee this morning? We haven't had a chance to talk much lately." They'd had nothing *but* chances to talk: right now, for instance, and the million times Zee swept past the sunporch pretending to be absorbed in the mail.

Miriam said, "Oh, lovely," and Zee said, "There's a chance I'll be waylaid by the dean."

And at ten o'clock, with Miriam waiting at Starbucks, with Case off at the doctor, chauffeured by Sofia, Zee drove back to the house and slammed her way into the silent, cold porch. Finished canvases leaned three deep against the walls, but the piece centered

on Zee's yellow cotillion dress was still in progress, laid out on the
floor like a corpse. The black swirls around it were finished—river
stones and coffee beans and checkers and an old Escape key and
barrettes. The dress was only half covered, in yellow but also orange
and little spots of brown and green. The green: It took a minute to
realize why the green looked so familiar. Here were the shards of her
mother's celadon vase, the one Case had knocked to pieces. Had
Miriam even asked to keep these? Had she stolen them that night?
Zee wiggled her thumb under the bottom of the hemline and
yanked up. Stones and scraps flew off, skittered across the floor.
Some of the fabric tore. It was only half a dress, really, as Miriam
had cut the back entirely away. But here were the words, the secrets,
just as Bruce had said. Zee left the dress attached by the left shoulder and read what she could of the black painted script below, ob-
scured by glue, bitten around the edges by the mortar and stones.

> *The hair just below*
> *Your navel*
> *Curls to the left*
> *Let me untwist it*

That was near the top. Farther down, below an unreadable swath:

> *Lick the scars*
> *Up your knees*
> *Taste what*
> *You drank*

And down by the hemline:

> *I forget to look*
> *In mirrors*

My guts have all
Sprung loose

She slapped the dress back down. There was an ugly satisfaction in finding what she'd known she would, despite the sudden light show behind her eyelids that was like the beginning of a migraine, but with a drumbeat.

Zee dragged Hidalgo from the big house. She got saltines from upstairs and sprinkled them all around, behind Miriam's trays of beads, under her papers. Then she shut him in. He might get free, but not before doing a lot more damage and clawing up the windows. He watched her leave, his eyes black and questioning. "Be bad," she said.

Her face, her smile, her breathing, would be fine at the coffee shop. If she could smile at Sid Cole, she could smile at Miriam. As she sped to town she developed the leaden sensation, though, that she hadn't just been right in her fears, but had actually caused something, yet again, to happen. That she'd willed this into being as surely as she'd brought about Cole's implicit confessions. She was getting everything she wanted, but also—like in a nightmare, where you're the author and also the victim—she was getting everything she feared: Miriam's crush, Doug's ineptitude, even the appearance of that stupid dress. She thought, *I need to be careful what I fear next.* And then she thought: *What I fear next is madness. What I fear next is madness. What I fear next is madness.*

31

I 'm so glad we can chat," Frieda said, though she didn't sound glad at all. Doug had gone on an absolute tear the past few weeks and finished the two new books, FedExing the diskettes and riding his bike triumphantly home from the post office.

"Something tells me I messed up." He sat down with the phone base in his lap.

"Well, we can fix it. It's not unusual that our writers find their voice and start embellishing a bit, and please take that as a compliment. You're a real writer."

"It was the eating disorder thing."

"The problem, in this case, is that it's the topic of the next book in the series, *What's Eating Molly*, which has already been written. And then—the Cece book is wonderful, you really have an ear for her, but we meant for the character of the neighbor to be peripheral. As it is, you've fleshed him out so much that I think readers would expect him to return."

"Right. Okay."

"What it boils down to, really, is that you've made uninvited changes to the world of the story. And you know, a little thing can have huge repercussions down the line. Someone discovers they're allergic to peanuts, for example, and then five books later—"

"I get it. How long do I have to fix this?"

Frieda sighed—an actual sigh, a rope around Doug's neck. "At this point, you know, you've been fabulous, but we have faster writers, ones who can do this in their sleep. I'm going to bring one of them in, and they'll split the payment."

Doug was surprised how upset he was. There was the money issue, to be sure, the four thousand dollars he'd counted on cut down to two or less, and there was the ignominy of being, essentially, fired. But moreover he felt a sense of failure, of stupidity. He'd messed up something that should have been a piece of cake. And for what? For trying too hard. When here sat his other project, the *real* project, for which he'd accomplished nothing at all beyond breaking and entering.

He poured yesterday's tepid coffee into his thermos. He was searching for milk when he heard Miriam sobbing again, this time from inside the rooms she shared with Case. He was about to make a silent joke about another dead Kennedy when he realized Case was in there with her, that the sobs were covering the rumble of an angry male voice. Doug heard the word *disaster*, and he heard *actually* and *Texas* and *forget it*. He waited longer than he was comfortable, listened for any reason to break down the door: slaps or crashes or sudden screams. But it was just this torrent of words and crying.

Doug started humming loudly as he dumped in a scoop of sugar and shook the thermos up. He gave words to the humming: *This is my cue to leave. This is my cue to leave.* Okay, then. He dug in his desk and found the diskettes that were Edwin Parfitt's prison, and he found the bound copy of his dissertation, and he found last year's research—Xeroxes and notes and outlines. He stuck them in his bag with the thermos. It had taken a punch in the balls from Frieda and Melissa Hopper, it had taken hysterical Texans spooking him from the house, but he would finally get to work.

And what was more: He was done being a baby. If there were files twenty yards away from him, he was going to help himself.

The fund-raiser was a week away, but that was enough time to plan the details. He'd have knocked on Miriam's door right then to tell her so, if she hadn't been indisposed. Instead, he headed out the door and into the rain.

In front of a library computer, he spread things out. He borrowed a stapler and some markers from the front desk. By the end of two hours, he had a plan for a new shape to the book, given that something, anything, could be found in the files. Parfitt was famous (if he was famous for anything, which he wasn't) for periods of hyperproductivity followed by long fallow stretches. This was often attributed to his depression, though Doug had never found any signs of the man's mood swings other than his offing himself—and Doug wondered if he could piece together some other theory, based on the poet's time at MacDowell and Laurelfield and his publication schedule. The MacDowell archives were at the Library of Congress, and maybe he'd be allowed access. Those librarians couldn't be harder to get past than Gracie. And the sickness Parfitt had mentioned in that letter to his niece—there might be something about that in the Laurelfield files. That he'd had to leave early, that he was depressed, that he had some condition like lupus that would have immobilized him for months or years. Perhaps he'd had, like Doug, an invisible troll sitting on his shoulders keeping him from his work—until, one day, the troll hopped off.

32

As the days grew short, as the ghost stories of the semester piled up in her dreams and (as fifteen-page papers) in her inbox, as she lay awake half the night and walked sleeping through the day, Zee began to wonder if her sanity, her residency in the rational world, wasn't a thin veneer. Something ready, all along, to crack.

She'd always believed she could read Doug like a book, but apparently this wasn't true. She hadn't even known what he was writing. She looked at him in the mornings and wondered who he was.

So what was real? And who was running the show? She used to think she was the one in charge. Now she began to fear this same thing.

She found herself pressing on the kitchen counter to see if it would give way, if it would turn to a liquid or a vapor.

The last weeks of November passed in a dull and angry blur. Chantal asked if she was feeling all right. "No," she said, and walked away.

In the bathroom of the English building, she noticed her arms had grown thin. There she was in the glass above the sink, still visible, fluorescently lit. What had once been a nice, symmetrical face had grown bony and shiny, like a cartoon of an unfortunate stepsister. As she stood at the hand dryer, the tiles on the floor began rearranging themselves, jumping to new spots. No. It was scraps of toilet paper, blown by the hot air.

Doug didn't seem to notice that she'd spoken maybe twelve sentences in the past week. She'd climb into bed and pretend to fall asleep immediately. He'd keep reading for an hour, his face glowing in the lamp and from some deeper contentment too. She found five hundred dollars in his sock drawer and figured he'd gotten it from those horrible books. She wondered if he was spending it on Miriam. She took a fifty from the stack, and used it to buy the bottle of vodka that lived in her office desk for the next week till it was empty.

She walked in to find her ghost seminar in deep debate. Sarah Bonheur was red in the face, practically shouting. "It would be a statement on how this school feels about women," she said. "Like, look at their date rape policy. Oh, excuse me, their *lack* of policy."

Chad Crosley, polo shirt and ratty cap, shorts despite the freezing weather, leaned back and said, with authority, "You know why they'll never fire him? He's an alum."

"*Exactly!* It's the old boys' network. The alum thing is a *male* thing."

Zee, setting down her papers, shook her head. "He's not, Chad. He went to Indiana." Fran was agreeing loudly with Sarah. "Look how long it took them to build sorority houses! Like we're some afterthought. If Dr. Cole is still here after Christmas, I'm transferring."

Zee—maybe it was the swig of vodka before class—snapped. "Look, Fran, you don't know the whole story. We're trying to teach you to think like adults, and you're jumping to conclusions like children." Fran stared, cowed. Zee wondered why she'd just defended Cole, without ever deciding to. "Professor Cole has *nothing* to do with your sorority house, Fran."

Chad, sullen under his cap: "I'm sure that dude's an alum."

Zee had no fondness for Case Breen, but she wanted to cry when she saw him. He lay on the downstairs couch, covered in ice packs, his neck swollen so his chin had nearly vanished. Miriam knelt by his side, and when Zee asked what had happened she lifted the ice packs to show how his face had swallowed his eyes, reduced them to slits.

"He was out walking," Miriam said. "Which he shouldn't have been. You know that bear statue, back in the woods?" Apparently Case, in an effort to avoid the trucks out front, the florists and caterers setting up for tonight's fund-raiser, had circled the rear of the property and taken a rest on the pedestal of the statue. (Zee, in her childhood, had named the bear Theo. She hadn't been back there in ages.) Bees began swarming out from under the thing, and Case, leaving his crutches behind, didn't get far enough fast enough. "He isn't allergic at least, but they took out forty-three stingers. And of course he hurt his ankle again."

"Good God. Really? Bees in November?"

Case made a noise from the couch, low and guttural. His arms were covered with white cream. Zee wondered if he could still talk, but then he said, "Leave me alone. Both of you. Go away."

33

There were two complications at the beginning of the fund-raiser, even after Miriam managed to prop the puffed-up shell of Case in the corner, a scotch in his hand, and leave him to his own devices. The first was that Gracie had recognized Leland, despite his Clark Kent act (shaved face, glasses). But Doug and Miriam had been standing far away, after sneaking him in through the garage, and Leland had preempted her question by saying, "I hope you remember me. I'm Jack Spence, whose life you so kindly saved by letting me photograph your attic. And I'm also a big Gore supporter. When I learned the event would be at your house, I couldn't resist!" Gracie had smiled warmly and introduced him to the lanky state senator holding court by the cheese table. Zee recognized Leland too, but only vaguely. "We've met before," he said, and before he could give her the second speech he'd practiced, she nodded and wandered away.

The second snag was when Zee pulled Doug into the closed-off hallway to Bruce's study, pushed him up against the wall, and unzipped his pants. In seconds he was growing full in her hand, and his brain had turned almost completely off. It was seven fifty-five, and he was supposed to meet Leland and Miriam outside the kitchen at eight o'clock, in the moments right before the speeches started. With every reserve of physical willpower, he peeled his mouth from hers and slid down the wall and zipped back up. "Not here," he said.

By the time he turned back, she'd been replaced by a blade of ice. She wrapped her arms around her stomach and glared so deeply into him that it seemed a serious accusation, an indictment. But he didn't have mental space left to decipher the look. She walked away, and he sat on the couch to wait out his erection.

At a minute past eight, Doug scooted past a scurrying caterer and planted a hand on Leland's shoulder. Bruce was clanking a glass already in the library. The quartet had stopped playing.

Miriam grinned up at Doug, all teeth. This was the happiest he'd seen her since before Hidalgo tore up her work. She had chosen a silver cocktail dress so she could be the one to handle anything dusty, afraid streaks would show on the men's black dress pants. She'd straightened her hair and pulled it back. Leland, meanwhile, was bouncing out of his skin. His pockets were full of the needles and keys he'd cadged from the same friend who'd been tutoring him all week on picking old locks. The three passed through the kitchen to climb the back stairs. The caterers paid no attention. No one was there as they made their way down the silent hall to the attic door. And no one heard as Miriam said, "We're like the Bloodhound Gang!"

And really, that was exactly what it felt like to Doug—that for the first time since maybe college, he had a cohort, and a pack mentality. Earlier, as the room had filled, Doug felt connected to them both by invisible strings. Their eye contact was loaded with a thousand reminders and encouragements.

Doug stood guard at the top of the stairs, and Leland told Miriam she should try the lock first. "I'm sure you have the steadiest hands," he said. There was no time for such gallantry, and Doug saw from the way Leland was rocking on his heels that he couldn't wait to take over, to show off his new skills. "Give me some light," Miriam said, and Leland produced his little pocket flashlight and held it right over her ear. Doug wondered if his heart might actually stop, if the sustained thumping he hadn't endured since his last real soccer game (twelve years ago? thirteen?) might simply kill him, if he might become the next ghost of Laurelfield: *The man who died for no reason in the middle of a party. They found his crumpled body at the foot of the stairs.*

But then he heard a click and a gasp, and he turned to find them both staring at the door, an inch-thick crack of darkness at its open edge. "Jesus!" Leland said. "God, that was impressive! I think I'm in love!"

Doug pulled out his own flashlight, and they passed the switch on the wall without flipping it. They closed the door, careful to test that it would reopen on the way out. "Oh, wow," Miriam said, climbing first, "don't you guys feel that? On the stairs? Don't you feel that presence?"

Leland said, "I can't believe that worked. I can't fucking believe it."

Doug climbed behind the other two, overcome by the unhelpful realization that he wanted out, that it was too much, that he'd rather be down on Bruce's couch getting screwed by his wife, or at the party listening to fund-raising news, or, better yet, in bed with a magazine and a beer. But no: The new Doug *did* things. For instance, the new Doug held the flashlight steady even when Miriam announced brightly, "Hey, there are micies! Don't worry, little guy! Oh, he ran away." And the new Doug was the one who navigated the maze of bed frames and dressers until he came, with awe and recognition, to the four file cabinets forming a crooked little quad by one of the moonlit dormers.

"Okay," Leland said, "say a prayer." And he pulled the top drawer of one cabinet. With a musical creak, it opened. He said, "Give me the light. Okay. Okay. Tisdale, Robin. Tollman, Harold. Tower, Rosamund."

Miriam squealed and threw her arms around Doug's neck, then hugged Leland from behind and tried to peer over his shoulder. They shushed one another and opened more drawers, announced the contents and shushed again. Two entire cabinets held the alphabetized colonist files, and the other two were a jumble of year-by-year records and correspondence. Miriam dove into those, instructed to search specifically through the twenties and thirties, and the men focused on the drawer that would contain both M and P. Because M came first, Leland dug through first. Doug restrained himself from shouting that the Parfitt research was the reason they were up here to begin with. He held the flashlight for Leland. Miriam pulled out files to read their labels by the moonlight.

"Moor, no *E*," Leland said. "Another Moor, no *E*. Christ. Oh, Christ. Marlon Moore? *Marlon Moore?* This is what they're going by?" He hefted an enormous file from the cabinet and sat with it on the floor. "Some douchebag named Marlon Moore. There's half a book here. No, literally. There's half a novel. And some idiot thought this was Marianne Fucking Moore."

"Can you scoot over?" Doug said. "We don't have time." He stepped across Leland and pulled the drawer as far as it would go. There it was: Parfitt, Edwin, a hanging file with a white label. It was alarmingly thin, though, and as he pulled it out he feared there would be a single piece of paper inside, an unpaid fifty-cent phone bill.

When he did open the folder there was, indeed, a single sheet, but that sheet was so bizarre he didn't have time to gape at its thinness, its singularity. He didn't say anything at all as he shone his flashlight around the edges. It was a photograph, taken outside. The more he looked at the background, the more he became convinced this was the back corner of the big house, the largest koi pond off to the right, and a bench. But the background was hard to focus on, because the subject of the photo was two men, both stark naked, both dripping wet. One was laughing, head lolled back. The other stared straight at the camera, his grin urgent and almost malevolent. Each man had a hand around the other's penis. And neither man was Edwin Parfitt.

Doug struggled for something to announce, but his brain had short-circuited entirely, and Leland was reading aloud from Marlon Moore's manuscript. *"Rose was mad with grief,"* he said. *"Yeah, I'm* mad with grief. Listen to this: *One who has not wandered under those titanic pines will scarce comprehend the weight of time that settles on the solitary philosopher seeking shelter 'neath their dripping arms.* The pages are out of order, too. Not that it matters."

"It's eight thirty," Doug said. "We need to load up."

"Did you find Parfitt stuff?" Miriam turned to him, eyes alarmingly bright in the moonlight.

"I'll show you later."

"I've got 1920 through '39, but each year is three inches of stuff. You have to pick."

"Pick for me. No, 1933."

She pulled two files from the drawer. Leland handed Miriam his suit jacket, then loosened the belt of his too-large slacks, and Doug and Miriam worked together to tuck the two thick 1933 folders and the flat Parfitt one into the waistband. Miriam secured the last and tightened the belt, and Leland wiggled his brows over her head at Doug. When he was retucked, jacket covering the bulges, he took a few trial steps.

"What about this, though?" Miriam grabbed a small green lockbox off the top of one cabinet. "This has to be interesting, right?"

Doug had noticed it in Leland's photographs, but he'd been so focused on the promise of Parfitt files he hadn't thought much of it. Now, though, he was willing to try anything.

"Just carry it out," Doug said. It looked natural in Leland's hand, like something he was supposed to be taking from a political fund-raiser. "Walk with authority."

The music started far below. Leland swore and Doug scooped

the Marlon Moore file back into its drawer. Miriam used the dust
cloth from Doug's pocket to wipe any sign of activity from the
cabinet tops.

Back at the party, with Leland gone right out the front door,
Doug and Miriam filtered into the living room, each grabbing
coffee and then talking loudly to each other about Bill Bradley.
There stood Case, alone next to the grandfather clock. He'd been
meant to find Clarence Mahoney, Bruce's friend with all the
connections—he'd been banking on it, in fact, on schmoozing
his way into a job tonight—but his drained glass and the fact that
he didn't seem to have moved were not auspicious. Doug wondered if he could even see the room, with his eyes swollen like
that. There was Bruce, cheeks and nose bright red, throwing his
arm around someone. There was Zee, keeping a narrow balance
as she crossed the room. She put her hand on Doug's tie and slid
it down to his navel. Her voice was flat, her face centimeters from
his own. "Where were you?"

"I stepped outside for a breather," he said, as planned. But it
was freezing out, he realized, and he was drenched with sweat.

Zee just smiled, and slowly turned to Miriam. "Miriam, what
did you think of the state senator? The one from the South Side?"

"Oh, the—wasn't he? He was great."

"And the one after him. What was his name again?"

"Oh, you're asking the wrong person!"

Zee said, "Yes. I am."

34

Zee was composing her final exam when Cole knocked on her office door. "Zelda, my one true friend!" he said. "I had to see for myself!" Every wall of her office was covered with pictures of nude men, which she'd had color printed at Kinko's. Some lounged on motorcycles, some touched themselves, some coyly pulled their jeans down to their knees. Cole stood in the middle of the room, turned a slow circle, emitted a long whistle. "They're not for the ladies, are they?" he said. "These pictures are for the fancy boys." Zee had taped them up on Monday, and by Tuesday Jerry Keaton had gone as far as he dared, sticking a postcard of a lingerie-clad Betty Paige on his office door. Ida Hayes, playing it safe but perhaps saying something more profound about the principles at stake, had copied Adrienne Rich's explicit "floating sonnet" for her classes. Golda Blum had come by to advise Zee that if she was being more flagrant than Cole she might expect starker consequences as well. But Golda was only exasperated and stressed. Zee knew when Golda was furious, and this wasn't it.

What Zee had realized, the day she snapped at Fran, was that her support of Cole had shifted from ironic and undermining to genuine. The first letters she wrote on his behalf were designed to make things worse. ("His jokes about wishing to date certain students have been largely misconstrued.") But around the time she realized what Doug was really writing, around the time he began mooning over Miriam, disappearing with her at the fund-raiser, she'd lost all interest in getting him Cole's job. The thought of Doug, undeserving, unambitious, sitting lovestruck in an office he didn't deserve—in Cole's office, the good little corner one, where that man had written real articles, had graded and conferred for twenty years—made her sick. And without Doug to root for, she found it harder and harder to root against Cole, especially when she saw the tenacity with which he fought his case, never once, never *once*, claiming the pornography wasn't his. She regretted, now, what she'd done, but it was a strange brand of remorse—more tactical than moral.

"And why, pray tell, do you possess a pistol cylinder?"

She tried hard to understand, and finally realized Cole was looking down at her desk. The metal flower, from the woods.

She picked it up and looked through the six perfect holes. She felt stupid—hadn't she seen them in a thousand movies?—but Cole didn't need to know that. "Souvenir," she said. "From my last shootout."

And there was Chad Crosley walking in to ask about his C-minus paper, beet red, hands around his eyes like blinders. He'd been warned.

35

Leland's apartment in Evanston smelled pleasantly of cigar smoke. The walls were lined with bookshelves, and an inordinate number of small, dim lamps lit the living room. The three of them sat on the floor, around the neat stack of files and the lockbox. It had been two days since the fund-raiser, but this was the first time they'd been able to meet. Doug had said he was going to the Northwestern library, and Miriam had invented a yoga class.

"Did you read the files?" Doug asked.

"I did better." Leland flicked the lockbox open, and Miriam applauded. "Well, my locksmith buddy did better."

"What's in it?" Doug lifted out the stack of papers and envelopes.

"Nothing good, sorry to say. It's just Gracie's stuff. We can't be this lucky with locks and get lucky with the content too. But you have your Parfitt file, right?"

"You really didn't look? That's amazing restraint." Doug ceremoniously opened the file to reveal the photograph: wet bodies, laughter, penises.

"Jesus God," Leland said. "Is that Parfitt?"

"Not even."

Miriam had gone bug-eyed, and some old rule flitted through Doug's mind, something about not being vulgar in front of southern women. But what she finally said was, "You know what's weird? They don't even have hard-ons. I mean, it's not *sexy*, you know?"

Leland turned it over. "Crap. Did you see this?" He pointed to the spidery handwriting on the back, the single slanted word and question mark: *Father?* "Someone thinks that's their father? It can't be Parfitt's father, right? The photo quality looks like twenties or thirties, at least."

As Leland and Miriam passed the photo, Doug flipped through the lockbox papers. The 1954 deed to a car. A 1955 marriage license for George Robert Grant and Grace Saville Devohr. A copy of Gracie's birth certificate.

"Hey, guys," he said. "How old did you think Gracie was?"

"Sixty," said Leland. "Maybe fifty-eight."

"Sixty-two," Miriam said. "Bruce is sixty-four, and she's two years younger."

"Look." He put the certificate on the floor. "1925. She's seventy-four."

They both squinted at it, with as much voyeuristic glee as they'd ogled the photo.

"So she had Zee when she was forty," Doug said. "But does Bruce really think she's younger than him?"

"Maybe that's why she didn't want you in the attic," Leland said.

Miriam said, "That's why she's afraid of getting put on the Internet! She doesn't want anyone doing the math."

They spent the next hour poring over the 1933 files, and the one major validation for Doug was the fact that at the end of the file lay a document with the heading "Confirmed Guests, Winter 1934," in which "E. Parfitt" was listed, alongside the note "(4th visit)." Although there was nothing he could immediately use, there was the promise of more. And the fact that the records were so detailed boded well for lists of who was there with Parfitt on his other stays, even minus anything meaningful in his own file.

The other artists might even have mentioned him in their own diaries and correspondence. It would be enough for a clever writer to build some analysis around, some stuff about influence—provided he could get back up to the rest of the files. They'd left the attic door unlocked, but they were sure Sofia, ever thorough, would have discovered it by now and said something to Gracie.

They ordered pizza and Leland dialed up his Internet. Their intent was to find Gracie, to see what was already out there about her. Leland had some vague idea that Doug could use her real birth date to his advantage, either by threatening to expose her or promising to protect her, though Doug doubted he had the guts to pull off either. They found a photo of Gracie as a toddler, blonde curls and a white dress; and another of her at eleven or twelve with her three younger brothers, all a bit petulant next to their dour grandfather, Augustus. It was, indeed, dated 1936. ("My God," Miriam said, "see, he's terrifying! Don't you think he murdered Violet?" "No, but I can see why she wanted out," Doug said. And Miriam said, "I'm glad it's her ghost and not *his*.") And then, following Leland's hunch, they looked up Gracie's father, Gamaliel, and studied his face.

"That *could* be him," Leland said. He was holding the photo of the two naked men next to the computer, comparing the stern businessman on the screen with the naked man on the right, the one throwing his head back in laughter. "It's a funny angle."

Miriam said, "And we don't have Gargamel's penis online, for comparison."

"I can't imagine the chain of events, though," Doug said. "Gracie finds this picture, recognizes her father, writes on the back, and then of all things she puts it in Edwin Parfitt's empty file folder?"

"Or," Miriam said, "she emptied the folder because she knew you'd get up there. And she put this there instead."

"Does she hate me that much?"

"Why else would this be the only file that's different? Like, where's his confirmation letter? Where's his application?"

They stared a bit longer at the online photo of Gamaliel. He was older, but the chin was right, the ears were feasible. Doug remembered that game from the senior yearbook, match the baby with the eighteen-year-old, and how it had been impossible, except for the one Asian kid. Impossible to identify the people who had been your whole world for four years.

It was getting late, but there was more to discuss: How to return the lockbox to the attic, for instance, before Gracie discovered it was gone. How to get the rest of the files.

Leland said, "Look, you don't need to sneak around anymore. You don't need to pretend you did nothing wrong. You can play your hand."

"I didn't know I had a hand."

"You have—you have some *tools* at least. You know Gracie's real age. You know her father might or might not have gone skinny dipping with a male companion."

Miriam said, "We know she either hates Doug or doesn't want him writing about Laurelfield."

"That's not really a tool," Leland said.

"*You're* a tool."

He pelted her with a pizza crust.

Doug added, "And we know her biggest fears. That civilization ends on the thirty-first, or that it doesn't and the Internet survives."

Miriam nodded slowly. "That's all you need, isn't it? That's all it takes to run the world. Knowing people's fears."

(The air between
our bodies

The miles between
intention
and act

The windows, eclipses, forgettings, doorways,
misses and losses and half-slept dreams

The shrinking space between now
And century's end

Here
Under stone
Overboard

I'll tell
the secret I have seen:
The ghosts live in
the space between)

On December 31 Zee and Doug walked to the big house, arms full of belated gifts. They'd spent Christmas itself at Doug's mother's house in Pennsylvania, and there, amid the hoarded statuettes and smoke-stained walls, Zee had felt almost normal again. They ate casserole for four days straight, and helped put in storm windows. It didn't feel like a return to stability or even a vacation, though, so much as a stay of execution. They had to come back to Laurelfield to face their lives and their marriage and the end of the millennium. Any number of explosive things.

Gracie had decreed that the millennium would go out with a late Noel, and that all presents must be wrapped in silver and blue to make Miriam more comfortable. ("I don't get it," Doug had said, and Zee had said, "Just because she's Jewish. My mother's an idiot." "Miriam's Jewish?" And when she'd stared at him in disbelief, he'd added, "I guess I just thought of her as Texan." "What, they don't have Jews in Texas?" "No, like 'Don't Mess with Texas.' Like that sort of overrides everything. I don't know." And she'd looked at him hard, trying to figure out if he was really this clueless, or if he thought he needed to pretend, this late in the game, that he hardly knew Miriam. She wanted to tell him he needn't bother.)

They gathered in the living room around the tree, Case and Miriam underdressed in jeans. Case still wore his boot, but at least his face had resumed its normal shape. The golden tan he'd shown up with that summer was long gone; replaced by a sickly gray. Sofia was off, the food she prepared yesterday already reheating in the oven.

There were flashlights and oil lamps lined up on the sideboard, waiting for midnight, and boxes in the kitchen full of food and aspirin and matches and batteries and vitamin C and toilet paper, alongside office-sized bottles of water and a kerosene stove. Bruce kept checking his watch. It was only six thirty, but every hour he turned on the TV to check the march of time and potential disaster. City after city survived. Electricity had stayed on in Beijing and New Delhi and Moscow and Paris. Bruce was convinced now that the real trouble wouldn't start until midnight hit the U.S. east coast, and so that's what they were waiting for: eleven o'clock central, when the Times Square ball would fall and so, presumably, would humanity.

Miriam scooted around the floor like a lithe elf to distribute the packages. For Bruce, a book on subsistence farming. For Gracie, an antique toast rack. When Miriam opened her present from Doug, Zee nearly gagged: a Ziploc bag of sea glass, blue and green and copper. It would have taken him weeks on the frigid beach to collect so much. Miriam said, "I know how I can work them in!" She meant the monstrous thing on the board in the kitchen, the vertiginous patterns she was laying down inch by inch in wet mortar, better than her other work only in that the pieces were tile and glass instead of garbage. Case gave everyone chocolate. Miriam began opening Zee's gift, which was truly awful. Three days ago, Zee had gone back to her office and grabbed the pistol cylinder. It was an antique, of sorts. It was interesting. It was also a nongift. It was, quite literally, an empty threat of violence.

But Miriam didn't seem alarmed. "This is amazing!" she said.

"I thought you could stick pencils in it."

"It has to be ancient. I *love* it."

Zee was chagrined that no one had to ask what it was. Even her mother, after a moment of silence, said, "Zilla, where on earth did you find such a thing?"

And Zee said, "Boston."

There were survival kits from Bruce, sweaters from Gracie, a collection of Marianne Moore poems from Miriam to Doug, with a bizarre inscription: *for walks under those titanic pines.* Doug turned pink. He smiled at his shoes.

And then—as if Zee had done it herself, as if her rage had flown across the room—the window behind the tree shattered into a million raining shards. They kept falling, with a sound like a xylophone, until nothing was left, just a rectangle of night and frigid wind. Gracie stopped shrieking and they all took shelter on the far side of the room. Miriam's arm was cut, and Doug's eyebrow, but not badly. Bruce checked his watch (only seven fifteen, not nearly time for the apocalypse), grabbed a poker, and headed out to make sure it wasn't a thrown rock—but they knew it wasn't, the way the glass had just disintegrated so gracefully, from everywhere at once. Gracie scampered to silence the burglar alarm.

They all moved gingerly for the rest of the night, in case another window shattered. After dinner, Zee cleared the table and snuck back to the living room. Bruce had duct taped a blanket over the window, but the frozen air still crept through. She poured straight vodka into her teacup, and let the tea bag diffuse and turn the liquid golden. She didn't care how it tasted. Bruce retreated to his study to watch the New Year hit whatever Atlantic islands were three hours ahead. Gracie stood in the kitchen, sorting absently through yesterday's mail, throwing away a late Christmas card from distant family in Toronto. "I don't know why they persist in sending these," she said. Back in the dining room, Miriam hovered over Doug's chair, inspecting his eyebrow. Her small breasts were inches from his mouth. "I'm worried there's a sliver still," she said.

Zee pretended to read Bruce's *Tribune* and then circled back to the dark living room again, her teacup empty. She'd already started to pour when she noticed Case standing silent with his crutches by the blown-out window. If she hadn't been numbed from the alcohol, she'd have screamed.

"Would you like a drink?" she said.

Case's face was ravaged, sunken, nothing but eye sockets and cheekbones. It was hard to remember the way he used to smirk at everything.

She tried again. "Case, I'm sorry about all of it. You've had terrible luck. No one deserves that."

"You know what's funny?"

She shook her head.

"As soon as someone says *luck*, you know we're not really talking about luck anymore. If it were luck, the coin would come up heads half the time. Right? It would balance."

"But it never does."

"I just think *luck*'s the wrong word. When we bother talking about it, we mean there's been a whole string of good things or a string of bad things. Like the coin keeps coming up tails."

"So maybe what we mean is fate."

"You know about her, don't you? You know about her."

"Oh. Oh, Case." It was terrible: She honestly hadn't given him much thought in all this. He had it worse than her, home all day to see it, no job. "I *do* know. Case, I'm sorry. I—everyone's going to get through this." She brought him a glass of vodka, which he took and held like he didn't know what it was for.

Case said, "She put her finger on my lips." He reached out one finger and actually pressed it right to Zee's mouth before she could move, before she could even register his words. His eyes were wild and green, fixed on hers. Zee took his hand as gently as she could and removed it from her face. "And you've seen her too, I know you have. She comes to you too."

Zee regretted the alcohol fog that wasn't quite allowing her to shift paradigms. He couldn't be talking about Miriam, could he? He looked like he might cry, actually cry. "Are you talking about Violet?"

He shrugged, humiliated, and didn't answer.

"Case, I think you need to see a doctor. This house can get to people, but no, I haven't seen—not *literally*. Not like that."

He was devastated, she could tell. However difficult it was for him to say all this, he'd been counting on her understanding, on some kind of validation.

"This place doesn't want me," he said. "It's rejecting me. Like a transplanted organ."

"You shouldn't be here. You should go back to Texas." She said it purely out of concern, and only afterward remembered that this was what she'd wanted all along.

He blinked down at the vodka. "Miriam won't leave. This is the happiest she's ever been. This is the best work she's ever done."

She wished she could tell him that it wasn't the house, that Miriam was only happy because she was in love with Doug, and it was the wrong kind of happiness. But she couldn't do that to him right now. "Tomorrow, if the world doesn't end. Bruce will loan you guys money, right? Go home and get healthy."

But now Gracie was in the doorway saying "*There* you are," and asking who would join Bruce for a spin in the '57 Chevy "before the streets get dangerous."

Case said he would, and he handed Zee the vodka and walked from the room like a broken marionette. Zee went back to the dining room, where Miriam and Doug both still sat. Their whispering stopped the moment she appeared. But she wasn't there for *them*, she wished they knew. She walked around to the back wall, to the portrait of Violet. If the artist had been less skilled, her great-grandmother might have remained as flat and uninteresting as any other ancestor. Instead, her skin glowed and her mouth hovered before some small movement, as if she were just now about to say something she'd held in these past hundred years. Zee tried to look at Violet straight on, but Violet was always looking somewhere else.

It was frustrating. Because (and maybe it was just the vodka) Zee needed that moment of silent communication. She had a question for Violet today, a hypothesis she wanted confirmed in this most unscientific of manners. *You aren't even the ghost,* she wanted to ask, *are you? Something drove you crazy in this house, and it's the same thing killing Case, and it's the same thing driving me mad. Everyone in this house is crazy. And look at the blown-out window, the strangling ivy. It isn't you. This is why I felt fine in Pennsylvania. Something's wrong with this house. Something's broken. Things don't work normally here.* (If the semester weren't over, she'd float the idea by her seminar: not a haunted house, a haunting house.)

But Violet avoided her eyes.

38

At ten thirty, fortified by bourbon, Doug asked Gracie if he could speak to her in the solarium. Gracie had been drinking champagne since six, and Miriam had made sure to refill her glass every time it was even halfway empty, till she was wobbly and glassy-eyed. Miriam ran interference now on everyone else, making sure they stayed in the den, where the TV replayed the celebrations from the International Dateline and points west. Doug and Gracie sat on the long white couch and he said, "I have an offer for you. A good one."

She looked skeptical. She said, "If this is about your employment situation, I can't do more than I already am."

"No. It's—I think you know that I've been in the attic."

Her hand fluttered to her forehead.

"I shouldn't have, I know, but please understand how important this is for me. Those archives are the whole meat of the book. But I'll get back to that." He pushed his fists into his knees. "While I was up there, quite by accident, I also found some personal papers of yours."

"Oh, Douglas." She started looking for her champagne glass. Doug found it on the floor and handed it to her.

"And I did figure some things out. I want to help you. In exchange—I mean, I know you're nervous about the Internet. I checked, and it's already out there. It says you're seventy-four. We can't change what's already there. But if it's important to you, there are ways to create alternate timelines, to get those circulated as well, to confuse things. I have a friend who does Internet stuff. I want to help you. I do."

Gracie leaned back, her eyes closed. She looked pale—fine wrinkles on top of tissue-paper skin on top of a sudden gray bloodlessness—and he felt he should be taking care of her, getting her a blanket, rather than tormenting her like this. But then she sat up and leaned toward him. She tapped his leg.

"Douglas, you're clever. And I'm smarter than I seem. I want you to know that."

"I'm sure we can strike a reasonable bargain." He was glad Miriam and Leland weren't there to hear how ridiculous he sounded.

"Those papers are just a joke. People with our kind of wealth, we need other documents sometimes. *Alternate* documents."

"But that would be illegal."

"Not at all. Bruce is smart with these things, and he has lawyer friends."

"Gracie, I'm talking about *old* documents. Long before you knew Bruce."

Miriam had told him just to stare Gracie down if he was at a loss. He pressed his thumbs together and looked right at her. She gave a high laugh, a sound like a teacup hitting the floor.

"Well. Are you trying to ask for money, Douglas? You've never been direct."

"I just want the colony files."

"What files?"

He said, with as much conviction as he could summon, with an edge of threat that surprised him when he heard it: "The Parfitt files. You know exactly what I mean, because you're the one who replaced them."

Gracie looked furious now, which was at least a development, if not an admission. She said, "I don't know what on earth you're talking about. *Replaced* them!"

"I went searching, and instead of what I should have found—"

"Douglas, I've been good to you."

"And that's why I know we can help each other."

"What precisely did you find?" The downside of her champagne consumption, he realized, was that she'd become difficult to read. He didn't want to anger her further by implying that her father was gay, so he tried to word things carefully.

"I found—I mean, you must know. It was those two people who—I don't know who they were, exactly. Two people, here at this house. Doing something very strange, very unorthodox. You *do* know what I mean. And please don't lie to me."

Gracie took a breath so deep that Doug worried about her ribs. "The world's about to end, isn't it? One way or the other." She was so small on the other end of the couch. She said nothing for a long time, and Doug wondered if the question wasn't rhetorical after all. Then she said, "But you have to understand that there was *no* point calling the police. Douglas, there was a lipstick mark halfway down the top of her dress. That's how far her neck had snapped. The car was like an accordion."

Doug had the horrible feeling that he'd jumped down the wrong rabbit hole, that the prospect of Edwin Parfitt was growing dimmer and dimmer as he fell. All he could think to say was "Oh."

"It was the worst thing I'd seen in my life." She was crying, he saw with horror. Her eyes were pink. He felt like hyperventilating himself, and it was only his utter confusion that kept him pinned to the couch, that kept him from breaking down over lipstick and accordions himself. "But you *do* know it was an accident. I'd die if you thought otherwise. Max would never have let him take the car if he knew Grace was in it. He didn't answer the phone—he wouldn't answer the phone—but he didn't know it was *her*."

There was a paper napkin in Doug's pocket, and he unfolded it and handed it to her and tried to rewind those last sentences, tried to guess whether speaking of herself in the third person was a rhetorical flourish or a sign of mental breakdown.

He said, idiotically, or perhaps brilliantly, "Max wouldn't have let him. If he knew Gracie was in it. The car."

"She was always *Grace*. Oh, she was a fool. No one got divorced in 1955, but still, I remember thinking there was something wrong with her that she didn't leave him. He was terrible. A *terrible* person."

Doug wished he had Leland on an earpiece, telling him what to say. He managed: "How so?"

"Oh, you know, a drunkard." She was still crying, but there was a gossipy edge to her voice now, a mean one. She spoke quickly. "That's why the family left them alone out here. They *never* came to check on her. Not *once*. They died not long after— the father, and then the mother a few years later—and the brothers didn't care for her a fig. But Douglas, that family! They made it easy for us, by not caring. Half the time she was hiding a black eye. He tried me, but I could handle him. I knew about drunks. My father was in *jail*, Douglas. Can you believe that? George never dared mess with me."

George was Zee's father, the gentle man who had taken Zee on the train to the Art Institute once a month. Doug knew he'd once had a drinking problem, but he'd never heard of any violence. And Gracie's father might indeed have been jailed once or twice—the Devohrs were never long out of the gossip columns in those days—but none of it, together, made sense. Hidalgo trotted in and stuck his nose in Doug's crotch.

"And what would we have done, if we hadn't stayed? The family would have come and covered the furniture with white sheets. They'd have been in no hurry to sell. We'd have been out on our ears. And Max would have died. It would have *killed* him to leave, I really believe that. He was a true gentleman. You should have seen how he turned the pages of the newspaper: He picked up the corner with his finger and thumb, and just lifted it over. Everyone I'd ever known turned pages with their whole palm, like something they were wiping away. It wasn't a *romantic* relationship we had. But it was better than most, and Zilla is something. We wanted her so badly. She was born ten years later, exactly. I always took it for a sign. Ten years."

Doug tried to think if he'd ever heard of someone named Max. He managed to push Hidalgo away and lock his knees against further attack. He said, "Who else knows all this?" As if he himself knew it, or understood it, or had any idea how much of it was a joke.

Gracie shook her head. She was looking at some spot near Doug's face, but not at Doug. "Max, until he died. I suppose the gardener knew. I always guessed Max bribed him, but I said I wanted no part of it. The hole for the greenhouse was already dug, but the cement wasn't poured yet. So it was all done the next day, just Max and the gardener. I hid upstairs, but I could hear the wheelbarrows crunching along the drive to the big house. *Wheelbarrows.*" She covered her nose and mouth with her hands and closed her eyes. The sound of wheelbarrows was apparently the worst part, to her. "And he fired the rest of the staff. *Big* tips, of course. More money than they'd ever seen. And hired new people."

Miriam poked her head in the door just then. If she'd overheard anything, it was only that last sentence. "Ten fifty-five. Five minutes till doomsday, east."

"We're just finishing up," Doug said, though he didn't know if that was true.

Miriam raised an eyebrow—Doug's face must have looked as ashen as it felt—and ducked out.

"I need you to know it hasn't been *easy*, Douglas. Especially at first. The research we had to do, the places we had to avoid. It helped that she'd *never* shown her face in town, and they'd only been here a few months. Those ridiculous sunglasses. And he was always off in Highwood, drinking. They looked nothing alike. George and Max. But it didn't matter a bit, in the end. People see what they expect to. And the rest can be handled with money. Still, if you think I haven't had a thousand heart attacks along the way. And the close calls, the parties where someone was from Toronto and I'd have to get sick and leave. It's stolen *years* from my life."

Doug took a risk. "So it's—under the greenhouse." He wasn't sure at all what he was referring to, but the remote possibility remained that it was something to do with Parfitt. Or else why the missing file? He looked over his shoulder, at the sliding glass doors that separated the solarium from the greenhouse. He could see a few geraniums out there, borrowing some of the indoor light.

"Yes. Both of them. Good lord. If you want the real ghosts of the house, it's those two, not poor old Violet."

"Those two, meaning—"

"They made that window shatter, you know. They've done it before."

And there was Bruce at the door, waving urgently. "Come on!" he shouted. "This is the big one!"

As they hurried down the hall after him, Doug realized he hadn't gotten a single answer about Parfitt. He didn't understand what she was saying, but he believed her. He just had no idea what it was he was supposed to believe.. What ingredients he'd just swallowed. He wanted to march Gracie back to the solarium and lock the door, to ask her fifty more questions, but first he needed to see if the world was ending. He was less certain of its survival than he'd been an hour ago.

Zee and Miriam and Case sat on the leather couch, staring at Dick Clark and the drunken masses in Times Square. No one on the screen seemed particularly panicked. They jumped around in the cold, kissing strangers.

Doug and Bruce and Gracie stood with their hands on the couch back, braced for some kind of impact.

The ball came down, and the world did not end.

President Clinton addressed the nation. Bands played, proposals abounded, and after a soothing update about the absence of nuclear meltdowns, the station switched over to the Chicago team and the depressingly anticlimactic forty minutes they had to fill until midnight Central from the floor of a balloon-filled ballroom.

Case said, "We're still here." Something odd about his voice, as if he wasn't entirely sure of the fact. Or as if he was disappointed to find himself still alive, still on the couch, the lights still on.

Bruce turned down the volume and spoke for the first time. "Well, you never know," he said. There was phlegm in his voice. "You never know what could still happen. But it looks like a lot of bullshit, doesn't it? It looks like a great deal of human folly here this evening."

"It never hurts to be prepared," Gracie said.

"And the things we bought—the car, the food, the water—they're not useless. I'd always wanted that Chevy, all my life."

They nodded. Doug was afraid Bruce would start weeping. He couldn't handle any more of that tonight.

"You know what else? We've lost sight of something, with all this millennium bullshit, with all the computer nightmare. We're forgetting that this is the end of a *century*. The worst century, I believe, in all of human history. Hitler, Stalin, genocide, the worst warfare in what, a million years of human life on this planet."

"But a lot of good, too," Miriam said.

Zee turned to face her. "Oh? Like what?"

"Penicillin? And all the art. Think of, you know, Georgia O'Keeffe. And jazz, and movies! And airplanes. All of it."

Gracie said, "It's the house's birthday. Did you know that? This house is a hundred years old now."

"I don't think they built it on New Year's, Mom."

"They started building in nineteen hundred!"

"What do you think, Doug?" Bruce's voice was a little off, a little too loud. He put down his rum with a clatter and undid his collar. "You're the writer here. Was the twentieth century a comedy, or a tragedy?"

"Or a tragicomedy," said Zee.

Doug said, "I don't know." He was still thinking about Gracie, and didn't trust himself to form a coherent sentence.

"Well, I think it was a tragedy," Bruce said. "An absolute and gruesome tragedy. The whole damn century would've made more sense backward. Where we've ended is worse than where we began."

Miriam said, "Maybe it was a love story."

Doug was so busy watching Zee sneer at Miriam that he didn't see Bruce collapse on the floor beside him. He heard Gracie scream, and there was Bruce, his right arm flapping, his face pale and wet.

Case ran to the phone, and for the five minutes it took the ambulance to get there, Gracie kept shrieking that someone should do CPR, and Zee kept calmly explaining that you could only perform CPR on a dead person and Bruce wasn't dead.

Doug monitored Bruce's pulse, which was weak but consistent, and tried to remember what other medical skills he'd been taught in his 1985 training for YMCA camp counselor. Hidalgo ran in circles and barked.

Miriam managed to let the paramedics in through the triple-locked doors, and as they carried the stretcher through the house Hidalgo lunged at it again and again with his front paws, until one of the men sent him flying with a knee to the sternum. Bruce was stable as they carried him out, conscious and wheezing and trying to lift his head.

Gracie rode in the ambulance. Once she was out the door, Doug suggested that Zee drive with Case in Gracie's car, and he and Miriam follow in the Subaru. "Someone needs to put Hidalgo in his cage," he said. The job would take twenty minutes of bribery and wrestling, and required at least two people. "We'll come right behind." Zee shot him a withering look he couldn't quite interpret, but she grabbed Case's elbow and steered him out the door.

Miriam held up her hand to show it shaking. If she'd been closer to her father-in-law he would have waited, but he couldn't hold it in. "You won't believe this," he said.

As they turned off the TV (seven minutes to midnight) and the lights, and constructed a trail of Milkbones to Hidalgo's kennel in the mudroom, he repeated what he could. He knew he was leaving things out, and he told her at least three times about the man named Max and the way he turned the newspaper pages.

"I was totally drawn in," he said. "I couldn't think straight. You'd have done a better job. Anyone would've."

Miriam spun in circles, trying to catch Hidalgo's red leather collar. "So basically her story is she can't be seventy-four because she's really some other person?"

"I believe that was the gist of it. She kept talking about 'Grace' like that wasn't her. So allegedly Grace died, I think? In the car crash. And someone else died too. I don't know if she said it was George, but that was what I got. She said 1955."

"Hmm. Those are the principles of a good lie. Tell a big one, and throw in details. Hidalgo! Sit! Hidalgo!"

"Right. So you—you think she was lying."

"She gave you one excuse for the papers, and when you didn't believe it she gave you another, complete with tears and melodrama. She told you *nothing* about the files?"

Doug felt like an utter idiot. He'd become a dimwitted televi-
sion viewer, sucked into a soap opera and too distracted by the
amnesia and stolen identity and ghosts to realize he'd just watched
five ads for laundry detergent. Gracie had warned him, hadn't
she? That she was smarter than she looked. But no, it had been
real. It had *felt* real.

"She was crying," he said. "I can't explain—it wasn't like she
was making something up. She was letting something out." He
got Hidalgo straddled for one second, but in the next Doug was
falling into the wall and Hidalgo was again circling frantically.

"It's insane. I mean, for many reasons. Not one person in the
whole town saw they weren't the real Grants? Not one family
member suspected something funny?"

"I didn't tell that part right. The woman, Grace, she always
had a black eye, because the husband hit her, and he was always
out drinking. So they didn't go into town. And the family didn't
visit." He wasn't sure if he was defending Gracie's story, or only
his own credulity, however fragile.

"I'm not buying it. Hidalgo! Biscuit!"

If Miriam didn't believe it, *Miriam*, who believed houses had
souls, who wouldn't write anyone a letter when Mercury was ret-
rograde, then was he the most gullible man in the world? But his
narration was flawed. Nothing new there. He had made uninvited changes to the world of the story.

In one ninja-fast move, Miriam wrapped her fingers through
Hidalgo's collar and pushed his backside until he stood, stunned
and whimpering, in his kennel.

"Impressive," Doug said. He checked his watch. "In fact, that
was officially the best dog-wrangling of the twenty-first century."

"Of the millennium!" Miriam said. "Happy New Year."

They sat with Zee a long time in the ER waiting room, watching
Ricky Martin gyrate soundlessly on the overhead TV. Case came

out at two-thirty to lead them to the ICU, where chairs lined the end of the hallway. Places for people to get bad news. Gracie was in one, her legs crossed at the ankle, her pocketbook clutched on her lap.

"He's still stable," she said. "It was a massive coronary. Doesn't that sound dramatic? But they've got the best doctors in there. Bruce and I are big supporters of this hospital, and not for nothing. Douglas is going to help me get some coffee now, because in my nervous state I can't pour a thing."

She held his arm all the way down the corridor and around the corner. She stopped and clenched both his shoulders in her hands. She was sharply sober. "It should go without saying," she said, "that what passed between us was privileged information." He feared for a moment that she'd guessed what he told Miriam. But no, it was just a warning. "You do know which side your bread is buttered on. If this information were to get out at all—*at all*—there would be Devohr cousins descending on us in an instant. Like locusts. *You'*d be homeless, among other things. Not to mention, it would kill Zilla."

He said, "I wouldn't dream of repeating—"

"Good. And I want you to know that while I wouldn't cheapen our relationship by paying you off, I do guarantee that if you hold your tongue, I'll make it worth your while in the long run."

He wanted to ask if there was some medication she'd been neglecting, and he wanted to ask if she thought he was a moron, and at the same time he wanted to tell her he believed every word. But here was his opportunity. "All I need is the colony files in the attic. Just the key to the attic, really." Doug saw dimly, through the fog, that he was demanding things from a woman whose husband was in Intensive Care. He was a bad person.

"Oh, for Pete's sake. Of course. Run and get me coffee, though. Cream and sugar."

Doug practically floated to the cafeteria, and although he told himself several times that he should be worried about Bruce, all he could think of was that key, and those files, and of how he'd relate Gracie's vehemence to Miriam later.

He returned with a thin cup of scalding coffee. Back in the ICU corridor, they were all standing: Zee with her hands on her hips; Miriam clinging to Case; Case pale and thin; Gracie with her hand to her forehead; two doctors, one tall, one short. As Doug approached the group, Zee turned and glared. "He's dead," she said. As if it were Doug's fault. As if Doug, in those five minutes, had betrayed them all.

39

That ridiculous cup of coffee, that flimsy prop. When it was obvious to everyone—humiliatingly, glaringly— that even in the midst of her crisis, her husband *dying*, Gracie had felt the need to drag Doug aside and upbraid him for his brazenness, for staying behind with Miriam to wait for midnight, to kiss her at midnight, to be with her alone in case the world ended, to leave Zee an abandoned fool at the end of the world. When Zee and Case had met her in the ER, Gracie had grabbed her arm so frantically, asking where was Doug, and Zee saw that she *knew*. No one could hide anything from her mother.

They went into the room, first Gracie and then Case and then all of them, and there was Bruce, still so pink, so sweaty, the hairs in his nostrils still wet, his fat hands resting so lightly on the sheet, that he couldn't possibly be dead. They should have waited an hour, till he was bluer and smaller.

The nurse said, "There's been a whole lot of heart attacks, the last few days. A lot of stress right now." As if it were all the rage.

Case, behind Zee, said quietly: "This is my fault." Zee turned and saw that Miriam was over near Doug—of course—and he must have been saying it just to her, to Zee.

She whispered back: "That's not true, Case."

"You know it is. I'm a lightning rod. I *told* you."

She pulled him away from the bed. The others were talking to the nurse. She said, "Case, I used to hate you, I really did, with your little car and your haircut, but—you didn't do it. It's not your fault." She should have stopped there. She didn't. "You just need to get away from that house. I mean, especially now. Why stay?"

Zee was asking herself as much as she was asking him, but he was the one who turned and crutched his way out of the room. She didn't follow.

Gracie leaned over the bedrail, gazed at Bruce's face with her blue eyes huge and dull, but she didn't make any noise. When Zee's father died, Gracie had folded up like a clever piece of origami, right in a hallway of this same hospital, and Zee stood there, twelve years old, stroking her mother's hair and waiting to feel something more violent, more physical, herself.

She marveled at the difference in Gracie's reactions, at her stolidity now, her asking the nurses what she needed to sign and how soon the body would be moved. But of course Zee's father had been her first love, and they'd been so *deeply* in love. And his illness had been drawn out—*protracted* was the word—and he'd been in pain for months, his body weakened by those early years of heavy drinking, his liver and spleen finally both giving way.

Her father was a good man, maybe the only good man she ever knew. He was gentle and quiet, and in third grade when her friend Ellen said he was just like Mr. Rogers, only smaller, Zee said, "You're totally right!" and wasn't offended at all.

He took her to the Art Institute and showed her the hidden woman behind Picasso's blue guitarist. He taught her to handle books like precious objects, never to dog-ear. He told her long, fantastic stories, and if she sat in his lap she could sometimes hear a coin clinking against his teeth.

What would he make of her life? He'd be proud of her work, she was certain, proud of her commitment to dissecting power structures and money and class. He who had vetoed the Chippeway Club. The grounds crew and maids he hired (of necessity, or the house would fall apart) were always starving artists who did a terrible job for which he overpaid them. He'd be sad at the spiral she was in. And he'd be disappointed that she'd abandoned her name. By twelve, the burden of the nickname Godzilla became too much, and so after his death she reduced herself to the sound of a single letter. He had named her, and she had lost her name, and for some reason this made her sadder than anything else. He had loved that house, and she had tried to come home, but it was destroying her. She began sobbing. She went for a walk through the halls.

When she came back, there were Doug and Miriam and Case in a little triangle. Miriam was saying, "You need to lie down. Why don't I drive you home?"

"Just dizzy," Case said. "I'm not tired." He looked up and saw Zee. His eyes were flat little plates that reflected no light at all.

Doug said, "Case, sit down. You're going to pass out."

He didn't move.

"You look terrible," Doug said.

Case didn't even look at him, just kept staring at Zee. She ought to have said something reassuring about the laws of the universe, about cause and effect. (The things she wasn't sure she believed in anymore.) But Doug kept talking.

He said, "I'll drive you."

Case said, "No, man, I'm good." Then he looked at Miriam, a terrible look, and said, "You can have it, Mir."

Miriam sat on the floor and put her head in her hands. Her shoulders started moving up and down.

Doug said, "What? She can have what?"

Case walked right past Doug, right past Zee, and out of the hospital.

In the big window at the end of the corridor, the sun was coming up on the twenty-first century. New nurses were starting the morning shift.

40

Though Case came back to town for the funeral and posted himself next to Miriam in the church, he wasn't staying in the coach house. Doug was reminded of Hamlet, skulking back to the graveside before heading into more tragedy. Doug didn't understand what had happened that night at the hospital, or the next day, when Miriam shut herself in the sunporch and Case packed things into duffel bags and headed off in a cab. He worried it was his fault, that something he'd said in the hospital hallway—what had he even said?—had broken their marriage in two.

Zee implied there was more to it, that she'd seen this coming. But Zee was always seeing things he wasn't.

Miriam moved slowly in the next weeks, fragile and unfocused—but she didn't have that wild look of someone who's reliving a shock again and again. Whatever it was that had gone bad, she'd already figured it out ages back. There were purple circles under her eyes, but Doug never heard her crying.

She worked only occasionally on the kitchen mosaic they'd come to call the Happensack, and spent most of her time on a series of Gothic mansions, cross-sectioned like dollhouses. She used bigger scraps and tiles, creating flaps that lifted to show secret rooms beneath. Sometimes there would be a second, smaller door behind the first. One piece was based on *Jane Eyre*: a mad face painted on a button, peering from an attic window. Another was *The Secret Garden*, another was *Rebecca*, and a fourth was Laurelfield itself, the big house and coach house, built from symbols of luck both good and bad: clovers, acorns, rabbit's foot keychains, broken mirrors, pennies, toy ladders, and—most disturbingly to Doug—hundreds of ladybugs she'd swept from the floor, their faded bodies forming the borders between the rooms.

Doug cooked dinner for all three of them every night, and Zee would take her pasta or soup back to her desk. She wasn't comfortable with grief. Doug ate with Miriam at the kitchen table, and when they talked it was about music or celebrities or *Semfeld*.

They watched *Bluebeard* again together, and she pointed out the scenes where Marceline Horn looked sick. They paused the movie to study her face, then fast-forwarded. At double speed, the two sisters ran to the tower to lock themselves away from Bluebeard. At double speed, Bluebeard beat down the door.

Both Gracie's story and the subject of the colony files had been put on ice for now. Nor could Doug claim the attic key yet. Gracie was barraged with a stream of visitors and fruit baskets and hadn't emerged much from the big house. And to bring up the story with Miriam would be to bring up New Year's Eve, the night that her world did, after all, come to a halt, even as the rest of the planet kept spinning. Doug promised Leland he'd fill him in when things settled, when he had time to digest the bizarre changes of fortune that had befallen everyone in the house. Everyone but Zee, really. She was the only one whose life wasn't massively altered for better or worse. But Zee had always been above the sways of fortune.

And so it was three weeks later that Leland finally came for dinner, and the Bloodhound Gang reunited. Zee was at a conference in New York, and Doug made flatbreads. As they opened the second bottle of wine, Miriam brought her materials up to work on the Happensack, and the men sat watching her and discussing Gracie's story. Doug had made sure this time to tell it slowly and accurately, hoping he could get Miriam to understand what it was he'd heard that was so persuasive. But when he finished, it was Leland who spoke. "What an amazing load of bullshit! Did Scooby-Doo pop out and rip off her mask?"

"I'm just saying it was convincing, the way she told it. At least she *thinks* it's true."

Leland took a long sip of wine. "She hears the wheelbarrows 'going off' to the big house, right? Meaning she was *here*, in the coach house. So she's what, a maid or something?" He hit the table. "Can you imagine Gracie in a maid outfit? Can you imagine her *cleaning*? Okay, and we have this Max, and we have a gardener. And Max has something to do with the car. And the phone. If it's 1955, how old is Gracie? If she's really sixty-two right now."

Doug calculated. "Eighteen."

Leland was having fun, it was clear. And possibly showing off for Miriam. She was inscrutable, though, focused on her tessellations. "And then there's Grace Devohr and George Grant. They're married, they've just moved here, right?"

"The colony closed at the end of '54," Doug said. "So it fits."

"And no one in the entire town knows them. And they get in a car crash."

"Somewhere close, I think," Doug said. "Like, on the property."

"So Max and the gardener roll their bodies away in wheelbarrows, and bury them under the greenhouse."

"Oh, *God*," Miriam said. "Can we not?"

"I'm just sorting the bullshit from the baloney here. And then follows the most brilliant identity theft of all time. Max and Gracie—whatever her real name is, Molly the Maid—become the Grants. So Zee's parents—Zee's the daughter of some maid and butler. Not a Devohr at all. I love it! And no one suspects anything for *forty-four years*. Eleven presidential terms."

Doug said, "Well, yeah. Yeah. But honestly, why *would* they suspect? Look, it doesn't have to be *likely*. It just has to be *possible*. I mean, we think it's hard to get away with crimes because we only ever know the stories where someone gets caught. So we think everyone gets caught. But we have no idea how much never comes to light."

"*Maybe*," Leland said, pointing a finger at him, and for a moment Doug thought he was serious, "maybe Gracie is really Marianne Moore. She'd only be about a hundred ten."

Doug said, "Look. Look around this town. You think *all* the millionaires in this town came by their money honestly? You think there were no Cayman accounts, no fraud? I'm just saying weirder things happen every day. And why would she make up a lie that's self-incriminating? When you lie, you make yourself sound *good*. Not like a felon."

"God," Leland said. "Suddenly you're a Baptist preacher."

They looked to Miriam for a verdict. She turned from the Happensack to face them, balanced in a squat. "I've been thinking about it. A lot. And no, I don't believe her. Because people don't reveal everything the first time you push them. If you think you're caught, you only tell *half* the story. Right? But that means whatever she's covering is *worse*, or more embarrassing. Something about the colony, maybe. Because that's the one thing she won't even talk about."

Leland said, "Who wants to bet the colony was a front for a sex club!"

"Sex club, arts colony," Doug said. "What's the difference."

But Miriam didn't laugh. She went back to her mosaic, and they watched in silence as she arranged a two-inch square section on a cookie sheet, using tweezers, and pressed a sheet of sticky contact paper to the top. She spread the mortar quickly on a new patch of board, then pushed the sheet of tiles into it, holding it in place a minute. When she peeled the contact paper away, the pieces were embedded. It was hypnotic: both the way she worked and the Happensack itself. Doug grew dizzy if he stared too long at the unending pathways, the shapes that were clear one second and dissolved the next into chaos. She had incorporated Zee's pistol cylinder into the bottom right corner, sticking a piece of glass in each compartment. It looked like a flower.

Miriam finally said, "For instance. Let's say the real Grants truly died. How do we know their deaths were accidents? It's much more likely the servants killed them."

Leland said, "Don't eat any food she cooks."

Miriam told him to stop.

Down on the sunporch, they turned on Miriam's computer. They were hoping for a wedding photo of Grace Devohr and George Grant, or any adult photo at all, really, but they had no luck. Doug had brought down the photo from Zee's dresser, the one of her reading with her father, its frame still showing the cracks he'd fixed back in grad school. But there was nothing to compare this picture with. She was about five, so George Grant (based on the marriage license) should have been forty-seven. This man looked closer to sixty—his hair gray, his face well carved. Even Leland and Miriam had to admit it. But then he had those puckish features that can make a man look either older or younger than he is.

Doug had always been drawn to his face, this father-in-law he'd never met. It was his wife's face, sharp and quick. Small eyes, round ears. He'd always felt he could picture George Grant moving, could hear his voice. Now, Doug tried to imagine this man starting life as someone named Max, someone in charge of the cars. The same driver he'd pictured so many times as he sat in the old Morris chair, the man dreaming of faraway lands. So perhaps Max had reached those lands, ending his days as master of the mansion, critic of the arts, father of a golden child. Doug wanted to believe that life could be like that.

Something had occurred to him: Zee's middle name was Devohr. It might have been a way to cement Zee's inheritance, if any questions arose later. It might have been a joke or homage or apology. But Leland and Miriam would only have used this information as proof of Gracie's lying—and he surprised himself by saying nothing, protecting the story as if it were his own.

"So what's next?" Leland said as he left. It was funny how they all assumed they'd reunite immediately. But it felt as natural as if these had been Doug's college roommates, back when "Where are we going tonight?" was not a presumptuous question.

Miriam rubbed her hands together. "Tomorrow's the day Doug gets the rest of the files," she said. "It's time."

With Leland gone, with the kitchen quiet, Doug was antsy. The little house was a boat in icy water. As he helped Miriam put away her tiles, she said, "I have to admit I'm a little freaked out."

"Don't let Leland get to you."

"It's not—it's just everything." She looked a little shaky. "Would it be weird if we camped here, in the kitchen? I've got sleeping bags. You could leave once I'm asleep. I mean, like, far apart sleeping bags, not—"

"It wouldn't be weird."

Miriam brought out the two shiny blue mummy bags she and Case used for camping back in Texas. They put one on each side of the kitchen table, separated by a little forest of chair legs. Lying there, the finished bits of the Happensack glowing in the light from the window, they talked for another hour.

"I think part of my skepticism," Miriam said, "a *small* part, is Gracie's sense of entitlement. Some of the things she *says!* Remember what she said about my teeth?"

"I don't know. Sometimes the people who think they deserve stuff are the ones who started life deprived. And then when they're lucky they feel they earned it."

"And all the things she'd have to have gotten away with! I just can't wrap my mind around someone having *that much* good luck."

"But can you imagine the same amount of bad luck?"

It was a mistake. He shouldn't have said it.

"Yes," she said.

"You look like a caterpillar in there."

"Good night, caterpillar."

"Good night, caterpillar."

Zee was a fraction of herself, a vertical fraction, and another sliver of her was still back in New York at the interviews, and another was in the mirror that spat her decaying face back at her, and another had curled up and died.

There was no one home in the coach house, and she left the door open to the wind. The bed, yes, she checked twice, was still short-sheeted. The jackass hadn't even made an effort to rumple the covers. Two wine bottles in the recycling.

All she'd needed, in the end, was physical proof. There had always been the possibility, however remote, that those words on Miriam's work had been about some other man with scarred knees. That they'd been wishful thinking. That nothing had happened yet, as thick as the air was with inevitability.

In the last weeks, their private jokes had grown more flagrant. "This is the greatest soup of the millennium!" Miriam had said, and Zee could only assume it had to do with the night they stayed back at the house, the night of the heart attack, when Doug would have stooped to kiss her at midnight, and Miriam would have tucked her head under his arm and said, "That was the greatest kiss of the millennium."

She threw things into two suitcases. Clothes and jewelry and shoes, medicine and family photos. Sofia could pack the books up later, could send them to New York.

She'd felt clearheaded in New York, but back here she was underwater again. She had to leave. Obviously, she had to leave. The only question had been whether to take Doug with her. They could have waited till summer. If she'd come home and found no evidence, that's what she'd have done. Broken the news slowly, convinced him he wanted to live in New York, and they'd be away from her mother and Miriam and Laurelfield, horrible Laurelfield, by July. But here was the evidence, and there was a spare room waiting for her in New York, and Doug was a stranger.

Or maybe it was as simple as this: She'd never been a hardboiled egg but a raw one—and Doug, Doug's solid devotion, had been the shell keeping her in. When that shell cracked, what else could a raw egg do but run?

Down on Miriam's sunporch, she found red acrylic paint and a firm, narrow brush. She took them back through the TV room—there were mountains of file folders there, probably something to do with Miriam's next ridiculous series—and up to the bedroom, and covered the wall with words.

Doug, you idiot.

You left a trail.

But I already knew, and I took a job in NY.

I never saw how ugly I was till you reflected it back
at me.

If Case comes home, tell him I'm sorry.

Tell him to run far away.

Tell Miriam that thing in the kitchen is the only
pretty thing she ever made.

She stood in the woods behind the big house, and she looked at it, at all the windows. She closed her eyes, but when she opened them the house was still there.

She stuck a brief resignation in Golda's box, ignoring Chantal. She might have said in the letter that the porn was her fault, but Cole wouldn't even have wanted that. He'd adopted this battle wholeheartedly.

She'd brought with her the photo of herself reading *Green Eggs and Ham*, the one where she looked so much like her listening father. She had another copy in her album, and she wanted to leave this part of herself, this sharp and innocent part of herself, here. But more importantly, she didn't want to keep the frame that Doug had fixed so long ago. She leaned it against Cole's closed office door, with a note. *Dear old bastard*, it said. *For you to remember me. Portrait of the Communist Heretic Zilla Devohr Grant, circa 1970. You're laughing at "Devohr," aren't you? That's my real gift to you.* Back in her office, she filled boxes with books and syllabi and handouts. Her diplomas, journals with her articles. She saved everything from the computer to disk. She wouldn't teach many of the same courses in New York—the school was so nontraditional that the intros and surveys didn't even exist—but she wanted all her files nonetheless. Gretchen, her roommate for one year of college, was hard-skulled and ironic, as perfect a department head as Zee could imagine, and her phone call had been a sudden shaft of light. Yes, Zee had said, she was very much interested in a job like that. Zee had told both Gretchen and the hiring dean the story of Cole (the official one, minus her interferences) over dinner, and—she knew it would be all right after the dean told about hanging Robert Bork in effigy on the Oberlin quad—she also told them what she was planning to do. It wouldn't affect her new contract, they assured her.

She'd been thinking a lot lately about the myths her father used to read her at night: Daphne, Philomela, Actaeon. She realized years later they were all stories of metamorphosis, and she wondered how much he needed these myths to affirm his own reinvention from alcoholic slouch to responsible father and art critic. She'd tried so hard to transform herself—Zee the earnest academic was not the same person as Zilla the privileged child—but she'd slipped. She'd ended up living at home, and sure enough her entire adult life had crumbled away.

She would do it properly this time, in a town where she knew exactly one person. As her father had done, leaving Toronto with his new wife, remaking himself in the grandest American fashion. Some things she could not escape: that gene for mental illness. The sharp and unattractive edges of her own personality. But in New York she'd be away from Doug, and from the self who'd been played for a fool. She'd be away from that house.

She marveled at the lucidity of her thoughts, then realized this was not a good sign. When did people do that, except when they were drunk? And she wasn't, she was fairly sure.

She took the boxes to her car, and she bought, for the last time, a grilled cheese sandwich from the co-op. It was the only thing they did well, and they did it exquisitely. It was half butter, and the toasted bread broke in your mouth and then melted like the thinnest sheet of ice. In an hour she'd be free. She needed to finish just this one thing first—to undo her damage, outscandal the scandal.

At two fifteen, as a class period ended, she stood in the middle of her office and took off her clothes, all of them, and folded them into her purse. Her flesh was pale from the winter, her arms and legs unrecognizably thin. She stuck another muscle relaxer on her tongue. She walked, with just her purse, into the hallway and down the stairs, past students she knew and ones she didn't, past

Chad Crosley, past Fran Leffler. If sound came from their open mouths, she couldn't hear. She walked past Jerry Keaton, who tried to grab her arm and then thought better of it. She heard Chantal calling out: "Zee! Dr. Grant! Can you—Oh, someone get her a—Zee, come *in* here!" Out onto the lawn the icy lawn, her feet in the slush. She didn't care if she fell, but she didn't fall. Past the administrative building, through parting clusters of students in parkas. She heard one say, "Where's my camera?" And another, "Oh, dude, it's about Cole! I get it, it's about Cole." And another, "Hey it's that math prof! Shane, wasn't that your math prof?"

Past the library, past the co-op.

All the way to her car. She couldn't feel her feet.

She drove off campus with the conviction, the finality, of someone driving off the entire planet.

42

Doug had started to see the world as reticulated. The way the colored pieces of any view fit together: windowsill, wall, sky, driveway, tree, roof. Shoe, carpet, book. If you looked long enough, the three-dimensional world flattened to a plane where every block of color was a tile, so tightly clicked together that no mortar showed at the cracks.

He stared at the Happensack for hours a day, whether Miriam was in front of it smoothing mortar over the top and scrubbing it off with a hard sponge, or whether he was alone at two a.m. as Miriam, similarly insomniac, worked downstairs on other things. They continued to sleep in the kitchen. The first night, he hadn't gone to bed at all. He'd been at the police station, and then slumped at Gracie's table. ("What did you *do?*" Gracie kept saying, until Doug worried the officers would think he'd strangled his wife.) The police traipsed through the coach house. "Talk about the writing on the wall," one said, unhelpfully, and even his partner didn't laugh. The second night, he'd been downtown meeting a private detective, and afterward he made it only back up to Leland's place, where he lay on the couch for five hours but didn't sleep. The third night, Miriam told him he needed to lie down. She zipped him in and brought him a pill and put a washcloth on his forehead, and then it was morning. And for fifty nights since then, he'd crawled in four feet away from her.

He worried the hard kitchen floor would ruin his back, but it didn't. Dr. Morsi agreed: Regardless of the disintegration of his heart and brain, his back had never been better.

Gracie had accused him, in those first weeks, of telling Zee what he knew. She said, "It would have pushed her over the edge. She *worshipped* her father." Doug might have asked *which* father, and who Zee's father even was, if her father was a chauffeur named Max, if her father had perhaps posed nude by the koi ponds. But his jaw was full of lead, and Gracie was in a dull and constant rage. He only encountered her now on the driveway, roaring past in the Mercedes. It was a miracle of good timing that Doug had gotten the files out of the attic the day before Zee left, or Gracie might never have handed over the key at all.

Although the Parfitt file was still conspicuously missing—he and Miriam wondered if it was actually Zee who'd replaced it with the photo, falling apart long before he knew it but one step ahead as always—the rest was a treasure trove. If he could have crawled into the files to live, and never had to worry about food or detectives or showering, he'd have done it. There were sheaths of correspondence between the longtime director, Samantha Mays, and the artists and writers and composers who saw her as their guardian angel. There were slides of paintings. Miriam pored over the Demuth ones, comparing them to prints in library books and calling a friend at the School of the Art Institute who drove up to borrow them, along with the Grant Wood slides and the files of artists Doug hadn't heard of. There were project proposals and sample work. There were letters of recommendation.

Miriam was most excited about the files of two female sculptors, Fannie Cadfael and Josephine Lizer. "I *knew* it" she said. "I knew it, I knew it, I knew it! The bear statue, in the woods! I *knew* that was a Lizer. I should've said so! White rabbits!" Even Doug registered, through his haze, that this made no sense. Miriam explained, her hands flying, that the White Rabbits were the women who had assisted the sculptor Lorado Taft before the Columbian Exposition in 1893. Taft begged special permission to use women, until the man in charge snapped that he could use white rabbits if they'd get the job done. Those women proudly clung to the name as they launched their own careers as some of the first successful female sculptors. A Josephine Lizer piece, even one covered with moss, was a big enough deal that it sent Miriam running for the phone.

Less valuable but more personally intriguing were the references, in the forties and fifties, to a colony caretaker named Maxwell Perry. "That has to be Max!" Doug said. "And he stayed after they kicked the artists out."

Miriam said, "Well, sure, that was probably really the driver's name, and he'd probably really been the caretaker. When people lie, they don't make up *all* the details."

Leland just said, "Any caretakers named Marianne Moore?"

Parfitt, it seemed, had stayed at least six times, and as late as 1941, just four years before his suicide. Some rosters listed his apartment on Rush Street in Chicago, and the earliest—in 1929—had a Philadelphia address that was news to Doug. The most useful detail was the fact that for every stay but the last, his lover, the artist Armand Cox, had been there at the same time. ("*Armand Cox?*" Miriam said. "That's his real name?") It meant their relationship started earlier than was thought. Doug imagined Parfitt writing at a Laurelfield desk, his partner down in a studio designing stage sets and drawing his magazine covers, his fadeaway girls. The two reuniting at the dinner table, discussing the day's work.

Even so, it wasn't enough. Doug tried his best, in the blur of weeks after Zee left, to imagine what a project centered around these scraps of information might look like. And then, the punch in the gut: In late March, a professor from Yale published a long article on Parfitt in *The New Yorker*, a rediscovery piece. The professor, said his bio, was about to publish a book on the lost modernists. It wasn't that his work entirely supplanted Doug's. It was that ten other people were now going to get the same idea, and do it better, and do it faster, and be more qualified to tell the story.

But Doug imagined he might write a nonacademic article about Laurelfield itself, or about artists' residencies in the 1920s. He could drive to other colonies, the places that still kept their records in dusty attics. He had a hell of a story for the introduction, at least: the first-person narrative of recovering the lost Laurelfield archive.

He spoke to the historical society about taking the files off his hands once he'd copied the parts he wanted.

These papers were the trails of the artists—and, in the cases of the most obscure visitors, these might have been the only remnants of their art. But what trail he himself had left, what had prompted Zee to choose that word, *trail*, for the wall, he still wasn't sure. Something told him it wasn't a trail up the attic stairs, but something that had led her to Melissa Hopper and her soccer tryouts, her babysitting gigs, her crushes—yet the trailhead was missing. He'd hidden every scrap of paper, scoured his desk every day before Zee came home. He felt stupid, or at least outsmarted. He had a thousand imaginary conversations with her. The speech evolved and mutated. It went through angry cycles, conciliatory ones, and there was a pleading phase. It grew shorter and more concise. Eventually it became a single and blanketing word, a one-breath mantra: "*No.*" With every step around the fish ponds, every thrash in his sleep. No to it all. No, this didn't happen. No, you couldn't have been in your right mind. No, I'm not the pathetic slug you think I am. No, I didn't want this. No, I don't take it back. No. No. No. No. No.

A package arrived in the mail: *Melissa Calls the Shots*, *Melissa Takes a Bow*, *Cece Makes the Grade*. He dumped them in a desk drawer. He spent the day wishing he could call Zee and tell her that the changes she'd made just weren't working for him. "You altered the universe," he'd say. "We're going to ask you to start over."

In April, a call from the detective: Zee was in rural New York. Here was her address. Here was her number. "Look, man," the guy said, "you could try and get her committed, but I haven't seen that work out so well. Seemed fine to me."

This was the afternoon of the same day Miriam filed for divorce from Case. Doug might have driven straight to New York that very night, but he couldn't leave Miriam alone right then. And moreover: If he was still sure of anything about Zee, it was that contacting her against her will would make things worse. He wanted to believe this was all that kept him back, that fear wasn't part of it. That a modicum of relief wasn't part of it.

Miriam wanted sushi, so they went out and Doug let her order for him. She told him, only after he'd swallowed and liked it, that unagi was eel. She told him that when she met Case she'd been so young that she'd taken the regular trappings of his adult life—his job, his car, his drawer full of polo shirts—as signs of maturity and stability. Here was someone who could support her while she made art, a steady rock on which to build her life. Really he'd been anything but. Every year had been worse, every day had been worse—and then they came here, and things got unbearable.

"I think I feel happy tonight," Miriam said. "Is that awful to say?"

Doug looked at the sushi on his plate. It, too, was tessellated: the wet pink rhombus of salmon, the grains of the rice, the thin edge of seaweed. He thought, *I am a different person now. I am someone who eats eel, and this small artist is my best friend. I am someone who has turned the TV room into a file-sorting station, someone who believes fantastical tales of identity theft.*

If everything else were still the same, he'd have felt Zee's absence like a gaping hole. But if he could continue to reconfigure his entire life, there would be no missing place where Zee had been. He thought of Parfitt's last published poem, "Proteus Wept." In Greek mythology, the sea god Proteus changed shape to avoid telling mortals the future. Parfitt had twisted it, though: Parfitt's Proteus changed to avoid remembering the past. It ended with a litany of the forms he took: *A lark, a crow, a spoonbill! / This sea-foam, rank and green.* Yet Parfitt himself ultimately chose death over reinvention. It was as if he wrote the poem to convince himself of future possibility, and failed. But Doug could do better.

He didn't drive to New York the next day, or the day after. He didn't call, and then he continued not calling.

What he did instead was ask Sofia to make him an appointment with Gracie. She had written Zee a letter once they had her address, and Zee had written a short note back that, by not expressing anger over car crashes and wheelbarrows, had put Gracie's mind at ease.

Hidalgo greeted him at the door, relatively sedate. Doug scratched him, just to steal a moment to fortify himself. It had occurred to him that the reason Gracie let him continue to stay in the coach house was that she thought he had far more information than he did. He had to choose his questions well, lest they betray his ignorance. He wasn't sure how to begin.

But, at the kitchen table, Gracie spoke first.

"Douglas, I've come to a place of peace," she said. "Either my daughter is crazy, or I raised her wrong, but I don't believe this was your fault."

He said, "I really didn't do anything, Gracie. Honest to God, I didn't."

They talked about the detective, and about leaving Zee alone awhile.

Then Doug said, "I hope you can help with something." He showed her the photograph, careful to keep a hand over the men's naked torsos. "Because I've appreciated your honesty. What I still need to know are these men's full names."

She put on her reading glasses and squinted down. "I haven't a clue. Is there a correct answer?"

"Theoretically."

"That's out back of the house, isn't it? It's the kind of thing Zilla's father would have known. Every few years, someone would call up asking about the colony. He'd rattle off who stayed here."

"But you don't know these men?"

"I've never seen them in my life. What are you hiding under there?"

He slid the photo back in its envelope and asked her blessing to transfer the files to the historical society. "They should be preserved," he said. "With acid-free folders. And there's nothing in there that would, you know, incriminate you. I've been through every inch."

Gracie folded her glasses. "Douglas, I've been a bit of a fool. When you cornered me on New Year's Eve—that's really what you did, you *cornered* me—I was in quite a state. Bruce had me convinced of the end of the world, for one thing. I can't quite remember all I told you. But I realize I might have said more than I needed."

Doug said, "I'd already been in the attic, remember. There were a lot of papers up there."

"I see." It didn't seem to bother her particularly, though. "The papers you want to donate—it's *just* the colony papers, correct?"

"I have no desire to get you in trouble."

She was quiet, and he worried he'd said the wrong thing. Finally she said, "There's actually something I need from you. I've made a decision, Douglas. With Zilla away, with Bruce gone, I think the time has come for me to move on. Did you know I have a sister? A half sister named Elizabeth, and I never stopped writing to her. She doesn't know quite where I am, just that I've had a good life. She writes me back at the post office. We got together in Colorado a few times, after Zilla's father passed, and before I met Bruce. She's moved to Sedona. It's beautiful out there. You know, it was the saddest part of leaving Florida, not knowing what would happen to my sister. She was only four, and leaving her was the worst thing I ever did, the worst thing in my life. But she got out too, and she was a teacher, and now she's divorced. I've been sending her money every month since she was old enough to cash a check. And I think it's time to be Amy Hall again, to go out and join her. Grace can't live much longer, and there's the matter of the Internet. The last thing I want is to become famous for being the oldest living person. Where would I be then? Max made sure from the start that we kept paying ourselves salaries. Every month I'd write a check from Grace Grant to Amy Hall, and I'd cash it at the bank in Libertyville. And Max did the same. I have quite a bit saved up, and that's all I need."

Doug tried to look skeptical, but found himself nodding instead. "Sedona is beautiful."

"Douglas." She put her hand on his. Veins like mountain ranges. "I want you and Miriam to take care of everything here. I've talked to my lawyers, and there can be a transfer of property and funds. To the two of you. Lord knows Zilla doesn't want it. Maybe she'll come back and maybe she won't. But the house will be yours. We'll keep Grace alive a few years, and then she'll die. These things can be arranged, with money to grease the wheels. It'll be my worry."

"You want us to take the *house?*" The squeak of his voice woke Hidalgo, who stood and hit his head on the table.

"I want you to reopen the colony."

He wasn't entirely sure what his face was doing. It was the most outrageous thing anyone had ever said to him.

"Don't answer yet. It's the right thing. The colony was shut down for bad reasons, for greed and spite. Max would tell me stories—artists by the ponds, writers under the trees. When I first showed up there were still cabins, you know, artist's studios, with skylights and sinks. I know I always spoke poorly of it, but that was—I felt I had to. He said it was quiet all day, everyone working, and then at night they all came together and made a racket and had dinner in the dining room. Can you imagine? And the work they made! We never could have reopened it ourselves, even though Max wanted to, he wanted to desperately. It would have brought too much attention. The Devohrs would have descended. But you and Miriam, you're so many layers removed. It would set the universe right."

"Wouldn't the right thing, technically, be to give it back to the Devohrs?"

"The Devohrs left Grace out here with an alcoholic husband, and they never once came to see her. Never once." She pointed a finger right at him, as if he were trying to argue otherwise. "We had a plan in case they did, a whole elaborate plan. But it never happened. They made it easy for me. It was easy because they never showed up, and it was easy because I never felt bad. And they don't need it, do they? Zilla's the one always talking about Marxism, and look! Here I am, little old me, redistributing the wealth!"

"Oh. God." There was still the possibility this was all a bribe, Gracie's chance to cover up something gruesome, to get out of town before Doug turned her in. That's what Miriam would have said.

"There's money to get it started. I know how much these things cost, I'm not naïve, and there's plenty. Of course it's mostly Bruce's money at this point, so he's the one to thank. I was nearly broke before he came along. And poor sweet Miriam can help you. She knows the art world. She'd know how to build a studio.

Why she married that pompous ass is beyond me but otherwise she's a smart girl."

Doug realized that in the time she'd been talking, every color in the kitchen had grown brighter. His mind was listing reasons why this wasn't a tenable plan, but it was thinking twice as fast of what would need to be done, planning where people would sleep, what grants could be applied for, what Leland could bring to the table. Doug would have a job. He'd have a life. He felt as if he'd stepped into the Happensack, into its vertiginous abundance.

Leland would tell him he was a sucker, and Miriam would worry Gracie was leaving them with a basement full of dead bodies or worse, but when you're drowning in the ocean and someone throws you a rope, you don't ask what it's made of.

He said, "I have to talk to Miriam. I'd have to tell her— I mean, what could I tell her?"

"Don't worry about it." She smiled, and he knew it must have been painfully obvious that he'd already told Miriam everything. "Go talk to her now."

And he got his things, and he walked back to the coach house.

No, look: He was running.

43

Summer and fall swept through with a cleansing, scorching heat, and when the students returned to campus, they eagerly told the few seniors returning from a year abroad the story of Professor Grant walking off campus nude.

There was Old King Cole. His Melville class applauded him the first day. For still being there, for still being Cole, for waggling those eyebrows and saying, "You don't kill an old virus *that* easy."

When students came to his office, he pointed to the little framed photo on the wall, the girl and her father. She was reading and she was happy. Each time he'd say, "That's a picture of the bravest woman in the world."

44

On June 10, 2001, a poet named Sara Calovelli pulled into the Laurelfield driveway in a dying Honda Civic with Ohio plates. Though eight more artists and writers and composers would arrive later that afternoon, she was officially the first resident of the Laurelfield Arts Colony in forty-seven years.

Doug and Miriam ran out from the office to meet her, and introduced her to Ben, who'd get her settled in the main house. Dinner was at six, they told her, and then there would be a bonfire out back. When Sara had disappeared through the front door with her suitcase, Miriam did a little jump and clapped her hands.

The chef had the grill going, Sofia and her crew were putting out soaps and towels, and Denise and Chantal worked frantically from the office that used to be the coach house TV room, dealing with all the last-minute things like medical forms.

Everything had fallen into place—money, staffing, town approval—with such ease and speed that Doug and Miriam kept waiting in vain for something to go terribly wrong. That winter, they'd received a donation from some Miss Abbaticchio, an elderly woman in town, that surpassed even the money Gracie had left. The desks from the attic were all still usable. The Illinois Arts Council came through nicely.

The buzz they'd built in the year of frantic work created a deep applicant pool, and Miriam and Leland knew the right people to rope into admissions panels and a board. An article in the *Tribune*,

"Refounding a Haven," came out the same day Doug learned that Zee was living with a sixty-year-old physics professor.

And it was the strangest thing: That night, as he lay in bed, he had to remind himself to feel sad.

His bed was downtown now, in an apartment above the bagel shop. Miriam stayed in the coach house, and Doug and Zee's old quarters had become a guest room and studio.

Gracie had sent them congratulatory flowers, delivered that morning. She wrote them occasional notes from Sedona, which Doug took to be some kind of proof. ("Her going where she said she'd go proves exactly nothing," Miriam said.)

They sat next to the driveway, and Miriam picked up a hand-ful of its smooth gravel: white and tan and black. She arranged the stones in a trail down her shin.

Doug said, "Are you tessellating yourself?"

She said, "I've had a funny thought all day. It seems like this is the only way things could have turned out. You know? Like all the bizarre and horrible things that happened, they pushed us both here. The colony was taken away, the house went back to the Devohrs, and after everything here we are, two people who aren't even Devohrs, opening it back up."

Doug laughed and said, "You think the house just really wanted to be a colony again? It missed all the artists, so it smashed that car and waited half a century?"

"I wasn't going to say the house," Miriam said. "I was going to say ghosts."

At some point they'd agreed that if he could believe Gracie's story, she could believe in her ghosts, and he wasn't allowed to laugh.

Doug said, "Last chance to dig up the greenhouse. Before that writer gets here."

"Ha."

"Just to prove I'm not a gullible ass."

"We'll never do it. It's such a great studio. If I were a writer, it's the studio I'd want." She cleared the gravel from her leg and it fell on the driveway with a sound like rain. "Even if we did," she said, "even if we found bones. What would it prove? You'll never know the whole story. You realize that, right? That you'll never know."

Doug looked at her, speechless. She was right. Like so much she said, it was a revelation. It was also an absolution.

Before dinner, there were cocktails in the library. The travel-weary artists revived, chattering and checking out the displays. Doug had filled the shelves with copies of all the books and musical scores he could find by the earlier generation of residents, and books of art prints as well. He'd even hunted down Marlon Moore's only published work, which seemed to have predated the attic manuscript. Moore turned out to have been a local writer, a professor in Zee's old department in the late twenties. The novel, *Jack of the Woods*, was truly awful, but Moore's spot on the shelf was one of Doug's favorites.

Doug had finally convinced Miriam that what would make the room complete was to put the Happensack above the fireplace, where Gracie's farmhouse painting had once hung. They'd wanted to install it before the guests arrived, but they ran out of time. There were so many little crises in those final days of preparation. For now, the spot was empty.

After dinner, the artists toured the grounds—the reconstructed cabin studios, the wood-chip path to the bear statue—and gathered at the bonfire, which Leland had roaring. Beside him on the ground was a stack of things to be burned.

Miriam explained it to the group. "There's been a lot of good and a lot of bad at Laurelfield since artists last gathered here. Those of us who've been working to make this all happen—we wanted to clear away the past to make room for the new, and the amazing, and the good. And so tonight we're going to burn some bad art."

The crowd laughed, and Doug held up the farmhouse painting, removed from its frame, and tossed it on the fire. It cracked
and hissed and then it blazed away.

Leland personally threw in, with great relish, some horren-
dous poems he'd written after a breakup five years back. Miriam
contributed what was left of the yellow dress piece—clawed to
scraps by Hidalgo, never really salvageable. Doug threw in three
slim paperbacks: *Melissa Calls the Shots, Melissa takes a Bow, Cece
Makes the Grade.*

"Oh, I used to love those!" said someone across the fire. "They
were terrible!"

As the night grew cool the artists gathered closer to the blaze
for a minute, and then they headed off. They had work to do:
canvases to prime, desks to arrange, poems to start.

Doug turned to Miriam and said, "Let's get the Happensack
right now. We'll be too busy tomorrow."

"We don't have anything to patch the wall with. We'll have a
gaping hole for days."

He shook his head. "I want it in the library when they come
down to breakfast."

Up in the coach house, they took turns hammering a chisel to
break the thick paint seal around the edge, then going at it with
the pry bar, getting behind each of the four nailed corners in
turn, a bit at a time.

Doug took a shift as Miriam held the edges of the board, ready
to catch its full weight if it came loose. He felt utterly happy. It
was a happiness beyond the colony, beyond the triumph of the
day. He didn't know, after all the disastrous things that had happened, why he should be so profoundly, overwhelmingly satisfied
with life. But he was.

The board gave a thrilling crack and Miriam wrested it backward, the nails sliding out, and Doug wasn't sure if he should grab

the board or catch her from behind. But moreover—in that exact moment, as he watched her stepping back, finding her balance, panting—he felt as if something had dislodged inside him as well. He said, "Put it down." He let the pry bar fall to the floor.

"No, I've got it."

"Please put it down."

"Why?"

"Put it down."

She did, she leaned it against the wall, and he stood and hooked two fingers into the collar of her shirt and pulled her, stumbling, toward him. In front of the gaping mouth of the wall, he kissed her. There would be time later to move the board, and time to shine flashlights into the wall, and time to replace the small orange tile that had clattered to the floor. He'd been waiting only three seconds for her, but he felt he'd been waiting a century, as if there were nothing more obvious, more necessary, in the world.

PART II

1955

After all, Grace had grown up with stories about attics. A *Little Princess*, and *Jane Eyre*, and a hundred campfire ghost stories. The one, for instance, about the bride trapped in the trunk on her wedding night. And that spring on the honeymoon she'd picked up Anne Frank's diary at the English bookshop in Paris. When George disappeared on the third day, she sat in La Rotonde with her open book, a glass of Chablis and a bowl of mussels. She'd brought the book as a shield, hoping she could pass for a young art student, a girl who dined alone once a week when she tired of the French boys in her sculpture class. She still looked twenty, it was true. The waiter called her *Mademoiselle*.

Her water refilled as if from an underground spring. The sun turned to twilight and then streetlamps, the crowd thickened around her, but the waiter never brought the *addition*, just more bread and then, with a wink, more wine. By then the book had plunged her into a world so vivid that the Paris around her seemed the fiction. She was Anne Frank, and this Paris street was a dream after death. She returned to the hotel around midnight to finish the book in bed. When George banged on the door twenty minutes later, his key lost forever, it was too easy to pretend he was a Nazi ripping the bookcase from the Annex door. She lay in bed and tried not to breathe. He shouted and kicked and tried to force the handle. Only when he went silent, presumably starting down the hall to wake the night manager, did she jump up and turn the knob.

"I was asleep," she said.

He steadied himself, his eyes swimming so fast that she knew he saw three of her. He smelled sweet and complicated—like whiskey and cigars and fifty women—and she unbuttoned his shirt. He knocked the door closed with his elbow.

She lay back across the bed. She'd bought a pale green night-gown that afternoon on the Rue de Rivoli. She pressed her white foot to his thigh. She said, "And I was alone all day thinking about you. You'll have to make it up to me."

So was it such a surprise back here, in this vast and disconsolate brick trap, when the smell of Paris had faded from her palate, when George's disappearances left her not ensconced in a café of strangers but humiliated in front of the staff, that she'd claim the attic for her haven? She figured she loved it for the reason we always love attics, for the reason they figure in our dreams: because they are the hidden rooms where we store our pasts. Where we stick the things we can't bear to throw away but hope we never have to see again.

And more practically—it had cooled with the fall air, and here she could sit, invisible, and see everything. The people below were tiny and featureless, dolls around a dollhouse: Max the driver, who claimed he'd been at Laurelfield twenty-five years, more than half his life. Mrs. Carmichael the housekeeper. Beatrice and Ludo in the garden. Rosamund, the cook. The mail-man, coming and going. The dairy man, coming and going. Peculiar little Amy, Max's niece, who showed up one day in July startled as a deer and just stayed and stayed. George, taking off in the Capri with Max or in the Darrin without him, or just lurking the grounds, leering at Beatrice as she bent over the squash bed, leering at Amy as she carried linens from the big house to the coach house.

Grace imagined bringing darts up here, perfecting her aim, and launching them at the unsuspecting dolls. One in Max's tire. One in Amy's round posterior. One right in the muscle of George's beautiful arm. One in the koi pond, one in the milk truck. Pop.

What she brought up instead was food, just a bit and stored it on the windowsill. A loaf of sliced bread, a pot of strawberry jam, five long and knobby carrots. She liked to calculate how long it would last her, if she decided to go missing. One week, she decided. And then down she would climb, skinny as a wraith.

On the tenth of October two strange things happened, and so she knew there would be a third.

The first was that a witch walked into the coach house. Not a real witch, this being the modern day and the rational world. Still, in October, to dress in flowing black like that, hunched at the waist against the wind, the woman was rather asking to be burned at the stake. She'd arrived by taxi from lord knew where, Salem perhaps, and darted into the coach house as if she belonged. Grace's first thought was that the witch was Amy's mother, Max's sister, come to claim her renegade daughter at last, but when Amy walked out toward the garden ten minutes later, untroubled and unhurried, she knew it couldn't be. Grace pulled her bird-watchers off the filing cabinet and trained them on the coach house's second story, above the two open garage doors. She could see them through the windows of the balcony door. The witch sat at the kitchen table, her hair in a low, gray chignon. Max sat across—there was his dark hair—his hands going up and down from the table to his mouth, eating or smoking or drinking. But that was all she could tell.

The scene brought to mind the only card she remembered from her tarot reading with George in the Marais. The others had all looked like playing cards, silly queens and princes, but then the old woman had flipped up the five of pentacles, and Grace had felt she'd seen the picture before, or maybe lived it: two beggars in the cold, outside the warm church. Locked out. She couldn't remember the woman's explanation for the card, but she knew she'd felt it in her bones. And she felt the same thing right now, watching Max. She was only a visitor at Laurelfield.

She remembered George's tarot better, only because it had seemed to trouble the old woman. As if it had revealed his problematic soul. She'd muttered her way through most of it, while Grace did her best to translate. George had wanted to know about the tower card, which looked terrifying: a turret struck by lightning, two naked figures jumping from the windows. The woman said, "*C'est pas si grave. C'est la change, seulement, la change soudaine.*" And then, as if this were just as important, the woman had explained that in the old Belgian decks, the tower had been a tree. "What's she saying?" George demanded. And Grace said, "It means don't go outside when it's raining."

Now she chose one of the tart green apples from her sill, one of the five she'd picked that morning from the trees behind the Longhouse (three adjoined artists' studios, inhabited now by raccoons), and ate slowly around the core. All the windows were open, no screens. She'd pulled those out so birds could fly through, though her only guests had been some skittish barn swallows who hadn't even made nests under the gable eaves as she'd hoped. She started to throw the core onto the driveway, but changed her mind and crossed the broad, loud floor to the back of the house. There were George and little Amy, near the yellowing catalpa tree. There was something odd in the way they stood—the very fact of their standing together, to begin with, but moreover the way he curved above her like a cobra—so that it wasn't even a surprise when George grabbed one of Amy's wrists and pinned it above her head, against the bark of the tree. Grace grabbed her birdwatchers. She held the last bite of apple in her mouth like Snow White, not chewing or spitting or choking, just watching as George undid the top buttons of Amy's dress and yanked it down below her left breast, and her brassiere with it so that Grace could see the pink nipple even from here. Amy's leg rose as if she were trying to kick him away but didn't know to aim for the groin. George lowered his head to Amy's breast and, since he was in profile to her, Grace could see even his tongue, circling the breast and then climbing slowly up Amy's neck. Amy pushed him away and tugged her dress back up, but she didn't run or scream, and that was what counted, wasn't it?

Well.

Well.

Grace, good literature major that she was, told herself this apple was a symbol of lost innocence, and that now, with the sweet pulp in her mouth still undissolved, would be the perfect time to feel shock and repulsion. And was it a failure on her part that she felt neither? Not shock, because she wasn't an idiot. And not true repulsion, either, not in the way she ought. This was the man she'd chosen. This was the reason she'd broken things off with Gunning Burke and Stanley Langhoff and Lionel because they weren't the kinds of men to do anything surprising or awful or awakening. They smothered her with their patience, and she'd felt locked in a windowless, velvety room with the smell of peppermint and nowhere to vomit.

Well.

This was not the second strange thing. Because really it was not so strange.

The figures below had parted, Amy trotting across the lawn to the kitchen door. Grace supposed she was heading in there just to burn the soup. Ever since she'd shown up the food was markedly worse, and Grace suspected Rosamund was trying to teach her things, letting her chop and make salad dressings. Poor, stupid Amy, probably in love with George and not able to understand that a year from now he wouldn't recall her name.

Grace was the only kind of woman George could ever have married, just as George was the man she'd waited twenty-eight years for, through parties and debutante balls and engagements and what everyone saw as spinsterhood. And then at the Governor's Ball in '53, up had walked George Grant, a pimentoed olive in his teeth, eyes like the Big Bad Wolf. He bit down so the olive split, half in his mouth, half tumbling to his palm. He walked a step closer and, right in front of Grace's father, jammed the olive half between her lips. "It's good for you," he'd said, and walked on to scoop his arm around the slim waist of the mayor's daughter.

Her mother, scurrying up: "Who was *that?*"

And Grace, quite drunk and melodramatic already that evening, had swallowed the olive and turned away.

A pleasant paralysis set over Grace as the afternoon wore on, and she watched the coach house as Max and the witch continued to talk. Amy reappeared at one point, walked to the big house, returned to the coach house with a pillow and blankets—and yes, there she appeared in the east rooms, opening the window and preparing a bed for the witch. Grace ought to have cared that yet another guest was being welcomed on her property without her consent. Her mother never would have allowed it, would have been horrified at Grace just sitting here, watching Max build a harem in that little house. Some harem: a witch and his niece. Only she wasn't really his niece. Grace knew.

After a long while, Max and the witch strolled together out of the coach house, behind the big house, and straight into the garden shed. They emerged twenty minutes later, and so did Ludo and Beatrice, the gardeners. Max and the witch walked them to their car and kissed their cheeks before the gardeners drove off, done for the day. The witch took Max's arm, quite formally, and they disappeared back into the coach house.

The sun was setting, and she ought to head down for dinner before they sent a search party.

Amy reappeared. She was a figurine from a cuckoo clock, circling forever in and out: coach house, big house, coach house, big house. But this time, as she crossed the lawn toward the kitchen door, the earth seemed to move behind her. No, it was rabbits. Grace counted at least seven of them, hopping along behind Amy as if out of Hamelin. She didn't seem aware in the slightest. And what irony! Seven cottontails, and not a bit of good luck for Amy—sad little, odd little, hungry-eyed Amy, who thought she was desired because George pinned her to a tree. The kind of girl to whom misfortune clung like moss. Grace stood and brushed the attic dust from her lap.

So it was two strange things now, two omens. If she only kept watching, tomorrow and the next day and the next, the third thing would come. And the third was always biggest.

She felt the house waking around her in the morning before she herself was fully awake. Windows opening, Ludo's rhythmic clippers outside, feet in the hall, wheels on the gravel drive. It was the same everywhere she'd ever lived: at home at Bealey Hall, with so many more servants than here, and her brothers shouting, and later her brothers' children shouting; in the college dormitory, where some girls were always up and running baths at the crack of dawn; in hotels, where someone had been up all night at the desk, where the maids arrived at four in the morning. She wondered what it was like to awaken alone in a little cottage on a quiet street, where nothing would stir until she did. Maybe a sleeping cat at the foot of the bed, and that would be all. But here at Laurelfield, there was something more in the mornings, a buzzing sensation about the whole house, as if it weren't the servants keeping it running but some other energy. As if the house had roots and leaves and was busy photosynthesizing and sending sap up and down, and the people running through were as insignificant as burrowing beetles.

She sat at the breakfast table with a book. George wasn't there yet. He'd begun sleeping in the small bedroom with the fourposter on nights when he returned home closer to dawn than sunset. He was either up there asleep or he wasn't, but wondering wouldn't accomplish much. She asked for eggs and toast, no meat, and opened her book to the middle. A romance. A college friend had sent six of them as a joke wedding gift—the whole *Ancient Passions* set, tied with pink ribbon, a calligraphed note: *For when that flame flickers!*—and Grace had ripped through two just since Paris. This one was set in an English manor house in the reign of Henry VIII. The poor servant girl and the second son were madly in love with little hope of marriage. She'd have imagined it finished badly for all, were this not the type of book that guaranteed a happy ending. How funny it would have been, what a great trick on the poor lonelyheart readers, if one of these stories ended terribly. Abandonment, shame, an accidental baby with six fingers on each hand. The heroine taking to the streets.

George arrived, unshaven. His hair a mat of black curls, his eyebrows mirrored by the dark circles beneath. He was even more beautiful like this than neatly groomed. She closed the book, but didn't bother hiding it under her napkin. He snorted at the cover and asked where the cook was. Grace forked some eggs onto her saucer and slid it across the table to him, and she poured half her coffee into his cup.

She said, "Do you know anything about Max's new guest, in the coach house?" She'd been going to ask him last night at dinner, but he'd taken a phone call and she ended up eating alone. "A woman."

He scratched behind his ears. "It's your house, Duck. Tell me what you want. You want me to bark at him?"

She considered. "No. I can handle it, certainly. I just wondered if he'd cleared it with you."

George laughed and tried to catch the cook's attention through the open kitchen door. "I think the fellow's smart enough to know I'm not the one to clear it."

"Well. In any case, there's a guest. A distinguished sort of witch, all dressed in black. Just so long as you don't go mangling her bosom."

George lifted a thick eyebrow, but the look on his face was all amusement. No denial, and certainly no apology. If he'd already been drunk for the day, he might have thrown his coffee cup at her face. As it was, he seemed on the verge of saying something slick and snide, but just then Rosamund, strapping, gray-eyed Rosamund, strode through the door with the coffee and a heaping plate of eggs.

Grace said, "I'll manage it all." Though she had no idea how to speak to Max, no desire to put her authority to the test.

George paused his bite in front of his mouth and said. "Your dear departed grandmother is staring me down. Can't we move her?"

She glanced over her shoulder at the portrait. "She's beautiful, I think."

"She makes my skin crawl."

"We can change seats."

"I'd rather have a ghost look me in the eye than look down the back of my neck."

"We can't take it down. Father would be mortified."

"You think he's going to see? You think he's going to visit us?

Grace. They're never going to visit. Don't you understand that yet?"

Back in the attic, she considered how to spend her day. Her favorite corner, the northwest one, was a most comfortable nest. She had covered an old, splitting Morris chair with a green blanket, and pushed it over to the file cabinets that formed a little cove by the dormer. She'd found a half-finished painting on a piece of rolled linen, and she'd carefully unrolled it and cleaned it of dust, and tacked it to the wall below the window. It was maybe meant to be an oak leaf, in intense close-up. She put a board across the arms of the Morris chair, and this became her desk for drawing and writing letters. It was exactly like an artist's garret in Paris in the nineties, she decided, somewhere on Île Saint-Louis, and when Amy crunched by on the path Grace pretended it was a fishmonger.

Today she would plan her greenhouse. Ludo was thrilled at the idea, and he'd promised to learn orchids. She sketched it out on the back of an empty folder from the cabinets—not the architecture of it, which was already determined, but the placement of the plants—and she used a second folder as a ruler. She penciled in the neat little shelves and pots. Here, along the eastern windows, tomatoes and lettuces. How heavenly, in January, to eat a soft, ripe tomato. There should be spinach, as well. She thought of a hot vegetable pie. African violets along the inner wall by the house, unless there wasn't shade enough. Phalaenopsis along the west, framing the view of the back lawn: white, purple, pink. Yellow lady's slipper, the small ones. Ferns all over the middle, a jungle of ferns, and a little copper mister. Ferns hanging from the ceiling, as well, and other things that would lilt down with soft tendrils and green threads of hair.

In another life, she'd have been a botanist, or a painter of plants. In college she took a whole course on the plant kingdom.

The professor, an ancient British woman, had cut an apple in half the wrong way—down its equator—and turned the halves out to face the girls, to show them the stars that had been hiding there, the carpels, the seeds cut through and leaking arsenic. Stars! In the apples she'd been eating for twenty years! Suddenly, that year, every tree had a name. When boys sent her flowers, she'd sit at her dormitory desk dissecting each one, pulling daisies apart into disc flowers and ray flowers, splitting the bases of lilies with her thumbnail to find the rows of neat, white ovules.

And what was she to do with all that information now? The French literature, too, and the appreciation for Dutch art, and the ability to write a theme on Chaucer. What were those skills but silent companions in the attic, ways to keep her mind from digesting itself over the next fifty years? She imagined her classmates amusing their husbands with their intelligence. When she'd tried talking to George in Paris about the architecture of the bridges on the Seine, he'd accused her of humiliating him.

Her boredom wasn't his fault. What had she done with herself from college to the age of twenty-eight? Precisely nothing. She'd traveled to Italy with her mother (educational, but none of the Italian stuck), she'd answered telephones in her father's office, she'd been engaged, or pretended to be, to two boys, which took a great deal of time and energy but little creativity. She'd been sick for an entire winter with pneumonia. She'd organized blood drives for the Canadian Red Cross. Never, in that time, had she impressed anyone with her knowledge of Chaucer.

Here came Amy, crossing the drive, arms empty for once. She walked with her nose down, as if someone had forbidden her from seeing anything beautiful in the world. Grace was not ready yet to confront Max, but she could talk to Amy. She could get her bearings.

By the time Grace got downstairs, Amy had disappeared. She looked for her in the kitchen (no Amy, but Rosamund had a

question about what vegetables Mr. Grant would accept in his
stew) and down by the linen closets. She finally looked out the
dining room windows and spotted her standing under the catalpa
tree, the same one where George had manhandled her. But she
was facing the tree, staring at its bark, and George was nowhere
around. So Grace walked outside despite the cold, and came up
slowly beside her.

"It's a northern catalpa," she said, and Amy jumped and gave
a rough little shriek.

"Mrs. Grant," she said. "I'm sorry. I thought—maybe you were
an animal or something."

"Well, I suppose I am. And that's a northern catalpa. It can't
be as impressive to you, coming from the south. But up here, it's
got the largest leaves of any tree, by quite a lot. It isn't always so
ugly." In early summer, it had been sublime in its inflorescence:
white flowers hanging like bridal trains, foot-long seed pods,
leaves as big as dinner plates. But now the leaves were sickly yellow, the pods brown and distressingly phallic.

"No, it's very pretty," Amy said. "It is."

"Don't lie."

"Oh."

Amy looked as if she might cry. Grace was tempted to push
her further, to see if she would, but instead she said, "Come
sit with me a minute." She led her to the bench by the koi pond.
She'd have to ask Max soon what was to be done with the
fish once the weather fully turned. She didn't know if they'd
be brought indoors, or if they continued to live here, sealed
beneath a sheet of ice. They sat, and Amy immediately buried
the toes of her saddle shoes in the leaves. She was a child,
Grace reminded herself. Max said she was eighteen, and she looked
it, but there was something much younger about her, something
stuck at seven. Grace said, "Your uncle has a visitor."

There was just the shortest flicker of confusion before Amy

said "Yes." Of course. Because Max, Grace had figured out weeks
ago, was not Amy's uncle. Max had been flawless in his story,
introducing Amy back in July with a proud hand on her shoulder,
including just the right number of details: "the daughter of my
sister Ellen," and "took the train all the way from Florida by herself," and "planned to stay with friends but it's all fallen through."
Grace had bought it completely. Why wouldn't she? She'd said
Amy could stay as long as she needed. And in August, when he'd
come to her again and said that Amy would really love to work,
that she could use the experience, Grace had thought of what her
own mother would do, the manners and generosity she'd seen
modeled for years before she learned, in history class, to call it
noblesse oblige. The housekeeper, Mrs. Carmichael, was ancient
and nearsighted and gouty, and Grace had been sure she wouldn't
mind the help. Amy could fill in wherever needed. Grace had
said, and Amy had broken her own outpouring of gratitude only
to say that she didn't have a green thumb at all, that she could
clean and help in the kitchen, but the gardeners would be better
off without her.

Then certain details started to needle Grace. There was
something so raw and low about Amy, a harshness to her vowels
that was separate from her southern accent. Her teeth were
crooked, she didn't know what a sideboard was, she bit her nails.
In asking Mrs. Carmichael how to reshelve the records in the library, she pronounced "Mozart" with a soft Z. Whereas Max was
a true Brahmin. Grace had no idea of his background. besides his
long attachment to the colony, but the man spoke fluent French
and subscribed to *Harper's*. It didn't fit that his sister would be
Amy's mother. And so Grace had devised a test. She found Max
in the garage one day in September, and said, "I'm thinking already
about Christmas. I know, here we are roasting to death—but it's
my first Christmas as a married woman. How did you celebrate,
Max? When you were growing up? I need inspiration." And he'd

told her about sticking cloves into oranges, about opening gifts by candlelight on the Eve, church service at nine in the morning, duck for dinner, carols and eggnog after. And then, the next day, Grace had come into the kitchen and asked the same thing of both Amy and the cook. Amy had swallowed hard and said, "Well, we always had bowls of nuts on the coffee table. That was a real treat." Grace pressed further and heard about turkey the night before, leftovers for Christmas dinner itself, a mad rush for gifts at dawn.

Grace was certain, then: There was no way a woman who'd grown up in the house Max had described would invent Amy's Christmas for her own children. It answered her question, but it raised many more: Who in heaven was this Amy Hall, and why did Max want her here, and what did she want from Laurelfield? There was something about her weakness that made Grace want to hurt her, to test how long she could hold herself together. Perhaps it was the same instinct that had led George to pin Amy to the tree. She and George were so similar, after all.

Grace said, "Who is she?"

Amy seemed relieved that the question was this easy. "Miss Silverman. From New York City."

"*Silverman*. And she—Miss Silverman is a friend? Of your uncle's?"

"I think so."

"Jewish. A name like that."

"Oh. I wouldn't know, ma'am."

"Had you met her before?"

"No, not before."

"She seems quite odd. Don't you think?" She leaned toward Amy and whispered, twelve-year-olds in the schoolyard. "She dresses like a witch."

Amy let out a short giggle.

"Is she still here today?"

"She went down to the Art Institute," Amy said. "On the train. I worried about her, going all alone, but I guess if she's from New York City she can find her way around."

"Certainly. And is she—*attached* to your uncle? In a romantic sense?" Even though the witch seemed older than Max. She was gray, and he was not.

"Oh, no! I mean, she hasn't seen him in years. That's what I gathered."

"Amy," she said, "one thing I admire about you is your power of observation. No one could have learned this place faster than you. I'm still learning it myself."

"Thank you, ma'am."

"I'm just trying to find out what I can, because I don't want to make your uncle uncomfortable. The truth is that he never asked to invite a guest."

"Oh, but he didn't know she was coming!"

"Are you sure?"

"You've never seen anyone so surprised. He—well, I don't know. He was upset that she'd come. It's really not his fault, I think."

Grace decided to be quiet until Amy said something else. This was one of her father's negotiation tactics, and she rarely had reason to use it. Perhaps she was still improving her mind after all. She stared at Amy, and Amy kicked the leaves and looked generally terrified. It only took a few seconds.

"I'll tell you what she said, though. It was after he got over his shock, and they'd sat down at the table, but I was still on the stairs. She said, 'I had to see for myself. You have no idea what I went through to get away.' And then they were quiet a long time, and I thought they were either laughing or crying."

Grace was impressed, despite herself, with the old-fashioned Yankee accent Amy had put on for Miss Silverman's voice. She was a good mimic. Why, then, did she so doggedly keep her wretched twang when she was capable of speaking properly? Grace would like to write out the ways Amy might elevate herself.

"I imagine she was referring to the colony," Grace said. "To the colony closing. Do you suppose it's an artist rushing here to see the damage?"

"She said—she said no one in New York knew where she was. I left that out. She said she'd told them all she was visiting her brother in Wisconsin."

"And where does she sleep?"

"Oh, not—not with—he asked if I wouldn't mind sleeping down on the couch in the mechanical room. And I don't. So she's got my quarters, and I don't mind at all."

"You're very helpful, Amy. You truly are." She hated the sound of Amy's name in her mouth. Such horrible vowels, such an egregious mangling of the French Aimée—*loved*, but who loved little Amy? Not her. Not George. Probably not Max.

"Thank you, ma'am."

Part of what bothered her about this girl was how much the two of them resembled each other. Both blonde, both with long eyebrows, strong chins. Though Amy was at least twelve years younger. And prettier, even discounting age. Grace, at eighteen, had not been as pretty as Amy at eighteen. It was only fair. Amy had been luckier in looks, and Grace had been far, far luckier in breeding. If she were Amy, though, she might find it odd that this woman, this sad and tired Mrs. Grace Grant, should be elevated so far above her, in defiance of the hierarchy biology itself had bestowed. In the court of femininity, looks trump all. The gorgeous lady-in-waiting can always smirk pityingly at the plain-faced princess. And *this* was what enraged Grace. She'd finally pinpointed it. That Amy pitied her. Their similarities invited comparison, and Amy must be measuring herself against Grace all the time. And pitying, and gloating, and letting George claw her by the tree.

Grace stood. She didn't want to talk to Amy anymore, even if she had more information.

Amy stood too. "Ma'am, if I might ask something."

"Certainly."

"Your eye." And she reddened as soon as she'd said it. She might have no manners, no sense of propriety, but she must have seen that Grace wanted to slap her.

Grace restrained herself, though, and touched her own cheekbone with two fingers. She was about to say that she'd slipped in the bathroom. But she felt like wounding Amy, and so she told the truth. She said, "George hit me with a large salt shaker. Thank you for your assistance, Amy."

She needed her coat before she walked all the way to see Max. Her mother had sent her an alpaca coat, and this was the first day it was cold enough to wear it. She walked back in through the kitchen, and was nearly to the hall closet when George (a whole herd of Georges) thundered down the front stairs and saw her and said, "You're coming with me. We're playing golf."

"Now?"

"We've been here five months. I want to get in one round before Christmas."

He could have gone without her, but the membership at the Chippeway Club was in her father's name, and she knew George was secretly terrified of being turned away at the door. Grace was his human shield. She'd been making excuses for weeks.

"I'm wearing slacks. I'm not sure of the dress code—"

"Well, change."

"I'll freeze."

He didn't answer, though. He was headed for the basement to scare up the golf bags.

In the end she kept her slacks on, half hoping it would get

them kicked out, though she could already imagine George screaming that she'd embarrassed him. She put on a cardigan and the alpaca coat, and she wore cat-eye sunglasses that didn't quite cover the bruising. By the time she came down, George was already in the back of the Capri, which Max had pulled up to the front door for loading the golf bags.

"Why don't we take the Darrin?" she said to both of them. "Max shouldn't have to come. He has a guest, after all."

Max looked startled, as if he'd hoped this fact had escaped her notice. He rested her bag on the lip of the trunk.

"I'm happy to drive," he said.

"What are we paying this guy for, if he never drives us anywhere? Come on, hop in."

Grace wanted to protest that this wasn't done, that people didn't need drivers to transport them one mile across town, that it wasn't 1920, but George would think she was lecturing him on cultured behavior. And perhaps it was safer to have Max along.

She leaned her head on the window as they rode. So many pretty houses. The maple trees were still red.

George was worrying his trouser knee. Someone had once told her that if a man sees the line of a woman's suntan—the strip of white peeking out beneath the strap of her bathing suit or the collar of her dress—he'll fall in love with her. Because he will believe he's seen her truest self, raw and pale, something no other man knows. And this was the reason she'd fallen in love with George: She could see the desperate nerves beneath the bluster. He came from nothing, and nobody, and nowhere. His parents were middle class, but they died when he was three, and he was shuttled between orphanages and aunts, and everyone robbed him till he was grown and lethally charming with no money at all. He'd survived childhood only by ingratiating himself to women, and as an adult it remained his leading skill. He showed up in Windsor at the age of twenty, and his only lie was an aristocratic British accent. Everything he said was technically true: orphan, penniless, et cetera. Once people heard that bit, they never pressed him on his background. He met a rich girl and seduced her and followed her to Toronto, where she introduced him to everyone and he dropped the accent. He went to a different party every night, spiraling up the social world, and he ended with everyone considering him a sort of relative, a crazy cousin to be endured. He'd pay a girl a lot of attention, get her father to give him a job, get her brother to loan him a bed, and then before they knew it he was on to another place. None of the girls loved him, though, so he didn't break many hearts. To his credit, he was always careful to pick out the adventuresses. He told Grace all these things, tearful and drunk, a few nights after they met. She should have been horrified by his crying, but instead it did her in, and she put his head in her lap and ran her fingers through his hair.

A Negro in uniform nodded them through the gates of the Chippeway Club, and another opened Grace's door at the front entrance.

She spoke before George could, before he could even get out of the car. "We're guests of a member," she said. "But he isn't with us. Could you direct us, please?"

He led them to the golf office while Max gave the bags to a caddy. She watched him out the office window, standing there by the car, waiting to see if they'd be turned away, and she wanted to tell him to leave, to stop caring about them and go back home to his witch. The man in the office gave them a tee time and welcomed them cordially. He asked if they'd like a drink on the back porch. Grace nodded, figuring at least on a porch it wouldn't be ridiculous to keep her sunglasses on. They followed the man. Max would have to figure out on his own that they were settled, that he was dismissed.

Everyone on the glassed-in porch was ancient, hunched over

bowls of soup and snifters of brandy. On the weekends it must be different, businessmen and their bouncy wives. In summer, it would be full of children. She knew there were women her age in town—she'd seen them at the pharmacy and the hairdresser, even if she did turn down the invitation from the Newcomers' Society—but they all had children, and nothing in common with her. She'd counted on neighbors, but the house to the south was vacant and the older couple to the north spent all their time in Virginia. Grace had no idea how to insinuate herself into a new town, and no pressing desire to. She was unaccustomed. Toronto society had simply flowed through her parlor, and her friends and beaux had appeared as naturally as wildflowers. George knew how to do it, but now that he had the house and the wife and no need for a job, he had no motivation to meet and charm anyone but the regulars at the Highwood bars, the men with loose and shady business ventures who could use an investor like George. Besides which, he wasn't interested now in social climbing so much as in having a good time. One Sunday, in an aborted effort to be sociable, Grace had gone to the Presbyterian Church, but she only wound up sitting alone in the back and trying to delineate the families, putting mental dividers in the pews. Four blond children, bookended by blond parents. Two teenage girls with pageboy cuts, and their graying mother. Grace hadn't been back. The last thing she wanted was someone who knew her name, who looked for her every Sunday, and then worried when she showed up with a purple jaw.

She looked out across the eighteenth hole to where three tee-pees stood in a row. It was simultaneously 1955 and 1800 out there.

George ordered them both gin and tonics, and the waiter already knew his name: "Yes, sir, Mr. Grant."

At the next table, an old man sliced into a cylinder of pinkish aspic.

She whispered to George: "We've checked into the geriatric ward."

"Your father picked a hell of a club."

"Oh, he hardly came. It was only a way to keep friendly with the locals when the colony was open. The artists were always making such a ruckus. He'd golf with the mayor, that sort of thing. I think his parents were members, way back."

George laughed too loudly. "That's why Madame Violet offed herself. Too boring at the old country club."

Their drinks arrived, with small wedges of lime.

After the waiter had gone, Grace said, "We can't very well charge these to my father."

"Are you going to take those ridiculous glasses off?"

"It depends if you'd like people to call the police."

"What you need is to be better with makeup. Makeup would cover that, if you did it right."

"Miss Georgia, the cosmetician."

George reached a finger across the table toward Grace's stemmed glass of ice water. He touched it as if he were about to say something about it, something important, but then he kept pushing, and the whole glass tipped slowly toward Grace, until gravity sped it up and the ice cubes and water tumbled into her lap.

She made a noise but managed to keep her lips closed. She stood and shook the ice to the floor, and the aspic-slicing man handed her a napkin and his wife rushed around the table to see if she could help. George stayed calmly in his seat, and Grace refused to look at him.

She said, to the older couple, "I'm sorry, I'm sorry," and she said it to the waiter, who had run over with a broom and dustpan to collect the ice: "I'm so sorry." She ran through the dining room and toward what she thought was the front door, but it was an empty banquet hall. She ran back around a corner and another corner, and yanked off her sunglasses to see better, and finally she found the door. She had no plan except to walk home, or maybe into town—but there, just a bit farther around the drive than where he'd dropped them, was Max, leaning against the Capri. He dropped his cigarette and squashed it with his toe. He opened the back door as if he'd expected her at precisely this moment.

"Mr. Grant won't be joining us till later," she said. Max put on his driving gloves and handed back a handkerchief.

He said, "I'll return for him. I assume he'll play the full eighteen?"

She couldn't very well question him about the witch now, even though she had him alone. That could wait till she was breathing evenly, till she wasn't riding in a vehicle he controlled.

When her father had made all the arrangements, he'd said Max would look after her. At first she worried he was meant to report back to Toronto about George's behavior, but Max was far too tight-lipped for that, besides which he and her father didn't seem fond of each other in the slightest. "I *can't* fire the fellow," is what her father had said, as if he wanted nothing more in the world. "He's been there longer than the trees." But Max seemed to be following some deeper imperative than just driving and overseeing the grounds. He acted, at times such as these, like Grace's appointed protector. Perhaps he was fond of her. But that made little sense, seeing as she and George had usurped the estate. This wasn't really the way it happened, but it was the narrative she knew the colony people had told one another: Old Gamby Devohr is shutting us down so he can hide his daughter and her drunken husband while her brother runs for Parliament. When really it was just a convenient confluence. The colony's death knells had been sounding for years, and yes, they wanted George far from Ontario, and they wanted Grace to live with her mistake, here in the suburban wilderness, till she recognized the error of her ways and came crying back, divorced and wiser. And her idiot brother had as much chance of winning that seat as he had of winning the Nobel Prize in physics.

Her mother's parting words: "You'll see, when you can't run him around Toronto shocking everybody. You'll see what he's like to live with. And you'll see how it is when no one cares that you're Grace Devohr."

That last bit was true: At both the beauty parlor and the florist, she'd slipped and given her maiden name, and there wasn't the slightest recognition. Of course, that same hairdresser, when she learned Grace was Canadian, asked, "Do you have a president up there now, or do you still believe in the queen?" This town was a vacuum. Well, she'd live with it. She'd have to live with it. And perhaps invisibility could be her great adventure.

Max dropped her at the front door, and she took the mail off the hall table and climbed immediately to the attic. A letter, in her mother's elegant hand: Father was a little better, but still coping with the gout, and short of breath with the autumn air. Wallace was growing discouraged in his infant run for Parliament, and it seemed the public saw him as a lazy gadabout (true, Grace thought), but he had a year and a half to change their minds. Uncle Linus had run off again, and no one was doing much about it. The maids dusted Grace's bedroom every day, and she'd be welcomed home on a moment's notice. Deer had eaten all the mums.

The rest of the mail was bills and a catalogue. It was odd that she never got mail intended for the colony, from far-flung artists who hadn't heard of its demise. But she supposed Mrs. Carmichael must sift that out. She ought to ask.

And now, again, she was facing a blank day. She couldn't plan the greenhouse much further without Ludo. Her brother Morton, or rather his personal secretary, had sent a Paint-by-Number kit for her birthday in July, and it seemed the most tedious and point- less exercise in the world—but then today was a tedious and pointless day. She laid out all the packaged supplies. Pots and pots of little oil paints, five brushes, turpentine, a cup. Three poster boards: Big Ben, the Eiffel Tower, the Leaning Tower of Pisa. She picked Pisa: Imminent gravitational tragedy suited her mood. There were several old easels with the colony furniture, crammed along with the beds and desks and bureaus into the two front wings, and she hauled one back to her northwest corner and set the little poster board up. The unpainted picture was fascinating, an unfathomable mess of pale blue lines, shapes that weren't shapes, full abutment, no spaces between.

She opened a pot of alluring gray-blue, and painted, with the smallest brush, a wedge of sky, until the number 8 was covered and the edges looked crisp. It was tremendously satisfying. The oak leaf painting was still tacked under the window, and Grace resisted the urge to reach down and daub some paint in the cor- ners, to finish the job. It was perfect as it was, though, even if clearly incomplete: the frilled, fleshy edges of the leaf blade, pink- ish brown, as if it were blushing, as if the artist had discovered, deep in the forest, a fallen leaf that was more vibrant after death. It ought to make her sad, to paint something segmented and pre- scribed so close to this delicate blurring, this confident restraint, but really she felt lovely just to be painting *near* it.

She worked for quite a long time, then set the brushes to soak in the turpentine. The afternoon was getting on, and she hadn't eaten lunch, but she wasn't ready to go down yet. She stretched, then leafed a bit through the colony files. She loved the names, and the old penmanship, and she loved the woman who, to compensate for a broken typewriter hammer, had written in all her *D*s with purple ink. There was even a novel manuscript in there that she'd once tried to read, until she found it was unrewardingly dense. Today she pulled out the chunk behind that, N through P. Earl Napp would not attend for the summer of 1939 after all. Alma Nellis wondered if she had left her valise. Samantha Mays, the director, wrote back: No, she hadn't, and they'd even checked at the train station for her, and they dearly hoped there was nothing of value inside.

A name she recognized, though she couldn't place it: Viktor Osin, a "maître de ballet," had stayed five times in the twenties and thirties. A recommendation glowed about his "kinetic vivacity." Then it clicked in place like a jigsaw piece. That spring, right after they'd moved in, that strange article in the *Tribune*. A choreographer who'd gone missing and turned up in Grant Park, a common wino. One of his own male dancers had found him, had recognized him through the grime and the beard. The dancer had washed him off and sobered him up. There'd been a photo of him, Mr. Viktor Osin, on the front of the Arts section, attending a performance of his own work, a version of *The Winter's Tale* he'd choreographed some twenty-five years earlier. But something was off about it all, and this is why Grace remembered, why she'd even read the accompanying article in the first place. Despite his suit, his shaved chin, his combed white hair, there was still something deeply wrong with the man and his hollow eyes—as if they'd reanimated his corpse just for the occasion. She remembered how she'd felt at her wedding. Everyone so falsely happy for her, congratulating her for—what?—for showing up, for existing. She wanted to climb into the newspaper, to tell Viktor Osin that she understood him, that she forgave him. And here in the letter: "kinetic vivacity"? She wondered what had gone wrong, what broke him.

A creak traveled across the attic floor, and shook her awake. She didn't know how long she'd been staring at that file, and she became disgusted that she'd spent her afternoon painting in someone else's version of the sky and dwelling on the minutiae of twenty years ago, when she might deal with Max. George was out of the way, and even the witch was off at the museum.

She rested the files on one of the cabinets, and got her coat from the hook at the top of the stairs. But here was Max, after all, coming to find her, knocking at the door below. Or at least someone was, and she assumed it was Max, not Mrs. Carmichael, from the quick confidence of the raps. She trotted down, but when she opened the door the whole hall was empty. She looked in the flowered bedroom on the right, and in the guest suite to the left, but there was no one. Ridiculous child, to get goose bumps on her arms. It was the acorns, of course. They'd been falling all week, pelting the windows and roof.

Without thinking she started back up, as if that had been her mission all along, and it wasn't till she got to the top that she remembered Max. But meanwhile the files had all spilled down from the top of the cabinet, onto the Morris chair and floor. She sorted what she could: the letters, some slides, a postcard from poor, luggageless Alma Nellis. Sticking halfway out from the top of a folder that read *Parfitt, Edwin*, was a photograph. She pulled it out. A *revolting* photograph, the kind she knew existed, the kind she'd glimpsed in boxes of postcards at the *bouquinistes* by the Seine, but it was never *men*, and never so *anatomical*. She dangled it upside down between her thumb and finger. There was nothing else in the Edwin Parfitt file, and nothing else that seemed to belong there. She turned the photo right side up so she could properly read the expressions on the two men's faces. The one on the left was grinning like the devil. The one on the right: Oh, oh, oh. The man on the right was her father.

Down in the library, she poured herself a glass of George's scotch. She preferred to taste something harsh and stinging just then. She didn't know what to do with herself, besides crawl out of her own skin.

She moved the little jade monkey from a bookshelf to the top of the bar, as if it were contemplating what to drink next. It was one of the few items she remembered from her childhood visits to Laurelfield, and she'd been delighted to find it still in the library. What she remembered was a plump, friendly woman pressing it into her hand, saying, "We haven't many toys here, but this might do."

She drank one more glass of scotch and waited til she could feel it in her cheekbones, and then she marched off to the coach house, the photograph in her coat pocket.

She found Max in the garage, washing the windshield of the Darrin. It was a ridiculous car, two seats only, pale yellow with a puckered grille in front, sliding doors and a sliding roof that always got stuck halfway open. And George had been one of the only saps in the world to buy the thing.

"Max," she said. "I want to inquire about your guest."

He stopped and folded the rag. "I do apologize. That's Miss Silverman. An old friend of the colony." But he wasn't apologizing at all, really, and his brazenness brought her up short. For such a tiny, quiet man, he was awfully sure of himself. "Are you feeling all right, Mrs. Grant? Perhaps you'll take a seat." He indicated the passenger side of the Darrin, but she knew she'd have to remain standing if she wanted to show any authority at all.

"So she's an artist."

"Just a friend of the colony."

"Then she must hate me."

He smiled far too kindly. "None of us bears you ill will, Mrs. Grant. You needed a place to live."

"Do you know the irony?" she said. "I'm the only one of my family who ever loved this place. I came here several times as a child. I remember the dog. Miss Mays, the director, had a wonderful sort of walrusy dog."

"Alfie."

"Yes! It was Alfie!"

"He's buried back in the woods."

"Oh, he's—Oh, now I'm sad and I don't even know why. You'll have to show me, sometime, where he is. You must have been here then yourself, but I don't remember."

"I was lower on the totem pole, at the time. Lawn care and such." He gestured, again, to the seat, and she wondered if she'd really gone that pale, or if maybe she'd smeared blue paint on her face without realizing. She gave in this time, and slid the little door, and sat. Max came around so he wasn't looking at her through the glass.

"And do you know, I always thought that when I was grown I'd come stay here. That I'd be an artist, and I'd show up with an assumed name, and no one would know. Sometimes I think it was a horrible mistake to tell my father so. What if he closed it all down just to spite me? And then sent me here to babysit the corpse. But I had to live somewhere. And I knew if I didn't come take it, he'd put it up for sale."

"There were offers," Max said.

"Max, do you suppose there's something wrong with him? With my father? I think I've just realized that I don't know him at all."

He said, "I can't speak ill of my employer."

"But how well do you know him? How *long* have you known him?"

"We were never great friends."

She put her head down on the dashboard. "Do you know what I want? I want to start all over again with a different name. I want amnesia, I think. I'd like to wake up in some city like San Francisco with no idea who I am."

He was quiet a moment and then quickly, as if he'd been working up the courage to ask it: "Have you heard of the poet Edwin Parfitt?"

Her blood reversed direction in her limbs. Yes, she'd heard of him not twenty minutes ago, and he was now committing an act of sodomy in her coat pocket. "Just recently," she said.

Max made a little cluck. "I'm surprised. He's horribly out-of-date. I have something for you. Please don't leave." And he scurried around the corner and up the stairs to the living quarters.

She worked out what she'd ask him when he came down, and the way she might hand the picture to him. But he was gone quite a long time, and when he finally returned the witch was behind him. When had she returned? Grace was upset with herself for missing it.

She climbed out of the car and struggled for balance.

Max said, "Allow me a belated introduction. My dear friend Zilla Silverman."

She extended a hand. "Miss Silverman," she said. "I do hope you enjoyed the museum."

And she immediately took it all back about this woman looking like a witch. Her eyes were kind and pale blue, a liquid blue, and there was something noble about her, the way she held her shoulders, the way she clasped Grace's hand. She said, "I'm absolutely taken with this little car behind you. It looks made of butter, doesn't it?"

Grace stepped aside so Miss Silverman could view it better. "It's pretty from the side, but from the front it has a pushed-in pig face. My husband paid far too much. It's made of fiberglass. Doesn't that sound like it would shatter from just a pebble?"

"What's it called? No, don't tell me. The Elegant Swine. The Zippy Creampuff!"

"The Gilded Lily," Grace said, and she was thrilled when Miss Silverman laughed. She found that she very much wanted this woman to like her.

"It does have the funniest face on the front. The Pucker-Up-and-Kiss-Me-Quick. What *is* it called?"

"The Kaiser-Darrin."

"Oh, it's German!"

"No, no, George would never." She knew what she was implying, what she'd often implied back in Toronto—that George had
served—when really he'd spent the war years scooping up young
widows like candy from a piñata. But she found that the implication excused his behavior somewhat. And if this Zilla Silverman
planned on staying for any length of time, she was sure, sooner or
later, to see George at his worst. It was true though that he'd
never buy a German car.

And then, because she wanted to change the subject, and
because the scotch was getting to her, she said, "You have the
loveliest teeth. Like pearls. It shows you were well raised. I've always said, if you want to know someone's lot in life, look at his
teeth." In fact there was a small space between Miss Silverman's
incisors, one of which was chipped, but the effect was all the
more charming.

"Well, that's a new idea. Fortune-telling by the teeth. Dento-
mancy!"

"Orthomancy," Max offered.

"Yes! I was just thinking it about poor Amy, the other day,
looking at her teeth. They're horrid, and you can tell she just
hasn't had a fair chance in life. I do wish she could get them
fixed." She'd forgotten about the ruse that Amy was Max's
niece—it was clumsy of her—but she could see now by the look
on Max's face that there was something far worse wrong
than that. He was looking past her shoulder, back toward the
door of the mechanical room. Grace just barely avoided turning
to see if Amy was standing right there in the doorway. It was
where Amy had said she was sleeping, and it was surely where she
was right now. Well, *now* there was another reason for Amy to
despise her, to glare. Grace was only glad she hadn't brought up

the photograph, with Amy hiding the whole time and listening like a little rabbit. "Well," she said. "Hadn't you better fetch George soon from the club?"

Max handed her a small, red book. *Edwin Parfitt: His Selected Verse.* He said, "I've marked the right poem with a paper."

She turned back, halfway to the door. "I meant to ask about the fish," she said. "What are we to do with them in winter? Do they just freeze solid?"

"I bring them in," Max said. His voice stayed as quiet as ever, though she was all the way across the garage. "They'll outlive us both." She was nearly out the door when he said, "Do you know what they like better than anything?"

"No."

"A root beer float."

"I don't understand." She thought over the words. It was like a riddle, but it made no sense.

"You don't?" He looked almost sad.

"Oh, don't worry, dear," Miss Silverman said. "I've never understood him myself!"

Grace stuck both the book and photo in the attic so George wouldn't come across them. Miss Silverman walked the grounds when Max took off to retrieve George, and Ludo raked leaves. Nothing else of note happened the rest of the day.

She was quite taken with the poem, which was about Proteus, and she was pleased that her recall of mythology and meter and rhyme were finally being tested. She appreciated certain lines, the "thickening, quickening night," and "Daphne's branches, sleeved in moss." She also understood the inversion Parfitt had accomplished: In his telling, everyone wanted to pin Proteus down to make him remember the past, not to tell the future. Though what he was so loath to remember she couldn't quite glean. Something about a lightning crash, and the bit about "paying to Charon his tongue-lidded coin," which she took to mean a death.

Most fascinating, though, was the short introduction written in 1950 by Edna St. Vincent Millay. *"Edwin Parfitt was not so much a giant of the poetic world,"* it read, *"as one of its forest elves, whose song lures us deeper into the wood—though we may neither recognize the tune nor ever find the piper."* It went on to claim that his classicism of theme and form had been horribly misread by the critics. At the end came an astonishing paragraph:

> It has been five years now since Eddie Parfitt, after an insurmountable personal loss, took his own life at Lake Glinow, Wisconsin. In accordance with his wishes, he was not buried but wrapped in white cloth and burned, his ashes set loose to the wind. Those of us in attendance took some small delight in knowing those ashes would find rest on far and unsuspecting plots of earth, that they would bless and fertilize their landing places. As, too, will these poems.

Grace wondered if this paragraph was the true reason Max had given her the book: if, after her outburst, he assumed she knew more than she did, and wanted her to learn what had become of her father's partner in sodomy. That didn't seem right, though. She scanned it again, wishing she'd find the words *fish* or *root beer*, wishing the paragraph would tell her where Amy had come from or when Zilla Silverman would leave. Perhaps this book could read her tarot.

Really she supposed Max had only given it to her because she'd spoken of starting over, and he had recalled the poem about Proteus shifting shape. But he must have misunderstood her, then. What Grace wanted to run from wasn't the past, or even

the future as the original Proteus had, but rather the present.
Here she was, crystallized in time, in a place where nothing ever
really happened, at least not to her, while the world marched on
without her back in Toronto. It wasn't so much the house that she
wanted to escape, or George, even as his charm faded like a suntan, but the feel of every moment being precisely *now*, with no
cause and no consequence. She supposed a Buddhist might appreciate it. But it wasn't for her.

On Friday morning (nothing around but sunlight and some
distant sounds traveling out the kitchen windows and back in
through the dormers), she sat in the attic in her robe and slippers
and read the introduction for the fifth time. It struck her only
then that Millay referred to Parfitt's "small dark eyes, and dark
hair, slickly parted." She crossed the floor and pulled out the file
she'd sworn she'd never open again. The grinning man on the left
had pale, wavy hair. Golden or light brown. No one would call
his eyes small. It couldn't be Parfitt. But neither could the man
on the right, who, she was more certain than ever, was her father.
His uneven shoulders, his chin. She turned it over, to see if some
perverse and helpful archivist had recorded their names for posterity, but there was nothing. Well. She'd do it herself, then. She
snatched up the pencil from her greenhouse sketch and, holding
the photo up to the window so she could see the image through
its paper, wrote "*Father*" right across his backside. It felt like nail-
ing him down, accusing him. On the reverse of the other man's
buttocks, she drew a question mark. Then she stuffed it back in
the folder, and the folder back in the cabinet.

Miss Silverman was gone, had been gone since yesterday, and
Grace was unduly bereft. A spectator with no spectacle. George
had disappeared for a day and then returned. The leaves were
gone, except on a few stubborn oaks, and the catalpa was all pods.
They made music in the wind, like maracas. It was freezing now
in the attic, and so she walked its perimeter, closing each of the

twelve dormers, and came to the northeast one last, the one closest to the coach house. Sometimes she thought this was where her
grandmother had done it. Her father would never talk about Violet, so most of the very little that Grace knew she'd learned from
her mother. Violet had killed herself at Laurelfield in 1906, when
Grace's father was only two. For this, she was never to be forgiven
by anyone in the family. Her name was never used for babies, her
grave (they'd taken the body by train all the way back to Toronto)
wasn't visited. When Grace and George first arrived, back in May,
Grace had asked Mrs. Carmichael which part of the house was
supposed to be the haunted bit. "Oh, the attic!" Mrs. Carmichael
had said, and then Grace had to endure fifteen minutes of ridiculous stories about flickering lights and doors that shut themselves.
"So that's where she did it, then?" Grace had asked. "Violet, I
mean. It was the attic?" Mrs. Carmichael had laughed. "I wasn't
here myself, ma'am. I couldn't tell you beyond what I've heard. But
the artists used to say so."

"And did she hang herself?"

Mrs. Carmichael put down her silver polish and looked puzzled. "It's funny. I don't know why, but I always assumed she
jumped."

Grace watched George take the Darrin out of the garage. Max
waved after him, and George backed out toward the big house,
then took off like a French racer through the gate. When he
drove like that, when he took the Darrin, it was a sure sign he
wouldn't be home the same day. Maybe he was headed to Chicago. To a whorehouse. She wondered what it would be like to
start life over as a whore, to show up on the step of a *house of ill
repute*, to live there entertaining the men, the handsome ones
only, until, one day, George would stumble in. And either recognize her, or not.

Max closed the garage door and disappeared inside, and then
there was absolutely no one left in the world but Grace. She

wasn't serious about it in the slightest, but before she closed his last window for the winter, she wanted to see what it felt like, if it was even possible. She stepped out of her slippers and up onto the sill, bracing her feet against the outer edges, clinging with both hands to the bottom of the glass. She had to crouch to fit inside the small, open square, and the wind rushed straight through her dressing gown. It didn't look far enough, really. You'd land on the grass, if you didn't hit the pine tree on your way down. You'd at least end up in a wheelchair, but you might or might not die, and someone wanting to do herself in would undoubtedly choose something more certain. Maybe she'd poisoned herself, after all.

Below, Max came out of the coach house, out the mechanical room door right next to the stone wall. It wasn't his usual way out, and there was something odd about the way he walked too: slowly at first, as if he were scoping things out, then very quickly, all the way along the wall to the gate. He had a leather satchel over his shoulder.

Perhaps this was the third strange thing, the one she'd been waiting for after the rabbits and the witch.

She ought to follow him. It was better than hanging out a window, and better than sitting here waiting for some five-act drama to unfold right on the lawn. She hopped inside and dressed quickly and retrieved her bicycle from the tree it had been leaning against, untouched, since July. She assumed Max must have walked toward town, and she was right: After a few blocks she saw him hurrying along the opposite sidewalk. He turned left, toward the college, and she hung back and followed as obliquely as possible.

He walked past the main gates, across a quadrangle, and through the side door of a Gothic building. Grace parked at a stand of student bikes and walked toward the same door, trying to look purposeful and collegiate. Inside, students milled and sat on hallway benches, and in all directions the classrooms were filling. The signs on the bulletin boards seemed history related. Max had vanished. She peeked tentatively through an open door, then another, and finally she spied the back of his head in a lecture hall. He took a notebook from his satchel, just as his neighbors were doing, and set it on the table in front of him. He turned and whispered something to the thin-shouldered blond boy on his right. A few more students brushed past Grace, and finally a professor strode to the front, with a ripped shopping bag instead of a briefcase.

"Have we spent every waking moment reading about the Bolsheviks?" he asked, and a laughing groan rose from the room. "Fantastic."

She shouldn't hang around, even though she might have liked to audit a class herself. An art class, perhaps. She'd adore a good course on the Dutch masters. She knew what would happen, though. George would find out, and then one day he'd storm in and drag her out of the class by the arm. And she couldn't abide the looks, the gawking undergraduates, and she'd never be able to return. So that was the end of that particular fantasy. She walked out of the building, smiling at the students: the girls in their sweater sets, the boys leaning and smoking and glancing with curiosity at Grace.

Back through town. She aimed her bicycle wheels at individual dead leaves, loving the crunch. She didn't particularly want to go home just yet. There was a beauty parlor with a bicycle stand in front, Matilda's House of Style, and she might as well follow her impulse inside. She had put ten dollars in her pocket, and this would at least be a place to sit down. The cycling had tired her quite a bit.

The woman at the desk told her there was a spot open in twenty minutes, and asked her name. "Amy Hall," Grace said.

And she smiled and tucked her hair behind her ears, and sat to read a copy of *Vogue*.

When they called Amy, she was ready—she'd prepared herself to respond to the name—and she had a shampoo and then sat in the chair while Matilda cleaned her scissors.

"I want it just below the ears," she said. "I need a new look." Matilda began combing, and told her she had lovely hair, just like Grace Kelly. "Oh, you're too sweet." She was trying out just a bit of southern accent, not a harsh one like Amy's but a refined version. "You know, I've just moved here from Florida. My husband Max and I. I thought I'd like a new cut to go with the new house."

"Oh, congratulations!"

"It's just a little one. You know, a starter home. It used to be the coach house of an old estate, but they've converted it. I'll tell you, though, I'm not used to this cold. And to think it's only October! I don't know what I'll do with myself this winter."

"Long underwear!" Matilda said. "That's my advice." She raked Grace's hair out in a straight line and chopped an inch from the end. "And maybe you'll start a family. Some meat on the bones will keep you warm."

To her surprise, Grace actually blushed. She'd sooner give herself a lobotomy than have a baby with George right now, but the newlywed Amy and her husband Max might indeed love to have a daughter, a little girl with soft cheeks and smocked dresses. She marveled at how readily she could feel the emotions of this invented self.

She was on her way through the front door when she saw rabbits. Just three this time, moving quickly along the front of the house. Not so much fleeing her footsteps as running toward a secret party. Grace wondered why on earth God or nature would put that puff of white on their rear ends, when everything else about the rabbit seemed designed for maximum camouflage. Their silence, their speed, their fur like dried grass. But then, at the back, this white target, this flash of light. And they'd never know, would they? Had any rabbit ever seen its own backside, seen the way it was trailed by its own demise?

She followed them around the house.

Outside the solarium, Ludo had marked the lines for the greenhouse with little flags. He'd made arrangements for a crew to come dig out the foundation before the ground got hard. He'd ordered the glass and cement, too, and was working with a friend who'd built greenhouses up and down the North Shore.

She couldn't see where the rabbits had gone. The ivy on the house had shrunk back a bit for fall, as slowly as a balding man's hair. Beneath, the bricks showed through. She found their regularity troubling, their strict overlapping. Something about the lockstep rigidity sickened her, and she thought she'd rather have the tangles of ivy back.

Back inside, she walked through the living room—she wasn't at all sure what to do with it, but maybe paint it over in coral—and the dining room, which, when empty, was so overwhelmed by her grandmother's portrait as to seem a shrine. Violet always looked a little surprised, as if Grace had caught her in the middle of some wildly inappropriate thought and she'd just managed to compose herself.

Grace heard someone across in the library, but when she got there it was empty. She loved this room best if only because there were still small relics of the artists who'd gathered every night for predinner drinks just a year before. Scribbled in the endpapers of an old copy of *Dombey and Son*, she'd found a ridiculous "List of Demands," added to over the years in different hands: head massages, a bugle corps, Chinese footmen, better weather, lullabies, resident astrologer. She'd hidden that book deep in the shelf to protect it, and she checked now that it was safe. The jade monkey was gone from the bar, though, and she wondered where it could have gone. She checked all the shelves, and she checked under the leather couches. She'd have thought George took it, but he hated the library even more than he hated the portrait of Violet— he'd seen strange shadows there the week they moved in, and hadn't set foot in it since. At first he had Mrs. Carmichael bring him out his drinks, but then he just began stocking his bureau as a bar. Grace would have, as a result, spent all her time in this room for the privacy, were it not for the windows between each set of shelves, on three sides of the room. It was an observation tank, and anyone walking from the driveway to the kitchen door would see right in. And perhaps that was what happened. Amy had looked in, on her walks from the coach house, envying the little monkey till she had to have it. But to make sure, Grace went first to Mrs. Carmichael, watering in the solarium, and to Rosamund in the kitchen, and even to Ludo and Beatrice, and none of them even knew what she was talking about, except Mrs. Carmichael, who was sure she had dusted it Friday.

It *must* be, then. Amy was a child, a greedy child. Grace had known this all along. She walked straight to the coach house, and up the stairs to the living quarters. The stairs came out in the small kitchen, and she had to orient herself to think which was Max's apartment and which must be Amy's. She knocked on Max's door first, to be sure he wasn't back, then walked into Amy's side without knocking. The outer room had a sitting area. Well-thumbed fashion magazines on a little table. Fashion! All Amy ever wore were those three cotton dresses, in rotation.

She moved silently to the next doorway. Amy lay on her bed, on her stomach. Grace said, "Amy, I do hope you plan to return everything you've borrowed."

The girl bolted up and straightened her blanket. "I'm—hello. Mrs. Grant."

"I expect my things returned before dinner."

"Only, I—which things?"

"Anything borrowed from the estate, including the jade monkey from the library. I don't think you'll be staying much longer, but you might yet salvage a letter of reference from me if you're forthcoming."

Amy stood and looked around the room frantically, as if checking that she'd hidden everything properly. "Ma'am, I truly don't understand. If I've done something wrong it was a pure mistake."

"Amy," she said. "I don't know who you are, except that you are not Max's niece. Maybe you're his lover, only I don't think so. That's not it, is it? You're a child, but you sit in judgment and you think you know how you'd act if you were me. You think George wouldn't hit you, that you'd tame him. Well, you couldn't."

"Ma'am, you're mistaken." There were fat tears collecting on her chin. "I'm sorry, but you're mistaken."

Grace felt Amy's pain in her own stomach, she did. It was a convulsion, like holding back a sob. But all she could think to do was make it worse, as if that would solve everything. She imagined this was how a killer felt, halfway through the job. Finish stabbing the fellow, so there was no one left to feel it. She said, "Here's what you don't know yet: So often in life, you get exactly what you look for. If you want a George, you'll get a George. The worst thing I could wish you is everything you want."

She meant to leave Amy standing there silenced and shamed, but as she turned Amy said, quietly, "Speak for yourself."

And Grace might have slapped her, she really might have, if she hadn't heard Max come up to the kitchen just then. She walked out and told Max she'd been wondering where he was.

"A quick trip to the doctor," he said, and smiled. "My old knee problem from the war. Can I drive you somewhere?"

"Oh!" she said. "No, but—what time did George take the Darrin out?"

"Around ten."

Grace glanced around the kitchen, and tried to find something to say. "We should get that fixed," she said, pointing at the big board patching up the wall. It was the wall shared with Amy's bathroom and closet, and it was painted yellow, like the rest of the kitchen. "What is it?"

"It's—I believe there was an electrical problem once. It doesn't bother me a bit."

"But you shouldn't have to live someplace all stitched together."

He set his satchel on the table. It looked so soft.

"I know there to be at least five layers of paint over that thing. Another five, and it will all come even. Really, it's not worth the disruption."

His ears were round, like little handles. Grace liked that about him, and she liked the way he sometimes looked almost in love with her. Perhaps he was. She felt wonderfully visible just then, as if something might happen to her, and not just in front of her.

She said, "All right, Max," and smiled in a way she normally wouldn't have, a way her mother never would have smiled at a servant. She trotted downstairs and waved to Ludo, who was pushing a wheelbarrow full of sticks back to the fire pile.

George was shaking her by the hip. He was saying, "What's that smell? What is it?"

Grace rolled over and tried to feel where the blanket had gone. "Is something burning?"

"No, it's you." He turned the light on, and when Grace managed to open her eyes she saw that he hadn't shaved all day, that the cleft in his chin was filled in with black stubble. He had a long red string tied around his neck, like an opera-length necklace, and she couldn't think why that would be. "Why do you smell that way?" He came back to the bed, though it took him a few tries to propel himself in the right direction. Grace sat up, and George stood over her and put his fingers in her hair. "Why did you cut your hair off?"

"The hairdresser did. I needed a trim."

"You think I want you looking like a boy?"

"George, I want to sleep." She slid down under the blanket. "What time is it?"

He pulled the covers completely off the bed and stood over her. "You smell like sex."

"That's ridiculous. I smell like the outdoors. I went for a bike ride."

He yanked her nightgown up to her stomach, and stuck his face between her legs and sniffed loudly. "You smell like you were fucking some fungus-covered hustler."

"*George.*"

She meant to pull him on top of her and turn it into sex before things got worse, but he had rolled her, with one push, to the edge of the bed, and he rolled her again till she fell. Her forehead hit something on the way down. It was hard and sharp, and it must have been the corner of the nightstand. Her whole head and neck throbbed, but especially above her left eyebrow, and when she put her hand there it came away covered in blood.

"George, *look!*"

"Oh, shit," he said. "Oh, Grace, come on. Don't—I'll get a towel."

And he did, one of the GGG monogrammed set from her Saville cousins, and it turned from powder blue to reddish brown in seconds.

"Please ring Max," she said. "I want to go for stitches."

His mouth was open, and he looked like a fish. He said, "I'll take you."

"The hell you will. Either ring Max or bring me the phone."

"What will you say?"

"That I fell off the bed."

"Grace, I love you."

"I know that."

"And you love me."

"Yes. Yes."

He sat on the ground and put his head between his knees, and started rocking like a little boy. Grace stood gingerly and went for the telephone herself.

Max took her in the Capri. There was Amy, owl-eyed at the coach house window as they crunched down the drive.

A hat with a little veil, combined with the sunglasses, hid the stitches and bandage quite well when she ventured out, even if she did look like an escapee from Hollywood. George disappeared for five straight days after that—he was gone by the time Grace and Max returned in the morning—and Grace passed the time by following Max on her bicycle. Now that she knew where he was headed she could hang behind quite a bit, and after he left the property he never seemed to look back.

Might she be in love with him? It was one explanation for this compulsion to follow his every move, but she doubted that was it. He wasn't the type she'd enjoy making love to—he'd be too polite, too quiet, which had been the problem with all the boys back in Toronto. She thought of Lionel, who had kissed her wrist and wouldn't stop asking what she wanted. "Do you like this? Tell me what to do. What do you want me to do?" The problem with George was that she could never be happy with a man who *wasn't* George. She searched herself to see if she held any sort of physical longing for Max, and really she didn't think so. But he was a nut she wanted to crack.

He was taking two classes: the one with the Bolsheviks (Grace thought for a while that it was Russian history, but one day as she listened at the door the professor talked about the Balkans, and she became less sure) and one on the novels of Thackeray and Dickens. She heard enough of that one that she became curious about *Vanity Fair*, which she'd never read, and scared up a copy from the Laurelfield library. Becky Sharp was a wicked heroine, and Grace loved her immediately. Becky was doomed, that was clear. No vice went unpunished in the nineteenth-century novel.

She never stayed more than ten minutes outside the classroom doors, afraid Max might one day head out to use the restroom and discover her. She found, though, that when she biked directly home, Max often didn't return for two or three hours. Certainly the classes weren't that long. In the English building was a smaller hallway off the main one, and she realized she could stand by the corner examining the framed map of Literary England without arousing much suspicion. She did that one Tuesday as the class let out. She was ready to run, but Max lingered by the door with the same blond boy he'd whispered to that first day in the history lecture. They walked together, shoulder to shoulder, down the stairs. Grace stayed and looked down from the window, and saw which way they walked: to the large building with ivy, talking together the whole time. After they'd passed through the double doors, she followed.

It was the library. She picked a direction and walked briskly past the front desk, only to find herself in a reference room with no one in it. She found a larger room with card catalogues, and a study area where the students sat smoking, but she didn't see Max. Upstairs were study carrels and shelves packed thickly together. She supposed if Max saw her she could always pretend she'd been looking for some book. It wasn't any odder for her to be here, after all, than for him to be.

A girl raced past and nearly knocked Grace over with her poodle skirt. Peering down a long aisle, Grace saw, on the far end, the blond boy, walking alone now. She went as far down the aisle as she dared, and managed to watch him through the last bit of shelf. He walked through a door and shut it. There were several such doors along the far wall, and through the open ones she could see very small rooms with desks. Her own college library had offered similar setups: for the girls who wanted no distractions, the ones with ambitious senior projects.

Not two feet in front of her, Max passed by, eyes down. He didn't notice her. She watched as he entered the same room, and as the door once again clicked shut.

If it hadn't been for that photograph, so fresh in her mind, it might have taken her quite a bit longer to figure it all out.

She stood there at the end of the aisle, just stood there, a long time, feeling like an all-around nitwit. She was humiliated that she'd been so fascinated by Max, that she'd liked how he looked at her. She wondered if the world were full of degenerates, Max and this boy and her father and the other man in the photograph, and who knew how many others, all around her, and she in the middle of it, blind and oblivious. Or maybe there was something connecting it all. Her father had told her that Max wasn't to be dismissed under any circumstance. And maybe it was only because Max and her father frequented the same dark bars, the same alleys and closets. Max and her father, her father and Max. Yet they didn't seem to care for each other a bit. Perhaps that wasn't a requisite, in these types of relations. Or maybe he was simply afraid of what Max knew about him.

She knew she ought to leave. If Max found her there *now*, her face would betray her. She thought about that boy, no more than twenty, and how maybe she oughtn't leave him alone there with a man twice his age, how the boy's mother would have preferred Grace to break down the door and send him home at once, his luggage following after.

She went back to the ground floor and sat on one of the smoking couches where she could see the stairs. She held the *Tribune* open in front of her face. Max came down alone, twenty minutes later, and though she expected the boy would follow a few casual paces behind, he didn't. Grace waited another twenty minutes, and then she walked upstairs and back through the aisles. She found the boy at a regular small study carrel, hunched over a textbook. There were other students, but not terribly near. She walked around the carrel, pretending to look for something, and she glanced at his face, at his prodigious eyebrows. He didn't seem distressed, or even guilty—just wholly immersed in his studies.

"Excuse me," she said, and he looked up. "I'm afraid I'm lost."

He gave a sly smile and gestured around the room. "It's the library," he whispered.

"Yes." She laughed. "And I—My husband is a trustee of the college, and he's left me to fend for myself while he meets the dean. I got here, and I don't even know what floor this is. All I'm looking for is the powder room."

The boy stood and nodded. "Pleased to help a damsel in distress." If she hadn't known better, she'd have thought he was flirting.

She followed as slowly as she could, so she'd have time to think what to ask. "You look like a senior," she said.

"Sophomore." He stopped and extended his hand. "Sidney Cole of Indianapolis. Sid."

"Amy Hall," she said. "Of New York." They continued walking. "And do you like it here?"

"Oh yes." But she doubted he did at all. How could he, the poor thing? Boys like that never lasted anywhere long.

"People are friendly?"

"Enough are."

She wanted to say something useful, but what? She had nothing to tell this boy about how to live his life. Besides, they had reached the ladies' room door. "Well," was all she could think of. "Thank you. Do take care of yourself, Sid."

The Darrin was back, parked in the middle of the driveway and waiting for Max to store it. Grace picked up the mail and went directly to the attic, and hoped George at least wasn't drunk enough to destroy things down below.

A letter from her college friend Harriet, tentative, curious if Grace would come home soon. Harriet had been one of the very few at the wedding, and—of those—one of the only ones not to pull Grace aside, to ask if she was *sure*.

She wouldn't write back. What was there to say?

By dinnertime, the Darrin was gone again, and a hard knot that she hadn't realized was in her stomach melted away. She'd have dinner alone, and she was getting rather used to it. She brought down *Vanity Fair*—Captain Osborne had just asked Becky to run away with him—and sat at the table.

After a long time, she heard a wail from the kitchen, a cry that wasn't sudden or surprised, more like part of an ongoing tantrum. There was talking—several voices, all female—and then a low, constant sob. Grace considered heading back there, but it was on principle that she didn't. Dinner was fourteen minutes late. The cook could apologize when she emerged.

The crying got louder before it stopped altogether. When Rosamund walked out, she didn't have a single dish in her hands. Her face was red, but Grace could tell immediately she hadn't been the one crying. She'd known all along, really, that it was Amy. Rosamund stood inside the door, her arms folded across her waist, and she said, "I can't do it any longer. I'd gladly stay on for you, but I won't work for *him*. I refuse."

"He's not even here tonight," Grace said. "He took the Darrin out again. And you haven't served him a meal in five days."

"Listen." She had lowered her voice, though she didn't come any closer to Grace. Why didn't she talk like a servant? None of these American ones did. "I apologize for my language. But, ma'am—he's raped her." Her nostrils flared and she put her hand to her earlobe, but she kept her eyes straight on Grace. All Grace could think of was throwing a plate right at Rosamund's mouth until she stopped talking, until she vanished from the earth. "She's been in there two hours, and she won't stop to breathe. Beatrice is giving her tea. He took her into the Longhouse and he forced himself on her."

"Well," Grace said. And she spoke on instinct, or at least she said what she imagined her mother might say, even though she didn't know what that would be till she heard it come out of her mouth. "I very much doubt that's true. If you must know, Amy lies and steals, and she's quite in love with George. He's had his way with her, I do know that, I'm not blind. But I've *seen* her. She was quite willing. I'm afraid she's played you for a fool."

"Now why would she do that?"

Grace stood from the table and left her chair out, and pushed past the cook into the kitchen. Amy was perfectly well clothed, her dress not even ripped or stained, except that someone had draped a kitchen towel around her shoulders. She and Beatrice sat side by side on chairs, Beatrice still in her gardening boots. Grace wanted to stick all three women into the Frigidaire and lock the door.

"Amy," she said. "Are you with child?"

Amy looked up with red, swollen little eyes. She choked out a whisper: "No, ma'am. I don't think the timing—no."

"Then I don't understand the change. It's all been fine with you up till now. Or perhaps it's because I caught you stealing. The thing of it, Amy, is that you aren't going to wedge us apart. If I leave George, or if George leaves me, it won't be because of some thieving girl."

Amy screamed into her hands and rocked forward, and Beatrice bent over her and rubbed her back. Beatrice said, "I found her outside the Longhouse."

"But you didn't hear her when she was *in* the Longhouse, did you? She must not have screamed very loudly. Beatrice, I haven't invited you into my kitchen."

Beatrice looked shocked, but then, as Grace had known she would, she nodded and walked slowly to the back door. She said, "Amy, I'll be in the garden cottage."

There was soup boiling on the stove, getting too thick, probably.

Grace said, "Amy, are you quitting your job?"

"No, ma'am."

"*I'm* the one quitting," Rosamund said. "And, forgive me, you ought to quit too, ma'am. You ought to leave this house and get back to Canada before he slices you to bits. And Amy ought to leave, and Beatrice ought to leave, and anyone with any sense should get out of here. But as it seems I'm the only one with a backbone, I'll be leaving alone tonight." She whipped her apron off, as if more drama were necessary, and left it behind her on the counter.

She was gone, and it was just Grace and Amy, alone in the kitchen.

Grace said, "You'll have to serve the soup then.'

"Yes."

She didn't know what to think. How could she possibly know what to think? But she did have one clear and horrible realization, as she sat back at the dining table. The drama she had sought in George, the lust and fire, would never involve her anymore, because she was the one married to him. He might gash her face, but he wouldn't ravish her, wouldn't focus his whole being on her seduction. The drama would always be, from now on, about other women.

Amy brought her the soup, clattering the bowl on the saucer and hyperventilating the whole way. Cream of squash, cooked to a gelatinous mess.

Grace wanted to sob until she flowed to the floor and out of the house and into Lake Michigan.

She said, "Amy, I'll want more water."

And when Amy brought her more water, she sent her back for another roll.

And when she brought the roll, she told her to take the soup away because it wasn't any good.

The next day there was a telegram from Toronto: FATHER GRAVELY ILL. TWO OR THREE WEEKS LEFT PLEASE COME HOME.

She wouldn't do it. She couldn't face him now. He'd see right through everything, he'd see that she knew about his degeneracy, and he'd see that he'd been right about George, and she'd break down screaming and she'd tear her clothes and move back to Toronto forever. And do what? And live how? And George would follow her there, and ruin everything for everyone, for her brother and her mother, and the whole city would see her as the girl who came home broken, rather than the girl who ran off for love.

And then she sat and cried all afternoon. Because if it was true that her father was dying, and if George was right that no one would ever visit her here, and if she was too stubborn to go home, then she'd never see any of them again.

Three days later, she went to the coach house when Amy was busy in the kitchen. Amy was cooking everything now, though Grace knew Beatrice snuck in there, whenever she could, to help. The food was dreadful: browned meat covered in sour cream and baked for an eternity; chopped celery covered in cheese and baked; sliced apples for dessert, smothered in a mash of cream cheese and powdered sugar. Grace wanted her gone, wanted her back wherever she'd come from, but she couldn't bring herself to do it, not least because Amy might go to the police then, might say enough that word would spread, as word always spreads, and word could reach Canada. It could reach her father on his deathbed.

But she did have a plan, and having one made her feel better. It came together just when the greenhouse plans came together, as if she were turning out, after all, to be the architect of her own life.

She found Max in the garage and asked him to walk with her to see the digging. "I want your opinion," she said, though it made no sense why someone would have any particular opinion about a hole in the ground. They walked to the far end of the house and stared into the rectangular hollow for the greenhouse foundation. Ludo and two Negroes and a red-haired man all stood in it, poking around the edges of the steps that currently led down from the door of the solarium. They'd have to pull out those steps like decayed teeth, and the concrete floor of the greenhouse would come even with the door. Max greeted the men and looked without great interest at their progress, and when she asked if she might speak to him on the terrace, he nodded and followed her around the corner. They sat looking out at the fountain and the paths that spread from it like rays, and the fire pile growing tall back by the woods, and the Longhouse, and the little studio behind that and, on the far side, the cottage studio that used to house composers and was now the shed for Ludo and Beatrice. Next to the cottage, Beatrice's vegetable garden was finished and brown.

Grace said, "Max, I'm going to ask a favor of you. Amy's been here quite a while now, and it's time for her to move on. You know she's become a terrible distraction to everyone. I think she's be-gun stealing things, as well."

"You'd be out a cook."

"She's no cook. And you've seen how unhappy she's been, these past few days." Max looked puzzled, and she wondered if Amy and Beatrice had managed to keep all the hysterics from him. "Don't you think you can send her home now?"

He rested his hands on his legs as if he were keeping them still only through great effort. "It would be difficult."

Grace reached into her coat pocket and brought out a key ring with four small keys. "I thought I'd offer you my keys to the artists' studios. You could use them however you'd like. You know—" and she was glad he was gazing out at the grounds in confusion, and not at her "—sometimes I think about those boys at the college. I worry about them, so far from home. If you meet any who are in need of a good meal, or a place to rest, you could invite them to visit you here, and they might even use the daybeds in the stu-dios. Surely there's someone who wants a quiet space."

She hadn't been sure, when she'd rehearsed this, what his reac-tion might be. Shame, perhaps, and a grateful exchanging of fa-vors. Or he might be angry and take it as blackmail, which would work as well. She wasn't prepared for him to turn and grin at her. She'd never even seen such an expression on his face. All the composure, all the reserve she'd come to know as Max, fell away in that moment, and she was looking at someone she'd never met.

"I already have keys," he said. "You should hold on to those."

"She's not your niece," Grace said.

"Not technically."

"But she'll listen to you. I don't imagine she's in *love* with you."

He laughed softly. "No. She's quite naïve, I think. She's not like you, she doesn't realize how I am, but she's fond of me. And Grace, I'll say quite plainly that I won't send her home." Only a moment later did she realize that he'd not only defied her, he'd called her Grace. And what could she do about any of it? Threaten to tell her father, when she had no idea what history lay between them? If she couldn't dismiss him, and he wouldn't do what she said, then it was quite obvious that he was really the one in charge. He said, "Some fellow brought her to Chicago, is what happened. He convinced her to leave Florida with him, which, from what I understand, likely saved her life. But it turned disastrous. As those things tend to. She's only eighteen. Do you know how she came to us? Beatrice found her outside the gate, peering in. She'd been knocking on every door down the street, looking for work. She's remarkably resourceful. In Chicago, before she left the man, she asked around where the nicest houses were, and someone said she ought to come up here. She told me she figured that even if she failed, no one in a small town would let her sleep on the street. Whereas in the city . . . She'd been to a hundred houses before she met Beatrice."

"How lucky that she found us." She was amazed, really, at how sharp her voice was, how mean. It was exactly like her mother's.

"This has always been a place for strays. The people who need to find Laurelfield always find it. Listen, Grace, she's got nothing back home. A horrible family. A whole family of Georges. I can't send her."

"Why don't you just marry her, then? If you care more about Amy than your employment here. Are you capable of being with a woman? It would be a happier marriage than some, even if it were a farce. And then you could keep her out of everyone else's business, and maybe you could leave alone poor Sid Cole of Indianapolis."

Max did look startled now, and perhaps Grace shouldn't have let on that she had Sid's name. He'd been impressed with her intuition, her worldliness, and now he knew she was just a snoop.

He stood, and at first she thought he was stalking off, but he came instead and knelt down in front of her chair, right on the stone floor, right in the dead leaves.

He said, "You don't look good."

It ought to have insulted her greatly, but it didn't. Maybe it was a relief to have someone in charge, someone who cared if she lived or died. He was trying to get her to look at him, right at him. That was why he'd gotten down so low. And she couldn't do it. She looked over his shoulder, out at the dry fountain.

"Grace," he said. "Aren't you the one who needs to get out of here?"

She kept staring until the fountain became a gray blur, no closer or farther than the trees beyond.

"Grace. We're similar, you know. Maybe it's something I shouldn't say, but it's true. Did you read that poem?"

"It didn't apply."

"The point is to reinvent yourself."

She felt like reaching out to touch Max's dark hair. She might push a small dent into it with her finger, and it might stay that way. Instead she stood to leave, while she still had some small remnant of dignity.

He said, "I'd marry you myself."

"That's very kind."

Saturday was Guy Fawkes Day. No one in the States seemed to celebrate it, but when George showed up at breakfast—Grace was mildly surprised to see him, as he hadn't slept in their bed—she suggested they do a bonfire that night. The burn pile was so tall.

George said, "That's a fine plan."

He was lit by the sun, black curls in every direction, eyes bright green and unclouded. She loved him at breakfast. If she kissed him she would taste like Listerine, and when he stretched his arms and back she could hear the cracks. In the morning he was like a small, clean snowball—one that would roll downhill all day, picking up rocks and darkness and growing enormous and sharp.

A shaking Amy brought coffee without looking at either of them. It smelled terrible, acrid and offensive, and Grace thought she might retch. She said, "Amy, can you take this away? There's something wrong with it."

George tasted his. "It's perfectly fine."

But Grace handed her cup to Amy, who hurried it back to the kitchen.

"If you drop dead from poison, I'll know who did it," Grace said.

Grace asked Ludo to plan the bonfire, and she thought she and George might even have dinner on the inner terrace, after the blaze was going. But by three in the afternoon George was roaring drunk, and he found her sitting on the bed with the telegram that had just arrived from Toronto. All it said was FATHER WORSENING, PLEASE ADVISE IF COMING, but she couldn't keep from staring at it, as if it would update itself every time there was a change, every time her father sat up to eat a bite of soup. George yanked it from her and she told him what was happening but that she didn't think she'd go.

"They're lying to you," he said. "He's not sick. They want to get you up there and lock you in a closet."

"That's not fair."

"No. Exactly."

"That isn't—George, what are you doing?"

Because now George was shredding the telegram, pouring the shreds into the ashtray on his bureau, and lighting them with a match. She thought of yelling or grabbing it, but then he might throw the whole thing, still on fire. So she waited till it had smoldered to nothing. Then she said, "That wasn't necessary."

"*Ha!* What do you do, all day long? You sit in that attic, moon-ing over your grandfather's precious files, then you sit at dinner staring at your lunatic grandmother."

"They aren't my grandfather's files."

"And where the hell are we? We're in a—we're on an *altar.* This place is an altar to your family. How is this supposed to be my house when it's the Devohr International Museum?"

She hooked her finger through his belt and pulled him toward the bed. "I'll make it up to you," she said.

But he pushed her onto the mattress and left her there, and then she listened for quite a long time as he stormed through the house opening and shutting doors, until it turned from storming to crashing. He must have drunk more in the meantime. And the sun was already going down.

She stood in the bedroom doorway and watched him come up the stairs, then stumble all the way down the hall to the open door of the attic steps. He disappeared, and came back a minute later with his arms full of file folders. The Parfitt book was bal-anced on top.

He saw her, but he didn't stop except to call out "*Remember, remember the fifth of November!*" And then, from halfway down: "What do you say, Duck? Fall cleaning!"

Grace ran to the attic door and thought of locking it, but the key was all the way down in the kitchen. She might have gone in and locked it from the inside, only George would just kick the door in, and what would that accomplish? She went into the flowered bedroom and watched from the window as he strode across the lawn, papers flying from the files. He rolled up the fold-ers and stuck each into a space between sticks. Ludo stood by the cottage, keeping quite a distance. Beatrice, she assumed, was in the kitchen helping Amy.

He was coming back, and she ran, while she still could, up the stairs to think what she might hide. He hadn't gotten to the middle of the alphabet yet, and so she scooped out the whole section that would contain the Edwin Parfitt file and its photographic contents and stuffed it all far back in the jungle of office furniture, between the mimeograph machine and the postage meter. She might have liked that photo burned, but she couldn't run the risk of George seeing it. He would do something horrible, she was sure, something that would finish off her father. Besides which she hadn't solved its mystery yet. She wasn't *done* with it yet. George was back, before she could get more files. She considered hiding, but when he appeared she was just standing by the cabinets, unable to move.

He saw her and said, "*What*."

"I was curious."

She ducked before he could push her aside, and he snatched the oak leaf painting from under the window, the tacks flying from its corners and skittering across the floor. He said, "Whose vagina is this?"

"It's—first of all it's an oak leaf."

He held it at arm's length. "That is a vagina."

"It might be valuable."

"Sure. What you need, Grace Devohr, is more money. All your problems will be solved." He rolled it and tucked it under his arm and scooped more files out. His hands were massive—it was the first thing she loved about him, that his hands were like bear paws—and he grabbed up six inches of folders in each hand. He stacked them against his chest, held them down with his chin, and Grace thought they might all fall, but only a few did

She said, "Here, I'll carry the painting."

"The hell you will."

He went past her, and down the stairs, and this time she followed him all the way out, watched him strip to his undershirt to stuff things into the pile. Ludo, when he saw her, retreated into the cottage. Max stood on the path by the catalpa, watching, hands in his pockets. She wondered if he recognized what was being burned today, if he cared as much as she did about these last relics of the colony. There were two faces as well in the kitchen window: Beatrice, Amy. Three gas cans near the pile, but it didn't smell like he'd used them yet.

She knew something right then. She saw George pushing those files into the sticks, saw him bent on destroying something. And not because he loved it but because he *didn't*. Because he didn't care at all. And she knew then that Amy had told the truth, that she hadn't offered herself to him.

George said, "I'm not leaving you out here alone," and he pulled her by the arm back to the house. They passed not five feet from Max, and she looked straight at him and tried to send him a message to rescue the painting, at least the painting, but he looked like a man trapped in stone.

In through the terrace to the living room, up the stairs, down the hall, letting go of her at last, and up the attic stairs.

And when he was halfway up, when she was still on the bottom step, he fell. He seemed to fall forward and then, mid-pitch, his body jackknifed and it turned to a headfirst backward dive. The stairs were steep. He landed above her and slid down and came to rest with his head, face up, at her feet.

Grace surprised herself by not screaming. She just stood there looking down, her heart a kettle drum, and a thousand different futures flashed in front of her.

But no: He was still breathing. Great, deep breaths, like a child asleep.

Even so. What if she just left him here? What would be the effect of staying at this downward angle after a blow to the head? What were the odds of his drowning in his own vomit?

All the tension had gone from his face, and all the anger. His forehead was smooth and unfurrowed. Grace crouched and ran a finger from his eyebrow to his hairline. It was an odd moment to think it, but what she found herself contemplating was how the forehead is one of the more sexual parts of the body, the texture of smooth skin over hard bone. She kissed his eye, his closed and upside-down eye. And then she ran to get Max.

Max, surprisingly strong for his size, got George splayed out on the bed in the flowered room. He asked if Grace wanted him to call an ambulance, but by now George was stirring, moaning a bit and reaching for his head. Max fetched an ice pack from the kitchen instead. Then he whispered, "What can we do?"

If she hadn't guessed already that he was talking about the files, she'd have known by the way he faced the window, ready to dive right through it and reclaim everything.

"He'll remember," she said. "He rarely forgets what he was doing."

"Can we restuff them? Can we put other things in the files?"

Grace scanned the room: the pretty old washbasin, the glass-shaded lamp. "There are the two phone books in the hall," she said, "but it won't be enough." Then she remembered the unreadable novel, still hidden with its neighboring files upstairs. She told Max to wait, and she ran to get it. "This isn't important, is it?"

Max looked at the name on the two files, and at the six hundred pages crammed inside. "Good lord. No, this is nothing. It's perfect."

Grace stayed with George, stroking his hand and making sure he stayed put, while Max ran to the burn pile. She craned to watch from the window as he worked first alone and then with Ludo, collecting the folders, yanking out the contents into one huge stack, and systematically restuffing each with a few pages of phone book or failed novel.

He put the rescued papers into Ludo's wheelbarrow, and Ludo wheeled it all into the gardener's cottage. Max met her in the hallway with just the painting and a bit of the novel ("I couldn't bear burning it *all*," he said). He told her Ludo would shelter the other papers in the cottage till Max had time to sort it. He said, "I remember most of these people. It shouldn't be hard to refile. He'll miss the painting, though."

Grace ran the novel remnants back to the attic, and stowed the painting behind a pile of colony mattresses. There was nothing to replace it. She looked at her poster board with the Leaning Tower of Pisa, and laughed. It would never roll. And it was the wrong size.

George rested till dinner, groaning and stirring and eventually sitting up to ask for food. Grace intended for Amy to bring him his dinner on a tray while she ate in peace downstairs, but she stopped just short. She wouldn't send the girl to be alone with him in that room. She wouldn't send the lamb to the lion. So Grace brought him a tray herself, bread and butter, whiskey and water. Then she sat alone at the dining table. Amy smiled so kindly at Grace as she put the baked carrots and cheese in front of her that Grace wanted to scream. She wanted to gouge the girl's eyes out for knowing what she knew, for seeing Grace dragged back to the house like a child. And at the same time she wanted to fold Amy up in her sweater, to rock her to sleep.

Soon after, George went out to the pile himself and came raging back to where Grace sat in the solarium. "Where did the painting go?" he said.

"I don't know what you mean."

He seemed to be summoning the strength to fly across the room at her, but Max and Ludo had followed him, and here they came through the terrace doors.

"The painting!" he said. "Your painting. You think I don't know what you're doing up there?"

"I didn't paint it."

"Mr. Grant," Ludo said. 'The painting is blown away. I am sorry. It—puff!—across the lawn while you sleep. I see it go.'

"Ha!"

"Let's start the fire," Max said. "While the night is young."

Before he followed the men back out, George pointed at her. "If I see that painting again. If I find that you—I don't like to be lied to."

"I wouldn't, George."

"If I see that painting again, I'll burn the whole place down. The whole house."

She watched as Ludo poured gasoline on the pile. George threw the match, and everything went up in a glorious blaze.

The next morning, as soon as George took off, Max came into the dining room where Grace still sat at breakfast. The oak leaf painting was in his hands, rolled. "Can't you give it to the college?" she said. "I'd put it in the bank vault, but George has a key."

Without waiting for an invitation, Max sat in George's seat. He unrolled the linen and touched his finger to the paint. "This ought to stay at Laurelfield," he finally said.

"We can't afford that."

"The artist would want this to stay at Laurelfield. There are simply some things that you don't remove from their natural habitats." Amy opened the door from the kitchen, saw Max, and turned back. Now she'd be eavesdropping, but Grace didn't have the energy to care.

"Even if we hid it in your personal effects—it's just that George—"

Max said, "I know what George is capable of."

"I imagine it's valuable."

"Yes. This is a very good artist."

"I do love it. I love the edges of the leaves."

"We could *reconfigure* it," Max said. "It would be a great joke."

"I don't follow."

"We could paint over it. And hide it in plain view."

"I couldn't destroy it!"

"You'd be preserving it, really." The idea seemed to tickle him tremendously.

Really, the thought of George seeing it every day, walking past it, having no idea—it was appealing. It was a modicum of revenge. And when they were both seventy, and she needed to trump him in some battle, she'd point to the thing and say, *It's been there the whole time. You've been taking your coffee beneath the vagina for forty years.*

"Would oil paint work?"

"It's all that would do."

That afternoon, using an advertisement for another kit from the back of the Paint-by-Numbers box as a guide, Grace painted it over with a farmhouse scene. It ended up not terrible for a rank amateur, and there was quite enough paint in the combined pots of Paint-by-Number oils that it covered the canvas thoroughly. She and Max carried it from the big house to the coach house together, each holding two corners of canvas.

Max knew where to get it framed, as soon as it was dry enough. Six days later, it was hanging in the library.

In the next week, Grace found herself struggling to rise from bed. The room would spin, and she'd lie back to sleep for another half hour, and eventually her hunger would bring her downstairs, if the smell of Amy's horrible coffee didn't keep her from the dining room.

Then she'd walk down by the little hill of ash where the fire pile had stood. She'd follow the paths in the woods.

George was sweet for a few days, until he wasn't.

She realized she ought to move the portrait of Violet, just to be safe. Max stored it in his own room. When George saw it was gone, he wasn't happy at all. He asked if she sold it, and even though she said she hadn't, he asked how much she'd gotten for it, and what she'd done with the money. He threw his glass past her head, and it shattered on the spot where the painting had hung, and for a moment water streamed in a thousand little rivers down the wallpaper. Beatrice served the rest of the meal, and said that Amy had gone to bed with a sudden bug.

She saw Max enter the Longhouse, and two minutes later Sid Cole of Indianapolis followed. They stayed in there an hour. It happened again the next day, and then three days after that.

She didn't want to sit in the attic now that it had been defiled, and so she tried perching herself on the huge, decaying tree stump between the coach house and the big house, her legs crossed. But she felt so strange and dizzy there. It might turn to a sinkhole and swallow her. She thought of the studios, but she couldn't go into the Longhouse. She walked to the little one behind that. It had been a darkroom, Max said. And indeed there were both blinds and shutters inside the windows, and when she closed them it was dark as death. She sat on the daybed and tried not to feel her limbs. She opened the shutters and stared at the floor. Five dead bees. A dead ladybug, its body bleached pink by the sun. A 1939 penny. Someone was happy here once. Someone sang to herself and made her prints and didn't notice when she dropped a penny.

A telegram from home: COME IMMEDIATELY OR NOT AT ALL.

That afternoon, Grace walked right up into Max's apartment and sat at the table and called his name. He appeared in his doorway, his shirt unbuttoned and untucked. He put himself together and joined her. She said, "Max, if anything happens to me, if I go missing, if I turn up drowned in the fish ponds, I need you to know that George did it."

"That—yes, I'm afraid that would be my assumption."

"And if that's the case, I want you to do to him whatever you must so that he doesn't get the house and all the money. Finger him, frame him, poison him, I don't care." She'd said it, and there it was, and once she heard the words out in the air, outside her own mouth, she was sure she meant them.

"You might get out of here before that happens."

"Well. Max, my father is very ill."

"Yes."

She shouldn't have been surprised that he knew.

"When George was lying there, at the bottom of the stairs, I thought for a moment he was dead. And I thought, if George is dead and my father dies, I might do what I like. And I felt a tremendous lightness. It was only the tiniest moment, though."

Max leaned across the table with an intensity she'd have been offended at a few weeks ago, before they became complicit together in the replacement of the files and painting, and in turning the Longhouse into a refuge for fairies. He said, "What is it you'd do?"

"I didn't think it through. Maybe I'd reopen the colony. I could, you know. If I poured my trust fund into it."

"You'd be starting from scratch." He looked glassy and sad. His cheeks had turned pink.

"Yes, well. But you'd help, wouldn't you? You've been here longer than anyone."

He said, "I suppose I'm the memory of the place."

"But it's all just fantasy, and I shouldn't let myself get ahead of my feet. Because what am I going to do? I'm not going to murder George."

Max laughed, a harsh little laugh. "All you'd really have to do is nothing. Not rescue him. Next time, you leave him lying there. Next time will be different. But there will be equivalents."

"Well. And divorce is the real option. I've not wanted to let myself consider it. But he—" She stopped herself a moment, so she wouldn't cry. "Max, do you know what he did to Amy?"

Max shook his head slowly, but she saw that she didn't need to explain it. Just as well, because now she was sobbing, a big heap on the table. "I hadn't believed it was true, or I *couldn't* believe, but then when I saw him with those files, when I saw him hurting something that wasn't me—Max, I've been a perfect *monster*. I want to do something for her. Will you find out what she needs? To get set up comfortably somewhere?"

"You need to leave him," he said.

"I think I might. I'm at least going back to Toronto to see my father. I've telephoned the travel agency to see if I might fly home. I'll know in the morning. I might be able to *go* in the morning, for that matter. Just to visit."

It was true. She wasn't lying. It just hadn't felt real until she'd said it.

"And then you'll leave him."

"I—yes. I think so."

"But you mustn't tell him."

"I do think he'd figure it out *eventually*."

Max chuckled—when was the last time someone had laughed at her joke?—and said, "Promise you won't get carried away and tell him so. You'll need lawyers first."

She nodded, but she imagined that part would really have to wait till her father was gone. If he was truly dying, the family lawyers would be tied up with the inheritances a while.

He said, "We'll figure it all out. We will. Grace, I don't want you alone with him."

"I promise."

_____

That same night, George got dressed to go out. He put on his sport coat and shaved. He'd made some friends, he said, at a bar in Highwood, and they had a business opportunity for him, a solid investment. He'd said the same thing back in July about a fellow he met down in the city. George wrote him a check for two thousand dollars and never saw him again. These new friends knew someone who would take the money to Brazil and double it. George had stayed sober for the occasion, and he danced around the bedroom as he gathered his wallet and hat. Grace lay on the bed in her yellow cotton dress, a wool cardigan on top. This was what she'd pictured, when she first settled on George: the two of them together in the bedroom before the dinner hour, George happy and energized, Grace with bare feet and a book. Only she hadn't imagined feeling like a ball of lead.

She put her forehead to the window and watched as he trotted to the coach house. Max backed up the Darrin and climbed out, holding the driver's door open for George himself.

Max disappeared into the garage, and George backed partway out, but then two things happened: He circled the car around to the big house door and ran inside—for his warmer hat, probably, as it was quite cold and the Darrin was a poor choice even with the roof up. And, at that same moment, down by the maple trees and all along the inside of the stone wall, the earth began to move again just as it had that day a month ago: rabbits and rabbits and rabbits. A swarm of rabbits, a plague of rabbits. Grace slid on her shoes and ran down the stairs and past George, who was rifling through the coat closet. She had to see if they were real, and if they were, she wanted to know what it was they were all doing here, surrounding the property like a hex or a blessing.

She was out the front door, and George was still inside, when

Sid Cole of Indianapolis walked right through the front gate. Grace ought to have told Max to have him come in the side gate at least, but here he was, hands in his pockets, shoulders hunched against the cold, heading straight down the drive toward the big house. The grass was wet and cold, and he probably wanted to stay off it until he reached the path to the Longhouse, but it made it look, Grace realized with horror, as if he were here to see her in George's absence. Her young date for the evening. She didn't have time to warn him without yelling out, and George was coming out the door behind her just now. So what she did instead was to turn and catch George by the waist and turn him toward her and the coach house at once—away from Sid, who seemed oblivious in his stride. She said, "Take me with you tonight. Let me come with you." She pulled him hard against her.

He put his hand on her posterior and said, "I'm meeting these fellows."

"I'll charm them."

He stepped back and looked her up and down, judging her presentability. It was true that for once she wasn't hiding a bruise. The bandage was off her forehead and the stitches were out, just a clean pink mark now.

She said, "It'll be fun."

"All right, Duck."

He opened the passenger door with an exaggerated bow, and as she stepped in she managed to catch Sid's attention. He was only ten yards away, but when he saw the warning on her face he darted back among the maple trees before George came around the car. He wasn't well hidden, but it didn't matter.

They shot down the drive, pebbles flying up and hitting the bottom of the frame like a mortar attack. Sid was a blur out Grace's window, his face calm and curious. He couldn't have understood that Grace had just saved his life as well as her own.

They took the back corner table at Pasquali's, and George nodded in passing to two swarthy men at the bar. "They'll join us when their partner's here," he said. Grace realized she'd have to sit quietly through whatever ridiculous scam they wanted his money for—she'd watch mutely as he wrote a check from their joint account—or else the night could go unpleasantly wrong.

There was a record on: Frank Sinatra sang "Ain'tcha Ever Comin' Back?" Everything smelled good, and Grace was ravenous. Amy would be getting dinner ready at home and wondering where Grace had gone.

Grace steeled herself to smile at George, but he wasn't paying a bit of attention. He looked at the two men, and the door, and the bartender, and the menu, and the next table. He ordered a scotch, plus a bottle of Chianti for Grace's benefit. The wine went right to her head, though, in a way it usually didn't. It had been a while—since Paris, really—that she'd had any regular amount of wine. But one glass in, she felt dopey and dizzy, and her mouth felt full of cotton.

She ordered lasagna.

"You're getting stout," George said, when the waiter had walked away.

"It's Amy's cooking," she said, though she wanted to argue, to tell him it wasn't true at all, it was only her bust that was suddenly a bit larger. And then, wall of ice: It was November 16. She'd bled in September, back when it was warm enough to walk to the pharmacy in her blue cotton dress. And that must have been the last time. She was an idiot. A dizzy idiot, with blackness closing around her head. She'd been so distracted. Right when the witch showed up, right when George pinned Amy to the tree—that should have been the next time. She'd spent the next month watching everyone and everything but herself, and meanwhile she grew slow and slept late, and the smell of Amy's coffee made her gag, and she began crying at the drop of a hat.

The waiter set her plate in front of her. A heap of lasagna, clots of red leaking out the frilled edges. George was talking about Quebec, about taking a motor trip in the spring

She wanted to think to herself that she'd never go on that trip because she'd be a free woman by then, but she knew it would be the opposite. She'd be at home with a watermelon stomach or a squalling baby, and maybe he'd be there too, or maybe he'd be off without her, but she'd never get free of him now.

The room blurred, and fell to little stars, and came back together in flashing colors and shapes. The shapes locked back to reality with a sickening little click. Just like the bricks of the house—everything cemented together, everything in order. Her entire life was like those bricks, she saw it now. And every attempt at escape just locked her further in. She'd tried to marry someone wild, and ended up in a prison. She'd tried to leave him, and ended up tethered to his child, growing inside her.

George was saying, "The man eats coins. Did you know that? I saw him put a nickel in his mouth, when he thought I wasn't looking."

"Oh. Who?"

"Max. The driver. I said."

"That can't be true. Did he swallow it?"

"No idea."

She managed to get a bite in. George was waving to the third man, who'd just entered.

Grace dropped her napkin on the floor and ran to the bathroom, and the vomit barely made it in the toilet. Look at the tiles on the floor. Look: a graph-paper grid. Her own private, tessellated map to her appointment in Samarkand.

Why should she be so surprised by it all? By getting exactly what she'd signed on for, no more and no less? Except that we become so used to the twists of chance and fortune. Sometimes the greatest shock is getting exactly what we've been promised.

Back at the table, George and the men were laughing. One scooted over and patted the bench next to him. But she stayed standing and said, "George, I'm ill. I'll call Max to bring me home in the Capri."

George nodded. "Sure, Duck."

She called the coach house line from the pay phone by the bar. It rang and rang and rang, and no one picked up. It was six thirty now, and they'd left the house at five. Soon Amy would give up on her for dinner, and Max would be finished with Sid Cole. She sat back at the table. The men talked about soccer. She couldn't imagine why.

She might have slept a bit, but now she felt worse. She tried the coach house again, and the main line too, and no one picked up. She came back and waited for a pause and said, "George, why don't I drive the Darrin home and tell Max to pick *you* up in the Capri?"

"We'll be done soon," he said to her. But she could tell that they wouldn't, and that it would not be wise to press the issue. He wouldn't let her drive the Darrin even under the best circumstances, and he'd never hand over the keys in front of these men. He was quite drunk now. There was another full scotch in front of him. She made her hands into a pillow on the placemat.

Finally they finished. There were papers on the table, and George took some of them, and one of the men took the rest. George said, "Okay, Duck, let's go." But when he stood, he caught his ankle on the table and nearly pulled the whole thing over with him. He righted the table but fell himself, and Grace propped him up by the elbow.

"He okay?" one of the men said, and another of them laughed.

"We're calling someone to drive," Grace told them, and

George didn't object. She led him to the pay phone and used the same dime, the same unlucky dime, to call the coach house. It was now nine o'clock, and either Amy or Max had to be home. The men, seeing she had the receiver to her ear, nodded and left the restaurant. George leaned against the wall.

The phone rang and rang and rang. Max should be home— Sid never stayed this late—but then he might be down in the garage. It might take him a while to hear the phone and get up-stairs to the kitchen. And where was Amy? George grabbed her arm. "This is ridiculous. Let's go."

She didn't hang up. "I'll drive," she said. "Or we'll call a taxi." She shouldn't have raised the issue earlier—he might have re-mained malleable. Now he'd never give in.

"Grace, let's go." His voice was louder than last time, and the bartender glanced in their direction. Next time would be louder, she knew, and all these people would look up from their spaghetti in dismay.

She listened for one more ring, and one more ring, and one more ring. The rings lined themselves up like bathroom tiles. One more, one more, one more. George took the phone and hung it in its cradle.

Outside, Grace tried to catch the valet's eye, hoping he'd fig-ure out everything wrong, call the police or a cab, but he just sent a boy out to bring the car, and the boy opened Grace's door for her, then struggled to slide it back. Everyone stared at the car, the strange and shiny car, and no one noticed the problem. George took off like they were being chased.

Down Sheridan Road, down the middle of it, really, with a sharp jerk to the right whenever another pair of headlights ap-peared. Grace hadn't been out at night since all the leaves had fallen, and she realized with wonder that for the first time since they'd moved here in the spring, she could see the houses—see into them, even, as George tried to light a cigarette and compensated by suddenly driving too slowly. Those homes always seemed so hidden and empty, no life but for someone out on the sidewalk. Now, every illuminated room was a perfect frame of yellow. Each frame both a revelation and a further mystery. She'd forgotten that November was such a strange, unveiling time of year—not a deadening but a quickening. In the smaller houses, closer to the road, she could make out a clock, a shelf of plants, an old woman, a refrigerator. In the bigger ones, behind stone walls, just an occasional upstairs hall light. She wanted to climb into each frame, to live in each for a year. But then George picked up speed again.

She might say something about it, might see if George understood even a little bit. And if he did, she might tell him, tomorrow, about the baby too. The baby might change him. Perhaps change was possible even while staying put, staying with him, staying in the house.

They turned, and the right-side wheels went up on the curb and down with a horrible jolt. Her nausea returned, from the floor of her stomach upward in a wave, and she grabbed the door handle. She was too dizzy, too tired, to work up the appropriate anger at herself for getting into this situation, when she might have wrested the key from him or passed a note of distress to the bartender. Surely there was *something* she might have done. Wasn't there always something to be done?

They turned again, and now he was going so fast that the lights in the houses were just blurs. She knew that if she asked him to slow down, he'd only speed up.

There was Laurelfield, dark and still, the gate open. George took the entry wide and fast and nearly clipped the gate. He turned toward the coach house without slowing. The gravel hitting up again, a thousand little bullets. "Look at that," George said, meaning she should look up before they went through the open garage door, look at the bright windows of the coach house kitchen and Max's rooms. "He's home after all. The bastard is home."

And she would have looked, she would have looked, but the gravel was still hitting too fast. The trees were coming too fast.

PART III

1929

IN THE FIELD: THE TRIBE

Zilla was a moving statue in the torchlight. If Eddie could, he would love her: her hair a black puddle, her teeth a broken necklace. Her white throat, thrust forward when she laughed. Viktor, though—Viktor Osin *did* love her, or else what was this filament between them, across the night?

There were only the eight: Samantha had stayed back.

Marlon Moore led them all to the teepees, which were just as he'd described: cloth cones in the field, big enough for all to squeeze inside just one. They passed the flask again. Vital to maintain the drunken state in which the plan was hatched, lest they sober up and discover themselves ridiculous. It was only a few drinks into the evening that Marlon had volunteered his story—dragged by a colleague's wife to last year's Chippeway Ball—and several drinks later that the joke had started: A true Chippeway Ball should feature more scalping and war whoops and nudity. The sun had set, additional bottles brought to the terrace, when it became a plan, when Viktor and Marlon and Eddie drove to the college where Marlon taught, and broke into the theater's costume shop and returned with headdresses and face paint.

Across the lawn, windows full of elegant locals. Long tables, candles.

The eight undressed in the open teepee by torchlight, laughing and shushing, leaving clothes in distinct piles to speed escape.

Zilla, muscled, flat as a board. Viktor—with his impossible limbs, his dancer's limbs—staring at her like a drugged man. Ludo, pale for an Italian, a thatch of dark fur on his chest. Fannie and Josephine, the White Rabbits: one doughy, one thin as rope. Armand Cox (preposterous name!), his whole being covered in golden hairs. Marlon with his little potbelly, stretching his legs to run. Two weeks ago, Eddie hadn't been able to keep them all straight. And now he imagined he'd know their voices to his dying day.

Another adjustment: All day long, in front of his pen or typewriter, he was as alone as he'd ever been. But at night, he was a "we." Something he hadn't felt since childhood, since he'd climbed in bed with his sister in the afternoons, since she'd let him wear her shoes. He was part of a first-person plural.

Some of them wore the headdresses, and the others stuck loose feathers in their hair. Their faces: red and black stripes, yellow down the nose.

Armand and Ludo, leading the parade, each grabbed one lawn torch to hold aloft.

Zilla started the war cry, hand pulsing on her open mouth, and the others joined and rode the wave of noise onto the club porch and through the open glass doors to the dining room.

The first thing Eddie saw, he told the others later, was the fat woman in the green dress, the way her fork flew from her hand, lettuce still speared on the tines.

The tribe whooped and screeched and circled the sea of tables three times. A great deal of anatomical flapping: some high, some low, all uncomfortable, all ridiculous in the electric lights, but wasn't this the point? As the rest of them flailed and beat their chests, Viktor did actual pirouettes. He leapt over the carving table, his legs straight out like wings. The evening-gowned ladies dove into their husbands' laps. Half the men laughed and clapped and the others stood to do *something* but then weren't sure what to do.

Someone screamed, "*Stop* them!"

Ludo shouted, "We come for squaws!"

Two white-haired men tried to block the path, but moved away quickly when Armand and Ludo didn't stop, as Armand even turned and shimmied backward toward them, posterior muscles twitching. The youths, boys and girls both, watched with poorly contained glee. Viktor planted a kiss on a squealing girl's forehead and left a perfect black lip mark. On the final circuit, Eddie grabbed a dinner roll and stuffed it in his mouth.

Back into the night: some of the tuxedoed men giving chase, but only halfway across the lawn, then posting themselves cross-armed between teepees and building, shouting, guarding against further invasion.

A loud voice thinned by distance: "This is *a private es ablishment!*"

Zilla wheezing with laughter. Armand, torch abandoned, turning a cartwheel.

The artists carried clothes in armloads and ran, some back to the waiting auto, some, with Eddie, into the woods where they dressed, and then found the path to the road, and then walked the road back to Laurelfield.

ZILLA IN HER STUDIO

She has assembled seven things on the table in the Longhouse: a potted geranium, a pile of gray rocks, a hair pin, a square of yellow cotton, a Mason jar, a feather, a dead bee. She has stapled a linen to the wall.

The choosing, the starting: It's a cliff to jump off.

She examines the feather, the way invisible hooks link each barb to the next. The way, when she pulls one strand from its neighbor, it leaves a clean gap that will not smooth together again. She doubts this cleaving can be conveyed in paint: the hooks that grip us, that tie us to each other. To place, to time. The ways we might come unhinged.

She walks to the wall and begins.

WESTERN UNION

AUG. 29-29.

SAMANTHA MAYS
CARE LAURELFIELD ARTS COLONY

HEARD OF DISTURBANCE STOP IN NY CITY
ON BUSINESS STOP ARRIVE LAURELFIELD
TOMORROW AFTERNOON STOP DO MAKE
PREPARATIONS=

   G W DEVOHR

SAMANTHA IN THE KITCHEN

It was raining all morning, dusk all morning.

From the windows of the director's house, the main house looked reflective, all windows and wet.

Samantha laid the telegram on the middle of her kitchen table so they all could read it: Armand over her shoulder, Viktor and Zilla leaning across. "He sounds furious."

Zilla said, "Everyone sounds furious in a wire."

They kept their voices low. Beatrice, Samantha's brand new office girl, was typing in the next room and needn't be alarmed. Samantha warned her the day she started that Laurelfield was hanging by a thread, that Gamby Devohr, newly in charge of his family's affairs, would take any excuse to oust them all.

Armand said, "We don't even know what disturbance he means. *Heard of disturbance.* He could think there are real Indians in the woods."

Viktor was playing with a spoon, spinning it on the oilcloth. "He's not the world's leading intellectual."

Samantha read it again, aloud. They turned on the floor lamp, the one with no shade, and dragged it to the table. As if more light would possibly help.

Zilla said, "What can he prove? No one took our photograph. I'm sure they weren't looking at our *faces.*" Zilla's voice was calming even when there was no cause for calm. Samantha had once thought of it as a liquid voice, but lately she'd refined the image:

Zilla's voice was mercury, a bubble of mercury in a phial. Liquid but metallic too.

"He can't expect me," Samantha said, "to keep everyone quiet in their rooms all night. We're not *bankers*. I think he'd like to run a banking colony."

Zilla said, "At least I'll meet the infamous Gamaliel Devohr."

"Gamby the Great," Viktor said.

Armand: "We'll meet Mr. Devohr as he's kicking us to the curb. We'll meet the bottom of his foot."

Viktor: "He can do that?"

Samantha: "It's his house, still. As far as the colony, he's just a member of the board. But he owns the property. If he kicks us out, we cease to exist."

"How nice for the Devohr family taxes," Armand said. "To turn your spare mansion into an artists' shelter."

"It's the only charitable thing they've ever done. Lord knows they aren't patrons of the ballet. And now they'd rather get the house back and sell it. I don't believe they've done well since the war."

"Oh, it's nothing," Zilla said. "I'm sure it's nothing."

Viktor stood and stretched—the man was a tree, his hands on the ceiling, pressing it away—and announced he was heading back to the Longhouse to work, and Zilla announced she would follow him. Armand and Samantha watched them go.

"Oh, Armand," she said. He sat at the table, and she put her head on his shoulder.

"They're in love, aren't they? Viktor and Zilla?"

"I should think so. She's married, though, and he's got all those dancers, and she hates that he's got his dancers. They always come here the same time, just to torture each other. I believe it's an excruciatingly chaste affair. They'd never moon around like that if they'd *had* each other." She folded the telegram up, as small as it would fold.

"We ought to lock them in her studio together and see what happens."

"It's fascinating to watch, except when it's painful."

"Mr. Devohr will love your new hair."

"Ha!" She touched what was left of the blonde curls. "He might run screaming. And end our problem."

"He'll take you for Amelia Earhart's younger brother. Tell me," he said, "now we're alone, about Eddie Parfitt."

"He's tremendously talented. Vachel Lindsay wrote his reference."

"I mean—he's been here two weeks. I'm late to the game. Is he, you know, *my sort of gentleman?*"

"Oh. Yes, I imagine. Ask Marlon. He'd know."

Armand laughed. "If Marlon knows, I'm far too late."

"He could use some bringing out of his shell, at any rate. I'll put you in charge of it. Only don't fall in love with him."

Armand looked hurt, as if she'd misread him completely. But she knew him better than he thought. It was only his first visit, but Armand had been her friend for years, since the days when he was sleeping on the floor of someone's studio in the Fine Arts Building. He'd been *so* young. Well, so had she. Later, when he finally had a bit of money, he'd bought her blue ladder painting. They'd worked together on the No-Jury show. And she knew, if nothing else, that he was quite similar to her. He believed that drawing the world would keep him at an ironic distance from it, keep him safe from caring deeply about things. When in fact it had the opposite effect. And she knew how Laurelfield had affected *her*, on her first stay—as an artist, long before she dug in her nails and managed to get hired. She'd felt exhilarated and confused, and she couldn't eat, and she couldn't sleep, and she mistook it all as love for an older poet, a man with a pipe and a wife. She'd thrown herself at him, and they were together awhile, until—later, back in the city—she realized she had no interest in the man at all. What she'd been in love with was Laurelfield, and everyone there, and her own work, and maybe even with *herself*, for the first time.

She saw that same wild look in Armand's eyes. He was looking for someone to love. He was a transitive verb with no direct object.

She said, "Just watch your heart."

Down at the bottom of the stairs, Alfie started barking. He ran all the way up and then all the way down, and Samantha followed him.

A woman struggled at the door, propping it open with her foot and hefting a wet valise through the frame. Behind her, a man unloaded trunks from a taxi straight into a puddle. The screenwriter wasn't due to arrive till tomorrow, but this was obviously her. She bore that distinct look of the arriving artist: disoriented, exhausted, profoundly relieved to be there. "I've arrived too early!" the woman said, only she said "arrifed," her voice thick with dignified German. Samantha scrambled to remember the name—Marcelina von Hornig, there it was, and she'd wondered if it would be a "Marcy" type or a "Lina," but clearly this woman was above shortening—and then, as the door closed behind her and Alfie was subdued and the woman looked up into Samantha's face, Samantha reeled. This was *Marceline Horn*, the film star Marceline Horn, in color, in three dimensions. The same high-bridged nose, the enormous eyes, eyelashes like window valances. She'd played Juliet and Charlotte Corday. She'd kissed Valentino. Samantha had gotten used, over the years, to speaking with artists and writers whose talent intimidated her. This was different, though, more like meeting Cinderella than the Brothers Grimm.

Samantha managed to say, "It's not a problem. The maid was already making up the room for you. You might have to work in the—in the library. Until it's done."

"Oh, of *course*. I need a few hours to screw my head back on."

"You've had a long trip."

"Vell, I vas in Chicago a veek."

"Yes." The address on this woman's papers—Beverly Hills, California—hadn't seemed odd, since she was coming to write two movie scripts. A letter of recommendation from L. B. Mayer, himself, of MGM. Samantha had convinced the rest of the file readers that this would be a novelty, that they'd be embracing a new form of storytelling. Mayer's letter said he'd worked with the woman in the past, but it said nothing of directing her in films, of their affair—wasn't there an affair? She remembered something, an item in *Picture Play*—just that she showed great talent and needed a quiet place. And for all Samantha could tell from the script sample, she was a natural writer.

Stupidly, her lips numb: "This is Alfie. A wirehaired pointing griffon. He's harmless."

Marceline bent to look him in the eye. "I'm a great friend of the dogs."

Samantha took in the woman's outfit: the green cloche hat, the slim black frock with pearls at the hip—all regular enough, if a bit formal for mid-morning—but below that, and above her black one-straps, she wore silk stockings appliquéd with green velvet snakes that appeared to climb her legs.

Behind her, Armand crouched on the landing, peering down. He was silent—which, Samantha knew, was his particular form of shrieking. Beatrice stood behind him, her fingers to her little chin.

"Armand," Samantha said, and he didn't answer. "Will you be a dear and see if Maisie has finished the yellow room? And the kitchen needs to know, as well, that there will be one more for dinner. You could help with the trunks. And Beatrice, the packet. For Miss von Hornig."

Beatrice vanished. Armand rushed past them both and out the door with no umbrella. It occurred to her that Armand might bang on everyone's door with the news before he bothered finding Maisie, that eight noses might be pressed to the wet window within minutes, but meanwhile she had her list of things to say, her regular and memorized orientation to Laurelfield—the quiet hours, and keys, and meals—and this woman looked as thirsty and tired as any new arrival. She invited Marceline to follow her up to the kitchen. She dropped the folded telegram into the dustbin and put the kettle on for tea.

Marceline stopped her, as she crossed the kitchen, and clasped one of Samantha's hands in her soft, strangely large ones. "I tell you, I feel like Shakespeare's Viola, vashed up on the shore of Illyria. And I can tell this is a blessed place. A *generous* place I feel it in my feet."

"You haven't even seen it all yet!"

"It is not something von *sees*."

LUDO AND JOSEPHINE ON THE LAWN

They look at the roof, the way the sun just now, at eleven, shoots a tentative ray over the top, the last rain turning to mist. In a minute, it will be too bright to look east.

Ludo says, "No, I don't believe. Back in Napoli, one time, I go to a séance. Is all tricks. All click-click and knocking sound and guess what someone wants to hear." He laughs. "Is same with my music, no? Knock knock, tell you what you want to hear. I used to write symphonies. Now I make rhymings and bouncings."

"No ghost appeared? At the séance?"

"The ghost is in our ears."

"Marlon *swears* he heard something in the night."

"I tell you what I learn: At a colony, there always come noises in the night. Howling, thumping, door slam, moaning, bang bang bang, you know. You know what is? Is not ghosts."

"What?"

"Is people making sex."

In Residence

UPDATED 29 AUG '29

Abbaticchio, Ludo (M)
Composer
*

St: Comp. Cottage
R: Southwest
*

Cadfael, Fannie (F)
Sculptor
Cleveland Hts, Ohio
St: Solarium
R: Blue
through 9/2

Cox, Armand (M)
Illustrator
Chicago
St/R: Longhouse E
through 10/4

Lizer, Josephine (F)
Sculptor
Cleveland Hts, Ohio
St: Solarium
R: Green
through 9/2

Moore, Marlon (M)
Writer
Lake Bluff, Ill.
St/R: Northeast
through 9/5

Osin, Viktor (M)
Maître de ballet
Chicago
St/R: Longhouse Cent.
through 9/16 (extended)

Parfitt, Edwin (M)
Poet
Phil, Pa.
St/R: Flower
through 9/27

Silverman, Zilla (F)
Painter
Madison, Wis.
St/R: Longhouse W
through 10/12

Von Hornig (Horn), Marcelina (Marceline) (F)
Screenwriter
Beverly Hills, Calif.
St/R: Yellow
through 9/20

Beatrice, please note:

Miss Silverman has asked use of attic
in addition to Longhouse W.

Miss Lizer and Miss Cadfael are in fact
sharing Green bedroom; trunks of both
are stored in Blue; Miss Cadfael has
that key.

Garden studio is empty if Miss Horn
prefers it to working in her room.

Please remember Mr. Abbaticchio not to
be listed on public documents.

WHAT WE'VE GLEANED FROM MARLON

Marlon Moore claims to know a woman who knows the Devohrs. It's impossible, Samantha insists, because *no one* "knows the Devohrs." You might know one Devohr, or another Devohr, but they aren't an entity. It's like saying you know all the feral cats in the woods. You've probably just seen the same one five times. Marlon counters that his friend knows the *important* Devohrs, the ones who've stayed sane, the ones with the houses.

Marlon has heard testimony, from some of the greatest living writers, that the best way to induce strange and inspiring dreams is to eat very strong cheese before bed. He himself keeps a crock of Roquefort on the windowsill in his room. He doesn't see the problem. It has a lid! "Yes," Josephine mutters, "but your mouth does not."

Marlon knows with great certainty that back home, Ludo, our own Italian fixture, became unnecessarily political for a composer. It seems Ludo was a great friend of the Communist leader Bordiga, and wrote a song lampooning Bordiga's rival, Gramsci, and (worse) Mussolini himself. Marlon believes he rhymed "Benito" with "finito." ("Let's ask if it's true!" says Armand. "I wouldn't," says Viktor.) And so (Marlon fingers his moustache, adopts a tone of epic narration), by 1926, both Bordiga and Gramsci were in jail, and Ludo was on a boat to New York under an assumed name, quotas and papers be damned. How he landed at Laurelfield, where he's stayed the past three years, is no great mystery. Bordiga probably phoned Samantha himself. Is Ludo sleeping with Samantha? Oh, everyone assumes so. Certainly. But that's beside the point. And now Ludo has a bit of a career stateside as well, writing show tunes. "Our gain," Fannie adds emphatically. Fannie is our greatest optimist.

Marlon can tell astrological signs with great accuracy. He pegs Zilla as an Aquarius, and she nods. We are duly impressed.

Late one night, Marlon starts giggling about Viktor Osin and his ballerinas. "They're all French," he says, "or Russian. Nineteen years old, eighty pounds each. Let me tell you: a line of twelve swans? He's been under every tutu." His giggling turns shrill. "Not a single bosom between them, but can you imagine the ways they stretch?" Zilla leaves the room.

Marlon wears a silk burgundy smoking jacket over his clothes. He is poised for great things.

Marlon has heard a rumor: Mr. Devohr is already on his way.

Civic Opera Company
Mary Garden, Director
430 South Michigan Avenue
Chicago

Aug. 28

Dearest Samantha—
   Dashing this off to say Gamby Devohr
has written to all the board. Received
my letter this a.m.
   Samantha, what's happened? Wishing I
could zip up but all is chaos here,
moving to the new space, Aida, etc.
Tell me if I should come, though. Do.
   Devohr is requesting ad hoc meeting
Sept. 3rd for what I fear are
apocalyptic purposes.
   Do advise if I can help, but as you
know I haven't much clout with the
other boardsters, I'm the artistic quack
not the purse strings.
   I'm worried, Sam. Tell me you're fine.
Tell me Laurelfield's fine.

   Oh dear lord,
   Mary

EDDIE IN THE LIBRARY

The hour before dinner, normally restrained—stretching writers, artists just scrubbed up, a shared bottle of gin—turned into an all-out soirée in everyone's effort to meet and impress Marceline Horn. The party continued after the meal, the artists reconvening to the library where Viktor mixed an enormous vat of orange blossoms and Ludo played the piano. It was fortunate Ludo was kept busy. Having seen Marceline as Scheherezade ("Just scarves! No other clothings!"), he couldn't speak to her without leering.

Viktor ladled a drink into a smudged glass for Eddie, slopping some down the side. Viktor was all arms and legs. A dancer and dance maker with hair of the most rebellious kind, each strand hating its neighbors with such static ferocity that his head achieved a perfect geometry of divergence.

Eddie sipped and tried to listen to the music, but it didn't help. He felt sick again: a chill that had vanished a few hours the night of the Indian raid, that the August sun baked away whenever he took lunch outdoors, but that returned the moment he reentered the house. Now the dizziness was back, the feeling that he needed to leave the house soon, or else he would fall into his bed and freeze to the mattress and never rise again. Fannie and Josephine had told him, his first night, to watch for the ghost, for the long white nightgown in the upstairs hall. They had giggled and shivered, and expected him to do likewise. But the chill, he knew, was not something he'd encounter in the corridor. It had already gotten deep in his bloodstream.

There was something wrong with the house. The windows gazed in on you instead of out at the world.

And now the White Rabbits had cornered Marceline on the davenport behind Eddie, and leaned in eagerly to tell the story of Violet Devohr. "She locked herself in the attic," Fannie said. "It's unclear why."

"Well, she was mad!" Josephine cried. "Why else does a woman lock herself in an attic?"

"And the old man, Augustus, the one who built the place for her, begged her to let him in, but he didn't go so far as to kick down the door. He was too genteel. And he didn't want the servants hearing."

"Scandal, you know."

"He figured she'd come out eventually. Every day he knocked, three times a day, and she told him to go away. And then he realized—"

"No, you forgot to say, it was five days! Five days she was up there. She had taken in the key. Did you say that part?"

"Yes, five days. And only then did he realize that she had no food or water."

"And so he broke down the door. Or he called a locksmith, I'm not sure. But it was too late. She wasn't dead yet, but she couldn't survive."

Zilla rejoined them in time to hear the end. "Are you trying to make her *leave*? She'll run off in the night!" But her voice was so soft and rolling that it was only a joke.

"Anyway," Fanny said, "that was Gamby's mother. Gamby is Gamaliel, the one who's coming to get us all in trouble. The poor dear, he was just two years old. It's no wonder he's always begrudged Laurelfield."

Over at the piano, Ludo had started one of his new songs, a

bouncy thing with a chorus designed to be joined by the flappers who, under more urban circumstances, would no doubt surround his piano. It had become a great joke to all of them in the past weeks that Ludo's English could be so tortured in conversation but so smooth in lyric. He sang with tremendous verve:

> Columbus spied the ocean shore
> He counted natives by the score
> He cried, "Exploring's such a bore
> When all of it's been found before!"

> Ohhhh—I tell you, gentle philosophers,
> In these modernest of times
> That history doesn't repeat . . .
> It merely rhymes!

There were so many layers of insulation to this one room. The leather-bound books, and then their shelves, and the walls themselves, and the outer bricks, and then the blanket of ivy that could swallow your whole hand, up to your wrist. And then the thick summer air, and the groves of mismatched trees—the legacy, apparently, of Violet Devohr's insistence on horticultural diversity—and then the stone wall, and then the woods. It should have felt safe, but instead it was smothering and cold at once.

Marlon leaned against a standing Eddie and settled his rear on the back of the davenport, just inches from Marceline's head. He wore, as usual, his smoking jacket, tied at the waist. He smelled of pomade. He said, "Do you believe in fate?"

"Sure."

"The moment I saw you, I felt certain I'd seen you before."

"I'm not sure that's fate so much as déjà vu."

"Ah. The French have no imagination."

Eddie found himself smiling back but ignoring whatever else

Marlon said. He watched Armand take a drink to Marceline. Armand dressed like a college boy, argyle sweater and bright argyle socks, knickers. The rumor of the afternoon had it that Marceline had been demoted from a lead actress at MGM, and sent here at the mercy of Mr. Mayer to try her hand at writing, to rework two old silent scripts into talkies. Her exquisite looks were fading, the sharp bob doing nothing for her nose, and that accent, it was true, would not go over now. Everyone was dying to ask about films, to ask if she knew Gary Cooper. Eddie heard her say to Armand, "You should go right now to Berlin. There are in Berlin the most vonderful pansy clubs."

In the corner, Zilla and Viktor, ignoring each other.

Samantha in tweed knickers and green broadcloth blouse, rubbing Ludo's shoulders, singing along.

Everyone coupling and recoupling around the room in laughter, like a formal dance.

Armand, hands on the White Rabbits' shoulders, swaying by the piano. His sleeves rolled up, his arms covered in dark golden hairs. The White Rabbits sang the chorus of a new song:

> Give me back my kiss,
> It wasn't for you to keep.

Eddie had languished in confusion for a full week before finally asking Zilla why the women were called White Rabbits. But he couldn't get it out of his head yet that there was some connection to their noses, both small and pink, or to their silvering hair, or to plump Josephine's buck teeth or wiry Fannie's quick little eyes.

He realized that behind him, below him, on the davenport, Samantha Mays was crying quietly, and Zilla was comforting her. He had thought of Samantha as the type of woman who didn't cry. There was something about her that was like a fourteen-year-old boy, all elbows and knees and a broad chin, and he'd always imagined she could fall off a horse and bounce. She said, softly, "But I didn't imagine he'd written to the *board*. Oh, I just don't know. He's been looking for the slightest justification."

Zilla's voice, low: "But we have a room here full of tremendously creative people. I'm sure we can think of something."

Marlon must have heard it too. He said, "Tell him we have a film star here! That'll grab his attention!"

Samantha looked up and laughed. "Oh. Oh, Marlon, don't listen to me. I'll just worry you. But no, it wouldn't help. If anything, he'll use it as proof we're a bunch of hedonists. We'll have to clean up. We'll have to hide Ludo. If anyone asks, Ludo's been gone two years."

At midnight, it was just Marceline and Armand and Zilla and Eddie. Eddie wanted to be in bed, asleep, but he didn't want to be alone yet in his little room at the top of the stairs.

Marceline was explaining that Los Angeles was a city without attics. "Why would you need them? Nothing is old there—not a single antique, except the ones brought in for display. And I am myself an antique, of course."

A clamor of protest.

Eddie had worried she'd be haughty, but he found he enjoyed this woman, the tenacity with which she was determined to move on past the end of her particular, silent art.

"How is the life in Chicago?" she said to Armand. Another thing to admire: the instinct to steer the conversation away from herself.

Though Marceline had asked the question, Armand seemed to address his answer to Eddie. "It's swell. I'm in Towertown, and really I think it's better than New York. Everyone interesting in New York is actually in Paris, anyway. But Chicago's copacetic. And there's a lot doing for artists. Poets, too. Eddie, do you know Harriet Monroe? I could introduce you. If you were ever in the city. And you ought to be! What does Philadelphia have? You're out of the loop there. And what life is there, even? For people like us? You ought to be in Towertown or on a boat to Florence."

Zilla said, "Oh Armie, you made him blush!"

It was true. He was blushing at how easily Armand had read him. At Armand's ready implications. *People like us.* But the heat in his face had started before that, at Armand remembering Philadelphia— at his remembering Eddie's name at all. Eddie had grown used to assuming he was the only one in the room taking note of everything, of everyone's habits and gestures, squirreling away the details they let fall about their lives. He'd learned long ago to reintroduce himself at least three times to people whose names and drinks and life stories he'd long since memorized. He wondered if the rest of the Chicago crowd was like Armand, like himself—not in the way Armand had meant, but wide-eyed, absorbent.

Eddie struggled for something quick to say, but just then the lamp on the piano crackled, and the room was dunked in blackness. Marceline screamed, and Zilla laughed. "There," Zilla said. "I don't know why the Rabbits had to go frightening you about the attic. When clearly the ghost is right here."

FRIDAY, 10:16 A.M.

Marlon stands on the wall by the road and aims his Leica at the director's house, what used to be the coach house back when this was poor, doomed Violet's estate. Armand Cox leans there, smoking. Alfie sniffs in quick circles nearby. The wall is narrower than Marlon expected, and it takes great effort to balance. He can't quite focus the lens on Armand, and so he trains it on the giant oak between the houses instead. After the photo but before he can hop down, a voice from out on the sidewalk: "What *is* that place, anyhow?"

Marlon looks down at the speaker, a young boy with a stick. He says, "It's an asylum for people who think they're artists."

Uncaptured by the lens:

Samantha staring from her bedroom window, listening to the calming clatter of Beatrice's typewriter. Behind her, the smell of something burning. She wonders what on earth could be burning.

Ludo in the composer's cottage, hitting his head on the piano keys in frustration.

Fannie and Josephine, lying like quotation marks in bed, the afternoon sun on their feet. Fannie tracing the lines of the room from one corner all around to Josephine's shoulder, thinking about shape as sound, about silence as negative space.

Viktor in the hallway, picking Zilla's blue earring off the rug and clipping it back to her ear, letting his wrist touch her neck, watching her eyes close. Zilla scrambling like an egg.

The bootlegger, driving slowly up the road, knowing he'll recognize Laurelfield by the number of autos out front.

Eddie Parfitt, on the second floor, trying to remember what he's writing and why he's writing it, wondering what cold and congealed substance his blood has become.

John and Ralph, the two brothers who work the grounds, oiling the old wheelbarrow.

Marceline, settled now in the yellow room, swearing in German at a script never meant for words.

Gamby on the train, his daughter curled against his lap, her yellow hair spilling down his leg, her whole body expanding with every breath.

SAMANTHA IN HER ROOMS

Eddie, not knowing to let himself in, had knocked patiently at the downstairs door till Alfie barked and found Samantha. She led him up through the kitchen, and into her own rooms rather than the office, so they'd have privacy from Beatrice. She gave him the Morris chair and took the rocker herself. Poor thing, so awkward and formal. He was particularly nervous now, sucking in the lips on his little face until he resembled a gargoyle. He looked around the room, at her desk, her file cabinets, the Chinese lantern, the row of green apples ripening on the windowsill.

He took a great breath and said, "I wasn't leaving till the end of September. But I think I might go tomorrow morning." His palms flat on the arms of the chair. It dwarfed him.

"Oh," she said. "Oh dear." But she wasn't surprised at all. He'd stayed in bed so much, was so silent at breakfast, and talked at dinner only in a rushed, anxious way. (Zilla, who noticed everything, had told Samantha to keep an eye on him. "He's twenty-one," she said. "Can you imagine, coming here right from school and expecting yourself to be brilliant?" "He's already brilliant," Samantha had protested. "He published two collections at Princeton, and everyone's talking about him." "Well, regardless, he's raw. And he's afraid of the house.")

Samantha looked at him now, the way his face had thinned

in the two weeks he'd been here. She said, "You can leave whenever you need. But I hope there's nothing wrong."

"I've been doing good work here," he said. "Really good work. I've finished twelve poems, and they're different from anything I've made before. They're darker, actually. I *never* work this fast. No one does! But that gets at the problem. I'm not— something's wrong with me. I feel this place is going to swallow me whole."

"The house can have an effect."

"It's nothing at all about the way things are run."

"Eddie, why don't you see how you feel in the morning? Just enjoy yourself tonight, relax a bit, and let me know tomorrow."

He dropped his shoulders and smiled. "I will."

"You'll be getting out just in time, too. Mr. Devohr arrives tonight. Lord knows what'll happen to us all in the morning. We'll be walking the plank, I fear." She said it lightly, but really she'd spent the past day calculating frantically: the new artists due next Tuesday, the impossibility of sending Ludo back to Mussolini, the number of trustees who might eventually support a reconfigured Laurelfield, maybe on a farm up in Wisconsin. The finished canvases she was still storing in the basement for a painter who'd left in June. The prospect of having no home. Gamby might give her a month to clear out. Or maybe it was nothing. Maybe she was panicking over nothing.

They stood and walked back through the kitchen.

"May I inquire what happened to your wall?" he said.

She'd already forgotten the ugly black hole beside the icebox, the size of a large fist. And around it a larger circle of blackened wall, a foot in diameter. "I'll have to cover it before Mr. Devohr arrives. I had a lamp with no shade, and it fell against the wall this morning. When I smelled it, I thought I must have burned my lunch—and then I remembered I wasn't cooking anything."

Beatrice's voice, from the office: "We ought to dig all the way through and install the world's shortest pneumatic tube!"

Eddie laughed. "The ghost has been at the lamps lately. She snuffed ours out in the library last night."

"That lets me off the hook, doesn't it?"

THE DISH ON MARCELINE

She gets up early to work. Some of us saw her notes on the first script, when she left them by the coffee pot. *The Aspern Papers*, from a Henry James story, a failure in its first filming and sure to fail as a talkie. Because the only real characters are the old woman, her plain spinster niece, and the man obsessed with obtaining the old woman's love letters. No part here for Clara Bow, no room for a WAMPAS Baby Star. Only, if Marceline is smart, and we think she is, she'll show the audience some scenes from the past, when old Juliana was young and in love with the writer Aspern. But no, some of us argue: The whole point is the burning of the papers at the end, the fact that our man will *never* know the truth about the love affair. It would ruin it all, to show the past!

The other script, the one Marceline hasn't yet begun, is *Bluebeard*. She told us at breakfast. No, not the pirate. His beard was black. Bluebeard was the killer. The one with all the wives. Remember, the key she can't get the blood off? That one has potential.

Someone has heard that Marceline Horn once lived in sin with Ronald Coleman. Only it's not a sin in Hollywood, is it? They have different gods out there.

Someone heard she spent two thousand dollars on a Chinese rug. We are disinclined to believe this.

ZILLA IN THE ATTIC

Up here, she could concentrate. It wasn't so much that she had heard Viktor's feet through the Longhouse wall, and his humming, and occasionally the phonograph, but that she could *feel* him there, and it made her cold and it made her blood vibrate and every day she shrank. Every noise might have been his door closing, or opening, or him tapping on her window, or a woman—one of his dancing girls, or that waifish poet who left last Tuesday—coming to see him, to untuck his shirt, to lead him to the bed in the corner. So Zilla asked Samantha for the attic key, and Samantha gave it without comment, though she knew, they all knew, who wouldn't have known? And so for the fourth day now she was working on a piece of linen that she'd tacked right to the floor, for lack of properly lit wall space. And also for the difference it made. To stand *above* it, to feel she was peering straight through the linen and into the rest of the house, Fannie's bedroom below, and what was below that? The dining room. It was a hundred degrees up here, but still she was freezing from the inside out.

She wasn't sure what this painting wanted to be. She'd tried for petallate, frilled, wet, but ultimately she found she couldn't, in her state, create something verdant and expectant. She found five fallen oak leaves outside, early jumpers, stuck together with rain, not brown so much as opally pink, blushing at their early demise. And this was what she wanted to express now: a stack of soft, lovely suicides.

She'd had a letter that morning from Lemuel, holed up in Madison, "drowning in silver baths and sulphite," trying to finish the prints for his show. He wanted her home. He wanted her to keep him safe from nightmares. He said he might go up in an airplane with Kneller, which she knew was meant as a threat, as he believed all planes crashed, and believed that he, in particular, was due a fiery death. If she could, she'd stay here forever. She'd be like Ludo, minus the marooning via political unrest. She'd beg Samantha to let her stay, and then stay longer, and stay longer, until she'd become a part of the furniture. Her room, like Ludo's, would be permanently blocked off on Samantha's color-coded chart. Except that Lemuel would die, he truly would. He'd stop eating, like Violet Devohr.

The leaves were working out nicely. There was something new, a depth she could normally achieve only with many layers of oil, but that somehow came through now with just the thinnest washes. Now that she was this far from him, she was painting, in a sense, for Viktor. Though she'd never admit it aloud. And if he visited her studio along with everyone else at the end of her stay, why would he assume this particular pile of oak leaves had to do with him?

When she'd walked, travel-weary, into the library three weeks ago and seen him there, sitting as always, cigar and drink, legs halfway across the rug, she'd been shaken to the core, but only in the most familiar of ways. This time, she'd have been more surprised if he'd *not* been there. This was the third stay for both, and the third time their visits had coincided. He didn't need to tell her he hadn't arranged it this way: The blanching of his face was enough. It wasn't Samantha's doing, either—Samantha, who, in '27, asked them in all earnestness if they'd overlapped before. Zilla had come to feel the house itself was responsible, a magnetic field drawing them both back at regular intervals.

In March of '25, right after her first solo show, she'd come here to recover, to try to make something she didn't loathe as much as the work she'd just stared at till she wished for blindness. When she first saw him, Viktor was arriving late to dinner. His walk from the train had half frozen him, and he hadn't shaved in days. His hair—she'd thought it was the ice freezing it out like that in all directions. He sat next to her and said very little. She asked him for the salt without even looking at him—an elderly playwright was holding forth on hermaphrodites—and Viktor took her hand and uncoiled her fingers, tilted the shaker so the salt poured slowly into her palm. She turned, and he locked up her eyes in some kind of cage with his own, so that she couldn't turn away. Everyone began laughing and thought it a great joke, but really something far stranger was going on, something to do with her spinal column and her entire future. Her hand grew heavy. The salt began to spill over the edges and between her fingers. It was a long time—a minute? five minutes?—till he gave the container a last shake and set it down, and there she sat, dopey, buried under a mountain of a million small things. She pinched a few grains off the top for her casserole, and sat there eating the rest of her meal with her hand still outstretched, still laden. She said nothing at all, and this became a source of tremendous amusement for the rest of the table. They tried to remember which Roman goddess it was she resembled, and whether there might have been, once, a salt-bearing oracle. For the rest of that stay, the whole group called her The Oracle. She resumed talking the next morning, and found she had become such an object of fascination to the other artists that they all wanted to hear whatever she said. They wanted to ask The Oracle their futures. "How burnt shall dinner be?" "When will my poems ever be done?" "Which painting will sell?"

But she was caught up, meanwhile, in watching Viktor. His clothes were always too small or too large, or both. His eyes bugged out, so dark a brown that you couldn't tell iris from pupil.

She'd thought him tremendously ungraceful for a dancer at first, until she understood his problem: He was meant to move in empty and infinite space, not to interact with chairs and lamps and soup spoons. Still, every muscle engaged in whatever he did. No movement was isolated to just the hand, or just the leg. Each action had behind it the force and eloquence of his entire body.

The next night there had been a storm, one of those violent Midwestern ordeals she was still unaccustomed to. They'd been gathered in the library after dinner, and midway through the first round of drinks Zilla had confessed how terrified she was of the thunder, of the lightning hitting her in bed as she slept. Viktor had rested his cigar in the ashtray, and left the room. They'd laughed about where he'd gone—he felt a dance coming on!—but twenty minutes later he was back, soaked like a shipwrecked sailor, teeth clacking, hair improbably still erect. He extended his palm, a wet, black acorn in the middle. He said, "For your windowsill. To protect you." It was a tradition having to do with Thor, he explained, being god of both the oak trees and the lightning. The whole crowd had laughed again, but this time with— she thought she heard it—an edge of wonder and knowing and general romantic envy. This man must be in love with this woman. *But we haven't yet spoken!* she wanted to say. Later they would speak. They'd spend hours on the terrace, always with others, laughing about failure and rent parties and a thousand other things.

She hadn't thought of it till now, but this must be why she'd chosen oak leaves to paint. Of course. How dense, not to realize.

A knocking below.

"Yes!" she called. "Yes, yes, yes."

And here, hurrying up, were Samantha and Ludo, and trailing behind was Armand, the illustrator, the sweet golden one with the odd teeth.

Samantha's eyes were bright and wet. "We'll need to hide

Ludo up here. Tonight at dinner, and after. You know Gamby thinks he's gone. I swore."

"You no mind?" Ludo said. "I leave alone your paint." He appraised the room.

Zilla took Samantha's wrist and led her gently to the rolling stool. "Sit down," she said. "Breathe great slow breaths."

She found chairs for the men and a crate for herself, and they sat by an open dormer, where an electric fan fought a losing battle with the heat.

Samantha said, "I'll offer Gamby the extra bed in the director's house, but I'm sure he'll stay at the hotel. Either way, Ludo should be safe to sleep in his room. I mean, just at night. I don't imagine Gamby will stay more than a day or two. Unless he kicks us out and stays *forever*."

"He won't," Ludo said.

"He will. He actually will."

Ludo was a frenetic little man. It had been two years since he and Zilla had made love (*love*, ha!) in the composer's cottage, since Viktor had hit him in the mouth with a dinner plate the next day—also, not coincidentally, the last day Viktor had spoken directly to her—and she could remember nothing at all about the feel of Ludo's body, his smell, his tongue. He looked at her with equal vacancy.

Samantha said, "This morning I wrote to the board. Some are my friends, but most aren't. I don't know how much sympathy we have."

Armand, quiet till now, let out a loud breath, a dragon puffing contemplative steam. "What would he take from New York? The Broadway, or the Twentieth Century? Well, no, it doesn't matter. They both get to the city in the morning. Let's say he's there now, he'll have to switch to the local, maybe he'll have lunch first. We have a few hours."

"To do what?"

"I haven't a clue."

Ludo said, "I quote you Ovid, but I don't know in the English: Fortune is not helping those who pray but those who act."

"Didn't Ovid get exiled?"

Armand said, "Stay here." He vanished down the stairs, and they all stared after him, bemused, and then in seconds he came running back. He put something on the windowsill: a little monkey, carved from green jade. Loopy arms, a manic grin. "It's the Lord of Mischief," he said. "A relic of my dissolute years in the Orient. He'll be our totem."

Samantha stared at the thing. "I thought you'd be coming back with an idea."

"Well, no."

Zilla rubbed Samantha's neck. She said, "We could either seduce him or kidnap him. I believe these are our options."

Armand: "We'll charm him."

Samantha: "It won't work. And what then?"

"Then, anything and everything. Desperation."

VIKTOR IN HIS STUDIO: THE WINTER'S TALE

It is a dance to be done to a wall.

On the stage, it will be a dance to a statue, to the frozen Hermione. Leontes will dance his grief, his longing, for the wife he betrayed and killed, and then—then!—the statue steps down, Hermione lives, and there is to be the most exquisite *pas de deux*, all the more wrenching for their sixteen-year separation, for the age of the dancers. If only he can create the thing. But for now, in the Longhouse, he lives inside Leontes' dance of despair, the score spread around him on the floor like icebergs. His feet bare. The music is in his head, and he dances to the western wall. Zilla is through that wall (Armand Cox is through the other) and there are times when he knows she's standing not two feet away, facing him, brush in her left hand, a brush in her teeth, painting on her thin cloth. If there were no wall, if there were no cloth, she'd be painting the same air he is dancing in.

In sixteen years, he will not need a statue to remember her body, her face.

He dances as far as the dance is written.

He presses his hips to the wall.

FRIDAY, 1:00

Armand and Ludo, hunting down the other artists, giving them their roles.

Josephine at the window, to Fannie: "It's one of the last good places in the world, isn't it? One of the last."

Viktor, walking Marlon around to sober him up. Marlon: "Have you seen those photos of Zilla? The ones her husband took? And exhibited in public! They're—let me tell you. Let me *tell* you." Viktor: "Yes. I've seen them."

Zilla and Samantha in the kitchen of the director's house, giggling like children, tearing at the thin plaster of the wall around the small black hole, until chunks come away in their hands and the opening is two feet square between the counter and the icebox.

"There, see? That cross beam back there," Samantha says.

They reach carefully into the hole with the bottles they've brought from the library, and line them up along the exposed beam: gin, bourbon, rye, scotch, vermouth, all new and full from the bootlegger's drop.

Zilla: "That's the ugliest speakeasy I've ever seen."

"It'll do."

They nail the square board over the hole, as gently as they can, so the bottles won't fall.

Outside, sunshine and wind.

ARMAND AND EDDIE IN THE FLOWERED BEDROOM

He found Eddie under the desk, tucked in a ball, writing in a small black notebook. Armand understood instantly, and wanted to tell him so: that it sometimes felt better like this, tucked into something solid, hidden from the world. Instead, when Eddie scooted halfway out, what he said was, "You look like a turtle."

Eddie laughed and nodded, but he didn't come any farther, so Armand sat Indian style on the floor.

"I'm sorry to interrupt," Armand said.

"I'm glad you did. I didn't like what I was writing."

Eddie was so controlled, so careful. His eyes, though—the way they pulsed around the room and then back to your face—it was as if they were taking in everything with such tremendous force, such thirst. A good chance *this* was the reason for his quiet. There was so much pouring in that nothing could come out.

Armand told him his role for the evening, and said nothing would go into effect till Samantha gave the word. "We might yet be wrong," he said. "He might be paying a purely social visit. To absorb some culture, you know. Perhaps he wants to learn to paint. Ha." Eddie didn't say anything. "It's not a full plan, I know, but it's something. God, I'd love to draw you under there. The lines are fantastic. It's just the desk and your head and your knees."

Eddie blushed. Everyone blushed when you said you wanted to draw them. It was perhaps the most flattering thing in the world.

Not the suggestion that you were beautiful so much as the implicit revelation: *I see you. I really see you.*

Armand said, "You're so quiet." And without knowing he would, he reached forward and grabbed Eddie's jaw and popped it open like he was giving a dog a pill. He pulled a nickel from his pocket and stuck it on Eddie's tongue. Eddie closed his mouth. Armand let go of him.

Eddie managed to say, "Why did you do that?" The coin still in his mouth. Armand heard it click against his teeth.

"I thought if I paid the nickelodeon it would make some noise. And see? It worked."

THE WHITE RABBITS APPRAISE GAMBY

Mr. Devohr has requested dinner at five—a bad sign, surely. There will be no drinks before, no gathering in the library. When they enter the dining room at four-fifty, Gamby Devohr is already there, Samantha at his side. She's managed to put on a dress.

Fannie whispers to Josephine: "He looks like a starfish. Stuffed in a suit and fitted out with a black wig."

Josephine to Fannie: "He doesn't resemble his mother one bit."

Fannie: "Not a bit."

They glance to where Violet hangs on the wall, darkly regarding her endless stream of uninvited houseguests.

"He's terribly young."

"He's twenty-five."

"Keep your voice down."

"He can't hear."

"He flunked out of Yale, Samantha said."

"But I thought he left to marry the girl. And seven months later, wouldn't you know, a baby!"

"It's amazing how quickly they grow them, these days."

"Look, someone's folded all the napkins like little sailboats. How swank!"

The artists file past to shake Gamby's hand, to thank him for his generosity. Armand has traded in his knickers for ludicrous Oxford bags, a facetious nod to formality, and as he introduces himself Gamby stares, confused, at what appears to be a floor-length skirt. When Samantha introduces Marceline, Gamby turns red. "Miss Horn," he says. "It's a great honor. I watched you in *Old Kentucky*, and you were just swell. Wasn't that you in *The Statesman*? In the dress, you know, that dress? I'd love to—wow, I'd love to hear some of your stories!"

Fannie can't look at Josephine, or they'll both laugh. Gamby is nothing more than a little boy in a suit. The silly nickname fits.

Marceline accepts the kiss on her hand. "The honor is entirely mine."

Fannie, whispering: "His father's been trying to boot Samantha for years, Zilla said. Only the board wouldn't."

"Augustus? That's the father?"

"And he had a stroke last year."

"He's got something to prove, then, hasn't he? Gamby."

"Show up at the old man's bedside and give him back the house."

"Look how smooth his hands are!"

"And plump!"

They sit to eat.

Josephine to Fannie: "Wouldn't we love to sculpt him?"

Fannie to Josephine: "I'd do it in mashed potatoes. With a little butter hat."

EDDIE AT DINNER

The food was elegant, a stretch for the cook: consommé julienne, roast Surrey fowl with bread sauce, hearts of celery, new potatoes in cream. Eddie struggled to eat.

Gamby asked them each, cordially, about their work. Armand said, "You've probably seen my magazine covers and forgotten them at once. I did a lot of fadeaway girls, when that was the style."

"I suppose they model for you!" Gamby said. "The girls."

"Certainly."

"And why does it help to be here in the woods? Don't artists thrive in the city?"

Zilla said, "We are like flowers, Mr. Devohr. We might exhibit ourselves in the city, but we grow best in the wilderness." She touched his arm with two fingertips. She wore all white.

"Huh."

Fannie said, "We don't even have a proper studio right now, Josephine and I. We're trying to make enough pieces here this month to last the rest of the year."

"What, to sell?"

"That *is* how artists make a living." Samantha must have realized how sharp she sounded because she took a long drink of water and looked around the table. She wanted someone to rescue her.

Marlon said, "I've written a tremendous amount, this stay. A *tremendous* amount."

Gamby listened patiently, and soon enough he was focused in again on Marceline, asking about the talkies. "Von must speak from farther up in the throat," she was saying. "Or it von't record vell. You do as if you vere talking into the telephone."

He said, "I heard they can do gunshots now. Isn't it true, they invented a slow-motion pistol just so it'll record?"

"Yes," Marceline said. "It opens many possibilities." Brave woman, chatting so amiably about the death knells of her own career.

Zilla, seated to Gamby's left, was the one responsible for figuring out how serious he was in his mission, how doomed they all really were. If anyone could get a man to give too much away, it was Zilla—her palpable empathy, the way she leaned into everything you said. Even Eddie relaxed when he talked to her, and the chill vanished. Being near Zilla was being near a small, smooth lake.

Eddie forced a bit of bread. He'd lost weight here. If he stayed any longer, he might vanish entirely. He heard Zilla, her voice a bit higher, more emphatic than normal: "Oh, but we can't even *interact* with the town! It's like an invisible fairy castle! This is my third stay, and I haven't set *foot* off the grounds but once, when I cracked my wrist and was rushed to the doctor. I don't suppose they think anything of us at all!"

A minute later, Gamby laughed for all the table to hear: "It goes without saying that if I'd decided to be an *artist* or a *poet*, or what have you—my father would have sent me over Niagara in a barrel."

"Yes." Zilla said it through her teeth. "We're awfully lucky to do what we do."

Viktor was rotating all the food on his plate to the left. Choreographing his vegetables. What must it have meant, Eddie wondered, to be accustomed to young dancers he could throw around—literally throw in the air!—and then to fall in love with a woman like Zilla? A woman so grounded, so unflappable (so *married* too), that he, Viktor, would inevitably be the one to bend and break. It would be unbearable, surely.

Gamby was saying: "So when you start a painting, do you arrange all your fruit and whatnot on a table, or do you just make it up?"

Eddie watched Armand and Marlon pretend to talk to each other. Marlon had removed his smoking jacket for once, and he might even have been sober. His moustache was waxed. Armand, beside him, his hair combed into golden waves. Armand's teeth looked as if each had been collected from a different man's mouth, a sort of harlequin set. Eddie remembered a toy Roman arch where, when the keystone was pulled, the entire thing collapsed. He imagined that if he pulled out Armand's incisor, something similar would happen, the splendors of the ancient world giving way all at once.

Eddie excused himself from the table as the orange layer cake was served, and said he must lie down with his headache. It pained him to be so rude, but his one task tonight was to sneak Ludo his dinner. And then he'd pack his trunk. He wanted to leave as soon as possible in the morning.

In the kitchen, Eddie picked up the covered plate from the cook and wove past the sinks to the back exit. A small blonde girl, no more than four, sat at the counter on a stool, staring disconsolately at a plate of peas. Her milk glass was empty.

"Mr. Devohr's daughter, Grace," the cook whispered. "I don't know what I'm expected to do with her."

When he returned from the attic with the empty tray, she was there still, and she glanced up with hopeful eyes, until she saw he wasn't her father. He wondered if anyone had considered her in the midst of all the planning. He didn't imagine they'd found a maid to watch her, to put her to bed. He said, "I have an important job to do. There are hungry fish out back, and I'm going to give them their supper. I don't suppose you know how to rip bread very, very small."

Grace gave him a deep, appraising look, like an old lady's. "Oh yes I do!"

"Well, you'll have to help me, then. I'm afraid I'm not very good at it. The fish are always complaining. Will you come along?" She hopped from her stool, and the cook, winking, handed Eddie two slices of the dinner bread. He put one in Grace's hand and said, "This one's too heavy for me."

"Are your arms very skinny?"

"Yes, quite."

They sat on the two big rocks by the largest koi pond, and Eddie showed her how to tear tiny pieces and throw them in. They watched the fish come to gobble the crumbs, their round mouths impossibly large.

"The spotted one is my best one," Grace said. "What is his name?"

"Oh, that's Elwood. A terribly distinguished gentlefish."

"Does he love bread the best of any food?"

"*Almost*. Almost. Do you know what he told me the other day? He wishes, more than anything in the world, for a root beer float."

Grace looked skeptical. "It would fall apart in the water."

"That's precisely the problem. He'll never get his wish."

"But I know how to do it! Take him out with a big scoop, and put him *into* the root beer float. He can eat it from inside it."

"Ha! You are an exceptionally wise young lady. I might make a poem about you."

She threw another crumb and thought a moment. "Face."

"I beg your pardon?"

"That's what rhymes with Grace."

He convinced her, miracle of miracles, to lie in bed with a book. He read her the story of Rapunzel from the Brothers Grimm she'd brought on the train, and he changed her into her white night-gown, and he tucked her into the spare bed in Samantha's house, in the room behind the office that Gamby had surprised everyone by accepting. He drew the blinds against the evening sun—it was only ten to six—and told her that back in Toronto, it was nearly midnight.

"Can you remember what I just read you? You can look at the pictures all over again."

"I can read words. I can even read the big words!"

"I shouldn't have doubted it. Did you know, if you lie very still and read the same story ten times, you'll have magic dreams?"

"Oh, I knew that."

"So someone told you the secret. And Elwood will dream about root beer, and I will dream about you."

Grace giggled and kicked her toes under the sheet. Eddie moved her water closer and kissed the top of her head. She smelled like sun and grass.

MARCELINE AT THE END OF THE WORLD

Zilla dropped her spoon on the table with a clatter, and said, a bit too loudly, "Oh, how *clumsy* of me!" Confirmation. That Devohr was here on a euthanasia mission. That he couldn't be charmed. Marceline hadn't caught his exact words, but then she didn't need to—the man's intentions were clear. And so: They all braced themselves, ran through their parts, such as they were, and tried to continue their several conversations as if nothing had happened.

Zilla took a breath to say something, but just then there came a loud knocking above them. A series of small, hard raps that seemed to travel the whole length of the house, ending over the window.

Josephine laughed—a nervous burst.

It happened again: hard and fast, on the roof—the dining room did stick out from the rest of the house—and trailed off as if it wanted them all to follow somewhere.

Devohr scanned their faces, blinking his little eyes again and again.

Marceline wondered if this was the misfiring of some effect they'd arranged for Devohr's benefit—akin to all the fireworks shooting off at once, before the grand finale. She perceived nothing but confusion all around her, though, and concern. Fannie and Josephine grabbed each other's hands.

Samantha said, finally, "It's the acorns. They're early this year."

So it hadn't been the plan. What had been the plan? Zilla was to have spoken. But she just sat there, ashen, the only one not laughing now, the only one who didn't seem relieved, and whispered into her cupped hands: "Good lord."

Marceline had simply been told to flirt, and this she had done expertly. The high art of pantomime—quite possibly her last performance of that art. She was unfortunately hazy on other details. But she could flirt till dawn.

Mr. Devohr stretched and stood. "We should end this soirée. I'll be heading back to Chicago quite early in the morning."

Samantha said, "We're finished." But it was a question, and they all knew she wasn't referring to dinner.

He sniffed. "You've had a good run, Miss Mays. I always say, it's important to recognize when the party's over. There's a fine art to it."

Armand said, out loud: "What in the hell do you know about *art?*"

Marceline thought for a moment they might all erupt into violence or weeping. Instead the energy slowly left the room. A leak in the balloon.

Zilla should have taken over now, but she was still glazed, still spooked.

Marlon finally spoke. "Well, what happened to the booze? If we're giving up here, can we at least make a good night of it?" The poor man. He was twitching, positively twitching. Marlon hadn't been in on the plan—he'd spent the afternoon sobering up, not rehearsing—but he'd inadvertently cut to the chase, skipping over Zilla's forgotten invitation to visit the studios, skipping the slow progression that would lead them all to a nightcap and then another and another. Which would all lead, somehow or other, to Gamby Devohr's heart.

"He's only joking, Mr. Devohr," Fannie said. "We don't drink a drop here!" Marceline supposed this was part of the script, a displaced line. She felt herself back on a rooftop in Fort Lee, those embarrassing summer flickers of twenty years past, costumes pulled from theater trash, directors who'd never directed so much as bicycle traffic. Devohr was about to laugh. Marceline— finally she knew exactly what to do—Marceline stood up next to him and slid her hand down the outside of his thigh. She cocked her head and let her eyelashes fall slowly down. "Please do join us for a drink," she said. "For a last bacchanal. How often, back in Canada, do you live like the artists do? The night is terribly young." And she could see in his dopey eyes the affirmation of what she'd learned on her very first picture: Sex trumps a poor script and poor players any day.

Marceline walked with him, arm in arm, trailing Zilla and Samantha and Armand back to the director's house and up the stairs. Marlon followed at a distance, apparently even less sure than Marceline of what was happening. Alfie circled their feet. They found Eddie alone at the little kitchen table, his finger to his lips. The girl, he said, was in bed.

Samantha got a hammer from under the sink and, turning it to the prong end, began prying the nails loose from the ugly square board behind her. Marceline kept Devohr talking and laughing while Armand took a turn, and then Eddie. The board broke loose from the wall, and then there was a great clatter as Eddie and Armand reached in and pulled out an improbable number of liquor bottles.

Marceline guessed from the proximity of the hammer, from the loose way the board was nailed, that this unveiling had been part of the plan all along. If Devohr thought they were letting their guard down—if he thought they'd given up entirely and were revealing their true selves—he'd maybe let his guard down, too.

Armand said, "The terrace! I'll bring cigars!"

Eddie stayed behind to make sure the child was asleep. Marceline pulled Devohr by the hand—down the stairs, down the walk that circled behind the big house. The sun was still bright and high. When she was sure he'd been propelled in the right direction, she let go and fell back with Zilla and Armand, five bottles between them, the dog at their heels.

"How does the plan go now?"

"That *was* the plan. That's as far as it goes."

ALL OF THEM

More acorns covered the ground than should have been possible. The oaks all grew in front of the house—the smaller ones off to the left, the majestic one between the director's house and the big house—but even so their helmeted seeds carpeted the lawn and terrace and paths out back like hail. Green still, and dangerous: Josephine went rolling forward, and Fannie caught her under the arms. "They're good luck!" Marlon said.

"Well, we need plenty of that."

Hazy and hot, the air still and heavy.

Viktor said, "Shall we build a fire? Back on the pile?"

"Oh, yes, yes!" Fannie said.

Everyone made it to the terrace. Even Ludo, with nothing more to lose, came down from the attic to slap Gamby on the back and say he'd teach him to drink like an Italian.

Armand took over one of the long, high tables and started mixing drinks. Someone broke into the kitchen and brought out lemons, and soon Armand was squeezing them into a glass and picking out seeds with his fingers so he could mix the juice with the gin and the precious Cointreau to make White Ladies. ("How ghostly!" Josephine cried, and Fannie rubbed her hands together. "Ooh, shall we bring out the Ouija? It's still in the library!")

Gamby said, "You don't believe in ghosts, do you? Tell me this. Why'd they all die violently? Where's the ghost of the nice old lady who died in bed from a tumor?"

"Resting in peace! It's *energy* that makes a ghost, unfulfilled energy. Anger, or fear, or—or—"

"Love," Josephine said. "Unrequited love."

Armand said, "There are more things in heaven and earth, Mr. Devohr, than are dreamt of in your philosophy."

Marlon and Viktor decided they were in charge of the bonfire. Marlon slipped his smoking jacket back on and ran around gathering extra sticks, while Alfie the dog scampered after in joyful brotherhood. Viktor became convinced the quality of the fire would depend on the number of matches used to light it, and took donations from the men's pockets.

Marceline and Zilla reclined on the terrace wall, legs stretched along it toward each other. Sylphic bookends. Samantha put a chair for Gamby right in front of them, at eye level with the legs. And she sat too, and she asked Ludo to open the solarium windows and turn on the Victrola. Soon there was music, "A Shady Tree" and "Was It a Dream," and soon Ludo was back and handing out Armand's cigars, and Armand was passing drinks. Marceline said, "I vent to such a lofely garden party last month, at the house of Mary Pickford. Mister Devohr, do you know her films?"

"Heavens, yes!"

She lowered her voice. "And I vill tell you the real reason she cut her hair."

Behind them, Josephine leaned against the ivy, and Fannie leaned against her, on her soft shoulder. She said, "What would we do without this place? What sort of world would this be, without refuges?"

In the distance, the fire pile began to glow. Small spots around the lower edges first, then a few thin arms of fire. Now the whole thing, a consummation. Marlon ran back to the terrace, to view his creation from a distance. "A fine fire," he said. "The best work I've done here." And it was true, he saw that now. He shouldn't have let himself sober up. He could suddenly see his whole book, the shape of it, the bulk of it. It was a monstrosity, a tangle, a snake swallowing its own tail. He took a White Lady from Armand, and with the drink he walked slowly back down the path, back to where Viktor stood staring at the blaze.

Up on the terrace, Armand filled Gamby's glass before it could get half empty.

Gamby didn't seem to doubt that the high spirits were genuine. That these women would naturally want to surround him and regale him with stories. That these artists were simply dying to share their liquor.

Somone did find the Ouija board, and Marceline climbed down from the wall, pulled a chair close to Gamby's, convinced him to press his knees into hers with the board between them. Here was some hope: If Marceline was as gifted an improviser as they all supposed, she might manage to nudge the planchette toward some helpful message. Something about ghosts of artists past, or the ghost of his mother. Saying she loved the art created here and wanted the colony to stay. But all Marceline knew of his mother was that horrible attic story, nothing personal that would shock him into compliance. She couldn't even recall her name.

From behind Gamby's head, Fannie mouthed it: "Violet! Violet!"

Josephine whispered, "Watch, she'll spell it with a W."

Gamby's short, stout, pale fingers on the planchette, Marceline's long ones. She said, "I haf done the Ouija von time before. At a Hollyvood party, vith my dear friend Lon Chaney. I vill tell you, he used the board to proposition me!"

Back by the fire, Marlon and Viktor. Marlon said to him, "I might burn the novel. The whole thing."

"Don't."

"It's a doorstop. I've sat here six weeks and made a doorstop."

"Then burn it." Viktor regarded him with something like spite, a look Marlon hadn't anticipated. "Did you know, you can't burn a dance? There are quite a few things you can't burn, unless you burn yourself, unless you jump into the fire *yourself*."

"Let's step away from the fire."

"Look at her up there, offering herself like—"

"Who? Sobriety doesn't suit you. Good God." Marlon handed over his own drink. "It's delicious," he said.

Viktor looked down at it. "I don't drink."

"You don't?" Marlon thought through the past weeks, and took back his glass. "You mixed the vat last night. And you're always dropping things. You're the drunkest man I know."

"I've never touched the stuff. I couldn't dance."

"But when you were younger?"

"I started training when I was eight." Viktor poked the fire with a long branch and said, "Tell me something. Tell me why I could walk down a street in the city and see two faces in the crowd. And one of them—a stranger—it might be a beautiful woman—for one of them I feel nothing, I remain intact. And the other, no more beautiful, no more spectacular: When I see her, I fall through the universe. And only because of our past, only because of some promise my idiot heart made itself years before."

"Why don't you try a drink."

"The truth is, there's no such thing as love. There's only *history*."

Zilla was pouring her drinks off the far side of the wall. She needed to stay clear.

Alfie ran yapping between the terrace and the fire, the terrace and the fire.

"The Ouija dates to Pythagoras," Ludo said.

Zilla said, "Ludo's our encyclopedia."

Gamby laughed. "That's funny, it says here *William Fuld Talking Board Set*. Was Mr. Fuld a follower of Mr. Pythagoras?" Marceline smiled up as if the two of them alone were in on the joke. Gamby addressed the board. "What horse shall I pick at Saratoga next summer?"

"No, no," Marceline said, and she attempted to make even that one word flirtatious. "Let us ask the spirit's name."

She aimed for the V. She was halfway there when Gamby jerked the planchette down to the bottom, to the number 2.

"Hell of a name!" Gamby said. Pleased with his own joke. "You should get your money back from Mr. Pythagoras."

Marceline said, "It must mean there are two spirits!"

Samantha closed her eyes.

Gamby said, "Are you men or women?"

Before Marceline had time to think, the planchette slid to the sun face on the top left, with the word YES beneath.

"Well played, Miss Horn." Devohr waggled his eyebrows. "One of each, male and female! Are we ourselves the spirits, by chance?"

"I am not mofing the pointer, Mr. Devohr. Are you?"

Fannie and Josephine swayed to the music. Ludo changed the record, and, returning to the terrace, did a shuffling little solo dance to "I'm Saving Saturday Night for You."

Samantha, next to Gamby but silent, relied on Marceline's and Zilla's social graces. She wrapped her hands around the iron arms of the chair, let the metal cool her fingertips. Or rather, her fingers transferred their warmth, electron by electron, into the chair. An important distinction. And when she was gone, when there was no visible trace of her at Laurelfield, when the lawn was filled with matrons drinking tea, her electrons would remain in the chair. That was something, and she pressed harder. That was something.

Alfie slept, at last, under her.

Zilla watched Marlon lead Viktor back to the terrace. She said, "There ought to be marshmallows."

Viktor said nothing. He swayed a bit. Marlon had never seen a man sway from sobriety. He led him to Armand. He said, "We need to fix this fellow up."

Marceline had asked again for spirit's name. They all watched.

G

G

G

The planchette circled the letter like a bee on a flower.

"I think you are writing your own name, Mr. Devohr." She wanted to push back harder on the planchette, but then the whole idea was for him to believe it had moved on its own.

"No, too many G's!" he said. "Gagog. It sounds like a caveman. Gagog the Horrible. Gilgamesh!"

Fannie said, "Ask how she—ask how it perished. The spirit." And they did.

S

C

R

F

C

"Scarface!" Marlon called, unhelpfully. Josephine aimed a plump elbow into his ribs, but he didn't understand. "Maybe they're two of the fellows Capone got! Ask if they died on February the fourteenth! Ask if the last thing they saw was a warehouse!"

Marceline tried to think quickly. "Perhaps it means *sacrifice*. Perhaps—it is von who sacrificed a great deal for, for the colony."

But she was going off course, wasn't she? Violet hadn't had a thing to do with the colony. She felt the looks around her, a net of disappointment. She said, "Vhen did you lif?"—not certain where she'd aim the thing even if she could wrest control.

NO

Gamby said, "Well that's terribly uncooperative! Tell us, brave spirits, when did you walk the earth?"

NO

NO

NO

GOOD BYE

The planchette stopped and stayed on that "good bye" at the bottom as if its motor had run out. Gamby lifted his fingers.

"But *NO* was on the moon picture!" Fannie said. "I think it meant 'Many moons ago!' Don't you?"

Josephine said, "It's useless."

Marceline said, "Let's gif it von more go."

Gamby sighed and looked down. "Well," he said. "I suppose there is one person I want to reach. It's just that she's been gone a long time. And she—BOO!" He slapped the board, and it flew across the terrace with the planchette, and Gamby erupted into boisterous laughter at the same moment that Fannie and Josephine screamed and Viktor fell back into the ivy. Alfie awoke and barked disapprovingly.

Ludo scrambled after the Ouija set. Marlon poured his own drink straight into Gamby's glass while he was distracted, then fetched himself a refill.

By the time Eddie joined the party, the little girl at last asleep, or at least pretending, there was no appeal to joining the drinkers. He'd never catch up, and they made it look so tiresome. Flushed faces and stupid, shouted conversation. He ought to pack, but his room would be hot. He'd wait till the air had cooled. He leaned against the ivy, next to the White Rabbits, and together they watched Gamby.

Fannie said, "Look at him there, surrounded by beauty. What did he do to deserve any of this?"

Josephine said, "What if we murdered him? What if we threw him on the fire?"

"*Josephine!*"

"We could forge letters back to Canada. He'd say how he was joining the artists, how he'd always wanted to be a painter."

"There's that little girl!"

"Well, I'm only *joking.* Eddie, I'm afraid Fannie takes me *awfully* seriously. And I don't deserve to be listened to for a single word."

"She's all nonsense, it's true."

Meanwhile Gamby had grown loud and shrill. "That's *ace!*" he shouted.

"He's going to lick her shoulder," Armand whispered. "Marceline's."

"Do you suppose he's corked?"

"He's fried to the hat."

Eddie watched Zilla, still perched on the wall, watched the way she never fully looked away from Viktor. He'd understood half of it before, but now he realized there was something he'd absolutely missed, something about the way her eyes sunk into themselves: She was bereft, or broken, or grief stricken. She stared at Viktor the way a woman on a boat stares at a man drowning in the ocean.

Marlon and Armand leaned on the makeshift bar, and Ludo soft-shoed around the terrace, but Viktor sat now, Indian style, an empty glass by one knee. He was looking out, either at Zilla or the fire. Maybe to him they were the same thing.

In one breath Eddie fished his Waterman from his trouser pocket and grabbed Viktor's hand. Viktor didn't seem to notice at all. He wrote across the veins, in dark blue: She loves you. He stepped in front of Samantha, in front of Gamby, in front of Marceline, who was talking about Hollywood ghostwriters and the confessional craze. He grabbed Zilla's hand—she at least looked at him, startled—and wrote: He loves you.

He capped the pen. It was a service someone had to perform,

he felt. A translation service, in a way. What *was* all this, but a modern tower of Babel? Here was someone speaking nothing but dance, and someone else speaking paint, and someone speaking poetry, and someone speaking music. And what were they trying to express, but the inexpressible? If there existed words, regular words, to say what they were aiming at, then why would they even need to do what they did? Why were they all living here, knocking so ineffectively at the doors of the palace? The ink was insufficient as anything else, but perhaps it was a start. If he'd been a sculptor, he'd have sculpted it for them: Look! There! Love.

Someone had appeared at the edge of the terrace: a small girl in a white nightgown. No one but Marceline noticed at all, until Eddie sprang across the bricks and knelt in front of her and said, "Let's have one more story, shall we?" And he vanished with the girl, around the corner of the house. Gamby, his eyes closed in laughter, hadn't even seen.

The sun was lower in the sky. It hovered over the trees a long time, casting long shadows toward the house.

Fannie: "If we could only slow down time, we could accomplish an infinite amount of work before this place gets the wrecking ball."

Armand: "I'll move very slowly when I'm near you. And you'll believe it's come true."

Josephine: "You have such an honest energy, Armand. You live very close to the skin."

And off Armand bounded, to pour more gin in Gamby's cup.

Zilla and Viktor both squinted at the backs of their hands like confused palm readers.

Marceline, a laugh like an oboe: "Vell, can you belief, ve all thought the talkies vould mean more vork for *theater* actors But instead they vant to pay youngsters something like seventy-fife a veek. And gif them leads! And star them!"

Zilla tried to focus on the same conversation: "But," she said, "*here* is a place—here we're so different from a place like Hollywood. They've built a city, an industry. And here we are in our studios. You understand it, don't you, Mr. Devohr? What it is we do here, and why it matters. A man like you, a man has everything he wants, autos and servants and land—what does he do next? He buys art!"

"I do!" Gamby said. His words were garbled. "I buy art! I'll buy it from you! You can paint me a picture of Marcelot. Of Marceline. Of—ha!—of Miss Horn."

Eddie returned. Things felt like they'd fallen apart—the Ouija long abandoned, even Marceline and Zilla's flirting strangely mechanical and overdone now. Samantha had turned to stone. He wished he could think of something to help. The magic words to save this place that he himself wanted nothing more to do with.

But Armand was staring at him, Armand was smiling at him, Armand was not looking away.

Any instinct on Eddie's part to hide had been wiped away by the catastrophe of Viktor and Zilla. Did he want to end up like them, made sick by what he wouldn't acknowledge? And so he stared back at Armand.

Ludo wove around them like a leprechaun. The music from the solarium was "Let's Fall in Love." Ludo pulled Zilla off the terrace wall with both hands, pulled her into a little waltz that didn't match the music at all.

He whispered: "Where is your camera? Don't you, somewhere, have a camera?"

"Marlon's got a Leica."

The August air, thick enough to climb.

Alfie, asleep again.

Eddie looked right at Armand. And—the bravest thing he'd done in his life—he slowly, slowly, stuck out his tongue to display the nickel he'd kept in his mouth since the afternoon, removing it only for dinner. Then he flipped it back in and closed his lips.

Armand did not look away. For the next five minutes, he did not look away.

Gin fractured the time. An encounter halfway down the lawn, Fannie tripping—how had they gotten there?—and one back on the terrace, surely later. Marlon would try to recall, the next morning. He'd had his smoking jacket, and then he hadn't. Eddie had been near. and then he'd been quite far away, and then there was a bathroom floor. And then there was the fire, still burning, though someone else was in charge. The sun was low but still hot, and Viktor was crying. Why was Viktor crying? What was wrong with the man?

Gamby stumbling down the lawn, grabbing at Marceline's chest. She was nimble. She held him by the elbow. Laughing and laughing.

Zilla had Marlon's camera.

"Everyone together! Quick, before the last of the sun—"

Fannie, trying. Josephine pulling at her arm. "Mr. De—Mr. Devohr. Your mother, and her death. Don't you think—don't you think, though, she'd have wanted all this? All this art?"

"Vell, the tap dancers are doing splendidly now of course. Who could haf guessed?"

"Eddie, what's wrong with him? Can you get Viktor some water?"

Samantha nodding to Armand. *Yes, go ahead, do it, whatever it is.*

"Miss Horn will join us, yes! And Miss Silverman as well! But—"

Armand's clothes off, Gamby's off, Zilla's off too. Marceline backing toward the house. The sun beginning to set.

"It's the way the natives fish!"

"Here, get your head up! Don't drown."

And the two of them, Armand and Gamby, out of the water. Who had kept the fire going? Laughing and laughing, and no one could stop laughing.

Armand, grabbing: "Look, I caught a fish!" Moving the other's plump hand: "Look, you caught one too!"

Laughter and the click of the Leica and the low red sun, and the light of the fire. No one could stop laughing.

It was dark so fast, and they couldn't remember how.

Viktor, somewhere out in the dark. No one could find him. They could hear him, but they couldn't find him.

In the humid night, some of them stumbled together, and some stumbled farther apart.

ZILLA IN THE DARKROOM, GAMBY IN THE DARK

First she points it at the back of the big house and clicks through the rest of the film. Thirteen photos of abandoned windows, lit orange by the setting sun. Up there, the room where she slept on her first visit, before there were beds in the Longhouse. The yellow room at the other end, where Viktor once stayed. The solarium studio, Fannie and Josephine's sculptures shining like living things. The dining room, where she's fallen in some sort of love with every artist and composer and writer who's ever sat across from her.

The sun is gone as she gropes her way down the path to the darkroom cabin. She's been developing Lemuel's prints for years, doing half his work, really, and even in this unfamiliar space it takes her little time to sort things out. All the chemistry she needs is here: a jackpot of not quite empty bottles left by departing photographers. Tanks and reels. An ancient ruby light, with a funny little door. But no photographic paper. No matter, if the negative is clear and convincing. She takes her time lining things up left to right on the counter. Developer, stop bath, fixer. She makes sure the sink works.

(At this same moment, back on the lawn: Gamby, somehow both drunker and more sober, lunges at Fannie. He says, "Hey, wait, where's your camera? Wait!" "Good gracious, it wasn't my camera," Fannie says.)

She turns off the electric lamp and feels her way back to the counter. It's a relief not to see her hands anymore, the upside-down script: *He loves you.* Well, yes. Eddie didn't know what he was doing, writing on them like that. He imagined he was pointing out something they didn't both already know.

(It has started to rain again, to pour. Marlon wakes up on the terrace and wonders why he's in a pool, why he's underwater, how he can breathe underwater. He goes back to sleep. Gamby is looking for Armand. He's shouting.)

Her hands are shaking so that she can't get the film hooked onto the reel. She has no idea if the light was enough. She has no idea if the shutter clicked at the right moment. If everything's a blur. At last she gets it engaged, begins reeling. One long strip of gray. The images hidden under that gray, waiting. Backward through time. This first half will be empty house. Somewhere in the middle here will be Gamby and Armand, the four shots she managed. The last bit should be Marlon's shots—yesterday, and the day before, and the day before. She finishes, and traps the whole thing in the aluminum canister, and hopes, as she pours, that the bottle of developer is correctly labeled, that it isn't someone's old supply of bathtub gin. It smells right at least. She closes the canister and turns the lamp back on. She sits on the counter to agitate. She goes by her watch to time the moving meditation—the front of her wrist, the back of her wrist—and the periods of rest.

(Eddie and Armand, behind the composer's shed, in the rain. The coin has been replaced by Armand's tongue. Eddie Parfitt, despite his considerable success, his poetry collections, his awards—Eddie Parfitt is twenty-one years old. He has lived a thousand years in those twenty-one. But he has never been in love.)

The stop bath, the fixer, the water. The water, at least, she can trust.

(Viktor, back in the house alone. Picking up the book Zilla

left in the library—Keats's letters—opening it to the middle: He smells it.)

She feels that Eddie broke something tonight. By writing it out, so starkly, so stupidly, on their hands.

(They are starting without her. Ludo walks Gamby in, drenched and confused, face like a mole forced above ground, and sits him in the solarium among Fannie and Josephine's sculptures.)

At last, she can allow herself to look at the negatives, to see the damage. She finds scissors first, a good sharp pair hanging from a nail. She opens the canister and slowly unspools the reel. The first frames, of the house, she snips off. A blurry shot of the two men, so unclear that they might as well be monkeys. The next one, yes, as she hoped: everything clearly visible, everything anatomical and precise. Gamby's face, as clear as a mug shot. And Armand's as well, and his body, and the sinews of his legs. The head of his penis, fat and soft.

(Samantha says, "You're a businessman, Mr. Devohr.")

She cuts the good shot loose and hangs it to dry. Then she spools back through the shots Marlon's been taking all week. A close-up of a daylily, meant to be artistic. Samantha on her balcony. The giant oak, the two houses, Armand smoking a cigarette. Eddie, smiling uncomfortably on the terrace. Fannie and Josephine walking by the fountain, but obviously posed. Perhaps because she's already in an agitated state, perhaps because of the awkward subjects, Zilla finds these photographs all unduly chilling. What should be so troublesome about two women walking the path? Only she can't shake the feeling that the photographs have existed all along, have been waiting in their canister for a thousand years, and that the people in them have lived their whole lives just to end up in these exact positions, just to hit their marks like dancers. Certainly this is what happened to Gamby, every moment of his life leading him right into this photograph, this trap. They got him to stand just so. They got him entwined with Armand. And he became the picture.

(Eddie's been summoned to the solarium as a bodyguard. All five and a half feet of him, arms like—well, like a poet's. Armand hiding in the library, for his safety. Eddie slips his coin back in his mouth, where it now belongs. Samantha, in a molten voice Eddie didn't know she had in her: "Mr. Devohr, Armand Cox is a known homosexual.")

Zilla realizes something, and it takes her a minute to wrap herself around the idea. She's always thought of Laurelfield as a magnet, drawing her back again and again. But that's just it: A magnet pulls you toward the *future*. Objects are normally products of their pasts, their composition and inertia. But near a magnet, they are moved by where they'll be in the next instant. And this, *this*, is the core of the strange vertigo she feels near Laurelfield. This is a place where people aren't so much haunted by their pasts as they are unknowingly hurtled toward specific and inexorable destinations. And perhaps it feels like haunting. But it's a pull, not a push. She doubts she can express it to anyone else, and she doubts she ought to.

(Gamby, no more blood in his face, sunken back in the chair, surrounded: "What in the hell do you people want?" Samantha still sitting, but she might as well be flying above him, Athena in the sky: "We want twenty-five years.")

Zilla hangs Marlon's shots next to the shots of Gamby. He'll be delighted that someone's done all the work for him.

(Grace, tossing in bed, turning the pillow to the cool side. Dreaming of Rapunzel and fish.)

But a moment later Zilla's sinking, and she realizes what's wrong, what it is. A lot of time has passed, and she's done her job, and Viktor hasn't followed her here. After Eddie wrote those words, there was a window of maybe half an hour when Viktor might have staggered through the dark, knocked on the door, called her name. But he hasn't, and the night air has hardened to impenetrable glass.

(Gamby's head between his knees. He says, "Twenty-five?" And he sits up to sign the paper they've made.)

Zilla and Viktor might pine for the rest of their lives, but that is *all* they will do. They will harden and soften into their old age, and she will paint him a hundred pictures and he will make her a hundred dances, but there will be no words, and there will be no coming together of bodies.

(It's not till Fannie has escorted Gamby back to the director's house that the solarium erupts in jubilation. Armand bursts in and says, "We changed fate! Do you realize what we did? It's— what is it? The victory of art over greed! It is! We reached in and we changed fate!" But Eddie says, "Did we?" Because this whole evening he's felt himself sucked into a whirlpool of inevitability. "Are you sure?")

Oh, stupid Eddie with his stupid pen. And stupid Zilla too, and stupid Viktor. She sits on the floor and stretches her legs. Lemuel is waiting for her, back in Madison. She can feel him, lying in bed awake, waiting. A different kind of magnet.

(Samantha turns a cartwheel, a full cartwheel, into the hall. The skirt of her yellow dress falls over her head like a parachute.)

After a while, the rain lets up.

And a while after that, the negatives are dry.

Dear Miss Mays,

Please, if it isn't too late, disregard my premature attempt to leave Laurelfield.

(And do pardon my slipping this under the door. It's early, and I'd hate to wake you.)

Everything felt wrong before, but now I know this is exactly where I ought to be, of anywhere in the world. I think I had hold of the place by the wrong end. Or it had hold of the wrong end of me. The point is, it's all changed now. It's right.

The batch of poems I finished—they were too dark. I'm not going to write that kind of thing again. They were haunted. I thought I was haunted, or the house was, but it was only the work. I'm going to start over.

Do you ever think of it, how as artists we can just start over? I don't suppose a businessman could throw out his business and start fresh. But we can begin again. And that's what I hope to do, if you haven't given away my spot.

Sheepishly, thankfully,

Eddie

THE GHOSTS

Samantha walked the grounds. She wanted to kiss everything. The grass was soaked.

She'd stayed hidden in her rooms when Gamby stomped out of her house at dawn. So it wasn't till noon, when she found Marlon smoking his pipe on the terrace, that she learned about the scene in the big house. Gamby had stalked in and dropped his little daughter off at the breakfast table, asking Josephine to tend to her. Josephine had told riddles, and Fannie went running around the house looking for things that might pass as toys: a pencil and paper, Armand's little jade monkey, a hair clip.

Gamby went through the house opening doors, startling Marceline half dressed. Marlon was heading back to his room for more sleep when he heard a noise above him on the attic stairs. A thundering, a crashing. He thought of the ghost. But no, it was Gamby, descending like an avalanche. Gamby braced himself in the doorway, panting. He said, "The attic may *not* be used for a studio."

"I'm a writer," Marlon said.

"Who the hell's been painting up there?" When Marlon didn't speak—he would have, if he'd known the answer—Gamby exploded. "The attic is a FAMILY space! It has not been offered to you!"

"I don't think it's a studio."

Gamby slammed the door and turned the key in the lock. He

regarded the key with a horror normally reserved for bloody knives. He slipped it in his pocket.

"I'm just a writer."

But by the time Marlon told this all to Samantha, Gamby was long gone. Beatrice, arriving for work, had been so cowed encountering him angry outside the director's house that she'd fetched him both the other copies of the attic key.

In the library that night, Zilla was disconsolate.

Samantha said, "We can pick the lock, I'm sure."

But this wasn't the problem. The problem was the acorns pelting her, the words fading on her hand, the sense that Viktor—look at him in the corner, folded up like an umbrella—was a fate she'd circumvented. And that she wasn't sure if this would be her salvation or her undoing.

Though, yes, the unfinished painting bothered her as well. She hadn't been able to work all day. She'd sat on the fountain, nearly overflowing from all the rain, and stared at the attic dormers, and considered that part of her soul was locked up there, as surely as Violet Devohr had been locked up there. Violet, Violet, dragged here against her will. Was *that* the magnetic force behind her haunting? She was pulled, and so she pulled others. Toward ruin, toward redemption, toward love, away from it. Why? Because she could.

Fannie: "Doesn't he recognize the irony? In *locking* the *attic!*"

Josephine: "I think he's truly that dense."

Outside, the storm was back—violently this time, lightning at all the windows. Marlon said, "In the English department, this is what we would call the objective correlative. Storms of all kinds, outdoors and in."

And on cue there came a shattering thunder unlike any they'd heard before. The glasses clattered on the table.

When the rain finally thinned, when they could count ten seconds between the lightning strikes and their crashes, a

delegation ventured out front: Zilla and Armand and Fannie—
and Alfie, who needed to relieve himself. At first they saw nothing.
Then Armand realized. "The oak," he said. And he pointed to
where the giant oak, the oldest oak, had stood, west of the director's house, taller than any building at Laurelfield, older than the
oldest living turtle. It was utterly gone. A ragged stump stood
maybe four feet high, and a thick mulch of branches and bark and
leaves had formed a carpet for yards and yards around. But there
was no piece thicker than an arm bone, no piece longer than a leg.
Alfie sniffed through it, barking and whimpering.

Fannie said, "Holy mother of God."

Zilla leaned forward at the waist as if she were retching,
though she wasn't. The rain hit her back.

Very late that night, when they were all asleep, she left Laurelfield
without saying anything. Since she hadn't worked in the Longhouse for days, those paintings were dry enough to roll. In the
morning they would find her studio empty, but for a little pile on
the table: rocks, a feather, a dead bee inside a Mason jar.

The attic would not, in fact, be reopened until August of 1954,
when, in those last, calamitous days of the colony, someone called
a willing locksmith and the able-bodied hefted the desks and office machines and cabinets with forty-two years' worth of files up
the stairs. A few files were expunged at that time. Ludo's, for one.
Eddie's, for another.

Zilla came the next year, to visit Laurelfield's grave. She got up
in the attic when Grace and George were out, but her oak leaf
painting—the one held prisoner all those years—was neatly
tacked beneath a window. Its absence would be noticed, and
there was no telling who'd be blamed. And so she decided it
ought to stay. If she couldn't return to Laurelfield, at least part of
her could always remain.

Out on the terrace at midnight, Marlon, terribly soused, his head finally clear: "Only oaks will do that. They always split or explode. And they draw it, they actually draw the lightning to them. *Beware the oak! It draws the stroke!*"

Josephine told him, fondly, to shut his mouth and write a book about it.

Viktor refused to speak.

In 1933, Zilla would watch him dance Albrecht in *Giselle*, his last performance before he vanished. She would sit in the second-to-last row and dart out at intermission.

From 1929 to 1954, forty novels, seven symphonies, fifteen dances, around three hundred stories, and over five thousand poems were completed at Laurelfield. Six times as many of each were begun or continued. Which isn't to mention the concertos and memoirs, the photographs and charcoal sketches. Seventy love affairs were begun, and forty-two were ended. One woman died in the bathtub. A poet hanged herself in the woods. A violin was hurled from the roof. Eight children were conceived. Between 1938 and 1945, seven Jewish artists from western Europe were allowed indefinite stays.

Some of this is a matter of record, the Laurelfield archives having been made public in the fall of the year 2000. Other stories, other sequences of events, are known only to Edwin Parfitt's Olympian gods (if they have survived our neglect) or to the fates, or to the ghosts who keep watch. Count it as the universe's cruelest irony that the ghosts, who alone could piece a whole story together, are uniquely unable to tell it.

One such tale: On October 18, 1944, Lieutenant Armand Cox, a photographer with the Army Signal Corps, climbed onto a barricade in the street outside the Hotel Quellenhof, in the bloody heart of the Battle of Aachen. His interest in the shot was journalistic, not tactical: just a German soldier up in the window. The frame, never developed, captured the soldier's arm mid-motion. The grenade killed Lieutenant Cox, not the eighteen-year-olds below him on the street. His camera landed near his right leg and was, in any event, crushed soon after. In the window boxes of the hotel, there were still geraniums.

A year later, sorting through Armand's things in their Rush Street apartment, Eddie found, in a box in the closet, a photograph of the love of his life, naked, laughing, on the night he first fell in love with him. One of the five copies Samantha had spread throughout the world to prevent Gamaliel Devohr from simply burning Laurelfield to the ground. That night Eddie made his way up Route 41 to Laurelfield, where he stood out back, at the edge of the woods, with a pistol to the flesh behind his chinbone.

He stood there an hour, until he couldn't feel his legs, until he'd become part of the earth, until he thought he might grow leaves. The upstairs lights came on, one by one, as the artists finished their drinks and returned to their work or their trysts. Someone staggered back to the Longhouse. It was a revelation to him, those lights, the shadows behind the curtains: There were artists still up in those rooms, making art. There was good in the world. And the world was worth living in, it truly was. It just wasn't worth being Edwin Parfitt. He had nothing left to write, and he had no one left to love, and he had nowhere left to go. His editor at Holt, himself just returned from the Pacific, had telegraphed that the public awaited his next work, his response to the war. The only thing that could make his grief even less bearable was feeling stared at, waited for. When all he'd ever wanted was to hide inside of something, to crawl inside a piece of furniture and become a mouse.

He wondered if he could move his finger on the trigger.

But look at those lights.

He lay on the ground and put the gun in the leaves. He slept, and as he woke at dawn he remembered a woman he'd met on his last stay, in '41. Armand was already off at training, and it was Eddie's first visit to Laurelfield without him. Her name was Alma Nellis. Hair like grapevine tendrils. This woman would shatter plates against the fountain lip, then mortar them back together in completely illogical ways. The final plate would be vaguely round, but jagged and jumbled. She destroyed and reconstructed an entire tea set this way. Cups no one would dare drink from. "Is it always china?" he asked, and she said, "Next will be a chair."

He wondered if a man, a broken man, could be reconfigured in the same way.

When the sun was up, he knocked at Samantha's door. She held his face in her hands as if he were returning from the dead, as if his had been the dog tags and left arm sent back from Aachen.

Her hair was longer now, wispy. She was softer somehow. She made him toast, and they sat at her table, and they talked about, of all things, the White Rabbits, and Josephine's new solo work, and how she'd taken over the same seventh floor studio in the Fine Arts Building where Armand had once camped out. "She's a worthy inheritor," Eddie said.

Samantha said, "Eddie, I'm dying. I have cancer in my breast."

He had nothing left—the night had drained him—but she understood. She didn't expect anything. After breakfast they walked the grounds. Eddie said, "You'll have to move the fish in soon."

"Eddie, it should be you. The board would hire someone awful. Why can't it be you instead?"

Eddie thought again of the smashed-up plate. He thought of Proteus, shifting shape and evading capture.

"Wouldn't you want to? Wouldn't you want to live here?"

When they finally stopped, at the bench by the pond, he said,

"We've pulled two tremendous stunts here. The Chippeway raid, and the trapping of Gamby Devohr. Let's do one more great and ridiculous thing."

"I doubt I have the energy."

"It's called The Death of the Poet Edwin Parfitt."

On October 29, a small circle of poets and artists and writers—some in residence at Laurelfield at that very time, some farther flung—gave testimony to the police about a drowning by suicide in Lake Glinow, Wisconsin, and the perverse funeral that followed. The artist Zilla Silverman and the composer Charles Ives together paid the hefty fine to the town hall that was all the police could come up with by way of penalty, after their fruitless inquest.

"Proteus Wept," published posthumously in *The American Mercury*, drew quite a bit of attention, as did the man's extraordinary suicide note.

Before her death the following spring, Samantha wrote a letter to Gamby reminding him of the poet Max Perry, "whose acquaintance you made in the summer of 1929. He was the one who took such fine care of your daughter Grace when you were incapacitated. I'm afraid he hasn't made much of himself as a poet since that stay," Samantha wrote, "but he is devoted to the arts, and would be an exceptional steward for Laurelfield. He also has possession of a file of particular interest to you. I expect his guaranteed employment and lodging as caretaker through at least the end of our agreement on September 1 of '54."

As for the artists who stayed there over the next ten years—a very few were friends who recognized him, but most were not. One writer, having been acquainted with Parfitt in Chicago and having mourned his death, wasn't sure if his heart would recover till halfway through his stay. No one left talking about him,

though—they all understood the charge of silence, and admission was, after all, selective—and so to everywhere that was not
Laurelfield, Edwin Parfitt remained dead.

Zilla Silverman, on the other hand: Zilla's was a real suicide. In
February of 1956, a note from Lemuel, saying simply that she'd
poisoned herself. Eddie knew it had nothing to do with Viktor.
By then there had been other men. She'd flung herself at other
closed windows. The windows never broke, but her heart, at the
end, was in splinters. (Nor had Viktor's breakdown had anything
to do with Zilla Silverman. Except that had he found one love,
one great love in his life, she might have kept him off the street,
kept him warm and fed and sane. And Zilla might have been that
love.) Eddie never learned what had changed for Zilla that particular February morning, beyond the obvious, beyond what one
can assume about every suicide: that her unhappiness, in the end,
had outweighed all the beauty of the world. Lemuel brought the
ashes to Laurelfield. Josephine Lizer carved the statue of a bear
that served as Zilla's only headstone—the sculptor's last completed work.

Eighty years after the oak tree exploded, the ground where it had
stood was an especially fertile bed for all those small flowers that
thrive in shade and rich soil: lily of the valley, trillium, Jack-in-
the-pulpit, dog violet, wood sorrel. And there was a little girl
named Emma Grace Herriot, whose mother and father ran the
place. When her parents worked late in the director's house she'd
gather whatever was blooming and tie it together with string and,
on tiptoes, leave the bundles outside studio doors. She had her
mother's curls, her father's half smile. She believed herself to be
in charge of the koi. She ran away silent from the studios, as she'd
trained herself to do. She hoped the surprised artists would believe the flowers were a gift from the ghost.

———

But it was still 1929. And we were in the middle of saying: The oak tree had been blown to toothpicks. When Fannie came back to the library, drenched to her slip, she tried to tell Josephine about it. "You'll see for yourself in the morning. I've never been so startled before by an *absence*, by a shaft of thin air! I wish we could sculpt it. But how do you sculpt something that isn't even there?"

SAMANTHA AT HER WINDOW

There went Ralph and John, on a *Sunday*, bless them, carting wheelbarrow after wheelbarrow of oak shreds back to the fire pile. Hours earlier there had been just a circle of ash, and now already there was a whole new heap to burn. Eddie was down there, for some reason, poking at the pile and talking to the men. He'd seemed utterly changed yesterday, pink and energized.

She plucked a ladybug off the windowsill and dropped it gently onto the leaf of her hydrangea, where it might be happier. There was a lot to do. The hole in the wall was still open, and she ought to give the maid the sheets from Gamby's and Grace's beds. The White Rabbits were leaving tomorrow, and three new residents would arrive the day after. She ought to telephone Zilla and make sure she was all right, that something hadn't happened to Lemuel. And with Zilla gone she'd need to make prints from the negatives herself, the ones they'd told Gamby they already had. At the very least she could wash out the Mason jar from Zilla's studio. She poured the dead bee into the dustbin, rinsed the jar, and left it to dry.

After lunch, as she walked Alfie through the mud, she noticed what looked like a water lily. A folded white flower, at the edge of a puddle. When she got close she saw it was paper. A poem, or part of a poem. Typed, with a few penciled marks. A marvelous line about a tree cased in ice. She smoothed it and took it with her to find Eddie—there were no other poets, it must be his—and then she remembered what he'd said about starting over. But he'd finished twelve poems, and surely he couldn't mean he'd abandoned all of them.

And then, as she and Alfie continued behind the house, she thought of the fire pile, the way Eddie had been lurking there. She trudged off the path and all the way back, till she saw, like ornaments on a Christmas tree, the white rolls stuffed between the splintered oak branches. She glanced around the grounds and saw no one—she could hear Viktor's phonograph, too loud, from the Longhouse—and began pulling them out. Some were hard to reach, and they were all damp, but she couldn't leave them. Eddie was prone to changing his mind, after all, and in a week he might be in tears over their loss. There were more than twenty pages. The endings were signaled by his initials and the date, the beginnings by hand-penciled titles now smeared with the wet. She found one more page off by the composer's cottage, and one by the catalpa.

She let them dry on her kitchen table, and when they were dry she resisted the urge to take them back to Eddie. She clipped them together and set them on the counter.

The next afternoon, when John and Ralph came in to nail the board back to the wall, she told them to wait a moment, and on a whim she folded the stack in half and rolled it to fit in Zilla's Mason jar. She screwed the lid on tight and set the jar in the hole, on the beam where the liquor bottles had been.

John held the board and Ralph nailed it. They'd seen enough strange behavior at Laurelfield that they'd stopped asking questions years before.

PROLOGUE

1900

Virgin land is a fine and great thing. The Irish farmer who'd sold it did nothing with this part, letting decades of decomposing leaves richen the soil. Augustus and his architect, Mr. Ross, walk apace where the trees will let them through. Where the way is narrow, Mr. Ross follows Mr. Devohr.

This plot feels auspicious, not like a place he's seen before but a place he's always been meant to see. What is the opposite of memory? What is the inverse of an echo?

"It's flattest just beyond," Ross says. They are less than a quarter mile back from the road, and Augustus originally imagined even more seclusion, a long ride down a private drive. Ross is right, though, about the space. They've stopped by a massive oak, a tree stately enough to anchor an estate. "Most of your landscape would sit behind the house, then," Ross says. "We might clear a whole pasture, or we might put trails through the woods."

"Violet will want some ornamentals."

A scrawny rabbit stares at them, petrified. Augustus claps his hands and the creature darts away. The snow is long gone, but the mud cracks in brittle, icy sheets under both men's boots. The century is only six weeks old.

Violet, after the long ride from the city, refused to leave the station. He left her sitting on the bench with her travel case, hunched against the cold, and tipped the stationmaster a dollar to keep watch, to see to her lunch. After his visit to Mr. Ross's office, the two men stopped to see that she was still there, a seated statue, hands in her muffler. She insists he's building her a prison in the wilderness. And isn't he? What other choice has she left him?

His own idiocy: the failure to realize, when she abruptly stopped referring to Billy, the boy she'd left behind in Surrey, the boy who'd given her daisies for her fourteenth birthday and swam across the river for her—that it might not be a good sign, an acquiescence to marriage, but a very bad sign indeed. A Dr. W. H. Lambert showed up in Toronto that same year, a fellow Briton, and Violet saw him for her heart, and her women's troubles, which were several in that year after the wedding. Her parents were dead before the newlyweds had even returned from Paris, and there was trouble in the grain market, and Violet lost two babies in the womb, and in short there was so much worry that Augustus was left apologizing for the Devohr curse, not thinking he ought to watch for more bad luck. It was at the Ambulance Association Ball last summer that Violet's brother, back in town, sidled up to Augustus at the punch bowl and nodded at the doctor across the room. "Imagine old Billy Lambert showing up here in Toronto." Augustus was a drowned man.

Mr. Ross is counting his paces, walking what he thinks might be the perimeter of the main house.

"I'd want a wall," Augustus calls. "If we're so close to the road."

"And you'll have neighbors eventually."

When he returns to the station he'll tell her the house will be perfect. He'll tell her that in this new century, on this untouched earth, they will start something noble and good. What will Billy Lambert be, but a memory? What will the babies be, but things that never lived? *For man is man and master of his fate.* All boys ought to memorize that one in school.

And he has made the money that has made escape possible.

Money is freedom, and he will explain it to her again, how this move is the triumph of money over fate and memory—which is, in turn, the triumph of hard work. For what is money but work made tangible and put into the bank?

He imagines he'll take her back to Toronto just for the spring, for the packing of the house, and then they'll stay in Chicago while the new estate is built. They might look, tomorrow, at the homes along Astor Street. Yesterday she said he wants to lock her up. And he said, "Would you rather I had your dear doctor shipped back in a barrel? I'm doing things the proper way."

She looked at him level and said, "You may shut me in, but I can shut you out. There are two sides to every door, Augustus." Her eyes were dark and sharp, and he felt, in that moment, like a lion tamer. Like a man who is only in charge because for now, for a few days more, the lions will still allow it.

He must forgive her. Billy Lambert had the prior claim on her heart. She cannot see Lambert for what he is, a fellow who deals in blood and urine all day, whose coat sleeves are always too short. And Augustus is not without sin.

Violet, maps of blue veins inside her wrists. But where can he follow them? Her eyes, too: windows to what, precisely? He thinks of the Sargent his father briefly owned—a small painting, not a great one, Mrs. de Somebody—how he himself, age twelve, would stare at her eyes, just dark and imprecise daubs of paint, and yet he *knew* her, he felt she might see that he alone loved her truly. And he knew what she was thinking, which changed daily. And now that he possesses a real woman, all her flesh, her eyes are nothing but opaque glass. He is slowly learning there might be greater honesty in art than in woman.

Ross has circled back. He says, "You couldn't do better. It's a fine plot."

"I thought you'd be chalking it off somehow. Something official."

Ross smiles, indulgent. "Why not break a branch to mark the front door?"

He shows Augustus the spot, and a scrubby little tree, leafless, doomed to die with its cousins when ground is broken. Augustus takes hold of a low branch, level with his own face, thin enough to snap but thick enough for the men to find again later.

"I ought to say auspicious words. Aren't we meant to throw wine and salt?"

Ross raises his hand as if lofting a goblet. "A full moon on a dark night, and the road downhill all the way to your door!"

"That should do." The branch breaks cleanly down with an echoing snap and hangs there, swinging, by a strip of skin. It is decided.

Ross says, "I'll come back to mark it. A red ribbon."

He pulls out his watch and shows it, grimacing, to Devohr. It is nearly half past three. The men sprint for the horses, and the horses, cold and unprepared, hurry as best they can back to town.

At the station, Devohr throws his bridle to Ross and dismounts and runs, but he sees, as he nears the platform, that the train is not inching to a stop but to a start. Men who have just disembarked hold their hats to their heads and wait to cross the track. And Violet is not on the bench where he left her. Instead there is a row of brown acorns down the bench arm, lined up and evenly spaced. She hoards small things, collecting them in columns and stacks: coins and pebbles and beetle wings. Once, he found it charming. Now he wonders what strange math she's doing with the trinkets. The world is her abacus. She is calculating against him.

He searches frantically for the stationmaster, but then he sees, gliding past above, more slowly than if she were walking, Violet's face in the window.

He shouts her name, and she looks down, but just a bit, and he isn't sure she's seen him. He refuses to run along the platform like a fool in a French novel. He can keep pace by walking, for at least a moment, and he thinks what can be done. He could take Ross's horse, but it's more than thirty miles to the city. He might track down an automobile. If nothing else, he can wire the Palmer House and make sure she arrives, make sure she's seen to.

The train picks up a bit of speed, and he'll trot, but just barely, not for much longer. Above him, she has put her white knuckles to the window and is knocking, slowly, listlessly. Looking straight at him now, with no expression at all. A cruel and pointless knocking: not to get out, and not to call him in. As if to demonstrate, simply, that the glass is thick.

He can almost hear the knocks, above the hiss of steam and the sound of the pistons. But he can't, he knows he can't. It's in his head. The train only gets louder, and it only moves forward.

He will see her tomorrow, in the city, but this feels for some reason like the last glimpse of her he'll ever get: staring through him, pale and inscrutable behind the glass.

Oh Violet, Violet, Violet! He wants to shout it, but he won't.

Let me in.

Let me in.

Let me in.

ACKNOWLEDGMENTS

This is a novel about, among other things, how much artists need a community. These are a few of the communities that have sheltered me during the writing of this book:

The wonderful people of Viking and Penguin: Kathryn Court, Lindsey Schwoeri, Scott Cohen, Veronica Windholz, Nina Hnatov, Nancy Resnick, and Kristen Haff; as well as Josh Cochran, who gave Laurelfield the red sky it needed.

The stupendous Nicole Aragi (the Queen of Pentacles) and Duvall Osteen.

A phalanx of early editors: the writers M. Molly Backes, Alex Christensen, John Copenhaver, Tim Horvath, Brian Prisco, and Emily Gray Tedrowe; and the readers (the world needs more readers like them) Shelley Gentle, Margaret Kelley, and Pamela Minkler.

The friends who let me bother them about technical details (and aren't responsible for my errors): the writer David M. Harris on series ghostwriting; the writer Margaret Zamos-Monteith and the photographer Matthew Monteith on photographic history and 1920s darkrooms; Edward McEneely on WWII history (so much work for so few words!); and my social media hive-mind for everything from the drying time of oil paint to oak stump decomposition to pry bars.

The Sewanee Writers' Conference, where the first chapters were encouraged, and where Christine Schutt's kind read convinced me to keep working on this book.

The colleges on Chicago's North Shore that have been kind enough, in the time since I originally drafted the first part of this novel, to welcome me to campus or let me teach. The college in this book is explicitly *not* based on any of those institutions.

The Ragdale Foundation and The Corporation of Yaddo, and everyone I met at both, whose work–from sonnets to paintings to smashed teacups–has inspired my last few years. What sort of world would this be, without refuges?

My family–Jon, Lydia, Heidi, Mom–who have been, variously, great editors and/or less requiring of diaper changes than they were three years ago.

Also, all five of the people I've forgotten.

This book started as a short story about male anorexia. I have no idea what the hell happened.

^{THE} Forbidden

Also by F. R. Tallis

(writing as Frank Tallis)

FICTION

Killing Time

Sensing Others

Mortal Mischief

Vienna Blood

Fatal Lies

Darkness Rising

Deadly Communion

Death and the Maiden

NON-FICTION

Changing Minds

Hidden Minds

Lovesick

THE
Forbidden

F. R. TALLIS

PEGASUS CRIME
NEW YORK LONDON

THE FORBIDDEN

Pegasus Books LLC
80 Broad Street, 5th Floor
New York, NY 10004

Library of Congress Cataloging-in-Publication Data is available.

ISBN: 978-1-60598-555-8

10 9 8 7 6 5 4 3 2 1

Printed in the United States of America
Distributed by W. W. Norton & Company

Acknowledgements

I would like to thank Wayne Brookes, Catherine Richards, Clare Alexander, Sally Riley, Steve Matthews and Nicola Fox for their valuable comments on the first and subsequent drafts of *The Forbidden*. I would also like to thank Brendan King for answering questions about J.-K. Huysmans's characters in *Là-Bas*, Owen Davies for answering questions on magic books and the capture of demons in glass, and Dr Yves Steppler for alerting me to the existence of TTX.

PROLOGUE

1872

Saint-Sébastien,
an island in the French Antilles

During the great siege of Paris I had worked alongside
one of the Poor Sisters of the Precious Blood. Her name
was Sister Florentina and it was she who had written to
me, advising of a vacancy that had arisen for a junior
doctor at the mission hospital on Saint-Sébastien. Perhaps it was because of the dismal autumn weather and
the heavy rain that lashed against my windows, but I
immediately fell into a reverie of sunshine and exotic
landscapes. Throughout the day, these images played on
my mind and I began to take the prospect of Saint-
Sébastien more seriously. I envisaged learning about rare
diseases, visiting leper colonies and embarking on a kind
of medical adventure. That evening, sitting in a shabby
restaurant with sticky floorboards and frayed tablecloths,
I looked around at my glum companions and noticed

that, like me, they were all regulars: two dowdy seamstresses, a music teacher in a badly fitting dress and a moribund accountant with greasy hair. By the time I had finished my first course, I was already composing my letter of application and, two weeks later, I was standing on the deck of the paddle steamer *Amerique*, a vessel of the General Transatlantic Company, bound for Havana.

The Saint-Sébastien mission hospital consisted of a low, whitewashed building in which the patients were cared for by nuns under the general direction of a senior medical officer, Georges Tavernier. Outpatients were seen in a wooden cabin just removed from the hospital, and next to this was a tiny church. Every Sunday, a priest arrived in an open carriage to celebrate Mass.

My new superior, Tavernier, was an easy-going fellow and dispensed with formalities as soon as we met. When I addressed him with the customary terms of respect, he laughed and said, 'There's no need for that here, Paul. You're not in Paris now.' He was a bachelor in his middle years, of world-weary appearance, with sagging pouches beneath his eyes and curly, greying hair. In repose, his features suggested tiredness, fatigue, even melancholy, but as soon as he spoke his expression became animated. He was a skilled surgeon, and during his ten-year residency on Saint-Sébastien he had acquired a thorough understanding of tropical diseases and their treatment. Indeed, he was the author of several important papers on the subject and had invented a very effective anaesthetic ointment that could be used as an alternative to morphine.

The hospital was situated some distance from the capital, on the edge of a forest which descended by way of gentle undulations to a mangrove swamp. Our only neighbours occupied a hinterland of scattered, primitive villages, so it was fortunate that Tavernier and I enjoyed each other's company. He often invited me to dine at his villa, which was perched high on the slopes above the hospital, an old plantation owner's residence that had seen better days – an edifice of faded stucco, crumbling pillars and cracked bas-relief. We would sit on the terrace, smoking and drinking aperitifs. The view was spectacular: a solitary road winding its way through lush vegetation down to Port Basieux, the busy harbour, boats swaying at anchor, the glittering expanse of the sea. As the sun sank, a mulatto girl would light hurricane lamps and bring us plates piled high with giant lobster and crab, mangos, pineapples, sapodillas and yams. The air was scented with hibiscus and magnolia and sometimes we were visited by armies of brightly coloured frogs or a curious iguana.

Tavernier was keen to hear about my experiences during the Paris siege, and he listened attentively.

'The winter was merciless. People in the poor districts – driven mad through starvation – were breaking into cemeteries, digging up corpses and making gruel with pulverized bones.' I paused to light a cigar. 'One evening, while walking back from the hospital to my lodgings, I came across a shocking scene. A building had been shelled and the road was obstructed by fallen masonry.

Through the smoke, I could see men rushing about, trying to put out fires. I climbed up the bank of rubble and, on reaching the top, saw a pale arm sticking out from the wreckage below. I scrambled down and began removing the bricks that were piled around it. The skin was smooth and it was obvious from the delicacy of the elongated fingers that they belonged to a woman. "Madame!" I shouted, "Can you hear me?" I took her hand in mine and pulled a little. To my great horror the entire arm came away. It had been detached from its owner by the blast and the lady to whom it belonged was nowhere to be seen.'

Tavernier shook his head and lamented the folly of war; however, his mood could change quite suddenly. The siege had exposed profound social inequalities and I was illustrating this point with a revealing anecdote. 'Along the boulevards, the best restaurants remained open and when the meat ran out, they simply replenished their stock with zoo animals. Patrons were offered elephant steak, stewed beaver and camel fricassée.'

Tavernier slapped his thighs and roared with laughter, as if the horrors I had only just described were quite forgotten. I came to realize that, although his clinical judgement was sound, in other respects Tavernier could be quite wayward.

Naturally, I had wondered why it was that such a talented individual was content to languish in relative obscurity. He was not devout and his specialist knowledge would have made him a valuable asset in any of

4

the better universities. I began to suspect that there might be a story attached to his self-imposed exile and indeed, this proved to be the case.

One night, we were sitting on Tavernier's terrace, beneath a blue-black sky and the softly glowing phosphorescence of the Milky Way. A moist heat necessitated the constant application of a handkerchief to the brow. Again, much of our conversation concerned Paris, but our talk petered out and we sat for a while, listening to the strange chirrups and calls that emanated from the trees. Tavernier finished his rum and said, 'I can never go back.'

'Oh?' I said. 'Why not?'

'My departure was . . .' he paused, considering whether to proceed. 'Undignified.' I did not press him and waited. 'A matter of honour, you see. I was indiscreet and the offended husband demanded satisfaction. Twenty-five paces – one shot, the pistol to be brought up on command.'

'You killed someone?'

Tavernier shook his head. 'He didn't look like a duellist. In fact, he looked like a tax inspector, quite portly, with a ruddy complexion. After agreeing to his conditions, I learned that he had once been a soldier. You can imagine what effect this information had on me.'

I nodded sympathetically.

'The night before,' continued Tavernier, 'I couldn't sleep and drank far too much brandy. When dawn broke, I looked in the shaving mirror and hardly recognized myself: bloodshot eyes, sunken cheeks, my hands were trembling. A thought occurred to me: *This time tomorrow you will be dead.* My seconds arrived at seven o'clock. "Are you all right?" they asked.

'"Yes," I replied, "quite calm."

'"Have you had breakfast?"

'"No," I replied. "I'm not hungry." Another gentleman, the doctor, was waiting in the landau. I shook his hand and thanked him for coming. When we got to the Bois du Vésinet, the other carriage was already there. I looked out of the window and saw four men in fur coats, stamping their feet and blowing into their hands to keep them warm. My seconds got out first, and then the doctor, but I found that I couldn't move. The doctor came back and said, "What's the matter?"

'I was paralysed. It was obvious that I wouldn't be able to fulfil my obligation. "I'm sorry," I said. "I'm not feeling very well – a fever, I think. I'm afraid we'll have to call it off." I was taken back to my apartment, where I spent the rest of the day in bed. In the morning I made arrangements to leave and have not been back since.' Tavernier gazed up at the zenith. A shooting star fell and instantly vanished. 'I disgraced myself. But at least I'm alive.'

'Honour is less important these days,' I said, 'now that the whole country has been disgraced. You could return, if you really wanted. And who would remember you? Ten years is a long time.'

'No,' said Tavernier. 'This is my home now. Besides, there are other things that keep me here.'

I didn't ask him what these 'other things' were, but I was soon to find out.

That year, the carnival season began late, and I was aware of a growing atmosphere of excitement. Preparations were being made in the villages and some of the patients were eager to be discharged for the festivities. I paid little attention to all of this activity, assuming that the season would pass without my involvement. Then, to my great surprise, I received an invitation to attend a ball.

'Oh, yes,' said Tavernier. 'The de Fonteneys always invite us.'

'The de Fonteneys?'

'They're local gentry,' he pointed towards the volcanic uplands. 'Piton-Noir.'

'Are you going?'

'Of course I'm going. I go every year. I wouldn't miss it for the world!'

It had been a long time since I had attended a social function and I felt increasingly nervous as the date approached. The de Fonteneys were a very old family, having settled in the Caribbean during the reign of Louis XIV. I was not accustomed to mixing with such people and thought that I would appear gauche or unmannered. Tavernier told me to stop being ridiculous. When the day of the ball finally arrived, we were allowed to use the mother superior's chaise, so at least we were spared the indignity of arriving on foot. We took the Port Basieux road and, on reaching the coast, began a steep ascent. A large, conical mountain loomed up ahead, rising high above the cultivated terraces. This striking landmark was La Cheminée; its sporadic eruptions, over a period of many thousands of years, had created the Saint-Sébastien archipelago. A ribbon of twisting grey smoke rose from its summit.

We reached a crossroads, at which point the chaise came to a juddering halt.

'Straight on, Pompée,' said Tavernier.

Our driver seemed uncomfortable. He began to jabber in a patois which I found difficult to follow. Something was disturbing him and he was refusing to proceed. He pointed at the road and jumped down from his box.

'For heaven's sake, man,' Tavernier called out. 'Get back up there and drive!'

More fulminating had no effect, so Tavernier and I alighted to see what Pompée was looking at. A primitive design had been made on the ground with flour. It consisted of a crucifix, wavy lines and what appeared to be a row of phallic symbols.

'What is it?' I asked.

'A vèvè,' said Tavernier. 'A bokor – a native priest – has put it here to invoke certain spirits. Pompée thinks we will offend them if we pass it.'

'Is there an alternative route?'

'No. This is the only road to Piton-Noir.'

Tavernier and his servant continued to argue and as they did so I heard the faint sound of a drum. Pompée stopped gesticulating and looked off in the direction from where the slow beat was coming. The sun had dipped below the horizon and the looming volcano made me feel uneasy.

'Are we in danger?' I asked.

'No,' Tavernier replied. 'It's just superstitious nonsense.'

He stomped over to the vèvè and scraped his heel through its centre. The effect on Pompée was immediate and melodramatic. He cowered and his eyes widened in terror. Tavernier kicked at the ground, producing a cloud of flour and red dust, and when the vèvè was utterly destroyed he turned and said, 'See? It's gone. I had expected Pompée to respond with anger, but instead, he now seemed anxious for his master's safety. He removed an amulet from his pocket, an ugly thing of beads and hair, and insisted that Tavernier take it. Tavernier accepted the charm with an ironic smile and we returned to the chaise. Pompée leaped up onto his box and struck the horse's rump. He was eager to get away, and for some obscure reason so was I. When the steady pulse of the drumbeat faded, I was much relieved.

We entered the de Fonteney estate through an iron gate and joined a train of carriages. An avenue of torches guided us to an impressive facade of high windows and scalloped recesses, and as we drew closer, the strains of a chamber orchestra wafted over the balustrade. We were announced by a liveried servant and welcomed by the Comte de Fonteney, who addressed us with the slow finesse of an aristocrat. With brisk efficiency, we were then ushered into a dazzling ballroom full of mirrors, gilt embellishments and the portraits of bewigged ancestors. The dancing was already under way. I proceeded to the other end of the ballroom and stood on my own, watching the revellers. In due course, a young woman appeared at my side and we began to exchange pleasantries. She was small and strangely artificial, like a doll. Her eyelashes were long and her ox-bow lips were the purple-red of a ripe cherry. I asked her to dance and she offered me her hand. Her name was Apollonie. Afterwards, she introduced me to her cousins, all of whom were of a similar age and dressed in lustrous silks. They surrounded me, like exotic birds, with open, quivering fans and asked me many questions about Paris: what were the society ladies wearing, where did they shop and which operettas were most popular? I allowed myself a little inventive licence in order to retain their attention. At midnight, the ball ended and I went outside with Tavernier to wait for our chaise. I had enjoyed myself and was reluctant to leave.

'Ah,' said Tavernier. 'You are thinking of that coquette I saw you dancing with. And why wouldn't you: she was very pretty. But I'm afraid it can't go any further. We are only welcome here once a year and, if I'm not mistaken, your little friend was the governor's daughter.' I sighed and he gripped my arm. 'Don't be downhearted. Look, there's Pompée. Might I suggest that we stop off in Port Basieux. I know some places there that I'm sure will cheer you up.'

We drove down to the harbour and kept going until we came to the docks. Behind the warehouses were some narrow streets. Tavernier ordered Pompée to stop outside a crudely painted shack and tossed him a coin. I could hear the muffled sound of carousing from inside. 'Wait here,' said Tavernier to the driver, 'and don't drink too much.' I followed Tavernier into the shadows, traipsing down alleys and passageways until we came to a shabby building with shuttered windows. We walked around to a side entrance, where, hanging from a post, was a candle burning in a red paper lantern. Tavernier knocked and we were admitted into the hallway by a plump middle-aged woman, wearing an orange silk turban and paste jewellery. She greeted Tavernier warmly and led us up a staircase to a small room containing only some wicker chairs and a small card table. We sat down, lit cigars and five minutes later two women entered, one a negress, the other a mulatto. They were carrying bottles of rum and wore no shoes or stockings on their feet. Tavernier reached into his pocket, took out Pompée's amulet and handed it to me with a wide smile. 'Here, take this.'

'Why are you giving that to me?' I asked.

'The last thing I want right now,' he said, 'is protection from wickedness.'

The following night, I found myself dining again with Tavernier. Nothing was said about the brothel: it was as though we had never been there. The heat was oppressive and I was being eaten alive by mosquitoes. After we had finished our meal, my companion leaned across the table and said, 'Why did you become a doctor, Paul?' He had been drinking excessively and his speech was slurred.

'My father was a doctor, as was his father before him. It was always assumed that I would uphold the family tradition.' I was not being entirely candid and Tavernier sensed this. His eyes narrowed and he made a gesture, inviting me to continue. 'When I was a child, perhaps no more than eight or nine, my father took me to an old church. It must have been situated somewhere in Brittany, which was where we usually went for our summer holidays. The nave was long and empty. On both sides were arches and, above these, high, plastered walls that had been decorated with some kind of painting. At first, all that I could see was a procession of pale figures, hands joined, against a background of ochre. It reminded me of that nursery entertainment. You must have seen it done: whereby artfully cut, folded paper can be pulled apart to reveal a chain of connected people. As my eyes adapted to the poor light, I became aware that every other figure was a skeleton. My father told me that the mural was called a Dance of Death. He crouched down, so that his head was next to mine, and identified the different characters: friar, bishop, soldier, constable, poor man, moneylender. "Everyone must die," said my father. "From the most powerful king, down to the lowliest peasant, Death comes for everyone." I was beginning to feel frightened and experienced a strong desire to run back to the porch. "But look at that fellow there," my father continued, pointing his finger, "the fellow wearing long robes, do you see him?" His voice had become warmer. "How is he different from the rest?" Where my father was pointing, I saw a figure, flanked, not by two skeletons, but by a man and a woman. He was the only human participant in the dance who was untouched by Death. "Do you know who he is?" my father asked. I had no idea. "He is the doctor. Only the doctor can persuade Death to leave and come back another day only the doctor has such power." From that moment onwards, my destiny was set.'

Tavernier's expression was enigmatic. 'What a peculiar child you must have been, to have found the idea of vanquishing death appealing: such vanity in one so young!'

I had never thought of myself as a proud person and was quite offended by the remark. 'You are being unfair, Georges,' I protested. 'I merely wanted to help others, to save lives.'

Tavernier smiled and said, 'Paul, you are such a romantic!' Then, taking a swig of rum straight from the bottle, he added, 'No good will come of it!'

Most Sundays, Tavernier and I made an effort to attend Mass – it was judicious to keep up appearances. One week, as the nuns were departing with their charges, we noticed that the priest had been delayed by one of the villagers, a short, wiry man, who was becoming increasingly agitated. Tavernier loitered and tilted his head. 'That's interesting,' he muttered.

'What is?' I asked.

Tavernier silenced me with a gesture and continued to eavesdrop. The exchange we observed was short-lived and ended when the priest issued a severe reprimand. He then climbed onto the open carriage, made the sign of the cross and set off down the Port Basieux road. Tavernier went over to the villager and struck up a conversation. I tried to follow the patois, but, as usual, found it incomprehensible. When Tavernier returned, he said, 'A young man passed away last week, his name was Aristide, do you remember?' It was custom for the recently bereaved to walk the local byways, proclaiming their loss like a town crier, and I did indeed remember a woman calling out that name. 'Well,' continued Tavernier, 'that fellow there,' he pointed to the receding figure, 'is Aristide's father. He came to ask Father Baubigny to pray for the release of his son's spirit.'

'I'm not sure I understand.'

'He believes that Aristide's soul is still trapped in his body. His son has become one of the living dead.'

'I'm sorry?'

'A spell was put on the boy and the day after his funeral, he was spotted in the forests below Piton-Noir.'

'How absurd,' I said. 'No wonder Father Baubigny was angry.'

'I'm afraid I must disagree,' said Tavernier. 'The people of this island believe many stupid things; however, the existence of the living dead is something that I would not dispute. Father Baubigny was wrong to castigate Aristide's father, who will now have to seek another solution – not that Baubigny's prayers would have done any good. Funeral rites, as practised by the villagers, consist almost entirely of efforts to make death real and lasting. In my opinion, they have good reason.'

I assumed, of course, that Tavernier was joking, but there was no light of humour in his eyes. Indeed, he spoke with uncharacteristic gravity. One of the nuns reappeared and called out to us. A patient had collapsed. Tavernier and I ran to assist, and our conversation was brought to a premature close.

The following evening, Tavernier returned to the subject while we were eating. 'That man who came to see Baubigny yesterday – Aristide's father – he's been down to Port Basieux. He consulted a bokor, who has agreed to lead a search party tomorrow night. They're going to find the boy and release his soul.'

'How do you know all this?' I asked.

'Pompée told me. He's related to the family and intends to join them. They're meeting in the village at sunset.'

'Why don't they just look in the grave?'

'They have. The coffin was empty.'

'Then the body has been stolen?'

'Yes, in a manner of speaking.'

'In which case, the family should inform the police. If a crime has been committed, then the perpetrator should be identified and arrested.'

'Someone removed the soil and opened the coffin. But that was the full extent of their grave-robbing: the thing that Aristide has become emerged from the ground without further assistance.'

'Come now, Georges,' I said. 'This joke is wearing thin.'

Tavernier looked at me in earnest. 'I know that there is nothing I can say that will persuade you. I was sceptical too, once.' He paused to light a cigar. 'But you don't have to accept my word. We could join the search party.' He blew a smoke ring which expanded to encircle his face. 'Then you could see for yourself.'

I was beginning to wonder whether he was not merely eccentric, but slightly mad. Even so, the intensity of his expression made me enquire: 'You're being serious?'

'Yes,' said Tavernier. His eyes glittered.

Removing a handkerchief from my pocket, I wiped the perspiration from the back of my neck. 'All right,' I said. 'I'll go.'

Something like a smile played around Tavernier's lips. He flicked some ash from his cigar and nodded once.

The next day, I began to have second thoughts. Tavernier had not, on reflection, been a very good influence. Although he had taught me a great deal about tropical medicine, he had also introduced me to the brothels of Port Basieux and now I too shared his proclivities: his appetite for dusky flesh and depravity. I did not like to degrade women in this way, to use them as objects of pleasure, and I frequently resolved never to return. But

I discovered that I was weak and the prospect of gratification was a siren call that I could not resist. Thus it seemed to me that I was about to take another step down a headlong path. Even so, as the hours passed, I did not make my excuses. Instead, I met Tavernier at the appointed time, and as the sun was setting, we accompanied Pompée to the nearest village. On our arrival, I saw men carrying torches, mothers and children huddled in doorways and a nimble man wearing a straw hat, cravat and ragged trousers posturing as he danced around a green and red pole. He was rattling something in his hand and anointing the points of the compass with water. I noticed the carcasses of two chickens at his feet.

Tavernier leaned towards me and whispered, 'The bokor from Port Basieux.'

Pompée marched over to the village elders, among whom stood Aristide's father. When Pompée spoke, they all turned at once and looked in our direction. Their expressions were not hostile exactly, but neither were they welcoming. Tavernier responded by raising his arm.

'Are you sure we should be here?' I asked.

'I took Pompée in as a child,' said Tavernier. 'He was only eleven years old. The people of this village know that I can be trusted.' His allusion to 'trust' made me feel uneasy and I wondered what confidences I would be expected to keep. The burden of complicity would weigh heavily on my conscience. I regretted not having acted on my earlier misgivings. Pompée returned and spoke a few words to Tavernier, who then said: 'We'll walk a short distance behind the party. We are guests and must show respect.' The bokor picked up a bamboo trumpet and honked out three notes, the last being extended until his breath failed. This signalled his readiness to begin the search, and when all the men were assembled, he led them down the road. Pompée, Tavernier and I fell in at the rear. A hulking, muscular giant stopped walking and stared back at us. There was something about his general attitude that I did not like, and I was not surprised when he spat on the ground. Pompée said something to Tavernier.

'Georges?' I asked, anxiously.

'Keep walking,' Tavernier replied.

As we drew closer, the man spat again.

'Georges? Why is he doing this?'

'Just keep walking!' said Tavernier, impatiently. The giant shook his great head, turned on his heels and loped away, quickly catching up with the other villagers. 'There, you see?' Tavernier added, forcing a laugh. 'Nothing to worry about.'

I was not convinced.

After travelling only a short distance, the bokor took a pathway which branched off into a forest. Our noisy arrival disturbed the sleeping birds. There was squawking, the beat of wings and a general impression of flight overhead. When the fluttering died down, the night filled with other sounds: frogs, insects and the rustle of larger animals in the undergrowth. We seemed to be heading across country in the direction of Piton-Noir, and in due course, when we finally emerged from the trees, we were presented with an awesome spectacle. The summit of La Cheminée was emitting a baleful red light, which rose up to illuminate the underside of some low-lying clouds. A sparkling fountain erupted into the sky, climbing to a great height before dropping back into the wide vent: at once both beautiful and terrible.

The bokor was not distracted by the eruption. He sniffed the sulphurous air and led us into another forest, so dense with convolvulus and wild vine that the men had to hack their way through with cutlasses. The heat was intolerable and my clothes were drenched with perspiration. Eventually, we came to a clearing. The bokor signalled that we were to be quiet and, crouching low, he crept across to the other side. I could hear what I imagined was a beast making noises, but as the sound continued I realized that the source was human. It reminded me of the glottal grunts and groans of a cretin. The bokor let out a shrill cry and the men sprang forward. We chased after them, through a line of trees, and then out into a second, smaller clearing, where we discovered a young man, not much older than sixteen, chained to a stake. He was naked but for a soiled loincloth, and his eyes were opaque – like pieces of pink coral. He held his arms out, horizontally, and began to walk. His legs did not bend at the knee and he achieved locomotion by swinging his upper body from one side to the other. After he had taken only a few steps, the chain was stretched to its limit and he was prevented from proceeding any further. His head rotated and he seemed to register each member of the search party. When his gaze found me, his body became rigid. I will never forget that face, those hideous, clouded eyes and the fiendish smile that suddenly appeared. It was as if he had recognized an old friend. I willed him to look away, but his fixed stare was unyielding. A low muttering started up and quickly spread around the clearing. There was something in its sonorous tremor that suggested unease.

'Why is he looking at me like that?' I said to Tavernier through clenched teeth.

'I have no idea.'

The bokor shouted, waved his hands and succeeded in capturing the young man's attention. His head swivelled round and I sighed with relief. The bokor then began to chant and shake his rattle while performing a ballet comprising of sudden leaps and awkward pirouettes. While he was doing this, I heard him say the name 'Aristide' several times. There seemed to be no question as to who this captive creature was. The boy bellowed like a bullock and, as he did so, his father fell to the ground, releasing a plangent cry of his own. My intellect recoiled, unable to reconcile the evidence of my senses with what I understood to be impossible. I was overcome by a feeling of vertigo and feared that I might pass out.

When the bokor had completed his ritual he was given a cutlass. I saw reflected fire on the curved blade. There was a sudden silence, a flash of light and the sound of steel slicing through air. Aristide's head dropped to the ground and his open arteries produced a shower of blood that fell around us like heavy rain. The decapitated body remained erect for a few seconds before toppling over and hitting the ground with a dull thud. I watched in dumb amazement as a gleaming black pool formed around the truncated neck. The men descended on the remains of Aristide like vultures. There was more chopping as the body was cut up into parts small enough to bundle into hemp sacks. When the butchering was complete, the men began to disperse, leaving no evidence of their handiwork, except for an oval stain.

'My God!' I exclaimed, grabbing Tavernier's arm. 'They've killed him.'

'No. He was already dead, or as good as.'

'But he was breathing, standing up – walking!'

'I can assure you, he wasn't alive in any meaningful sense of the word.'

'Georges, what have we been party to!'

Tavernier grabbed my sopping jacket and gave me a firm shake. 'Pull yourself together, Paul. Now isn't the time to lose your nerve.'

I was about to say more but he shook me again, this time more violently. His expression was threatening. I spluttered an apology and struggling to regain my composure, said, 'Let's get away from here!'

We set off at a quick pace, stumbling through the undergrowth. I had not taken the trouble to get my bearings, and assumed that Pompée would negotiate our safe return. Eventually, we came to the location overlooked by

La Cheminée, and once again our progress was arrested by its infernal magnificence. The low-lying cloud was now fretted with purple and gold, and a thin rivulet of fire trickled down the mountain's steep slope. There was a sound, like the crump of distant artillery, and a halo of orange light flickered around the summit. Some burning rocks rolled down the leeward slope and a column of billowing ash climbed into the sky.

There was some movement in the vegetation and, when I turned, I found myself looking into the crazed face of the bokor. He jumped forward, brandishing a knife, and at that same moment I was seized from behind.

'Georges?' I cried out.

Tavernier raised his finger to his mouth. 'Be quiet. And whatever you do, don't try to escape.'

I could sense the size of the man standing behind me, and guessed that it was the giant who had demonstrated his contempt for us by spitting on the ground as we were leaving the village. The bokor rose up on his toes and pressed his nose against mine. His stinking breath made me want to retch. Out of the corner of my eye I saw glinting metal and was fully expecting to be stabbed. But instead I felt a sharp pain on my scalp as the bokor grabbed a tuft of my hair. He then brought the blade up and deftly cut it off. Still keeping his face close to mine, he hissed something incomprehensible and then barked at Tavernier.

'He wants you to know,' said Tavernier, 'that if you tell anyone what transpired tonight, you will die.'

'Yes,' I nodded vigorously. 'Yes, I understand. I won't tell anyone.'

'He wants you to swear,' Tavernier continued. 'I would suggest that you invoke the Saviour and name some familiar saints.'

'I swear. I swear in the name of Our Lord, Jesus Christ, Saint Peter and Saint John, and the Blessed Virgin Mary. I swear, I will tell no one.'

The bokor withdrew, taking a few steps backwards, then, pointing a wrinkled, thick-boned finger at my chest, he suddenly screamed. His cry was so loud, and chilling, that even the giant flinched. The bokor's eyes rolled upwards until only the discoloured whites were exposed, and he began muttering the same phrase, over and over again.

'What is he saying?' I asked Tavernier.

Tavernier sighed. 'He's says that if you break your oath, you will be damned – and that you will go to hell.'

The muttering abated and the bokor fell silent. His irises reappeared and he drew his hand across his mouth in order to remove some foamy saliva. For a few seconds, he seemed disorientated, but he quickly took possession of himself and signed to his accomplice. The powerful arms that were restraining me relaxed, and a few seconds later the bokor and the giant were gone.

Anger welled up in me. 'What in God's name . . . ?'

'I'm sorry,' said Tavernier.

'"Sorry"? You said that there was nothing to worry about! You could have got us both killed tonight!'

'No,' said Tavernier shaking his head. 'I don't think so. You are not known to these people, and what happened back there . . .' Tavernier gestured into the trees and then shrugged. 'The bokor was simply anxious to be assured of your discretion. Please, my friend, I have no wish to argue. We are both tired and the sooner we get back, the better.' He then instructed Pompée to proceed, and reluctantly I followed. When we reached the church, Tavernier said, 'You look like you could do with a drink.' His face was flecked with dried blood. 'You'd better come with me.' I wanted to storm off into the night, but I also felt a pressing need to make some sense of what I had witnessed, and Tavernier was the only person I could talk to.

'Yes,' I replied, swallowing my pride. 'I think you're right.'

Seated on Tavernier's terrace we gazed out over the balustrade at a swarm of fireflies. The trembling points of lights were strangely calming. Even so, it took several glasses of rum to restore my customary disposition.

'Well,' said Tavernier. 'You can't say I didn't warn you. I did tell you that such things existed.'

'I don't understand. You have always said that their religion was nonsense.'

'Gibberish! Of course it is.'

'Then how . . . ?'

'Allow me to explain.' Tavernier handed me a cigar, and then, after lighting one for himself, he leaned back in his chair and exhaled a cloud of smoke. 'A feud has existed for many years between Pompée's relations and another family who live in one of the Piton-Noir villages. Aristide was accused of stealing one of their goats and, shortly after, he became very ill. A rumour quickly spread that he had been bewitched by the Piton-Noir bokor and, sure enough, the boy became very ill and died. But his death was – how can I put this? – an imposture. In fact, he had been given a poison which paralyses the diaphragm and retards respiration. Under its influence, the heart slows and the pulse cannot be detected.'

'An asphyxiant?'

'Indeed. It can be derived from many sources: the skin of the puffer fish, certain lizards and toads, the venom of the small octopus, and it is many times more potent than cyanide.' Tavernier poured himself another glass of rum. 'The anaesthetic ointment I invented uses the same substance. In very small quantities, applied topically, it has a numbing effect. The bokors have been using it to engender a death-like state in their victims for nearly two centuries. Of course, they pretend that they have achieved their ends by sorcery, that they can kill by sticking pins into effigies and that they can raise the dead, but the truth is more commonplace. Their magic is chemical, not supernatural. Needless to say, more often than not, they miscalculate dosages and when they open a coffin they find only a rotting corpse inside; however, very occasionally they meet with success. The victim has survived and the poison has begun to wear off. The bokor can then command the occupant to climb out and he, or she, will obey. Living dead are remarkably docile, having suffered significant brain damage due to lack of oxygen.'

As Tavernier was speaking, a question arose in my mind. 'If the bokors are anxious to maintain the illusion of their possessing magical powers, then I must suppose that they also guard their secrets closely. How is it, then, that these mysteries were revealed to you?'

'I introduced one of them to morphine and when he was addicted, I told him that I wouldn't supply him with any more unless he explained how the deception was accomplished.' Tavernier produced a wide grin. 'It was child's play!'

'Why were you so interested?'

'Soon after my arrival here, a young woman with whom I was acquainted died, and the following week I saw her stumbling around behind the brothel where she formerly plied her trade.' He adopted a frozen attitude, raising his eyebrows theatrically. 'It gave me quite a shock, I can tell you, but I'm a sceptic by nature. I knew there would be a rational explanation and immediately began to make enquiries.'

I was unnerved by Tavernier's matter-of-fact manner. Unwanted images kept on invading my mind: the rain of blood, the decapitation, the mob dismembering the fallen body, the fitful orange light around the summit of La Cheminée.

'What's the matter? asked Tavernier.

'We have just witnessed a murder,' I said, flatly.

'No, Paul, you are quite mistaken. We have just witnessed the liberation of a soul. Aristide had become the slave of a bokor. Can't you see what that means to the villagers? For them, there is nothing worse than slavery. It is a fate worse than death.' A drum began to sound and its jaunty rhythm was almost immediately supplemented by another. 'See?' Tavernier continued. 'They're celebrating. Aristide is free now. He can join the ancestral spirits.'

I stubbed out my cigar and said, 'Perhaps we should report what we saw to the authorities.'

Tavernier laughed. 'The authorities? Go on then, go down to Port Basieux and tell them what happened. Do you honestly think that they'll be the slightest bit interested? Now, if a horse had been stolen from one of the plantations, that would be a different matter . . .' He waved a languid hand in the direction of the drums, leaving a trail of cigar smoke. 'The life of a villager has no monetary value. It is of little consequence to the authorities.' He stood up and strolled over to the balustrade. 'Anyway,' he continued, gazing out into the darkness. 'It wouldn't be such a good idea for you, having made a promise to the bokor. You promised to say nothing. If you break that promise, you'll go to hell. That's what he warned. Remember?' When Tavernier turned round, he was grinning like a maniac and his head was surrounded by darting points of light. Unsurprisingly, I did not find his irony amusing.

PART ONE

Damnation

1

AUTUMN 1873

Paris

I returned from Saint-Sébastien to a Paris that, although
not quite recovered from its humiliating defeat, was
starting to show signs of restored confidence. As soon as
I had found somewhere to lodge, I wrote to my father,
and we met shortly after to discuss my prospects. I was
becoming increasingly fascinated by the nervous system
and was keen to learn more from an expert. Indeed, ever
since that fateful night when I had witnessed the murder
of Aristide, I had become preoccupied with the brain and
its workings. I wondered to what extent consciousness
was preserved in the living dead? What – if anything –
did they experience? These sober reflections prompted
broader philosophical inquiries, concerning the mind and
its relation to the body.

'Duchenne,' said my father. 'That is who you should
work with.'

This seemed an absurd suggestion. Guillaume Duchenne de Boulogne was the leading authority on nervous diseases. He had been an early advocate of electrical treatments, had made advances in the field of experimental physiology and was the first doctor to use photography as a means of recording laboratory and clinical phenomena.

'Why should he employ me?' I asked.

My father then explained that we were distantly related. A letter was written, and a week later I received an invitation to visit Duchenne's laboratory. He was of sage appearance, possessing a bald, flattish head, thick eyebrows, strong nose and long, bushy side whiskers that stopped just short of meeting beneath his chin. I learned during the course of our conversation that his son, Émile, had died during the Paris siege after contracting typhoid. Émile had been Duchenne's assistant and the old man had made no attempt to find a replacement. Perhaps he was feeling lonely, or maybe our distant kinship influenced his thinking; whatever the cause, Duchenne was disposed to offer me the position formerly occupied by his son, and I accepted without hesitation.

Shortly after commencing my work with Duchenne, I read his handbook on batteries, pathology and therapeutics. Needless to say, I was already aware that electrical devices were routinely employed to treat a variety of medical conditions, but had never before come across examples of their use to resuscitate. I was surprised to learn that Duchenne had been conducting experiments in this area for almost twenty years. One of his earliest case reports concerned a pastry cook's boy, a fifteen-year-old who – because of some imaginary trouble – had imbibed a large quantity of alcohol before climbing into his master's oven, where he fell asleep and became asphyxiated. He was found the following morning and his apparently lifeless body dragged out. As luck would have it, the doctor lodging above the bakery happened to be Duchenne. The boy had stopped breathing and no pulse could be felt with the hand, although a feeble murmur was heard through the stethoscope. A battery was swiftly brought down from Duchenne's rooms and an electrical charge was delivered to the boy's heart. After a few seconds, slow and weak respiratory movements appeared and in due course he gave a loud cry and began to kick. His circulation and respiration were re-established, his colour returned and he was soon able to answer questions.

Other attempts to resuscitate are recorded in Duchenne's handbook, but he was careful not to exaggerate his achievements. He offered a balanced review. Most of the cases he reported were only partial successes: temporary recovery, followed by the final and complete loss of vital signs. Even so, I was fascinated by these findings and wanted to learn more. Duchenne was an obliging mentor and demonstrated his method using rats as experimental subjects. Each animal was chloroformed until it stopped breathing and general movements ceased. Then, electrodes were touched to the mouth and rectum, until convulsive movements and twitching provided the first evidence of reanimation. As with human subjects, outcomes varied. Most of the animals did not respond at all to electrical stimulation, some enjoyed a brief recovery which lasted a few minutes, but one or two rats from each basket were successfully brought back to life.

In his middle years, Duchenne had become interested in the physical mechanisms underlying the expression of human feelings. He had shown that, by applying electrodes to the face, it was possible to stimulate muscular contractions and manufacture emotion. His photographic record of these experiments was reproduced in a landmark publication, *The Mechanisms of Human Facial Expression*. It is a masterpiece of medical portraiture. For the work of a man of science, Duchenne's preface begins with a surprisingly unscientific assertion. He states that the human face is animated by the spirit, and I suspected that, although he had ostensibly been engaged in identifying the muscle groups that excite the appearance of emotion, the true nature of his project was somewhat deeper. For Duchenne, there was no tension between religion and Enlightenment values. The presence of God could be felt as strongly in the laboratory as in a cathedral. He was not really studying facial expression, he was studying the soul.

Duchenne's notebooks were filled with observations and ideas which were worthy of more extended treatment. I suggested that some of this material might be incorporated into academic articles that I was willing to draft. He did not object and we worked together on several papers that were eventually published. One of them took the form of a comprehensive review of the literature on resuscitation.

At that time, I made no connection between Duchenne's pioneering attempts at resuscitation, which began in the 1850s, and his subsequent book on facial expression, which appeared some ten years later. Had I been more astute, I would have discerned a natural progression. There was a reason why Duchenne wanted to study the soul, but I would not discover that reason for several years, and then only on the night that he died.

I chose to work late and when my labours were completed, Duchenne would invite me into his parlour, where we would sit and talk until the street sounds diminished and there was silence outside. On one such occasion, we were discussing a rare form of palsy, when Duchenne suddenly said, 'There's a fine example just admitted into the Hôpital de la Charité. Let's see how the poor fellow's getting on.' He rose from his seat and went to fetch his coat.

'What?' I replied, 'Now?'

Duchenne looked at me askance. 'Yes. Why not?'

And so it was that I discovered my mentor's peculiar habit of visiting hospitals at irregular hours. He did this so often that his appearance on wards at two or three in the morning was usually greeted with indifference by the nurses. On arriving, he would usually check up on his patients and then look for interesting cases. He was permitted such liberty, not only because of his considerable reputation, but also because of his impressive virtue. If he discovered an impoverished patient with a painful condition who could not afford to continue treatment, Duchenne invariably offered his services without charge. I remember him moving between the beds on the wards, a gaunt figure, passing in front of the faintly glowing gaslights, head bowed as if in prayer, administering drugs with the gentle authority of a priest giving Communion.

We were particularly welcome at the Salpêtrière, because the chief of services and recently appointed chair of pathological anatomy, Jean-Martin Charcot, was a former pupil of Duchenne. Under his canny stewardship the Salpêtrière, previously an insignificant hospice, was already on the way to becoming a neurological school of international renown. More like a city within a city than a medical institution, the Salpêtrière consisted of over forty buildings arranged around squares, markets and gardens. It even had its own church, a baroque edifice with an octagonal cupola, large enough to accommodate over a thousand congregants. Although Charcot was a proud man, whenever we encountered him he always treated Duchenne with the utmost respect, and if accompanied by an entourage of students, he would introduce his old teacher (a little too theatrically, perhaps) as 'the master'.

After a year as Duchenne's assistant, I had settled into a very comfortable routine. The possibility of finding employment elsewhere had never occurred to me. However, one day, Duchenne informed me that Charcot was looking for someone young to fill a post at the Salpêtrière and he advised me to apply. I protested, but Duchenne was insistent. 'I cannot be responsible,' he said, 'for holding you back. This is a splendid opportunity and I will be mortified if you do not take it.' He sent a letter of recommendation to Charcot and, such was his influence that news of my official appointment, when it arrived, was a mere formality.

As a junior doctor I was obliged to attend Charcot's Friday morning lectures, which at the time of my appointment were still relatively modest affairs. Long before his arrival, the auditorium would begin to fill, not only with physicians, but also with curious members of the public: writers, artists or journalists. The platform was littered with posters mounted on stands, showing enlargements of microscopic slides, family trees and different categories of neurological illness Brain parts floated in jars of preservative next to dangling skeletons with deformed joints. The doors would fly open, revealing Charcot, accompanied by an illustrious foreign visitor and a troop of assistants. He would ascend to the podium, pause, allow the silence to thicken and then start his address in sombre tones. Occasionally, he would stop and illustrate his observations with skilful drawings on a blackboard, or ask one of his assistants to man the projector, and images would suddenly materialize on a hitherto empty screen. Charcot was never a great orator, yet he knew how to manage a performance and compensated for his deficiencies with solid, reliable stagecraft.

I was never entirely comfortable in Charcot's presence. I found him too self-conscious, too obviously the author of his own legend. He was humane, told jokes, and abhorred cruelty to animals, but essentially he was an authoritarian. None of his interns dared to question his theories. It was common knowledge that some of our predecessors had been dismissed for voicing imprudent objections. Irrespective of my reservations concerning his character, our professional relationship was friendly and collegiate. He was favourably disposed towards me, probably because of Duchenne's letter of recommendation, and our meetings were always agreeable. I was accepted into Charcot's inner circle and began to receive invitations to his soirées; these became, like his Friday lectures, an obligatory fixture in my diary.

Charcot lived in a cul-de-sac adjoining the busy Rue Saint-Lazare, situated between the train station and the Church of the Trinity. It was a substantial if not particularly striking residence, which belied his prosperity. He had married a young widow who, in addition to inheriting her deceased husband's fortune, was also (being the daughter of a highly successful clothier) independently wealthy. This shrewd connection ensured Charcot's complete financial security and guaranteed his admission into the upper echelons of society.

38

The Salpêtrière was an energetic hospital and its corridors reverberated with academic debate. There was a kind of fervour in the air, fuelled by the constant thrill of discovery. Although my feelings towards Charcot were mixed, it would be churlish to deny that he was an inspiration. Because of his patronage, I was introduced into a talented fellowship and profited greatly from the lively conversation of my peers. When I was sufficiently established, I accepted more clinical responsibilities and the additional remuneration I received enabled me to secure better rooms. Life was good, but for one sad event: the death of my old teacher, Duchenne de Boulogne.

When I received news of Duchenne's illness, I immediately sent a message, informing him that I was at his disposal. He declined my offer of assistance but requested that I visit him at my earliest convenience. This note of urgency filled me with apprehension. He had obviously determined that his remaining days were few in number. An arrangement was made for me to call on him the following evening, which – as Duchenne had suspected – proved to be his last.

A storm broke as I travelled to his apartment. Thunderclaps preceded a downpour of exceptional ferocity. My driver had to stop twice: once to don his oilskins, and a second time in order to calm the horses. When we arrived at our destination, I thanked him for persevering. A maid escorted me to Duchenne's bedroom, and when I entered I was shocked by his appearance. He was sitting up in bed, his back supported by pillows, a frail, desiccated creature, with grizzled side whiskers. As I closed the door, he began to stir.

'Paul, is that you?' His voice was barely a croak.

'Yes, it's me.'

I crossed the room, sat at his bedside and noticed that he was clutching a wooden crucifix. He released the object from his grip and reached towards me, whereupon I took his hand in mine and squeezed it gently.

'Thank you so much for coming,' he said. 'It's a terrible night. Listen to that rain.' Then, twisting his neck so he could see me better, he added: 'How are you? Are you keeping well?'

His solicitous remark brought me close to tears.

'I am very well.'

'Good. I wish I could say the same. But, as you can see, I am very weak. Indeed, I fear that I have little chance of making a recovery. Still . . .' He left his sentence unfinished, and shrugged, suggesting that he was confronting the prospect of death with equanimity. He did not dwell on his predicament, but instead made some polite enquiries about my duties at the Salpêtrière. When I had finished answering his questions he closed his eyes and became very still. It seemed that he was no longer breathing: a flash of lightning transformed his face into a collection of hollows and cavities. My anxiety subsided when his eyes opened again and he whispered, 'Lately, I have been troubled by certain matters that I now wish to talk to you about.' He paused and seemed a little uncomfortable, even embarrassed. 'The first of these concerns my son, Émile. I am sorry to say that I misled you. He did not die during the siege. He became ill . . . mentally ill. It was necessary to have him interned at the asylum of Saint Anne in Boulogne-sur-Mer. He is still there today.'

'Do you want me to visit him?' I asked, 'Check that he is being properly looked after?'

'No, no. Provision has been made for his care. Besides, I would not dream of burdening you with such a commitment. You understand, I hope, that I do not wish to die with a lie on my conscience.'

'It is perfectly understandable that you should—'

'That is the first matter,' Duchenne interjected, raising his hand to silence my protest. 'There is also a second.' He swallowed and moistened his dry lips with his tongue. Another flash of lightning was followed by a colossal thunderclap. 'Paul, you were always interested in resuscitation.'

'Indeed.'

'It is regrettable that resuscitation by electrical stimulation is rarely attempted. The field has hardly progressed since the publication of my early reports, yet I still believe that this is a branch of medicine that promises to be of the greatest benefit to mankind. I can envisage applications beyond the remit of clinical practice. Batteries might prove to be a kind of philosophical tool.'

I supposed that he wanted to hear that I intended to continue his work, and I offered him some bland promise, to the effect that, if the opportunity arose, I would certainly resume a programme of laboratory experiments. As I spoke, he seemed to become impatient and he interrupted me again. 'No, Paul. There is more. Please, allow me to finish.' He sighed and added, 'I have struggled, not knowing whether it is right or wrong to . . . God created a lawful universe. If science lifts the veil . . . it is revelation, and revelation is divine.' His speech became incoherent and I wondered if he was slipping away, but another clap of thunder seemed to bring him back. 'Paul?'

'Yes, I am still here.'

'Do you remember case number six in my book on therapeutic applications?'

'The woman asphyxiated by carbonic oxide?'

'I lost her, but when stimulated, her respiration was restored. In my summary, I stated that she regained her intelligence and that she was able to give me information about what had happened to her. A few hours later she sank into a coma again and died.' He pointed at a jug on the table and I poured him a drink. He took a few sips from the glass and then continued. 'My summary is incomplete. When she regained her intelligence, it is true that she gave me information about what had happened to her, but it was not information about her symptoms. In fact, she spoke of an experience.' A faint smile appeared on his face, and retrieving the wooden crucifix, he pressed it against his heart. 'A remarkable experience.'

I was unsure what he meant by this. 'What? She recollected something from her past?'

'No. Between going and returning she saw things.'

He seemed to be making such an extraordinary claim that I thought it prudent to seek clarification. 'Between going and returning? You are referring to the time that elapsed between the woman's death and her being revived?'

'Precisely!' He found some last reserve of energy and beat the blanket with his clenched fist. 'Yet she saw things.'

'Some kind of hallucination?'

'No. What she saw was no hallucination. She was entirely lucid and the very specific terms she employed to describe her experience persuaded me of its authenticity.'

As he spoke, I felt as if the world outside was receding; the cascade that tumbled from the gutter, the keening wind that rattled the window panes all of these sounds became a distant murmur. Even now, I can remember his lips moving, the sense of being drawn in – a tremor of excitement passing through my body, scepticism becoming interest, and interest becoming wonder. That night, my life was changed forever.

2

Duchenne's death had made me more contemplative, more inward-looking. Instead of dining with friends, I preferred to go for solitary walks by the river. I would steal into empty churches and sit, deep in thought, until the light faded and the gloom intensified. I sought out booksellers who stocked works of theology, and found myself buying copies of Augustine and Aquinas. What I had previously dismissed as sterile debate, pointless sophistry, I now approached with interest.

It was about this time that I first encountered Édouard Bazile. The circumstances of our meeting were unremarkable and I did not suspect that one day we would become close friends. He had engaged me to treat his wife, who was suffering from progressive loss of hearing. Prior to seeing me, she had consulted a number of doctors, none of whom had been able to improve her condition. I had been recommended to the Baziles by one of my former patients, a librarian with peripheral nerve disease. After examining Madame Bazile, I decided to use one of Duchenne's electrical therapies – a risky undertaking because the tympanic membrane is very delicate and stimulation with strong currents can cause total deafness. I advised Madame Bazile of the dangers, but she was insistent that we should proceed, and, after six administrations, her hearing was fully restored. Needless to say, I did not expect to see the couple again.

Several months passed, during which I moved to pleasant rooms on the ground floor of an apartment block in Saint-Germain. The great church of Saint-Sulpice was only a few streets away, and this remarkable building, magnificent and austere, became my habitual refuge. I familiarized myself with its interior, the Corinthian columns, grand arches, carved dome and chapels, the gilded pulpit, the exquisite statue of Mary as the Mother of Sorrows and its trove of curiosities.

One evening, as I was leaving Saint-Sulpice, I heard someone call my name, and when I looked up I saw a short, stocky man, with longish black hair and an untrimmed beard and moustache. He removed his hat and I immediately recognized Édouard Bazile. We shook hands and I enquired after his wife. There had been no recurrent problems and he thanked me again for my help. Our exchanges were cordial and I mentioned, in passing, that I had just moved to the area and was fond of visiting the church.

'Well,' he said, 'you must let me show you around the north tower.' I had a dim recollection of his occupation having had some connection with ecclesiastical life, but its exact nature escaped my memory. Indeed, it is possible that he had never been very precise. He detected my confusion and added, 'That is where Madame Bazile and I live. I am the bell-ringer.' We arranged to meet by the chapel of Saint Francis Xavier the following afternoon.

Bazile was already waiting when I arrived at the appointed time. Removing a key from his waistcoat pocket, he unlocked the door, invited me through, and we commenced our ascent up a winding staircase. Eventually, we came out onto a narrow wooden ledge. I was suddenly overcome by anxiety. I felt disorientated, unsteady, and feared that I would fall.

'We're a long way up.'

'About halfway.'

Shafts of light entered the tower through tilted panels. I looked down, and saw a complex arrangement of joists and beams that descended into darkness. Among the lattice of timbers was an array of enormous bells. They were oddly fascinating. Bazile directed my attention upwards, where I saw yet more bells, floating magically. I noticed bright patches on the inside of each one, where the surface had been repeatedly struck by the clapper.

'Glorious, aren't they?' said Bazile. 'For me, they are much more than pieces of metal. They are like people; each bell has its own personality.' He smiled and added, 'Did you know that they are baptized? It is a Church tradition. And as they grow older, their voices change, mellowing with age.'

I felt the air move, a ghostly caress on my cheek. The woodwork creaked and the bells began to rock.

'In the Middle Ages,' Bazile continued, 'bells were cast

by itinerant founders who would travel all over France. Villagers would throw their valuables into the boiling bronze, their jewellery, candlesticks and family heirlooms – the things that they loved most – thus creating a unique alloy which gave the bell its individual voice. The bell embodied the virtue, the generosity of the people, and its chime was supposed to comfort the sick and repel evil spirits. It is no coincidence that when we think of home, the place where we were born and raised, more often than not, we think of an area which corresponds roughly with the sounding of a particular church bell.' He brushed a cobweb from his sleeve and added, 'There is more to see.'

Another climb brought us to the stone arches beneath the roof of the tower. We were in a rotunda, the floor of which was perforated by a circular hole surrounded by rusty iron railings.

'You can lean over, monsieur. It's quite safe.' I peered into the abyss. 'Would you like to go all the way to the top?' Bazile pointed at another staircase.

'Not today. Thank you.' I was still feeling a little unnerved by my attack of vertigo.

Bazile was an erudite man. As we talked, it became apparent that – at least with respect to the church and its history – he was extremely knowledgeable. I asked him how it was that he knew so much, and he replied, 'When I was younger I wanted to be a priest. I was admitted into a seminary, but left after only a few years. I suppose I had a . . .' he hesitated before adding, 'crisis.' I was tempted to press him for more information but resisted the urge. Bazile's eyes widened and I thought he was about to disclose more, but suddenly he turned away and spoke over the void. 'I came to Paris and became the assistant of a scholarly priest at Notre-Dame. He was a very wise man and taught me a great deal. Indeed, I learned more about Church history and theology from him, than I'd ever learned at the seminary.' He paused again and stroked the rusty rail, dislodging a few red flakes. 'Although I had decided against taking Holy Orders, I still wanted to maintain a connection with the Church, to serve God daily, but I wasn't at all sure how I would achieve this. Then, quite by chance, I came across several works on campanology in the priest's library – *De Campanis Commentarius* by Rocca and *De Tintinnabulo* by Pacichellius, wonderful books – and it occurred to me that bell-ringing might be just the solution to my predicament. I served an apprenticeship, right here, in Saint-Sulpice, and when the old bell-ringer died, I took his place.'

The gentle breeze outside was now gathering strength, and an eerie wailing filled the rotunda. I raised the collar of my coat. 'Ah,' said Bazile. 'You are cold, monsieur. On our way down – if you are not in a hurry – we could, perhaps, visit my rooms. I'm afraid I can't offer you a brandy, but I have some very good cider.'

Bazile's lodgings were located directly beneath the bells. We entered a spacious parlour with rough stone walls, semi-circular windows, and a vaulted ceiling. The floor tiles were partly covered with a faded rug and the furniture was rustic in appearance. A stove stood in the corner. Its thick pipe crossed the ceiling and disappeared through a canvas sheet that had been used to replace a broken pane of glass. Next to the stove was a bookcase packed with volumes. The air smelled of cooking: not a stale smell, but homely and pleasant.

Madame Bazile appeared, and, to my great mortification, delivered a lengthy eulogy. The term 'miracle worker' was used. I objected, but she would not be contradicted. When her stock of superlatives was finally exhausted, she produced a ceramic pitcher full of cider and two tankards. Bazile and I sat at the table, where we smoked, drank and continued our conversation. It was to be the first of many, for we were, in a sense, kindred spirits, and soon recognized in each other a common sensibility. There are those who discern in felicitous meetings the hand of Providence, and, I must admit, the timely entry of Édouard Bazile into my life did feel as if it had been arranged for my benefit. I had become preoccupied, isolated, and needed to unburden myself. I needed someone to talk to about theology, mysticism and the meaning of existence, a believer, but a believer for whom faith did not also mean the disavowal of reason. Bazile was such a man. He embodied these qualities and possessed many more that I would learn to appreciate as our friendship deepened.

From that day forward, whenever Bazile discovered me, either seated at the back of the nave, or pacing the aisles of Saint-Sulpice, he would greet me and we would start a conversation that could only be satisfactorily concluded several hours later, seated at his table in the north tower. We agreed to meet on a more regular basis. I would arrive with a leg of lamb for Madame Bazile to cook, and she would prepare it beautifully with a purée of turnips and caper sauce. After dinner, Bazile would light his pipe and we would talk until the candles had burned down and the sconces were overflowing with wax.

For many months, I remained silent on the subject that I needed to speak of most and when finally I confided in Bazile, I did so almost by accident. We were discussing, as I recall, logical proofs for the existence of God.

'What could be more convincing,' said Bazile, 'than the moon, the sun and the stars? Or this room, with me and you sitting in it? There is something here,' he struck the table with a rigid forefinger to emphasize his point, 'when, so easily, there might have been nothing. Aristotle informs us that all effects have their causes. It is a universal principle and utterly irrefutable. God's effects are the proof of his existence. There must have been a first cause, and that first cause was God. Of course, some would say that logic has no place in theology. It is not a view I subscribe to, but one must recognize that the human mind has its limits. We cannot expect reason to supply answers to all of our questions.'

'My teacher, Duchenne de Boulogne, would never have accepted such a position. He was a scientist, but also deeply religious. He studied facial anatomy, because he believed that our expressions are animated by the soul, and he believed in the soul because—' I stopped myself mid-sentence.

'Yes?'

'Because he knew that something of us survives death: he had no doubt about this, and his unshakeable conviction was based on strong evidence.'

'He dabbled in spiritualism?'

I shook my head. 'Do you remember the machine I used to treat Madame Bazile – the battery? It can also be used to resuscitate '

'What?'

'It can be used to bring patients back to life after they have died.'

Bazile took his pipe from his mouth and looked at me in disbelief.

'If the heart fails,' I continued, 'a jolt of electricity can sometimes start it beating again.'

'I did not realize medical science was so advanced.'

'The method is far from reliable and most patients are afforded only a temporary reprieve. Typically, those who have undergone the procedure report nothing. Death is experienced as a loss of consciousness, like dreamless sleep; however, there was one exception, a woman who claimed to have had what might best be described as an encounter.'

Bazile could see that I was hesitant, and poured me another drink. I thanked him, sipped the sweet liquid and said: 'She told Duchenne that her soul had risen up from her body, and that she had found herself floating just beneath the ceiling. Looking down at the lifeless person below, she registered the closed eyes and bluish pallor – the right arm hanging limp off the side of the bed. She observed Duchenne, dashing out of the room and returning with a battery. The woman was not frightened. On the contrary, she felt very calm and pitied the doctors and nurses, who appeared agitated and distressed. She wanted to say to them, "Do not worry, there is no need, I am perfectly comfortable and happy." The hospital melted away and the mouth of a tunnel materialized in front of her. She glided, without effort, into the opening and coasted towards a light that was emanating from the other end. Her speed increased, she was drawn rapidly through space and expelled into an expanse of uniform brilliance. It was not light as we understand it, but rather something far more wondrous and pure. She said it was like being irradiated with love. This experience was utterly overwhelming: rapturous, ecstatic. She sensed an immanence in the light and presumed that she must be in the presence of a higher being, an emissary.'

Bazile frowned. 'An emissary? What did she mean by that?'

'The woman remained in this state of blissful suspension for an indeterminate period of time. Then, quite suddenly, she was pulled by a powerful force back into her body. Duchenne was standing over her, removing the electrodes from her chest. She felt no joy, only a terrible, crushing sadness. She wanted to return to the light. When her condition had stabilized, she told Duchenne what she had experienced. Two hours later, she became comatose and died; however, at the moment of death, Duchenne observed something very strange. She smiled. And her smile seemed to be directed at someone, or something, quite invisible.'

The creases on Bazile's forehead deepened. 'Extraordinary, a fascinating account, but . . .' He hesitated before adding, 'Deathbed visions are not so uncommon. Ask any parish priest and he will tell you such stories. How the blacksmith's wife claimed to see the Virgin Mary or the baker's daughter heard a heavenly choir. They might, or might not be, authentic. We can never know. Is it not possible that Duchenne's patient was simply hallucinating?'

'Édouard, dead people do not hallucinate. Her heart had stopped and there was no blood circulating through the arteries of her brain. There was no breath in her lungs. Only a living brain is capable of dreams and hallucinations. Moreover, her observations of Duchenne's activities, made while she was unconscious, were entirely accurate.'

'Ah,' said Bazile. Removing the now-extinct pipe from his mouth, he tapped it against the table leg in order to dislodge a plug of tobacco and fell into a troubled reverie, during which he worried the tangled mass of his beard with restless fingers. After a very considerable interval, he said, 'If I am not mistaken, you have just recounted the most compelling evidence for life after bodily death ever reported. Would it not be appropriate, therefore, to inform the scientific community of Duchenne's remarkable discovery?'

'It was Duchenne's dying wish that I should continue his work and offer the world irrefutable proof of the life hereafter. He hoped that the provision of such evidence would change the hearts of men: that if people knew, with absolute certainty, that they would one day be judged by their Maker, they would not stray so easily from the path of righteousness.'

'And did you agree to do as he asked?'

'I did.'

Bazile pressed his palms together. 'A grave responsibility.'

'Indeed. And thus far, I have done nothing.'

3

1876

I began my programme of research using animals: rats, initially, and then stray cats. There was no shortage of equipment at the Salpêtrière and I had use of the very latest chloride of silver batteries. Death was 'administered' by means of chloroform intoxication. A particularly successful trial resulted in one of my cats being revived after an unprecedented four minutes. She was very weak, but over the next two days she regained her strength and was able to chase a ball of paper tied to a piece of string. As far as I could tell, she had retained all of her feline faculties. On the morning of the third day I gave her a dish of milk and a sardine that I had saved from my breakfast, and released her into the hospital grounds. She scampered off and soon disappeared from view.

Only two opportunities arose where I could attempt the electrical resuscitation of humans. Both were patients with epilepsy whose vital functions ceased during particularly violent seizures. The first of these, a middle-aged man, never regained consciousness; the second, a young woman, 'awoke' in a delirium that lasted for thirty minutes before she fell into a coma and passed away. Even so, I was not discouraged. The results of my experiments on animals were very promising, and I had in mind some procedural modifications that I was eager to test on human subjects.

I continued to visit Bazile, and my research was a frequent topic of conversation. He was usually excited by news of any developments, however, one evening, his reaction was somewhat muted.

He chewed the stem of his pipe and seemed ill at ease. 'It is not possible to know the mind of God and I would not presume to do so. Be that as it may, it seems to me that the finality of death communicates something of His purpose. If He had meant there to be traffic between this world and the next, then would He have troubled to erect so great a partition?'

'That is a problematic argument,' I replied, 'because if you apply it consistently to all natural phenomena, you arrive in great difficulty. Take illness, for example. If God had meant us to be in good health, then he wouldn't have permitted diseases. It follows, therefore, that the practice of medicine must be irreligious. No one, however, would endorse such a view. Indeed, healing the sick was fundamental to Christ's ministry.'

'But death seems so . . .' Bazile paused, searching for an appropriate word, 'decisive! To reanimate a dead body, to snatch a departed soul back from eternal rest, might seem to many Christians to be something,' he winced before adding, 'unnatural.'

'When holy men perform miracles they are made into saints. What is a miracle, if not unnatural? The Church has always rewarded the violation of natural laws!'

'Resuscitation is indeed miraculous, but it may not be miraculous in quite the same way, as, let us say, the feeding of the five thousand.'

I smiled mischievously. 'Perhaps not, though surely it bears comparison with the raising of Lazarus. And are we not told, even as children, to learn from Christ's example?'

Bazile conceded the point, but I could see that he was still uneasy.

Months passed, autumn became winter, and I received a letter from a surgeon at the Hôtel Dieu (at that time, this the oldest hospital in Paris was being rebuilt, and the new building – situated next to the cathedral – was nearing completion). He had recently read my review of the literature on electrical resuscitation – the one I had co-authored with Duchenne – and there were several technical matters that he wished to discuss with me. These were too numerous to be addressed by post, so I agreed to meet Monsieur Soulignac at a private dining room above a restaurant on the Boulevard Saint-Germain.

The man who greeted me was in his mid-forties and immaculately dressed. He had blond hair which glistened with a generous application of pomade, blue eyes and a neatly trimmed beard and moustache. His questions were not difficult to answer and the next few hours passed agreeably. By the time the brandy and cigars arrived, we were in our shirtsleeves and feeling very much at ease.

Soulignac spoke candidly: 'Surgeons have been slow to take advantage of electrical devices. The old methods of resuscitation are still favoured by nearly all of my colleagues. Inflate the lungs, apply pressure to the abdomen, and then start praying!' He exhaled a cloud of yellow smoke and shook his head. 'I have been using batteries for nearly a year now, and without doubt, more of my patients survive crises as a consequence. I have been able to revive patients whose hearts were barely beating and would otherwise almost certainly have died. But I have yet to save a single patient whose heart was already stopped. And I have tried on many occasions.'

'Perhaps you should acquire a more powerful battery,' I suggested. 'Duchenne used to swear by his volta-faradic apparatus. It was heavy and cumbersome, but could still be carried in an emergency, and its graduating tubes could measure the weakest doses as exactly as the strongest.' I told Soulignac about my animal experiments and the cat I had returned to life after four minutes. He declared the result 'extraordinary'.

The atmosphere in the room became hazy with cigar smoke, almost conspiratorial, and I found myself talking about my father and that long ago day in Brittany when he showed me the Dance of Death and I had resolved to become a doctor. It transpired that Soulignac had had a similar epiphany when he was much the same age, coinciding with the tragic and horribly premature death of his mother.

'One of my patients told me something. . .' said Soulignac. He seemed to become lost in deep introspection.

'Oh?' I responded, reminding him of my presence.

'A civil servant . . . I really thought there was no hope. He wasn't breathing, but I detected a faint beat – not even that, a murmur – an undertone. I stimulated his heart, his pulse returned, and, remarkably, he regained consciousness a few minutes later. He was very feeble, but he reached out, gripped my arm and was insistent that I listen to him. "It's all true," he said, "all true," and he proceeded to describe a visionary experience.'

The account that followed corresponded exactly with the testimony of Duchenne's case number six. As Soulignac described the tunnel, the light and the sublime being, I was, at once, both excited and disturbed.

'Now, I do realize,' Soulignac continued, 'that the whole thing could have been the product of a brain starved of oxygen and nutrients, but I can't bring myself to believe that. Perhaps you will consider me foolish, but I think there was more to it. You see, this gentleman, he was a down-to-earth fellow. During his convalescence, I visited him many times, and we discussed his vision in minute detail. He said that what he had experienced was nothing like a dream. Indeed, he maintained that it was the very opposite – a more immediate and vital reality. He confessed that prior to his resuscitation he had been a lifelong atheist. Yet, when he was discharged, he went directly to a monastery with the intention of dedicating his life to Christ.'

I did not respond and Soulignac mistook my silence for disapproval.

'You will say it was a hallucination,' he added, somewhat embarrassed.

'Not at all,' I said plainly. 'One of Duchenne's patients, a woman resuscitated after carbonic oxide asphyxia, reported something very similar.' I told him of my mentor's deathbed confession. When the waiter appeared, more to impress upon us the lateness of the hour than to be of service, we ignored his dyspeptic expression and ordered more cigars.

It became clear to me, as the night wore on, that Soulignac's interest in electrical resuscitation was as much motivated by spiritual curiosity as a desire to advance medicine, and that our ultimate purpose was identical: the provision of scientific evidence for the existence of the soul and its survival after bodily death. We both recognized that, by combining our resources, this objective could be realized more readily. I, a neurologist and erstwhile assistant of the great Duchenne, had access to a variety of batteries and was already embarked upon an impressive programme of animal experiments. Soulignac, a surgeon habituated to the frequent loss of patients in the operating theatre, had ample opportunity to test the new procedures I was developing. Those successfully brought back to life could be asked about their experiences, and we might, over time, collect their testimonies together for publication. The appearance of such an article in a respected professional journal would cause a sensation. When we finally made our way downstairs and out onto the deserted street, we did so flushed with alcohol and exhilarated by the audacity of our ambition.

Three months after our initial meeting, an amputee whose heart had stopped for almost a minute was resuscitated by Soulignac using the chloride of silver battery I had been using on my stray cats. The man awoke from his temporary extinction and informed Soulignac that he had been to a world of brilliant light and while there he had conversed with his dead wife. The man died two days later, but not without having first provided his surgeon with a comprehensive account of an astounding voyage to the frontier of eternity.

The first time I saw Thérèse Courbertin was at one of Charcot's soirées. We were introduced and exchanged only a few words before Henri Courbertin, an associate professor, swept her away, keen to show off his pretty new wife to the other guests. His behaviour occasioned some mischievous comments the following day. Courbertin was a decent man – artless, amiable, with a cheery bedside manner – but he was ageing badly. Thin strands of hair, raked across his crown and fixed by unguents, did little to disguise the fact that he was almost bald, and his bulging waistcoat struggled to contain a hefty paunch.

Courbertin had returned to his home town in order to find a wife, and, I imagine, by backwater standards, he must have cut an impressive figure: the distinguished and prosperous physician from the big city. One could appreciate how his reputation, generosity and solid virtues might appeal to a certain type of woman, eager to escape the tedium of provincial life.

After an initial burst of social activity, Thérèse Courbertin was seen less and less, and once the Courbertins' son Philippe was born she wasn't seen at all. When questioned about his wife's health, Courbertin replied that she was well and enjoying motherhood. In fact, she was suffering from depression, but this – I would later discover – was something that Courbertin found difficult to come to terms with. I suspect that he blamed himself (rather than a post-partum disturbance of metabolism) for his wife's unhappiness. Doctors are notoriously bad at coping with illness when it arises in their own homes.

Several years passed before Thérèse Courbertin started to appear in public again. The Charcots had crossed the Seine and now occupied a wing of the Hôtel de Chimay, a mansion on the Quai Malaquais. I can remember watching Madame Charcot as she guided a tall, elegant woman around the parlour, drawing her attention to particular pieces of art, and suddenly realizing that this fine lady was none other than Thérèse Courbertin. It was remarkable how much she had changed.

On a subsequent visit to the Hôtel de Chimay, somewhat bored by the company, I excused myself and found a solitary spot by one of the full-length windows where I could look out and enjoy a view of the river. I became absorbed by the play of light on the water and was startled when I heard a female voice say, 'It's beautiful, isn't it?' I turned, and there was Thérèse Courbertin, standing right next to me. We began a conversation but I have only the vaguest recollection of what was said. I can only recall the smoothness of her skin and the luminosity of her eyes.

We tended to seek each other out at Charcot's soirées, and if we found ourselves standing apart from the others, our talk soon became peculiarly intense. She had become interested in spiritualism and frequently referred to the seances she had attended. I was sceptical, but curious, and always encouraged her to tell me more. She spoke of ectoplasm, objects materializing out of thin air, and messages from the dead. We were once overheard by Courbertin, who moved closer and said, with strained affection, 'Thérèse, my darling, Monsieur Clément isn't interested in such things.'

'Oh, but I am,' I protested. 'The great questions of life and death are endlessly fascinating.'

Courbertin laughed, slapped me on the back and said,

'I hope she hasn't made a convert of you!' He steered me away and whispered in my ear, 'Thank you for humouring her, Clément, you're a good chap.' He then urged me towards an imposing gentleman surrounded by a group of bespectacled young doctors. 'Now,' he continued, pausing to catch his breath. 'Let me introduce you to Monsieur Braudel. His recent article on hereditary ataxia is set to cause quite a stir – a man worth knowing.' It was Courbertin's way of showing gratitude. He was relieved that someone was willing to keep his wife 'amused'.

One sunny afternoon, I saw Thérèse Courbertin in the Luxembourg Gardens. She was sitting on a bench and little Philippe was playing at her feet. I approached, and when she saw me, she stood and waved.

'Where is the professor?' I asked, looking around.

'At his club,' she replied, a note of irritation sounding in her voice.

We began a conversation which became increasingly intimate. She spoke of feeling dissatisfied, unfulfilled and, although these remarks arose in the context of some broader point she was making concerning the human condition, it was obvious to me that she was really talking about her marriage. When we parted, she offered me her hand and allowed my lips to linger.

At the next Charcot soirée, I thought that it would be wise to avoid Thérèse Courbertin. I feared that if we spoke, our mutual attraction would be so obvious that others would notice. It is ironic, therefore, that as I was preparing to leave, Courbertin approached me with Thérèse on his arm.

'What, going already?' he said jovially. 'We've hardly had a chance to speak.'

I can't remember how it came about, but a few minutes later we were talking about music. The Courbertins were supposed to be going to a concert the following evening, a rather refined affair at the home of Le Coupey, a professor at the conservatoire. The performer was a young woman called Cécile Chaminade and the programme was to include a selection of her own piano works and songs. Courbertin was lamenting the fact that he could no longer go, on account of Charcot, who had just informed him of an impromptu committee meeting which he was obliged to attend. Then, all of a sudden, his eyes widened and he exclaimed, 'Just a minute! If you're fond of music, why don't you take my place?'

'Oh, I couldn't,' I replied.

'Of course you could.' He turned to face Thérèse. 'There you are, my darling. That is the solution. Clément will be your chaperone.'

'We cannot impose on Monsieur Clément in this way,' said Thérèse.

'Nonsense,' said Courbertin. 'He wants to go. Don't you, Clément?'

I made a submissive gesture. 'You are too kind.'

'There. You see?' Courbertin chuckled. 'That's settled then.'

The concert was delightful. Chaminade – who was

much younger than I expected, barely in her twenties, in fact – had short curly hair and soft, rounded features. She looked a little like a milkmaid, albeit a very serious one. When her hands touched the keyboard, she produced enchanting music, although its spell was never powerful enough to make me forget Thérèse Courbertin, whose closeness had become a kind of torment. She was wearing a tight-fitting dress of black silk, striped with satin and faille. At one point, she changed position and her hem rose up, revealing a sparkling stocking of peacock blue and a petticoat trimmed with cream lace.

After the concert, I hailed a cab and we sat, side by side, talking mostly about Chaminade, with whom Thérèse was well acquainted. They had met at a seance and had since become friends. I was informed that the young composer was a strict vegetarian, preferred to work at nights and was much more interested in music than suitors. As Thérèse told me these things I began to feel light-headed with desire. I seemed to enter some altered state of being in which every detail of the world was magnified: a dewy reflection on her lips, the powder on her cheeks, flecks embedded in the green transparency of her eyes; suddenly, restraint was no longer possible, and she was in my arms, submitting to my kisses.

That was the start of it: the secret notes, the deep-laid plots and 'accidental' meetings in the Luxembourg Gardens, the play-acting, the lies and deceit, all leading to a shabby little hotel in Montmartre, where we finally consummated our passion.

As I watched a droplet of perspiration evaporating from her body, I said, 'I want you to leave him.'

She sighed. 'I can't.'

'Because of Philippe?' I enfolded her in my arms and she nestled into my chest. 'Then what are we to do?'

'I don't know,' she replied. After a lengthy, thoughtful pause, she was only able to repeat the same, disappointing words.

Soulignac and I continued to question patients who had survived resuscitation. After a year, we had collected five accounts similar to the one given to Duchenne by his case number six. Of our five cases, I was responsible for resuscitating only one, a stable boy who had sustained a serious head injury. He was surprisingly eloquent and his description of communing with the infinite was deeply affecting. Sadly, his recovery was fragile and he died later from a brain haemorrhage. There were other patients, returned to consciousness from serious illness, whose breathing had slowed and whose hearts had almost – but not quite – fallen silent; however, none of this group said anything about tunnels or light. Most reported nothing, and a few described vivid dreams. Some of these dreams were religious in nature and featured radiant angelic beings, but Soulignac and I were never tempted to confuse them with what we now recognized as authentic contact with the numinous. A simple rule was emerging: the greater the loss of vital signs, and the longer the duration of their absence, the more likely it was that a resuscitated patient would subsequently report a spiritual experience.

Shortly after Thérèse and I became lovers, I told her about the research I was undertaking with Soulignac. She was amazed. 'Why didn't you tell me before?'

'There was never the opportunity.'

'But we have always discussed matters of the spirit.'

'Yes, at the Hôtel de Chimay, where anyone might have overheard what I was saying.'

'And what if they had?'

'As far as my colleagues are concerned, I am trying to refine electrical resuscitation techniques and nothing more. If Charcot knew what I was really embarked upon I would probably be dismissed. He is a staunch anti-cleric, a low materialist.'

'But isn't your project scientific? I thought that was its purpose: to prove, beyond doubt, that death is not the end.'

'I need evidence.'

'You already have it.'

'Yes, but not enough. And in the meantime I have my reputation to consider. '

She raised herself up on an elbow, stroked my forehead, and said in a hushed half-whisper, 'You will be famous.'

The seed was planted. Ambition fed on the compost of my vanity.

I imagined myself eclipsing Charcot, installed in a

mansion on the Rue du Faubourg-Saint-Honoré, feted, entertained by ambassadors, kings and potentates, lauded in the society pages – the modern Odysseus – and in this fantasy, always, Thérèse Courbertin was by my side.

An idea arose in my mind that floated, kite-like, above my everyday thoughts. At first it seemed too fanciful a notion to be taken seriously, but the more I reflected on it the more I persuaded myself that a favourable outcome was not unlikely.

'Interesting,' said Soulignac, 'but what you are proposing could never be accomplished. The risks are too great.'

'When I was working at the Saint-Sébastien mission hospital, I learned of a poison that paralyses the diaphragm and slows the heart. It is found most abundantly in the skin of the puffer fish.' I explained how the poison had been exploited for centuries by the native priests of the Antilles. 'A precise quantity – determined through experiments on animals - might produce a temporary suspension of vital functions in a human subject. And then, such a subject could be returned to life in the usual manner.'

Soulignac pulled at his beard. He looked sceptical.

'I know this poison is effective,' I continued, 'I once saw . . .' It had been a long time since I had thought of Aristide's murder. Images of blood and fire tumbled into my mind. 'I once saw a village boy who had been declared dead, risen from his grave – breathing and walking.'

'What were the circumstances?' asked Soulignac.

I hesitated. The bokor had made me swear never to reveal what I had witnessed. I remembered his bony finger poking my chest, his chilling cry and the discoloured whites of his eyes.

Soulignac was still frowning at me. 'Well?'

Tavernier had said that the magic of the bokors was chemical, not supernatural, and that their religion was nonsense, gibberish. What was there to fear?

I lit a cigar and began to describe the events of that terrible night: the meeting in the village, the journey into the jungle and Aristide's decapitation. Recollecting the rain of blood still sent a shiver down my spine. When I had finished, Soulignac produced a lengthy exhalation and said, 'That is a very remarkable tale.'

'And every word of it is true.'

My companion tapped his fingers on the table and said, 'Where would you get this poison from? We are a long way from the Antilles now!'

'Indeed,' I replied. 'But we are not so very far away from a zoo.'

The head keeper was most obliging. He was a widower whose wife had suffered a painful death. When I told him that I was trying to develop a new anaesthetic compound, he was eager to assist. There were puffer fish in the aquarium, and in the reptile house I found a tank of frogs from the Saint-Sébastien archipelago. It was relatively easy to isolate the poison by filtration, and I soon had enough to begin experiments on animals. The poison had several interesting properties. It was consistent in its action, making it easy to establish a clear relationship between dosage and effect. Moreover, the arrest of functioning it produced was more easily reversed by electrical stimulation than the arrest of functioning produced by chloroform. Thus, I achieved a higher number of successful resuscitations, particularly after extended periods of lifelessness.

'Think of it,' I said to Soulignac. 'For millennia, men have dreamed of voyaging to the other side, and returning. And now it is possible. Indisputable proof of an existence beyond the grave: not the makeshift proof of the theologian with his unconvincing arguments and dusty authorities, or the groundless proof of the priest exhorting us to pray for the gift of faith, but the strong, unshakeable proof of direct experience. It has fallen upon us – you and I – to penetrate the mystery.' Then, trembling with excitement I added, 'I want to go.'

When I told Bazile of my intentions, he was silent for a very long time. Then, removing his pipe from his mouth, he said, 'The Lord forbids self-slaughter.'

'I won't be committing suicide,' I responded, 'just submitting my body to a state of temporary suspension.'

'But at the moment when you stop breathing and your heart stops, you will be dead.'

'Yes, but only for a minute or so. Then, I will be brought back to life.'

As I said these words, I realized that I had become like a bokor; I now exercised fearful powers.

'Dear God,' said Bazile. 'What you are about to do is so very extraordinary.'

Before entering the Hôtel Dieu, where Soulignac had prepared an operating theatre, I paused to look up at the great towers of Notre-Dame. Clouds were racing across the sky and the light was just beginning to fade. 'Father,' I whispered, 'into thy hands I commit my spirit.'

4

I lay on the operating table, stripped to the waist, my
bare feet pressed up against a metal footplate. A trolley
was positioned next to the table and on the trolley were
two batteries: a new chloride of silver, and beneath it,
an older, volta-faradic apparatus. Soulignac produced a
syringe and injected me with morphine. Its purpose was
to ease the distress caused by the poison, which was
already coursing through my veins and causing my lungs
to labour. A pleasant warmth spread through my body
and I began to feel detached from the world. I heard
Soulignac say, 'Good luck, my friend.' His voice sounded
distant. The hiss of the gas jets and buzzing of the batteries seemed to get louder and when I closed my eyes, I
started to feel sleepy. I was aware of pain in my chest,
the inflexibility of my ribcage, and the effortful exertion
of my weakening heart, but all the time, my consciousness was dimming, until at last, all that remained was a
flickering sense of self, trembling at the very edge of
oblivion, and then, non-being, nullity, absence.

There was no slow awakening, no gentle return of
intelligence, but a sudden and disorientating jolt. I did

not, as I had expected, find myself floating beneath the ceiling, looking down at my body. Instead, I was hovering in the air, high above the hospital. Beyond the river, I could see the rooftops of the Latin Quarter and the dome of the Panthéon. I drifted out, over the parvis, turning in space until I was facing the cathedral. Its Gothic detail was bathed in a soft red light emanating from above. Veils of luminescence circled above the central spire, blushing and shimmering, dissolving into points of slowly descending brilliance: the phenomenon was in a constant state of flux, the dissolution of one veil presaging the appearance of another. Delicate tendrils of crimson lightning spread through the entire system, defining its awesome height and circumference. I was so entranced by this wondrous sight, so entirely emptied of thought by its hypnotic beauty that it was only when I passed between the blunt towers of the cathedral that I realized I was being drawn towards its core. Below, I could see a row of gargoyles. Winged, devilish creatures, staring balefully over the city.

I rose up through a crackling mist and halted directly above the spire. The copper statues, ascending the slope where the nave and south transept connected, looked as if they had been sculpted from blocks of ruby. I began to rotate in synchrony with the clockwise motion of the cloud, and through glittering sheets observed every compass point of the horizon. Suddenly, awe became fear and I screamed, and the scream was so all-consuming that I was, for a moment, nothing but the medium for its raw expression. I was no longer a person, recognizably human, but a scrap of terror, confronted by forces beyond my comprehension. And then I plummeted into darkness.

It seemed that I was falling down a shaft. sunk deep into the earth. This impression was reinforced by the appearance of an oval aperture, faintly glowing at some abysmal remove. The aperture expanded, and, dropping through its centre, I found myself disgorged above a pit of astounding immensity: a funnel of concentric tiers that shrank, step by step, towards its lowest point. It would have been impossible to discern the geography of this benighted landscape were it not for various incendiary events: conflagrations, eruptions, winking fires and thin reticulations of scarlet.

My descent continued. I saw jagged mountains, lakes of filth, blasted forests and plains of ash, and when I descended further still, sufficient to discriminate the motion of figures on a human scale, what I saw next made my soul convulse with horror: a stampede of naked men and women, stumbling, slipping and scrambling, pursued by winged, reptilian creatures – hopelessly attempting to evade capture. Those at the rear of the herd were lashed with chains, flayed and beaten until their bodies were reduced to a bloody pulp. From my elevated vantage I could see demons in flight, hunting prey, swooping down to impale their quarry on pitchforks. Victims were tossed into the air, mercilessly butchered and eviscerated with indifference.

The beat of leathery wings alerted me to two devils rising up from below, a struggling woman in their clutches. I glimpsed her contorted face as the fiends took hold of her arms and legs and began to draw apart, until all four limbs popped out of their sockets and what remained of her fell back to the ground. I watched the head and torso shatter, producing a burgundy sunburst.

My trajectory changed and I came to a desolate place, of narrow ravines and volcanic dust. It seemed to me that I had arrived in some dismal hinterland, set apart from the principal thoroughfares of damnation. The cries receded and the ground came up to meet me. My long descent ended when, with the natural precision of a snowflake, I landed on an expanse of black and magenta pumice. I had, until that instant, seemed discarnate, but now I was embodied. I could feel heat on my skin, smell foul vapours rising from vents in the earth and taste the bitter iron of fear in my mouth. My whole person was shaking and I was seized by an animal instinct to seek safety and find cover. I ran towards a fissure in a basalt outcrop and entered a narrow channel that proceeded between two smooth, glassy walls. I had not gone very far when I heard someone groaning, and looking up, saw an old man, hanging from the rock face, arms outstretched. Nails had been driven through his hands and feet. A bird-like creature was sitting on his shoulder, pecking at one of his eyes. It inserted its long beak into the socket and pulled out a grey-pink floret of brain tissue. I gasped: the bird swivelled its head around, fixing me with a curiously intelligent gaze. I ran the length of the channel and out onto a charred wasteland littered with boulders. This bleak arena was illuminated by pools of magma that coughed molten pellets into the air.

I had not been there for more than a few seconds when I heard a woman shrieking, and as the noise became louder, I also heard other voices. These were low, guttural and punctuated by rough barks. I crouched behind one of the boulders and peered around its edge. A troop of demons appeared over the nearest ridge, one of them carrying a young woman slung over his shoulder like a sack of coals. Her pale buttocks made a lunar circle next to the demon's hideous, leering face. As they advanced, I drew back and waited for them to pass, but they halted before reaching my hiding place. I heard them, close by, yawping and growling, while the woman continued to shriek. Occasionally, the demons made a sound which was like laughter, a rasping cackle. There were hammer blows, rock splintered and the woman's shriek became a howl of pain.

When I peered around the side of the boulder again, I saw that she had been nailed to a flat rock and her legs were hanging over the edge. There were five demons, all of them holding pitchforks. Their wings, when folded, arced elegantly from hooked prominences above the shoulders to tapering points beside their ankles. When spread out they resembled the ribbed and scalloped wings of a bat. The demons were standing in a loose group, jeering and making lewd gestures while the woman writhed in agony.

One of their number parted the woman's legs and positioned itself between her thighs. I saw it lunge forward, the woman juddered and she let out a piercing scream. The demon began to rut, its haunches moving backwards and forwards as its tail thrashed the ground, raising columns of grey dust. Its body was scaly and powerfully built, and each brutal thrust made me wince. The other demons stamped their feet, shook their forks, and flapped their wings, producing a ghastly parody of human applause.

The rutting demon raised its arm, revealing three great talons. It drew them across the woman's belly, opened her up, and dragged out a length of colon. Looping the entrails around its neck, it looked to its audience for approval. The phosphorescence of the magma pools was reflected in the blood which splashed around the demon's feet. Another demon vaulted over the woman's body, leaving its pitchfork behind in her smashed ribcage, but she did not stop howling. There was no end to this torment, no release – because, of course – she was already dead. Moving with the slow grace of a python, the loop of colon was already beginning to free itself from the rutting demon's shoulders. It climbed over the demon's head, dropped onto the woman's thighs, and insinuated itself back between the ragged lips of her abdominal rupture. I saw the woman's blood defying gravity and flowing slowly back into her torn arteries.

She was being reconstituted, renewed, so that her suffering could be sustained in perpetuity.

It was then that one of the demons, a fierce-looking monster with prominent forward-projecting horns, broke away from the group and sniffed the air. I saw its wide nostrils flaring. Its malevolent expression changed, and insofar as I could interpret its significance, confusion turned to surprise. It grunted and started towards my boulder. I drew back and cowered, naked, vulnerable, my bowels loosening, and terror – indescribable terror – rendered me insensible. I stood, jabbering, wringing my hands together, as I listened to the pumice breaking beneath its heavy tread.

Its eyes were yellow – evoking something putrid – and broken by thin, vertical ellipses. The retraction of its lips produced a smile of cruel intent, made more sinister by the length of its fangs and the slithering of its forked tongue. There was still something like disbelief lingering in its expression as its wings rose up and it positioned itself in readiness to pounce.

There was a mighty pull, as if I was being yanked backwards The demon's eyes seemed to stay with me for a moment, then they vanished; such was the magnitude of the impact that followed that I might have been hit by a steam train.

Soulignac was shouting: 'Breathe, Clément, for God's sake, breathe!' He pressed electrodes against my bare chest and I felt a painful electric shock. My back arched and fell back heavily on the operating table. 'Speak to me, Clément! Can you hear me? Say something!' My torso felt as if it had been wrapped in metal hoops. 'Come on, take a breath.' I gasped, and my lungs seemed to fill with fire. 'That's it, and again.' Soulignac's expression was wild and his forehead glistened with perspiration. I opened my mouth and sucked at the air. 'Well done, Clément. Keep going.' Gradually, my breathing became regular and Soulignac gripped my hand, 'You've been gone for three minutes. I thought I'd lost you.' He wiped his brow. 'You're not out of danger yet. I'm going to stimulate the phrenic nerve.' I nodded, and closed my eyes, submitting to his ministrations. 'No, Clément. Keep your eyes open. Stay awake.' Several minutes passed before he removed the electrodes and helped me to sit up. 'Well,' said Soulignac, 'what did you see?'

I shook my head and replied: 'Nothing.'

PART TWO

Possession

5

For the next two weeks I was confined to my bed. Soulignac, who nursed me through the initial stages of the sickness, wanted to consult a specialist in respiratory disorders.

'Don't do that,' I said. 'It's unnecessary.'

'But I am concerned,' Soulignac implored. 'The poison may have caused some bronchial damage.'

'A few more days,' I responded. 'I'm sure I'll be better in a few more days.'

Bazile came to see me and was obviously disturbed by my appearance. He rearranged my pillows and set a vase of flowers by my bedside. 'A present from my wife,' he said, pulling the curtains apart.

'No,' I called out, covering my eyes. 'The light gives me headaches.'

'I'm sorry,' said Bazile, quickly drawing the curtains again. He sat down and lit his pipe. 'Well, my friend, what happened?'

'Nothing,' I replied. 'I lost consciousness – died – and was brought back to life. I saw nothing, only darkness. It was like going to sleep.'

Bazile stroked his beard and after a lengthy silence said, 'We know already that not all patients who are resuscitated are granted a preview of eternity. One must assume, therefore, that such experiences – the tunnel, the light, encounters with divine presences – do not follow automatically from death, but are afforded only to those who are in some sense ready.'

For a while, he elaborated on this theme, but thereafter our conversation was rather stilted. I was too tired to talk, and realizing this, Bazile stood to leave. 'You are exhausted, poor fellow. If you need anything, anything at all, let me know and I'll return as soon as I can.' I thanked him and he left the room.

Turning my head to one side, I gazed at Madame Bazile's flowers: white amaryllis, chrysanthemums and sea lavender. I felt curiously numb, incomplete, as if my resuscitation had been only partially successful, and that a part of me, perhaps the most significant part, was still dead. Reaching out, I took a petal between my thumb and forefinger. The sensation was pleasurable and familiar, but strangely deficient, as if I were observing someone else performing the action, rather than feeling the velvety softness directly for myself.

I dozed off and was beset by bad dreams. I saw demons rolling rocks over a heap of squirming bodies, cavorting with prodigies that crawled from fissures in the earth; I saw a great vortex made of wailing humanity, spinning across a boundless flatland and leaving in its wake a trail of gore. I saw myself standing behind a boulder, naked, incontinent, shaking uncontrollably, knees knocking together, hands clasped protectively over my genitals, mouthing gibberish. And then I awoke, still yammering, the bedclothes soaked in perspiration, the awful vision of my utter helplessness still impressed on the darkness, persisting until its gradual dissolution released me from a suffocating terror.

Night had fallen and my head was throbbing. I heard the bells of Saint-Sulpice and thought of Bazile pulling on the ropes in the north tower, performing his sacred duty. The sound had a soothing quality, and with each chime the pain became less severe. When the ringing stopped, I felt oddly restored. A question arose in my mind: *Why did you lie to Soulignac and Bazile?* But I could not give myself an answer.

I spent the next two hours tossing and turning, unable to get back to sleep. Dawn was breaking and a gap in the curtains admitted a strip of light that fell in disjointed sections across the rumpled bed sheets. There was enough illumination to see that Madame Bazile's flowers had wilted. Many of the petals had dropped off and were now scattered around the vase. Scooping up a handful I inspected them closely. They were shrivelled and brown at the edges.

Soulignac was puzzled by my swift recovery. I was soon walking every day, down to the river and as far as the cathedral. A few of my symptoms were tenacious, particularly my excessive sensitivity to sunlight, but the solution to this problem proved simple enough. I was able to obtain some 'eye-preservers' (pince-nez with blue-tinted lenses) from an optical instrument shop on the Rue de Tournon, and, subsequently, morning and afternoon excursions were relatively painless. Returning from one of my walks, I found a letter from Thérèse Courbertin. She had learned from her husband that I was recovering from a chest infection (a plausible fiction supplied to Charcot in order to explain my absence) and her brief missive was sympathetic and tender. It was obvious that she wanted to see me and the desire was mutual. Employing one of our usual devices, we arranged to meet at 'our hotel' in Montmartre.

I had never disclosed my intentions to Thérèse Courbertin. She knew nothing of the experiment. By withholding the truth, I was not seeking to prevent her from worrying about my safety, but rather indulging in a childish conceit. I had wanted to succeed first, so that I could then surprise her with the astonishing revelation, that I, Paul Clément, physician and neurologist, had made the ultimate voyage, and had now returned to change the world. In my vainglorious fantasy, I imagined her overwhelmed by the magnitude of my achievement. Of course, this dramatic scene would no longer play out as I had planned. However, my disappointment was moderated by a consoling thought: Thérèse would not be asking me any difficult questions.

When I entered the hotel room I found her already

waiting. She took off her hat, which was adorned with a fresh orchid, and allowed her sable wrap to slip from her shoulders. I closed the door, advanced and encircled her supple waist with my arms. We kissed, and when we parted I began to undress her. I loosened her fastenings, unlaced her corset and, when she was naked but for a pair of stockings, she fell back onto the eiderdown. Her arms were thrown back above her head and her luxurious writhing communicated readiness. I removed my own clothing with clumsy haste and flung the garments aside.

There was something about her scent, a fragrance of extraordinary sweetness, that seemed to create in me a state of unbearable excitement. With every inhalation my want of her increased until I was possessed by a furious urgency. She tried to calm my agitation by touching my face and whispering the word 'gently' in my ear, but her scent was maddening and I could not stop myself.

Afterwards, as we lay together, our limbs still entangled, she said, 'I thought you were supposed to be ill?'

'I'm feeling much better now.'

'Obviously,' she retorted. Her hand travelled over my chest and stomach. 'You've lost weight.' Before I could respond, she added, 'I've missed you.'

'Yes. I've missed you too.' She turned away and I curled to accommodate the curve of her spine. 'You're wearing a new perfume.'

'No I'm not.'

'It smells stronger. Sweeter.'

'Don't you like it?'

'I like it very much.' I kissed the nape of her neck. 'I want to see you more often.'

She sighed. 'Paul . . .'

'I was thinking of renting a room for us – in Saint-Germain – somewhere discreet.'

'That would be too close.'

'Not necessarily. Not if we're careful. It would make things easier.'

'Would it really?'

'Yes. I think it would.'

When we were dressed and getting ready to leave, Thérèse picked up her hat and wrinkled her nose.

'What's the matter?' I asked.

'My orchid.' She plucked the flower from the brim and held it out to show me. 'It's dying. And I only bought it this morning.' I had put on my eye-preservers. 'What are those?'

'Spectacles made with coloured glass.' Thérèse's expression became quizzical. 'To soften the light. I'm still getting headaches.'

'They make you look . . .' she hesitated and smiled coyly. 'Rather interesting.'

I resumed my clinical duties at the Salpêtrière and was immediately given new responsibilities. Charcot was becoming increasingly interested in hysteria, a condition that had mystified physicians since ancient times, and he was determined to systematize its study. To that end, many junior doctors, including myself, were instructed to collate various measurements. These included thermometry, respiration and pulse. Tables were compiled, graphs plotted and the effects of different treatments meticulously recorded.

Dramatic presentations of hysterical illness are frequently connected with some religious idea or the symbolism of the Church, and one of our patients, a humble washerwoman, had contractures that resulted in a form of muscular crucifixion. Her arms would extend and gradually become rigid, her ankles would cross and she would maintain this position for hours. She was completely unresponsive and could be lifted or leaned up against a wall like a statue – a spectacle that Charcot delighted in demonstrating to visiting professors.

Bazile was always fascinated to hear accounts of such phenomena: 'When the contractures ceased, what did she say?'

'She described a blissful transport. Ecstasy, rapture.'

'Hallucinations?'

'Yes.'

'But how do you know that? How can you be sure this woman did not commune with the infinite?'

'She responded to Charcot's treatment. Compression of the ovaries released her from the fixed attitude she had adopted.'

Bazile was sceptical. 'I once saw a stigmatic in a religious retreat, a kind, devout man who had about him an air of profound spirituality. I saw for myself the wounds of Christ in the palms of his hands, and I do not believe, cannot believe, that he was, in fact, a species of lunatic suffering from psychosomatic haemorrhaging, and that baths, electricity or applying pressure to his body would have caused those divine injuries to heal over. I fear that if Monsieur Charcot had encountered the great stigmatics, Saint Francis of Assisi, Saint Catherine of Sienna or Saint John of God, he would have locked them away and subjected them to all manner of indignities. The faculty of reason is God-given and sets us apart from the rest of creation. But we must use it wisely. It seems to me that the ruthless logic of scientists frequently takes us further from, rather than closer to, some of the essential truths.'

In addition to religious visionaries, there were also demoniacs at the Salpêtrière, and these, too, Charcot counted as hysterics. The wretched individuals complained of sharp pains, clawed at their throats, grimaced and leered, spat, cursed and shouted blasphemies. Although they ate little and had wasted physiques (some were almost like skeletons), they were also extraordinarily strong and had to be kept in restraints, for fear that they might damage themselves or cause harm to others.

One morning I was conducting hourly examinations – taking and noting temperatures – when I heard, coming from an adjacent ward, a crashing sound followed by a scream. This in itself was hardly unusual, but the scream was interrupted by pleas for mercy and as I listened I thought I recognized the voice. It belonged to Mademoiselle Brenard, a young nurse admired for her cheery manner and tireless industry. I dashed to her assistance and found a chaotic scene. A bed and trolley had been tipped over and the floor was covered with tablets and spilled syrups. Some of the patients had hidden themselves under their bed sheets while others were cowering in corners and crying out, 'God help us, he'll kill us all.' One of my colleagues, Valdestin, was standing in front of Mademoiselle Brenard, who was being held captive by Lambert, a demoniac who had apparently managed to remove his straitjacket. Lambert was holding a scalpel against the nurse's throat and grinning. His other hand cupped one of her breasts.

'That's enough, Lambert,' said my colleague. 'Let her go.'

'No, monsieur. She's mine now, mine to enjoy.' Lambert bumped his crotch against Mademoiselle Brenard's rear and produced a hideous cackle. 'All mine. Come any closer and I'll open her up.' He licked the nurse's face. 'I like them this fresh. Don't you, monsieur?' I saw the poor girl flinch when the maniac whispered some unspeakable obscenity into her ear. 'Isn't she a peach? Ripe and succulent, I'd like to peel her, taste her pulp, her lovely, delicious sugary pulp.'

'Please let me go.' whimpered the nurse. 'I beg you.'

'I must insist,' Valdestin commanded, taking a step forward, 'that you release Nurse Brenard at once!'

The demoniac nicked the nurse's throat, causing her to scream.

'Shut up!' he shouted, grabbing a handful of her hair. He then pulled her head back to expose a bead of blood that grew slowly before trickling down to the collar of her uniform. Valdestin froze. The demoniac studied the red trail, which was particularly vivid against the paleness of Mademoiselle Brenard's skin, and traced its length with the tip of his finger. Sucking the blood off, he said, 'As sweet as they come.'

Valdestin turned to me and asked: 'What on earth are we going to do, Clément?'

It was then that Lambert noticed me. He fell silent and his head began to jerk – a series of nervous, bird-like movements. His expression was still typical of derangement, wild staring eyes and hair standing on end, but his brow seemed to compress under a weight of anxiety. Something seemed to have shaken his confidence.

'Ah,' said Lambert. 'Forgive me. I did not realize. Please, take her – a token of my respect.' Releasing Mademoiselle Brenard, he pushed her in my direction. She stumbled and fell to the floor. Lambert waved the scalpel magnanimously. 'She's all yours. I meant no disrespect, all yours.'

I quickly interposed myself between the sobbing nurse and the demoniac. Fear had made my mouth dry and I was barely able to utter, 'Put the knife down, Lambert.' These words sounded thin and he immediately sensed the unsteadiness of my resolve. Whatever it was about me that had made him give up his prisoner could not be relied upon for sustained effect. He was clearly having second thoughts concerning his impulsive act of surrender. Not wishing to lose my advantage, I advanced and repeated my order, this time, more firmly. 'Put the knife down!'

Lambert studied the glinting blade and then transferred his attention back to me. I was expecting him to lunge at any moment, and was preparing to leap out of the way, when he smiled, obsequiously, and whined, 'Of course, of course. Anything you say.'

He dropped to his knees and, making a great show of his willingness to comply, placed the scalpel on the floor just in front of my feet. I kicked it out of his reach and he squealed, 'Please, don't punish me.' Then, lowering his head, he began to kiss my shoes while imploring me to take pity on him. I stepped back, disgusted, and as I did so, he started to retch. The position he assumed made him look like a huge insect: sharp elbows, bent and pointing upwards, plates of bone and vertebrae clearly visible beneath taught, grey-green skin. He rocked backwards and forwards until the contents of his stomach gushed out of his mouth and splashed on the tiles before forming a wide pool. The stench was appalling. My disgust was amplified when he pushed his hands through the steaming vomit and picked up something which he held up for my inspection. His expression communicated that he was eager for me to take it. At that point, some stocky porters arrived, accompanied by an associate professor. They dragged Lambert to his feet, and twisting his arms behind his back, frog-marched him off the ward with the professor in attendance. I remember how Lambert kept turning his head to look back at me. He was still looking when I lost sight of him.

Valdestin was already dressing Mademoiselle Brenard's wound.

'That was strange,' he said. 'The way Lambert suddenly changed his mind.'

'Yes,' I said. 'We were lucky.'

Mademoiselle Brenard's injury was more serious than I had realized and a significant amount of blood was seeping through the bandage. The poor girl was distraught, tears streaked her face and her chest was heaving.

'Mother of God,' she cried, 'I thought I was going to die.'

I took her hand in mine and squeezed it gently. 'You were very brave, mademoiselle, very brave. But please, calm yourself. You are quite safe now, and Monsieur Valdestin will look after you.' In order to deliver my reassurances I had knelt down beside her. She was wearing the same perfume as Thérèse Courbertin. My gaze lingered on the nurse's lips and the swell of her breasts. Annoyed by my own impropriety, I made some excuse and moved away.

Other doctors were arriving and peace was quickly restored. An orderly was mopping up Lambert's vomit and as I walked past he stopped me and said, 'What shall I do with this?' His fingers opened, revealing something in his palm.

'Where did you find it?'

'Just here.'

It was the object that Lambert had wanted me to take.

'Let me see.' The demoniac had obviously dropped it when the porters had manhandled him out of the ward. 'I'll look after it. Thank you.'

The orderly carried on mopping and I found that I was holding a bronze statuette. It was clearly supposed to represent the female form, and, although I am no expert on such matters, I estimated the thing to be very old. I had seen fertility charms that looked very similar in books about pagan civilizations. Where, I wondered, had Lambert obtained this little Venus? It was not uncommon for demoniacs to swallow objects and to regurgitate them later, but their provenance was usually obvious. This was quite different and emanated an aura of authentic antiquity. I looked around the ward and when I was sure that no one was watching, I slipped the figure into my pocket.

At the end of the day I returned to my apartment, where I discovered a letter from Soulignac. It was not the first. There had been two others, almost identical, containing the same parting request for us to meet again soon. I had previously claimed that Charcot's hysterics were taking up all of my time, but as I opened the third letter, already certain of its contents, I recognized that I could not defer Soulignac indefinitely. With some reluctance, I wrote a brief reply, suggesting that we might dine together at a restaurant on the Boulevard des Italiens.

We had hardly finished our oysters when Soulignac said, 'Well, what are we to do now? It seems to me that we have reached an important juncture. Although we did not accomplish our ultimate objective, we have nevertheless developed and tested a method for probing the greatest of all mysteries, and, we have collected together a series of case studies which appear to demonstrate the independence of personality from the brain. Perhaps it is time for us to publish?'

'But I experienced none of those things reported by our patients. There was no tunnel, no light . . . nothing.'

'Indeed, a disappointing result, but one which was not entirely unexpected. We were both fully aware that this might happen. Remarkable phenomena are not reported by all resuscitated patients. Be that as it may, our experiment could easily be replicated by others. That is how science proceeds. I assume that you have no desire to repeat the experiment yourself.'

'No.'

'Good. Frankly, I don't think I could be party to such a dangerous venture again.' The waiter arrived and set about removing our oyster shells. 'So, what do you say to a publication?'

I prevaricated. 'You are a distinguished surgeon and I have a position in the world's finest department of neurology. The scientific community will not be impressed by six cases, most of whom are dead and can say nothing more in support of their testimony. It would be foolish to risk our reputations.'

I urged circumspection, restraint and the more rigorous interrogation of patients. Premature publication might cost us our careers, our livelihoods. We argued through two fish courses, until, eventually, Soulignac conceded defeat. 'I suppose you're right. And in this matter your wishes must prevail. It was you and not I who very nearly made the ultimate sacrifice.'

Outside the restaurant we said goodbye to each other and I watched Soulignac as he marched off into a haze of rain. Why could I not tell Soulignac the truth? I attempted to reflect on my behaviour, but found it impossible to do so. My thoughts resisted connection and my motivation remained obscure.

6

Thérèse Courbertin continued to raise objections to my suggestion that we find rooms in Saint-Germain. She seemed to have developed a superstitious attachment to our hotel in Montmartre, believing that as long as we continued to meet there we would never be found out. Yet, to me at least, it was self-evident that the existing arrangement was unsatisfactory. The hotel was too far away. Her opposition did not prevent me from investigating alternatives, and I soon discovered somewhere more suitable. The concierge, accustomed to handling delicate matters, made it known to me that a small gratuity would be enough to secure his confidence, and after only a few visits, Thérèse grudgingly conceded that I had been right all along. It was now much easier to conduct our affair. The apartment was perfectly situated, tucked away in a quiet cul-de-sac and in easy walking distance from our respective residences. Moreover, the interior, if a little dreary, was tolerably furnished.

Intimacy with Thérèse no longer felt like an optional indulgence but, rather, something necessary, vital: a form of sustenance that I could not do without. Inhaling her sweet, heady fragrance, I would lose myself in her beauty, become enraged by desire and batter her with my body until it seemed that her bones might shatter. Her eyes would show alarm, but then, quite suddenly, her expression would change as she abandoned herself to my fevered clutches. Something in her nature, something dark and aberrant, was gradually awakening in response to my need. Months passed and she became increasingly compliant. She was obviously excited by my violent passions and I interpreted her passivity as a form of consent. I knew that I was hurting her, but she did not protest, and the cast of her face, half-closed eyes, parted lips, cheeks flushed with pleasure, and the little moans that issued from her mouth encouraged me to further excesses. After these ravishments, these assaults on her flesh, I would make a token apology. 'I want you so much. You don't understand what it's like, not having you – as a wife – completely. It's unbearable.' But I was play-acting, feigning remorse and fully conscious that Thérèse was a willing accomplice.

As I lay on the bed, smoking a cigar, admiring Thérèse's exquisite body, its planes and intersections, its loose-limbed perfection, she turned to show me her outer thigh. The skin was marred by five oval bruises, corresponding with the fingers and thumb of my left hand. 'Look what you've done!'

99

'Forgive me,' I said, raising myself up and kissing each blemish. 'I got carried away.'

'What if Henri was to notice?'

If only, I thought to myself. If only he were more observant!

I still begged her to leave him. My constant appeals had not swayed her in the past, but I persisted nevertheless. She tried to mollify me with bland assurances: her marriage was sexless, they lived like brother and sister, she was always asleep by the time he came to bed, but none of it had any effect, because I was not jealous, as she seemed to think. I did not view Courbertin as a competitor. He was much less than that, a nuisance, a handicap, an obstacle, and why Thérèse should be so resistant to the dissolution of their disastrous marriage was beyond my comprehension. There was Philippe's welfare to consider, I understood that – of course I did – but Courbertin was not a vindictive or malicious man. He would not seek to remove the child. Everything could be resolved amicably. Thérèse had long since tired of hearing my opinions and increasingly her typical response was a heavy, impatient sigh. The ensuing silence was always tense and intractable. I suppose it was inevitable that my resentment would build and eventually find expression.

Circumstances had prevented us from meeting for two weeks and I was desperate to see her again. I went to the apartment early, hoping that she would make efforts to do the same, and passed the time drinking rum and pacing the well-worn carpets. When she finally entered, at the exact hour we had prearranged, I leaped out of my chair and threw my arms around her. I kissed her face, stroked her hair and started fumbling with the hooks of her dress. Her perfume was stronger than ever, almost overpowering. She put up some slight resistance, and when I did not stop, she twisted out of my embrace. 'Let's sit and talk,' she said. 'We don't talk as much as we used to.'

I did not want to talk. Even so, I attempted to comply and sat with her on the couch, holding hands, making conversation. It was difficult to concentrate, given the urgency of my desire. Before long, I was once again kissing her neck and reaching round to unfasten the back of her dress.

'No!' Thérèse cried, pushing me away. 'I don't want to. Not today.'

'Then why on earth did you bother coming?'

'To be with you!' Her eyes flashed angrily.

The tense exchanges that followed quickly escalated. Accusations were followed by counter-accusations, voices were raised and yet, even as we argued, my wanting of her did not diminish. I found her denial completely unreasonable, petty, callous and spiteful. Eventually, she burst into tears and laying a hand over her abdomen, informed me that she had a 'stomach ache' and was in considerable pain. I realized at once that she was speaking euphemistically.

The situation was beyond repair. We sat in uncomfortable silence, until Thérèse bid me a frosty adieu. I did not try to prevent her from leaving.

That evening, I found myself ordering absinthes in a dingy cafe near Saint-Sulpice. I poured water over the trowel, and with studied restraint, watched the sugar crystals dissolve and the green liquor turn opaque. I was aware that my thoughts were not as they should be, but I could not divert them from their course. I imagined Thérèse, in bed, with Courbertin beside her, his bloated face embedded in her hair, his arms around her waist. It was so unfair. Everything was on her terms.

Stumbling out of the cafe and onto the pavement, I hailed a cab and said to the driver, 'Take me to the Folies Bergère'. Until that instant, the idea of going to the theatre had not crossed my mind, and some part of me was still lucid enough to register mild surprise. The words had tripped off my tongue in the absence of any accompanying desire to be amused or entertained, yet I did not reflect on my impulsivity and simply climbed into the vehicle without thought.

The facade of the Folies Bergère was brightly illuminated and many carriages were parked outside. I went to the box office, bought myself a ticket, and made my way through the milling crowd. The auditorium was stifling, the air not merely warm, but hot. In front of me, the stage was only visible between columns of smoke that rose upwards, perpetually feeding a layer of cloud that hung like a stormy sky beneath the wide dome. I took my seat and gazed over bald heads and feathered hats at a man and woman performing a trapeze act. They were succeeded by a magician and then by a pretty chanteuse who practised her art in a state of semi-undress. The heat was overpowering and I decided to venture out into the garden: a covered space, planted with yew trees, resounding with the splash of fountains. It was a great relief to step through the doorway and breathe the cool night air. Couples sat at zinc-topped tables, heads tilted towards each other, almost touching, sharing drinks and stealing kisses; others sat alone, solitary gentlemen whose dark, hungry eyes feasted on the spectacle of so many whores gliding beneath the boughs and dispersing fragrances with their fans. I was captivated by their method of locomotion, which involved a languid swaying of the rump. Sitting down at an empty table, I called a waiter and ordered an absinthe. I don't know how many absinthes I had drunk earlier, but this additional glass, even though of modest size, was the one that finally interfered with my powers of perception. Everything became luminescent, fantastical.

Two of these whores were looking at me, one of whom had black hair, the other brunette. I tipped my hat at the latter and she came forward. Her face was caked with white powder, her eyes artfully elongated with a pencil and her lips were the brightest red. A smile opened cracks in her cosmetic mask: 'Buy me a drink, monsieur?'

'Of course, mademoiselle, my pleasure. What would you like? '

'A grenadine?'

'Certainly. Waiter?' I snapped my fingers. 'A grenadine.'

She sat down beside me and we made some small talk, which evolved into a pathetic, artificial flirtation; however, she quickly tired of this game and bluntly stated her terms. It was evident that she was anxious to clarify my intentions so as not to waste any time. Subsequently, we found ourselves in a grubby brothel a short distance from the theatre. I was still feeling angry with Thérèse, resentful, affronted, and some of this bad feeling was transferred onto my companion. 'If you want to be rough,' she scolded, 'there are specialists. Places you can go to.' Afterwards, she stood in front of a full length oval mirror, looking over her shoulder, inspecting her back. There was a small scratch. 'I'm sorry,' I said. 'This should make amends.' I tossed a pile of coins onto the eiderdown and when she saw the extent of my generosity, she rushed across the room and planted a kiss on my cheek. 'Just cut your fingernails next time, eh?' she laughed.

I emerged into the thin light of a grey dawn and managed to get a cab back to Saint-Germain. Throughout the night I had not felt at all tired, but as the sun began to rise I experienced a sudden, deep exhaustion. I longed for sleep.

Before retiring, I picked up the little figure that the demoniac had regurgitated and wondered where Lambert had got it from? As I handled the bronze, I noticed my fingernails. The whore had been right to admonish me. They were long and sharp, which was curious, because I had not neglected my toilet. I found a pair of scissors and gave them a trim, finding the activity more of an effort than usual. The substance of my nails had thickened. When I had finished, I drew the curtains and listened to the bells of Saint-Sulpice. I experienced a flicker of guilt, but the emotion was dull and muted. Standing by the window, I seemed diminished, an echo of my former self.

The whore's rebuke played on my mind. 'If you want to be rough, there are specialists. Places you can go to.' Even when I was living a dissolute life on Saint-Sébastien, visiting the brothels of Port Basieux with Tavernier, the pleasures I craved were never unorthodox: excessive, yes, but not exceptional. I was feeling increasingly frustrated, as if I was being denied an entitlement. The prospect of obtaining proper and full satisfaction proved a temptation impossible for me to resist, and, after making judicious enquiries I learned of an establishment situated in the Marais that had gained a reputation for accommodating patrons with very particular requirements. It was frequented by men of a certain type, effete, foppish individuals with slow mannerisms and drawling voices, many of whom claimed to be poets. I made their acquaintance in the waiting room, which was cavernous and lit by an iron chandelier. The wallpaper was made from red satin, embossed with Egyptian hieroglyphs, and the floor was littered with hookahs. Large Venetian mirrors reflected images of women sprawled on banquettes, their dressing gowns loosely tied, or falling open to reveal enticing glimpses of lace underwear or a silk stocking. Something about their disposition created an impression of exotic flowers with heavy heads, drooping in the humid heat of a conservatory. Occasionally, the madam would circulate, offering the sleepy clientele strawberries soaked in ether. On my first visit, she seated herself beside me, and after making some witty remarks, said, 'So, monsieur, what are you looking for?' We had a curious, elliptical discussion, and at its end, she said, 'If I'm not mistaken, monsieur, you'll be wanting to spend some time with our Lili.' She directed my gaze across the room to a diminutive figure, encased in a cocoon of smoke that issued in spirals from the bowl of an enormous pipe. The stem of the pipe was long and its ceramic bowl supported by a cage-like contraption containing an oil lamp. 'I can promise you, monsieur, Lili is very willing.'

The madam must have been a perceptive woman, because, although I did try some of the other girls, none of them was able to satisfy my desires as much as Lili. I would take her tiny hand and lead her to one of the upstairs rooms, where she would stand before me, swaying slightly, her ribs protruding through rice-paper skin, her nipples erect, her stomach a shadowy hollow.

'Do whatever you want with me, monsieur,' she would say in a voice made hoarse by her addiction, before advancing like a ghost, weightless and sacrificial. When we were coupled, I would abandon moderation, she would wrap her flimsy arms around my shoulders, pull me closer, and whisper enticements in my ear.

On one such occasion, my nostrils were filled with the sweet perfume that I had hitherto associated with Thérèse. It was unusually strong and, inhaling deeply, I became more and more intoxicated, losing all of my inhibitions and entering into a state of rapturous abandon. My hands travelled over her body, grasping, squeezing, until, wildly excited, my nails sank into her flesh. I raked them down her neck and chest, but was too transported, at first, to notice the injury I had inflicted. Then, I saw the three red trails, the blood welling up, the formation of glistening droplets that eventually trickled away. The air was suddenly as fragrant as honeysuckle and I found myself kissing and licking the broken skin. It was not iron that I tasted, but the sublime essence of the perfume that had tormented me for so long. Pressing my mouth against the wounds, I sucked and sucked until I was overwhelmed by an ecstatic swoon and lost consciousness completely.

When I awoke, Lili was sitting on the edge of the bed, inspecting the large white rose that she had previously worn in her chignon. The edges of each petal had darkened. Then, turning her smudged eyes towards me, she said, 'Are you all right? You collapsed on top of me. I had to struggle to get out from under you. You're very heavy – heavier than I thought.'

I reached out and touched the scratches on her neck.

'Forgive me,' I said. 'I don't know what . . .'

Looking down, she saw how I had scored her body; however, she merely blinked and assumed her habitually vacant expression.

What was happening to me? For the first time since my resuscitation, I experienced a reawakening of self-disgust, dismay at my own depravity. I could still taste the sweetness in my mouth, but it had turned sickly. Getting up from the bed, I picked up my jacket and went through the pockets until I found my cigarettes. The tobacco was soothing, but I still felt queasy and feared that I might throw up.

'I'm sorry,' I said to Lili, raising her chin with a crooked finger. But even as I said those words, the accompanying remorse had already begun to diminish.

I was still finding it difficult to sleep at nights. With the arrival of evening, I became restless and when I retired, the pillow quickly became hot and the mattress uncomfortable. I felt trapped, anxious and agitated, needful of open spaces. The apartment became airless and the walls seemed to close in on me. Not wishing to inconvenience the concierge, I would climb out of the window onto the pavement and walk the streets. These nocturnal excursions were mostly aimless, and I would wander from district to district without any notion of reaching a particular destination. More often than not, I found myself standing in front of Notre-Dame, looking up at the western facade, humbled by the upward thrust of the stone, the three sculpted portals, the Gallery of Kings, the circular perfection of the rose window and the delicate arches of the open colonnade. It had become strangely fascinating to me. I would circle the great edifice, studying its intricately carved exterior, impressed by the span of the flying buttresses which leaped audaciously from the ground to the roof and urged the eye to ascend even further: to the spire and the saintly statues that surrounded its eminence. And I was reminded of that night when I had looked down on those same statues from my impossible vantage point before plummeting through the cathedral, the earth and the pit.

Early one morning. I happened to see a priest unlocking the door to the north tower. He disappeared inside and a few minutes later reappeared, clutching some books. He then dashed off, his stride widening to hasten his progress. The sky was only just beginning to glow in the east. I crossed the road, opened the door and started to climb the spiral staircase. Although some candles had been lit, the interior was gloomy and it was necessary to navigate partly by sense of touch, feeling the walls for safety and guidance. I emerged abruptly onto the viewing platform above the colonnade. The panorama was breathtaking; roofs, domes and steeples receding in all directions, and the steel-grey river flowing beneath the arches of the Petit Pont and the Pont-Saint-Michel. In the distance I could see plumes of smoke rising out of factory chimneys and the purple masses of the surrounding hills. The parvis was empty, but the streets were coming to life. I could hear the sound of stallholders greeting each other, the rattle of carts and the whinnying of horses.

Clinging to the parapet were the famous gargoyles or 'chimera' of the cathedral: mysterious veiled birds, sleek predatory cats, goats, grotesque apes, dragons and semi-human things that were the stuff of nightmares, abominations that combined the characteristics of several species, freakish and unnatural. Open beaks and gaping jaws suggested a petrified dawn chorus of screeches, screams and mocking laughter. The balustrade was an infernal menagerie. Only one representation of humanity was included in this unholy assembly, a bearded sage, whose stone face expressed fear and speechless horror.

I found myself drawn to the most striking of all these creatures, a curiously melancholic personification of evil whose elbows rested on a cornerstone, and whose hands, distinguished by long fingers and sharp, tapering nails, supported a massive blockish head. His great, folded wings curled forward over his shoulders and two stump-like horns projected from his forehead. His eyes were deep cavities, his nose broad with flaring nostrils, and a swollen, lascivious tongue protruded from his open mouth. He seemed to exude indolence and lechery. Standing next to this Satanic likeness, I was reminded of the temptation of Christ.

It is recorded in the Holy Bible that the Devil showed Our Lord the kingdoms of the world, and said, 'All this will I give unto thee if thou wilt bow down and worship me.' Jesus did not question the Devil's right of possession. Evidently, the Devil's terms were valid, for when, as proud Lucifer, the Devil had been driven out of heaven by the archangel Michael, God decreed that the earth should be his domain. It has always been understood that the Devil is master here.

Looking out over the sprawling city, this proposition seemed incontestable. Here, surely, was the new Babylon: Paris, renowned for its vices, its tens of thousands of whores, its alcoholics and opium addicts, its voluptuaries, thieves, cut-throats and degenerates – a turbulent city of barricades and revolutions, blood and execution, of cruelty, lust, disease and madness. The melancholy demon was well placed to see it all, and I imagined him deriving much pleasure from observing the various permutations of human iniquity. Feeling uneasy, I returned to the stairs and, after descending to the street, made my way directly to the hospital.

After losing a night's sleep, I found it very difficult to function the following day. I felt drained of energy and had to put on my eye-preservers to prevent headaches. The problem of my abnormal sleeping habit was partially addressed by changing my working practices. Hysterical patients were monitored at regular intervals around the clock and I started volunteering for the unpopular night shift. This not only allowed me to catch up on lost sleep (when the rest of the world was going about its business), but it also pleased my colleagues and impressed Charcot. It was not possible for me to work every night. That would have been conspicuous. Even so, the compromise that I pursued was quite satisfactory.

I had not touched a battery for many months – not since before my period of infirmity. The day came, however, when I was referred an elderly gentleman who suffered from muscle weakness and I decided to treat him using electrical stimulation.

'Will it hurt, monsieur?' he asked.

'No. Not at all,' I replied.

The old man was not reassured. 'I was talking to Monsieur Fromentin, do you know him? He suffers from the same indisposition, and he said that he found the procedure quite painful.'

'Please,' I said, placing a friendly hand on the old man's knee, 'You have nothing to fear.' I switched on the battery and it began to buzz. Lifting up the rods, I passed them over the old man's exposed legs. 'See?'

'I can feel a prickling sensation,' said the old man, anxiously.

'Well, that's all right, isn't it?'

The old man nodded, but he did not look comfortable. He then said, 'It's getting hot.'

'Come now,' I responded tetchily. 'You are thinking too much about what Monsieur Fromentin told you.'

'No, it really is very unpleasant.'

The battery started crackling and there was a loud bang which made both of us jump.

'What on earth was that?' cried the old man. A ribbon of smoke was rising up from the machine and it had stopped buzzing.

'I am very sorry, monsieur, the device seems to be faulty. I'll have to get another one.' I went to the store-room and on my return found the old man inspecting his legs.

'I've been burned.' he complained.

I inspected his skin and a few blisters had indeed risen.

'That is most unfortunate,' I said, 'but it won't happen again.'

I set the second battery down next to the first and switched it on. There was no buzzing sound. I tried the switch again and turned the dials but the machine was stubbornly inert.

'Is something wrong, monsieur?' asked the old man.

Again, I was obliged to apologize and went to get a third battery. Thankfully, this device was in working order and I was able to administer the treatment without further difficulty. The events of that morning set something of a precedent. Thereafter, I kept on having problems with electrical equipment. Batteries became temperamental in my hands. On one occasion, I was attempting to treat a hysterical contracture and the battery 'died' almost immediately. Yet, when Valdestin took the rods from me they promptly came to life again.

'You're jinxed,' he said, laughing.

'Yes,' I replied, pretending to enjoy the joke. 'It certainly looks that way.'

I was accustomed to receiving one letter a year, always around Christmas, from the mother superior of the Saint-Sébastien mission. Consequently, its unseasonal appearance among my mail immediately struck me as odd. On opening the letter, I learned that my old colleague Georges Tavernier was dead. He had fallen ill quite suddenly and his health had rapidly deteriorated. His assistant had been unable to treat the condition (which my correspondent neglected to identify). Tavernier must have been delirious at the end. Instead of calling for Father Baubigny to administer the last rites, he had requested the services of the Port Basieux bokor. That evening, sitting in a dingy restaurant with rotten floorboards, I raised a glass of rum to Tavernier's memory and took from my pocket an ugly thing of beads and hair. It was the amulet Tavernier had given me in the brothel we visited after the Piton-Noir ball. I worried the charm with my fingers and finally placed it on the table. The world is not always intelligible. When I left the restaurant, I did not pick it up. I left it there, an alien object, wedged between the pepper and the salt.

*

The examination room was painted entirely black and hung with etchings by Raphael and Rubens. Charcot had taken a personal interest in its refurbishment and had created a darkly atmospheric space in which he could initiate his disciples into the mysteries of differential diagnosis. When I arrived, a large number of my colleagues were already gathered there, among them, Henri Courbertin. We had not encountered each other for some time and he greeted me with characteristic warmth.

'Clément, my dear fellow, what a pleasant surprise!' He clasped my hand, smiled benevolently, and began talking about a monograph he had recently obtained on cerebral localization. Although I showed no interest and may have even stifled a yawn, he somehow managed to suppose that I was eager to read it.

'My dear fellow,' he continued, nudging me with his elbow. 'Why don't I lend it to you?' Before I could reject his offer he was saying, 'I'll leave it in my office for you to collect. I'm sure you will find it absolutely fascinating. Please,' he raised a finger, mistaking an emerging objection for gratitude. 'It's my pleasure.'

Charcot appeared in the doorway and marched through the assembly, distinguishing some of these present with curt acknowledgements, before taking his seat behind a bare table. The rest of us had to stand. He took off his top hat and angled his cane over his shoulder like a soldier's rifle. After he indicated his readiness to proceed, the drone of lowered voices heralded the appearance of a morose woman who was escorted out onto the empty floor.

Her hospital gown was removed and a flush of shame made her upper chest and face glow. Valdestin read aloud the woman's history and after a lengthy silence (broken only by the drumming of Charcot's fingers) our chief spoke directly to the patient: 'Madame, I would be most grateful if you would come forward.' He beckoned and she obeyed. He then raised his hand, 'Stop. Now, please turn around and walk back again.' Charcot touched his ear. 'Gentlemen, I want you to listen carefully. Now, madame, would you please walk backwards and forwards, just as you did before.' When she had done this, Charcot thanked her and continued in a more pedantic style of speech, 'If the ankle flexors and extensors are affected, as is sometimes the case, the foot will be absolutely flaccid. As the patient walks, she overflexes at the knee joint and the thigh lifts upward more than it should. As the foot hits the ground, the toes hit first and then the heel so that you can quite distinctly hear two successive sounds. The ataxic patient thrusts her leg forward in extension with almost no flexion of the knee joint; this time, the foot hits the ground all at once, making only a single sound. Here,' he gestured at the woman, 'we have a very typical example of the latter.' It was only then that he turned to see if we were impressed by his powers of observation. Some discussion followed, the woman was given a diagnosis, and the next patient was summoned. This procedure was repeated until noon, when Charcot rose from his chair, bade us all 'good day', and departed in the company of an associate professor and four junior doctors.

Those of us remaining filed out of the examination room and loitered in the corridor in order to enjoy a cigarette before resuming our clinical duties. It had become a point of etiquette to express disbelief at Charcot's brilliance before talking of other things, and for a brief duration the air was humming with superlatives. Once again, I found myself standing next to Courbertin, who, after honouring this servile obligation, spoke with jovial fluency about a number of inconsequential topics. It was only when I heard him say that he intended to take his wife and son to Venice in September that my attention was fully engaged.

'And how is your wife?' I asked.

A shadow seemed to pass across his face. His complexion was pasty and he was breathing heavily. 'She . . .'

'Yes?'

'She hasn't been very well lately.'

'Oh, I'm sorry to hear that. Nothing serious, I hope.'

His reply was hesitant, faltering. 'No, no. It's just . . .' He raised his arms and let them fall. 'Women!' Then, suddenly recognizing the impropriety of this exclamation, he pretended to make light of it. 'Enjoy your liberty while you can, Clément! With marriage comes great responsibility.' And with those ill-judged words, he set off down the corridor, pausing only to remind me of his prior commitment. 'I'll leave the monograph in my office. Tomorrow.' I watched him recede – a fumbling, perspiring fool.

That night, I could not stop myself from thinking about Thérèse Courbertin. I imagined how she might look in Venice, wearing a pale short-sleeved summer dress, carrying a parasol, crossing Saint Mark's Square or standing on the Rialto Bridge. And I imagined Courbertin, at her side, consulting his guidebook, his handkerchief permanently pressed against his damp brow. I imagined them returning to their hotel, a former merchant's palace with marble floors and gilded stair-cases – in bed together, listening to the sound of mandolins and lapping water. These flights of fancy made me aware of how much I still wanted Thérèse Courbertin. Indeed, I wanted her more than ever.

We had not spoken or written to each other for several months, not since our ridiculous argument. If Thérèse was as miserable as I suspected (a reasonable suppos-ition, given Courbertin's remarks) then I was hopeful that the cause of this misery might be our separation.

The next day, I concealed myself in a doorway oppos-ite the Courbertins' apartment block. At half past ten, Thérèse appeared and walked off in the direction of the Luxembourg Gardens. I followed her through the gates but kept my distance. She sat down on a bench over-looking the octagonal pool, the edges of which were surrounded by nurse maids and small boys launching toy boats. The sun came out from behind a cloud and its brilliance made my head ache. I put on my eye-preservers and drew closer to my quarry. It was obvious that Thérèse was in a reflective mood. She wasn't looking at the palace or the blooming flowers, but staring blankly out into space. I took one more step and sat on to the bench beside her. She was so self-absorbed that she didn't even notice my arrival and it wasn't until I had spoken her name that she turned around and gasped, 'Paul!'

'I'm sorry,' I said. 'I am so very sorry.'

'Not here,' she responded coldly. 'We can't speak here.' She got up to leave but I grabbed her arm and pulled her down again.

'No. Don't go,' I said. 'I won't let you. Not before you have heard what I must say. Please.' She stopped trying to escape and I released my grip. 'I behaved inexcusably – I know that – intolerably – but I beg you, please, please, take pity on me. I have been selfish and now recognize the magnitude of my stupidity. I adore you. I cannot go on without you. Please forgive me. I promise that I will never demand anything of you again. I love you – I do not deserve you – but I love you all the same and will always love you.'

Her eyes had begun to fill with tears, but she did not respond sympathetically. Instead, she stood up and took a few uncertain steps towards the balustrade. 'We can't talk here. Not like this.'

'Then let's go somewhere else.'

'No,' she sobbed. 'I can't do that.' She started to move away from me. I willed her to stop and, remarkably, she came to a sudden halt, jolting, as if she had reached the end of an invisible leash. Then, glancing back she said,

'I'll write,' before descending the steps that led down to the pool. I watched her marching through the perambulators and squealing children until I lost sight of her.

Thérèse kept her word. She did write me a brief letter, full of hurt and anger. I wrote back: wretched, penitent. Soon, we were corresponding regularly, engaged in a subtle process of negotiation, the outcome of which seemed – with increasing likelihood – to be some form of reconciliation. For this to happen, however, it was necessary for me to make certain promises, one of which was never to ask Thérèse to leave her husband again. Needless to say, I accepted all of her conditions, and we were subsequently reunited in our secret apartment. There was some awkwardness at first, but in no time things were just as they were before.

7

Autumn 1879

Bazile opened the door, smiled broadly and shook my hand, 'Ah, Clément, what a pleasure it is to see you again. Forgive me for not responding to your note more swiftly, but I've been away. A family matter. In fact, Madame Bazile is still in Normandy.' I entered Bazile's parlour and had to pick my way through piles of books on the floor. 'I'm sorry,' Bazile continued 'without Madame Bazile to keep things in order . . .' He drew my attention to the chaotic consequences of her absence. In addition to the scattered books, I saw a bicycle frame, some thick coiled rope, a lectern and a box of garden tools. There was also a small ginger kitten scampering around the room. Bazile scooped it up with one hand. 'I found him outside and thought I'd bring him in to keep me company.' The animal's ears drew back, its mouth opened wide and it hissed, apparently at me. 'Now, now, that's not how we welcome our guests,' laughed Bazile. He then put the kitten back on the floor, whereupon it darted under the sideboard and crouched, peering out from its shadowy retreat with glinting eyes. 'He's usually more sociable,' said Bazile, pulling a chair out from beneath the table. 'Please sit.' He then excused himself, and returned carrying a bottle of cider and two tankards. 'How have you been?' he enquired.

'Very well,' I replied. 'Apart from a little eye-strain.'

'You still look very pale.'

I shrugged. 'I haven't been out in the sun much, that's all.'

Bazile poured the cider and took his seat on the opposite side of the table. Our initial exchanges were, perhaps, a little more mannered than usual, but we were soon talking with the easy familiarity of old friends. 'So,' said Bazile, lighting his pipe and assuming a more serious expression. 'What next? The result of your courageous experiment was disappointing, but by now you must have given the matter much consideration and I have been wondering how you intend to proceed.' I explained to Bazile that he was mistaken, and that since recovering from my illness and returning to the Salpêtrière all of my time had been taken up by Charcot's hysterics. 'A shame,' said Bazile; however, he did not press me to reveal more and surprisingly allowed the subject to drop from our conversation.

The frequent replenishment of my tankard had brought me close to inebriation. Bazile, who was also guilty of over-indulgence, had digressed some distance from his initial topic, and was talking about the bells of

Notre-Dame. 'Emmanuel is the sole survivor. All the others were seized during the Revolution and melted down to make cannons. Guillaume, Pugnais Chambellan, and Pasquier. John and his little brother Nicolas. Gabriel and Claude and the ladies, Marie, Jaqueline, Françoise and Barbara, who, like her saintly namesake, was reputed to have had the power to deflect lightning. Gone forever! Oh, what heavenly music they must have made.' He paused to imagine their lost voices

'Why are there so many gargoyles on the cathedral?' I asked.

Bazile's reverie was so deep that he did not hear me properly. 'I'm sorry,' he said, blinking. 'What did you say?'

'The gargoyles,' I repeated. 'Why are there so many of them?'

'Strictly speaking, a gargoyle is a rain spout, albeit a rain spout that has been made to look like a monster. There are indeed many of these adorning the cathedral, but I suspect that you are, in actual fact, referring to the chimeras – the statues on the viewing platform.'

'Indeed.'

'They are not authentic, of course, but recreations in the medieval style, commissioned while the cathedral was being restored. Even so, there have always been hordes of hellish creatures on the balustrade. The originals were weathered away or removed when they became dangerous, but their claws and feet survived.'

'Dangerous?'

123

'By the end of the last century the cathedral was so eroded that it was not uncommon for the most dilapidated statues to fall off.' Bazile bit the stem of his pipe and spoke through his teeth. 'That must have been a sight, eh? Demons raining down from the sky and shattering on the parvis!'

'But why so many?' I persisted.

'There are certainly more devils on Notre-Dame than on any other building I can think of.' He took the pipe from his mouth and began to enumerate. 'There are the gargoyles and the chimeras. Then there are the carvings on the portal of the Last Judgement, which show sinners being led to hell in chains by demons. And on the north portal you can find Théophile kneeling before Satan.'

'Théophile?'

'Théophile, a seneschal who was supposed to have made a pact with Satan to secure advancement. He was saved from eternal torment by the intercession of the Virgin.' Bazile opened his mouth and released a cloud of smoke. 'The men who built the cathedral were keen to remind onlookers of the infernal domain.'

'Why so?'

Bazile looked at me as if I had failed to grasp something very fundamental. 'Because the cathedral is dedicated to Our Lady, and as her cult became more widespread, she was revered, not only as the queen of heaven and earth, but also, the queen of the underworld.'

'Our Lady is the queen of hell?'

'Yes,' said, Bazile insistently. He saw that I was doubtful and cited his source. 'When I first came to Paris I became the assistant of a scholarly priest of Notre-Dame. Do you remember, I mentioned it once before? His name was Father Ranvier and he was greatly interested in the carvings and statues of the cathedral. He was so knowledgeable that his opinion was frequently sought during the restorations. He had embarked on a fascinating history of the building that, after all these years, is still incomplete. I was his amanuensis.'

Placing a cigarette between my lips, I said, 'I was on the viewing platform recently. I hadn't been up there for years, and found myself quite intrigued by the chimeras.'

'In my humble opinion they are masterpieces.'

'Especially the winged demon.'

'Ah yes, the strix. I adore its melancholy expression, don't you?'

I lit the cigarette 'The strix?'

'A name – of classical provenance – that has become associated with the winged demon because of the artist Charles Méryon. It was he who made the famous etching. You must know it: the winged demon, swooping crows, the tower of Saint Jacques in the background? Why it was that Méryon borrowed a name from Roman mythology is unclear, but in all probability his choice was somewhat arbitrary. He lost his mind and died in an asylum. Father Ranvier corresponded with him but Méryon's replies were unintelligible.'

Bazile tilted the bottle over his tankard but found it empty. Scuttling off to the kitchen he returned with yet more cider. We continued drinking and talking, but the subject of hell arose again in relation to a theological point, and I found myself speaking intemperately.

'Can any sin merit such a punishment? If Christian doctrine is correct, and such a place exists, then I must question our trust in absolutes, the reassuring polarities of good and evil, because a god who consigns his errant children to the pit cannot be meaningfully described as benign.' Looking across the table at Bazile, I saw in his eyes a combination of disapproval and compassion. 'I'm sorry,' I added. 'I have offended you.'

He sighed and said, 'Perhaps the disappointing result of your experiment has shaken your faith.'

I shook my head. 'I never had faith. Not really. That is why I sought to prove.' There was bitterness in my voice. 'People with faith have no need of evidence.'

Bazile made an ambiguous gesture. 'Perhaps we have had too much to drink.'

'Yes,' I agreed, pushing my tankard away.

As I was leaving, Bazile took something from his pocket and held it out for me to take. He tipped a silver cross into the palm of my hand. I was surprised by its weight and Bazile must have noticed. His brow furrowed momentarily before he declared, 'A small token of friendship. Let it be a reminder – you are always welcome here.'

I thanked him and motioned to leave, but hesitated in

order to ask a final question: 'What does it mean? Strix? You never said.'

'A strix is a nocturnal bird of ill omen,' Bazile replied, 'but one which feeds on human flesh and blood. A kind of vampire, I suppose.'

8

I had promised Thérèse Courbertin that I would never again ask her to leave her husband, and when I made that promise, it was one that I was confident I would keep. But as soon as our meetings were re-established, the urge to issue the same ultimatum returned, perhaps even stronger than before. Even so, I managed to exercise restraint and made an effort to talk to her in much the same way as I had at the very start of our relationship. We talked about events that had transpired during seances she had attended, spirit communication, inexplicable noises and the levitation of objects, the writings of Allan Kardec and many other subjects of esoteric interest. I wondered how she reconciled her spiritual aspirations with an illicit affair but, needless to say, I was not so stupid as to challenge her. What passed as her morality was clearly both idiosyncratic and pliable, a fragile system of values that would not bear the weight of too much scrutiny. It seemed to me, however, that at this particular juncture she was happier than she had been in a long time, insofar as an individual with Thérèse's constitution, so full of contradictions and prone to episodes of melancholy, could ever be described as happy.

I remember her so clearly, her supple body encased in a tight satin dress, her fur coat, the warm collar of which brushed my cheek as she offered me her neck, the sapphires that hung from her ears and the wisps of blonde hair that escaped from beneath her hat, her gloves, which, when raised to the lips, seemed to be saturated with her essence – the sudden ignition of her eyes and her glistening teeth.

Perhaps as a result of our temporary separation, Thérèse had come to appreciate the special nature of our union, our unique, if somewhat deviant, compatibility.

In order to increase our pleasure I introduced her to morphine, which had become fashionable among certain ladies, principally those who either hosted or frequented salons where stained glass, draped silk and the attendance of artists was obligatory. Medical suppliers were quick to profit from this craze, and small but beautifully finished enamel syringes were soon being manufactured to meet the demand. I was able to obtain a fine example, encrusted with pearls and lapis lazuli. Included in the purchase price was an attractive case made of ebony with a lining of black velvet. Thérèse was naturally inclined towards experimentation and curious about altered states of consciousness. Moreover, one of her spiritualist acquaintances, a woman who I guessed was eager to associate herself with any new fad, had already acquired an enamel syringe and shown it off to her friends as if it were a new bauble. Under such favourable conditions, the task of persuasion was not very difficult.

Consigning Thérèse to oblivion was such a rare delight: slipping the needle beneath her skin, depressing the plunger and watching her face become serene, her eyelids heavy. After removing the needle, a bead of blood would well up from the puncture, unusually bright and red – like rose petals or rubies – and I would touch the droplet with a trembling finger and surreptitiously transfer it to my tongue. I could not stop myself, for the temptation was too great, and even though later I might reflect on my behaviour and be troubled by its implications, the pleasure of the moment far outweighed all subsequent considerations. There was something singularly appealing about Thérèse's bouquet, for it was at once both sweeter and more subtle than that of other women. It collected beneath her tresses, where I would bury my head and inhale deeply, and as I thrust myself into her, with savage insistence, her honey-like effusions incited brutality. I wanted to mark her flesh with my nails, but was forbidden to do so, and the frustration that I felt was insufferable.

When our love-making was over – for that, I suppose was what it was – she would curl into a ball and sleep, and I would feast my eyes on the gentle contours of her form, the arc of her back and the regularity of her buttocks. Through her translucent skin, I studied with some fascination the branching pattern of her vessels. I was strangely obsessed by the notion of her interior, and imagined Thérèse transformed into a medical wax-work, with her muscles and ligaments exposed. This exer-cise did not dampen my passion. Quite the opposite: contemplating her carnality (rump, flank and tenderloin) made her even more desirable. These meditations were increasingly associated with a creeping sense of unease, but I knew that it would pass. The feeling of not being wholly alive would return, and with it, a consoling anaesthesia.

One afternoon I was engaged in my habitual study of Thérèse in post-coital repose. She was sprawled out beside me, like a slumbering goddess, her arms angled either side of her head, one leg bent at the knee, the other extended. The sun was shining and a shaft of light disclosed flecks of gold among the chestnut curls of her pubic delta. I then noticed that the air was full of wink-ing motes, and lazily raised my arm, fingers outstretched, intending to catch a tiny blazing world. My open hand threw a shadow across Thérèse's chest. I made a move-ment and was puzzled by a curious phenomenon. The motion of my hand did not correspond precisely with the motion of its shadow. There was a slight delay. I wiggled my fingers to confirm my observation, and as before, the silhouette lagged behind. My professional instincts inclined me towards a neurological interpre-tation. Perhaps I was witnessing further evidence of damage to my nervous system? But such thinking was automatic and unconvincing. The shadow of my hand, now hovering over Thérèse's breasts, seemed to have an independent existence, being somewhat displaced from where I had expected it to fall. I abruptly closed my fingers, so hard that they produced a snapping sound, and, a fraction of a second later, their shadowy counterparts curled into the compact roundness of a clenched fist. Thérèse's eyes sprang wide open, the lids rolling back to such an extent that her irises were surrounded by gleaming whiteness. She gasped and clutched at her heart, struggling to draw breath.

'What's the matter?' I asked. She did not register my presence so I shook her and asked again, 'Thérèse, what's the matter?'

Her gaze gradually focused and she replied. 'It hurts, here.' She then began massaging her sternum. I took her pulse, which was racing, but there were no other symptoms.

'Did you have a bad dream?'

'No.'

'Then it's probably just cramp, a spasm of the intercostal muscles. You were asleep and the sudden pain woke you up with a fright.'

'No.' She rocked her head from side to side. 'I wasn't asleep. It felt like something was touching me,' she paused before adding, 'inside.'

I lay down beside her and drew her close. 'Cramp. That's all it was. There's nothing to worry about.'

'But the pain was so . . . bad.'

'Indeed. Cramps can be very unpleasant.' I stroked Thérèse's hair and whispered endearments into her ear, until once again she was asleep, or at least very close to it. The light faded as a cloud drifted in front of the sun, and my thoughts, although troubled, were also strangely excited.

As time wore on, my desire to take complete possession of Thérèse Courbertin – to have her as mine, and mine alone – grew so intense that my thoughts became fevered and my head filled with lurid fantasies. I imagined how it might have been, had we met in different circumstances, another life perhaps, in which Henri and Philippe had never existed, and in which I was free to do with her as I pleased.

There were rare moments when my conscience seemed to revive and protest, and then I would feel authentic emotions once again, self-loathing and disgust at my repellent daydreams. I thought of the nerves that connect the tongue and nose to the brain, and considered how oxygen deprivation might have affected their functioning. And how was it, I wondered, that for me, love and inflicting pain had become so hopelessly confused? I rationalized and rationalized, until, exhausted by an interminable and utterly sterile inner debate, I would fall into a state of torpid indifference.

Thérèse would sometimes say something that suggested the operation of a higher perceptual gift. She seemed to sense a presence in the room; however, her female intuition did not allow her to understand its nature or the extent of its influence and malignancy. On one of these occasions she became uneasy and restless.

Wrapping her arms around her body and shivering slightly, she said, 'I feel like we're being watched.'

'That's ridiculous,' I laughed.

'I never feel like we're truly alone.'

'What, do you think the concierge is spying on us? Do you think he peeps through the keyhole?' She shrugged and I continued, 'It's the morphine. It can create false impressions in the mind.'

She nodded, but her expression remained apprehensive.

We usually left the apartment separately, Thérèse first, and I a few minutes later. I did not always go home. More often than not, I went straight to the hospital or wandered the streets, brooding. I had managed to remain silent on the subject of Thérèse's marriage; I had made no more demands, but my resolve was weakening. Something in the core of my being felt tense and ready to burst.

Shortly before dusk, I found myself on the cobbled path that follows the river Bièvre. The air smelled rank and the surface of the bilgy water was mottled with green scum. Everywhere I looked there was refuse, broken pots, metal drums and heaps of decaying food infested with vermin. Men in flat caps were hanging pelts out to dry over wattle fences: they had just finished skinning animals and the workers' shirts were rancid. Other menials were unloading leather hides from a cart and throwing them into enormous vats.

I came to a shanty town of huts and beyond these were taller dwellings that seemed to have been con-

structed by simply piling one hovel on top of another.
They leaned across the river towards each other, the
upper storeys almost touching and compressing the sky
into a fine, luminous strip.

An old woman, dressed in rags, was dangling her feet
in the water. She was singing a sentimental ballad
and took inebriate liberties with rhythm and pitch.
When she heard me coming, she turned abruptly and
whined, 'Charity, monsieur? A few coins, that's all I ask.
I'll remember you in my prayers.' Her lips retreated
to reveal a few blackened teeth. I walked on without
acknowledging her plea and she immediately launched
into an abusive tirade. A coughing fit cut short her string
of insults.

After choosing a path that led away from the river, I
entered a network of alleys that brought me to a dingy
street enlivened only by the presence of a tiny cafe. It
was getting cold, so I went inside and ordered a brandy
from a moribund waiter with a drooping moustache.

The situation was intolerable. It couldn't go on. One
way or another, I would have Thérèse Courbertin all to
myself.

When I stepped out onto the street again, a full moon
had risen above the rooftops. Looking up at the bright
white disc, I felt a gentle heat on my face.

Two weeks later, I happened to be walking past the
Courbertins' apartment, when I was overcome by a strong

desire to see Thérèse. My feet began to drag and I found myself rooted to the spot. I knew, at some level, that it was madness to contemplate paying her a visit, but I was not deterred. Indeed, the longer I remained stationary, the more it was that I became determined to pursue what, ordinarily, I would have identified as a reckless course of action. A single thought came to dominate my mind: *You shall not be denied.* It was curiously resonant, like a spoken command.

I crossed the road and on entering the building asked the concierge for directions. There was something about his expression, his narrowed eyes and jutting jaw, which suggested suspicion; however, whatever doubts he may have harboured regarding my character, he answered, 'Madame Courbertin? Second floor, first on the left, monsieur.' I climbed the stairs and, as I neared the top, saw my double, rising and approaching from the opposite direction. A floor to ceiling mirror had been mounted on the landing and the person who confronted me was pale and haggard. I removed my eye-preservers and dropped them into one of my pockets. On the second-floor landing, there was yet another mirror, identical to the first, and once again I stopped, and after further consideration of my appearance removed my hat and combed my hair.

The Courbertins' apartment was easy to locate. I rang the bell and the door was opened by a fresh-faced maid.

'I have come to see Madame Courbertin.'

'Is she expecting you?' asked the maid.

'No.'

She raised her eyebrows and waited for some further explanation. Perplexed by my silence, she coughed nervously, and asked, 'Whom should I announce?'

'Monsieur Clément,' I replied.

The maid led me into what appeared to be a waiting room. Like most associate professors, Coubertin saw his private patients at home. I did not sit down, but instead examined a fine dry-point etching of a chateau beside a lake. The apartment was very quiet, although I could hear a muffled exchange taking place not very far away. A carriage clock chimed. The maid reappeared and requested that I follow her into the parlour, where Thérèse had situated herself by the fireplace. I bowed and said, 'Good afternoon, Madame Courbertin.'

She was wearing a grey dress with a pink blouse, and her hands clutched the edges of a tasselled shawl that she had thrown around her shoulders. I registered the potted plants, the photographs in silver frames, the leather sofas and the upright piano, the trappings and emblems of a comfortable, conventional existence.

'Monsieur Clément,' she replied, acknowledging my arrival with a tight smile. Then, addressing the maid, she said, 'That will be all, Isabelle.' The maid curtsied and left, but Thérèse waited for the girl's footsteps to fade before she asked, anxiously, 'What is it? What's happened?'

I turned my hat over in my hands. 'Nothing has happened.'

She appeared confused. 'Then why . . . what are you doing here?'

'I wanted to see you.'

'What?' Her features hardened and she glared at me.

'I wanted to see you,' I repeated.

'Dear God,' she paced up and down in front of the hearth. 'What are you saying?' She stopped abruptly and touched her brow. 'And what . . . what am I going to tell Henri? Have you taken leave of your senses?'

I sighed and said, 'I know that I shouldn't be here. But I hope that you will understand, when I say that I had no choice in the matter. I could not act freely. My heart. . .'

She made frantic movements with her hands, beating the air with downward movements while making hushing sounds. 'Must you speak so loudly?' Then, taking control of herself, she added with precise emphasis, 'Please leave.'

I shook my head. 'We can't go on like this. I am not prepared to—'

'Enough!' Thérèse interrupted. 'Henri will be returning shortly.'

I took a few steps forward but Thérèse retreated into a corner. Her expression, which had been stern and resolute, suddenly changed, becoming by degrees more uncertain. The colour drained from her face, she began to sway and I thought that she was about to faint. Moving forward, I took her in my arms and whispered to her in low, urgent tones, professing my love and begging her to put an end to our unhappiness. 'Have courage,' I said. 'It is in your power to release us from this wretched existence of secrecy and lies.' Her eyes glinted like those of a frightened animal and her bosom heaved with emotion. Emboldened by her fragrance I stroked her cheeks and kissed her neck. 'No, Paul,' she whimpered. 'No.' But I did not stop, even when she tried, weakly, to push me off. I felt invincible, excited by the fact that I was having my way with Courbertin's wife in Courbertin's parlour, and it seemed to me that, with every caress, I was demonstrating the insubstantiality of the psychological partition that Thérèse had erected to keep the different areas of her life separate. With every touch, I was forcing her to accept that the dissolution of her marriage was both inevitable and necessary. Courbertin was my inferior in every way. A feeble old man and a third-rate intellect.

'Please, Paul,' she ducked and escaped to the centre of the room, where she checked that her hairpins were still in place and repositioned her shawl. 'You must go now.'

I walked around the sofas, occasionally bending to inspect a framed portrait. When I reached the piano I noticed that there was some music on the stand. It was not a published piece, but an original composition copied out in black ink. Beneath the title, 'Serenade', was a dedication, 'For Thérèse'. The composer was Cécile Chaminade.

'Is this your piano?' I asked.

'Yes.'

'I didn't know you played. How strange, that we've

known each other all this time, and I didn't know that you played.' Thérèse's hand had risen to her mouth and her eyes were wide and staring. I turned the first page over and wondered how the music might sound.

'I would so love to hear you play. Would you do that for me? Would you play for me? It's only a short piece.'

Thérèse did not respond, but maintained her fixed position. The silence that followed was lengthy, eventually broken by the sound of a key turning in a lock. Someone had entered the hallway. 'Henri,' whispered Thérèse, folding the shawl around her body as if the temperature in the room had suddenly plummeted.

Courbertin called out, 'Thérèse, my dear?'

I could see that for a fleeting instant Thérèse had contemplated not replying, but on realizing that this would serve no purpose, she answered, 'Henri?'

We both listened to Courbertin's heavy approach. The door opened and on entering the room he caught sight of me and froze. I noticed that he was sweating and his breath was laboured. He glanced at his wife, who looked terrified, and then back at me. Dropping his medical bag to the floor, he cried out, 'Clément, what on earth brings you here?' He strode across the Persian rug with his arm extended.

'Your copy of Monsieur Varon's monograph,' I replied as we shook hands. 'I was passing and remembered that I should have returned it.' Reaching into my coat pocket I produced the volume and gave it to Courbertin. 'Charcot will be discussing cerebral localization at the research meeting tomorrow. I thought you might want to reacquaint yourself with some of Varon's theories.'

'Thank you,' said Courbertin. 'You're always so considerate, Clément. But really, there was no need.'

I gave Courbertin a conspiratorial look. 'The professor is not familiar with Varon.' It was generally accepted that an opportunity to impress Charcot should never be missed.

'Yes,' said Courbertin, slowly registering the implication. 'I see what you mean.' He tapped the monograph and smiled. 'Good man.' Then he turned to his wife who was still standing somewhat dumbfounded in the centre of the room, and said, 'My dear, you haven't offered Monsieur Clément anything to drink?'

Before she could respond I said, 'You are mistaken, monsieur. Madame Courbertin has been most hospitable; however, I am running a little late and must now be on my way.'

'Very well,' said Courbertin.

Facing Thérèse, I said, 'Good day, madame.'

She lowered her head and responded, 'Good day, Monsieur Clément.'

Courbertin placed a kindly hand on my back and guided me into the hallway. 'A fascinating study,' he said, raising the monograph up as if it were sacred – Moses presenting the Ten Commandments to the Israelites. He then mentioned some obscure point of interest and sought my opinion on the matter. The answer I gave met with his approval. At the door, we shook hands once again and bid each other farewell.

I was due back at the hospital by eight o'clock and had several hours at my disposal. The thought of returning to my apartment was not very appealing so I walked to the river and smoked cigarettes on the quayside. I could see the cathedral, gilded by the setting sun, and, before long, I found myself crossing the Pont de l'Archevêché, responding to a silent but irresistible summons. I came to the rear end of the building and rounded the complex jumble of pinnacles and buttresses. Looking upwards, I saw that my progress was being monitored by a host of gargoyles. They protruded from the stonework at various levels of elevation: smooth muscular creatures, with extended necks and whose jaws, stretched wide open, evoked the din of hell. Their horizontal thrust was forceful, carrying with it a strong impression of exertion, as if they were straining to break free and at any moment might leap out into the void and take flight.

I arrived at the north portal and paused to study the stone reliefs and statuary. Three concentric arches, occupied by angels, maidens and learned men, enclosed a rough triangle in which many figures congregated on three levels. The lowest of these levels, the lintel, seemed to depict episodes from the infancy of Jesus Christ. The second level, however, was quite different. I had passed beneath the tympanum of the north portal on numerous occasions, without ever troubling to look up at these strange dramas, but now, having been made aware of their significance by Bazile, my curiosity was aroused.

The seneschal, Théophile, was shown five times, each appearance representing a stage in the telling of his story. Most of the figures had been splattered with white bird droppings, endowing the scenes with an eerie, wintry quality. In the first, Théophile was shown kneeling in front of the Devil. An earnest man stood by his side, holding the pact that the seneschal had evidently just signed, the terms of which promised worldly power in exchange for his soul. The second scene showed Théophile in prosperity. As he distributed pieces of gold with his right hand, a little demon was surreptitiously slipping more into his left. The next two scenes showed Théophile repenting and his subsequent salvation – a war-like Virgin Queen descending upon a vanquished Satan. Finally, in the upper register of the tympanum, Théophile was shown holding his head and marvelling at his good fortune.

I set off for the hospital but found walking more strenuous than I should have. An object in one of my trouser pockets was dragging me down. It turned out to be the silver cross that Bazile had given me. When I reached the Pont de l'Archevêché, I leaned over the railings and tossed it into the river. Thereafter, I made much better progress.

The night that followed was largely uneventful. I made hourly observations of Charcot's hysterics and was obliged to examine an epileptic patient who had had a seizure. Other than this minor incident, I was left to my own devices. Just before sunrise, I went for a stroll around the hospital grounds, and on my return felt unusually tired. I had some business to attend to in the plaster cast room which, being full of moulded body parts, resembled an art gallery or museum. The human form was not celebrated in this dusty depository, but maligned; all of the exhibits were twisted, deformed and diseased. I noticed that there was a chair in the corner. It looked welcoming, so I sat between its broad arms and was overcome by exhaustion. I closed my eyes and started to dream.

I was standing on the viewing platform of the cathedral, next to the statue of the strix. The sky over Paris was a flickering aurora of red light, broken by thick bands of black cloud. Fiery meteors dropped from the firmament, leaving incandescent trails and exploding with great violence when they reached the ground. On the horizon, I saw a conical mountain belching smoke and ash. It reminded me of La Cheminée. Most of the buildings in the vicinity had been reduced to burned-out, smouldering carcasses, and the river had become a channel of filth. I saw broken cupolas, crooked spires and mountains of rubble. In the middle distance was a strange edifice that I didn't recognize, a tangle of iron girders that might have risen to a great height before its destruction. Winged creatures wheeled around the burning remnants of the tower of Saint Jacques and I could hear their screeches, carried on a searing wind. It seemed that I was witnessing the last judgement, the final chaos.

It was then that I heard a voice.

'Behold: the divine plan.'

I turned slowly and discovered that the strix was looking at me.

'Do you want my soul?' I asked.

He licked his lips, leered and replied. 'No. It's mine already.'

I awoke with a start. The dream had been so vivid that it took me some time to recover. I could see the objects that surrounded my chair – a gnarled hand, a club foot and a bucket rimed with hardened plaster – but they all seemed less substantial than the apocalyptic images that refused to fade from memory. I raised my sleeve to my nose and thought that I could smell acrid smoke and flaming timbers. When I finally stood up, my legs were stiff and my temples throbbed with a painful beat. I had been asleep for more than an hour.

The research meeting was scheduled early and, after attending to my toilet, I went straight to the conference room. I was surprised to discover that most of my colleagues were already present, standing like sentinels around the large oval table. The associate professors had taken their seats and were gabbling convivially. There was some accommodating movement, a general repositioning of bodies, and I found myself looking down at Courbertin's bald head. He must have sensed my presence, because he interrupted his conversation to offer me a tacit greeting.

When Charcot entered, the associate professors stood to attention and they did not sit down again until he had invited them to follow his example. Consulting a sheet of paper that an assistant had helpfully placed in front of him, Charcot read out the agenda. Before discussing some new findings relating to cerebral localization, he wished to review the hysteria project.

'Gentleman,' said Charcot. 'I cannot emphasize enough the importance I ascribe to measurement. Some of you will no doubt remember the case of Justine Etchevery.' The associate professors produced a low, vaguely approving rumble of assent, but even the most junior doctors were conversant with this celebrated patient's history. 'Her retention of urine resulted in severe distension of the abdomen, and her survival, without developing any of the signs of uraemia, seemed to defy the laws of science. When the possibility of imposture was eliminated, some authorities suggested we were witnessing a miracle.' This provoked a ripple of sycophantic laughter. 'Gentlemen: measurement solved this mystery. Etchevery's vomit was found to contain urea, thus demonstrating an alternative pathway for excretion, and hysterical ischuria was distinguished from its rapidly fatal organic form.' Charcot proceeded to summarize some of the data that I had been partly responsible for collecting and then speculated on the potential significance of certain trends. A brief discussion followed, although none took issue with his largely unverified conclusions.

Our chief lit a cigar and whispered something to his assistants. The curtains were drawn, a screen erected, and the projector was switched on. A broad beam of light travelled over the heads of the seated professors and a photographic image of a naked woman appeared on the screen. Contractures had forced her hitherto supine body into the shape of an arch, supported only by the tips of her toes and the top of her head. Her buttocks were elevated some distance from the ground and she appeared to be thrusting her hips towards the ceiling. Charcot continued talking, and more images appeared. Gaping mouths, bulging eyes, bared teeth; a veritable gallery of human chimeras.

I was standing close to the projector, with my chin gripped in my right hand, and my right elbow cupped in my left hand. I noticed that I was casting a shadow on the back of Courbertin's jacket. Detaching my right hand from my chin, I opened my fingers, creating the illusion of a dark, spider-like form that, with a little encouragement, ascended Courbertin's spine and came to rest between his shoulder blades. The progress of the shadow had been slow and fractionally delayed. Charcot's voice sounded thin and remote: 'Gentlemen: it is important to recognize that hysteria has its own organizing principles, just like any other nervous ailment originating from a material lesion.' Tendrils of smoke rose from his cigar. 'The ultimate cause still eludes our means of investigation, but it expresses itself in ways unmistakable to the attentive observer.' As he elaborated, his words became less and less distinct until all that I could hear was a faint murmur.

My focus of attention was entirely on Courbertin. How absurd he looked. I considered the wispy strands of hair that had been raked across his head, the roll of flesh that hung over his collar, his short neck, his capacious trousers and flabby haunches: a man of modest abilities, who, by stubborn, bovine persistence and shameless ingratiation, had managed to secure a place at Charcot's table; a fraudulent man, anxious to please others and win their favour lest they should turn against him and expose his mediocrity; a man of nervous smiles and perspiration, clinging undergarments and wary confidences; and of course, a lucky man, who by an accident of chance, happened to come from a provincial town where a beautiful woman saw in him a means of escape. That such a pathetic specimen should represent an obstacle to the satisfaction of my desires was scarcely believable.

I lowered my hand and the shadow nestling between Courbertin's shoulder blades dropped a short distance. In my palm, I could feel something, a barely perceptible fluttering, like the wings of a trapped moth. I closed my eyes, and the trembling sensation became more intense, its definition increasing until it achieved a distinct periodicity. There could be no doubt as to what this curious phenomenon represented. I did not respond with shock, horror or surprise, but fascination. My tentative fingers closed around what I knew must be Courbertin's heart. I could feel its regular, vigorous beat – valves opening and closing, blood entering the atria, the ventricles contracting. The rhythm was hypnotic. Then, quite suddenly, the sensation vanished. Opening my eyes, I saw that Courbertin had shifted in his seat and positioned himself out of my shadow.

The photographic slide on the screen showed a cross-section of the brain. Charcot was gesticulating at certain structures with his cane, but I could not hear a word he was saying.

I altered my position and the shadow of my hand reappeared on the back of Courbertin's jacket. Once again, I felt his heart beating against my palm. The same thought that had provoked my rash actions the previous day sounded in my mind with identical declamatory resonance: *You shall not be denied.* I closed my fingers and began to squeeze. Immediately, Courbertin sat up straight. He began rubbing his chest and looking around the room. I squeezed harder, and harder still, until I felt the beat in my palm accelerate. Courbertin produced a handkerchief and mopped his brow. He was shaking, and it took him several attempts to stuff the handkerchief back in his pocket. His sweat tainted the air and I could smell his panic. He muttered something to the man sitting next to him and then stood up. Our eyes met briefly as he hurried into the darkness between the projector and the door. He had looked nauseous, sickly, and his forehead was covered in glistening droplets. Charcot registered the disturbance and threw a glance in our direction, but his delivery did not falter. 'With respect to the management of hysterical young women, I recommend extra, that is to say, punitive cold showers, beyond five or more per day if they are to be mastered.' My hearing was now totally restored. I could hear Charcot's voice and, behind me, the door being opened and softly closed.

When the research meeting ended, I went straight to my apartment and slept soundly for the rest of the day. In the evening, I returned to the hospital, and met Valdestin, who was just leaving.

'Did you hear about Monsieur Courbertin?' he asked.

'No,' I replied.

My colleague shook his head and produced a heavy sigh. 'Died this morning – a heart attack – on his way home in a cab.' Valdestin made a helpless gesture. 'The driver thought he was asleep.'

The feeling of not being wholly alive seemed to rush into my body and its coldness made me numb and unresponsive. Valdestin mistook my impassivity for grief. 'I'm sorry, Clément. You were better acquainted with him than I.' Then, attempting to console, Valdestin added, 'He always spoke very highly of you.'

A thought formed out of the nothingness in my skull: *She is mine now.*

9

The Salpêtrière was well represented at Courbertin's funeral. Charcot and Madame Charcot were present, as were most of the associate professors and a respectable number of junior doctors. Thérèse looked beautiful in black, tall, slender and alluring, her widow's veil endowing her with an aura of mysterious glamour. One of her hands rested on Philippe's shoulder. Standing next to Thérèse was a man who reminded me of Courbertin. He was clearly a relative and I supposed that he must be a brother or a close cousin. At his side was a dowdy wife with dull, lifeless eyes.

The priest swung his censer over the coffin and mumbled prayers. Birds sang. The sun was bright and my skin started to prickle, so I edged into the shade of a mausoleum.

Some distance from the principal mourners stood a tight knot of people who I suspected might be members of Thérèse's spiritualist circle. The women sported enormous hats festooned with black ribbons, and one of the men was wearing a cape so long that it touched the ground. A frail old lady, who sat on a portable chair in the centre of the group, kept on staring at me. Whenever our gazes coincided, she quickly looked away.

After Courbertin had been buried, the crowd began slowly to disperse. I watched Charcot go over to Thérèse and offer his condolences. Valdestin, who was standing in front of me, turned round and said, 'Do you think we should say something too?'

'No,' I replied. 'I think we should leave now.'

I had already written to Thérèse – twice, in fact – and on both occasions I had endeavoured to be sympathetic without also being hypocritical. Thérèse did not love Henri Courbertin, perhaps she had never loved him, and, although I expected her to show some outward signs of grief, I did not expect his death to affect her very deeply. The replies that I received were measured and gave me no cause to suspect that I might be wrong; however, when we finally met, three days after the funeral, Thérèse was clearly troubled.

'What is it?' I asked.

'Henri must know now,' she replied.

'Know what?'

'How I deceived him. I keep on imagining Henri, on the other side, heartbroken, appalled.'

Taking her hand in mind, I tried to console her, 'You placed your domestic responsibilities before your own happiness. That was a selfless thing to do.'

'There was nothing selfless about my behaviour,' she responded. 'I was frightened of losing Philippe, that's all.'

'You cannot blame yourself for what happened, and if, as is commonly supposed, the newly departed are obliged to examine their consciences, then Henri will appreciate that he too was at fault. He neglected you, patronized you and made no real effort to understand you.' A long silence ensued and I added, 'What's done is done. He is no longer with us and we are now free to do as we please.'

On hearing these words, Thérèse's expression became anxious and some lines appeared on her brow. 'We cannot be together. Not yet. It's too early and people are sure to talk.'

'If they wish to gossip,' I said, sweeping my hand through the air with scornful disregard, 'let them, I really don't care.'

'Perhaps not,' said Thérèse, 'but I do. A woman has good reason to concern herself with the opinion of others.'

'Then perhaps we should leave Paris altogether, start a new life in a spa town. Lamalou-les-Bains, perhaps? I could get a position in the sanatorium where Charcot sends his patients for the thermal cure.'

'What about Philippe?'

'What about him?'

'Are you prepared to—'

'I'll treat him like a son,' I interrupted. Something in my voice, a strained note of impatience, must have betrayed my insincerity.

Thérèse looked down at the floor and said, 'I think we need to consider our situation very carefully.'

We did not make love that day; however, when we met again (for the second time after Courbertin's death) Thérèse responded readily to my tentative caresses, throwing her head back to expose her long neck, welcoming each advance with a tremulous, breathy sigh. As my passion mounted, I found myself treating her roughly, my nails digging into her skin, the urge to tear and rip so powerful that I only stopped when she emitted a cry. I removed my hand, but she drew my fingers back to her flesh. 'More,' she whispered. 'More.' Her invitation was so exciting that my passion found its ultimate expression prematurely. Such was the violence of my paroxysm, and so depleted did I feel after, that I was completely unable to recover my potency. I was still lying on top of her when Thérèse said, 'I attended a seance last night.'

'Oh?' I responded.

'I received a communication from the realm of the spirits.' She hesitated before adding, 'From Henri.'

'Did you?' I rolled off her body and reached for my cigarettes. After lighting one, I said, 'What did he say?'

'He said that Philippe and I were in great danger.'

'How, exactly?'

'The medium, Madame Gravois, was unable to be more specific. She said that the communication was very faint.'

'I don't think you should go to these seances any more. I'm not sure you are in the right frame of mind.'

'Do you think it was him? Coming through?'

'I don't know.' I stroked a damp strand of hair from her forehead and wanted to say something more comforting, but all I achieved was a flat repetition of the same sentence.

The question of when we should make our relationship known to the wider world was raised intermittently, although with decreasing frequency. Since Courbertin's demise, it no longer seemed quite so necessary that we should live under the same roof. The proximity of a child would, I realized, very likely dampen our ardour and we had had insufficient opportunity to enjoy our newfound liberty. One rainy afternoon, Thérèse asked the inevitable question: 'Do you still want to marry me?'

'Yes,' I replied, without making eye contact.

Her instincts must have served her well, because she had the good sense not to press for a date.

Weeks became months and we continued to meet in secret. The Saint-Germain apartment, which had always had a dusty, mouldering atmosphere, was now looking distinctly shabby and ill-used, and something of its character seemed to have found a corresponding weariness in Thérèse's soul. Her movements had become slow and languid, her gaze unfocused. This may have been because of the morphine, which she now injected on her own as well as in my company. Even so, there was something about her lassitude that seemed to require more than just a chemical explanation. When I contemplated her malaise, my brain supplied an apposite image: a wilting flower. Yes, that was what she had become, a wilting flower, with petals turning brown at the edges.

Thérèse continued to encourage my excesses. She permitted me to tug at her hair and bite her so hard that impressions were left in her flesh, to rut on her back like an animal. She would get down on her knees at my command and, taking me into her mouth, prolong her humiliation until I found release. She was incapable of disobeying me and exquisitely responsive to my needs. Indeed, there were moments when it seemed that I had only to think of a novel transgression and she was at once positioning herself for my convenience.

This willingness to comply with my wishes seemed to extend into other areas of her life. It occurred to me that she had not mentioned her spiritualist circle for some time and I pointed this out.

'I stopped going,' she replied.

'Why?' I asked.

She coiled a lock of hair around her finger and pouted. 'You were right. It just made me upset.'

Beyond the walls of our retreat, the city went about its business, and when we emerged, we would join the flow of pedestrians and blend into the anonymous traffic. I would usually go to the hospital, and she would usually go home, and so it went on. Although I often crossed the large open square in front of Saint-Sulpice, I no longer ventured inside the church, and rarely spared a thought for my old friend the bell-ringer, but a chance encounter quite literally brought us together again. We were both rounding the Fountain of the Four Bishops, and neither

of us was paying very much attention to his surroundings, when we stepped into each other's paths and
collided.

'Paul!' Bazile took my hand and shook it vigorously.
'How good it is to see you again. Where have you been?'

'I'm sorry,' I replied. 'The hospital, you know how it
is – Charcot works us like mules.'

'Why don't you come inside for a cider?' He gestured
towards the north tower. 'Surely you can spare a few
minutes?'

'That is very kind of you, but I must decline. My day
has been very demanding.'

'Then next week, perhaps?'

He was insistent and did not let me go until I had
committed myself to a dinner engagement. At the time, I
felt quite irritated by Bazile's tenacity, but in due course
I would be grateful.

Memory is not reliable, and a distinctive event can easily
erase the impressions that preceded it. Consequently I
have only the poorest recollections of Thérèse's arrival
at the apartment and what happened immediately after:
skirts and stockings on the floor, my thumb on the
plunger of the syringe, writhing limbs, parted lips, tears
rolling down her cheeks, leaving gritty black trails of
mascara. But what followed, I remember all too clearly.

She was lying on the bed, her body curled around a
pillow that she clutched against her breasts. On her back,

I could see the imprints of my barbarity, scratches, bruises, bleeding traces, and I experienced a certain creative pride in my accomplishment. She was exuding her inimitable fragrance in copious quantities. It seemed to fill the room like a thick, scented fog. I imagined its restless movement, pouring out of her wounds, flowing over the bedclothes, cascading to the floor and creeping into corners and crevices: the oil of the damask rose, figs in honey, sweetmeats, glazed fruit, lavender, civet and bergamot: all of these things combined, and yet so much more – luscious, heady, delight – beyond description. I brushed my mouth against her lacerations and licked the blood off my lips. With eager fingers I tore a scab from her shoulder and examined it closely: a red-black crystal that when held up to the gaslight seemed to glow like a garnet with a dancing spark imprisoned at its core. I placed the scab on my tongue, and, as it dissolved, my palate was suffused with new registers of sensation. My body was electrified and I was filled with a profound sense of well-being. The skin where the scab had once been darkened and a bead of blood appeared, ripening until it reached its natural limit of expansion, before trickling from one shoulder blade down to the other. I licked at the rivulet of blood, and licked again, until my mouth was pressed against the source and I was sucking with the concentrated energy of a newborn baby. Thérèse stirred and made a mewling sound, but her personality was submerged in a bottomless opiate sea. The blood was intoxicating, and when I had sucked the capillaries dry, I raised myself up, my knees sinking into the mattress as I became upright.

Thérèse's neck was exposed and beneath its gleaming surface I could see the pulsing of her carotid artery. I was seized by a desire to slice it open and quench my thirst: a thirst that was suddenly urgent and demanding.

She is yours, now – all yours. The thought was sonorous and persuasive. *Yours to enjoy.*

Thérèse was very still, so still that even her breathing was impossible to detect. Only the pulse on her neck indicated that she was alive. My thoughts progressed logically: *Her surrender excites you. The ultimate surrender is death. Therefore, in order to experience the ultimate pleasure. . .* I raised my hand and a faint shadow crept across the spoiled surface of Thérèse's back. At once, I could feel the moist heat of her interior, the throbbing of her heart. My fingers closed and I began to exert pressure. A rasping sound emanated from Thérèse's throat as she struggled to take in air.

The bells of Saint-Sulpice rang out, their peal oddly transformed into a harsh, plangent clangour.

I looked towards the window and what I saw made me freeze. A paralysing horror robbed me of the power to move. In the glass, I did not see a copy of myself, but a demon, a hideous creature, leering, salivating, grinning maniacally, its arm lifted high, displaying a set of lethal talons. Its eyes were yellow, eyes that I recognized – eyes that, once seen, could never be forgotten – poisonous eyes radiating malice and wickedness. I felt as if I were standing on the edge of an abyss. The sweetness in my mouth turned sour and I screamed. Leaping off the bed, I ran to the washstand, where I coughed a thin stringy liquid into the bowl. Thérèse said something, a soft murmur, but she was still asleep. I saw clearly what, until that moment, I had been blind to. The cuts and bruises that covered her body were no longer pleasing to look at, but repellent. She looked pitifully thin – wasted, broken. I stepped towards the window, my whole body quivering, but all that I saw was my own ghostly reflection suspended in darkness.

10

That night, I had bad dreams: awful, vivid dreams of hell and damnation. In the last of these, I found myself returned to that bleak arena of boulders and belching magma pools, and once again witnessed the arrival of a troupe of demons. As before, the leader was carrying a naked woman and, when he threw her onto a rock and began hammering nails through her hands, I realized that it was Thérèse Courbertin. She was writhing, shrieking, straining to break free, begging for mercy, while all around her the demons flapped their wings and created an infernal din. I was not frightened, but excited by what I saw, and utterly indifferent to Thérèse's ordeal. She squirmed, twisted and cycled her legs furiously in the air, all the time, wailing and screeching. I drew closer, close enough to catch her ankles, pull them apart, and hunker down between her thighs. She was yelling, 'No – please – no,' but I was deaf to her cries. I leaned forwards, punched a hole through her ribcage and ripped her heart out. Then, I held the organ up, a grisly trophy. the aorta dangling, before crushing the ventricles over my open mouth and squeezing the blood out like water from a sponge. The fragrant liquid scattered over my face and trickled down my gullet. I stretched my wings, howled at the roiling sky and awoke with a bestial moan still issuing from my mouth. The bed sheets were clammy, and during the course of my troubled sleep I had torn them to shreds.

I was haunted by images of Thérèse, fleeting impressions of her flesh, her curves and crevices, the neatly folded pleat of her womanhood, all of which made me eager to see her. I knew, of course, that I must resist the urge, that if we met again she would be in mortal danger. But exercising self-control only seemed to increase the urgency of my desire, and a prolonged inner struggle ensued. It was as if my mind had been divided and I was no longer a single person, but two antagonistic personalities: one permissive, encouraging me to satisfy my needs, the other prohibitive, demanding abstinence. My head swam, I felt sick and dizzy; I vacillated between states of acceptance and denial, insight and confusion.

What was I to do? Find a church and pray? Ask the all-knowing God to intercede? He, who created everything and watched, impassively, as the ripples of cause and effect spread from His person, bringing evil and suffering into being – our Holy Father and architect of hell. I sank into a quagmire of theological debate, becoming desperate for the reassuring certainties of science. Once again, I tried to make sense of my experience with reference to peripheral nerve damage, and, once again, the demon had cause to celebrate another victory.

A week later I kept my dinner engagement with Bazile. He and his wife welcomed me with their customary warmth and, after aperitifs and some cheery exchanges, we all took our places at the table. Madame Bazile had prepared a succulent belly of pork served with vegetables and a creamy sauce. The cider, however, was rather sour and I was unable to drink very much of it. 'No more,' I said, placing my hand over the tankard, 'I really should stop.'

'But you've hardly had any,' pleaded Bazile.

I feigned embarrassment. 'Last night . . .' My expression communicated remorse.

'Oh, I see,' said Bazile. 'You over-indulged? That is most unfortunate, because my dear wife returned from Normandy with several bottles of my favourite cider, a speciality of the region where she was born. You really must try some! I asked her to pack an extra bottle, a very heavy one, might I add, just for you!'

'Don't listen to him, Monsieur Clément,' said Madame Bazile, 'It was no trouble at all.'

Bazile excused himself and returned to the table with another jug, but the new cider tasted no different from the old – again, the same sourness, an acrid undertow. I doubt that I was able to disguise my dislike of the beverage, because Bazile said, 'Being uncommonly sweet, it is something of an acquired taste, but persevere and I'm sure you will learn to appreciate its virtues.' Not wishing to upset my hosts, I was obliged to drink the whole lot while making dishonest remarks about its vitality. It made me feel quite ill.

When we had finished eating, Madame Bazile retired for the evening. Bazile lit his pipe and our conversation soon became more serious. Before long, we were engaged in one of our deep philosophical discussions, but as the evening drew on, I was gradually overcome by a creeping sense of despair. Great rifts of nothingness seemed to be opening up inside me.

'What is the point of prayer?' I asked. 'God is supposed to be unchanging. Even before a prayer is recited, He must have already decided whether or not He will answer it.'

'There is no contradiction,' said Bazile. 'Prayer is not separate from the causal order of the world, but an essential part of it. We bring about by prayer those things that God has already determined should result from prayer.'

I found the circularity of his argument irritating: 'If human beings are not free to make choices, then there can be no such thing as morality. We are only good or bad insofar as God wills it so. Either God is all-knowing, in which case we are not free, or we are free, in which case God is not all-knowing.'

'The God in whom I believe is perfect,' said Bazile gravely, 'and all-knowingness is a fundamental condition of His perfection.' The bell-ringer pressed more tobacco into the bowl of his pipe. 'All-knowingness and freedom need not be considered irreconcilable. Just because God knows that you will do something does not mean that he is responsible for your actions. Rather, God has fore-knowledge of what it is that you freely decide to do.'

'Sophistry,' I said, shaking my head.

Bazile sucked on the stem of his pipe. 'Yes, to an extent. I accept that charge. Complex ideas do not lend themselves to easy expression. Perhaps we have reached that point at which language itself is no longer service-able and, as a consequence, arguments appear more suspect. Indeed, one must suppose that, ultimately, God is unknowable because the human intellect is of limited capacity. You would not try to scoop up the ocean with a thimble, so why do you expect your mind to encompass the infinite?'

'If God is unknowable, why conclude that He is per-fect or benign? Why make any assumptions about His goodness? The Bible exhorts us to be kind, but the world, with all of its manifest imperfections – injustice, cruelty and disease – does not look like the handiwork of a loving Father.'

Bazile frowned. 'As a doctor, you must have seen many children being subject to painful medical procedures?'

'Yes.'

'A very young child cannot understand why it must suffer. It is incapable. But such suffering is necessary. Evils may be the price we pay for the greater good that outweighs them.'

'You truly believe that this is the best of all possible worlds?'

'Yes. How could imperfection arise from perfection? The existence of injustice, cruelty and disease do not demonstrate that the world was not perfectly created. These things are requisite, unavoidable, in ways that perhaps we will never fully appreciate.'

I was not impressed by any of Bazile's arguments. They seemed facile, slippery, specious, an uneasy attempt to gloss over the glaring inconsistencies and stark contradictions that lay at the very heart of his religious convictions.

What had I been hoping for? The prospect of redemption? To be persuaded that I could still alter my destiny? As our dialogue continued, the rifts inside me widened, and despair was replaced by a feeling of desolation.

'I do not understand how you are able to sustain your faith,' I said to Bazile. 'It is beyond me.' The tone of my voice was contemptuous. I might as well have called him an imbecile.

The atmosphere in the room became tense and uncomfortable. Bazile affected indifference, but it was obvious that I had offended him, and our subsequent efforts to revive the conversation stalled.

'It is a curious thing,' said Bazile, yawning, 'but for some time now, whenever we have been together, I have become very tired: unnaturally so.' He turned his eyes on me. There was something disturbing about the probing intensity of his gaze. 'Intellectual rigour!' he added with a wry smile. 'Perhaps I'm not used to it any more.

Madame Bazile is a devoted wife and an excellent cook, but relatively untroubled by the great mysteries.'

'I think I had better go,' I said, rising abruptly.

'If you wish,' Bazile replied.

'Please thank Madame Bazile for an excellent meal. The pork was exceptional.'

Bazile took his own coat as well as mine from a peg on the wall and we descended the bell tower together. Outside, the pavements were glassy with rain. Before I made my departure, we shook hands, albeit rather stiffly.

'Goodbye,' said Bazile.

I nodded, put on my hat and marched across the square. When I reached the other side, I turned to look back and fancied that I could still see the bell-ringer standing beneath the mighty colonnade, a barely discernable figure in the shadows. I quickened my step and headed off into the night, giving scant consideration to my route or destination.

My black mood worsened and I began to feel totally divorced from my surroundings. I did not see the shopfronts, cafes and advertisements. The city made no impression on my senses. I was in the world, but set apart from it, estranged, alienated and alone. Grief and bitterness curdled in my stomach. Everything seemed futile, a divine joke, a preordained pantomime without meaning or tangible purpose.

I had died, travelled to hell and returned, possessed by a demon: a predatory evil that had discovered pathways of easy influence along the soft grain of my many flaws and weaknesses, my arrogance, lechery and self-pity. I had been a willing accomplice to murder, lending the demon my shortcomings and deficiencies so that it might perform its heinous deed. And, inevitably, I would be its accomplice again, my debased love providing it with the means and opportunity to destroy Thérèse. I recalled her scarred flesh, her languid movements, the emptiness in her eyes, and realized that her descent into depravity must also be counted as one of the demon's accomplishments. It had reached into her mind and cultivated latent proclivities to ensure our mutual ruin.

A demon has many goals – to corrupt, to defile, to propagate suffering – but all of these are secondary to its principal goal, which is to take souls to hell. Well, my demon had already achieved this end. I was not, at that moment, in the hell of fire and brimstone but in another hell, a far worse hell, the hell of my own guilt and desperation.

An angry voice: 'Get out of the way!' A carriage was coming towards me, lamps glaring. 'Monsieur!' I dodged the vehicle but was drenched with spray when its wheels rolled through a puddle. The driver swore and shook his fist.

I was standing on the Pont Neuf.

How could I justify my continued existence? If I lived, the demon would surely prevail and Thérèse would die. I climbed onto the low wall and looked down into the black water. My death had brought the demon into the world, and my death might also be the means to expel it. I was already damned, so what did it matter if I took my own life? At least Thérèse would survive, and in the end all choices are sanctioned by God!

I launched myself into the void and was surprised when, instead of falling forwards, I fell backwards. Someone had grabbed my coat, and I found myself lying on the pavement, gazing up at low, faintly glowing cloud. Bazile's face appeared. 'If you kill yourself,' he growled, 'it will become more powerful than you can possibly imagine.'

11

I can remember little of what transpired immediately after, a general impression of passing through familiar streets, rain, Bazile at my side, occasionally grasping my elbow to make me turn left or right, fragments of speech – 'poor fellow', 'be strong', 'you are no longer alone' – and finally, Saint-Sulpice coming into view, flat and unreal as if painted on a curtain at the opera. It seemed that one minute I was on the bridge and the next seated in Bazile's parlour nursing a bowl of steaming tea.

'How did you know?' I asked.

'There were indications,' replied the bell-ringer. 'Certain signs.' He struck a match and lit his pipe. 'However, your evident discomfort drinking the cider this evening confirmed my suspicions. I had added holy water.' Bazile gestured in such a way as to suggest that he was unhappy about having deceived me. 'The small quantity you drank revived your conscience, gave you the strength to put up a fight; however, a demon is a subtle adversary, and even the best intentions can be subverted to serve its aims.'

'I was trying to . . . thwart it.'

'Indeed,' said Bazile, 'but self-slaughter is a sin, a sin born of despair. A demon feeds on misery, nourishes itself on negative emotions. Tonight, had you succeeded in ending your life, not only would you have insulted your Maker, but you would have also empowered the very evil you sought to frustrate! No longer obliged to cause suffering by exploiting the frailties of its host, the demon would have been liberated, free to do its mischief without constraint.' Bazile produced a small cross attached to a thread-like chain. 'Put this on. Now, my friend, you must tell me everything.'

I made my confession. I told him of my time on Saint-Sébastien, how I had witnessed the murder of Aristide, and how I had carelessly sworn to tell no one, and how I had broken my oath. I told him what had really happened on the night of the experiment, and how I had journeyed to hell and witnessed unspeakable horrors. I told him how I had been resuscitated and how I had awakened a changed man: sensitive to sunlight and the smell of blood, alert at nights and tired during the day, my fingernails grown thick and sharp. I told him about the demoniac and the little Venus, my affair with Thérèse, the brothel in the Marais, the death of Courbertin and the image of the demon in the window. And when I was done, I broke down and wept.

'These tears are precious,' said Bazile. 'For many months, your soul has struggled to resist spiteful tyranny, your natural emotions smothered by a suffocating malevolence and now, at last, your humanity is restored.'

'What am I to do?' I asked, pathetically.

'We will consult with Father Ranvier.'

'Who?' The name sounded vaguely familiar.

'My old mentor,' replied Bazile.

'But I am expected at the hospital.'

'I will send word of your indisposition.'

'Will he be able to help, this priest?'

'I am sure he will.' Bazile rose from his seat. 'Would you like some more tea?'

'Yes,' I said placing my head in my hands. 'Thank you.'

I heard Bazile leave the room and sounds coming from the kitchen. As I waited, the cross hanging from my neck seemed to grow heavier and heavier until I was experiencing considerable discomfort. I slipped my fingers beneath the chain and lifted the tiny links off my skin, but as I did so, my nails caught the clasp and released the fastening. The cross and chain dropped onto the table top. I immediately felt relieved and straightened my spine, but only temporarily, because relief was quickly superseded by panic. The walls seemed too near, the temperature too hot; I felt trapped, entombed, and it became difficult to breathe. All that I could think of was getting outside, where I could fill my lungs with the cool night air. I crept over to the door, opened it and immediately set off down the stairs. Darkness prevented me from making a quick escape and I had not got very far when I heard Bazile calling my name and chasing after me. His hand landed on my shoulder and he spun me around, 'Paul!' I detected some shadowy movements and once again I felt the weight of the cross and the bite of the chain. 'Where are you going?'

I felt dazed, bemused. 'I don't know . . . It's stifling up there.'

'Why did you remove the cross?'

'I didn't.'

'You must have.'

'It was an accident.'

Bazile took my arm and said, 'Come now. The tea is made.' We ascended the stairs in silence and as soon as we were back in the parlour, Bazile locked the door and removed the key. 'I'm sorry, Paul. But I would not forgive myself if anything happened to you. Dawn is nearly upon us. Please, sit down and drink your tea.' He excused himself and I heard him speaking to his wife. When he reappeared, he pointed at the window, which was grey with the first light of the new day. 'The sun is up,' he said with a kindly smile. 'We must go.'

After leaving Saint-Sulpice, we went directly to my apartment in order to collect the little Venus. 'Father Ranvier will be most interested in this figure, I am sure,' said Bazile. I wasn't very hungry, but my companion insisted that we stop at a cafe and I managed to eat a few rolls. The bells of Saint-Sulpice rang out and I threw a questioning glance at Bazile. 'Madame Bazile,' he said, smiling. 'And very skilled she is too!' Rising from his chair, he dropped some coins into an ashtray and indicated that it was time for us to depart.

'The cathedral is this way,' I said.

'We are not going to the cathedral.'

I was surprised, given that Bazile had described his mentor as a scholarly priest of Notre Dame. 'Where does Father Ranvier live?'

'Lately, in the Hôtel Saint-Jean-de-Latran.' Bazile paused, and I could see that he was considering whether or not to elaborate. 'I regret to say that Father Ranvier has never been properly appreciated by the Church. The Bishop considers some of Father Ranvier's views,' again Bazile paused before adding, 'unorthodox. Perhaps I should be more respectful, especially where a bishop is concerned, but in my opinion, Father Ranvier has been denied the privileges he deserves.'

When we arrived at the Hôtel, the vestibule was empty and we went straight up to the second floor.

'Shouldn't you have sent a note?' I asked. 'It is still very early.'

'Given what has transpired,' said Bazile, 'I am sure that Father Ranvier will forgive us for neglecting formalities. Besides, I know the hours he keeps. He rises at four thirty every morning and has done so for years.'

We came to a scuffed door and Bazile knocked three times. After a short interval a frail voice called out, 'Who is it?'

'Édouard.'

The door opened and standing before us was a

venerable gentleman whose seamed face was surrounded by a tangled mass of wisps and curls, made all the more striking on account of their whiteness. He squinted at us through oval spectacles with watery grey eyes so pale that they were almost colourless. It was difficult to estimate his precise age, but I fancied he must be at least eighty. Embracing my companion, he cried, 'Édouard, Édouard.' Then, taking a step backwards, he acknowledged my presence with a shy inclination of his head.

'My friend, Monsieur Clément,' said Bazile.

'The nerve doctor?'

'Yes.'

'Please come in.' The room we entered was spacious and resembled a library. Tall bookcases lined the walls and the air smelled of wax, dust and leather. 'Fetch more chairs,' said the priest. Bazile did as he was instructed and we all sat around a table, the surface of which was covered in statuettes of the Virgin, star charts and astronomical calculating devices. 'So,' said the priest to Bazile, 'what brings you here at this early hour?'

'Monsieur Clément,' said Bazile, 'is greatly in need of your assistance.'

'Really?' said the priest, exchanging the spectacles he was wearing for another pair.

Once again, I was obliged to tell my story. It was, perhaps, a little easier on this second occasion and, as I spoke, the priest listened intently. His expression was sympathetic and the creases around his eyes deepened when distress or embarrassment made me falter. When I reached my conclusion, the priest exhaled and whispered, 'Astonishing!'

'The figure,' said Bazile. 'Show Father Ranvier the figure.'

I took the little Venus from my pocket and handed it to the priest. He produced a magnifying glass and, closing one eye, peered through the lens.

'Do you know what it is?' asked Bazile.

'Yes,' said the priest.

'It looks very old.' I interjected.

'It is very old. Third century BC, or thereabouts, and almost certainly the work of the Parisii, the Celtic tribe who occupied the Île de la Cité before the Romans came.'

'You don't think it could be a copy, a replica?'

'No.' The priest turned the figure over. 'What we have here is a sacramental object, probably used to propitiate Cernunos, the horned god – their god of the underworld.' He put the magnifying glass down and continued, addressing his remarks to me rather than Bazile. 'Unlike other Celtic tribes, the Parisii rarely produced representations of animals and warriors. They were much more likely to make effigies of women and . . .' his lips twisted before he completed the sentence, 'demons.' The priest picked up the figure and handed it back to me. 'Nearly two hundred years ago, workmen digging beneath the choir of the cathedral unearthed four stone altars, now presumed to have been part of an ancient temple. The face of Cernunos is carved on one of these altars, and an individual unfamiliar with the old gods would probably say that it is the face of the devil.'

I felt confused and unsure of what the old priest was implying. He must have detected my confusion, because he leaned forward and his expression softened. 'It will all become clear, monsieur, I promise.' Then, touching his fingertips together, he continued: 'Our city has an exceptionally bloody history. No other capital in Europe has witnessed so much violence and cruelty. It is as though there is something bad here, a pernicious influence that makes men turn against each other. And, invariably, when they turn against each other they also turn against the cathedral. For hundreds of years, the mob has congregated in front of Notre-Dame, brandishing weapons and flaming torches. United by a common savage instinct, they have repeatedly attempted to raze the cathedral to the ground. In 1793 they put nooses around the twenty-eight kings and pulled them off the facade, roaring with delight as each one fell. The statues were then decapitated, smashed and thrown into the Seine. Between 1830 and 1848, Paris was barricaded almost thirty times by its rebellious workers and, every time, the cathedral was attacked. And you will recall, no doubt, the most recent uprising, when the cathedral was set on fire and the archbishop executed. Why should this be?' The old priest sighed. 'Why is Paris such a violent city, and why is it that the mob nearly always directs its ire at the cathedral?'

I recognized that these questions were rhetorical and remained silent.

'Many of our churches are built on sites already associated with worship, such as holy wells, shrines and sacred caves. Those who have studied Hermetic philosophy suggest that these sites are, in fact, spirit portals, locations where the partition between this world and other worlds is weak or ruptured. At Notre-Dame, the partition is at its weakest between our world and the underworld, and by the underworld, I mean Sheol – Tartarus – hell. That is why the Parisii worshipped a horned god. They had knowledge of demons and sought to propitiate them through human sacrifice, usually a young female. In subsequent generations, men whom we would now describe as magicians succeeded in repairing the breach, thus preventing demons from gaining entry into our world. However, the partition is imperfect, and the malevolent powers that inhabit the underworld can still extend tendrils of influence, inciting violence and inducing the rabble to attack the blessed stones that now protect the portal. For reasons that I cannot explain, when you conducted your extraordinary experiment, your soul was able to pass through the partition and, of course, when your soul returned, it was no longer alone – but accompanied.'

It was evident from Bazile's neutral expression that he was familiar with Father Ranvier's startling cosmology. I, on the other hand, had enormous difficulty assimilating what I was being told. Although I was prepared to accept the reality of my own demonic possession, what I was now being asked to believe was strange beyond imagining. Yet there was something very persuasive about this priest, who spoke with calm confidence and whose scholarship did not rely on ponderous citations or frequent lapses into Latin and Greek.

'Please,' said Father Ranvier, 'may I see your hands?'

I held them out and he lowered his head to inspect my fingernails. They had not been trimmed since the previous day and had already grown long and sharp.

'You will recall,' said Father Ranvier, 'that the most celebrated chimera of Notre-Dame, the winged demon, also possesses very long fingernails.' Ranvier glanced at Bazile. 'You see? Poor Méryon understood the significance of this. Demons have a predilection for blood. They modify the physiology of their hosts to make them better instruments for the satisfaction of their need. That is why Méryon titled his etching of the winged demon "The Strix". Poor, poor man. Baudelaire thought he was possessed. I fear the poet may have been right.'

The fatigue that typically came over me during daylight hours was hindering my ability to concentrate. Father Ranvier and Bazile continued talking, but I was not always able to follow their exchanges. They spoke about a thirteenth-century treatise on diabolical manifestations, and then Marcel, a bishop of Paris reputed to have battled with vampires in the fifth century. When their conversation returned to my situation, Bazile said, 'Well, Father? Do you think you can help Monsieur Clément?'

'Yes,' replied the priest. 'Yes, with your cooperation,

Édouard, I can help Monsieur Clément. But I must make one thing perfectly clear,' he glanced from Bazile to me and back again. 'The undertaking that lies ahead of us is highly dangerous. The demoniac who ran amok at the Salpêtrière – or at least the thing that had seized control of his faculties – recognized the presence of a superior power. Our adversary occupies an elevated rank in the infernal hierarchy. One does not confront such an entity with anything less than extreme trepidation. To do otherwise would be folly.' Father Ranvier tapped the ends of his fingers together. 'I can perform an exorcism and, by the grace of God, the demon will be cast out; however, that will not be the end of it. The demon will continue to exist in our world and retain its capacity to do harm.'

'Why can't it be sent back to hell?' asked Bazile.

'Once,' replied Father Ranvier, 'there were books containing rituals for that purpose. But now they are all lost.'

'Then what are we to do?' I asked, desperation making my voice ragged.

'We must attempt to confine it.'

'You mean to imprison the demon?'

'Yes,' said the priest. 'The Holy Roman Emperor Rudolf II is reputed to have acquired a demon in glass which he subsequently exhibited in his museum of oddities. At that time, the practice of trapping spirits in glass and gemstones was quite common among the magical elite.' Father Ranvier got up and shuffled over to one of the bookcases. He ran his finger across a row of spines and when he had found the tome he was looking for he returned to the table. The text, faded to ochre-brown, was dense and annotated throughout by different hands – some cramped, others more broad and flowing. Father Ranvier began to read: 'Procure of a lapicary good clear pellucid crystal. Let it be globular or round each way alike and without flaws. Let it then be placed on an ivory or ebony pedestal . . .' The priest raised his head. 'Édouard, can you obtain the keys to the crypt of Saint-Sulpice?'

'Yes. Of course.'

'Then let us meet there tomorrow, at dawn. I must make preparations. Do not eat or drink anything, except water, and keep a close eye on Monsieur Clément. He must not be left alone for a second.'

12

Bazile and I spent the rest of the day in the north tower of Saint-Sulpice. He had taken the precaution of locking the door, but this really wasn't necessary. As the day advanced, I became tired and subsequently fell into a prolonged, dreamless sleep. When I awoke, it was past ten o'clock and the sky beyond the semi-circular windows had turned from grey to black. After attending to my ablutions, I sat down at the table.

'Can we go for a walk?' I asked Bazile.

'No,' he replied. 'I think that would be most unwise.'

He handed me a book of religious meditations and suggested that I read them.

'Where is Madame Bazile?'

'I've sent her away.'

'Normandy?'

'No: just round the corner. She's staying with a friend – a widow.'

'I'm sorry.'

Bazile raised his eyebrows, 'What for?'

'This imposition. Your inconvenience.'

He shrugged, dismissed my apology with a gesture

and lowered his head over the open pages of a Bible that he had evidently been studying while I was still asleep. The room was poorly ventilated and I was soon feeling extremely uncomfortable. 'Édouard,' I said, 'I need some air. Please, let us go outside, just for a few minutes. I am . . .' I paused to find the right words, 'quite sane. I can assure you, I won't try to run away.'

Bazile sighed. 'Can't you see what it's doing, Paul? Please, rest and ready yourself.'

I tried to read through the meditations but found the piety of the authors overblown and their blandishments vaguely irritating. My discomfort increased and I loosened my collar. As my fingers brushed the chain around my neck, I was reminded of the cross that hung beneath my shirt, and I noticed that it was not merely warm, but hot, as if the heat from my body was accumulating in the metal. I glanced across the table at the top of Bazile's head, his thick black hair divided by a makeshift parting. He was so engrossed in the Gospel of Saint John that his nose was almost touching the page. I looked from his crown to a large silver candlestick, and the idea of connecting one forcefully with the other entered my mind with a kind of casual indifference. The cross was now burning with a fierce heat, yet the pain was curiously cleansing. I pressed my palms together and offered Bazile my hands. 'You should tie me up. I am having thoughts. Unwanted thoughts.'

Bazile's eyes widened as he registered the implication of my appeal. 'It seems then, that the battle has already begun, but the very fact that you are able to make such a request clearly demonstrates that the first victory has been yours. No, I will not bind you. Let my belief in your innate goodness serve to strengthen your resolve.' He then recited the Pater Noster, raising his voice on reaching the words, 'deliver us from evil'.

The night wore on. I experienced more unwanted thoughts, some accompanied by obscene images of degradation, others by violent urges of increasing intensity. Bazile suggested that we kneel and pray together, but prayer had little effect. Disturbing thoughts and images continued to assail my mind and it was only after the middle hour of darkness had come and gone that finally I detected a subtle change, a shift in the balance of power, the gradual reduction of the demon's influence.

Bazile filled two oil lamps and lit the wicks with a match. 'Are you ready?' he asked.

'It isn't dawn yet,' I replied.

'The sun will be up within the hour,' said Bazile. 'Come.'

We descended the stairs of the tower and made our way directly to the crypt. As the door opened, a breath of air carried with it the smell of damp stone. I could not see very far ahead; indeed, it seemed as if we were walking through a void. The rich acoustic, however, betrayed the crypt's unusual size, its unseen vastness. Eventually, we came to a rectangular area defined by columns and arches.

'The remains of the original Saint-Sulpice,' said

Bazile, 'The present church was built on the site of this earlier building, a modest house of prayer where parishioners worshipped for more than five centuries.'

I judged that these crumbling remnants must be of medieval origin, although they might just as easily have survived from a more distant past: Roman times, or perhaps even earlier. Bazile and I smoked, paced up and down and engaged in some desultory conversation, and in due course my companion consulted his pocket watch and said, 'I'll see if Father Ranvier has arrived.' He picked up one of the oil lamps and marched off, soon disappearing from view. I peered into the murky distance and listened: a key turning in a lock, a door closing, the lock again, and then silence.

Almost immediately, I experienced an irrational terror of abandonment and my breathing became irregular. This 'attack' was far worse than any I had experienced before and came with a chilling suggestion of premature burial. I thought of Saint-Sulpice, directly above my head – its baroque bluffs and cliff faces, the immense dome above the transept crossing, all of that colossal weight, bearing down on the columns of the old church – and had to wrestle with a strong impulse to chase after Bazile. I imagined the vault collapsing, entrapment and a slow, agonizing death. Shadows leaped across the walls and I was overcome by a profound sense of being alone. It came as a great relief, therefore, when a few minutes later, I heard Bazile returning with Father Ranvier: footsteps, and the reassuring strain of human voices. The two men emerged from the gloom, Father Ranvier holding the oil lamp aloft, and Bazile struggling to manage what looked like a portable table under one arm and a canvas bag under the other.

'Monsieur Clément,' said Father Ranvier. He stood in front of me, gripping my arms above the elbow. 'A difficult night, I hear. Still, by God's grace you have survived the ordeal and by His grace we will be triumphant.' Placing his hands on his hips, the priest looked around at the columns and arches before adding, 'Hallowed ground! We have this to our advantage. Édouard, set up the table here, and then clear away anything that can be moved.'

In spite of his age, Father Ranvier went about his preliminaries with surprising vigour. He took a white cloth from the canvas bag and spread it over the table, pressing out any creases with his palm. Several items were laid out: a crucifix, two candles and a lead-capped wand – unwrapped from a handkerchief of blue silk. It did not seem right that a crucifix, the principal emblem of the Church, should be placed next to an object commonly associated with stage magic, and Bazile's remark about the Bishop not valuing Father Ranvier's scholarship came back to me. Suspicion was swiftly displaced by curiosity when the priest produced a sphere of glass so heavy that lifting it out of the bag made him grimace. I came forward and offered to help him, but he turned on me and said with unexpected ferocity, 'No, monsieur. You must not touch this.' He positioned the sphere on an ivory base some distance away. On his return, Father Ranvier ran a length of cord around the table, making minute adjustments as he did so to ensure its circularity. He chalked various words and symbols around the circumference and drew a complex triangular figure inside; then he lit seven candles, which he placed at regular intervals equidistant from the table so as to create a 'greater circle' of light. Next, Father Ranvier produced a straitjacket and a leather strap. Naturally, I associated such restraints with lunacy and incarceration. Perhaps all doctors who specialize in the treatment of brain disorders have a fundamental fear of suffering the same fate as their patients.

'I can't.' I said. 'Absolutely not!'

'But, monsieur,' said Father Ranvier, 'you have already experienced the demon interfering with your mind, is that not so? And there will be worse, I am sorry to say, much worse, before our work is done. Our enemy will not relinquish its claim on your soul without contention, and when it is forced to accept the sovereignty of Christ, it will be enraged, disposed to perform acts of violence. If you do not wear these restraints, you will be placing all of us in terrible danger.'

I could not argue. There was no logical objection and I duly submitted. After the jacket had been fastened, I sat on the ground, and Bazile bound my ankles together. 'Have courage, my friend,' said the bell-ringer. 'Have courage.' But I could see that he was troubled.

Father Ranvier and Bazile stepped into the circle, after which the priest instructed Bazile to touch the ends of the cord together and to seal the break with candle wax. 'Édouard,' said Father Ranvier, 'you must not step outside this circle. Whatever happens, do you understand?' Bazile nodded and Father Ranvier handed him a black leather volume. 'Let us begin.'

The two men knelt on the ground and began a series of invocations, beginning with the Litany of the Saints. A psalm preceded an antiphonal appeal on my behalf.

'Save this man your servant.'

'Because he hopes in you, my God.'

'Be a tower of strength for him, O Lord.'

'In the face of the enemy.'

'Let the enemy have no victory over him.'

'And let the Son of Iniquity not succeed in injuring him.'

When the invocations were concluded, Father Ranvier and Bazile stood up for the summoning.

'Unclean Spirit! Power of Satan! Enemy from hell!' The priest's voice was resolute. 'By the mysteries of the incarnation, the sufferings and death, the resurrection and the ascension of Our Lord Jesus Christ; by the sending of the Holy Spirit; and by the coming of Our Lord into last judgement, make yourself known to us!'

I had imagined that the ritual would proceed without effect for some time, that there would be a certain amount of waiting before the demon was compelled to respond; however, when the summoning was ended, I felt a 'change', subtle at first, almost imperceptible, but gradually intensifying until the reality of the phenoma god releasing a thunderbolt. Stamping his foot, he roared, 'I exorcize you, Most unclean spirit! Invading enemy! Filth! Be uprooted and expelled from this creature of God.'

My head felt as if it had been struck by an axe. I experienced blinding, white hot pain, and then there was darkness, oblivion.

enon was beyond question. Glances were exchanged and it was obvious that Bazile and Father Ranvier could also sense it: a presence, seeping into the atmosphere, nowhere and everywhere, a hiss beneath the silence, bringing to each of us an acute and almost painful awareness of our human frailties – the softness of flesh, the frangibility of bone, the precarious equilibrium of the mind. Its essence was threat, a wordless but unmistakable threat to the self. I tensed my muscles as if in readiness to receive a blow, and it seemed that this reflexive, physical reaction was complemented by some inner psychological equivalent: a contraction or shying away at the very core of my being.

Father Ranvier made the sign of the cross and cried out, 'God, Father of Our Lord Jesus Christ, I invoke your holy name and humbly request that you deign to give me the strength to expel this unclean spirit that torments this creature of yours.'

There was a strange abrasive noise, like two rocks being scraped together, and a dusty shower of granulated mortar fell from above. I stared up at the vault and saw nothing remarkable, apart from a billowing sail of spider's silk. My fear of being buried alive returned and I called out, 'The vault is unstable. Quick, release me. We must get out!' Bazile and Father Ranvier looked at me with blank expressions. 'Didn't you hear it?' I implored, my voice becoming shrill with exasperation.

'Hear what?' asked Bazile.

I rolled my eyes upwards. 'The stones shifting!'

'I heard nothing,' said Bazile.

'Nor I,' said Father Ranvier.

'Please. We must get out at once.' I struggled hopelessly to break free.

'Monsieur Clément,' said Father Ranvier. 'It is the enemy, interfering with your mind again.'

I could not accept this. The mortar was real. 'Édouard, help me. Please.' Bazile winced and repeated his earlier exhortation: 'Have courage, my friend, have courage.' As he spoke these words, I noticed that his breath was clouding the air. It was getting colder and a shiver passed through my body.

Father Ranvier began to recite the twenty-third psalm. 'The Lord is my shepherd, I shall not want; He makes me lie down in green pastures. He leads me beside still waters; He restores my soul.'

I felt a curious loosening of the constituent parts of my character, a loss of integrity, a shift towards disintegration. Bazile was looking nervous.

'Even though I walk through the valley of the shadow of death, I fear no evil . . .' Father Ranvier faltered as the temperature plummeted. 'For Thou art with me; Thy rod and staff, they comfort me.'

The impression we all shared, I am sure, was of approaching menace, inestimable power, and I was overcome by a visceral, bowel-gripping fear. My teeth chattered and the world around me seemed to pitch and roll. When Father Ranvier had finished the psalm, he threw his arm out, fingers outstretched, as if he were

a god releasing a thunderbolt. Stamping his foot, he roared, 'I exorcize you, Most unclean spirit! Invading enemy! Filth! Be uprooted and expelled from this creature of God.'

My head felt as if it had been struck by an axe. I experienced blinding, white hot pain, and then there was darkness, oblivion.

13

On opening my eyes, I was aware that a period of time had elapsed, but could not judge how long. It could have been minutes or hours. I was lying on my side some distance from my previous location. Two of the candles in the outer circle had been knocked over; my body ached and my thoughts were sluggish. Father Ranvier was chanting and Bazile was crouched at the edge of the circle – although still within it – studying me closely.

'Clément, are you back?'

'What happened?' I asked. 'Is it over?'

'No, my son,' said Father Ranvier. 'It is not over.'

'I am still . . . possessed?'

'You are,' said the priest.

'What happened?' I repeated.

'You lost consciousness,' answered Bazile.

'Indeed,' I replied, annoyed that he was merely stating the obvious. 'But what happened while I was gone?'

Bazile glanced at Father Ranvier and something passed between them: an unspoken request to proceed received reluctant approval.

'You were raving – speaking gibberish – and . . . It spoke to us. A voice, coming through you.'

'And what did it say?' Bazile shook his head. 'Tell me!' I demanded.

'Horrible things, obscenities.'

'You must tell me what was said!'

'It spoke of your friend, Madame Courbertin.' Again, Bazile consulted the priest, who sighed and indicated that he should continue. 'It said that she will not live long, and, very soon, it will have the pleasure of tasting . . .' Bazile shuddered, '. . . tasting her blood in hell'.

'The enemy is a liar – the great deceiver!' cried Father Ranvier. 'We must take no heed of what it says.'

I tried to sit up. 'Help me? Please. I can hardly move.'

Bazile started towards the circle's edge but Father Ranvier grabbed his arm and pulled him back. 'No! You must not!'

'But Monsieur Clément is in pain. Surely I can. . .'

'No!' The priest cried. 'You will stay in the circle!'

Bazile looked down on me, his expression full of pity. 'I am sorry, Clément.'

The priest returned to his table and began to recite a formal chastisement of the demon. He began in hushed tones, but was soon invoking the 'word made flesh' and delivering urgent reprimands. My head throbbed and I felt nauseous.

'You are enjoined in His name! Depart from this person whom He created! It is impossible for you to resist!'

As the priest's haranguing of the demon went on, the pain in my head became intolerable. I passed out several times, and on regaining consciousness found myself first on one side of the circle, then the other, feeling worse and worse on each successive reawakening, until everything became confused and blurred. I can recall, however, a brief interlude during which I seemed to recover my mental faculties and reasoned thus: you damaged your nervous system during the experiment and have since been suffering from delusions and hallucinations. You did not go to hell and did not return possessed. Courbertin died naturally and, because of your guilty conscience, you imagined it was you who had killed him! You cannot trust your memories: they are adulterated by fantasies and dreams. Charcot is right. Demoniacs are hysterics and hysteria is a condition of the nervous system.

I called out to Bazile, 'Stop! No more! I have misled you! I see it all clearly now. I am insane. I need sedation, electrical therapy, the water cure. Please, I am sick. Take me to the Salpêtrière! Take me to Charcot, I beg you.'

'Ah, Monsieur Clément,' said Father Ranvier, 'the enemy is now at his most dangerous. Do not be seduced by superficially attractive arguments. Even if you doubt the existence of God, our foe can yet be beaten, but if you doubt the existence of the Devil, all is lost.' His words resounded in the recesses of the old church, returning 'all is lost' as a portentous echo. The columns began to waver like fronds in a stream and I sank into a prolonged delirium.

I saw lurid visions: Thérèse, writhing luxuriously beneath a grotesque incubus, the winged demon of the cathedral taking flight and Courbertin climbing out of his grave and walking the streets of Montparnasse with the stilted gait of the living dead. I saw medieval townsfolk dancing with skeletons, oceans of fire and the discoloured eyes of the Port Basieux bokor.

It seemed that I was in this fevered lunatic frenzy for an eternity, time enough for the great pyramids of Egypt to become dust. And when finally I awoke, rising up through the cloudy medium of my disordered imaginings, my body welcomed me with blinding pain: no longer restricted to my head, but spread through every burning nerve. My face was pressed against the ground, but I could see the cloth of the straitjacket, scuffed and torn. In my mouth, I could taste blood, not sweet and fragrant, but sharp and metallic.

Bazile and Father Ranvier were looking at me with horrified expressions. They were both sitting cross-legged and breathing heavily, as if they had recently completed a task that had required sustained physical exertion. Father Ranvier looked tired and dishevelled – his spectacles were tilted at a steep angle across his nose and his purple stole was unceremoniously wrapped around his neck like a scarf. The cold was unbearable. I rolled onto my back. On my forehead beads of perspiration had turned to ice, and the air smelled faintly of sulphur.

'What happened?' I croaked.

Bazile stood up at once. 'Thank God! You're alive. I

thought it had killed you.' He looked up at the vault, then down to me, and I guessed that he was estimating the distance I had been raised and dropped. Turning towards Father Ranvier, Bazile said, 'We must stop now. Monsieur Clément may be injured. We can't go on.'

'No. That is not possible.'

'But he might be in urgent need of medical attention. And this abomination, this hideous thing . . .' Lost for words, Bazile waved his arms in the air. He swallowed and continued hoarsely, 'This is not what we expected.'

'We have no choice,' said the priest. 'We are bound to finish what we have started.'

'Bazile,' I cried. 'You really must help me.' I coughed up a clot of blood and spat it out.

The bell-ringer was about to step out of the circle, when the priest lunged and took hold of his leg.

'Édouard!' cried the priest. 'It is not safe.'

'Monsieur Clément may be dying.'

'Indeed, and we must save his soul. That is our principal obligation.'

The priest stood, raising himself up by pulling on Bazile's coat.

'I cannot stand by and watch him suffer!' said the bell-ringer.

The priest's eyes were ablaze with fanatical zeal. 'Have faith, Édouard!'

I remembered Bazile once talking of some spiritual crisis he had experienced in his past, and I sensed that a much greater struggle was taking place than was readily apparent. 'Have faith!' demanded the priest again. Bazile made an abrupt movement and shook off the priest's determined grip.

'It cannot be right,' said Bazile, 'To abandon him. Not like this.'

'And what about your wife?' the priest responded. 'Is it right to abandon her? If you step out of this circle, then the husband whom she next meets may be a very different man to the one she married.'

The riposte was well chosen. Bazile was torn, uncertain, and Father Ranvier, observing his indecision, seized the opportunity to carry on with the exorcism. 'Get out, impious one! Get out! Out with your falsehood! He who commands you is He who dominated the sea and the storms. Hear, therefore, and fear, Satan! Enemy of the faith! Enemy of humankind! Source of death! Thief! Deceiver!' Each accusation felt like a cudgel landing heavily on my skull. 'Depart this person!' bellowed Father Ranvier. 'Root of evil! Warp of vices!' He shook his fist and bared his teeth. 'Out, out! In the name of Michael, most glorious prince of the heavenly army! In the name of the blessed apostles, Peter and Paul, and all the saints! In the name of Jesus Christ, God and Lord! And in the name of Mary, mother of God, immaculate virgin, queen of heaven and hell: I cast you out! Be gone, demon, be gone!'

Father Ranvier's frame sagged. It was as though this final invocation had sapped all of his remaining strength. He looked impossibly old, like an ancient tree, desiccated and encased in cracked bark. A clump of hair had dropped over his forehead and his slack mouth resembled a hastily sewn suture. His gravitas had withered away, leaving nothing in its place but a suggestion of weary dotage, or even worse, senility. The silence that followed was exceptionally dense. Like the silence after snow at night – layered, unearthly – and I watched with horrible fascination as each candle began to dim, each flame dwindle to a faintly glowing point of light. From somewhere in the darkness came the sound of respiration: moist, low-pitched and reminiscent of a large animal. The in-breath was short and harsh, like a gasp, the out-breath long and accompanied by a liquid rattle.

'What is that?' whispered Bazile. But the priest did not reply.

The presence, formerly experienced as an abstract threat to the self, was now more substantive and possessed recognizable attributes: predatory intelligence, a savage disposition and malign purpose. It seemed, though – and I am not sure how, exactly – that it impinged upon the senses primarily as a noxious stench, vile and fetid. My empty stomach contracted and I began to retch. The will to destroy and obliterate was so fundamental to its nature, that proximity alone was sufficient to stress the fault lines of the mind and encourage fragmentation. A descent into madness seemed imminent. This effect was not confined to the inner world of the bystander. Once again, I heard stones shifting and felt a sprinkle of mortar on my face. It was as if materialization had placed an unbearable strain on the physical universe. Everything, from the bones within my aching body to the vault above my head, seemed in danger of being torn apart by indiscriminate and wayward forces. And at the centre of this 'system' was a molten core of hateful intent, a desire – no, more than that: an insatiable craving, lust – for human torment. I could sense its excitement, the registration in its consciousness of our vulnerability, its salacious hunger for flesh and its thirst for blood.

There was a ruffling of leathery wings and a loud snap, like the sound of a loose awning in the wind. The candles went out and we were plunged into darkness.

'Father?' said Bazile. Instead of the old man's voice, I heard a clop – as if a horse were tentatively testing the ground with its hoof. 'Father Ranvier?' Bazile persisted, but the priest seemed to have fallen into a kind of trance.

The bell-ringer struck a match and I saw his disembodied face floating above the ground as he searched desperately for the oil lamps. He found one, lit the wick, and adjusted the regulator to produce more light. When he looked up again, he screamed, the same scream that had issued more than once from my own mouth when confronted with the incomprehensible. The demon had emerged from the shadows. It moved quickly: stance forward-leaning, like a bull preparing to charge, septic eyes, eager and luminescent, horns tapering to points of precise and deadly sharpness. A snarl revealed fangs and the slithering fork of its tongue. It lashed its tail, whipping up a spray of stone chippings that stung my face. Terror, indescribable terror, made me jabber and weep. To see it again, at close quarters and unquestionably real, reduced me to mewling idiocy.

Father Ranvier, who had until that moment been immobile, seemed to recover his senses. He snatched the wand from the table and aimed it at the demon, muttering something in a language I did not recognize. Then, at the very top of his voice, he yelled, 'Adon, Schadai, Eligon, Amanai, Elion.' Bazile had fallen to his knees, both hands clamped tightly over his mouth. 'Pneumaton, Elii, Alnoal, Messias, Ja, Heynaan . . .'

The demon halted at the edge of the protective boundary and glared at the priest. I saw its arms rising, talons opening out in the lambency of the oil lamp, and slowly Father Ranvier began to ascend. He gained height, until his head almost touched the ceiling and then drifted out of the circle. At first, his limbs flailed around, but he was soon overcome by superior forces and his attitude became stiff and erect, like a soldier standing to attention. There was a ripping sound, and the priest's cassock and underclothes dropped to the ground in shreds, revealing a scrawny physique. Bereft of dignity, his shrivelled genitalia retracted into a wiry nest of grizzled hair. He began to rotate and his wrinkled buttocks came into view. When the turn was complete, his bladder failed, and a stream of urine trickled down his thighs and dripped from his calloused feet. The demon raised its arms for a second time and brought them down forcefully, emitting an effortful aspiration. What I saw next was so horrible, so utterly repulsive, that I very nearly swooned. Father Ranvier's skin was stripped from his body. It came away in one piece, like the slough of a snake, and for a brief moment stood on its own – a papery, hollow man – before collapsing. The priest shrieked and I flinched at the thought of so much pain: shrill, howling, bright-hued pain, incandescent scalding agony. His exposed muscles looked raw, lobster red, and glistened as if coated with a reflective laminate. Father Ranvier's face, although hideously transformed, was still recognizably his own. A few tufts of white hair still adhered to his bleeding scalp and his pale eyes were as distinctive as ever. His jaw trembled and the muscles attached to it began to bunch. He was evidently making a supreme effort to speak. After a few unsuccessful attempts, I heard him croak the word, 'Tetragrammaton.' And, a second or two later, his body burst into flames. Instinctively, I curled into a ball to protect myself from the scorching heat.

My terror had reached a limit beyond which there was nothing except mute vacancy. When the conflagration had exhausted itself, I straightened my back and peered through a veil of thick smoke. Father Ranvier's incineration had been total, and nothing remained of him except the smell of cooked meat and charred flakes in the air. The triumphant demon had not budged. It swung its head round and looked at Bazile, who was cringing and repeating, 'Merciful heaven, preserve us!' Then, reversing the movement, it fixed its eyes on me.

A faint white light had appeared, softly glowing in the middle distance. Its gentle insinuation dispersed like milk in water. I was too much in the thrall of those venomous eyes to be distracted. However, the light grew brighter and I realized that its origin must be the sphere of glass. The demon's expression altered and – insofar as one can interpret the rearrangement of such crude features – the alteration suggested wariness or caution. Shafts of brilliance were soon shining through the hazy atmosphere and the light became so bright that I could no longer look at it directly. I heard the demon snort, a deep growl, and then a stuttering, scraping sound, as if it were digging its talons into the ground to resist traction. There was more shattering of stone and I realized that a struggle was taking place. I was buffeted by a blast of air as the demon beat its wings, and then it roared: an appalling expression of towering rage. There was more lurching, and crashing, and I thought the vault was finally going to come down on our heads. But instead, there was a strange rushing, experienced more in spirit than through the senses, followed by an abrupt and total silence. The bright light was suddenly extinguished and for some time the ground shook – a soft, prolonged tremor. When I looked up, the demon was gone.

Bazile stepped out of the circle and walked towards the glass sphere. On reaching his destination, he craned forward, examined the object and drew back suddenly.

He made a hurried sign of the cross, removed his coat, and threw it over the sphere in a single movement. On returning, he knelt and helped me to get out of my restraints.

'Are you all right?' he asked.

'I don't think anything is broken.'

He nodded and whispered, 'God in heaven!'

Both of us were in a state of shock.

As I sat, with my back against one of the columns and rubbing my sore legs, Bazile lit more candles and started to clear up Father Ranvier's materials. He collected all of the items together, including the sphere (which he kept wrapped in his coat), and put them in the large canvas bag. He then turned his attention to Father Ranvier's remains. Although he was able to handle the shredded clothes, when it came to picking up the priest's skin he baulked, and I saw him turn away. After composing himself, he made another attempt, but the 'bundle' he had lifted unravelled, revealing its human outline. Bazile's face crumpled in disgust and only after several more endeavours did he manage to fold the skin into a shape that would fit into the bag. Finally, he erased the chalk marks with the heel of his shoe and I was reminded, curiously, of my old associate Tavernier, destroying the vèvè on our journey to Piton-Noir.

When I looked at my pocket watch, I thought it had stopped. 'What is the time?' I asked. Bazile consulted his own timepiece, and we discovered that only an hour had passed since our arrival. Clearly, the materialization had violated so many natural laws that even the flow of time had been affected. We climbed the stairs of the north tower and stumbled into Bazile's parlour. Taking our usual places at the table, we sat, dazed, saying nothing, until the morning was well advanced, and even then, all that we could utter were short declarations of horror and incredulity.

'When you depart, you must take the crystal with you,' said Bazile.

'I don't want it!'

Bazile sighed. 'I am sorry, Clément, but it is your . . . responsibility.'

'I can't.'

'I am afraid you must.'

'We could destroy it. Yes, let us do that.'

'And risk the release of what is now trapped inside?'

'Then I shall bury it!'

'And what if someone digs it up?'

'I'll take it somewhere remote. A distant country.'

'Wherever you go, it won't be safe. The glass might break.'

'What are you suggesting, Édouard? That I carry this abhorrent thing around with me for the rest of my life?'

'Yes. And perhaps at some point in the future you will find a solution to your predicament. But until then . . .'

'And what if I die before that is possible?'

'You will have to make some form of provision. I am sorry.' Bazile glanced over at the canvas bag.

'What are you going to do with Father Ranvier's remains?'

Bazile stood up and went to his sideboard. He removed a large scissors and set them down by the stove.

'One cannot expect the authorities to believe us. If we implicate ourselves in Father Ranvier's disappearance, then we will both become suspects in a murder investigation.'

Again I was reminded of my time on Saint-Sébastien, and how Tavernier had urged me not to go to the police. I was visited by a sense of déjà vu.

Bazile removed Father Ranvier's skin from the canvas bag and unfolded it on the floor. It looked like a slumbering ghost, transparent and slightly greenish. The priest's beard and most of his wild white hair were still attached and served as a vivid reminder to us that only minutes earlier this ghoulish sheath had been occupied. The bell-ringer squatted, opened the stove door and began cutting. I saw him detach Father Ranvier's right hand, now a drooping glove, and toss it onto the flames. The skin began to crackle and the room filled with a smell not unlike roasted pork. Bazile closed the stove door and said, 'I think I am going to be sick'.

14

I spent most of the following two weeks lying on my bed, looking up at the ceiling, smoking, thinking. Although I had not broken any bones, I had sustained some superficial injuries and I was suffering from exhaustion. Be that as it may, I felt quite changed – restored – much more my former self. Like the rest of humanity, when the sun had dropped below the horizon I began to feel tired, and when the sun rose I felt refreshed and alert. My fingernails grew at a normal rate and I was able to discard my eye-preservers. Even my nightmares were different: no longer vivid, fiery visions, but dark reflections, like moonbeams on water. I was still haunted by impressions of recent events, particularly the exorcism, but I also experienced episodes of giddy excitement when I remembered that I was now free of the demon's influence.

During this period of convalescence, I wrote several letters to Thérèse, declaring my affection and expressing my desire to see her again soon. I received only one reply which was short and apologetic: our next meeting would have to be postponed, because Courbertin's cousin was in Paris and she was occupied with the settlement of some family business. I thought nothing of this. Later that afternoon Bazile arrived with a selection of cold dishes prepared by his wife. We ate together at my dining-room table, but our conversation was subdued. It is said that shared adversity brings people closer together, but in our case something indefinable seemed to have come between us.

'Where have you put the crystal?' he asked.

I pointed at a chest of drawers. He nodded and his expression became pained.

I said, 'Father Ranvier's end was so unexpected. I am concerned that he meant to do something more. I worry that the ritual was not finished.'

Bazile chewed his lower lip. 'I cannot say for certain, but as far as I know, there was nothing else to be done.'

'Was there anything in Father Ranvier's bag to suggest otherwise? Items that he had not made use of?'

'Additional candles, a book of prayers,' Bazile replied. 'Nothing significant.'

I was mildly reassured. Even so, a general state of anxiety persisted. I wanted to know more about what had happened during the exorcism, particularly when I had been unconscious, but Bazile would not be drawn. He simply paraphrased Father Ranvier. 'Lies. All lies and wicked deception. You do not need to know such things.' He was clearly relieved when I allowed him to change the subject.

That evening, I devoted my thoughts entirely to Thérèse. I was undecided as to whether I should give her a full account of my remarkable history. She was open-minded, inquisitive and fascinated by the supernatural, yet I imagined that even she, on hearing such a fantastic narrative, might doubt the storyteller's sanity. Moreover, such an account would necessarily be incomplete. How could I explain what had happened to Courbertin? Although I was not, strictly speaking, responsible for his death, I had wanted to be rid of him and suspected that my ill-will had played a significant part in his demise. Remembering Courbertin filled me with grief, for he had been a kind, generous man.

I yearned to see Thérèse again, ached to see her face, touch her cheeks and kiss her lips. I conjured consoling images: Thérèse rising in the morning, laying out her towel and stooping to pick up a sponge, droplets glistening on her wet thighs and sunlight in the tangled mass of her hair. I wanted to cradle her in my arms, stroke her brow and hear her contented sighs. Another life suggested itself: a country practice, my new wife tending roses in the garden and little Philippe paddling on the shore of a wide blue sea.

When Thérèse's second letter arrived I could hardly believe what she had written. She was very sorry, but after much soul-searching, she had come to the conclusion that our relationship must end. We had not made each other happy. Now that Courbertin was dead, Philippe must be her priority.

I remembered the last time we were together, her body covered in cuts and bruises, and supposed that her decision must be connected with my acts of violence. Immediately, I went to my bureau and scrawled a frantic reply. I pleaded, grovelled, begged her to reconsider, confessed my faults and promised to change. But her position became entrenched and it soon became apparent that she was very angry with me. She blamed me for her 'moral decline' and declared, using forceful language, that she now meant to recover her 'dignity' – something that, for obvious reasons, could not be achieved if our 'association' continued. I resolved to see her that instant, to tell her the truth, to tell her everything; however, as I was running down the street, coat-tails flapping in the rain, common sense prevailed. How would presenting myself on her landing, drenched and raving like a maniac about demons help my situation? I stopped running, turned round and walked back to my apartment, where I composed another hopeless letter.

The following Monday I resumed my duties at the Salpêtrière. Charcot was delighted to see me back on the wards again and made some polite enquiries about my health. I told him that I had caught a chill and that my old respiratory problem had returned. He made some sympathetic remarks, patted me on the back and departed, dispersing papal benedictions with one hand while twirling his cane in the other.

I could not stop thinking about Thérèse. I missed her terribly. Indeed, I missed her so much that my mind began to play tricks on me. One morning I awoke and saw her standing at the end of my bed. She was wearing a dress of black silk and crimson lace and her eyes were abnormally large and bright, like emeralds set in white marble. Even though I realized she wasn't really there, her name escaped from my lips and I reached out my hand. The hallucination faded and joy was replaced by misery. I took to loitering outside her apartment, and after several weeks of agonizing indecision, I finally entered the building. I climbed the stairs and knocked on her door, which was opened, not by a maid, but by a man who looked vaguely familiar. It was the gentleman who I had seen at Courbertin's funeral, the one who had been wearing a long cape. I introduced myself and asked to see Madame Courbertin. The man shook his head. 'I am afraid she is not receiving visitors today.' He then shut the door in my face. Thereafter, all my subsequent letters were returned unopened.

A few months later, gripped by the same impulse, I walked to Thérèse's apartment again. I informed the concierge that I had come to see Madame Courbertin.

'She doesn't live here any more,' he replied, stubbing out a cigarette. 'She's moved away.'

'Where?'

'She said something about going back home to live with her parents. Her husband died, you know. Dreadful shame.'

'And where do her parents live?'

The concierge shrugged. 'How should I know?'

Everything around me seemed to go dark.

'Are you all right, monsieur?'

'Yes,' I replied, touching the wall to steady myself. 'Thank you.' I left the building, muttering, 'I have lost her.' But then I remembered that Courbertin and Thérèse had come from the same town. Over the next few days I made some discreet enquiries at the hospital and established without much difficulty that Courbertin was a native of Chinon. I nurtured a fragile hope that, with the passing of time, Thérèse might forgive me. This prospect, however unlikely, became the single most important reason for my continued existence.

The season changed. I busied myself at the hospital and worked hard. Charcot took me aside and informed me that my valuable contribution to the hysteria project had been 'officially' noted. Occasionally, I met with Bazile, but we were no longer at ease in each other's company. Life seemed dull and empty. Most evenings were spent alone, reading works of hermetic philosophy and ritual magic, but none of them contained what I was looking for.

On the Boulevard Saint-Michel is a shop that stocks plain, hard-wearing furniture. I had been meaning to go there for some time. When the opportunity finally presented itself, I stepped into a warm interior that smelled strongly of beeswax and sawdust. Down in the basement, I discovered several chests, one of which was made from solid oak. I asked the proprietor if it could be reinforced.

'There is no need, monsieur,' he replied, rapping the wood with his knuckle. 'It is virtually indestructible.' Ignoring his objection, I told him of my requirements. He listened heedfully and then said, 'Lead? Iron plates? But you won't be able to move it, monsieur. It'll be too heavy.' I dismissed his remark and negotiated a price. He was still shaking his head when our business was concluded. As I was preparing to leave the proprietor asked, 'What do you intend to keep in it?'

'Family heirlooms,' I replied.

'They must be of great value.'

'Indeed.'

'Well, rest assured, monsieur: they will never be stolen. It would be easier to rob a bank!'

One day, I was speaking to Valdestin and he asked me if I knew of anyone who might be interested in an unusual appointment. A friend of his, a neurologist named Trudelle, had agreed to become 'house physician' to a wealthy Touraine family. Unfortunately, only weeks before he was due to leave Paris, he had met a factory owner's daughter, fallen in love and decided that his interests were best served by remaining in the capital. The family were very disappointed and Trudelle, overcome with guilt, felt obliged to help them find a replacement.

'Well?' said Valdestin. 'Do you know anybody who would be interested in such a position?'

'Yes.' I said. 'Me.'

'Have you gone mad? Charcot always rewards industry, and, given the way you have been working lately, he will almost certainly recommend your advancement next year.'

'I could do with a change.'

'Clément! Don't be absurd!'

'Tell me: where can I find Trudelle?'

Valdestin said that I was being foolish, but I was insistent, and in the end he handed me one of Trudelle's cards. I think I had already made up my mind to get away from Paris. The same restlessness that had preceded my sudden departure for Saint-Sébastien had taken hold of me and I had been simply waiting for the right opportunity to present itself.

I visited the Du Bris family at their hotel, a fine establishment situated near the opera house. Gaston Du Bris was a big man, ruggedly handsome with longish hair and a pock-marked face. His wife, Hélène, was pretty and courteous. They had with them the eldest of their three children, Annette, whose delicate features and winning naivety made her appear somewhat younger than her twelve years, and Hélène's brother, Tristan Raboulet – a man in his mid-twenties whose dress and casual manners were perhaps a little too informal given the occasion. Both Annette and her uncle suffered from epilepsy and their seizures were becoming more frequent. I examined the two patients, discussed their symptoms, and enquired as to what treatments they had so far received. Their local doctor and a so-called 'specialist' at the hospital in Tours had prescribed largely inert substances. I was broadly in agreement with Trudelle, whose prescribing habits were at least more current. Nevertheless, he had neglected to consider the full range of options and I advised accordingly.

'With respect,' I said to Du Bris. 'I am not sure that you need to employ a house physician. Perhaps you should see first how your daughter and Monsieur Raboulet respond to the new medications?'

Before Du Bris could answer, his wife said, 'No.' She wrapped her arms protectively around Annette. 'The seizures are so terrible. Only last week I thought . . .' She shook her head and her eyes moistened.

'It is always very upsetting,' I said with sympathy, 'to see those whom we love in distress. But the seizures are likely to be less frequent and certainly less severe.'

'Even so', said Hélène. She glanced at her husband – a silent appeal for support.

Du Bris nodded and said, 'Monsieur, you seem to be suggesting that we can expect to see an improvement, but the new medications are not a cure. Have I understood you correctly?'

'Indeed.'

'Then I agree with my wife. Having a doctor – a colleague of Charcot, no less – accommodated at Chambault would be very desirable.'

Hélène breathed a sigh of relief.

We discussed certain practical matters and an arrangement was made for me to visit their estate in due course. As I was leaving, Raboulet sidled up to me and said, 'Monsieur Clément, would you be so kind as to recommend a good play?' He looked excessively disappointed when I was unable to. So much so, that I felt obliged to tell him about a concert I planned to attend that very evening: piano pieces performed by a Russian virtuoso. He promptly scribbled the details on the cuff of his shirt, seemingly indifferent to his brother-in-law's disapproval.

I had not expected to see Raboulet at the concert, he seemed too feckless and disorganized; however, during the interval, we met in the foyer and he enthused about the music. 'Thank you, monsieur. A thrilling programme. I am so glad I came.' He was a talkative fellow and I learned that he had a wife called Sophie, and a baby daughter called Elektra after the protagonist of his favourite Greek tragedy. 'I can't think why you would want to leave Paris for the country, monsieur,' he said, making flamboyant gestures. 'There really is nothing to do. You don't get heavenly concerts like this in the village! Still, if you're mad enough to forgo such pleasures then I will be overjoyed. You have no idea how much I crave educated conversation.'

The following week I travelled to Chambault. It was an extraordinarily beautiful chateau, surrounded by exquisite gardens. On my arrival, Annette handed me a little watercolour of a gentleman in a frock coat carrying a black bag.

'For you,' she said.

It was surprisingly accomplished and I recognized myself immediately.

'Thank you, Annette. The likeness is astonishing.'

'Please come and live with us,' she said, her brow tensing. 'Please come and make me and Uncle Tristan better.' Her appeal was so direct, so earnest, that I was quite moved.

I was introduced to Annette's brothers, Victor and Octave, and Du Bris's mother, Odile – a formidable old woman whose presence was quite oppressive. Hélène hovered in the background, quietly observant and slightly agitated. She was clearly anxious that I should find everything to my satisfaction. Du Bris showed me the suite of rooms that would be mine if I chose to accept the appointment. They were spacious and adjoined a massive library. As we were walking through, I stopped to read the titles and discovered that many of the books were about esoteric subjects.

'Are you a student of the occult?' I asked.

Du Bris laughed out loud. 'Me, good heavens, no! I'm afraid I'm not much of a reading man. Riding, shooting – yes; but not reading!'

'Then whose—'

'Almost all of the books you see here once belonged to Roland Du Bris – my great-great-great . . .' he stopped to calculate the precise relationship, but gave up and said instead, 'An ancestor who lived here hundreds of years ago.' He seemed impatient to proceed. 'Come, monsieur. You must see the dining room. We have a tapestry on the wall that once belonged to the first King Louis.'

That night I stayed in Tours, meaning to get the early

train back to Paris the following day. In the hotel parlour, I discovered a map of the area. I traced the course
of the river Loire, from Tours to Candes-Saint-Martin,
and then moved my finger from left to right until it came
to rest on Chinon. 'Not far,' I thought to myself, 'not far
at all.' Before retiring, I asked the porter for some paper
and wrote a letter to Du Bris accepting his terms.

I was ready to leave Paris before the onset of winter. I
said goodbye to Bazile and later that same afternoon
walked to the cathedral. The sun was setting and the
stone of the western facade was ablaze with red-gold
light. Looking up at the central portal I saw devils and
demons, endless permutations of human suffering: an
eviscerated sinner trailing his insides, another tumbling
headfirst into a boiling cauldron and an erring bishop
with the clawed feet of a succubus digging into his shoulders. I saw cascades of intertwined bodies, naked and
vulnerable, descending into torment, leering grotesques,
prodigies, instruments of torture. Among all of this obscene cruelty one scene in particular stood out: a woman,
upside down, with toads and serpents biting her breasts,
a hook in her belly, about to have her loins devoured by
lascivious demons. I remembered the exorcism, Bazile's
stunned voice, 'It spoke of your friend Madame
Courbertin . . .' I wanted to pray for her, but the words
stuck in my throat. How could a perfect, all-knowing
and all-powerful God permit the existence of hell? I had

not found an answer to this question and doubted that I ever would.

My first winter at Chambault was mild. Both of my patients responded well to the medication that I had prescribed and further improvements were achieved with regular herbal infusions. Raboulet had only two seizures between Christmas and Easter, while Annette had only one. The family were extremely appreciative and I was treated more like a guest than an employee. I had plenty of free time, most of which I spent in the library, and when I wasn't reading, I went out riding by the river. Once or twice, I was tempted to take the road to Chinon, but I managed to resist. Life at Chambault was delightful. The estate was a little Eden and I had slithered in like a serpent.

PART THREE

Redemption

15

SUMMER 1881

Chambault

The sun had climbed to its highest point and the white facade of the chateau shone with a radiance of exceptional purity. We had gathered at the edge of the lawn beneath the boughs of a wild cherry tree. Hélène Du Bris was seated at my side, paintbrush in hand, carefully introducing stipples of vermillion onto the green wash of her watercolour. Raboulet was lying on his back, vacantly gazing up through the overhanging branches, and behind him, sitting on the grass with her back against the trunk, was his wife, Sophie, their sleeping infant cradled in her arms. Odile Du Bris had covered her legs with a woollen blanket and was also asleep; I could hear her stertorous breathing. Mademoiselle Drouart, the governess, had organized a game for the children, and Victor, Annette and Octave were chasing up and down the steps which led to the ice house, their voices shrill with excitement. As usual, Du Bris was absent.

Earlier, the cook – Madame Boustagnier – had brought us a basket of freshly baked bread, goat's cheese and apricots. Only a few hollow crusts remained. She had also packed two bottles of wine from the cellar. The red from the estate – distinctive and spicy – had acted on my brain like a potent soporific and my limbs felt swollen and heavy. A butterfly settled on Hélène's easel. Its transparent wings trembled and opened to reveal markings of exquisite delicacy, a network of dark lines against a background of vivid orange. Hélène turned to see if I was looking, and when our eyes met, she smiled and said, 'Do you know what it is, monsieur?'

'No,' I replied, 'I'm afraid I don't.'

'So very beautiful . . .'

'Indeed, madame, and probably quite rare.'

Hélène continued painting, and perhaps because of the wine, I found myself incautiously staring at her. She was wearing a close-fitting gown of blue silk, cut to show the suppleness of her figure. Her arms emerged from short sleeves trimmed with white lace, and I noticed that her skin had darkened during the course of the summer to a sensuous olive. Her hair was piled up loosely on top of her head and held in place by a set of ivory combs. The nape of her neck was visible through a faintly glowing haze of blonde down.

'Monsieur Clément?'

It was the old woman. She had woken up. I rose, a flush of embarrassment warming my cheeks.

'Yes, madame?'

'Would you get me my blanket? It has dropped to the ground.'

'Of course.'

I picked up the fallen mantle and laid it across her legs. When she said, 'Thank you', I thought I detected a certain coldness in her voice. If she had observed me gaping at her daughter-in-law, there was nothing I could do. I made some solicitous remarks and returned to my chair.

Raboulet stood and brushed some grass from his trousers. He lit a cigarette and, addressing no one in particular, said, 'You know, I heard something quite extraordinary the other day. A fellow from Bonviller is supposed to have sold his wife. Apparently, he sold her along with all the furniture in his house for a hundred francs.'

'Who told you that?' asked Hélène.

'Fleuriot,' Raboulet replied. 'He told me that the notary refused to register the sale but the people involved decided to carry on regardless. They signed a document before three witnesses in the marketplace.' The old woman grumbled disapprovingly. 'Now, that can't be right, can it?' Raboulet went on, 'I mean to say, a man can't just sell his wife, surely? What do you think, Monsieur Clément?'

'Parties can agree to conditions without recourse to

law, and often do. I recall there was a similar case reported in Rive-de-Gier, not so long ago.'

'Who would have thought it?' said Raboulet.

'These peasants are brutes,' said the old woman.

'Let us hope,' I said, 'that in the fullness of time, compulsory schooling will have an improving effect.'

'Education is all well and good, monsieur,' snapped the old woman, 'but it will not be enough. The peasantry suffer from a moral weakness. I have lived here all my life and know what they are like. Believe me. They are godless and intemperate.'

'Oh, madame,' said Raboulet, extending his arms and tacitly begging the old woman to reconsider her judgement. Her unforgiving expression did not soften and she turned her head away sharply.

Undaunted, Raboulet continued to inform us of the latest gossip: an argument involving the blacksmith, the appearance of gypsy caravans by the river. His chatter was mildly diverting and occasionally prompted some frivolous banter. Thankfully, the old woman fell asleep again, so we were spared more of her scolding piety. When Raboulet had exhausted his stock of stories, he strolled around the cherry tree a few times before positioning himself between two moss-covered statues of cherubs. He gazed out over the lawn and waved at the children, who stopped their game to return his signal.

'I think I'll join them,' he said. 'They look like they're having fun.'

He picked up a straw hat and stepped out of the

shade and into the fierce midday heat. He was dressed in a pale summer jacket and baggy trousers. His gait was shambolic, as if his limbs were connected to his body only by threads of cotton, and his rangy, uncoordinated step reminded me of a marionette. The children became boisterous at his approach, and I could hear Mademoiselle Drouart attempting to calm them down.

Hélène leaned back in her chair and considered her watercolour. She had only included the southern tower of the chateau, with its conical roof and ornate chimney stack; however, the building supplied a vertical line which divided the picture into pleasing and complementary parts. I said, 'The fallen leaves are particularly well executed.' Hélène was so modest that my praise baffled her. 'No. Really, madame,' I persevered, 'I think it's rather good.'

'You are very kind, monsieur, but I am perfectly aware of my limitations.' She paused and a line appeared on her brow. 'Did you meet many artists when you lived in Paris, Monsieur Clément?'

'Yes, a few, but none of renown: the closest I came to artistic genius was to stand in the same room as Gustave Doré. We were never introduced. He was pointed out to me – a distant figure standing next to the punch bowl – by one of my medical colleagues.'

'You must find life at Chambault very slow, monsieur.'

'Not at all.'

'I worry that we will lose you one day: that you will

get bored with us and our provincial ways and return to the city.'

'I wouldn't dream of it.'

She looked at me in disbelief.

'I am very happy here,' I continued, eager to reassure her. 'I adore the peace, the tranquillity.' Directing my gaze to the noisy group on the other side of the lawn, she raised her eyebrows. I laughed. 'They don't disturb me when I'm in the library.'

'How are your studies proceeding, monsieur?'

'It is a privilege to have access to such a collection.' My response was a subtle evasion and I was relieved that it passed without notice.

Suddenly, the children were racing towards us, pursued by their uncle. Mademoiselle Drouart was following behind, unhurried, striking a graceful pose with her parasol. 'I won, I won,' shouted Victor, as he passed between the two mossy cherubs and collapsed on the ground. I was aware that Annette had purposely decreased her speed so as to allow both of her brothers to beat her. This little act of charity was strangely touching. She had inherited her mother's hair and eyes, and her face, although still that of an innocent, could communicate emotions of surprising depth and maturity. Raboulet arrived next, grinning and coughing after his exertions. He slumped down next to his wife, who looked at him with mock exasperation. Mademoiselle Drouart collected the children together and led them to an adjacent tree, where she began reading to them from a volume of fairy stories.

I closed my eyes and listened to the soft murmur of her voice, the humming of an inquisitive honeybee, and the gentle rustle of Hélène's skirts. I must have dropped off, because when I opened my eyes again, Annette was standing in front of me, a bracelet of tiny flowers in her outstretched palm.

'That is very pretty,' I said.

'I made it for you,' she whispered.

'Thank you.' I replied. 'It is too small for me to wear, so I shall keep it on my desk.' The child gave me the bracelet and I placed it in my breast pocket, making sure not to break any of her carefully constructed links.

'The demoiselles wear flowers.'

'Who?'

'The demoiselles. The fairies of the forest. Madame Boustagnier told me about them.'

'Is that so?'

Raboulet stirred: 'Ha! The doctor doesn't believe in fairies, my dear. He is a man of science, which means that he doesn't believe in anything that he cannot touch or see.'

'But you can never see the demoiselles,' said the child. 'It is impossible. They disappear if anyone gets close.'

'There you are, monsieur,' said Raboulet. 'Science's problem in a nutshell. Although there is no evidence to suggest the existence of certain phenomena, belief in them will persist forever because they cannot be refuted.' Raboulet liked to remind me that he had read one or two volumes of philosophy. 'This is why,' he continued, 'science will never replace the idiocy of religion.'

Hélène swivelled round to make sure that Odile was still unconscious. Anxiety became relief and she waved a cautionary finger at her brother.

'I could see she was asleep from here,' said Raboulet.

'Is that true, monsieur?' asked Annette. 'You do not believe in anything that cannot be seen or touched?'

'No,' I said, stroking a wisp of hair out of her eyes. 'That is not true. Thank you for the bracelet.'

A light breeze, carrying with it the perfume of roses, made the boughs above our heads creak. Some leaves fell and their descent was accompanied by birdsong.

Earlier that summer, I had written a letter to Thérèse. I did not know her address, but had assumed, correctly, that Chinon was so small a town that an envelope carrying her name would not present the postal service with too great a challenge. I had been half expecting her to return the letter unopened, so I was mentally unprepared for her reply, which arrived only two days later. The script was jagged, forward leaning, and in some parts made almost illegible by trails of splattered ink. It was not necessary to read the words to gauge the strength of Thérèse's emotion. She had apparently committed her thoughts to paper, without pause, and in a blind rage: 'I never want to see you again. What you did to me was unforgivable and every day I suffer as a consequence. Perhaps it is only right that a woman who neglected her son and deceived her husband should be punished. Why do you persecute me so? Please, leave me alone. Please, go back to Paris.' I would sit in the library, reading and rereading this letter. It was not her anger that I found so upsetting, but rather her pleading. News of my arrival in the Loire had reduced her to scrawling desperate entreaties: 'I beg you to respect my wishes. Please, please be merciful.' To think of her so frightened and wretched filled me with sadness.

Old buildings are said to make noises, but Chambault was remarkably quiet at night. I folded Thérèse's letter and slipped it into a volume of alchemical writings. When the dogs started barking, I assumed that they had been disturbed by a mouse or a wild cat, but they did not stop, and after several minutes I too detected the sound of an approaching trap: whip cracks, the jangling of the bridle, the rattle of wheels on the village road. The court-yard gate was closed and the vehicle was obliged to stop outside. There were raised voices and someone rang the bell. Louis, one of the servants, called down from a window, a door slammed and there were hurried foot-steps. I tidied my things and slotted the alchemy book back into its space on the shelf. The commotion grew louder and I decided to investigate. When I stepped into the antechamber, I was confronted with Du Bris, entering from the other side. He was in his dressing gown and clutched a rifle in his hands. Keeping pace with Du Bris was Louis, still in his nightshirt, and holding up an oil lamp. They were followed by Father Lestoumel, the curé, and a burly man from the village carrying a girl in his arms. Even from a distance I could see that her limbs were shaking.

'Quick,' I said. 'This way, please.'

At the opposite end of the library was the door to my rooms. On entering the study, I lit some candles, ordered the man to lay the girl out on the divan and commenced my examination. Her head was rolling from side to side, she was uttering incoherent phrases and her face was lacquered with perspiration. Lank black hair was plastered across her forehead. I asked Louis to hold the lamp higher, and as he did so I saw that the girl's skin had a bluish hue. There were blood stains down the front of her smock and her breathing and heart rate were rapid.

'How long has she been like this?' I asked.

'Allow me to introduce Monsieur Doriac,' said the curé, 'the girl's father.' He invited the man to step forward. 'Speak, Thomas. Answer the doctor's question.'

'She's been poorly for weeks,' said Doriac. He was a big, awkward fellow with lumpy features.

'Indeed,' I said, 'but how long has she had this fever?'

'Two days.'

'When was the last time she had anything to drink?'

'I don't know. My wife's been looking after her.'

'Why didn't you call Monsieur Jourdain?'

'We did. He came on Tuesday and prescribed some pastilles. They didn't help, so my wife . . .' Doriac became uncomfortable and he did not finish his sentence.

The curé bowed and spoke confidentially into my ear, 'I went to fetch Monsieur Jourdain earlier this evening, but unfortunately I found him indisposed.' What he meant was that the reprobate had, yet again, drunk himself into a state of insensibility. 'I'm sorry, monsieur, but there was nothing else I could do. I didn't want to risk driving her all the way to Bleury-en-Plaine.'

I listened to the girl's lungs and heard exactly what I dreaded: a horrible crackling as she drew breath. Du Bris must have observed my reaction. He clapped a hand on Doriac's back and said, almost jovially, 'Come, monsieur, let's leave the doctor alone, we mustn't distract him. How about a cognac? You look like you could do with one, and you, Father Lestoumel? Would you like to join us? No? Very well. Come, monsieur.' Du Bris steered Doriac towards the library and beckoned Louis. It was obvious that he fully understood the gravity of the situation. I emptied some water into a bowl and tried to cool the child's forehead with a damp flannel. I then prepared a solution of salicin. While I was dissolving the powder, I asked Father Lestoumel the child's name, and he said that it was Agnès. Positioning myself so that I could raise her up a little, I held the glass to her lips. Her breath was fetid. 'Agnès,' I said, 'listen to me. Keep your head still. You must drink. It is important that you drink.' The poor creature was delirious. I tilted the glass but she didn't swallow anything. The liquid came straight out of her mouth and cascaded down her front.

The curé caught my eye and said, 'When Jourdain's pastilles didn't work, Doriac's wife rode out to Saint-Jean to see Madame Touppin.'

'Who?'

'Madame Touppin. She is reputed to be a healer. In reality, she is nothing but an ignorant hag who sells charms and potions to the gullible and superstitious. She told Madame Doriac to slice a living white dove in two and to place the palpitating halves on the child's chest.' When the curé saw my expression, he added, 'Yes, I know: you wouldn't think it possible in this day and age, but I promise you, monsieur, it is true. Unfortunately, I didn't hear of this obscenity until today, otherwise I would have acted earlier.'

'Are you suggesting that the Doriacs actually . . .'

'Followed Madame Touppin's advice? Yes, and Madame Doriac was willing to wait indefinitely for the treatment to take effect. Naturally, as soon as I saw Agnès, I realized she was in need of urgent medical help, and set about persuading Monsieur Doriac to think again about Jourdain.'

'Really, Father, it is not acceptable that a doctor should be so regularly – as you say – indisposed.'

'Yes,' said the curé, bowing his head. 'You are quite right.' But I could tell by the defeated croak of his voice that he had no appetite for further arguments with the village council.

Taking pity on him I said, 'There is only so much that a priest can do.' He sighed and showed his appreciation with a grateful smile.

'Agnès,' I persisted. 'Drink. You are unwell and must

take some medicine to get better. Please, Agnès, you must try.'

It was futile. When I removed the glass from her lips, it was half empty, and she had imbibed nothing. The stream of nonsense issuing from her mouth continued unabated. Her forehead was burning and I could feel the heat coming off her body in waves. The effect was like standing close to a stove. I set the glass aside and removed the girl's smock, manipulating her arms and pulling the garment off over her head. The revelation of her naked flesh made the holy man cover his eyes. I soaked the flannel and began wiping away a layer of filth, and as I did so, her shivering became more violent. It seemed to me that her skin was a deeper blue than it had first appeared. The curé overcame his scruples and, after a minute or so, lowered his hand.

'Are we too late?' he asked.

The child looked pitiful. She was wasted and her ribs were clearly visible. Foamy sputum, flecked with clotted blood, oozed from her mouth. Wiping it away, I found it difficult to be anything other than frank: 'I am not very hopeful.'

Father Lestoumel nodded. 'Yes, I feared as much. Doriac will be devastated.' He searched in the folds of his cassock and produced a small bottle of holy oil. 'May I?'

I gave my consent and he began to administer the last rites. Rising, I crossed the floor and removed a hypodermic syringe from my bureau. It was my intention to deliver an anti-pyretic intravenously. If the child's fever could be reduced, then there was a slim possibility she might pull through. I could hear Father Lestoumel praying as I busied myself with my bottles, but then something changed. It took me a few moments to identify what was different. Agnès had stopped mumbling.

'Monsieur Clément?' The curé's voice was timid, uncertain. I rushed back to the divan and grabbed the child's wrist. There was no pulse. 'Has she gone?'

'Yes.'

The curé made a cross in the air and continued with his prayers.

Had I hesitated for the briefest interval, I would probably have done nothing, but instead I impulsively ran to the cupboard where the batteries were stored and removed one at random. Placing the mahogany box on the floor next to the divan, I raised the lid. The cells elevated and the elements were instantly plunged into a reservoir of dilute sulphuric acid. I made some adjustments to the coil and the device began to emit a soft buzz. Picking up the electrodes I held them over the child's heart.

'Monsieur,' the curé stirred from his ritual. 'What are you doing?'

Two glowing lines of liquid energy, like miniature bolts of lightning, bridged the gap between the electrodes and Agnès's body. The curé gasped as the girl's eyes opened and her chest heaved. A muscular spasm caused the child's back to arch, and she maintained this position for a second or two, her stomach thrust upwards, before she became limp and fell back. The impact of her landing seemed to knock the air from her lungs, which escaped in the form of protracted, rattling sigh. A further charge had no effect, and when I raised the electrodes, I saw that they had left behind two burn marks. Although Agnès's eyes had opened, and remained open, I was only too well acquainted with the glassy vacant stare of the dead – that chilling emptiness. She was beyond help now. With precise movements, I altered the position of the metal rod within the coil, pushed the electrodes into their cavities, and closed the lid. The buzzing ceased, creating a paradoxical, roaring silence.

'She seemed to come back,' said the curé, 'I have never seen such a thing. I didn't know that . . .' his perplexity rendered him speechless. Nervously worrying the beads of his rosary, his gaze travelled slowly from the dead girl to the battery. 'What is this machine?'

'An electrical device.'

My voice sounded alien, strained and distant. Perhaps it was the peculiarity of my delivery that made Father Lestoumel transfer his attention from the machine to me, and his strong pastoral instincts made him reach out to rest a solicitous hand on my shoulder. I should have acknowledged the gesture, but instead, I stood up and returned to the cupboard from where, among my pharmacological preparations, I took a bottle of rum. I didn't trouble to offer the curé a glass. Sitting down at the table, I rubbed the bristle on my chin and stared across the room at the corpse.

'You are a good man,' said the curé, 'and good men are always welcome in my church.' Emboldened by some inner sense of conviction, he added, 'There is nothing that God cannot or will not forgive.' He could be remarkably perceptive for a country priest.

I finished the rum and said: 'Shall I tell Doriac, or will you do it?'

16

I was preparing an infusion of passionflower and skull-cap when a rap on the door was followed by a tentative enquiry.

'Monsieur?'

I called out, 'Come in,' and Raboulet entered. His hair was mussed and a crumpled linen jacket hung loosely off his shoulders. He hadn't attached a collar to his shirt and he had neglected to shave. I indicated that he should sit, and he slumped down on a chair, extending his legs and placing his hands behind his head.

'Shame about the girl,' he said. 'I just heard; Hélène told me. Was it pneumonia?'

'Yes.'

'Poor child, why on earth did they drag her all the way out here?'

'Monsieur Jourdain was indisposed.'

Raboulet nodded. 'I slept through the whole thing.'

'There wasn't anything you could have done.'

'Like a baby. I thought you'd reduced my bromide.'

'I have. But even small doses have a sedative effect.'

I stirred some honey into the infusion and passed him the glass. 'How have you been feeling?'

'Not too bad.'

'No unusual experiences . . . sensations?' The young man shook his head. 'Good.'

'I was thinking of taking a boat out, later today. No one wants to come with me. I was wondering . . .'

'You can't row on your own.'

'But I've been doing so well.' He took a sip. 'How about you, monsieur? Can I tempt you out onto the river?'

'Not today, thank you.'

'Ah, yes. Forgive me. You must be tired.'

Raboulet stood up and crossed over to the window. Beyond the formal gardens, a carpet of wildflowers stretched off into the distance; aspen quivered on the horizon.

'I get so bored,' said Raboulet. 'There's so little to do.'

I felt sorry for him. 'Perhaps you'll be able to get away from here one day.'

'Do you really think so?' His voice was eager.

'I can't make any promises, but if things continue to improve . . . who knows?'

He finished his infusion and we sat and talked for a while. We smoked some cigarettes and played a game of bezique. When I declared two hundred and fifty I still had two aces. For several weeks, I had been letting Raboulet win, and judged that it was probably about time for him to lose again. Raboulet grinned and vowed to take his revenge. I was to expect, so he declared with counterfeit theatrical anger, 'a humiliating defeat'. As I put the cards away, he asked, 'What do you keep in there, Clément?' I looked up and saw that he was gesturing towards my wooden chest.

'Delicate scientific instruments,' I replied, 'and new preparations that I have yet to test.'

He responded reflectively. 'Yes, of course.' The tone of his voice carried an underlying implication of self-reproach, as if he was thinking: how stupid of me to ask such a question, a doctor can't leave expensive equipment and dangerous substances lying around the place. 'Oh well,' he added, rising from the chair and glancing at my table clock, 'I suppose I'd better leave you to your books and potions. Will you be dining with us this evening?'

'I'm not sure.'

'If you do decide to join us, don't forget the cards, eh?'

My mind was still clouded with memories of Agnès Doriac. After the curé's departure, I had stayed up for most of the night, drinking the remainder of my rum. Had I been less distracted, I might have responded more warily, but I let Raboulet leave, without asking any questions, as if nothing out of the ordinary had happened.

I spent the rest of the morning in the library. Madame Boustagnier, ever solicitous, brought me some soup and bread at midday. Just after two o'clock, the bell rang, and Louis came to inform me that Monsieur Doriac had returned. He wanted to speak with me.

239

'Shall I tell him that you are otherwise engaged, monsieur?'

'No!' I snapped. 'I'm perfectly happy to see him.'

'Very good, monsieur. He is waiting in the courtyard.'

'Why?'

'He wouldn't come in, monsieur.'

'Did you ask him?'

'It was his preference to remain outside.'

I put on my jacket and made my way downstairs. The dogs were barking and I was annoyed that nobody had taken the trouble to calm them down. Doriac was standing by the well, holding a wide-brimmed hat in one hand and a basket in the other. He started towards me, his upper body swaying as he lumbered across the cobbles. Damp patches were visible beneath his arms.

'Monsieur Doriac. Please, why don't you come in?' He looked down at his clogs. They were coated with white dust and he was clearly concerned that he would bring dirt into the chateau. 'You can clean your clogs in the kitchen.'

He shook his head. 'No. I can't stay.' He extended his hand and offered me the basket. I took it from him and peering inside, saw that it was full of straw and eggs. 'Thank you for trying to save my daughter. Father Lestoumel told me you tried very hard. I know it isn't much, but it's all that I have.'

I didn't want to deny him or his family their supper, but I had to accept his gift; to do otherwise would have been churlish, or even worse, insulting.

'Thank you, monsieur,' I said, inclining my head.
'You are most kind. Agnès was very sick. I am so sorry.'
Doriac took a step backwards. Now that he had accomplished his task, he seemed anxious to leave. I looked
about the courtyard and, noticing that it was empty,
asked, 'Where is your trap, monsieur?'

'I don't have a trap.'

'You had one last night.'

'The curé . . .' Doriac's explanation did not proceed
beyond naming the person who had obviously obtained
the vehicle.

'You walked?'

'Yes.'

'All the way?'

'Yes.'

'You must be exhausted. Please, allow me to drive you
back to the village.'

'No,' Doriac replied assertively. 'I can walk.'

I thanked him again for the eggs and he put his hat
on. He looked up into the blueness of the sky, turned,
and began his long walk home. The large wooden gates
had been left open and he was able to leave through the
archway that usually admitted carriages. I watched him
pass the little fountain and take a pathway that veered
off to the left. He didn't look back and proceeded slowly,
head bowed, his ponderous tread suggesting the grim
determination of an ox. When Doriac had disappeared
from view, I went to the kitchen, where I found Madame
Boustagnier chopping vegetables. I gave her the eggs,

informed her that it was my intention to dine alone, and requested an omelette.

'Where did you get these, monsieur?'

'They were given to me by Doriac.' She looked at me quizzically. 'The man who came here last night with the curé.'

'Ah, yes,' she replied. 'The girl's father.' Her face became anguished and she made the sign of the cross with fluid dexterity. 'God rest her soul.'

'The omelette must be made with these eggs,' I said, 'And these eggs only.'

'What? All of them, monsieur?'

'Yes,' I said. 'All of them.'

She reached into the basket, lifted one out, and inspected its speckled surface with interest.

'It's cracked.'

'That doesn't surprise me, Madame Boustagnier. Monsieur Doriac came on foot, carrying that basket all the way from the village.'

'I'll remember him in my prayers.'

I shrugged. 'If you think it will help.'

Cradling the cracked egg in her rough pink hands, she placed it back in the basket with affecting tenderness.

I had just finished giving Annette her infusions when her mother appeared in the doorway. Hélène was wearing a black dress and a silver necklace, her hair was tied back and two garnet teardrops hung from her earlobes.

'Are you finished with Annette, monsieur?'

'Yes, madame.'

'And is she well?'

'Very well.'

The child addressed her mother: 'Monsieur Clément put only one spoonful of honey in my medicine.'

'Oh, why was that?' asked Hélène.

'He said that I am sweet enough already.'

'Monsieur,' Hélène said in mild reprimand, 'you will give Annette an inflated opinion of herself!' I was somewhat embarrassed by the child's disclosure, and made some light-hearted remark before pretending to rearrange my bottles. I could hear Hélène's skirts sweeping the floor as she crossed to the window. 'Monsieur,' she continued, her voice a little strained, 'My mother-in-law has asked Father Lestoumel to say a Mass for the repose of Agnès Doriac's soul, and she was anxious that you should be informed. The service will be held tomorrow afternoon, in the chapel.'

'Please thank Madame Du Bris for her kind invitation; however, I must decline.'

Hélène nodded.

'Monsieur Clément?' I turned and saw that Annette was standing beside my wooden chest.

'Yes?'

'What do you keep in here?' She dragged her hand over the lid, creating a channel through the dust.

'Why do you ask?'

'It is so very large.' She caressed the padlock and insinuated her finger into the keyhole.

'Dangerous substances,' I said. 'Chemicals.'

The child seemed satisfied with my answer.

'Come, Annette,' said her mother, 'you have an English lesson with Mademoiselle Drouart and we mustn't keep her waiting.' Annette moved, but her hand seemed to linger on the lid, delaying her departure, for a brief moment before she succeeded in pulling away.

Hélène regained my attention. 'Will you be dining with us tonight, monsieur?'

'No. I intend to retire early.'

'As you wish, monsieur.'

I stood at the doorway, watching Hélène and Annette as they walked through the library. Even then, as my thoughts raced, I could not stop myself from admiring Hélène's figure and her graceful carriage. When they had reached the astronomical globes, I called out, 'Annette.' Mother and daughter stopped and turned to face me. 'Annette, would you come here, please.' I beckoned, and the girl returned. Lowering my voice, I asked, 'Annette, have you been talking to your uncle Tristan about what's in my chest?' She shook her head. 'Perhaps you were playing some sort of guessing game?' Again she shook her head. I smiled and added, 'Oh, I forgot to give you this.' I produced a boiled sweet from my waistcoat. 'Thank you, monsieur,' she said, before running back to her mother.

When Hélène saw what I had given Annette, she cried, 'You spoil her!'

I made a gesture, communicating my helpless affection for the child. Mother and daughter performed a pleasing synchronous revolution and marched into the shadowy antechamber. I needed to think and decided to go outside for a stroll.

Chambault did not possess a single large garden, but a number of relatively small gardens, all exquisite examples of the horticulturalist's art: intimate, scented spaces in which to sit and meditate or find solace in beauty. I crossed the courtyard and walked out into the Garden of the Senses, a system of concentric perennial beds rippling out from a central fountain, and from there entered directly into the Garden of Healing – a favourite haven of mine, planted with medicinal herbs. Sitting on a bench beneath a willow tree, I inhaled the calming fragrances. The sun was setting and the pale turrets of the chateau turned pink in the pastel light. I did not move until the sky had darkened and some precocious stars had appeared above one of the conical roofs.

On my return, I informed Madame Boustagnier that I was ready to dine, and a tray was brought to my rooms: an omelette, some bread, a dish of strawberries and a bottle of fruit brandy. As I ate, I was troubled by a peculiar sense of having stumbled across some important fact, but I was unable to say what it was, exactly. This feeling seemed to be connected, in an obscure way, with Doriac's eggs. When I had finished eating, I took off my collar and waistcoat and lay on the divan. For over an hour, I smoked and stared at the chest, trying to persuade myself that the curiosity expressed by both Raboulet and Annette concerning the contents was nothing more than a bizarre coincidence.

Raising myself up, I went over to the table and lit another candle. It was then that I noticed something different. I went down on my knees, and saw a line on the floor, just to the left of the chest. On closer inspection, I realized that the line was created by an edge of dust. The cause was obvious: dust had collected around the chest, and the chest had been moved approximately four centimetres to the right. There were no scratches on the floorboards. The chest was a very heavy object, made from solid oak, trimmed with brass, and lined with lead: the underside was reinforced with iron plates. When I arrived at Chambault, six powerful men were needed to carry it up the stairs. Although the chest had been displaced by a relatively small distance, this could not have been the result of an accidental knock, and nobody in the chateau was strong enough to push it. I was overcome by a feeling of dark foreboding – cold, obstinate dread.

For several hours I paced around the room, before going down on my knees yet again to examine the line of dust. No matter how many times I looked at it, I was obliged to reach the same conclusion. The chest had moved. I retired to my bed, but did not fall asleep for several hours. When finally I drifted off, I dreamed of Madame Boustagnier in the kitchen: a residue of memory from the previous day. She was inspecting one of Doriac's eggs, just as she had in real life. Once again, I heard her say, 'It's cracked.' Her voice sounded so loudly that I awoke. The meaning of the dream was all too apparent. Now I understood the cause of that insistent nagging feeling, of having encountered some important but unidentifiable piece of information. I imagined the pitch-black interior of the chest – a flaw in the glass, a hairline crack, spreading. My heart was beating wildly in my ears. I would have to open the chest to assess the damage, for that was the only explanation. It hadn't been opened in over a year, and the prospect of doing so filled me with horror.

17

I came upon Odile Du Bris just as she was leaving the chapel. A veil covered her face and a wrinkled hand clutched Louis' forearm for support. On hearing my approach, she looked up and said, 'Ah, Monsieur Clément. Do you have a moment?' She dismissed Louis with an imperious gesture and permitted me to escort her back inside. The space we entered was roughly circular and dominated by an ancient plaster altarpiece. The relief figures and ornamentation were crudely executed and painted in faded reds and gold. In front of the altar was a small table, entirely covered in blue brocade, on which rested an open prayer book. The deep, rounded depressions in the well-worn hassock showed where two protruding kneecaps were frequently accommodated.

Odile Du Bris lowered herself onto a chair and indicated that I should close the door. I performed the task and stood before her, my hands clasped behind my back. She looked me up and down and then said, 'Did Hélène invite you to the service, monsieur?'

'Yes,' I replied.

'You did not come.'

'No.'

She took a deep breath and expressed her disapproval with a lengthy sigh. Then, lifting her veil, she fixed me with a cold stare.

'How is my granddaughter?'

'Very well, madame.'

Odile's expression softened slightly and she fussed with her lace shawl. 'I worry about her.'

'There is no need to be unduly concerned.'

'She doesn't act her age,' Odile sneered. 'She doesn't comport herself as a young woman should.'

'Madame, she is only—'

'She talks nonsense about fairies and goes about as if she is in a dream. It is not right, monsieur.'

'Annette is very imaginative – a thoughtful child. It is her nature.'

'Thoughtful, monsieur? There is a difference between thinking and wool-gathering.' I did not want to argue with the old woman. When she spoke again, her voice was less confident and trembled slightly with emotion. 'You must make Annette better, monsieur. You must.' Her eyes moistened and she pretended to adjust her veil. When she had completed the manoeuvre she allowed the gauze to drop in front of her face. She was a proud woman and it was all too easy to forget her age and infirmity. I took a step forward and rested my hand on hers for a fleeting moment, just enough to communicate that I was aware of her distress, and then withdrew. Odile nodded and assumed her stiff attitude. When she spoke again, there was metal in her voice. 'I never approved of the marriage. But my son is headstrong. Had his father been alive . . .' She straightened her back, and drew obvious satisfaction from some imaginary scenario. A half-smile appeared and then faded as reality reasserted itself on her senses. 'There's something in their blood,' she added with contempt.

'I'm sorry?'

'The Raboulets. Look at Annette's uncle.' She shook her head. 'And there were others. Old Raboulet was just the same.'

'It is quite true, madame, that there are certain constitutional vulnerabilities that can be passed down from generation to generation. But if a condition can be managed, then individuals so afflicted can expect to live a full and happy life.'

Odile snorted. 'Annette will not be a child forever. What hope is there for the girl when she reaches maturity? She's not far off it! How many suitors can we expect?' Odile pushed out her chin defiantly. 'A good match with a local family is out of the question. Even if we send her to Paris, enquiries will be made and, I can assure you, people talk. If she could only be more sensible, more womanly, at least then there might be a chance.'

'Your granddaughter is kind and has many endearing qualities. There is nothing deficient in her make-up. Indeed, in many respects, I think she exhibits sensitivity and intelligence in advance of her years.'

Odile tutted and looked away. 'Monsieur. Would you be kind enough to call Louis?'

A filigree candelabrum had been placed on the altar next to some pots of dried lavender. The air was laden with scent and the light that passed through the stained-glass windows created pools of amber on the flag stones. I had been dismissed.

I passed from the Garden of Healing into the Garden of Intelligence, a delightful assortment of yellow and blue blossoms surrounded by pergolas of rose and humming-bird vine. The path led me to an uneven staircase which I climbed until the Garden of Silence came into view: a rectangular lawn, contained by low box hedges, with a Roman urn standing on a pedestal at its centre. Beyond the terraces which dropped away at my feet, the cor-belled turrets of the chateau emitted a warm glow in the early light, as if the sun's rays were being refracted through honey. I inhaled the morning air, which was cool and fragrant with lilac and the white chocolate undertow of clematis. A pallid wafer moon floated above the chimney stacks, more like a recollection, a thing imagined, than another world.

As I walked around the Garden of Silence, I felt strangely cleansed and began to feel more hopeful. There was no need to act rashly. Perhaps it was a temporary phenomenon. I should be patient and review the situation pending further developments; if there were none, it would be wise to leave the chest alone. The death of the Doriac girl had probably upset me more than I had realized. Attempting an electrical resuscitation had been ill-judged. Undertaking the procedure was bound to bring back bad memories. I should have left the battery in the cupboard and allowed the girl to die naturally. The whole episode had unsettled me.

On returning to my rooms, I enjoyed a breakfast of freshly baked rolls, fruit conserve and a brackish, aromatic coffee of exceptional strength. The walk had sharpened my appetite and I ate with relish. I spent the remainder of the morning in the library reading Montaigne, most notably, his essay titled 'How our Mind Tangles itself Up'.

It occurred to me that I had spent most of the year either cooped up in the library or riding around the estate. Perhaps it would be appropriate for me to spend some time away from Chambault? Raboulet and Annette had not had any seizures in over six months and I broached the subject with Du Bris.

'How long will you be absent?' he asked.

'A week or so,' I replied.

He turned his palms outwards and smiled. 'That seems perfectly reasonable. Where are you going?'

I heard myself reply: 'Chinon.'

18

Louis drove me to the village and it was there that I caught the diligence. The journey was not arduous and I glimpsed Chinon for the first time in the late afternoon. It was an impressive sight, ramparts and towers on a low ridge, the pale stone blushing as clouds passed in front of the sun. The approach road was well maintained and the vehicle made very good progress. Within minutes of crossing the river Vienne I was standing in the market square.

It was relatively easy to find an inn. I was shown a room which, although not spacious, was comfortably appointed and, after a short rest, I ordered some bread and cheese. This I ate outside, beneath a canopy of bright red flowers. I then went for a stroll.

The crooked medieval streets were mostly deserted. Apart from an old woman sitting in a doorway and a mangy stray dog, I saw no other living creature. I turned off the main thoroughfare and ascended a steep cobbled path that rose higher and higher until it reached the town's lofty fortress. From this vantage point the view was quite spectacular. I gazed south, over a patchwork of rooftops and timbered gables, beyond the river, where fields and vineyards rolled away to the shimmering horizon.

'She is down there', I thought to myself. 'Somewhere.'

The impulse that had made me travel to Chinon was obscure. I wasn't wholly sure what I was doing there. Of course, there were superficial justifications – reconnaissance, information-gathering, testing my nerve – all of them quite ridiculous. In reality, I wanted to find Thérèse and tell her how much I loved her. I wanted to take her in my arms, feel her warmth and touch my lips against her hair. I hoped that when she looked into my eyes she would see the torment, anguish and remorse, recognize my plight and take pity on me. Even though I could no longer believe in an all-knowing, all-powerful God of love, I was still prepared to believe in love itself. In a universe without certainties, love had become my rock, my pole star, my still centre. Love was all that I had left.

Over the next few days – I cannot remember how many – I wandered the streets, anxious, expectant, my heart racing whenever I saw a woman in the distance. One evening, and one evening only, I drank myself into a stupor. When I awoke the following morning I went to the post office, but a headache prevented me from making the relevant enquiries. Instead, I sat in a cafe, where I overheard two men talking about market day. Later, I asked the waiter on which day of the week market day fell, and he replied, 'Thursday.'

In a town the size of Chinon, all of the inhabitants

would be out on market day, buying provisions, gossiping, meeting friends. She would be there: a tall, well-dressed woman, conspicuous among the hoi polloi, moving from stall to stall, graceful, poised. The image persisted in my mind like a premonition.

I slept badly on Wednesday night and when I awoke on Thursday morning I felt agitated and fearful. Breakfast was served in my room but I hardly touched it. I went to the market square early and watched the stallholders laying out their produce and wares. People began to arrive, money changed hands and acquaintances gathered together in small noisy groups. I circulated around the square, studying the merchandise: wicker baskets, glazed pottery, brightly painted plates, goat's cheese, cured meats, quince jelly, pickled samphire, almonds and prunes stuffed with marzipan. A gypsy was trying to sell a piebald horse. One of the stalls was covered with a chaotic jumble of household items and I caught sight of myself in an oval shaving mirror. I looked unkempt, even disreputable. How would Thérèse react if she saw me like this? I straightened my hat and tried to look calm and dignified.

A mass of dark cloud was building overhead and the temperature began to drop. I had been patrolling the market for over an hour and was about to give up, when the crowd parted and I saw a gentleman dressed in a brown jacket and trousers. His skin was tanned and he sported a large bushy moustache. He was holding the hand of a child. Although the boy had grown, I recognized Philippe immediately. For a moment, I froze, but then I stepped forward and, making a show of glad surprise exclaimed, 'Philippe. Good heavens! Philippe, my dear little friend! Do you remember me?' The boy's expression remained blank, so I continued, 'Surely you remember me!' I then offered the old gentleman my hand, which he shook with unexpected firmness.

'Monsieur Arnoult. And you are?'

'Monsieur Clément.' I paused to see if the name meant anything to him, then added, 'I was a colleague of Philippe's father.'

'A doctor?'

'I worked with Henri at the Salpêtrière. Dear Henri; he is sorely missed.' I narrowed my eyes and looked from Arnoult to the boy, and back again. 'You must be Philippe's grandfather – on his mother's side?'

'Yes,' Arnoult replied. 'That is correct.'

'And how is Madame Courbertin?' I asked, attempting to sound natural, but my voice came out strained and hoarse.

Arnoult winced and stroked Philippe's hair. 'Not very well, I'm afraid.'

'Nothing serious, I hope.'

'Unfortunately, she is very ill.'

'Very ill?' I repeated. 'What is she suffering from? I do not wish to pry, monsieur. I only ask in order to establish if I might be of service.'

Arnoult turned Philippe towards a knot of gabbling women. 'Go and help your grandmother.' The boy ran off and the old man readied himself to answer my question. 'She had a condition, a stomach complaint, and took morphine to control the pain. Unfortunately, she was not very good at regulating her medicine and often took more than was good for her. Our doctor, Monsieur Perrot, tried to get her to reduce the amount she was taking, but this proved very difficult. She had temper tantrums, bad dreams and screamed like a mad woman in the night. The boy was terrified.' Arnoult shook his head. 'We couldn't go on like that. It was impossible. My daughter resumed her habit and became weaker and weaker. Her heart is not strong.'

There was a rumble of thunder and it started to rain. The people around us began to scatter.

'I am sorry,' I whispered.

'You knew her well?'

'Yes,' I replied. 'Henri was very good to me.'

'What was your name again?'

'Clément. Paul Clément.' It still meant nothing to him.

Philippe was standing next to his grandmother. She indicated her intention to find somewhere to shelter by placing a hand over her head.

'Excuse me, monsieur,' said Arnoult, 'I must go.' He advanced a few steps and then stopped. Looking back, he said, 'We live by the river.' He recited an address. 'If your business detains you in Chinon . . .'

'Thank you. I would very much like to see her again.'

'Then come this afternoon,' said Arnoult. 'I would appreciate a second opinion.'

Arnoult pressed his hat down to ensure that it would stay on and hurried off in pursuit of his wife and grandson.

At one o'clock I walked to the embankment and followed the river until I came to a house that was set back from the road. It was a substantial property with peeling paintwork and faded green shutters. I rang the bell and the door was opened by Arnoult, who invited me in and introduced me to his wife. Madame Arnoult was a handsome woman with strong, regular features. Her smile was an exact copy of Thérèse's.

'How is she?' I asked.

'Not good,' Arnoult replied. 'Her condition has deteriorated. We called Monsieur Perrot when we got back from the market. He is with her now.'

I ascended a staircase and was shown into a musty bedroom. When I saw Thérèse, my legs gave way and I would have fallen to the floor had not the old man grabbed my arm. 'Monsieur?'

'I'm all right,' I said, 'I'm sorry.'

He released his grip. The woman lying beneath the eiderdown was hardly recognizable as my beloved Thérèse. Shadows gathered where I expected to see her eyes, and her angular jaw bone defined the precise limit of her chin. Her skull was too present, too eager for exposure. She was wasting away.

Arnoult drew my attention to a middle-aged gentleman standing by the window. 'Monsieur Perrot,' he said. I nodded, moved to the bedside and sat on a wooden chair. Lifting Thérèse's limp hand, I noticed that her fingers were blue. I was vaguely aware of Arnoult continuing: 'Monsieur Clément was a colleague of Henri, they worked together at the Salpêtrière.'

'Thérese,' I whispered. 'Thérese. It's Paul. Can you hear me?'

Perrot came forward. 'She lost consciousness an hour ago.'

Arnoult spoke again. 'Monsieur Perrot? Monsieur Clément? Something to drink?'

'An anisette,' said Perrot, 'mixed with water.'

'And you, Monsieur Clément?'

I looked up. 'Nothing for me, thank you.'

Arnoult left the room and Perrot asked me if I had been informed of Thérèse's medical history.

'Her father mentioned morphine,' I replied.

Perrot lowered his voice. 'She had a long-standing addiction. The old man thinks that it all started with a stomach complaint.' He shook his head. 'I did everything I could to get her off it, but without success. She has been very ill for several months now. Very ill.' He tapped a stuttering rhythm over his heart and looked at me knowingly. 'She saw a cardiologist in Tours. He wasn't very optimistic.'

Thérese coughed and emitted a low groan. Her lips were cracked and a white residue had collected in the corners of her mouth.

'Do the family know?' I asked.

'I think Arnoult understands. I'm not sure whether his wife does.' Perrot removed his stethoscope. 'Were you close?'

'Yes,' I replied, turning away to conceal my grief. 'We mixed in the same circles – in Paris.'

'Poor Philippe,' Perrot continued. 'First his father, then his mother. Dreadful.'

Arnoult returned and handed Perrot his anisette. The doctor drank it while making some bland remarks, before picking up his leather bag. 'Well, I must be on my way. Madame Musard has a fever and I promised to see her again.' Looking over at Thérèse, he added, 'I'll be back as soon as I can. Stay where you are, Arnoult, I'll see myself out.' We listened to Perrot descending the stairs and the front door opening and closing.

'What do you think?' asked Arnoult. 'Is there any hope?' I couldn't answer him. My throat was too tight. Arnoult sighed and said, 'I thought as much.' He sat on the opposite side of the bed and bowed his head. After a few minutes, he stirred and said, 'Why Chinon, monsieur? What brings you to our town?'

I told him a little of my circumstances and said that I was taking a short holiday. He then asked me some questions about my life in Paris and I exaggerated how well I had known Henri. Arnoult's questions were innocent enough, but he clearly found it curious that his daughter had never mentioned me. I found the pretence tiring and wanted Arnoult to leave. I wanted to be alone with Thérèse.

It was an overcast day, and by mid-afternoon the room was quite dark. Arnoult lit some candles and then dozed off. He was relieved by his wife, who took his place. She asked me the very same questions and I repeated identical falsehoods. Perrot returned at eight o'clock and undertook another examination. He offered me his stethoscope and I was obliged to listen to the irregular beat of Thérèse's heart.

I remembered our apartment in Saint-Germain: the shadow of my hand on her back, her rasping as my fingers closed. Was this my fault too?

When Perrot left the room I could not restrain myself any longer. I wrapped my arms around Thérèse's neck and sobbed into her lank hair, 'I'm so sorry – so very, very sorry.' She felt flimsy, insubstantial, and I feared that if I handled her too roughly her ribs might snap. Withdrawing a little, I kissed her forehead and then her lips. 'Please forgive me,' I pleaded.

There were footsteps on the landing. I quickly found my handkerchief and wiped away my tears, but this clumsy attempt to hide my emotion proved futile. My voice was thick and my eyes were still prickling. Arnoult's expression was sympathetic, but I also detected a hint of suspicion.

'Would you like something to eat?' he asked.

'It is kind of you to offer,' I replied. 'But no, thank you. Perhaps I should go now. I do not wish to intrude.'

Madame Arnoult arrived with Philippe. She guided the sad-looking boy around the bed and said, 'Say goodnight to your mother, child.' Philippe planted a kiss on Thérèse's cheek and recited a touching prayer – an entreaty to the Blessed Virgin.

As he was leaving I stopped him and made him stand squarely in front of me. 'Philippe, your mother is very ill, and she has not been well for a long time. Illness changes people. But we will remember her how she was, when she was healthy and happy. She loves you, Philippe. She told me so on many occasions. She loves you more than any-thing – anything in this world.' I let him go and his grandmother took his hand. At the door, he paused, and said, 'Goodnight, monsieur.' But there was no warmth in his voice.

When Philippe and his grandmother had departed I sat in silence with Arnoult until the sky turned black. The old man drew the curtains and I said, 'May I come tomorrow?'

'If you wish,' he replied.

The following morning Thérèse was no longer at peace. She was in an agitated state, plucking the eider-down and mumbling. Occasionally, her eyes would open, but she registered nothing. Her fingers were freezing and I rubbed them incessantly to keep them warm.

Perrot appeared just before noon.

'She's uncomfortable,' he said. 'I think she needs sedation.' He gave me the opportunity to object, but he was her physician and I did not want to interfere.

Hours passed. I went for a walk and returned when it started to rain. Madame Arnoult had prepared a meal for her husband and Philippe. I did not join them, knowing that while they ate together I could be alone once more with Thérèse.

She was lying very still and her breathing was shallow. Quite suddenly, her eyes opened and she seemed to focus on me. I clasped her hand. 'Thérèse,' I cried. 'It's me, Paul. Do you see me? Oh, Thérèse, my darling, how I love you: how I love you! ' I saw the light of recognition flare in her eyes. Then surprise turned to fear. She was terrified. Beneath my thumb, I felt the last movement of blood in her veins. Her eyes remained open, but she was dead.

I sat on the embankment indifferent to the downpour. The surface of the water became choppy as an unseasonably cold wind gained strength. I remembered the demon's prediction: Thérèse would die and it would have the pleasure of tasting her blood in hell.

Father Renvier and Bazile had insisted that this vile taunt signified nothing, but they had clearly underestimated the demon's power.

I stayed out until nightfall and, after returning to the inn, I slept in my wet clothes. The next morning I caught the diligence back to the village. My muscles ached and I shivered all the way. I paid a farmer to take me to the chateau in a trap, and on my arrival went straight to bed. Although the weather was now perfectly pleasant, the sheets felt like ice and my teeth chattered. Louis came to see if I wished to dine with the family, but I was feverish and by that time quite unwell. Raboulet came up after dinner to see if I needed anything, but I sent him away.

'I have an infection,' I said. 'I should be left alone.'

'But you must eat,' Raboulet protested.

'Get Madame Boustagnier to leave some bread and water outside my door. That will suffice for now. If I need more I will call Louis.'

I was burning and my mouth felt as if it had been packed with hot ashes. Even after taking salicin my temperature remained perilously high and my mind was invaded by vivid memories and epic nightmares. I saw myself handing Thérèse an enamel syringe and saying, 'For you: a special gift.' I saw a funeral cortège marching solemnly behind a white coffin carried by leering demons and I saw Thérèse trailing torn cerements, wandering vulnerably across the fiery expanses of hell. It is impossible for me to describe my misery. I wept and wept until I seemed to have no substance.

The illness lasted for two weeks, after which I began to feel a little stronger. One day, towards the end, I awoke to find Annette sitting next to my bed.

'What are you doing here, child?' I asked.

'I came to see you,' she replied.

'Please. You must leave now or you will become unwell too. Does your mother know you are here?'

'No. She told me that I shouldn't come.'

'Then you had better go before she notices that you are missing.'

'It isn't right.'

'What isn't right?'

'You being here, all on your own.'

'I am perfectly happy.'

'No. I don't think so. I think you are sad.' She pointed to a glass on my bedside cabinet. 'I have made you a hot sugar and lemon drink. Madame Boustagnier said that it is good for chills.' She stood and pressed her cool palm against my forehead. Imitating my attitude and manner she said, 'Yes, a definite improvement.'

'Clean your hands before you leave,' I said with stern emphasis.

Annette walked over to my washstand and poured some water. Dipping her fingers in the bowl, she said, 'Are you very ill, monsieur?'

'No. Not very ill.'

'Good. I prayed for you in the chapel. I prayed that you would not die.'

'Thank you. That was most considerate.'

'Why does God listen to some prayers and not to others?'

'I don't know. Perhaps you should ask the curé.'

She considered this advice and then said, 'Yes. Perhaps I should.' After drying her hands she walked to the door. Her movement was so smooth it seemed to arise in the absence of any friction. 'Don't forget your drink, monsieur.'

'No,' I replied. 'I won't.'

She raised her hand, her expression coy.

'Goodbye, Annette. And thank you.'

I listened to her steps receding and when she was gone, for the first time since my return from Chinon I was aware of the birds singing outside my window.

My recovery was slow. A month later I was still quite weak; however, my old routine was eventually re-established. I monitored Annette and Raboulet's health, administered medicines, went riding by the river and read late into the night. But I was not the same man. I was altered. Something of my former self had died that day in Chinon: something essential, something that would never again be revived. A particular image suggested itself when I reflected on my inner desolation: my heart, shrivelled up like the head of a dead rose.

On the days when I was feeling more robust, I would go on lengthy excursions up into the hills where the cave-dwellers lived. They were poor farming folk who had created homes for themselves by digging into the soft tufa cliffs. Their infants were often sick and many would have died without my care. Why was I doing this? It is difficult to say. But if I had any reason at all, it was simply to spite God.

19

SEPTEMBER 1881

Mademoiselle Drouart had entered the antechamber and I saw her hesitating on the threshold of the library. She was about to knock on the door jamb when I called out, 'Please, mademoiselle. Do come in.'

Her heavy heels sounded loudly on the floor as she marched towards me.

'Good morning, monsieur.'

'Good morning, Mademoiselle Drouart.' I drew a chair out from under the table and the governess sat down. She was young and in possession of a flawless complexion, yet she was habitually serious and had a tendency to frown. Her chestnut hair was tied back and she wore a pair of spectacles that made her look like a spinster. She was carrying a portfolio. I took the seat opposite and noticed her stealing a quick glance at the book I had been reading.

'I am sorry to disturb you, monsieur, but I need to tell you something. It concerns Annette.' She placed the portfolio on the table, untied the ribbon and opened it out. 'Yesterday, we drove down to the village in order to make some drawings of the church.' Sorting through the loose papers, she selected a few for my consideration: pencil and charcoal sketches of Saint-Catherine's steeple, executed in a free hand and rich in detail. Mademoiselle Drouart registered my tacit appreciation and added, 'I think Annette must have inherited some of her mother's talent.'

'It would certainly seem that way, mademoiselle.'

'She is quite accomplished,' said the governess, 'which is why I felt it necessary to speak with you.' She offered no further clarification so I gestured for her to continue. 'In our lessons, I have always stressed the importance of being true to the eye. Paint what you see. That is what I say, and that is exactly what Annette does. However, yesterday, she introduced something into her sketches that wasn't really there. Now, if her brother or sister did this I would think nothing of it, but where Annette is concerned, I am mindful of her condition.' Mademoiselle Drouart selected two more sketches from the portfolio and pushed them across the table. I saw what she meant immediately. The spire of Saint-Catherine rises out of a square tower, and leaning over the indented parapet was a figure in silhouette – a winged creature with horns projecting from its head. I did not respond and Mademoiselle Drouart, assuming I had not identified the aberration, added helpfully, 'The gargoyle, monsieur. There is no such thing. Yet, it appears in all of the sketches Annette made while looking up at the steeple from the south side of the church.' More pictures appeared in front of me, all showing the same winged figure. 'There are two gargoyles at the rear of the church, but these are quite different from the one shown here. They are simple and stylized. Unembellished. Clearly, Annette has not confused them. When Annette used to have seizures, a few days before, she would sometimes refer to people and objects that I could not see. I wondered whether the gargoyle in these sketches represents something similar, something medically significant.'

I rubbed my chin and attempted to remain calm.

'Did you talk to her about it?'

'No. I wanted to seek your opinion first. I didn't want to berate her for something over which she has no control.'

'Very wise, mademoiselle.'

'Nor have I said anything to Madame Du Bris. I did not wish to worry her unnecessarily.'

'You are most considerate, mademoiselle.' I searched one of the drawers and found a cigar. In order to conceal my trembling hand, I turned away as I lit it. 'Annette is an imaginative child, mademoiselle, and even though she has not, to date, been inclined to introduce imaginary elements into her drawings, it is, I daresay, the most likely explanation. Her condition has been controlled for many months and I have not noticed anything that would lead me to conclude that she is about to have another seizure. Even so, one can never be too careful, and I am most grateful that you have brought these sketches to my attention.' I drew on the cigar and continued, 'I might give her an additional infusion tomorrow. Just to be on the safe side. It is in my nature to err on the side of caution.'

'What should I do with these?' The governess traced an arc in the air over Annette's drawings.

'Could I keep them?'

'Certainly.' Mademoiselle Drouart stood and, glancing at my book again, said, 'Ah, Montaigne, he is such good company. I am very fond of his essay on the education of children.' She took off her spectacles and, wiping the lenses clean with a starched handkerchief, quoted the great essayist: 'Only fools have made up their minds and are certain.'

'Indeed,' I replied. 'In life, the correct course of action is rarely obvious.'

She placed her spectacles back on her nose, smiled and said, 'Good day, monsieur.'

I bowed my head and remained in that position, looking down at my shoes. Outside, two birds started a fitful chirruping that became increasingly fluid until the library was filled with their song – a melodious duet of startling complexity.

After lunch, I saddled up one of the horses and rode to the village. Saint-Catherine's spire came into view long before I reached the market square and I immediately began to feel anxious. I knew already that I would find nothing there to alleviate my fears, but I kept going, nevertheless. Having travelled so far, I was reluctant to abandon hope entirely. The main road, which passed through the centre of the village, was empty, and most of the houses had their shutters closed. I dismounted, and a cloud of white dust rose up as my feet hit the ground. I proceeded directly to the church, where I took one of Annette's drawings from my pocket. Shading my eyes, I looked upwards, and compared her artwork with the original. There were no gargoyles leaning over the parapet, nor was there anything that might be mistaken for a gargoyle. I walked around the tower in order to view it from several different perspectives, but the architectural lines remained stubbornly simple. There wasn't even the consolation of a mysterious shadow.

My legs felt weak and I made my way unsteadily across the square to the inn. The door had been left open and, when I stepped inside, it took a few seconds for my eyes to adapt. Fleuriot was washing glasses and his only customers were Pailloux and a young man with sharp features whom I did not recognize.

'Good day, monsieur,' said Fleuriot.

Pailloux turned around, revealing his red swollen nose and saluted me. His companion grinned.

I ordered an anisette and sat at the counter. As Fleuriot prepared my drink he said, 'Have you seen the gypsies, monsieur?'

'No.'

'They're back again: camped out by the river. If you go up the hill,' he jabbed his thumb backwards, 'you can see their caravans. One of them came here this morning – big fellow, as brown as a berry – carrying an enormous pair of scissors. He went around all the houses asking the women if they'd sell him their hair.'

I must have looked puzzled because Pailloux called out, 'Wigs, monsieur. The gypsies collect sackloads of hair and take it north. The wigmakers offer a good price.'

There then followed a conversation about irregular transactions, during which Pailloux claimed to have known a man who was once offered a diamond in exchange for his teeth by a dentist. The young man was suddenly distracted by something outside and, reaching over the table, he pinched Pailloux's sleeve. With a discreet nod he directed the drunk to look through the window. My curiosity was aroused and I shifted position to get a better view. Du Bris was standing in front of the church, talking to a woman.

'Oh, he's a bold one,' muttered Pailloux. 'Look at him – in broad daylight too.'

'That's enough,' said Fleuriot.

Pailloux shrugged, 'What difference does it make?' The young man continued to grin inanely. 'It's hardly a secret any more.'

I looked at Fleuriot inquisitively and he waved his hand in a manner to indicate that I should take no notice. The drunk went on. 'Some men are never satisfied. It's not as if his wife isn't a beauty.'

'Pailloux!' Fleuriot's voice had hardened.

'What?' asked the drunk.

'Enough!' Turning to address me, Fleuriot added, 'I'm sorry, monsieur,' and then quickly changed the subject. The atmosphere thereafter was somewhat strained.

I finished my anisette and when I walked out into the sunlight there was no sign of Du Bris. Both he and the woman he had been talking to were gone. Before leaving the village, I took one last look at the church, then mounted my horse and rode back to the chateau.

As I entered the courtyard Hélène Du Bris was coming out of the kitchen, carrying a basket full of fruit.

'Ah Monsieur Clément!' she exclaimed, 'You have returned. Why don't you come and join us? We're sitting by the cherry tree.'

'Thank you,' I replied, 'that is most kind.'

I left the horse with the stable boy, brushed my jacket and walked through the Garden of the Senses. Massive purple flowers shaped like the bells of trumpets blocked my path, and a swarm of pale blue butterflies flew in all directions as I pushed the blooms aside. The air smelled of citronella. I made my way through the fragrant jungle and stepped out onto the lawn. Raboulet was lying on the grass, reading a book, and his wife Sophie was marching up and down, trying to get their infant to sleep. Hélène was sitting at her easel, painting, and Annette was standing next to Odile, passing her slices of fruit. When I reached the cherry tree, greetings were exchanged, and Hélène offered me the vacant chair at her side.

'Where are the boys?' I asked.

'With Mademoiselle Drouart. She has taken them up into the forest.'

I leaned forward to examine Hélène's watercolour. The subject was one of the moss-covered cherubs spaced at regular intervals around the edge of the lawn. I glanced from her reproduction to the original and was impressed by how she had managed to duplicate the various shades of green.

'You are a fine colourist,' I said.

With typical modesty, she responded, 'The light is very favourable today. Would you like some fruit?'

'Thank you.'

Hélène addressed her daughter, 'Annette: Monsieur Clément would like some fruit.' Annette picked up a basket – the one I had seen Hélène carrying on my return from the village – and brought it to me. She tilted the rim, revealing an assortment of apples, grapes and pears. I took an apple and Annette returned to her grandmother.

The sun was low and bright. On the other side of the lawn a wild cat was stalking lizards.

'One of the fountains has stopped working,' said Hélène.

'Has it?' I responded.

'Yes. Monsieur Boustagnier says that there must be an obstruction.'

'Will he be able to undertake repairs?'

'Not without digging up the Garden of Intelligence.'

Our conversation about the fountains became more general, and before long Hélène was enthusing about a new project. There was a field behind the Garden of Silence that was rather wasted – a large area of weeds and wild flowers. She was thinking of building a maze on it. 'I have always been peculiarly fascinated by mazes,' she said, emphasizing the cherub's capricious disposition with a skilful touch of her brush. 'Perhaps my father is to blame. He had a great love of Greek myths and when I was a child he often repeated the story of Theseus, the hero who ventured into the great labyrinth and killed the minotaur.'

'Yes, mazes are indeed fascinating,' I mused. 'They have about them a delightful air of mystery; however, I am inclined to believe that their universal appeal owes much to their symbolic significance.' Hélène gestured for me to continue. 'Consider how we negotiate a maze: we set off on a journey, not quite sure where we are going. We choose to go this way or that way, up here or down there. Some of our choices are good, others bad. Sometimes we progress towards our goal, but we are frequently frustrated or get lost. It seems to me that mazes are very much like life itself.'

Hélène turned to face me and I saw that my comments had unsettled her. She looked sad, distraught. 'That is so very true, monsieur. We make decisions without knowing what lies before us and we are obliged to accept the consequences. There is no way out.' Her eyes moistened. 'Is it any wonder that . . .' She stopped herself and seemed embarrassed.

To save her from further embarrassment, I gallantly pretended that I had just remembered something important: in fact, a trivial costing error on a pharmacist's invoice. The ruse worked and Hélène's customary good humour was restored; however, I could not help but connect her sudden emotion with Pailloux's indiscreet remarks. The thought of her being wronged made me feel quite angry, but there was nothing to be done. It was not my place to intervene with respect to such a private matter.

Our conversation petered out and my thoughts returned to Annette. She seemed no different: still the same girl, the same innocent creature whose smile was perhaps the last thing in the world that could raise the ghost of my lost humanity. I watched her closely, saw her straighten Odile's blanket without fuss, such that her little ministration went completely without notice – which of course was her intention. Once again, I succumbed to the seductive comforts of self-deception. 'Yes', I said to myself. 'One must not jump to conclusions. The drawing of the gargoyle might well be a pathological phenomenon, the result of a freak electrical discharge in the brain.' But I was soon to be shaken out of my idiotic complacency.

Odile had been telling Annette stories from the Bible, most of which included examples of divine retribution on a grand scale: plagues, floods, the destruction of cities. Presumably, the old woman's purpose was to instil in her granddaughter some of her own God-fearing piety.

Odile's noisome monologue was interrupted when she paused to take some refreshment. Annette lifted the fruit basket and Odile detached some lustrous grapes from an already half-eaten bunch. It was then that Annette said, 'Could God create a stone so large and heavy that he could not lift it?'

The old woman answered with irritation, 'What sort of question is that, child?'

Annette was puzzled by her grandmother's response. 'You said that God is all-powerful.'

'Well, so he is! He can do anything!'.

'But if he made a stone that he could not lift, he would no longer be all-powerful. It would be something that he could not do.'

'Don't be foolish, child!'

'Actually,' Raboulet set his book aside and sat up, 'that is an extremely interesting question.'

'Tristan!' Hélène threw a cautionary glance in her brother's direction, but he was not discouraged.

'No, really. It's rather clever. What do you think, Monsieur Clément?' He winked mischievously. 'Could God create a stone that he could not lift?'

'It is a question that has troubled theologians for many centuries', I replied. 'What made you think of such a thing, Annette?'

'I don't know,' she replied. 'It just came into my head.'

'In which case,' the old woman scolded, 'you should think more carefully before opening your mouth.'

Raboulet ignored Odile and said, 'Are you serious, Clément? Have theologians really considered this question.'

'Yes. It is sometimes referred to as the omnipotence paradox.'

'And what did these wise men conclude?'

'They concluded that the question is invalid.'

'Well,' he said, smirking, 'I can see why. The question seems to admit only two possible answers, both of which are rather disconcerting,' he paused and added under his breath, 'for believers.'

'Enough of this talk,' said Odile, glaring at Raboulet. 'The child is already confused enough. She should not be encouraged to ask absurd questions.'

Raboulet inclined his head, 'My apologies, madame. You are quite right. Thinking too much never did anyone any good – particularly young women.' His sarcasm was lost on Odile, who raised her chin, inflated her chest and engaged in some self-satisfied preening.

That night I could not sleep. I got up and walked through the gardens. Monsieur Boustagnier had suspended rocks from the almond trees and they knocked together as I passed. These weights bent the branches and made them produce more fruits.

Annette had wanted to know what I kept in my wooden chest. Then she had seen a gargoyle on the church. And now, one of the most problematic questions known to the medieval church had simply popped into her mind. I could no longer deny that something very strange was happening.

The world turns and we move from light into darkness, from darkness into light. With light comes warmth, with darkness, cold. Everything that lives and breathes depends on the light for its continued existence. All growth is stunted by darkness. When light is plentiful, the earth is fertile, but when light is scarce, the winter months bring death and corruption. From the earliest times, light has been associated with good, darkness with evil.

I had made my decision. The chest in my study could only be opened during the day, and preferably when the light was at its strongest. To attempt to open it at night would be folly. I went to the kitchen and informed Madame Boustagnier that I did not require lunch, and on my return bolted the first antechamber door, the second antechamber door and the door between my study and the library. I then found a jar full of keys that I kept hidden at the back of the cupboard. Tipping the keys onto the floor, I selected two from the jumble. I unlocked one of my desk drawers and removed a metal cash box. This too, needed to be unlocked. Inside was a third, more substantial key, its blade a complicated knot of serrated projections.

The time had come.

Light streamed through the windows, illuminating a

swirl of glittering motes, and I tried to steady my agitated nerves by observing their slow, circular motion. The attempt was futile. My heart felt swollen and heavy – my breath came in gasps.

Like a condemned man, I walked over to the chest, knelt down and inserted the key into the padlock. The key did not turn at first, and I had to use considerable force before a loud snap signalled that the shackle was free. I removed the padlock and, gripping two leather straps, heaved the chest open. Immediately, the trapped air inside escaped, carrying with it a stale, musty fragrance.

The interior was full of thick, brocade curtains: a top layer of neatly folded squares and beneath these a second layer of densely compressed bundles. There was also a third layer of folded squares at the bottom. I could remember packing the chest myself, and how I had endeavoured to arrange the cloth in order to diminish the destructive effects of any knocks or collisions. Any damage – if I found any – must have arisen, not because of mishandling, but because of internal violence.

I removed the folded squares and considered how best to proceed. It would be madness to unravel the bundles. Even a glimpse of what lay underneath might result in a weakening of my mental powers. I imagined a distorted, reptilian eye – seen through the convexity of the glass, magnified, bulging – and shuddered. A supreme act of will was required to fight a sudden urge to slam the lid down and flee. Looking away, I saw the bracelet of flowers that Annette had given me and was able to draw strength from the memory of her little act of kindness. I slipped my hands beneath the brocade and, bracing myself, extended the tips of my fingers. Like the sensory apparatus of an insect, they made trembling contact with the curved crystal. I knew, instantly, that my misgivings were justified. The glass was warm. I caressed the sphere and explored its surface. My hands began to hurt, and tendrils of pain crept up my arms. And then it occurred to me that to undertake a proper inspection I should surely push the curtains aside and take a look at what I was doing. It was not my thought, of course. The very substances of my brain were being tampered with. I was in dreadful peril and had to accomplish my task quickly. The pain worsened, I felt sick, and my vision blurred. *Just pull the material aside . . .* The thought had acquired the qualities of a command. *Go on. It's quite safe.* I closed my eyes. A momentary lapse of concentration and I might have found myself yanking the curtains away.

'You will not have control of my mind,' I said aloud. My denial was followed by a retaliatory wave of nausea. 'And you will leave the girl's mind alone too.'

I pressed on with my examination and discovered an irregularity on the otherwise smooth surface. It was just as I had imagined – a crack – like Doriac's egg. I moved the soft flesh of my fingertip along the fracture to gauge its length, felt a stinging sharpness, and quickly drew my hand away. I opened my eyes and saw blood welling up from a cut. With great care, I put the curtains back in the chest, shut the lid and fixed the padlock.

20

I placed the heavy volume in front of Du Bris and opened it up.

'The first of twelve library registers,' I said. 'This one was compiled by your ancestor, Roland Du Bris. The handwriting might even be his.' Du Bris peered blankly at the faded ink. 'The first eleven registers are complete; however, it would seem that towards the end of the last century, interest in the library waned. Thereafter, not all the acquisitions were catalogued.' Du Bris poured himself a brandy and indicated, without speaking, that he was prepared to fill a second glass. I declined and continued: 'The final register is very inferior. Hardly any of the nineteenth-century publications have an entry. Would you permit me to make the necessary emendations?'

Du Bris shrugged. 'It sounds like an awful lot of work.'

'I would not find the task onerous.'

'Well, Clément, if it makes you happy, then please feel at liberty to do so. I have no objection.' He paused and added, 'Do you mean to say, you've looked at every book in the library?'

'I have.'

'And have you found anything . . . valuable?'

'There are many valuable books in the library.'

'Yes, I know. But have you found anything of exceptional value?'

'I am sure that there are dealers in Paris who would be anxious to acquire many of these books.' I passed my hand over the register. 'Even so, it would be a tragedy if such a unique collection was broken up.'

Du Bris took a sip of his brandy and said, 'We're not great readers.'

'But future generations, perhaps . . .'

'My grandfather used to take me into the library and read me stories. I never really liked him – or the stories. I much preferred playing outside.' He looked towards one of the windows.

'May I ask: have any of the books been removed from the library?'

'I beg your pardon?'

'Are there, for example, any library books in your private apartment?'

'No. Why do you ask?'

'See here.' I pointed to a particular entry, '*Malleus Daemonum* – The Hammer of Demons – by Alexandro Albertinus, published in 1620: a treatise on exorcism. Now, just below, see, it says once again, *Malleus Daemonum.*'

'A second copy?'

'No, another Hammer of Demons, but this time one

written several hundred years earlier, by the great alchemist Nicolas Flamel.' I tapped the page. 'Unfortunately, it is missing.' Du Bris thrust out his lower jaw but said nothing. 'I believe that it may be the only copy in existence.'

'Which would make it very valuable?'

'Valuable and of incalculable interest to scholars. I have examined all the standard reference works, and nowhere is there mention of Flamel's Hammer.'

'Then perhaps old Roland made a mistake. Perhaps there was no such book.'

'I very much doubt that a man as fastidious as your ancestor would have made such a blunder.'

Du Bris raised his hands, as if to say, 'Well, what am I supposed to do about it?'

I closed the register and continued, 'I do not feel that it is for me to ask Madame Odile to look through her effects. I fear that she would consider such a request improper.'

'Oh, I see,' said Du Bris, laughing. 'That's what all this is about. No, I quite understand, Clément, of course. I'll explain the situation and get her maid to have a look. Her wardrobe is a veritable treasure trove – you never know what might turn up!'

'Thank you, monsieur.'

He stood, stretched out his arms and yawned. 'Did you go to the village yesterday?'

'Yes, I did.'

'I thought I saw the grey mare. I was there too – some

business.' He smiled and then asked, 'How is my daughter?'

'Mademoiselle Drouart brought a small matter to my attention, a disturbance of vision; however, I am not unduly worried.'

'Good. Good.' He shook my hand. 'And Raboulet?'

'In excellent health.'

'We are all greatly indebted, monsieur.'

I went straight to the library, where I immersed myself in magical writings: I read of ointments, philtres and potions, the consecration of lamps, wax, oil and water; of precious stones, secret seals and celestial correspondences – the twenty eight mansions of the moon – the preparation of amulets and talismans, incense and powders; and the characters that should be engraved on a protective ring. I applied myself to the *The Devil's Scourge*, *The Sworn Book of Honorius*, *The Key of Solomon* – all the time amending the notes that I had been keeping for well over a year. Oblivious to the passage of time, I only registered the lateness of the hour when the fading light made it difficult for me to continue reading.

There was a knock on the door.

I gathered my papers together and stuffed them into a drawer before calling out, 'Come in.'

Hélène entered. 'Good heavens, monsieur, I can hardly see a thing. Where are you?'

I stood and lit some candles. 'I am sorry, madame, I must have dozed off.'

She made her way to my table and I pulled out a chair. 'Thank you, monsieur.' She pinched her dress and raised the hem a little before she sat. 'The books you were reading couldn't have been very engaging.'

'No,' I said, returning to my own chair. 'They weren't. I was refreshing my Latin.'

She smiled somewhat nervously and made a few unconnected remarks about her own reading habits. As she spoke, I noticed that her hands were in constant motion, one revolving around the other. Eventually, she looked at me directly and said, 'Monsieur Clément, I wondered if I might discuss something with you in confidence.'

'Of course.'

'I am worried about my brother. He is talking of Paris.'

'Oh?'

'When he was younger he was always talking of Paris. He wanted to live there. In reality, he could never have made such a move because of his condition. He always knew that. But now, things are different. Your medicines have been very helpful and, once again, he is dreaming of theatres and the company of fashionable young men. He imagines that, very soon, he will be able to take Sophie and Elektra to the capital – that he will rent some rooms and support all three of them by writing articles.'

'The life of a man of letters is notoriously insecure.'

'He says that he is bored. I am sympathetic, of course, but he can't go to Paris, can he?' Her voice had acquired a pleading tone.

'No,' I answered. Hélène let out a sigh of relief. 'But

in the fullness of time, if he continues to enjoy better health . . .'

Her face fell. 'I would miss him.'

'I am sure you would.'

'Without Tristan's amusing conversation, life here at Chambault will be very . . .' her sentence trailed off and after a beat of silence she added, 'I fear I am about to embarrass myself again.'

I feigned ignorance. 'Again? I don't know what you are referring to, madame.'

In the candlelight, her eyes looked particularly large. She bit her lower lip. 'I haven't been sleeping well lately. Is there something you could make up for me? An infusion, perhaps?'

'Certainly.'

As I began to rise she said, 'No, monsieur. You do not have to prepare one now.'

'But it is no trouble at all.' I went into my study and mixed some camomile and lavender oil. When I returned, Hélène was standing by one of the shelves, examining the titles. I handed her the glass.

'Thank you, monsieur.'

'A very mild sedative. If you need something a little stronger, then let me know.'

She looked around the library. 'So many books.'

We stood together, surveying our surroundings. It felt to me as if she was delaying her departure because she had something more to say and was struggling to overcome a scruple. I never discovered if my presumption was correct, because at that moment the silence was broken by a strange, plaintive cry. It had come from the antechamber. We both hurried in that direction but slowed as we neared the interior doorway. Something was standing in the shadows – small and pale. I felt Hélène's fingers close around my arm and her grip tightening. Then, we heard a child's voice: 'Are you real?'

Hélène stepped forward and whispered, 'Annette?'

'Are you real, Mother?'

'Of course I am real. What is the matter, my dear?'

The child was obviously confused and I said, 'She has been sleepwalking.'

'Monsieur Clément?' said Annette, 'Is that you?'

'Yes, Annette.'

'I heard a voice, telling me that I should get out of bed and go to your room. It was peculiar, like my own voice, but different. I didn't want to get up, but the voice was very stubborn. I climbed the stairs . . . but then I woke up – and found myself here – and I couldn't tell whether I was still dreaming or not.'

'You have been walking in your sleep, Annette. It happens sometimes.' I turned to address Hélène. 'I think you had better take her back to bed. I'll get you a candle. It is quite dark now.'

On my return, Hélène glanced from the flame to the other side of the antechamber and the black emptiness of the entrance. 'I don't know how she managed to find her way here in the dark. She could have fallen and injured herself.'

'No,' said Annette. 'I was quite safe. The voice told me which way to go. It can see in the dark.'

Hélène shook her head and wrapped a gentle arm around the child's shoulders. 'Come on, my dear. Let's get you to bed.' Hélène looked at me and delivered a mute request for reassurance.

'Really, madame,' I said calmly. 'There is nothing to worry about.'

When they had both gone I went back to my table in the library. Hélène had left her infusion. I picked up the glass and drained it without pausing to take breath.

21

The following morning I received a note from the curé. One of the villagers had been involved in an accident. The man was in great pain and the curé begged me to come quickly. I dashed to the stables, saddled the grey mare and set off at a gallop. The address I had been given was not far from the market square and easy to find: a low building with a yard full of clucking hens. As I arrived, a door opened and the curé emerged. 'Oh, monsieur,' he cried, pressing his hands together and shaking them backwards and forwards. 'Thank you, thank you. Thank you so much.'

I dismounted and said, 'Where is Monsieur Jourdain?'

The curé sighed. 'He was not at home.'

'You mean that he didn't come to the door when you knocked.'

'That is a possibility.'

'Father Lestoumel,' I said sharply, 'something must be done!'

'Yes,' said the curé, 'you are right and I am sorry.'

We entered the building and I was immediately confronted by a curious sight. A woman was comforting two small children, but this charming little group – this artist's impression of a domestic ideal – was mitigated by the presence of a bullock. The beast was poking its head through a hole in the wall, and behind it, I could see the low roof of a thatched barn. I was momentarily stupefied.

'Please,' said Father Lestoumel, tugging gently at my sleeve, 'This way, monsieur.' He led me into the next room, where I discovered my patient lying on bed sheets soaked through with blood. 'Monsieur Ragot,' said the curé, indicating the poor wretch. Another woman, considerably younger than the first and whom I supposed to be the man's wife, was seated on a stool, mumbling prayers.

'What happened to him?' I asked.

'Some barrels fell off a cart,' whispered the curé. 'His legs were crushed.'

The man struck the mattress with a clenched fist and called out, 'Saints preserve us! The pain is unbearable!'

I opened my bag, took out a pair of scissors and cut away the sopping wet fabric of his trousers. The lacerations I exposed were ragged and deep – so deep, in fact, that one could see down to the bone. 'Madame,' I said to the woman. 'I will need some warm water and towels.'

'Will I lose my legs?' asked Ragot.

'No,' I replied. 'I don't think so. Providing the injured parts are kept clean.'

'Thank the Lord,' said Ragot, tracing a cross in the air above his chest.

I filled a syringe with morphine, pushed the needle

into Ragot's arm and, before the plunger was fully depressed, watched his jaw go slack and his eyes glaze over. When his wife returned with the water, I bathed Ragot's wounds, dressed them with lint soaked in carbolic and finally wrapped both of his legs in bandages. Turning to address Madame Ragot, I asked her for some wine. She blushed and answered, 'Forgive me. I'll get you some.'

'It isn't for me, madame,' I said, anxious to correct her mistake. 'I need wine to make a preparation for your husband, something for him to drink later – to ease the pain.' She excused herself and came back with a bottle that had already been opened. I poured the dark liquid into a glass and added a teaspoon of morphine. 'Give this to Monsieur Ragot when he wakes. By the time its effect wears off, I am sure Monsieur Jourdain will be able to assist.' I glanced at the curé and he shifted his weight uncomfortably from one foot to the other.

As we were leaving, Madame Ragot thanked me and said she would remember me in her prayers. I replied, 'You would do better, perhaps, to pray for the swift recovery of your husband.' It was an ungracious remark and I instantly regretted it.

I untethered the horse and strode off towards the market square. The curé caught up with me and said, a little breathlessly, 'Monsieur, I will make sure that you are fully compensated for your services. There is a small charity fund that I manage and . . .'

'That won't be necessary,' I said brusquely.

'But I insist,' said the curé. 'It is only right that you should be paid.' He paused, before adding, 'Especially so, given your other good offices.'

'Oh? And what might they be?'

'You have been seen up in the hills, monsieur.'

'I enjoy the views.'

'Entering the caves and carrying your bag.'

'Who told you this?'

'Fleuriot.'

'Perhaps your informant was mistaken.'

'On the whole, experience has taught me to trust his sources. Well? Is it true?'

'Some of the children were very ill.'

'I imagine some of the medicines you require are very expensive, and I would be happy to . . .'

Again I cut in: 'With respect, Father, there are better ways of dispersing your funds – better causes than my remuneration.'

The curé raised a placatory hand. 'You are very kind, monsieur.'

We walked on in silence, and a woman appeared at the end of the road. As she drew closer, I recognized her face. It was the same woman I had seen talking to Du Bris. She was young, pretty and dressed rather well for a villager. When she saw the curé she crossed to the opposite side of the road and, as we passed each other, she looked away, dramatically straining her slender neck and raising her chin in haughty defiance. I sensed Father Lestoumel bristling.

'Who is that?' I asked.

'Mademoiselle Anceau.' I could see that he was undecided as to whether he should say more. After a few moments, he glanced back and added, 'She has something of a reputation.' He underscored his disapproval by tutting loudly.

We reached the market square and I tied the mare to a post. I was about to bid Father Lestoumel adieu, when his face lit up and he exclaimed, 'I know! Why don't I show you the church.' Before I could voice an objection, he added, 'I am sure you will find the interior very interesting.'

He seemed eager to please, and I was conscious of the fact that during our time together my manner had been somewhat surly. I remembered the discourteous remark I had made earlier to Madame Ragot, felt ashamed, and suddenly found myself consenting to Father Lestoumel's suggestion. The curé clapped his hands together and cried, 'Excellent! Excellent!'

We marched across the square, entered the church, and Father Lestoumel began a summary of the building's history. It was much as I had expected: a medieval structure built on earlier foundations, destruction by fire and subsequent restorations. Features were pointed out to me, such as the carvings on the baptismal font, some ornate candle-stands and a faded remnant of a twelfth-century fresco – none of which excited my curiosity. However, in due course we came to a stump of stone mounted on a pedestal. It was evidently a religious effigy, but almost all of its surface detail had been worn away. Only the petrified folds of a gown were now visible.

'That looks very old,' I said.

'Not as old as you might think,' replied Father Lestoumel. 'It is a statue of Saint Clotilde at prayer and believed to possess healing powers. For over a century, villagers have been scraping the stone and mixing the powder in their food as a kind of medicine.'

'Do you approve?'

'It was reputed to have been a very fine piece of sculpture. No, I do not approve. I do not want the entire church to be scraped away and used as a cough remedy.' His eyes sparkled and he ventured a wry smile. Crossing the transept, he continued: 'Joan of Arc may have stopped here once. Or so they say. In actual fact, many of the local churches have been linked with her legend. She couldn't have visited all of them!'

We came to a stained-glass window, the central lancet of which showed a priest reading from a large red book. This hefty volume, fitted with gold hasps, was held up by a demon that had evidently been forced into an attitude of servile compliance. Diagonal shafts of sunlight passed through the colourful illuminations, creating a submerged, watery effect, dappling the floor with patches of luminosity.

'That gentleman,' said Father Lestoumel, pointing up at the window, 'was one of my predecessors. His name was Gilbert de Gandelus. When the Ursuline convent at Séry-des-Fontaines was plagued with demons in 1612 it was Gandelus who cast them out. His fame spread far and wide, and he was subsequently called upon to conduct exorcisms all over the country. I believe he was once summoned by the Bishop of Paris.'

I noticed that the demon did not have claws, but human hands, with long fingers and tapering nails.

The curé moved on, indicating a fifteenth-century likeness of the Virgin and the fragment of a Roman tomb embedded in one of the walls. We had completed a circular tour of the church and had arrived back at the font. The curé pushed the door open and we stepped out into the square. I thanked him for showing me the church and made some comments preparatory to our parting. Just as I was about to say goodbye, he said, 'You are an intellectual, monsieur. Educated. Well read. And I am but a simple country priest. I daresay, you cannot conceive of any benefit arising from associating with a man like me.' I was about to make a polite rebuttal, but he raised his finger and shook it. 'No, monsieur. It is true – and I make no judgement. All that I ask is that, should you find yourself requiring assistance, you will at least remember that I am here. I am not foolish enough to believe that you will ever want my counsel. But I have much local knowledge and perhaps one day this may be of some use to you.'

'Indeed.'

He smiled. 'And do not fear, I will not try to convert you: you are a doctor, a man of science. Reason is your religion and I will respect that.'

'You think me an atheist?'

'Well? Aren't you?'

'No,' I said. 'Far from it.' I turned and walked away, leaving Father Lestoumel standing outside the church with his frown deepening. The door of the inn was wide open so I went inside and sat at a table.

'Will Monsieur Ragot keep his legs?' asked Fleuriot.

'Yes,' I replied. 'He will.'

'Good.' Fleuriot poured me a beer and began a story about an amputee he had known as a child, who was so fast on his crutches that he could race against able-bodied men and beat them.

On returning to the chateau, I went to the library and found a work on witchcraft that contained an account of the Séry-des-Fontaines possessions. The mother superior had been the first to succumb. She had fallen to the ground, shouted blasphemies and lifted her petticoats without shame. Others followed her example, and within a few weeks the convent had descended into chaos. Nuns were running around the cloisters naked and the chapel was despoiled. Several attempts at exorcism failed and the Church authorities became desperate. It was at this point that Gandelus appeared. The demons were vanquished and order was quickly restored. Nothing is recorded of Gandelus's life prior to the Séry-des-Fontaines possessions, and his sudden transformation from parish priest to 'God's hammer' was identified by some as miraculous.

I shut the book and walked to my study. Sitting at my

desk, I smoked until a paring of moon peeped through the window. I then crossed to the chest and tested the lid with the palm of my hand. It was warm. I spat out the words 'Damn you!' and went to bed.

The next day, I was once again invited to sit with the family beneath the cherry tree. Everyone was present except for Du Bris, who had gone shooting with Louis, and we could hear the intermittent crack of his gunshots coming from the woods. It was a humid afternoon and our indifferent conversation was punctuated by long silences. Victor was speaking. His words intruded upon my thoughts, but not enough for me to register their meaning. Even so, a note of shrill excitement jolted me out of my reverie. The boy was pointing and squealing, 'Look at Annette! She has seen something!'

Annette was standing in the middle of the lawn, her head tilted back, looking up into the sky. She raised her hand, fingers pressed together, and shaded her eyes from the sun. Very slowly, shifting one foot, then the other, she began to rotate.

'Can you see anything, Monsieur Clément?' asked Hélène.

The sky was blue and cloudless.

'No,' I replied.

It was as if the child had become fascinated by something circling overhead.

'Is she dancing?' asked Victor.

'I don't think so,' Mademoiselle Drouart replied.

Annette gathered momentum, extending her arms, revolving faster and faster, until her skirt fanned out and she began to resemble a ballerina performing a pirouette.

'It is not right,' said Odile. 'A girl of her age!'

'Annette!' Hélène called out, 'Stop it! You'll get dizzy.'

'Yes,' shouted Victor. 'You'll make yourself sick.'

But Annette did not stop.

I jumped up from my chair and started off towards her, quickening my pace with each step. Her hair was whipping through the air, her feet barely touching the ground.

'Annette?' I said, 'Annette? What is the matter?'

I reached out to grab her shoulders, and when I did so she became tense and toppled to the ground. She lay there for a few seconds, before her limbs started to jerk. The movements were violent and uncontrolled. I stuffed a handkerchief in her mouth and raised her head. When I looked up again, I saw Hélène, Raboulet, and Mademoiselle Drouart gathered around me, staring down at Annette with worried expressions.

'Is it a seizure?' said Hélène, kneeling down beside me.

'Yes,' I replied. 'I am sorry.'

Mademoiselle Drouart's expression was transparent. I could see that she was thinking about the day when she had shown me Annette's drawings, and I had told her that I was not unduly concerned about the child's health.

She was not judging me unkindly, but rather exhibiting surprise that I had been so badly mistaken.

'Was it the spinning that brought it on?' asked Raboulet.

I rested my hand on Annette's forehead: 'That is a possibility.'

The jerking gradually subsided.

'Shall I take her inside, monsieur?' said Raboulet.

'No,' I responded. 'Not just yet.'

Annette had bitten her lower lip and I removed some spots of blood from her chin with the handkerchief. As I was doing this, her eyes flicked open.

'Monsieur Clément?' She tried to get up but I did not permit her to move.

'You have had a seizure, Annette. You must rest here for a few minutes.'

'My head hurts.'

'I know. I will give you something to relieve the pain.'

'I saw a bird – a great bird flying in the sky.'

'No, my darling,' said Hélène. 'It was something you imagined.'

'With enormous wings,' Annette continued, 'going round and round.'

'Hush now,' said Hélène.

I stroked the child's brow and she closed her eyes again. Mademoiselle Drouart returned to the cherry tree to tell the others what had happened, and in due course Raboulet picked Annette up and carried her to the chateau, accompanied by Hélène and myself. The poor child was changed into her nightclothes and put to bed, where she slept for most of the afternoon. I sat by her side, with Hélène.

At six thirty, Du Bris arrived.

'Where have you been?' asked Hélène.

'I had to go into the village,' he replied.

'Again?' Her voice was tart.

'Yes.' He turned to address me and said, 'How is she, Monsieur Clément?'

'As well as can be expected.'

'My mother tells me that before she collapsed she was spinning like a top.'

'It was most peculiar.'

'Does it signify anything?'

My cheeks burned as I lied: 'I don't think so, and there is nothing unusual about her current condition. She is exhausted and has complained of headaches. That is all.'

'She thought she could see something in the sky,' Hélène interjected.

'A bird,' I said.

'That is why she was spinning,' Hélène continued.

Du Bris shrugged and came forward. He crooked his index finger and brushed the knuckle against his daughter's lips. Her eyes opened and she smiled. Du Bris returned the smile and said, 'Well? How are you?'

'Tired,' she replied.

'Yes,' he went on. 'You would be.'

There was something curiously touching about this

little exchange, the light of recognition in Annette's eyes and the unsentimental affection of her father.

'Do not look so worried,' said Annette. 'Monsieur Clément is looking after me, and nothing very bad can happen when he is here.'

It was at that point that I decided to leave Chambault. Annette's faith in me, her innocent trust, was breaking my heart. Travel arrangements could be made by the end of the week and I might be gone within a fortnight. I stood up and said, 'The crisis has passed and you will no doubt wish to be alone with your daughter. I will be in the library if I am required.'

'Thank you,' said Du Bris, inclining his head.

I spent the rest of the day reviewing my notes, particularly the material I had collected on protective charms. The Seal of Shabako caught my attention, an all-purpose amulet of very ancient provenance favoured by the inhabitants of Abydos. It was sometimes carved on Egyptian stone coffins and supposed to help the dead negotiate their perilous journey through the underworld. I took a square of parchment from the drawer of my table and, using a compass, drew a perfect circle, within which I then copied a precise arrangement of hieroglyphs. I repeated the procedure and placed both amulets in my pocket. When the opportunity arose, I would give one to Annette and tell her to keep it about her person at all times. It would be our little secret.

Just before sunset, Madame Boustagnier had some chicken stew sent up to my study. It was fortified with the red wine of the estate, and the pale meat was saturated with its spicy bouquet. When I had finished eating, I smoked a cigar and walked around my apartment, making an itinerary. Transporting my possessions to Paris would be straightforward enough. But then what would I do? I saw my life stretching out ahead of me: a pitiful, lonely existence, wandering from place to place, unable to settle, always fearful of the demon exerting its wicked influence on those to whom I might become attached. There was much I would miss: Annette's sweet smile, idle conversations with Hélène beneath the cherry tree, card games with Raboulet, and of course the library. I had always hoped that I would find the answer to my predicament somewhere in Roland Du Bris's remarkable collection. But there were thousands of books, and, the longer I chose to stay, the more likely it was that Annette or some other member of the household would be placed in mortal danger.

It was past eleven when I heard someone crossing the library. There was a knock on the door, and when I opened it, I found Hélène standing before me, holding up a candle.

'You are awake,' she exclaimed. 'Thank God!'

'Is Annette all right?'

'Forgive me. I did not mean to alarm you. Yes, Annette is well. We put a truckle bed in her room and one of the maids, Monique, is spending the night with her.' Hélène stepped over the threshold. 'I am sorry to trouble you at this late hour, monsieur, but last week you were kind enough to make me a sleeping draught – although I never drank it. I think I must have left it in the library when I took Annette back to her room.' The skin around her eyes was swollen and I suspected that she might have been crying. 'Again,' she continued, 'I am finding it difficult to sleep; perhaps I am worrying too much about Annette. The attack was horrible – one forgets.'

'Yes. It was most distressing.' I paused for a moment and felt some strange compulsion to invite harsh judgement. 'I fear that I may have been complacent, too willing to believe that I had developed a cure, when in fact my achievement was much less impressive.'

'Do not talk like that, monsieur! Annette and Tristan are so much better than they were.' She reached out and somewhat awkwardly took my hand and pressed my fingers. I had not been touched like that for a very long time and I was disturbed by a sudden frisson of desire.

'I will make up the infusion,' I said, pulling away from Hélène, although my withdrawal was delayed by a slight tightening of her grip. It was as if she didn't want to let go. I went to the cupboard, took out some bottles and set about mixing the ingredients. Outside, the dogs began to howl.

We looked at each other and Hélène said, 'What a noise! I hope they don't wake Annette.' She sat down on the divan and I saw that she wasn't wearing any shoes. Through the thin silk of her red stockings I could see her ankles and toes. I tried to stop myself from stealing glances but found it almost impossible. She did not notice this liberty because she had turned away from me and was gazing directly at the chest. After a few moments, she started and said, 'I beg your pardon?'

'I said nothing, madame.'

She seemed a little disorientated and when she noticed that she wasn't wearing any shoes, she stood up abruptly and shook her skirt to ensure that her feet were properly covered. I pretended not to see what she was doing and kept my head bowed. When I had finished, I handed Hélène the infusion.

'Thank you,' she said, 'I will drink it before I retire.' She picked up her candle and walked to the door. The howling of the dogs had grown louder and she tutted before saying, 'What is the matter with them?'

'I don't know, madame.'

'They often bark, but I have never heard them howl like this.'

She stepped into the library and glided through the darkness like a ghost. When she had gone I marched over to the chest, slammed my hand down on the lid, and hissed 'Stop it! Stop it! Leave them alone!' An image flashed into my mind: Hélène Du Bris lying with her legs spread apart, naked but for a pair of red stockings. I withdrew my hand so quickly the lid might have been a hotplate.

22

The following morning I went to see Annette. She was in fine spirits and seemed almost recovered. I had wanted to give her the amulet, but Monique was hovering, and I decided that it would be wise to leave it until we were alone. Although I was hungry, I wanted to clear my head, so I went for a short walk around the gardens before returning for breakfast. As I entered the courtyard, I saw Louis and Monsieur Boustagnier lifting one of two large trunks on to the back of the trap. Du Bris came out of one of the rear doors; he was smartly dressed and propelled himself forward with a cane. There was something about his confident swagger that reminded me of Charcot.

'Good morning, Monsieur Clément.'

'Good morning,' I replied. 'Are you leaving us?'

'Yes, just for a few days. Tours.' He paused, deliberating whether to say any more, then added, 'I have to sign some documents.' The smell of his cologne was somewhat overpowering. It occurred to me that he had taken more care over his appearance than was customary for an appointment with a notary. Du Bris straightened the carnation in his buttonhole and asked, 'How is Annette?'

'Very well. There are no complications.'

'Good. Good.' He then looked at me as if to say, 'Anything else?'

'I was wondering,' I began, affecting a casual manner, 'did you get a chance to talk to Madame Odile?'

'What about?' A trace of impatience had hardened his voice.

'The book I mentioned.'

'Oh that! No. I'm sorry, I didn't. I'll ask her when I get back. Now, if you don't mind, Clément, I really must go. I need to catch the diligence.' He climbed up onto the box and Louis tugged the reins. The trap rolled off and Monsieur Boustagnier threw me an amused glance.

After eating breakfast in the kitchen, I went to Annette's room, meaning to give her the amulet, but when I arrived she was not there. I discovered from Mademoiselle Drouart that Annette was feeling much stronger and that she had gone for a walk with her mother. On returning to my study I wrote to a hotel in Paris, before sifting through my belongings, separating those things I must take with me from those that I might leave behind.

Louis had returned from the village with some letters, and among them was one addressed to me from Valdestin. We had maintained a very occasional correspondence since my departure from the Salpêtrière. This opportune communication would add legitimacy to the story I was concocting in my head, concerning the receipt of bad news of a personal nature and the regretful necessity of my return to Paris. I had resolved to make my announcement the next · day, and for that reason found it impossible to dine with the family. Once again, I ate in my rooms alone and, as the sun was setting, ventured out for what I imagined would be my very last walk in the gardens of the chateau. As I was making my way through the Garden of the Senses, I heard the dogs starting to howl, just as they had howled the previous night. A few minutes later I entered the courtyard and saw Louis standing by the kennel. The dogs were kept in an enclosure consisting of a low square wall, on top of which were high iron railings.

'I don't know what's wrong with them,' said Louis, removing a cigarette from between his lips. 'I've never seen them like this before.' Two of the dogs were standing on their hind legs, making a plaintive wailing noise, while the other three were crawling in circles, crouched low and whimpering. I shrugged, said, 'Goodnight,' and entered the chateau through the kitchen door. After passing through the dining room and parlour, I ascended the stairs and entered the library, where I took my seat at the table. I then went through my notes, checking my early transcriptions for accuracy – particularly those passages concerned with the construction of magical weapons. This was a demanding task, and the verification of hieroglyphs and symbols occupied me until the early hours of the morning.

It was only when I paused to smoke a cigar that I registered the silence. The dogs had stopped howling.

I should have been glad, because they had been making a frightful din, but instead the silence made me feel uneasy, as if every living thing had departed from the world and I was totally alone. The landscape beyond the library walls had become, in my imagination, a desolate, empty expanse. Opening my mouth, I released a cloud of smoke and watched it roll over the cracked pages of an illuminated manuscript. The minute hand dropped on the clock face and I noted the time: ten minutes past two. A faint pattering sound broke the silence, and I assumed that it had started to rain, but when I looked up at the window I saw no trails or droplets, and as I listened more closely, the sound became louder and clearer. Someone was running up the stairs. A moment later, I saw the glow of a candle and a figure wearing nightclothes entering the antechamber.

'Monsieur?' It was a young female voice, and belonged to Monique. She was obviously surprised to find me sitting up in the library.

I stood and marched towards her, 'What is it? Not another seizure I hope!'

'No. The little mistress is well.' The maid's hair was uncombed and stuck out horizontally in matted bunches. 'Madame Du Bris sent me.'

'Why? What is wrong with her?'

'I don't know. Annie wanted me to sleep in her room again tonight – and I did – and I was asleep, but Madame Du Bris woke me up and told me to get you at once. She looked . . .' the girl hesitated, 'not herself.'

This was a peculiar turn of phrase and she seemed a little uncomfortable. She looked past me into the library, and I could see that she thought it most irregular for a gentleman to be reading in the middle of the night.

We rushed down the stairs and Monique led me through a series of connected rooms until we came to an elongated chamber that served as a kind of hallway, with doors running along either side. The maid indicated one to our left, and glanced, rather anxiously, down an adjoining corridor. I gathered that she was worried about Annette.

'It's all right,' I said. 'You can go now, if you wish.' She thanked me and scuttled off.

I was standing outside a room that I had never been in before. It was not where Hélène and her husband usually slept. I was familiar with the marital apartment because Du Bris had come down with a chest infection the previous winter, and naturally I had spent some time at his bedside. I straightened my neck tie, combed my fingers through my hair and knocked on the door. There was a lengthy pause, and I was about to strike again, when Hélène called out, 'Come in.' I turned the handle and entered. The room was lit by a single oil lamp and smelled of lavender. Medieval tapestries hung from the walls, and the furniture – a large wardrobe, a dressing table and a chest of drawers – was solidly built. I could not see Hélène because she was concealed behind the drapes of a four-poster bed.

'Madame?' I said tentatively. One of the heavy brocade

curtains moved aside and I saw her, sitting up and supported by a mountain of embroidered pillows. 'Madame?' I enquired. 'What is the matter?' I stepped forward and peered through the opening in the drapes. Hélène's eyes were half closed, the lids drooping, her hair a tangle of loose curls. She was wearing a nightdress, the neckline of which was low and revealing.

'I could not sleep,' she said. Her speech was slurred, as if she had been drinking, but I could not smell alcohol on her breath.

'Do you want another infusion, madame?'

Hélène continued as if I had said nothing. 'And I have a pain . . .' She touched her sternum and traced circles on her chest. 'Here.' Her legs became restless and her body seemed to twist and contort; her writhing did not suggest discomfort, however, but rather sensual abandon. Her other hand toyed with her curls before it disappeared beneath the counterpane, producing a wave in the crochet that rolled over her belly and subsided between her thighs. The small movements that followed were exploratory, and my head filled with images: a risen hem, an index finger curling between folds of flesh. I fancied that I could hear the whisper of silk and for no good reason supposed her to be wearing the same red stockings she had worn the night before. Desire ignited in the pit of my stomach and my loins burned.

'Come closer,' Hélène spoke softly. She reached out and pressed the palm of her hand against my tumescence and I gasped with astonishment. I knew that by submitting to her caresses I was acting dishonourably, but my admiration for her had always been complicated by deeper feelings. To be touched in this way, after so long, made her invitation to transgress almost irresistible. Yet, even as I stood there, trembling with expectation, I was also uneasy, and not only because of my guilty conscience. Since the dogs had stopped howling, everything that had happened had seemed unreal, like the disturbing events of a bad dream, and particularly so with respect to Hélène's extraordinary behaviour. 'Come closer,' she repeated, the words carried on a falling sigh.

She looked up at me and I recoiled in horror. There was nothing behind her eyes, only a terrible, submissive vacancy: a submissive vacancy that I recognized. I shook her shoulders, hoping to rouse her from the trance. 'Madame, wake up – wake up!' But it was no use, she simply fell back onto her pillow, moistened her lips with her tongue, and continued her sinuous movements. Once again, she touched her chest. 'It hurts,' she said. 'It hurts.'

I drew back, both fascinated and frightened by the spectacle of her sensual delirium. Her hand travelled through the air, the fingers making little grasping movements, as if she was hoping to attach herself to my person. Stepping backwards, I tripped on the rug and fell against the wardrobe. I did not know what to do and raced to the door, which I opened and slammed behind me. Before I had had a chance to compose myself, candlelight preceded the reappearance of Monique.

She gave a little cry when she discovered me standing in the dark.

'Monsieur!' She placed her hand over her heart. 'You made me jump!'

'Forgive me. I didn't mean to startle you.'

'Have you seen Annie? Did she come this way?'

'No.'

'She isn't in her room. I've been looking for her.'

'Was she gone when you returned?'

'Yes. I looked in the nursery, the chapel and the schoolroom. I couldn't find her anywhere.'

The door behind me opened, and Hélène stepped out. She had put on a night-coat and tied her hair up with a ribbon, but she still looked dishevelled and dazed. 'Monsieur?' she croaked, rubbing the sleep from her eyes, 'What is happening?'

'Annette is missing,' I replied.

'Missing . . .' she repeated.

It seemed that she had no recollection of what had just transpired between us.

'Yes,' I continued, 'however, I think I know where she might be.' Hélène allowed me to take her lamp without protest and I marched off towards the stairs. 'Monique,' I called back. 'Please carry on searching for the little mistress down here.' I retraced my footsteps through the connected rooms, my soul full of dread. When I reached the bottom of the stairs, I heard Hélène calling out, 'Monsieur Clément. Wait!' She had followed me and I turned to see her emerging from the gloom.

'This way,' I said, beginning my ascent.

'Where are you going?' she asked.

'To my rooms.'

'But why? Why would Annette go to your rooms. And at this time!'

'She is sleep-walking — as before. Forgive me, madame, we must hurry.'

When we reached the antechamber my pace quickened, and on entering the library I started to run. As I passed the terrestrial and celestial globes, the door to my apartment came into view. It was, as I had expected, wide open. The child had made her way through the chateau in total darkness. 'Annette?' I shouted. 'Annette?'

I burst into my study and what I saw brought me to an abrupt halt. My heart seemed to rise up and stop in my throat.

The lid of the chest had been raised and the neatly folded squares of fabric strewn across the floor. I saw a jar on its side, an upturned cash box and the glimmer of discarded keys. Annette was standing next to the chest, arms outstretched, the crystal in her hands. She was staring into its core, entranced by the thing inside — her features lit by a red luminescence that shone out from the crack on its surface. A distorted yellow eye looked at me from within the glass, and the sickening force of the demon's malice made me stagger. The eye blinked and vanished as Hélène caught up with me. I gestured for her to stand back.

'Annette,' I spoke gently. 'Annette, put it down.' She

did not hear me and continued to stare into the crystal. 'Annette,' I pleaded. 'Listen to me. It is very important that you listen to me.'

'What is she holding?' asked Hélène.

'Madame – please,' I pressed a rigid finger against my lips and took a cautious step towards the child. 'Annette? It is Monsieur Clément speaking – your friend, Monsieur Clément. It is so very important that you listen to me, so very important – Annette?'

I took another step.

'Annette!' Hélène called out. 'Listen to Monsieur Clément, he is talking to you!'

She was only trying to help, but it was enough to startle the child. Annette dropped the crystal and when it hit the floor the glass shattered. There was a flash of red light, a whiff of sulphur and a sudden rearrangement of the darkness – as if all the shadows in the room had rushed towards Annette. The child's legs gave way under her and she fell to the floor, unconscious.

I set the lamp aside, scooped her up and laid her out on the divan. Her breathing was shallow, her pulse fast, and when I lifted her eyelids I saw that her pupils had contracted to two pinpoints. I tried to rouse her, but she did not respond.

Hélène was standing by my side. 'Monsieur, what is wrong with her?'

My answer was redundant and evasive: 'She has lost consciousness.'

'Yes,' said Hélène. 'But has she had another seizure?'

'No.'

'Then what . . .' her sentence stopped abruptly and her brow furrowed.

'Madame,' I replied. 'Perhaps you should sit down.' Hélène withdrew a little and I continued with my examination, but a worried mother is never silent for very long.

'Monsieur? What was Annette holding when we entered this room?'

'A glass receptacle.'

'Yes, but what was it? I recall you once said that you kept dangerous chemicals in your chest. But . . .'

Annette began to mutter something and Hélène fell silent. When I listened closely, I detected snatches of Latin and Greek.

'Is she all right?' asked Hélène.

'Yes, for the moment.' I stood up. 'Madame, you must excuse me.'

'Where are you going?'

'Just next door. I won't be long.'

I went into my bedroom, sat on the mattress and buried my head in my hands. It had succeeded once again. It had taken me to hell.

Rage boiled up inside me. I clenched my fists, looked up at the ceiling and directed a stream of abuse towards heaven. But such was my despair I then fell on my knees and joined my hands together in prayer. I was prepared to try anything for Annette. I was even prepared to entertain the slender hope that Bazile's theology was true, and that ultimately there was no other choice but to abandon reason and place one's trust in an incomprehensibly higher authority.

'Please, God,' I prayed. 'Do not let her suffer more than she must. I beg You.'

'Monsieur Clément?' Hélène's muffled voice came from behind the door. I got up and re-entered the study, where I saw Hélène standing over Annette. The child was mumbling louder than before.

'Listen,' said Hélène. 'Listen to what she is saying.' I crouched down and heard a string of obscenities. 'Why is she talking like that? I did not think she knew such words.' Hélène glanced across the room and stared at the splinters of glass that sparkled in the lamplight. 'What did Annette take from your chest?'

'It is difficult to explain.'

'When she dropped the . . . receptacle, I thought I saw things.'

I opened my mouth but seemed to lose all powers of expression.

Hélène continued, 'What is happening, monsieur? Please tell me.'

'What did you see?' I asked.

'There was a flash of light and then the shadows seemed to gather around Annette.' She shook her head and I surmised that she had seen something more, something even stranger. Even so, she clearly doubted the evidence of her own senses and did not continue. The sound of footsteps made us both turn towards the library.

Monique came through the doorway and when she saw Annette lying on the divan she clapped a hand over her mouth in shock.

'She collapsed,' I said to the maid. 'It sometimes happens when sleepwalkers are surprised. I am looking after her now. Go back to bed, Monique; there is nothing you can do to help.' I was anxious for her to leave before she realized what Annette was mumbling. The two women looked at each other, and Monique's raised eyebrows betrayed her thoughts. It was not acceptable for the mistress of the house to be in the doctor's study wearing only her nightclothes. Hélène understood the meaning of the maid's stony expression and said, 'Monsieur, I will return after I have attended to my toilet.'

'As you wish, madame.'

The two women departed and I was left alone with Annette. I placed my hand on her forehead and discovered that it was hot. 'You think that you have won,' I whispered under my breath. 'But I will fight you.'

As if in response, the dogs began to howl.

When Hélène returned, Annette was quite delirious. The pitch of her voice had descended several octaves and she was growling blasphemies. It was disturbing to hear such deep tones issuing from the mouth of a child and the language she employed was exceedingly crude. Occasionally, her features would contort into a lascivious leer and she would clutch at her genitals. I had to prise her fingers away and hold her arms down, until a shudder passed through her body and the agitation abated.

318

Hélène had positioned herself behind my desk and looked on in horrified silence. As I recovered from my exertions, Hélène stepped forward and stood behind me. 'Monsieur,' she said, 'is my daughter possessed?'

'Yes,' I replied directly. I heard a small gasp. She had been hoping, no doubt, that I would say something different, that I would chastise her, perhaps, for being absurd and offer her a rational, scientific explanation. But I could give her no such solace. I remembered the curé and his suggestion that if ever the need arose, I should call on him for help. He was, by his own admission, only a country priest, but I badly needed someone to confide in. I found myself saying, 'We must send for the curé at daybreak,' and when I turned, Hélène was looking at me intensely. The dogs were making a noise that sounded uncannily like grief-stricken human beings.

'Monsieur Clément, you must tell me what is happening. And what was that thing . . .' She swept her hand over the broken crystal. 'The thing that Annette dropped?'

'Please sit down, madame.' I stood up, indicated a chair, and crossed the room. Shards of glass cracked and splintered beneath the leather of my shoes. I then opened the cupboard, took out a bottle of rum and poured myself a large measure. Staring into the dark transparency of the liquid, I set about answering her questions, although with little reference to my actual history. The prospect of a full confession was simply too daunting. Instead, I improvised an episode of biography only loosely related to real life, which served the purpose of communicating some essential facts – but nothing more. I told Hélène that while living in Paris I had mixed with students of the occult and that among their number was a scholarly priest who had given me the crystal to look after. It was his claim that the glass contained a captive demon. The priest had gone travelling, had never returned, and I had become its custodian. I explained that I had only recently discovered a flaw in the glass, and that this discovery had coincided with Annette's deterioration and the occurrence of strange phenomena such as the howling of the dogs. 'As soon as I realized that the crystal was dangerous,' I concluded, 'I began making plans to leave Chambault. But it was already too late, madame. I am so very sorry.'

Hélène squeezed her lower lip between her thumb and forefinger. It seemed to me that she had accepted what I had said as true. Or perhaps she was simply too stunned – too bewildered – to think of any more questions. Eventually, she shook her head and glanced over at Annette, who was beginning to grumble obscenities once again. 'Demonic possession,' said Hélène. 'It is difficult to believe.'

'But you saw something,' I responded. 'Is that not so? When the glass broke?' She nodded and shivered as if a draught of cold air had chilled her to the marrow. Yet she did not elaborate and I did not press her. 'It – the demon – took control of Annette's mind,' I continued. 'That is how it managed to escape from its prison; and you too,

were, for a time, in its power.' She looked at me quizzically. 'Do you remember waking Monique?'

'When?'

'Tonight. You went to Annette's room, woke Monique,
and asked her to fetch me.'

'No,' she brushed a strand of hair away from her face.
'It was a dream! I dreamed that I was unwell, and . . .'
After a few moments of discomfiting reflection, her neck
and face reddened and she turned away. The embarrassment both of us felt made it hard for us to look at each
other and an awkward silence ensued. In due course,
Hélène sat up straight, and, trying hard to recover her
dignity, said, 'What shall I tell the others? Tristan,
Sophie?'

'Tell them that Annette was discovered walking in her
sleep. Tell them that she collapsed when we tried to wake
her, and that shortly after Monique left us, Annette had
another seizure.'

'Why not tell them the truth?'

'Your brother will not accept the truth. He will dismiss whatever it was that you saw as an illusion and he
will question my judgement.'

'Could it have been . . . an illusion?'

'No, madame. You saw a demon, and I do not want to
argue with Monsieur Raboulet. If you have any doubts,' I
gestured towards Annette, 'consider what your daughter
is saying.'

'But what if Tristan wants to see Annette?'

'Tell him that I have given strict instructions that

Annette is not to be disturbed. Tell him that her condition is critical and I have forbidden visitors.'

'We have always been honest with each other – Tristan and I.'

'These are exceptional circumstances, madame.'

Hélène rose from her chair and walked over to the divan. She looked down at her daughter and said, 'When will she recover from this . . . state?'

'I do not know.'

'Then how will she eat? Or drink?'

'While she is like this, eating and drinking will not be possible.'

'So what is to be done, monsieur?'

'We must consult the curé.'

'And what will he do?'

'Advise us with respect to the ritual of exorcism.'

'And once Annette has been exorcized: will she be well again?' Hélène observed my hesitation and said, 'Monsieur?'

'I hope that she will be well again, yes.'

'Hope?' Hélène's eyes were suddenly bright with anger. 'Monsieur, whatever made you bring such an object into our home!'

I could not justify myself and made another apology, but this time my voice quavered with emotion. Hélène registered my distress and her expression changed. I did not need further confirmation of her fine qualities, her kindness, her generosity of spirit, but that is what she gave me. Her anger seemed to melt away and her face exuded pity, as luminous as the aura surrounding a saint in a religious painting. 'Forgive me, monsieur,' she said, 'I spoke too harshly.'

'No more than I deserve, madame,' I replied, bowing my head.

Annette's body suddenly convulsed, her hips thrusting upwards, her torso and limbs describing a perfect arch. Her head was hanging down from her neck and I saw only the whites of her eyes. She opened her mouth wide and a jet of vomit hit the wall with remarkable force. It seemed to sustain itself beyond the point at which her stomach should have been emptied.

'Wake Louis,' I barked at Hélène. 'Send him to the village. The curé must come as soon as he is able!'

By the time I reached Annette she had become limp again and she was lying flat on her back. She licked the vomit from her lips, the corners of which curled upwards to form a hideous, leering smile.

23

Louis returned with the curé shortly after the sun had risen. The dogs had stopped howling, but they started to bark as soon as they heard the trap approaching. Hélène received the curé in the courtyard and conducted him directly to my study. She had evidently advised him of Annette's condition, because as soon as he came through the door, he barely acknowledged my presence and marched straight over to the divan.

Annette had been relatively peaceful since the break of day. Even so, she looked pale, drawn and exhausted. Her cheeks were hollow, her hair lank and her skin had turned a sickly grey-green colour. The air around her smelled faintly of ordure. Father Lestoumel gazed down at the child for several minutes. Finally, he turned and said, 'Monsieur Clément, I have been informed by Madame Du Bris that you believe this child to be possessed. Would you care to explain?'

We sat at my desk and I described how the drama of the previous night had unfolded, although for Hélène's sake, I omitted any mention of what had transpired in her bedchamber. I then informed the curé of how I had come to own the crystal, repeating the same half-truths. Father Lestoumel listened, showing increasing signs of discomfort, and when I had finished he asked Hélène a number of questions, quite clearly testing the accuracy of my report. As I listened to his gentle inquisition, I noticed two flies revolving around each other just beneath the ceiling. A third joined them, introducing an element of eccentricity into their orbits. I was mesmerized by their movements, the complexity of their mutual influence, and was startled when I felt Father Lestoumel's hand on my shoulder. 'You will excuse me a moment,' he said, tightening his grip. 'I am going to the chapel and will return shortly.'

Hélène and I waited for him in silence, and when he reappeared he was holding a small silver box in his hand. He lifted the lid and removed a communion wafer. Then, looking at Hélène, he said, 'Madame, what I am about to do may cause you some distress.' He brushed Annette's hair off her face and pressed the wafer down on her forehead. The child immediately screamed, as if in pain, and her limbs flailed around wildly. Father Lestoumel tried to restrain her without success and called out, 'Quick! Clément! Help me!' and I jumped to his assistance. Together, we managed to hold her down, but only with great difficulty. We were both surprised by her enormous strength, and, if she had continued kicking and punching for very much longer, our efforts to contain her movements would have failed. Fortunately, the attack subsided and Father Lestoumel silently drew my attention to the communion wafer, which had fallen to the floor. A red weal had risen up on Annette's forehead, its circularity and size corresponding exactly with the host.

Hélène was standing on the other side of the room, her hands crossed over her bosom. She seemed on the brink of tears. A fly landed on the child's cheek and I brushed it away.

'Madame,' said the curé, 'you must be very tired. Go and rest. In due course our needs will be better served if you are refreshed.'

'What are you going to do, Father?' asked Hélène.

'Nothing, for the moment; however, I would be most grateful if you would permit me to speak privately with Monsieur Clément. There are some matters concerning the provenance of the crystal that I wish to clarify. I will then decide how we shall proceed.'

Hélène did not want to leave, so I made a show of examining Annette, checking her pulse and temperature. 'Her condition is stable,' I said reassuringly. 'Perhaps you should do as Father Lestoumel suggests. Take the opportunity to rest while you can.' She nodded and went to the door, where, before leaving us, she glanced back at her daughter with tears spilling down her cheeks. The sight of Hélène in so much anguish made me feel utterly wretched.

'Thank you, monsieur,' said the curé, and we both sat down again at my desk. Father Lestoumel created a steeple with his hands and let it bounce against his pursed lips. After a long thoughtful silence, he said, 'I would like to begin by asking you one or two questions about these occultists you met in Paris. Were they members of—'

'Father Lestoumel,' I interjected. 'I regret to say that the story I told of how the crystal came into my possession was largely untrue.' The curé tilted his head to one side and eyed me quizzically. 'I did not wish to frighten Madame Du Bris with my true history.'

'You were not acquainted with any magical sects?'

'No.'

'And there was no scholarly priest?'

'Well, in that respect, I was telling a partial truth. His name was Father Ranvier. But he did not give me the crystal to safeguard in his absence. Nor did he fail to return from his travels.'

'What happened to him?'

'The demon . . .' I shuddered at the recollection of Father Ranvier's grisly end.

'Monsieur Clément,' said the curé, making the sign of the cross. 'Perhaps the time has come for you to unburden yourself.'

For a very long time, I stared at the surface of the desk, trying to order my thoughts. It was difficult to determine where I should begin, but eventually, I found myself saying, 'After the great siege, I travelled to the Antilles to work at the Poor Sisters of the Precious Blood mission hospital on the island of Saint-Sébastien.' And once I had begun, I continued, the words coming more easily, the momentum of the narrative demanding an ever-faster delivery. I told the curé everything: I told him of Duchenne, the experiment and my subsequent descent into depravity. I told him of Courbertin, the exorcism in the crypt of Saint-Sulpice and of Father Ranvier's horrible demise. It was only when I tried to describe my trip to Chinon that a lump in my throat made it impossible for me to go on. I extended my arm, as if I could push the memories away, and rushed to the cupboard to pour myself more rum. When I sat down again, Father Lestoumel rested his hand on mine and said, 'My son, how you have suffered.' I had not expected such a response and I was deeply moved by his sympathy.

Lifting the glass to my lips, I took a sip of rum and said, 'If it is God's will that I should suffer, then so be it; however, I cannot understand why Annette must suffer too. It is incomprehensible. Why does He allow such things to happen?'

'Wiser men than I have attempted to answer that question with less than satisfactory results. But our inability to penetrate God's mysteries does not mean that He is indifferent to our suffering.'

'I wish that I could believe that.'

'Our Lord was assailed by doubts, monsieur. When he was being crucified, did he not cry out, "My God, my God, why hast Thou forsaken me?" No one is without doubts.'

I looked across the room at Annette. 'She is such a sweet child. I cannot bear to think of what torments she is being subjected to, even now – as we speak. I cannot bear to think of what the demon is doing to her.'

Father Lestoumel withdrew his hand. 'Consider this, my friend: if an evil man were possessed, how would we know it? Both he and the entity that had taken control of his mind would share the same objectives. Consequently, the man's behaviour would not change. Now, look at Annette! Her soul is not yielding. The demon is unable to manipulate her. In spirit, she is not a helpless child, but a power to be reckoned with.'

'That may be so. But she cannot be roused and she cannot eat or drink. We must act promptly, Father, or she will die.'

'Of course.' He took off his biretta and used it to swat at one of the flies. 'The demon must be cast out, and soon.'

'Have you ever performed an exorcism before, Father?'

'No.'

'Are you sure that . . .'

'I am equal to the task? All priests are Christ's foot soldiers. All priests are exorcists.'

There was little point in observing small courtesies at this juncture and I pursued my theme, 'Father Ranvier was a distinguished scholar. He had made a lifelong study of the cathedral in Paris and its lore. Yet he was no match for the demon.'

'Do not worry, monsieur,' my companion replied, 'I will not underestimate our adversary.'

I took one of the parchment seals from my pocket and handed it to the curé. His eyes narrowed as he examined the hieroglyphs. 'It is an amulet. I made it for Annette, but unfortunately I did not give it to her in time. For over a year now, I have been studying the books in the library.'

'An intriguing collection.'

'And I have good reason to believe that this seal will give you some protection.' The curé turned the parchment over and held it up to the light. I thought I detected a certain wariness in his manner. 'Father Lestoumel,' I continued, 'some believe that Joseph, the son of Jacob – who interpreted dreams – was a practitioner of Egyptian magic. Moses too. You will recall that the lawgiver carried a staff. It could also be described as a wand. Not all magic is bad, Father. And some spells have been used against the forces of evil from the earliest times. Please keep the amulet.'

The curé inclined his head and tucked the amulet into his pocket.

'Thank you,' he said. 'But I am already protected.'

'By your faith?'

'Indeed.' His conviction did not strengthen my confidence. On the contrary: if anything, it weakened it. 'Do you think the child can travel?' he asked.

'Yes, I suppose so. Why? Do you want her brought to Saint-Catherine?'

'No. I was thinking of somewhere further afield.'

'Where?'

'Paris.'

I was so stunned that I could only respond by making inarticulate noises.

'It may surprise you to learn,' the curé continued, 'that I am not entirely ignorant of the occult sciences. Indeed, I would go so far as to say that, for a country priest, I am quite well read. Before your appointment, after celebrating Mass in the chapel on special Saint's days for Madame Odile, I would very occasionally spend a few hours in the library. I may not be a scholar, but I have a reasonable understanding of what might be termed the elementary principles. And in my opinion the exorcism should take place in the cathedral. That is where this began, and that is where this must end.' I stuttered an objection but the curé dismissed my utterances with a wave of his biretta. 'Now, I wonder whether your friend Monsieur Bazile would be willing to help us? We will need to be in the cathedral at dawn, and we must have access to a secluded area where we will not be disturbed.'

'I have not corresponded with Monsieur Bazile since my departure from Paris.'

'Then we must hope that he still occupies the same position.'

The curé stood up and circled the desk, pulling at his chin and talking very quickly. He was not addressing me, but rather thinking aloud. 'We must leave as soon as possible to make use of the daylight. Louis will drive us. If we set off soon, we may be able to make the capital shortly after sunset.' I wanted to know why, precisely, he had determined that the exorcism should take place in the cathedral, but he was not very forthcoming. He offered me some vague generalizations and, when pressed, spoke only of symmetries, sympathies and correspondences. Eventually, he dismissed my requests for clarification with an impatient gesture and his monologue resumed. 'After my departure, you must inform Madame Du Bris of our plan. She will, of course, want to travel with us. I would suggest we assemble outside Saint-Catherine at one o'clock.'

As Father Lestoumel aired his thoughts, I became increasingly unsure whether I had made the right decision concerning his involvement. I was not convinced that he fully appreciated the terrible dangers we would face; however, I had no alternative but to follow his lead. He was a priest, and a priest was needed to conduct the exorcism. Our eyes met on one of his turns around the desk, and he must have seen my uncertainty, because he paused and gave me a strange little smile. 'Faith,' he said, before starting up again, 'have faith.' But I did not find this exhortation in any way reassuring.

When the curé finally ceased talking, he stood by the divan and removed the wooden cross that hung from his neck. He looped the leather lanyard over Annette's head and placed the sacred object on her chest. Then, touching the red weal on the child's forehead, he said, 'Be strong. May God protect you.' We shook hands. 'One o'clock, monsieur. Outside Saint-Catherine.' He pulled his biretta back on and vanished into the library.

I sat next to Annette and gazed down at her face. Her expression was serene and the colour had returned to her cheeks. She seemed calm and her breathing was regular. Outside, the birds were singing and the sun was high. A mechanical whirring filled the air before the clocks in the library and study began to chime. It was noon. Before the last note had faded, Annette's eyes flicked open. I was startled and gasped. Her head rolled to the side and she said, 'Monsieur Clément.' The voice was her own.

'Annette!'

'Monsieur, I am thirsty. May I have something to drink?'

'Yes, of course, of course.' I leaped off the chair and emptied a jug of water into a cup. Returning to the divan, I helped Annette to sit up and placed some cushions behind her back. I held the cup to her lips and she gulped the contents.

'I have had such bad dreams, monsieur.'

'Have you?'

'A foul creature, like the one on the church spire, came to me and would not leave me alone. It teased me and hurt me and called me names.'

'Annette, I am so sorry,' I took her hand in mine and held it tightly. I noticed that her nails had thickened.

'And there were fires and people screaming and monsters that came out of the earth.'

'Do not think about it.'

She frowned: 'Am I unwell again?'

'Yes.'

'Am I dying, monsieur?'

'No.'

'The creature said that I would die soon.'

'It was only a dream, Annette.' Her eyes glazed over and her head fell forward. 'Annette?' I cried, 'Annette?' But she was insensible. I heard a low growl, coming from the back of her throat, which was sustained and then inflected to produce obscenities. 'Annette?' She was gone. I removed the pillows, one by one, and ensured that she was lying comfortably. 'Take me!' I shouted in anger. 'Take me! Not her. I won't resist. Take me now!' But the demon did not accept my invitation. The hell that I occupied was far worse than the hell of fire and brimstone, and it wanted me to stay there for as long as possible.

I wiped away my tears and rang for a servant. It was Monique who came, and I told her to go and wake Madame Du Bris immediately. 'But do not alarm your mistress,' I called after her as she descended the stairs. 'Tell her that Annie is well.' A few minutes later, Hélène stepped into my study. She anticipated my apology and said, 'I was not asleep.' Looking about the room, she added, 'Where is Father Lestoumel?'

'He has gone back to the village.'

'And when will he be returning?'

'He won't be.' I gestured for her to sit and told her of the curé's plan.

'But why must we go to Paris? To Notre-Dame?' Hélène asked.

'It is a very holy place,' I replied. She did not appear very satisfied with my answer and I felt obliged to add, 'We must place our trust in Father Lestoumel.'

While Hélène sat with Annette, I searched for Louis and found him in the kitchen. I told him to pack a small travelling bag and to prepare the two-horse carriage for Paris. Years of service had accustomed him to obeying orders and he hardly blinked when I added that we intended to leave in half an hour. On my way back to the study I encountered Raboulet. He was wearing a dressing gown, a pair of oriental slippers, and held Elektra in his arms.

'Clément, what is going on? I can't find Hélène anywhere and Madame Boustagnier tells me that Annette is very ill.'

'Yes, I'm afraid that what you have heard is correct. Multiple seizures . . . through the night.'

'How dreadful.'

'I have done all that I can, but it is not enough. I have decided to take her to Paris, to see Charcot.'

'Charcot?'

'If anyone can help her, it will be the chief of services of the Salpêtrière.'

'Do you want me to come with you?'

'No, that won't be necessary. Madame Du Bris will be accompanying me on the journey.'

'Can I see Annette?

'Now? I'd rather you didn't – she's sleeping. The poor child is exhausted.' Elektra insinuated a tiny finger into her father's mouth and laughed. 'Forgive me, but . . .' I indicated that I needed to get past and Raboulet stepped aside. Thanking him, I hurried through the connected rooms and ascended the stairs to my study.

335

Hélène was still sitting beside the divan and she informed me that Annette had been silent and calm. In turn, I recounted what I had said to Raboulet concerning the pretext for our imminent departure. Hélène then left to make her own preparations for travel and I washed and shaved. Even though the windows were closed, there were flies everywhere, and I supposed that there must be some connection between their increase and the demon. Anger welled up in me and I slapped one hard against the mirror. As I removed my hand, the squashed insect fell into my shaving bowl and sank beneath the suds.

When I heard the horses neighing and the rattle of the carriage, I picked up Annette and carried her down to the courtyard. In the bright benevolent sunlight she looked much the same as she always looked: a beautiful child, sleeping. It was fortunate that the hour of the day favoured the forces of light over the forces of darkness, because Raboulet was waiting to see us off and I did not want him to see his niece speaking in tongues or mouthing obscenities. Hélène got into the carriage and Raboulet helped me to lift Annette onto the seat. We settled her head on her mother's lap and covered her body with a blanket. Raboulet stroked her hair and noticed the red mark that Father Lestoumel had made with the host.

'What's that?' he asked.

'A rash,' I replied. He looked a little perplexed but made nothing of it. He then jumped down from the carriage and handed me my medical bag and a battery I had sent down earlier. I was already thinking the unthinkable.

Louis mounted the box and as soon as we were beyond the gardens I instructed him to stop outside Saint-Catherine. We arrived at the village shortly before one o'clock, but Father Lestoumel was not waiting for us. I entered the church and found the curé kneeling before the altar and praying. By his side was a large leather satchel. It was unfastened and appeared to contain a Bible, several candles and a rolled-up stole. He heard my approach, made the sign of the cross and rose to greet me. 'Is it one o'clock already?'

'Yes,' I replied. What little confidence I had in him suddenly evaporated. He looked small and slightly befuddled. 'Father,' I continued, 'are you sure you want to proceed?'

'Of course'

'If you had decided otherwise, I would not think ill of you.'

'The child's life is in danger.'

'Yes, and so is yours, Father.'

'Indeed, but I am not frightened.'

'You should be.'

'I do not want to die. But if God wills it . . .' He shrugged and repeated the same empty injunction that I had heard so many times before, and now served only to deepen my despondency: 'Faith, my friend. Have faith.' He smiled and added, 'Come over here. I want to show you something.' I followed him down a side aisle and we stopped beneath the stained-glass window of Gilbert de Gandelus and the demon. The image was so arresting

337

and colourful it was easy to overlook the rusted metal plate in the wall below it. Plunging his hand into the deep pocket of his cassock, the curé produced a key, and it was at this point that I realized what I was looking at: not a plate, but a door. Father Lestoumel pushed the key into the lock and, when he turned it, the sound of the bolt's release echoed through the church. He pressed his finger into the small gap between the metal and the stone wall and pulled the door open. Then, he reached into the dim compartment and removed a large book which he held out for me to examine. It was bound in red leather and the hasps were made from gold. My eyes oscillated between the book and the glowing image of its double in the stained glass. The curé showed me the spine and indicated the title: *Malleus Daemonum* – the Hammer of Demons.

'This, my friend,' said Father Lestoumel, 'was the secret of Gilbert de Gandelus's remarkable success. It was given to him by Roland Du Bris, an ancestor of the family you serve, at the time of the Séry-des-Fontaines possessions. The author of this volume is none other than the great alchemist Nicolas Flamel, who lived not very far from the cathedral in Paris. You will already know, of course, that he is reputed to have made a philosopher's stone and to have discovered the elixir of life. This remarkable tome, which has, for obvious reasons, escaped the notice of scholars through the centuries, contains a ritual of restitution – a ritual that can send demons back to hell. Flamel suggests that, where an exorcist can identify the portal through which a demon came into the world, that is where the ritual is most likely to be effective. I have long wondered why it has fallen upon me, a simple country priest, to be the custodian of this hidden treasure. But now I think I know. The Almighty has a plan, you see? I have my small part to play – just as you do, monsieur.' He handed me the book. 'Come now,' he concluded. 'We must make haste. It is past one o'clock and the road to Paris is long.'

24

Little was said in the carriage. The curé closed his eyes, sat very still and only the occasional movement of his lips, accompanied by a whispered invocation, indicated that he was at prayer. Hélène rested her head on the woodwork and gazed out of the window at the rolling countryside. I studied her reflection in the glass and watched the clouds passing behind her image. The situation in which she found herself was so far removed from the gentle routines of the chateau: her expression was blank and her jaw tensely set. Apart from the occasional grumble, Annette was relatively quiet. At regular intervals I took her pulse and found no change. Consequently, I was able to spend much of the first half of our journey perusing the *Malleus Daemonum*.

It was a remarkable piece of scholarship and contained chapters on a wide range of subjects: the provenance of demons, the demonic hierarchy and the names of the princes of hell; words of power; summoning demons and commanding them to do one's bidding; the making of pacts; capturing demons in glass, precious stones and rings; the demons of the Middle East, or djinni; the classification of demons according to Raban the Moor; incubi and succubi; magical weapons; exorcism; and finally, sending demons back to the inferno. I was astonished when I discovered a map of Paris, showing the location of what Flamel called 'openings' between our world and the 'infernal region'. Each was represented by a black circle, and the largest of these was located on the Île de la Cité, next to a miniature illustration of Notre-Dame. The ritual of restitution was decorated with figures representing the exorcist in various attitudes, and superimposed on mathematical diagrams. An explanatory footnote suggested that Flamel's geometry was originally developed by Daedalus, the engineer who designed the labyrinth in which the legendary minotaur was imprisoned.

We made good progress, stopping only twice to water the horses; however, I was conscious of the sun's steady descent, and as the shadows lengthened, Annette became more restless. There were bursts of obscene language and her fingers toyed with the hem of her smock. An hour or so before sunset, I noticed another curious phenomenon: Annette's skin seemed to become unnaturally smooth, making her face look like a tight-fitting mask. I did not want to worry Hélène, and said nothing, but eventually the effect was so pronounced that she also noticed and said, 'Monsieur? What is happening to Annette's face? She looks like a doll.'

'Dehydration,' I replied.

The curé caught my eye and continued his prayers.

He knew perfectly well that the phenomenon was supernatural, but, like me, he did not want to alarm Hélène unnecessarily.

And so the day passed, and we arrived at the southern tip of the capital in darkness. I got out of the carriage, joined Louis on the box, and directed him through the streets. Louis had only been to Paris once before, as a young man, and he could not believe how impatient the other drivers were. 'They are all lunatics, monsieur!' he cried, as a cab carelessly swerved in front of us and a crude imprecation resonated in the air. The old retainer gawped at the advertisements, shop windows and painted whores, who showed us their ankles and blew us kisses. After the peace and sleepy charm of Chambault, Paris was indeed like a madhouse.

As we came to a halt outside Saint-Sulpice, the bells started ringing. I prayed that it was Bazile, and not one of his assistants – or even worse, a new bell-ringer. The door to the north tower was unlocked and I climbed the stairs. Only a glimmer of light filtered down from above. Eventually, I came to Bazile's apartment. I knocked on the door, which was immediately opened by Madame Bazile.

'Monsieur Clément!' She cried. 'Good heavens! Monsieur Clément! Do come in, do come in!' I stepped into the parlour and my head filled with recollections of talk and sweet cider. 'Let me take your coat,' said Madame Bazile, fussing around me. 'Édouard has just rung the hour. He will be down in a moment.'

342

'How is he?' I asked.

'Well,' she replied. 'And you, Monsiuer Clément? How have you been?'

Before I could answer, the door opened and Bazile stepped into the room. He started and looked at me as if I were a ghost. 'Paul?' he said, a note of doubt creeping into his voice. The sight of my old friend touched me deeply and my eyes became hot and moist. He came forward, extending his arm, but when I took his hand, I drew him towards me and we embraced.

'It isn't over, then,' he said.

'No,' I replied.

'I knew you would come back, one day,' said Bazile, slapping my back. 'What took you so long?'

We carried Annette up the stairs of the north tower and put her to bed, after which I dismissed Louis, telling him to return with the carriage an hour before dawn. Up until that point he had accepted all of his instructions without question; however, before making his departure, he hesitated and said, 'Does the master know we are in Paris?'

'Yes,' I replied. 'Monsieur Raboulet promised to send a note.'

Louis gave a curt nod and began his descent of the stairs, but a trace of mistrust lingered in his eyes.

On returning to the parlour I found Bazile poring over the Hammer of Demons, with Father Lestoumel sitting at his side relating its history. Hélène and Madame Bazile were in the bedroom, watching over Annette. I was surprised to discover that Bazile was acquainted with the name of Gilbert de Gandelus. He even knew of the holy man's victory over evil at Séry-des-Fontaines. The curé was most impressed. When I showed Bazile the map of Paris with its many circular 'openings', his face shone with excitement. 'There it is!' he cried, pointing at the illustration of the cathedral. 'Proof that Father Ranvier was right!'

I tried, as best I could, to summarize what had transpired at Chambault – the cracking of the glass and the sequence of events leading to Annette's possession – although, once again, I felt obliged to protect Hélène's modesty and did not mention what had occurred in her bedchamber. Nor did I say anything about Thérèse Courbertin.

Bazile listened in his customary fashion, smoking his pipe and frowning. When my story was concluded he shook his head and said, 'We are up against a fearful adversary!'

'Indeed,' said the curé, 'it is a member of the hellish aristocracy, a grand duke of the infernal kingdom.' He drew Bazile's attention to the final chapter of the Hammer of Demons. 'What we must do,' said Father Lestoumel, 'must be done in the cathedral. That is what Flamel advises. Can you help us?'

Bazile bit on his pipe stem. 'The bell-ringers of Paris are – as it were – a brotherhood, and if the need arises, we can call upon each other for favours. I will consult

with Quenardel, the chief bell-ringer of Notre-Dame.'
Bazile stood up and lifted his coat off a peg on the wall.
'There is a room in the north tower of the cathedral that
will suit our purposes. I will return with the key as soon
as possible.' And the next instant, he was gone.

After ten minutes or so Hélène appeared in the doorway that connected the parlour to the rest of the
apartment. She leaned against the jamb and seemed so
frail and weak, I feared she might be about to faint.
'Father Lestoumel, Monsieur Clément,' she said, her
voice quavering. 'Please come quickly.'

She led us to the bedroom, where Madame Bazile was
placing pieces of incense in small dishes. It was cold and
the air was tainted with the smell of ordure. Annette was
very still, but the skin of her face seemed to have shrunk
even more tightly around her skull: it had a glazed quality, like porcelain, and seemed just as likely to shatter.
Although her mouth was closed, I could hear a steady
stream of obscenities, articulated in the unnaturally low
register I had heard the previous night.

The curé knelt by the bedside, took Annette's hand
in his own and began to pray: 'Soul of Christ, sanctify
me. Body of Christ, save me. Blood of Christ, exalt me.'
Madame Bazile held a lit match against the incense and
the room soon filled with the fragrance of sandalwood.
'Water from the side of Christ, wash me. My good Jesus,
hear me. Within your wounds hide me. Never permit me
to be separated from you. At the hour of death, call
me.' The demonic voice faded, but it was still present – a

persistent growling. I listened to Father Lestoumel, his gentle delivery, and found some comfort in the rhythm and cadence of prayer. But I was still incapable of accepting such sentiments. I was still paralysed by reason: if God is love, then He would not permit a demon to torment an innocent child. Therefore, God cannot be love. I could not think beyond the logic of this proposition. Father Lestoumel continued, 'To you do we send up our sighs, mourning and weeping in this valley of tears.'

I watched the smoke rising from the incense dishes and noticed a strange discrepancy. Above one, the smoke was dissipating in the usual manner, whereas above the other the smoke seemed to be accumulating. Grey wisps and filaments collected in the air, becoming more and more condensed as the sandalwood burned. For a fraction of a second, the play of lamp light on the cloud made it look like a head with projecting horns, and then, a moment later, there was nothing to see except a haze of expanding tendrils. I threw glances at the others, Father Lestoumel, Hélène and Madame Bazile, but none of them had observed this sudden transformation.

What I had witnessed was no phantasm of the brain, but a demonstration of power. I was being mocked, taunted. Although the room resounded with prayer, the demon was showing me how it could easily reach out and manipulate the material world. I sensed that something very terrible was about to happen.

Annette's hand moved so fast, all that I could detect was a blur. Father Lestoumel cried out and fell backwards, gagging on the wooden cross that had been jammed into his mouth. I heard Hélène scream, and then, Annette's body, as rigid as a plank, levitated. She rose up off the bed and began to spin. I was dimly aware of Madame Bazile kneeling beside Father Lestoumel and leaped over the priest's body. Grasping Annette's smock, I pulled on the material, but my efforts met with strong resistance and my feet almost left the ground. As soon as her back touched the eiderdown she began to thrash about and I had to use all of my weight to restrain her movements. The voice started up again, close to my ear, and embedded within a continuous stream of ugly babblings I detected a single intelligible sentence: 'For her soul I shall defile and her flesh shall I use for my satisfaction.' I was sickened and hoped that Hélène had not heard this. Annette's limbs started to jerk. She was no longer trying to break free, but in the throes of another seizure. Her spasms were so violent that I began to fear that her spine might snap. When the bucking stopped I wiped the foam from her chin and checked her pulse, which I found to be slow and weak.

I turned round and saw Hélène standing in the middle of the room, eyes wide open and biting her knuckles. She looked like a woman teetering on the edge of derangement. Madam Bazile was squatting next to the curé dabbing blood from his lips. I hurried over to examine his injuries. Two of his teeth had been knocked out and the roof of his mouth was deeply scored.

'Do you want something for the pain?' I asked.

He shook his head, and for the first time I saw self-doubt in his eyes: recognition of his own limitations and the fact that good does not always triumph over evil. Although we were armed with Flamel's Hammer of Demons, our victory was by no means certain.

'Don't worry about me,' Father Lestoumel replied, 'Take care of the girl.'

I returned to Annette, who was now still and quiet, and with Hélène's assistance washed away some soiling and changed her clothes. Hélène worked quickly and efficiently, but her hands were unsteady and her eyes unnaturally bright.

'Madame,' I said, 'you do not have to watch with us. You are exhausted. Please, go next door.'

She did not reply and gave me a hard look: a look that pierced my heart, because her eyes were accusing me. 'This is your fault,' they said, 'this is all your fault.' I pulled a chair from beneath the dressing table and added, 'At least sit down.' She did as I asked, but did not thank me.

Annette's breathing had become very shallow and her skin was completely drained of colour – a terrible, inanimate white: the white of chalk or alabaster, as if all the vessels in her body had been sucked dry. Sitting by her bedside, I heard an abrasive noise and noticed dust on my sleeve. I looked up at the ceiling, warily, but said nothing to the others.

An hour passed and Bazile came back, brandishing the key to the north tower of the cathedral. He had, no doubt, been expecting a warmer reception – handshakes and congratulations. But his smile disintegrated when he saw our grim expressions.

'What has happened?' he asked.

Father Lestoumel took his arm. 'Let us go into the parlour. I will explain everything there.' The curé did not want Hélène to hear his account. He, too, was worried about her mental state.

Annette's pulse was weakening, and by the time Father Lestoumel and Bazile returned, I could hardly find it. The curé resumed his prayers: 'Glory be to the Father, and the Son, and the Holy Spirit. As it was in the beginning, is now, and shall be, for ever and ever. Amen.'

Bazile appeared at my side.

'Are you all right?' he whispered.

'Yes,' I replied.

But his dark eyes registered my apprehension.

Annette gave a little sigh, and when the exhalation was complete, her pulse faltered and stopped. She was dead.

I did not move. Time halted with the cessation of her life. The moment I inhabited was infinite, and it seemed that I had an eternity in which to commune with Annette's impassive features. But then a tremor passed through my body and I was seized by rage, 'No, no!' I shouted. 'You shall not have her!' The emotion that animated me was exceptionally pure: complexities could not survive its fierce intensity. Suddenly, the world was a simpler place, my mind was emptied of redundant philosophy, I was not a player in some preordained drama in which the forces of good were pitched against the forces of evil. God and his mysterious intentions were completely irrelevant. What mattered now was this: the demon should not be victorious. Excepting myself and my enemy, the universe was now void.

I opened my medical bag, removed a scalpel, and cut down the front of Annette's smock.

'What are you doing, monsieur?' cried Hélène.

I did not reply and heaved the battery onto the bed. I raised the lid, adjusted the coil and the machine began to buzz. Placing the electrodes over Annette's heart, I delivered the maximum charge. Her body convulsed, but when I laid my ear against her chest, there was no heartbeat. 'Damn you!' I shouted, and again I applied the electrodes. Two threads of brilliant blue light dropped from the rods and scorched her skin. A second convulsion: but still nothing. Cold flesh and silence. I brought my clenched fist down on her sternum with such force that Annette's body bounced several times on the mattress. A pocket of trapped air stimulated her vocal cords and she emitted a pathetic whimper. 'Come back!' I yelled. 'You cannot die, you must not die!' Again, I placed the electrodes over her heart and – ignoring the smell of cooked flesh – did not remove them until her third convulsion came to an end. The pitch of the buzzing ascended and there was a loud report. A flame danced around the blackened coil and then went out. I threw the rods aside and pressed my hand against the side of Annette's neck. 'She's alive,' I cried. 'She's alive. Her heart is beating again.' Then, addressing Father Lestoumel, I added, 'We cannot wait until dawn. We must go to the cathedral now.'

'But the demon is at its most powerful at night,' said the curé. 'That would be most unwise.'

'The battery is broken,' I continued, 'and if Annette's heart stops again, I will not be able to revive her. Father Lestoumel, we must go to the cathedral now or she will die!'

Hélène swooned and Madame Bazile rushed to her assistance.

'Very well,' said the curé, 'let us go.'

I did not stop to examine Hélène. Instead, I picked up the child and strode towards the door.

'But what about Madame Du Bris?' asked Madame Bazile.

'The ritual we are about to perform is extremely dangerous,' I replied. 'It is just as well she will not be present.'

The bell-ringer's wife looked up at her husband. 'Are you going with them, Édouard?'

'Yes,' said Bazile, nodding his head vigorously.

'It is not necessary,' I said. 'Father Lestoumel and I can perform the ritual on our own.'

'I am afraid,' said Bazile, 'that my mind is made up. Come now, my friend, this is no time to quibble.'

We did not have to wait very long outside Saint-Sulpice before the lamps of a cab emerged from the gloom. The driver looked alarmed when he saw the girl in my arms.

'I am a doctor,' I said. 'This child has had a seizure and is close to death. She has already received extreme unction,' I nodded towards the curé. 'Please, take us to the Hôtel Dieu.'

'Put her inside,' said the driver. 'I'll get you there in five minutes.'

25

The cathedral loomed over us, its communities of saints, angels and demons ascending in energetic elevations towards a low vault of heavy cloud. Bazile unlocked the door of the north tower and, when he pulled it open, light spilled out from within. The interior had been hung with oil lamps. 'Quenardel,' said the bell-ringer. 'He is most thoughtful.'

We ascended the spiral staircase and came to a cavernous room littered with pieces of masonry and the decayed parts of statues. I had passed through this space before – it seemed a lifetime ago – when I had climbed up to the viewing platform and observed dawn breaking over Paris in the company of the chimeras.

'Is this the place?' asked the curé.

'Yes,' said Bazile.

Father Lestoumel looked around and smiled. 'You have chosen well, my friend.' He then produced some candles, which he lit and fixed to the floor with melted wax. I made myself as comfortable as possible, sitting with my legs crossed and cradling Annette's head in my lap. Her breathing was barely perceptible. 'Please hurry, Father,' I said.

'Monsieur Bazile,' said the curé, 'would you be so kind as to hold the book for me?'

The bell-ringer positioned himself in front of Father Lestoumel, holding the Hammer of Demons open so that the curé could read the text. There were no preparatory remarks. Father Lestoumel simply cleared his throat and began to chant. Some of the words were familiar, being either Latin or Greek; others, however, were in a language I did not recognize. As Father Lestoumel chanted, he moved his hands through the air, tracing the outlines of figures. At first, the shapes were simple – squares, triangles, circles – but then the movements became more complex, and it was no longer possible to identify specific forms.

Annette's face was now like a death's head. She had become a strange ceramic effigy. Her thin blue lips were pulled back to reveal two rows of even teeth and a blackened, swollen tongue protruding between them. The fetid exhalations that rose up from her mouth smelled like rotting fish. She rolled her head and spat out words that sounded like an Arabic curse.

'Hurry, Father!' I cried, fearful that we might lose Annette at any moment.

The curé did not acknowledge my appeal. Instead, he maintained the steady metre of his chant and continued to divide the air with graceful, sweeping gestures.

When I returned my attention to Annette, her eyelids

rolled back revealing only white, bloodshot membranes. 'End this now,' she growled. 'If you send me back, you know who I will seek.' I felt as if I had been splashed with acid. 'I will befoul your strumpet and violate her – rip her belly and make a garland of her bowels. I will undo her and feast on her yielding parts.'

'Do not listen to it!' shouted Bazile.

I looked into Annette's empty eyes, fighting to overcome a wave of nausea and terror, and said, 'Your time in this world is over.'

The demon responded with a horrible, grating laugh: 'Have you found faith?'

'No,' I replied. 'I have found hate, and with it, singularity of purpose.'

'You make my work so easy,' the fiend replied, before producing a series of harsh barks that managed to express merriment.

'Do not speak to it!' screamed Bazile, making frantic gestures. 'Do not let it into your mind! Nothing can be gained by engaging with the deceiver!'

'You think it is over?' said the demon, a note of amusement animating its gravelly monotone. 'Think again, fool. It is only the beginning.'

Bazile was right. Even though our exchange had been brief, it was enough to empower the demon. With each sentence, it seemed to find communicating easier. Moreover, its parting remark, delivered with such supreme confidence, weakened my resolve. As I swayed on the edge of some inner precipice, confused, shocked, enfeebled, I was startled by an electrical crackling; a short distance from where I sat, beyond Annette's feet, the darkness was infiltrated by a soft red glow. Veils of luminosity folded and dissolved into shimmering sprays of light. The portal was opening.

Father Lestoumel's hands fell by his side and he began to recite the ritual of exorcism. Not the Rituale Romanum, but a translation of an eighth-century Galician manuscript favoured by Flamel: 'I accost you, damned and most impure spirit, cause of malice, essence of crimes, origin of sins, you revel in deceit, sacrilege, adultery and murder! I adjure you in Christ's name that, in whatsoever part of the body you are hiding, you declare yourself, that you flee the body you are occupying and from which we drive you with spiritual whips and invisible torments. I demand that you leave this body which has been cleansed by the Lord. Let it be enough for you that in earlier ages you dominated almost the entire world through your action on the hearts of human beings.'

Annette's limbs began to jerk.

'Father!' I called out. 'She's having another seizure. It's trying to kill her. Please hurry.'

The curé and Bazile came forward and the two men knelt beside me. Annette's jaw snapped shut and a stripe of bright blood appeared on her lip. I clasped her mouth and made sure that it remained closed.

'Now, day by day,' declaimed Father Lestoumel, 'your kingdom is being destroyed, your arms weakening.

Your punishment has been prefigured of old. Through the power of all the saints you are tormented, crushed and sent down to eternal flames.'

The candles began to flicker. We felt the flow of chill air against our cheeks, and a moment later the curé's biretta blew off his head and rolled across the floor towards the portal. Air was being sucked from our world into some empty vastness.

Father Lestoumel looked around anxiously before laying both of his hands on Annette's forehead. 'Depart, depart!' he cried, 'Whencesoever you lurk, and nevermore seek out bodies dedicated to God.' I could hardly hear his voice above the rushing wind. All the candles had blown out, but we could still see each other, our faces bathed in the radiance of the portal. Bazile lifted the Hammer of Demons higher so that the curé could read the text more easily. 'Let them be forbidden to you forever, in the name of the Father, the Son, and the Holy Spirit.'

This final affirmation of the trinity was like the last chord of a great symphony. Father Lestoumel allowed himself a small, triumphal smile. There was nothing more to do. He took the book from Bazile, closed its covers and held it against his chest.

Almost immediately, Annette stopped kicking. Her skin seemed to loosen around her skull – the hardened, smooth-textured contours became less reflective and softened as her features filled out. I watched, astonished, as the frozen thing she had become, thawed with the returning warmth of her humanity. Her face was so tranquil, calm and harmonious that I was suddenly fearful that she might be dead. I pressed my fingers against her neck. 'Dear God,' I cried. 'Please. I beg you . . .' And there it was – a faint perturbation, buried deep in the flesh. The movement of blood: life. I let out a sigh of relief, kissed her hair and thanked the Lord for His protection.

When I looked up again, I saw that something had interposed itself between our small, huddled group and the portal – a dark, nebulous mass. Against the glittering red light, I glimpsed the scalloped edge of an enormous wing, claws, two horns, the glint of polished scales. Each of these parts appeared momentarily before disappearing. The demon was clearly attempting to materialize. Was this supposed to happen? Fear gripped my throat and I could barely breathe. Then, quite suddenly, the demon was drifting backwards, its efforts frustrated by energies of unimaginable magnitude.

I was overcome by a kind of inebriate madness. Shaking my fist, I shouted, 'Go back to hell! You have been defeated! Go back to hell and never return! It is over! Do you hear me? Over!' The wind was still whistling above the crackling accompaniment of electrical activity. 'Go back to hell!' I yelled above the noise. 'You foul, pathetic creature! This child is free – and you will never have possession of her again!'

There were no more materializations, and the formless darkness receded through the twinkling veils.

I had always been the weaker party. But now, as the balance of power shifted, I became drunk with excitement. I wanted to taunt, mock and gloat, to revel in my victory. I let go of Annette, stood up and screamed abuse into the void. 'You have been defeated and I have won!'

Bazile and Father Lestoumel were scrambling at my feet. Then, I saw Annette's supine body sliding away. She was travelling fast, her legs slightly raised, her hair trailing, as if being dragged. I choked on my own words as she passed through the shimmering divide. My adversary was no longer visible. But neither was Annette.

The despair that I felt is impossible to describe. It fell upon me like a weight of marble: a devastating, crippling despair that I knew I could never live with. Bazile guessed my intention and grabbed my arm. He hauled himself up and hollered into my ear. 'No. Don't do it, Paul!'

'Let me go,' I protested.

'The portal will close and you will be trapped there forever.'

'Let me go, I say!'

'For the love of God, Paul. You can do nothing now.'

I prised his fingers from my arm, pushed him away and ran towards the threshold. The wind was at my back and I almost took off as I passed through the undulating waves of luminescence. I ran and ran, through glowing nebulae and cobwebby threads of light, and kept on running, beyond where the wall of the tower should have stopped my progress. The strength of the wind lessened and I found myself charging blindly through a sulphurous mist. I could feel pumice breaking beneath my feet, and the surface over which I travelled became uneven. 'Annette?' I called out. 'Annette?' The atmosphere thinned and I recognized an all too familiar landscape: a black sky riven by crimson lightning, an expanse of cinders giving way to a massive staircase of congealed lava, crags and smoking vents, belching pools of molten rock.

There was a loud detonation, and a tower of flame climbed to a great height. The blast sent me sprawling onto a carpet of hot ash. I quickly jumped up and waved my scorched hands in the air.

Unlike the occasion of my first descent into the pit, when I had arrived naked, this time I was still wearing clothes – the same clothes that I had put on in my rooms at the chateau two days earlier. They had travelled with me between worlds; however, the blisters that were already rising on my palms confirmed that, in one other respect, my circumstance was very much the same. I was fully embodied, with blood and organs and nerves that had the capacity to thrill with pain.

The smell of burning leather made me leap off the ash and I proceeded between two boulders, both of which bristled with large, flat-headed nails. Manacles hung down from rusty hooks and medieval instruments of torture lay abandoned and half buried in dunes of volcanic dust.

'Annette?' I cried. 'Annette? Where are you?'

I emerged into a shallow depression of shattered stone,

and saw a tiny crumpled figure lying on the ground a short distance ahead. I hastened down the incline and slid to a halt, falling on my knees at the child's side.

'Annette?' I whispered, lifting her face off a pillow of cracked granite. The blood on her lip had dried, but there were fresh lacerations on her cheeks. Her smock was torn and parts of her hair had been singed. I touched her lips and said, 'Annette? Can you hear me?'

Her eyes opened. 'Monsieur Clément?'

'Yes, Annette.'

'Have I been unwell again?'

'Yes. I'm afraid so.'

'Why is the sky black? Why is the sky on fire?'

I tucked a loose lock of hair behind her ear. 'Hush. We are going home.'

'Home?'

'Yes. Can you stand?'

'I think so. Where are we?'

'Annette. Take my hand. We must go now.'

But I did not move. There was a trickling of scree and a shadow fell across Annette's smock. My heart was hammering against my ribcage, and my courage drained into the earth. I was paralysed, unable to even turn round. Instead, I watched with weird fascination, as Annette's pupils dilated and her mouth opened wide. There was a beat of silence, before the scream came.

The demon had positioned itself on the boundary of the depression. It looked immense, silhouetted against a delta of blazing reticulations. Its great wings unfolded and it stood, legs set apart, proudly surveying its domain. I was in no doubt that we were in the presence of a true prince of hell, and my instinct was to prostrate myself and beg for mercy. I withered in its sight. The demon threw its head back and roared. A clap of thunder shook the ground, new vents opened, and the horizon burst into flames.

Annette's fingernails were digging into my skin.

'Monsieur Clément, Monsieur Clément . . .' she repeated my name, again and again.

'Run, child,' I said. 'Quick. This way.' I tugged her upright and we bounded up the incline, back towards the portal, but the loose stone was treacherous and we kept on slipping. I looked over my shoulder and saw the demon loping after us, horns thrust forward. 'Quick, Annette, you must run faster.'

'I can't, monsieur. I can't.' She had already fallen several times and blood was streaming from the cuts on her knees.

'You must!' I hauled her over the top. We ran between the boulders and out, into the open space beyond. I paused to get my bearings. The wide flat steps of lava were clearly visible, as were the bubbling pools of liquid rock. In the distance, I could see the coruscating mists of the portal. 'Not far now,' I said to Annette. 'Just over there.'

We set off again, giving the hot ash a wide berth. A meteor landed close by and we were showered with debris. Annette yelped with pain. 'We cannot stop,' I said. 'We must go on.' It was then that the air filled with a harsh barracking and a flock of demons soared into view. They glided over the lava steps and circled above us. One by one, they dropped to the ground, forming a ring that made our escape impossible. My old adversary appeared between the boulders and snarled some commands. The horde stamped their feet and waved their pitchforks, shrieking and grunting in their infernal language.

'What will they do to us?' asked Annette. I could not give her an answer. The thought of how these devils would abuse her made me feel quite sick. I could feel Annette trembling beneath the thin and filthy material of her smock. 'Is this a dream, monsieur?' she continued. 'A nightmare? Tell me that I am dreaming.'

The demon fixed its venomous eyes on Annette; its lower jaw sagged and its tongue slithered out. It tasted the air and the cast of its expression became eager and lascivious. Then it raised its arm, and a single talon sprang up, its curvature suggestive of beckoning without the necessity of movement.

'No,' I cried. 'You shall not have her!' A pitchfork hissed through the air and pinned my foot to the ground. I wrenched it away and enfolded Annette in my arms. The troop flapped their wings and jeered. More demons were landing on the lava steps; one of them was carrying a decapitated head which it tossed in the air and kicked. The head flew through space and descended into a pool of magma, where it sizzled and evaporated.

Annette was sobbing into my shirt. I held her close and said, 'Dear child. Know this. Whatever happens, you were loved.' She would be tortured for all of eternity and it was my fault. I was to blame! It was only right that I should burn, that I should be skewered and roasted. But I could not countenance the suffering of a stainless innocent. 'I am so sorry,' I said, tightening my embrace. 'So very, very sorry.' Tears streamed down her face and, out of habit, I searched my pockets for a handkerchief. How curious, that this reflex, this vestige of normality, should find expression, even in the depths of hell. My fingers made contact with something papery. It was the amulet: the amulet that I had copied in the library – the Seal of Shabako.

The demon lunged forward, and as it did so, I removed the parchment from my pocket. As soon as the charm came into view, the creature drew back. Its thick brows came together and it produced a lengthy sibilance. The amulet was emitting a bright, golden light. I whirled round, brandishing it like a torch, and our tormentors were thrown into disarray. Some opened their wings and took off, while others covered their eyes.

Here was old magic: power that required no faith or belief in an all-knowing God to have its effect; a power as morally neutral as magnetism.

'Get back!' I commanded as the monsters fled. 'Get back!' The ruddy luminescence of the portal was fading. 'Come,' I said to Annette. 'We are running out of time.' At that moment, my adversary chose to pounce. It leaped high and was almost upon us, its fangs bared and claws extended. Without thinking, I raised the amulet and shouted, 'Away!' A bolt of lightning streaked from my fist and exploded against its chest. The demon spun backwards and crashed into the hot ash, raising a column of grey cloud. I did not stop to enjoy the spectacle, but simply clutched Annette's hand and shouted, 'Run!'

I held the amulet high, and its radiance repelled the swooping demons. Pitchforks rained down and thrummed after impact, producing a strange, metallic counterpoint. The glittering mists of the portal lay just ahead of us. We ran, faster and faster, until we were swallowed up, and could see nothing but a wall of dense fog. There was no way of determining direction in this featureless expanse, and I wondered if it were possible to get lost in the spaces between worlds. Would we be there forever, trapped in a state of eternal transition? The lights were dimmer and it occurred to me that the portal might already be closed.

The acoustic changed and the ground became level.

'Keep going,' I said to Annette. 'We are almost home!'

I could hear the skittering of pebbles on flagstones. The fog parted, and its dissipation revealed a solitary shimmering veil. Through this ghostly partition, I saw two flames – oil lamps – the welcoming light of our own world.

'This way,' I said to Annette.

Although we were now sprinting, the distance between ourselves and the veil was not diminishing as fast as it should. The very fabric of space seemed to be stretching, denying us progress proportionate to our effort.

My lungs were aching and I was overcome by a terrible feeling of tiredness and fatigue.

'It cannot end here!' I cried out, and miraculously my anger released some last reserve of strength. Pulling Annette along behind me, I accelerated. It felt like running up an impossibly steep hill. Soon, the veil was floating in front of me – but its edges were contracting. I yanked Annette forward and pushed her through. Her body seemed to meet some resistance, and the child let out a cry. I pushed harder and saw her fall to the ground on the other side. Two figures rushed out of the darkness: Bazile and Father Lestoumel.

The bell-ringer was peering through the glare, as if trying to make out something distant or indistinct. 'Édouard!' I yelled, but he could not hear me. I saw him reaching out and his fingers penetrated the veil. Each digit became elongated and moved slowly, like the tentacles of a sea anemone. Concentric rings of light rippled outwards from the rupture as I leaned forward with my right arm extended, straining until we touched. Our fingers found mutual purchase and interlocked. Bazile pulled hard, and I was drawn closer to the veil; however, I could not make the transition. Then, dismayed, I realized that it was no longer Bazile who was dragging me through to his side, but it was I who was dragging him through to mine. His attenuated wrist and forearm were now clearly visible.

'Let go!' I cried. My friend held fast. 'Let go!' I struggled to free myself, but Bazile was strong and determined. He did not give up. I felt a sharp pain in my shoulder and imagined the tearing of ligaments, the ball of the joint being torn from its socket. An old memory surfaced: climbing a mountain of rubble during the siege and seeing a pale arm sticking up from the wreckage – tugging at the hand – feeling the whole limb come away. Had I been offered a cruel presentiment of my own end? A foreshadowing of my own dismemberment and demise? Had my doom been decided upon before the stars were scattered across the void?

'No!' I screamed – and jumped.

When my feet left the ground, there was a subtle change in the interplay of forces. Bazile's grip tightened and I seemed to be passing through a medium much thicker than air. Enormous pressures built up around me and I feared that I might be crushed. There was one more burst of red lightning – then nothing.

I must have lost consciousness, because the next thing I remember is Bazile's head, eclipsing the high Gothic ceiling.

'Paul,' he said. 'Are you all right?'

'Yes,' I replied. 'Where is Annette?'

'Just here.'

I sat up. Annette was lying close by, Father Lestoumel beside her.

'Is she alive?'

'Yes,' he replied.

I let myself fall back. 'Is it over now – do you think?'

'Yes,' said Bazile, making the sign of the cross. 'It is over.'

26

Annette slept for several days and I did not leave her bedside. When she awoke, she talked of 'bad dreams'. It was obvious to me that she was not speaking freely. Gentle coaxing had little effect: she remained reticent, and I could not persuade her to unburden herself. In the end, I was forced to recognize my limitations and cede authority to a superior healer: time. Father Lestoumel took me aside and offered me some consolation. 'Do not underestimate goodness,' he said. 'The child is more resilient than you think.'

I did not return to Chambault. When I spoke to Hélène of my intention to remain in Paris, she said, 'If that is what you want, monsieur.'

'Would you be so kind,' I asked, 'as to arrange the transfer of my possessions to the Hôtel Saint-Jacques?' I gave her a card. 'Much of what I own has already been packed.'

'Of course,' she replied.

I scribbled some prescriptions: 'Give these to Monsieur Jourdain. I am confident that Monsieur Raboulet and Annette will continue to benefit from my preparations; however, I would strongly recommend that you appoint another house physician. As you are probably already aware, Monsieur Jourdain is frequently indisposed.'

On the morning of her departure, I asked Hélène what she was going to tell her family. She replied that she had discussed the matter with Father Lestoumel and he had agreed to talk to Du Bris, Raboulet and Madame Odile on her behalf. He must have also told her much of what had transpired in the north tower of the cathedral, because she added, 'Monsieur: what you did for Annette – it was a very brave thing. We will be forever in your debt.' The directness of her gaze was unnerving.

'No.' I did not expect, or even wish to be forgiven: 'You owe me nothing.'

Hélène sighed and offered me her hand. I raised it to my lips and did not look up again until she was gone. A beam of sunlight slanted through a gap in the curtains, and I stood alone, breathing the lingering scent of her perfume.

The following week I wrote a letter to Charcot, requesting – with due humility – that he consider me as a prospective employee, should any suitable positions become vacant at the Salpêtrière. I was summoned to his office by return of post. He was perfectly civil. 'So, country life didn't suit you, eh? I didn't think it would. And yes, Clément, of course you can come back. There have been some very exciting developments.' The hysteria project was still Charcot's principal preoccupation and much progress had been made in my absence. It had been discovered that the symptoms of hysteria could be reproduced using hypnosis: a phenomenon of great theoretical and practical significance.

I had imagined that returning to work at the Salpêtrière would feel strange. But I was quite wrong. In fact, it felt very natural and I soon settled into a routine of ward rounds and research activities.

With the exception of Charcot's soirées, I did not see very much of my colleagues outside the hospital. Even so, I did not crave company, and there was always Bazile. I often found myself walking to Saint-Sulpice with a joint of lamb clamped under my arm,. which Madame Bazile would later cook. And after we had dined, Madame Bazile would retire, and Bazile and I would smoke, drink and talk.

It was just like old times.

We revisited the same theological problems, the same arguments: 'I cannot believe in a perfect, all-knowing God, because a perfect God would not have created hell. Nor would He, by virtue of foreknowledge, have condemned so many souls to such a dreadful fate. The best we can hope for, I fear, is a good but flawed deity: a creator unable to exercise control over His creation, who battles with the forces of evil, much the same as we do.'

Bazile would listen patiently, and when I had finished he would doggedly reaffirm his faith. 'We are like insects, crawling over an edition of Montaigne's essays. With our limited sensory organs and minuscule brain, what do we perceive? A flat surface? Perhaps not even that. Montaigne's wisdom is right there, beneath our feet. But it is not accessible. And no matter how hard we try, we will never understand the great man's thoughts on virtue, indolence and cruelty – or benefit from his opinions concerning Cicero, Democritus and Heraclitus! Montaigne, and the complexities of human life, are utterly beyond us. Yet Montaigne's wisdom exists! The human world exists! And that flat surface is very misleading. One should never confuse evidence with reality, or facts with the truth.'

Our exchanges were always good-humoured. Bazile was no longer offended by my provocative remarks and I was no longer frustrated by his intransigence.

There were other pleasures: the smell of freshly cut grass, sunsets, bright stars on a cold night. Naive delights. But none of these pure, cleansing experiences ever dispelled completely the darkness I carried within my heart. My thoughts always returned to Thérèse Courbertin, regret and sadness.

Occasionally, I would receive a letter from Father Lestoumel. My replacement at Chambault, a young doctor from Orléans, did not stay for very long. Both Raboulet and Annette had stopped having seizures and there was very little for him to do there. He became bored and resigned his post.

I missed the gardens: the blossoms and the pergolas, the lawns and the box hedges, the statues and the forest. And I wondered whether Hélène Du Bris had realized her ambition of building a maze on the empty field behind the Garden of Silence. I imagined her wandering alone through its intricate avenues.

Years passed. I published many articles in international journals and wrote a well-received book on the diminution of the will in hysteria. In due course, I was promoted and became an associate professor. Ostensibly, life was good: a top-floor apartment on the Rue de Medicis, holidays in Italy, invitations to society gatherings on the Boulevard Malesherbes. I was even more comfortable in Charcot's company.

Then, one Sunday afternoon, late in the spring, I was strolling around the Luxembourg Gardens when I saw two women emerging from the crowd ahead. Their arms were linked and there was something about them that made me stop and stare.

'It can't be,' I whispered aloud.

Hélène looked much the same, but Annette was utterly transformed. She was no longer a child, but an elegant young woman of striking appearance. Mother and daughter paused to watch a little boy launch a boat on the octagonal pool. They were both dressed in fashionable red velvet and did not look at all like visitors from the provinces. Hélène made a humorous remark and Annette laughed. The toy boat sailed across the glittering water, listing in the breeze.

I felt curiously light-headed.

Hélène and Annette turned to face me, and I observed my own disbelief reflected in their changed expressions. The world fell silent and it seemed as if we were separated from the hubbub. I saw Hélène mouthing my name, the double pursing of her lips.

There they were! Occupying the foreground of a perfectly judged composition. Behind them, I could see the Luxembourg Palace, flowers in bloom and an immaculate sky. I might have been having a vision.

Annette rushed forward and, demonstrating a comprehensive disregard for convention, threw her arms around me.

'Monsieur Clément, it is you! I knew it!'

Something caught in my chest and I fought hard to overcome my emotions.

Annette stepped back and I shook my head in defenceless admiration. 'My dear child. How . . . extraordinary!'

I took Hélène's hand and kissed it.

'Madame Du Bris. What brings you to Paris?'

'We live here now,' she replied.

'You have left Chambault?'

'Yes. And our circumstances are somewhat altered.'

She spoke without a trace of self-consciousness. Du Bris had behaved dishonourably and their marriage had been dissolved. Subsequently, she had brought the children to Paris at the invitation of their uncle. Raboulet had pursued his writing ambitions and was now a successful journalist. So successful, in fact, that he had been able to afford spacious accommodation near the observatory.

'And you, monsieur?' asked Hélène. 'What is your news?'

I told them a little of my situation, but did not want to talk about myself.

'We still take your medicine,' said Annette, resting a hand on my arm. 'And it still works.'

'I am very glad,' I replied.

'Mother,' said Annette, 'can we invite Monsieur Clément to dinner?'

I glanced at Hélène. 'Really, madame, I would not want to impose . . .'

'What a good idea!' Hélène cut in.

Annette's expression intensified. 'There are some things I would like to talk to you about, monsieur.'

'Things?' I enquired.

'Yes, things that I remember – from when I was very ill.'

'And I am sure,' continued Hélène, 'that Tristan would be delighted to see you again, Monsieur Clément. It is you who have made his dreams possible.'

We exchanged addresses, said goodbye and I watched Hélène and Annette ascend a staircase and disappear from view.

The Greeks inform us that Pandora's box contained all the evils of the world, and that when she opened it these evils were released. There was, however, something left at the very bottom: Hope. Standing there, in the Luxembourg Gardens, among the bank managers and their wives, the lawyers and the seamstresses, the nurses and the children, I recognized that myths survive because they express the deepest of truths. And, miraculously, I found that I could hope for meaning and purpose once again.

Concerning Influences, Historical Figures and Sources

The Forbidden began as a homage to J.-K. Huysmans, whose *Là-Bas* is a firm favourite of mine; however, as the plot developed, other French novels began exerting an influence, most notably *Justine*, by the Marquis de Sade, and *Bel Ami*, by Guy de Maupassant. Saint-Sébastien is fictional, but owes an inestimable debt to another literary island – Saint-Jacques – as described by Patrick Leigh Fermor in *The Violins of Saint-Jacques*. As an adolescent, I consumed the black magic novels of Dennis Wheatley; readers conversant with his work – now a guilty pleasure for ladies and gentlemen of a certain age – might hear his voice echoed occasionally (although I have stopped short of the Imperial Tokay wine and Hoyo de Monterrey cigars). Wheatley was also a great fan of J.-K. Huysmans: in fact, *Là-Bas* was one of the volumes included in a series published as the Dennis Wheatley Library of the Occult, from 1974 to 1977.

Historical Figures

Many of the characters who appear (or are mentioned) in *The Forbidden* are real:

CÉCILE CHAMINADE (1857–1944) was a composer and pianist who achieved considerable fame in her day. The recital

375

described in *The Forbidden* took place at the residence of Le Coupey on 25 April 1878. She was greatly interested in spiritualism.

JEAN-MARTIN CHARCOT (1825–1893) was a pupil of Duchenne and is now regarded as the father of modern neurology. He was chief of services at the Salpêtrière and became known as the 'Napoleon of the Neuroses'. His reputation spread worldwide and his soirées attracted many of the scientific, political and artistic elite of the late nineteenth century. Many of the descriptions of Charcot and the Salpêtrière in *The Forbidden* were based on material that can be found in *Charcot: Constructing Neurology*, by Goetz, Bonduelle and Gelfand.

GUILLAUME DUCHENNE DE BOULOGNE (1806–1875) was a pioneer of electrical resuscitation techniques and was an experimental physiologist. The resuscitation cases described in *The Forbidden* are authentic and taken from *Localized Electrization and its Application to Pathology and Therapeutics*. Duchenne's most celebrated work, *The Mechanisms of Human Facial Expression* – ostensibly an experimental study of facial musculature – reflects his preoccupation with the soul as the origin of human emotions.

JUSTINE ETCHEVERY – a notorious 'case study' – was admitted to the Salpêtrière in June 1869.

CHARLES MÉRYON (1821–1868) was an artist who produced an atmospheric etching (which he titled *Le Stryge/The Strix*) of the winged gargoyle on the cathedral of Notre-Dame. He died young in the Charenton asylum. Baudelaire wrote of him: 'a cruel demon has touched M. Méryon's brain.'

Other Influences and Sources

The neurotoxin TTX (tetrodox) is found in the skin of the puffer fish, certain fungi and other creatures indigenous to the French Antilles. It can induce a death-like state and is thought to be the means by which bokors create zombies.

Near-death experiences (NDEs) are a relatively common phenomenon. Today, one in ten resuscitated patients – if asked – report core elements such as the tunnel and the light.

Chambault is loosely based on the small but magical chateau of Chatonnière and its exquisite formal gardens (37190 Azay le Rideau). It is one of the Loire's best-kept secrets.

The relationship between the cathedral of Notre-Dame and all things demonic is long and curious. The Celtic tribe who worshipped on the present site produced an uncommon number of demonic figures, and in 1711 workmen digging beneath the choir discovered four altars, one of which bears the image of a horned god. The north portal of the cathedral shows the legend of Théophile, and it is perhaps the earliest representation of a Faustian narrative. Some of the stone used to construct the cathedral came from beneath the Rue d'Enfer – Hell Street (which an old prophecy identified as the site of an infernal abyss). The cathedral is most famous,